C000060573

ISLA'S REACH

THE BREATHS AND DEPTHS DUOLOGY
BOOK ONE

FRANCISCA LILIANA

This is a work of fiction. All the names, characters, businesses, places, events and incidents in this book are either the product of the author's imagination or used in a fictitious manner. Any resemblance to actual persons, living or dead, or actual events is purely coincidental.

Isla's Reach
Book One in the Breaths and Depths Duology
Copyright © 2023 by Francisca Liliana
All rights reserved.

No part of this book may be reproduced in any form or by any electronic or mechanical means, including information storage and retrieval systems, without written permission from the author, except for the use of brief quotations in a book review.

ISBN 979-8-9880829-0-3

Cover art by Felix Ortiz
Cover design by miblart

For those who live with loss.
Come on out. The sun is beautiful today.

Contents

Iona

Edewor

ESHE WILLOW WOOD

Birny

Rya River

Soleil Citade

SOL

Cel

BENA MOUNTAINS

♟ Verbena

Idris Stream

⬦ Nashua Pass

D A T T A D R I   G R E E N S

Elm Lake

🍎 Ciar

Omya River

W A S T E

⬦ Farron Port

⚖ Reva

ia Sea

PART ONE

PRELUDE

THE BATTLE AT ELM LAKE

20 YEARS AGO...

The welling of blood is much like the blooming of a flower. Glistening and sanguine, blood planted and grew into the floor of the wooden steel ship, sprouting from the bodies that lay dead on the deck above. Caia stowed beneath the battle above her, listening to screams of the dying, the undulating death throes of her people. The enemy never made a sound. Rain of steaming water, swirled with blood, dripped from the wooden panels above her.

She sat crossed-legged, with one hand gripping Varsha's glowing scale and the other palm up towards the chaos. Beads of sweat dripped over her brow as the metal around her creaked with the boiling lake's surrounding pressure. Varsha was a stubborn creature, barring her consciousness from Caia. She struggled to connect with the dragon, gritting her teeth against the impassable wall she'd built. The air was so slick with heat that her breath felt as though it were fog in her lungs, weighing her down.

"Caia!"

She opened her eyes to find her husband, Eliam, standing before her with one foot on the steps that led to the surface. His face was lined with streams of blood; some was his and some was not, it was impossible to tell. The shadows within the hull danced along his features, making the blood look black and tar-like.

"I can't reach her," she yelled over the shouts, "She won't let me in."

"We need you out there. Slaughtered is too kind a word for what they're doing to us," his voice cracked as a dark stream of heated water burned its way down his slender nose. His once bright hazel eyes were as black as the sky and her heart leaped out for him. This was her fault. She should've stayed with Varsha. But she wanted to be close to him, to protect him. The vision she had seen before the battle revealed to her how her life would end, but she thought she may yet save him. The cry of a raptor shrieked through the ship, echoing down into the hull, the great eagles rejoicing in their kills.

She hesitated as she looked at the scale in her hand, straining to connect with her bondsmate again. Caia beat against the mental barrier Varsha had built until the dragoness could no longer hold her at bay. She opened her mind to Caia, filling her thoughts with the rumblings of her tumultuous voice.

Where is your spine? If the fault must lie with you, then it lies with me as well. Help them! There is wind under my wings yet.

Caia caught a glimpse of red wings from Varsha's eyes. Chao's claws gripped her leg, as her own were wrapped around his long, thick neck. His piecing single eye bore into her as he snapped and growled. Her bright tail whipped his jaw and he let her go in a fury of blazing white that stained the sky in her silhouette. On Chao's back, a figure held a long broad sword towards the sky. It shone bright, like a bolt of lightning in the storm clouds that gathered around them. The rider's eyes glowed red without any white and held a murderous gleam that even Varsha, the embodiment of passion and savageness, could not fathom.

Blood pumped from her leg wound, but it only fueled her temper. She felt Caia in her body, giving strength to her injury.

No!

4

Caia was ripped from Varsha's mind and brought back to her own body. She held the scale in both hands and closed her eyes, trying with all her strength to regain the connection. Eliam's hand fell on her shoulder, squeezing with urgency. She shook him off, gripping the scale as she would her own beating heart.

"Depths drown us," she cursed, meeting Eliam's confused expression. "She is warring with Chao. Cinaed is with him. That's why she's obstructed our bond."

She was filled with immediate regret for her decision to stay behind. As the last remaining Viden, there was a concern for her safety and protection. *No, not the last*, but she and only a precious few knew that. She thought Cinaed would meet her down on the battlefield. That she would have a greater chance of victory if Chao and he were separated. It seemed he enacted a similar tactic. She thought he would lead his army, but she thought too highly of him. Now that she considered it, it was foolish of her to believe he would behave in any way that would be deemed honorable. The man was mad after all. She looked at her husband, whose concerned expression matched her own. It was for those eyes she stayed. She had to do it. She had to save him. The guttural sounds of those choking on their own blood above her were a clear sign of their stance in this last great battle. They were losing.

"Let me help you." Caia's rage tempered into a low growl, mimicking her bondsmate. Varsha's deep voice radiated that same rage as she spoke.

THE EFFORT IS TOO GREAT. I CAN'T KEEP YOU AND IT'LL GET ME KILLED. HOLD TO MY SCALE AND FIGHT THE TONGUELESS TRAITORS.

Caia stood, and Eliam touched her cheek with a tenderness that had no right to be in battle. She breathed in and let the world fall away, focusing on the gift of Iona's Breath in her lungs. When she breathed out, a silver-blue, shapeless fog swirled in front of her, dancing like it had just discovered it had feet. Eliam's eyes followed her Breath, spinning wisps wrapping around his head, tousling his sweaty hair. She cradled the Breath and spoke into it. It swirled in her hand and when she finished, it burst from her grasp, disappearing in-between the cracks of the ship.

She touched his hand and held it at her side before following him to the hatch. The door creaked as if fighting against a gust of wind and swung open. Three Reticent in black jumped over the stairs leading down to them. The men brandished their blades, staring at her and Eliam with empty eyes, voided of what once had made them men. One was missing an eye, the hole in his face fresh and stripped like ragged cheese, melding into the rest of his scars. The other had a raised scar that cut through his bottom lip, while the last had loose strands of dark hair, sticking to the mass of open cuts crossing his entire face. It was as though the same whip had caused their malformed features, though Caia knew it to be the ravenous claws of their raptors. She'd seen the dark-haired man before, but he looked younger in her vision. That man had the stride of someone in the prime of their youth, but the battle could age any person beyond their years.

Eliam squeezed her hand before dropping it with a shout. He raised his sword over his head, the Reticent missing an eye meeting his blade. Caia held onto Varsha's scale, light pulsating from it like the soft beat of a firefly. The man with the scarred lip lunged towards her, and she bent at the waist under his reaching arm. She lifted her fist, drawing upon the shared strength within the scale. The Reticent's innards collapsed against the might of her fist. He doubled over, spitting blood as his body was thrown against the wall, denting the metal that held the ship together. His skull opened with pieces of bone and brain, painting the hull in sheets of crimson. She pulled out her belt knife and moved to strike his dark-haired companion, but he jumped to the side and held out a knife he pulled from his sleeve. She spared a glance at Eliam, who was pushed against the wall by the one-eyed man, his sword at her husband's throat. Eliam held him at bay with his arm, the sword cutting into his flesh as he cried out in pain.

Caia reacted without thought. She rushed at the dark-haired Reticent, thrusting her blade low at the man's leg. He blocked the maneuver with his dagger, but it caused him to lean forward. She gripped a handful of his hair and struck his head with her knee. His mouth opened to reveal a tongueless mouth, his pain a silent scream. She threw him aside and pulled another blade from her belt, throwing it at the one-eyed man whose sword had sawed through Eliam's arm to the bone. The knife burrowed into the man's temple, and he swayed as though just becoming aware a knife protruded from his head. The Reticent bled tears, smiled, and cracked his forehead into Eliam's face before finally sinking to the floor, dead. Eliam's eyes rolled back and fell to the floor with him, blood pouring from his nose.

The remaining Reticent regained his footing, fingering a small dark stone hanging around his neck. He bared his teeth, bloody spittle spraying as he thrust his blade at her chest. She spun her knife with the hilt facing towards her and blocked the attempt. The blades scraped against one another with a screech that nearly drowned out the screams of the dying. The Reticent snarled soundlessly, tossing the blade to his other hand and slashing it across her own. She sidestepped as he did, matching his footsteps. She swung her body backwards as he rent the air with the weapon. When she righted herself, he was within arm's reach. She grabbed his wrist. His shoulder crashed into her chest, muscle and bone screaming against the blow. She turned from him slightly, crouching to slash the back of his knees. He caught her arm, forcing her upright.

Inevitable. It was all so inevitable.

Pain blinded every thought she ever had. She'd seen this, yet she could not escape it. She arched her back and forced her head back. The base of her skull met with his chin, and she was torn from their violent embrace.

Eliam stirred on the floor, sitting up with a groan. He met her eyes and stared at her in horror, his expression mad with regret. That, she had not seen. The anguished grief ripping through it all, as though he had woken to her already dead. Her hands had gone numb, and she dropped her blade.

She looked down and saw the knife protruding from her

ribs. The steel buried all the way into her body, muscles clinging to the grooves of its serrated edge, cutting her from the inside. She plummeted to her knees, staring at the handle, gasping. She fell onto her back, questioning all she'd done to end up here. Who was she to think she could change anything? Foresight was not a gift meant for mortals who feared their own ends. She'd felt the edges of her mind already fraying, unable to cope with the inevitability of losing all she loved.

"No!" Elaim's voice was raw, as though he shouted through blood. A sudden jolt vibrated the floor and a rhythmic thrum beat like a viciously assaulted drum. With effort, she lifted her head and saw Eliam straddling the Reticent who stabbed her, striking him over and over. She heard the crunch of bone and the clatter of teeth flying.

Her vision blurred and she stared at the ceiling of the ship. She could hear the boots of the people above her fighting for the right to live, for the freedom of their people, and above that, she knew Varsha, in the sky, could feel what had happened to her. She still held to the scale, but Varsha's strength was waning in the hours she had spent fighting Chao. There was not enough to heal her as fast as she needed to be. She felt the tired wings at Varsha's back pumping to keep her in the air.

COWARD! I SEE YOU, BETRAYER! KINSLAYER! BONDBREAKER!

Varsha's anger was as hot as lightning and as strong as the wind that blew around her. Her wings were beaten and bruised; she wanted to rest, but there was no such luxury in battle. Chao licked his bloodied teeth and growled a grimace as he flicked his thick tail. He was so much bigger than her. She was a water dragon, slender and long. Beautiful and graceful when swimming, sleek and quick in the air, but it was not enough. How did she ever think she could take on a mountain dragon as muscled and old as he?

You must end this. I've not long left.

Caia's voice was riddled in agony and Varsha could feel in her own stomach the blade that pierced her bondsmate. It did not affect her physically, but the connection made the pain almost real. It had come to pass. Varsha wished it wasn't true, but the choice was to either test the threads of fate or risk both of them dying in the sky. Still, Caia might yet be saved.

HOLD ON. I AM COMING FOR YOU. BARE YOUR TEETH AT DEATH. YOU'VE NOT MY LEAVE TO DIE. She replied with as much gentleness as fierceness. This was it. The last battle and the boiling lake beneath were all she had left to her advantage. She and Chao were the last of their kind. He made her kill them all. She didn't know how he'd done it, made dragons go mad, killing their own bondsmates. It was the reason she and Caia decided to separate during the battle. Should Cinaed destroy her mind, Caia would be safe. But it didn't matter now. They were all gone. Her grief matched her hatred and she roared in the face of the red dragon.

YOU WILL DIE SCREAMING, DECEIVER. She roared again before reaching out her claws at the dragon.

When she gripped his wing, her claw lifted and bent with a loud crack, breaking. She bellowed her pain and released, flying over him to see Cinaed on his back. The night was so black, he almost dissolved into its darkness.

"There is bravery in you, Varsha. A fierce opponent you make for Chao," Cinaed said, his voice calm, but brazen.

His dark armor gleamed in the stormy night, a black cape billowing behind him, shredded like vapor serpents. His red eyes were wide, and a gleaming, terrifying smile etched his — by human standards — perfect features. That was why Chao was so strong. Cinaed would keep him close at the end, she should've known.

I SEE YOU ARE TOO CRAVEN TO MEET WITH CAIA ON EVEN GROUND CINAED. YOU CANNOT HAVE HER. She growled and snapped her jaws. His loud laughter boomed into the empty sky, and he placed a hand over his heart, as though listening to a tragic story.

"Oh Caia. She knows nothing, and neither do you, dragoness. I do not want her. All I want," he gestured to the elm, the great trees' branches bending to the will of the torrent wind, but not losing a single leaf, "is silence." He spat the word as if he'd bitten into rancid meat.

They were doomed from the start. Varsha thought that she and Caia had planned for this. Not even Eteris, the first and mightiest dragon, could have remained unbroken by Cinaed's cruelty. Madness reigned in his mind and who could fight against the decay of reason?

WHAT COULD YOU USE SILENCE TO GET THAT YOU HAVE NOT ALREADY TAKEN BY BLOOD AND MURDER?

"Everything else," he said, mimicking Chao's snarl. He lifted his sword and Chao growled in approval.

He dove down, heading towards the elm firmly planted in the middle of the lake. Its roots were a maze of bark and dirt, making a solid little island in the boiling lake. *Protect the elm.* It was her single thought, her echoing memory. The task she and all Videns were appointed with the protection of all of Iona. Varsha dove after him and with her slender body blocked his path to the giant tree. Chao roared in frustration; his cruel, graveled voice filled every void across the land.

SHAMEFUL HATCHLING! I WAS OLD BEFORE YOUR SIRES WERE BORN. I WILL CRUSH YOUR SKULL WITH MY FANGS AND DRINK YOUR BLOOD!

He bent his head and snapped at her neck, but she twisted, flapping her wings to spin above him. Cinaed threw down his sword and missed slashing her belly open by mere breadths.

IT SEEMS AGE HAS MADE YOUR WINGS SLOW, OLD ONE. YOU USED TO BE THE SCOURGE OF PREY, THE SCALED WINDSTORM, BUT ALL I SEE IS A MAW FULL OF BROKEN, DULL FANGS THAT CANNOT PIERCE EVEN THE HIDE OF A MUDDY BABI BOAR.

She didn't wait for his response. She flew straight down, wrapping her long tail around one of Chao's wings as her jaws shut on his shoulder. The dragon bellowed and buried his claws into Varsha's belly. She felt Caia's mind within hers, wrought with pain, fighting for breath—dying. In turn, Varsha heaved with weariness as her wings struggled to keep flight, straining to uphold Chao's massive bulk. They joined within each other to create one dragon, one Viden. She had to act quickly, or the connection would break, and she would lose her opportunity. Varsha's strength peaked, and she tightened her tail until a thunderous crack snapped the red dragon's wing in two. Blood sprayed across the sky, tendons and stringy meat connecting the crimson stars.

Cinaed screamed as he felt the break with his own connection to Chao. He looked down at his dragon, trying to speak with him, but the roar of Chao's pain was too great. He clutched the spike at the back of his dragon's neck, flipping through the air down towards the raging, boiling waves. He lost his grip and was thrown with an angry scream into the mass of roots that disappeared within vapors and steam.

You will burn with me! Chao snarled as he ran his claws across her wings, shattering the glass-like membrane into a fall of white, bloody crystals.

Varsha bit down harder as she fell with him. She lifted her claws and dug them into the bottom of his jaw. He roared before she twisted her legs, breaking his neck with a snap that could've been mistaken for thunder. His body went limp in her grasp, and she continued to fall, losing Caia's consciousness as the steam from the lake reached for her. The shape of a large ship formed clearer as she tried and failed to advert her descent.

Caia laid on the ground of the ship, her white eyes still staring at its wooden ceiling. It was done. Varsha did it, but she was falling—falling towards them.

She couldn't change it. She couldn't save them. Eliam would be crushed, and Varsha would burn in the lake. What knife in her gut compared to what she knew and failed to stop?

"Caia?" Eliam's soft voice echoed in the room. He crawled towards her, leaving the fleshy pulp of what used to be a human behind him. The man's scarred face was caved in and unrecognizable, a corpse of disfigured bone and blood. Elaim's fingers were bent and broken from the effort. He clutched them close, grimacing as he hovered above her. She could feel the back of his palms on her face as he leaned over her.

"She did it. Cinaed is dead. Chao too."

Eliam's rough, handsome features returned somewhat as he smiled and laughed at the news.

"You both did it. There is nothing without the other."

"We won." She coughed, blood coloring her teeth as she spoke. He smoothed out her dark hair with his shattered hand and looked up as the battle raged on above them.

"We should probably tell everyone then."

She chuckled, but groaned as the knife shifted inside her. The noise of war gave into terrified shrieks and boots running in all directions. There were even some splashes and screams of men and women jumping only to burn in the lake. Eliam's mouth opened into a confused gasp, and he tried to move Caia to bring her to see what was happening. She shook her head, staring into his eyes.

She said nothing. She should've prevented this, left him in Reva to meet her fate. As heartbroken as she was to see understanding grow in his dark eyes, she couldn't prevent the comfort she felt at not dying alone. It was selfish, she knew it, and tears fell from the agony of being in between such feelings. His own eyes brimmed with tears as he brought down his forehead to hers.

"You saw this?" He held no judgment in his tone as he gestured towards the knife in her belly. He lifted his head, looking into her fully white eyes with the gaze of a man whose loyalty knew no end. He never feared her eyes, and she loved him for that.

"I did," she whispered. It was getting harder to speak as her mouth filled with blood.

"Was that breath for Nakesha?" He brought his forehead back to hers and wrapped an arm around her neck, lifting her against him. She grimaced against the fading pain as her vision began to flicker.

She nodded into his chest. She could warn her, at least. She could do that much for her friend.

"I thought I could change it. I thought I could save you." She buried her face into the curve of his neck, savoring the feel of his naked skin on hers. "I'm so sorry."

He held her close, and they wept together.

"Meric." His voice ripped through their son's name as if the child were a limb torn from his own flesh.

"I know," she whispered.

She recalled his little hands and big sunset-colored eyes, so much like hers used to be. His face filled her mind's eye as impending doom descended upon them. The ceiling of the ship buckled and gave way to a sky of white scales and steaming hot vapor. Eliam covered her body, trying in his own futile way to shield her from the bone searing water of Elm Lake. The force of the waves broke them apart and all she could see was black as she was dragged beneath the surface.

She was burning, and then she was nothing.

CHAPTER 1

A NEW WOMAN

Evelyn stared out the window of her room, smelling the floral scent of oncoming spring. The Eshe Willow Wood to the east was beginning to bloom. She caught a glimpse of the sun's rays reflecting off the fresh snow. The small house was a humble home with only two rooms: one for her and one for her grandmother, Tansey. Evelyn liked to believe she was keeping an eye her, but the old woman was anything but dependent.

"Evelyn," Tansey said a low, aged voice.

She knocked on the door twice before entering. Tansey was a tall, thin woman who had dark hair like her own, but speckled in grey. Her brown eyes matched Evelyn's and she thought that if they were the same age, their differences would stand out more. Many of the villagers commented on how similar their appearance was, even if Evelyn had a hard time seeing it in its current state.

She groaned as she fell onto the bed, placing a pillow over her face. Tansey chuckled and laid down next to her. Evelyn removed the pillow, staring up into the wooden ceiling, following the lines of weathered cracks from the years spent keeping out the snow.

"I had a dream," Evelyn said, following a crack in the ceiling to the window.

"Tell me," Tansey said.

Evelyn watched the light snowfall, remembering what she could. There was a house in her mountains radiating with the kind of warmth she knew to be barren in the frozen land she loved so much. Its stone structure was built into the mountainside as though it had been carved with a tender hand. The groves moved seamlessly with cracks and caverns made centuries ago, becoming a part of the mountain instead of claiming its individuality. Flowers grew from in between the cracks, personifying the life that seemed to glow from the inside of the house. The scent of petals beckoned her, moving her to action as she walked into the mountain. Evelyn looked about the room, surrounded by petals. There were no whole flowers or stems, just perfectly white petals, as if birthed in the air. A sense of belonging and contentment enveloped her. Strong arms looped around her waist, the embrace creating a world where she was whole. She was happier than she had ever been. A child laughed in the distance. She reached out to touch a petal, but she woke before she could.

It was a Viden's gift and burden to dream. It was nothing so special, until those dreams came true. They were small dreams at first, the way she dropped her comb, or the familiarity of walking through a certain mountain pass. Then they grew as Evelyn got older. It represented the potential for greatness—however great Evelyn felt she could be. She could go anywhere, yet knew, somehow, her village was as far as she'd get. Tansey pursed her lips when Evelyn had finished.

"Too cheery for my taste, but it's your Viden dream." Tansey's wrinkled hand cupped her own, rubbing her palm in a soothing, rhythmic way.

"I am not Viden yet. I still have yet to meet Oretem." Evelyn's voice quaked at the sound of the dragon's name. No matter how much she was taught that dragons were the soul and heart of who she was to become, it was still somewhat daunting to meet a beast that could burn her alive.

"It is no different than any other courtship. A few fanciful words and he'll be eating out of your hand rather than swallowing it." Tansey slapped her hand on Evelyn's thigh and kissed her forehead as she stood up. She opened the door, looking back at her with adoring, but nervous eyes. "Happy name day, my love."

Evelyn dressed and walked to the kitchen as Tansey held a cup of hot tea, sitting by the fireplace. The wooden floor was cold, chilling her as she picked up a steaming cup that Tansey had left out for her. Evelyn grabbed a seat from the table, sitting next to Tansey as the flames warmed her feet. They remained in silence for a moment before Evelyn lifted her chin from the cup.

"I'm going to find Nakesha and go out with Birdie for a hunt." She took a sip, savoring the warmth.

"It's your feast, Evelyn. Let the others hunt," Tansey said as she lifted her hand in a dismissive wave. "We should go over what to expect when we travel into the mountains."

"Gran, if I have to practice dragon etiquette or meditation one more time, I might serve you at the feast," Evelyn said, jesting, but also entirely serious. Tansey nodded in the way old people do when they were disappointed.

"I suppose I have been training you into the ground, but can you blame me?"

Evelyn averted her eyes, remembering the reason for Tansey's iron will. Her mother, Nakesha, brought Evelyn to Verbena with the last bit of strength she had. Sou the Ferryman carried her mother to Tansey's doorstep, cold and dying, but Tansey always left that part of the story out. The journey was too much for her and she died only a few hours after arriving. Evelyn was only a child and had no memory of the journey or the war her mother was running from. Its violence never reached her small village in the mountains. Cinaed sought to *cleanse* the world of Videns and dragons. Reason was lost on the mad and Evelyn had only ever heard the man as being entirely deranged. His effort to destroy the great elm within the boiling lake was averted, though his motives were never learned. With his death and that of the rider Caia and her dragon Varsha, Cinaed the Decayed was merely remembered as a bloody madman. As the last Viden, Evelyn was to be kept safe in her mother's own home village, a place that barely existed in the outside world. She often thought of what Nakesha would think of her as she was now.

"I know, gran," Evelyn said, hoping to avoid another retelling of the tale.

She touched her grandmother's hand as she, too, felt the void Nakesha's absence left. But she had heard the story so many times she was desensitized to its melancholy. She mourned, but not in the way Tansey did. How could she miss what she never had?

"You are as dear to me as my own flesh. I am so proud of you this day. Twenty years I have watched you grow into the strong woman I see before me. Nakesha would be proud."

Tansey smiled and turned her head back to the fire.

"Well, I might foresee a bad blizzard every now and again, but I doubt there will be any adventure to be had in little Verbena, gran," Evelyn chuckled, happy to change the subject.

When she bonded with Oretem her power of foresight would strengthen, as all other Videns had before her. Her strength and reflexes would improve, and she'd gain a gift from the dragon. Although, from what she had been taught, it came at a cost. The dragon's gift had something to do with the wind, with Iona's Breath. The spirit that ebbed throughout the world—not a goddess, but a feeling, a way of simplicity and being. As far as she was told, every Viden's connection to the Iona's Breath was different. Some could shape it into solid objects and others could use it to fly alongside their dragons. Her great-grandmother, Arlisa, could breathe Iona's Breath into a person and heal them. It was a gift Evelyn hoped she would inherit. That could be of great use in her village. She wanted to be of use, but she felt ill-equipped to take on the responsibility. She hadn't experienced enough and worried at how much the bond would change her.

Videns and dragons had been extinct for so long, she had to rely on Tansey's memories of Arlisa for lessons. Tansey was a kind of knife-wielding ambassador in her time. She fought alongside Evelyn's great-grandmother in negotiations and some battles during the war. Of course, this was before Tansey married her grandfather, when dragons and Videns were common and the Venandi were allies. But the times had changed, and Evelyn feared she knew too little.

She looked at her hands and feared that the opportunity for her to receive Oretem's gift would be dismissed by what she had already possessed. The heat from the fire warmed the room and when she breathed out, the air spun as if from an open window. Evelyn quickly cut off the flow and looked to Tansey, who didn't seem to notice the fire dimming from the breeze she'd created. Since she was a child, Evelyn had been able to control the wind around her. She kept it secret all her life, knowing there would be only one reason why she possessed this ability, and she feared the sickened look on Tansey's face should she discover it. Evelyn had a suspicion as to where she obtained the power, but there was no way she could ask about it.

The Vagu were people of the Eshe Willow Wood who were rumored to converse with the dead through the wind. They were known to bare false prophecies for profit and cheat money out of grieving families. They were feared for their ability to control Iona's Breath, but more so for the superstitious belief that they spoke to the dead. Evelyn was inclined to dismiss that superstition; she'd never heard so much as a whisper of voices within the breezes she controlled. Her mother certainly wasn't Vagu so there left only one other option. It explained why Tansey never spoke of Evelyn's father, but it didn't stop her from wondering, no matter her decision not to ask. Once she bonded with Oretem she'd be expected to control Iona's Breath and would no longer need to hide it. Her grandmother sipped her tea, unaware of Evelyn's brief anxiety.

"Adventure will find you, I'm sure. Now run along and find Nakesha. I'm sure she will be most happy for a hunt," Tansey said with a wave of her hand. She stood and took the cup from Evelyn before she had finished it.

She opened her mouth to protest, but Tansey was already in the kitchen, dumping the cups into a bucket of soapy water. She strode behind her grandmother, wrapping her arms around her slender waist. The woman was not frail and weak, as her age would suggest. Her body was tight with muscle from training Evelyn in combat every day. Tansey was the embodiment of a woman who'd lived a thousand lifetimes and was still seeking the mysteries of life. She was a woman Evelyn aspired to be.

"I love you, gran," she spoke against her shoulder. Tansey raised her hand and touched Evelyn's cheek before replying.

"Oh, I've something for you before you go."

She strode over to the opposite wall and opened the closet where most of the winter coats were kept. She bent over and carried a green bundle back with her. A wrinkled smile cracked across her face, in what might've been a road map of her life. She handed Evelyn the bundle, then sat down on a chair at the table, nodding her head and urging her to open it.

Evelyn unraveled the cloth and a long green cloak of soft fabric swayed before her. She looked at Tansey with open speechlessness. It was exquisite. Her current one was muddy and frayed, a dim reflection of its former self from all the years she'd had it. She opened the wooden clasp that had the etching of a throwing knife on it and threw it over her shoulders. Not only had it looked to be hand-made for her figure, as the fabric reached just above her ankles, but the neck of the cloak was spun and ruffled into a scarf that fell over her shoulder, with a deep hood at the back. When she reached inside the scarf, she found a pocket. Immediately, she knew what she would keep within it. She bent over and embraced Tansey in a tight hug that could do little to express her true gratitude.

"Gran, I don't know what to say. It's wonderful! Thank you. How did you ever manage to find a cloak so beautiful?"

There was no such shop in the village to have such elegant attire. So far into the mountains they were, she doubted many people beyond their town knew of its existence. Tansey must've bought the cloak from an outsider.

"Do you remember the peddler that came through a few months back?" Tansey said as she rested her chin on her hand, salt and pepper hair falling over her forehead, giving her a youthful appearance.

"Jaspar, the man with the full head of hair. Yes, I remember," Evelyn said in a playful tone.

The older man came through the village with objects from cities as far as Reva and had an eye for her grandmother. They spent many nights at the local tavern, talking and drinking. Evelyn had to tell Tansey to be home at a reasonable hour, like she was the parent, although she never gave Tansey a hard time about it. Evelyn's grandfather died long before she was born, and Evelyn always wished for Tansey to find happiness in another man after so long.

The relationship she hoped for never came to fruition, but she had never seen Tansey more carefree than when she was spending time with Jaspar.

"Well, he was sweet on me and after an exchange I finally accepted the cloak as a gift." She winked and covered the blush that rose on her cheek. Evelyn raised her eyebrows, refusing to move until she knew what the old woman had given the peddler.

"I gave him a lock of my hair," Tansey said as she twirled a finger around her beautifully aged locks.

The relationship must have been more serious than Evelyn had previously thought. She decided she wouldn't press her anymore, but she was certain they would see the kind peddler again.

"You should use your wiles more," Evelyn said as she laughed.

"Only on those worthy of it." Taney's eyes drifted, as if recalling a memory. Evelyn felt a pang of sadness watching her upturned smile dissipate into something akin to loneliness.

"We may see him again."

Tansey's smile returned as Evelyn bent over to embrace her. She felt strong fingers rubbing her back in response before pulling back. Tansey tapped Evelyn's chin in the only way she could imagine a mother's touch to be and nodded.

"You are a new woman. Cloak and all. Be home in time for the ceremony and don't think you've gotten out of knife training. That is non-negotiable."

Evelyn kissed her cheek, sat back in the chair, and tied her thick, furred boots on. She went to the closet and grabbed her small pack of throwing daggers, placing them in the pocket of her new cloak. Tansey watched, eyes bright with approval before Evelyn burst from the front door, knowing she'd return this night a different woman.

Her breath froze in the air and the snow crunched beneath her feet as she walked towards the edge of the mountain pass. The village was alive with those setting tables and cooking meals for the Oathbearing. Men, women, and children were running around, talking with one another in soft tones as she passed them by.

Most treated her no different. The villagers smiled as she walked on, greeting her for the morning as they had done her whole life. Few others looked to the ground in an effort to not make eye contact. Some people had forgotten what being Viden meant, and they were afraid of the unknown. Once, Viden's were beacons of goodness, symbolic to the nature of Iona. Their presence insured peace and their justice was honorable in times of unrest. Their desire rested not in power or land, but in using their gifts for the good of the many. Evelyn had spent her entire life in Verbena and some of the villagers, in the weeks of her upcoming twenty second year, had stopped talking with her altogether. She didn't blame them, but hoped to earn their trust by using her position to help and ease whatever pain she came across.

"Just because you are some highborn now doesn't mean you can be late. Is that a new cloak?" A familiar voice called out.

Birdie walked up beside her, fists curled around her worn and tattered cloak, bouncing on her heels like a child. Her blonde hair was plaited in a single braid across her shoulder.

Evelyn lifted her arms to show her friend, the wind tousling the fabric like waves on the Omya. Birdie glided her fingers across the cloth as if it were some artifact of old that needed to be handled with the utmost care.

"It was a gift from Tansey, and don't call me highborn." Evelyn narrowed her eyes at Birdie as she withdrew her hand.

Birdie was much shorter than Evelyn, wearing thick woolen clothes under her cloak and a skinning knife at her hip, reflecting the frost. Her face was as pale as the snow around them except for the splash of freckles the sun would bestow upon her every now and then. They'd known each other most of their lives and always went hunting together. They had an unspoken language that made them an unstoppable force when tracking a babi.

"Of course, mighty Viden," she bowed her head slightly and Evelyn pushed her to the side in jest.

"It will not change anything."

Evelyn knew this wasn't true, but she felt the need to say it anyway. Everything changed with time, but she welcomed the development with anticipation. Her friendship with Birdie would never end, but evolve into something that would overcome whatever trouble may arise.

"Yes, it will, but don't worry, I'll still be better at the hunt than you," she said, a confrontation prepared in her bright eyes.

She threw a snowball that she had hidden in her scarf and sprinted towards the mountain pass. Evelyn gasped with laughter through the freezing frost coating her cheeks. When she caught up with Birdie, she was out of breath and punched her in the arm.

"After today, I'll be able to avoid those little ambushes of yours," Evelyn breathed in, heavy and loud. Birdie laughed and leaned against the mountain face that rose to be lost in the foggy sky.

"Oh, you know it won't stop me from trying. Call Nakesha and let's get started. Blasted beast will not come to me. Even though we've known each other just as long." She breathed out a sigh that turned into a white puff of frozen breath.

Evelyn pursed her lips and blew a tuned whistle. It was a soft note that lifted and fell into a song that only Evelyn knew and only Nakesha would answer. After a few moments, she heard the soft crunch of the white wolf's large paws. She peeked her fluffy head over a large boulder, running up to Evelyn with the fierceness of a glorious predator.

The bena wolf was giant and had fur long enough to be braided, especially around her neck. During the wintertime her coat was white, blending in with her surroundings. But in the summertime, she would turn pitch black that was perfect for nighttime hunting. Since they were in-between seasons, Evelyn could see patches of black beginning to peak beneath Nakesha's white coat.

There were many wild bena wolves in the mountains, but only a few had been trained since pups to assist her village. They used the animals to hunt babi boars, which were their main source of food. Her people would never dream of chaining the extraordinary creatures. They were free to roam and find their own pack to live as Iona intended. The other tamed wolves had returned to Iona many years ago; Nakesha was the only one left. She'd only just reached maturity and hopefully would mother a litter within a few years to be trained.

Evelyn couldn't remember her mother. There was a lingering guilt when she listened to Tansey's stories of her, but she never felt the emptiness of that loss, only the faint echo of loneliness to constantly remind her of what she never had. It was clear her grandmother still mourned for her daughter, but Evelyn had only known Tansey's love and care. The pit that grew in her stomach at the thought of losing Tansey was the only comparison she had. She liked to believe that her mother watched over her somehow. When she was gifted Nakesha as a pup, she immediately felt the spirit of her through the eyes of the wolf. There was no grief, but for the first time, Evelyn felt the empty part of her heart that her mother had left with her death. She always connected the two and so she named Nakesha after her.

"Hello, beautiful. Your spring coat is coming in. I know it's your preferred look, vain one," she said, combing her fingers through her soft fur with a rough tug.

The animal blinked in agreement and nuzzled her head in Evelyn's hands.

"You have your daggers?" Evelyn asked Birdie. Her friends' blue eyes sparkled as she tapped the inside of her sleeve and nodded. "Would you like to hunt, Nakesha?"

The wolf let out a small whine, impatient to proceed and laid down so Evelyn and Birdie could climb onto her back. Evelyn clutched the tuft of long hair at the wolf's neck as Birdie wrapped her arms around her waist. Nakesha howled in excitement as she broke out into a swift, but graceful run. Evelyn savored the cool air as they were carried deeper into the wilds of the Bena Mountains. There was still so much unexplored.

The last time someone wandered too far, they found a dragon.

Chapter 2

The Peddler Who Belonged

Maun sat by the fire wrapped in a pelt of onni fur. It wasn't as warm as what a babi pelt could offer, but it was all he had. The snow at his feet crunched, giving away with every move as it thawed against the fires light. He missed sand and its yielding disposition as he sat on frozen snow over a rocky terrain. Leaving the Order was a decision he didn't regret making, but it wasn't one he had planned. Even as the wind blew ice into his eyebrows, there was no other feeling than that of freedom. He had timed his departure with Tacet Devu's assignment to Reva. It was his mentor's task to bring a Child of Fortune to the Order, an untainted recruit to train and join the league of assassins.

Devu taught had him well. She taught Maun to be the most rational, the most silent—however much that was possible—and the cruelest. There was not much Maun wasn't willing to do in his pursuit. He glanced at the blood that peeked from the snow just behind his leg.

He turned, looking down at the body of the man whose fire he stole. He was old, but seemed to have a full head of hair despite his age. His hands were still clutched at his throat where a deep, red gash lined in between the folds of his neck, blood crystalizing around his head like a stained-glass halo.

Maun turned back to the fire and picked up his bloodied

dagger. The weapon was small and could cut through the wind as silent as he. The old man hadn't seen what happened, only that he was finished. He had fallen to the ground, ripping at his collar, and gasping into the air. The sight was pathetic, but Maun had grown used to it over the years. The blood had frozen in bubbles, as he was in the middle of humming when Maun's blade had caught his throat. The tune echoed in the back of his mind, a poem he'd heard a hundred times. Maun hadn't noticed before when he had done the deed. All he could think of was the warmth of the fire. Now, as he sat next to the old man's corpse, he wondered what the man had been thinking at the end.

Maun wiped the dagger against the snow and sheathed it onto his belt. A shriek shot through the sky and he looked up. Saiya must've made a kill. He took comfort in the idea of her eating well. The Bena Mountains held little vegetation and much of the wildlife was too large for her to take as prey. The old man would make her happy should she find whatever small creature she devoured unsatisfying.

The cart the old man had been pulling laid undisturbed beside the fire. Maun stood to inspect what he was transporting. Inside were trinkets and fine clothes from Reva, metal pots and spices from Solov. He was a peddler. There was a small town not far from where they were that must've been his final destination. Peddlers belonged to no one. They had no home, no one to miss them. His presence would go undetected.

Maun walked to overlook the old man; fingers curled around the collar of his cloak instead of his throat. He pulled the old man's arm down with effort, as the cold had started to harden his limbs. He reached into his collar and pulled out a necklace with a plain, wooden locket dangling. There were no etchings or distinguishing features as to its maker. The peddler must've carved it himself.

Maun opened the locket to discover a lock of hair, curled as if a coiled snake within its egg. It was dark brown with light touches of grey. He *did* belong to someone. In his moments before death, he reached for the locket as if it were the branch to break his fall. He was headed home. It made no difference.

Maun snapped the locket shut, dropping it to the cold ground with little expression. He pushed his thoughts out as he contacted Saiya to return. He felt her wings tremble in the air, throat contracting as she swallowed a rabbit. She wasn't far from the sound of her answering screech. He was warm enough. The snow would bury the peddler.

He reached into his pocket and felt the two stones resting together. Celosia's Glare traveled with him far and beyond where he had first found them. He'd lost count of how many times he'd reached into the pocket. As if there were any being in Iona capable of stealing them.

Behind him, the tumble of small rocks reverberated across the silent snow. He turned around and saw the sway of a cloaked figure disappearing in the distance. The stranger was too far for Maun to see any peculiar details except for a heavy limp. He doubted the figure saw him either. Maun didn't crouch or hide behind a boulder as he watched. He never hid, he only waited. There was nothing worth waiting for in the stranger and Maun watched as the snowfall covered their departure.

Following the cloaked figure wouldn't help him in his search for vengeance. It was compulsion that drove him. Blood for blood was all that would satisfy the loss of his mother. Even if it was years ago, before he earned his raptor. When he wasn't tongueless and scarred. It was time for retribution, and it started with finding that dragon.

CHAPTER 3

A PILLAR OF SMOKE

Nakesha's body stilled with anticipation beneath Evelyn. She knew the wolf could smell the boar before she saw it. With her hand inside her cloak, Evelyn reached for her daggers, feeling the smooth hilt across her fingertips. Nakesha's muscled shoulders held her form still as she lowered into a crouch; eyes fixated on her target.

Evelyn tensed, catching the bright, curved tusks of a babi boar against the boulders of the surrounding mountain. They curled inwards towards the head and back out around its elongated mouth. From its bottom jaw, huge incisors peaked to better rip rocks and roots from the frozen tundra. The boar wasn't quite as large as Nakesha but stronger, built for lifting boulders twice their weight. This one, considering the size of his tusks, was male.

His short legs upheld a massive frame of pure muscle that, without the element of surprise or the assistance of her wolf, would be impossible to overpower. As he came closer, the babi grunted, shifting the rocks as he used his enlarged cloven hooves to search for small rodents and roots. The animal's short, brown fur made for a perfect cloak, hiding within the shadows of the mountain's many caves.

Birdie hid herself behind a boulder a hundred paces from where the babi was digging. She stared at the beast, her finger tapping the hilt of her dagger. She lifted the blade to her chin, her grip placed expertly on the hilt. The blade was longer than Evelyn's, but thinner for less air constriction. Shadows danced across her friend's face, as though the light reflected the concentration and prowess Birdie exhibited. She was the perfect portrait of a huntress, mirroring Nakesha's crouching stance.

The wolf lifted her paw and Evelyn knew she was ready. She always trusted Nakesha to know when the best moment to strike was. After all, she had the most practice. Evelyn tightened her hold on Nakesha's fur and released a small puff of air against the wolf's ear, letting her know she was braced.

The wolf took a step and then broke out into a run, her broad paws burrowing into the snow as she pressed forward. Evelyn tightened her thighs and kept her head still as the predator sought out its prey. Frost burnt her face as she blinked away tears.

The boar lifted his head and, for a moment, stood still as Nakesha's fur blended in with the surrounding frost. His nose shifted, catching the wind as the wolf's scent filled the air. He jumped on the boulder he'd been trying to lift, disappearing behind it.

"Ha!" Evelyn shouted as Nakesha leaped, following the babi as he ran only a few leaps ahead.

The wolf panted as they got closer, her tongue lapping down her jaw. Evelyn pulled out a dagger, her arm stretched behind her. She only needed to be a little closer. The boar was bouncing from the mountain walls and over boulders, grunting and squealing. He tried to turn, attempting to trick Nakesha into thinking he was headed in one direction before quickly shifting in another. The wolf wasn't fooled and blocked every attempt at escape, herding the frightened beast in the direction Birdie was hiding. As the animal swerved around the bend, Birdie, without even the whispered sound of a breath, threw her dagger.

The blade buried itself into the neck of the boar, precisely where its main artery laid, but the babi's muscle was too thick.

The dagger stuck itself firmly into the boar's neck, causing the blood flow to trickle instead of pouring out as it should've. The babi unleashed a violent grunt and kept running down the path. Birdie let out a frustrated yell and threw her arm out to let Evelyn know to keep up with the injured beast.

She passed Birdie with a quick glance and headed around the bend, leaning far and close to the ground as Nakesha skidded on the ice. She could see blood dripping into the snow as Birdie's dagger sheared deeper through the boar's neck. Nakesha didn't lose her stamina, powerful legs pounding against the ice as primal instinct took over. Evelyn smiled as the path ended against the cliff wall, the only escape a far cry fall from the edge. The babi tried to climb, but his weight was too heavy, hooves renting the rockface, releasing the boar without compassion to his imamate fate.

Nakesha growled, pacing in front of the boar as he let out a wild squeal and bent his head forward with his tusks pointed straight out. This was the moment Evelyn always felt her heart leap into her throat. A cornered babi was the savage of the mountain, its tusks able to stab a grown man through. Many hunters died when cornering an animal as tough as this, and she'd seen the revolting display of their work on a human's body.

Evelyn held her breath as the boar charged forward. She never felt fear for herself. Her first concern was always Nakesha. Those tusks would skewer her beloved wolf and Evelyn would never recover from such a death. She let out a short whistle and Nakesha bared her teeth as she leaped against the mountain wall, rising above the boar as he ran through where they once stood. In midair, Evelyn ran her hands across the air, feeling the wind wrap around her fingers. The jump was too high, and she feared Nakesha would break a leg landing.

She pulled the wind up under the wolf and glided her forward above the babi. Her chest heaved and Iona's Breath wrap around them in an embrace. It consumed her, the power that spread from her fingertips, filling her with a sense that flying wasn't an impossibility. It was inevitable. Evelyn basked in the warmth of its freeing elation, then looked down at the boar beneath her, throwing her dagger straight down into the head of the raging beast. The animal grunted and tripped as his momentum carried him forward before he skid to a stop.

He was dead before Nakesha's paws found the snow. Iona's Breath dissipated from Evelyn's hands, and she was brought back to the reality of her life on the ground. She jumped from Nakesha's back, walking towards the river of icy blood that trailed from the babi's wounds. Birdie came running down the path, her breath coming out in puffs of cold air.

"Brilliant," she panted. "I only saw that last bit, but that was brilliant. When did you learn that? I've never seen Nakesha jump that high before."

Controlling Iona's Breath was not something Evelyn had any proficiency over as she hardly could practice without announcing it to the whole village. She kept it to herself and never told a single soul. Not Birdie or even Sou, who she shared almost everything with. Discussions of the Vagu inevitably led to the topic of the Evandis, the great war that drove dragons mad and caused the extinction of both beast and Viden. The Vagu had always been a mysterious people and with the end of the war, retreated further into their homeland of the Eshe Willow Wood, leaving behind further superstition for those who fear what they cannot understand.

Evelyn had seen a Vagu once when she was a child playing next to the river on Sou's land. The woman was beautiful. She had long, dark hair that was covered by a blue hooded cloak. Her face was angular and sharp—graceful like a snow fox. She was tall, but being only a little girl everyone was tall to Evelyn. Now that she remembered, the woman couldn't have been more than a youth. She was paying for passage on the Omya River to Reva. She waved a delicate hand at her and stared at Evelyn as if she were the first child she'd ever seen. Evelyn thought she wanted to play. So, without the caution she later adapted, she raised her hand, and a light breeze blew the hood down.

In the moment between the young woman's surprised

expression and her swift reaction of replacing the hood over her head, Evelyn caught a glimpse of the Vagu's signature slanted eyebrows. When Sou bade her to return to the village, she told Tansey of what she saw. Her grandmother, contrary to what she should've expected, was not at all pleased and left her in the care of Alen the village elder. When Tansey returned Evelyn was never allowed to go see Sou alone again. Tansey would always accompany her if she didn't sneak away to visit on her own. Evelyn never understood why there was such hostility around a people she found to be so much like her. In any case, all she had was within her village and no matter the love that surrounded her, prejudice had the capacity to be stronger.

"It was nothing. Nakesha and I practiced it," she said, giving the wolf a rub behind her ear.

That was at least partly true. Nakesha was the only living creature who knew everything about her. Evelyn was skilled in the art of knife throwing, but without a teacher she had little chance to perfect her wind prowess. Nakesha's quiet presence made it easier to access her own technique when practicing. The wolf's white fur shifted in all directions and she leaned into Evelyn's touch, salivating at the sight of blood pooling beneath the boar.

"Clever girl," Birdie praised as she patted Nakesha's mane.

Evelyn walked beside the boar and brought out a large carving knife from her boot. She tied her cloak into a knot behind her as she cut into the back leg of the babi, hearing the crack of the joint as she twisted it free from the rest of the carcass. She carried it over to the hungry wolf, waiting patiently for her share.

She rested her head on Nakesha's nose, her moist snout cold against her forehead.

"Thank you, vain one," she said as she kissed the side of her maw. Although the wolf couldn't speak, Evelyn could see satisfaction in her dark eyes, as well as hunger.

She dropped the leg as Nakesha bit into the meat, dragging

it away to the side of the mountain, growling the entire way. Evelyn knew better than to disturb her while she ate.

She turned around to see Birdie already halfway through skinning the beast, her bare arms covered in gore and blood. Evelyn crouched beside her as she assisted cutting up the babi into sections, then tying them in rope to keep them together. After the butcher, they buried the meat beneath the ice to stop the flow of blood and sat down together on a boulder overlooking the valley where their village lay.

The sun was lowering, its rays painting the landscape with orange and red, lighting her little village below in fire and warmth. The Omya River flowed beyond the horizon, leading to Reva and the soft transition of winter to spring. She often thought of one day accompanying Sou to the city. She heard of its modern streets and elegant people, that it was a place of progress and hospitality.

It was a daydream if nothing more. She loved her life. She loved the mountains and the cold. She could never leave Tansey, or Birdie. She especially couldn't leave Nakesha, who would wither in a big city like Reva.

"You could do it, you know," Birdie said, eyeing Evelyn with her cloak billowing in the wind.

"Do what?"

"Go somewhere."

Evelyn laughed and hugged her cloak closely around her.

"I would miss this too much," she said in truth. She could see herself reveling in the adventure, but knew she'd soon crave the simplicity her life was now.

"You're *Viden*," Birdie said, emphasizing the word as though it had the same cadence as *Lord* or *Lady*. "You can do anything you want."

Evelyn shook her head. Birdie always favored the dangerous because she couldn't do most of the things she wanted. Her father and mother died of fever not two years ago and so Birdie cared for her little brother, Maysom, who would not be of age for some time. She knew her life would be here for the foreseeable future and ever since, she had been encouraging Evelyn to spread her metaphorical wings.

"It's quite the opposite, actually," Evelyn said as she clasped her hands together.

Her whole life, she had lived in the shadow of her mother —in the echoes of her dying wishes. When she died it was as if Tansey thought drilling Evelyn with lessons and constant supervision were ways to keep her daughter close, to keep her alive. Tansey was insatiable in that regard. She loved the old woman with all her heart, but Evelyn hardly knew who she was without the title Viden. It was all she was ever told to be.

Birdie could see her inner struggle and patted her arm before glancing down at the village. The fire from the pit for the expected boar was a spec of daytime starlight. Their very own northern star. "Well, how could you want to leave a place so beautiful anyway?" she said as she extended her arm to the yellow horizon. The setting sun reflected flames across the snow laden land, blazing it alight with colors outsiders had no concept of imagining. The hues unique to the Bena Mountains, belonging only to Evelyn and her people.

"Nakesha is about done. We should pack it up and leave," Evelyn said as she glanced at the wolf licking blood from her white chops.

Birdie slapped her legs as she stood and jumped from the boulder. Evelyn rose but noticed in the distance, farther up the mountain, a pillar of smoke from a doused fire. Beside it was a piled mound of snow with some kind of animal moving on top. It was clearly eating, but the campsite was much too far to make out any distinct details.

"Birdie. Do you see the smoke?" she asked without turning around.

She heard her friend grunting as she carried some of the meat over to Nakesha.

"I saw, but I figured it was just a passerby," Birdie said.

"Do you think they need help?" She noticed a cart next to the campsite. The owner was nowhere to be found.

"I am sure they only went to piss. I doubt they'd want help with that. Would you get down and help *me*?"

Evelyn took one last look, then thought Birdie was probably right. It was a rare thing to have an outsider in their mountains, yet it wasn't unheard of. She helped Birdie tie up the meat on Nakesha's rump, hanging on her like bloody leather packs, then climbed on her back. The wolf let out a howl and ran down the slope. Evelyn soon forgot the smoke and the missing owner of the cart.

Birdie laughed behind her as the wind numbed their faces and Nakesha panted in excitement at the speed of going downhill. Evelyn joined in Birdie's laughter, whooping and screaming as Nakesha skimmed the edges of the cliffs. Out of everything that was bound to change that day, she hoped it was moments like these she could hold onto.

CHAPTER 4

THE WISDOMS OF A FERRYMAN

When they reached the bottom of the mountain Evelyn heard the shouting of children playing in the snow. Like a pack of pups to their mother, they screeched and ran towards Nakesha. Birdie jumped down from the wolf's back as she gripped the rope holding the meat, bits of blood staining the back of Nakesha's rear.

One of the cloaked children was Maysom. As Birdie's eight-year-old brother, he was always determined to be as troublesome as possible. Under his tight, furred hat, blonde curls peeked above big, blue eyes. He stuck his tongue out through gapped teeth and pulled on the rope that Birdie carried. The meat unraveled, falling to the ground with a hard crack.

"Maysom! I'll leave you out to sleep in the snow like the annoying creature you are!" she shouted as Evelyn laughed.

The boy was far from where he had started, a few of his friends shouting as they ran with feigned fear. The other children were petting Nakesha, and Evelyn felt the wolf hum in pleasure. Nakesha was as wild as she wanted to be, but Evelyn and her people were her pack. It was a relationship that balanced on trust and mutual respect. There were times Evelyn wouldn't see her vain one for days, but in the end Nakesha always returned and she always answered her call.

"It's all good laughter when you're an only child," Birdie said as she kneeled to tie the meat back onto the rope.

"Thank the Breaths and Depths for that."

Evelyn wished she had siblings. As much as Birdie fought with her brother, Evelyn could see how much they relied on that relationship, especially since their parents died. Evelyn was grateful to have Tansey, but sometimes she had thoughts that she alone had to bear. Birdie was as good as a sister, but they were still separated by the knowledge that if it came between choosing her or Maysom, her brother would be the immediate choice. Evelyn would never fault her friend for that. She only wished she had the privilege of loving someone that much.

Just as she was about to dismount, Tansey appeared, walking towards them. Evelyn let out an involuntary groan and looked behind her at the mountain pass. She was trapped. Either way was going to lead her to a place she wasn't sure she was ready for.

She looked ahead at the open plain. Alight with snow, it beckoned without limits on its horizon. A barren landscape that expected nothing of her, not even the concern of her survival. Her eyes met with Birdie's, and she crouched to better speak with her.

"Snow down the dragon?" Evelyn asked, imploring her with raised brows.

"Oh, come now. She's only helping," Birdie said as she glanced at Tansey, who was nearly within speaking distance.

"I can do whatever I want. I'm Viden, remember?" Evelyn smiled as Birdie rolled her eyes.

"Don't you think we're a bit old for that?" Her brows furrowed as she lowered her voice, "Also isn't that a little disrespectful, now that you're going to be bonded to one and all?"

Evelyn huffed and flicked her friend on the forehead. Birdie gasped, rubbing the spot between her eyes.

"Precisely why it should be done."

"You're fortunate I'm the only one who can care for

Maysom. Tansey can't kill me," Birdie pursed her lips. "Well, go on. Be back by dark, young lady."

Birdie pointed her finger as if she were giving an order to a child and Evelyn's lips curled into a grateful smile. There was nothing she couldn't rely upon Birdie for. Evelyn gripped the fur on Nakesha's neck, preparing for a quick getaway. Tansey waved her arm, her voice chilled in the cold air.

"You're back early. That's good, we have time—"

"Back away, beast!" Birdie bellowed, holding a compact ball of snow in her gloved hand. The old woman started at her sudden outcry, but realization swiftly overcame her surprise.

"You cannot be ser—" Tansey stopped midsentence as the snowball hit the side of her head. Birdie jumped up and down in childish triumph, her braid swaying across her shoulders.

"The dragon has been snowed down! Victory belongs to the brave!"

Tansey staggered back, thrusting her hands in the air as she tried to maintain her balance. Birdie glanced at Evelyn with a mischievous smile and ran with the meat in the opposite direction. The weight of it caused her friend to sprint as elegantly as an overfed bird. Before Tansey could gain her bearings, Evelyn whistled and the wolf beneath her leaped into a run, away from the verbal beating she was sure she would have endured had she stayed a moment longer. Tansey shouted, but the wind drowned out her words.

As Evelyn gained ground, she looked behind her and the village was barely more than a raised line on the horizon. She faced the setting sun in front of her, reveling in the cool breeze that blew past. She was unsure if that was her doing or Nakesha's pace, but either way, she loved the feeling.

Sou's little hut on the bank of the Omya River was small with piled stone walls and a tin roof that pinged whenever it rained. In the summer, the snow would make way for small patches of grass and wildflowers. Sou liked to keep a garden near the hut, but it was nonexistent now. The small port where he ferried supplies was at the fork of Nashua Pass that led into Idris Stream, dividing it from the Omya that she and her people relied upon for travel. The heat from the boiling water in Elm Lake kept the river from freezing over and baring the way into Reva. Without the Omya it would take a month to reach the city. Verbena depended on the river for supplies and goods that peddlers or Sou might bring in.

His boat was big enough for a cart to be brought over, but had no hull beneath or room for a large number of people. A small helm stood strong and a single sail swayed slightly with the calm churn of water. It was the perfect size for a little village that barely existed. As Evelyn rode closer, a man peered out from the hut in a light furred coat and thinly wrapped leather boots. When Nakesha reached the pier, Evelyn untied her cloak and rested it over her arm as she dismounted.

The wolf jumped, spraying snow in the air as she ran towards Sou. The old man laughed, and his eyes crinkled under a wide smile. He knelt as Nakesha fell on her back, presenting her belly with enthusiasm. He obliged and rubbed her stomach, burying his face into her thick neck. A cord of leather strapped to a clear vial hung from his throat, hovering above the wolf. She nipped at the necklace, which he placed back within the folds of his shirt. He patted her a few times more before rising to meet Evelyn at the end of the pier where his boat floated. The wolf followed him, panting with the hope of more pets.

Sou's head was wrapped in a brown cloth that kept his longer grey hair out of his green eyes. His jaw was stubbled in grey, and he had a familiar, long, shapely nose that suited him.

"Happy name day, lass!" he said with open arms. "Prepare for an embrace worthy of a fearsome Viden." She embraced him with a contented sigh. Sou was a thin man with the upper body strength of someone whose endurance was shaped by long distance rowing.

Like the ice that refused to form on the river, Evelyn was relieved of her burdens when she visited Sou. The old man was a calming presence that she couldn't find anywhere else. She held one arm across his back as he circled her shoulders, parting as they sat down next to each other, feet dangling over the wooden platform.

"It is a big day. *The* day," Sou said, rubbing his old knees. He was somewhere in his early sixties although Evelyn wasn't quite sure.

She shrugged, knowing no matter how hard she tried to hide her fear, Sou would be able to detect it. He always seemed to know how she was feeling before she did.

"What is it, lass? This is something you've waited your whole life for. Are you nervous?" His tone held no judgment, only concern.

"Something Tansey has waited her whole life for."

"What do you mean?"

Evelyn rubbed her hands together as she tried to find the words to speak her mind.

"How do I know I'll be any good at it?" She caught her troubled features reflected in Sou's clear, green eyes.

"Well, you don't. Breaths and Depths, let me have a go. I'll sure as sunrise be better at it than you, for certain." He lined his lips as if cross and Evelyn smiled.

"You would run this town into relevance, and all would flock to Verbena to see the idiot Viden and his flower garden." She gestured towards the barren tundra by the hut.

"Gardening is a man's venture for nurture and growth. If you ever go mad enough to have children, then I hope you would teach them that."

"I'll leave that to the expert." She pushed him lightly with her shoulder.

"Truth be said, lass. What's troubling you?"

Evelyn felt a pang of remorse as she looked at Sou. The old man was so kind and understanding. Most of the time she used Sou as an excuse to get out of lessons as she did today, and whenever she visited him, she felt as if she only came with problems. The closer the Oathbearing got, the more ill prepared she felt.

"Do you think I might come with you to Reva after the

Oathbearing?" It wasn't the question she planned to ask, but the one she felt scream the loudest in her heart.

Sou pursed his thin lips, rubbing his jaw as though considering.

"Aye, after the Oathbearing there isn't much anyone could deny you anymore. The rest of Iona will eventually find out of your existence soon enough. You'll have to travel eventually, and maybe a small trip to the city would be a good start to that." Sou put a hand on her knee and patted her leg as he looked over the river. It sparkled in the setting sun as the sky was growing darker by the minute. "There's no need to fret. It will be all be explained to you tomorrow morning, I promised you."

Evelyn raised her head, looking at Sou in confusion.

"What will be explained tomorrow?"

He removed his hand from her knee and cocked his head to the side, perplexed by her own confusion.

"Everything that your gran and I promised you." He paused. "She's not said anything about us speaking, has she?"

"This is the first I am hearing of it. What is it?" Her voice was tinged in worry.

She couldn't help it. The day after the most important day of her life, and the two people she cared for most in the world wanted to sit down with her. Two people who could hardly stand the sight of each other. The world was going to end. She was sure of it.

"No, lass. No, it's good news, I assure you. You're gran and I are fine. There are just some truths that need to be spoken. It may be hard for you to hear, but it is my hope you will understand why we kept silent." He touched one of the lines of cloth from his headband in a nervous tick.

"Why would Tansey not speak to me of this?"

It wasn't the first time Tansey had hidden the past from her. Evelyn hadn't known that Sou was the one who brought her and her dying mother home. He saved their lives, and it wasn't until Sou told her at fourteen had she found out. She didn't talk to Tansey for days she was so angry.

"Your gran has her reasons. I can't say I agree with her, but I can understand. However, no matter what she says you come here first thing tomorrow. With or without her I will tell you the truth."

"About what?" she said, exasperated.

"I'm sorry that I put this on you before your Oathbearing. It's not fair and I can't say I wouldn't be angry too."

Evelyn softened her expression, placing her head on his shoulder and spoke in a soft voice. "I'm not angry. I just don't understand why I must wait. Why I've had to wait these past twenty years without even a word of whatever secret pact you've got with Tansey."

The boat in front of them dipped up and down with the waves. The movement was soothing and helped alleviate Evelyn's breathing to slow normal breaths.

"It would not be safe to tell you until after your bonding. Your gran and I may disagree often, but we do agree that this was your mother's wish. It would dishonor her death if you were to be discovered before your bond was made. It is what she died for."

What in the Depths could warrant secrecy for so long? Was it something that had to do with her Oathbearing? No, surely they would tell her beforehand. It had to be another detail of her mother's death she didn't know. This revelation was doing nothing for her confidence and everything to fuel her temper. She lifted her head from his shoulders, feeling the air around her chill with her mood.

Sou's not too often serious face looked older as he faced her. She cast her eyes down as she took in his words and solidified them in her mind. If Sou said it, then it must be true. She looked at the rise and fall of the boat again and regained her composure, resigning herself to patience.

"How is it you and Tansey never got along? You've known each other as long as I've been alive. How can twenty-two years not be enough to reconcile? I mean you never..." she trailed off.

It was a question she often thought about. When she was

younger, she would imagine Tansey and Sou finding themselves in a romantic entanglement, giving her the parents she so desired. But as the years passed, their animosity strengthened and that dream died with her childlike thoughts.

"Oh, lass," he laughed as he tried to continue, "First, you'd seen but two name days when I brought you to your gran, so I've known her less than that. Second, from what I've heard there was but one man for your gran and death was his only way out."

Evelyn opened her mouth to protest, but Sou lifted his hand to stop her.

"I know, I know. He was a good man, I heard. But I brought her daughter as good as dead to her doorstep. I'm a walking reminder of what she lost." He bowed his head in reverence, then lifted it again. "I was only poking fun because, Breaths and Depths, lass, your gran and *me*? She throws punches for kisses and strangles for hugs. Besides, I'd met the love of my life already. There's no other woman that compares."

Sou bent his leg and rested his chin on his knee while swinging the other over the platform. She'd never heard Sou talk about a woman. For as long as she'd known him, he lived alone. She looked around the landscape and hut, trying to find any kind of feminine touch. She found nothing.

"You've never spoken of her. What's her name?"

He paused for a moment and looked into her eyes. The way Sou looked at her then, it was as if she were someone else.

"Her name was Lyn."

Was. She bit her lip, regretful at the inconsiderate way she'd asked him. Sou's face was not made for frowns and hard lines, it was difficult to see him in any state of distress.

"I'm sorry."

His melancholy broke as he smiled. Crinkled eyes returning to their bright green color as though forgetting every misfortune they'd ever seen.

"Oh, it was a very long time ago. No need to feel sorry, lass. She was an incredible woman that I had the privilege to love. It was painful to lose her, but I'm a better man for having loved her."

"Tansey says that love is a pain you ache to feel, even if you're broken."

"Especially if you're broken," Sou said as he nodded in approval. "Your gran is a wise woman, even if she can be as stubborn as a babi. Did you come here to avoid her?"

Evelyn averted her eyes as she heard the tone of his voice. She felt more ashamed of the sound of his disappointment than the expression in Tansey's face as she escaped from her.

"I just—just," she stammered, "I needed to clear my head."

Sou stood, holding out a hand to Evelyn to help her up. As she stood, he knocked on her head a few times, pretending she was a door.

"All clear up in there? I think I see some fog coming out of those ears."

She slapped his hand away with a laugh and glanced at Nakesha laying down on the snow at the head of the pier. The wolf's head rose, ears pricked for the departure she could sense was coming.

"Yes, it's clear. Thank you." She smiled as he pulled her in for another hug.

"Oh! I nearly forgot. You'll need this for tonight."

He reached into his pocket and pulled out a thin leather necklace. It was long and tied with a knot at the back. In the middle was an empty socket surrounded by brass, branch-like coils. It wrapped around a narrow space for something to be held.

Evelyn took the necklace from Sou and held it in her hand. The coils had little dents in the metal that gave it a rugged, appealing feel. Sou smiled secretively.

"Bring it with you to your Oathbearing. You'll know what it's for."

She thanked him and he followed her to Nakesha, who nuzzled her face against his chest. The wolf loved him just as much as she did, coating his hands in her slick saliva. Evelyn lifted her cloak and clasped it around her shoulders before mounting. Sou patted Nakesha's head, wiping his fingers through her silky fur to rid himself of the sticky drool.

"Stunning creature, you are. A slobbering mountain queen," he said, grimacing. Nakesha licked his cheek with appreciation, urging him to continue with his flattery and proving his point at the same time.

"Will you not come to the feast tonight?" Evelyn asked, already anticipating the disappointment of his answer. He glanced up at her, a heavyhearted smile creasing the wrinkles around his mouth.

"I've a feast large enough for a simple ferryman here. In any case, babi meat has never agreed with my stomach and I'm long past the age of youthful dancing." His voice was in jest, but Evelyn could detect the longing at the edges of his tone. Tansey wouldn't welcome his presence and she knew that he stayed away so that the festivities would not be ruined on her name day. Evelyn inclined her head, looking over the chopping river water. Sou said goodbye one last time before Evelyn gave the whistle for Nakesha to run.

With the moon rising behind her, she could see faintly in the distance torches lighting her village, twinkling as if reflecting the night sky. The smell of the cooking babi became stronger as she got closer. The fire beneath the boar becoming the star that lit her way home.

CHAPTER 5

THE CLIMB

"What is the proper bow when greeting a dragon?" Taney asked as Evelyn stood on one hand, her legs erect in the air. Her other hand was out, holding a dagger as sweat beaded off her forehead onto the ground below.

"There isn't one. You hold eye contact until the dragon looks away," she grunted, almost losing her balance. "I thought you said we'd only practice knife throwing."

Evelyn focused on the plank of wood in front of her, its surface scratched and chipped from all the years it had suffered her abuse. The X that Tansey carved into the trunk was deep and scarred, but seemed to grow smaller the longer Evelyn was upside-down. The old woman played with the laced leather bracelet on her wrist before answering.

"Disappointment builds character, as running from lessons creates consequences." Tansey lifted her foot and kicked Evelyn under her arm. Her upside-down figure swayed as she fell on her back, but not before throwing her knife, landing it perfectly inside the X.

The cold snow froze through her clothes and she sighed in relief at its refreshing frost. Tansey's face peered over her, the skin on her neck creasing with age. The old woman smiled and held out a hand. Evelyn grabbed it but Tansey, with more force than she had anticipated, lifted her off her feet and down onto her face before the old woman's scuffed, snow-stained boots.

Evelyn pushed herself up, rolling onto her back before feeling the ground rumble next to her cheek. Tansey's foot had burrowed itself into the snow so deep, flecks of frozen dirt dotted the tundra. It was a favorite lesson of hers to have a spontaneous fight in the middle of teaching.

For one as old and thin as Tansey, she was as nimble as any young fighter. Not that Evelyn sparred with anyone else, but she couldn't imagine a more agile partner.

"Where did dragons come from?" Tansey said, throwing out her arm. Evelyn stood, curling her hands around the old woman's wrists.

"Through the making of the world as Celosia sunk to the Depths," Evelyn said as Tansey twisted out of her grasp. She came at her with a series of quick jabs and punches that left her with bruised and sore arms. Evelyn was able to deflect most of the blows, but only barely. Tansey reached inside her cloak for her daggers and Evelyn pulled her arm behind her back.

"Good," Tansey said, panting. "How long is a dragon's memory?" The old woman couched, spinning beneath her arms. She grabbed Evelyn's wrist, bent it against the joint and pulled down. Evelyn cried out and reached up to grab the daggers from Tansey's cloak, her fingers straining against the woman's iron hold. The blade sung as it glided out of its sheath as if thanking her for being of use. Tansey bent her hand harder, dropping Evelyn to her knees. Her legs and one arm were free, but the pain that emitted from her bent wrist blotted out all sense of logic.

"As far back as their race has lived," Evelyn gasped, "Forever—"

Instead of trying to block out the pain, Evelyn embraced it. She let it consume her body and her back arched with the intensity of its power. A moment of clarity broke through the haze, and she growled a controlled scream, letting go of the dagger. She grabbed it with her other hand, lifting it to Tansey's throat with the flat of the blade against her skin.

Her grandmother released a breath as she let go of Evelyn's wrist. The ache in her joint pulsed with blood returning to her hand. She flexed her fingers as the pain receded and flipped the knife around, holding the carved hilt to Tansey.

"Well done," the old woman said as she sheathed the dagger, walking away.

Evelyn followed Tansey into the main square of the village. The smell of the boar roasting in the pit filled the air with its sweet aroma. The moon held high in the sky as the village gathered around the pit, their forms animated in carefree celebration. Evelyn could hear laughter and music as the night's festivities started. It was almost time.

An old man hobbled towards them, his thick boots sliding instead of stepping. Alen's beard hovered above a neck that folded in on itself with cavernous wrinkles. His eyes sagged as if weights were attached to the skin. The oversized maroon tunic he wore fell over padded pants, as the grey scarf around his shoulders grazed his boots. Alen was the village elder that surpassed most lifespans in their little town. He shuffled in small steps with the assistance of a simple wooden cane that rose to his hip. He was the last remaining man who conducted the Eteris Oath as far as she knew. *An old friend to the dragon,* as he had said to her many times during their discussions on the Oathbearing ceremony.

"The sun has set, and Iona's Breath has spun. It is time." His voice was gentle and held a youthfulness that didn't match his outward appearance. His smile was kind as Evelyn breathed in a heavy sigh. Tansey touched her shoulder and kissed her cheek.

"I will be with you—every step," she said.

Evelyn nodded with gratefulness. She could do it alone, but was relieved that she didn't have to.

The villagers lined up along the path that led into the mountains. They were simple folk who hadn't stepped one foot outside of the mountain's view. All they knew were the hardships of bitter winters and the scarcity of hot meals. They loved fire and the companionship of their neighbors. These were her people. There were no grand gestures or outcries of happiness. They only smiled at her, and she felt their strength renew her own. This was where she belonged.

Birdie stood with Maysom in front of her, one arm clasped over the boy's chest. Her eyes were bright as the fire danced across her features. She held out her hand and gently squeezed Evelyn's fingers as she passed through. Maysom looked down at the ground disinterested, not fully understanding the historic moment that was to take place.

Evelyn left the village as they entered the Bena Mountains. Tansey walked a little behind her and Alen, slowing down to accommodate the elder. The old man hummed to himself as they walked through paths and around boulders. The sky had darkened further from the village and Tansey handed out a few torches she carried for the journey. She lit the tips with her flint, fire leading the way into the night. Alen giggled to himself as they walked. Evelyn glanced at the elder, wondering what was on his mind, but deciding not to ask.

"It is a funny thing to grow old," he said as he shuffled along.

Evelyn slowed, concerned for the lack of stamina in the old man. "We can rest if you need to."

"No, child. This is a privilege I thought to be lost to me. I'll not dawdle the anticipation." His face glowed with excitement in the fire light.

Alen was as much a part of her life as her grandmother. She always remembered him with the same lines in his face, the same drooping eyes. He was an eccentric old man that spoke in ways that left the wisest of people puzzled. He was not one to give out complete thoughts, but rather pieces of it for the listener to put together themselves. He was beloved in the community for his strange, but kind ways.

"Tansey says it is a privilege to grow old, which is why she never complains—or so she says."

Alen laughed as he looked back briefly at her grandmother.

"When Tansey was about your age, she claimed to have found a cure for the ailment," he said, running a hand through his beard. "She insisted that partners brought on an early death. That their foolish recklessness aged the men and women who cared for them. That is why she said she'd never marry."

Evelyn chuckled and imagined her gran as a young woman, shrugging off all men in her attempt to remain young.

"You can imagine my surprise when she married Kalen only a few weeks later. I suppose the chance to grow decrepit together was too much a temptation." He showed a somber smile, "So few of us get the chance. I had hoped your grandmother to be one of the exceptions."

Evelyn responded with mournful silence. She never met her grandfather, but what she had heard about him exceeded expectations of the man. He loved to hike the mountains and repair homes, mending broken roofs or leaking walls. He was a simple man, who grew up not three homes down from Tansey.

She had traveled with her Viden mother for most of her life, only vaguely remembering the man as a boy she once played with when she returned. She never gave him a second thought until he asked her to hunt with him. They killed a boar together and hadn't separated until the day he fell from a roof and cracked his head. *It was quick*, her gran said. *He didn't feel any pain, but it took him four days to die.* Evelyn didn't believe he couldn't feel, but she'd never tell her that. There was no need for anyone to tell her Tansey was never the same after his death. She could see it every day in the bearing of her shoulders or the far-off stares into the hearth. There were times late at night when Evelyn woke to the voice of Tansey speaking to Kalen. She'd sit by the door of her room and listen to her grandmother talk about her day. How she feared Izel would burn her breakfast bread yet again or how the small shed keeping the firewood dry was leaking. Most of her conversations consisted of happier memories shared between the two before he died. Evelyn recalled the times she had to act as if she hadn't heard Tansey's stories before, feeling like a carrion bird that had taken a bite of meat not rightfully hers.

"What was she like before?"

Alen lifted his head and gripped his cane tighter as the mountain grew steeper.

"She was ice and fire incarnate," he said with a tone of wonder, "but a slow ember burning, deep under the tundra."

"I have a hard time imagining that or, to be honest, understanding either." Evelyn watched the old man suck on his teeth and smile.

She always pictured Tansey as a whirlwind storm that burned everything it came across. She was passion and flame. Evelyn had difficulty thinking of Tansey as someone who was quiet and still.

"Imagine what you will. The memory of an old man is long, but can still be relied upon. As long as you don't ask what I broke my fast with this morning. I've no room for such trivial moments."

"Is it also the way of the old to speak in such convoluted responses? I asked a simple question and you answered with a riddle."

Alen tapped on his cane and lifted his chin, feigning offense to her words. The torch light darted across the boulders, creating shadows of imaginary creatures.

"It is required of me as elder to answer questions with more questions. How else will the young learn?" He cackled as the torch revealed the dark shape of a large cave opening just up ahead. "You've only as far to look as your own nose to know what your gran was like in her youth."

Evelyn opened her mouth to disagree, but when she turned around, and looked upon the sturdy form of Tansey, she found herself unable to speak. Her body shape and hair length were exactly like her own. The thin shape of her nose and her full cheeks were familiar. Even the movement of her hands as she walked was like looking upon a reflection, just older. Evelyn wondered how she hadn't seen it before. They were the same in almost every way.

"Is it so hard to believe?" Alen said as he watched her realization become truth.

Evelyn was suddenly aware of her path and the implications of what that might mean. Was she doomed to repeat the same choices as her mother and Tansey? To experience the same pains and wounds? There was a shadow that loomed over her life in the form of Nakesha, reminding her of the life she gave to allow Evelyn to live. Could she eventually burn bright enough to dissipate its existence, so that she might thrive without its constant canopy?

They stopped just outside the mouth of the cave which ventured on becoming a crater. The blackness consumed the inside, leaving no light to be seen. Everything she knew was lost in that abyss as if she hadn't prepared at all.

"Do you believe the mistakes of the past linger for those left in their wake?" Evelyn whispered.

Alen lifted his hand to her chin and turned her away from the consuming darkness. His clear eyes brought a sense of solace, and she was able to compose her thoughts again. Tansey stood behind her and Evelyn was comforted by her fortifying presence.

Alen gently let go of her chin, commanding attention with his gaze. "We like to believe we have control over our lives, but we are only one catastrophe away from being different people."

He tapped his cane once more before leading them into the void where all was black.

CHAPTER 6

WAITING

The heat of the bonfire warmed Maun from where he waited beside a small house at the edge of the clearing. The villagers were celebrating with music and dancing. Most were of the older generation and talked amongst themselves while chewing babi meat. A few of the younger women were dancing with their hands lifted in the air. Their thick woolen dresses billowed around them as they spun and laughed.

The younger men watched them with a quiet fear. The fire reflected their insecurities as the women stared back unabashed. They had no idea. There was no anxiety or paranoia, nothing to indicate that they were being watched. As he stared from the shadows, Maun felt a primal glee in his observations. It made it that much more enjoyable when the instinctual awareness of being hunted washed over those he surveyed.

He heard the celebration while searching in the mountains and thought he might find a way to grab an easy meal. Saiya was able to catch an extra rodent a few days back for him, but mostly was only able to hunt for herself. He was capable of tracking and killing a boar, but the fire to cook it would announce all to his presence. Who he was required stealth and secrecy.

Unless he was amongst his fellow Reticent, he was a black blade in the dark. His scarred face would insight questions and when asked, he'd be unable to answer, which would announce his loyalties immediately. Even though he had left the Order to pursue his own goals, he still had a reputation to uphold. At the moment, there was no reason to disrupt the festivities and the people celebrating. It could always change, but for now he sat and waited.

As Maun continued to observe them, he was stunned by how simple they appeared to be. Their primitive lives had no conception to the dangers he possessed. They might think their mountains protected them from the worst of the world, when in reality, he'd never come across a town so exposed. Their homes were little more than huts. He hadn't even seen a blacksmith's forge when slipping into the village.

It was a small town filled with small people.

His stomach ached as the smell of the roasting meat rose and fell with the cold wind. It would disappear just as his hunger pains receded, then make his mouth water with the turn of the breeze. From around the house, a small, high-pitched screech resounded just beyond his eyesight. The cracking of the snow reminded him of the pitter patter of birds as a group of three children ran towards the bonfire.

They were all very young, no more than ten years of age. A little girl with long, black hair smiled brightly at a similar-looking older woman, her thick dress wrapped in an apron. The other two were boys. They pushed each other in the attempt to get some of the roasted babi meat first. The older man, who was cutting the boar, yelled something indistinguishable and immediately the boys ceased their fighting.

They each turned around with a plateful of meat in their hands. The platter was too big for their small frames, and they wobbled on unsteady feet. Maun licked his chapped, frozen lips as the swell of a breeze brought a shiver through him.

The boy with a thick cap sat on the snow next to the other, whose coat of fur was much too big for him. They exchanged words and bit into their meal, grease running down the sides of their mouths. Maun knew he would have to wait for the villagers to retire before he could take a slice of the boar. There were just too many eyes.

He watched the boys eat and imagined what a full belly felt like. He hadn't had one in so long. Involuntarily, his fingers reached for the pocket where he kept the stones. He touched nothing. He sucked a short intake of breath and pushed further into the pocket — nothing. He tore his gaze from the boys, leaned forward and looked down to see himself reaching into the wrong pocket. He closed his eyes and felt the smooth rocks in the one just above it. His breathing leveled out and Maun sighed in relief. He was too hungry. He was skilled in his covertness and weapons prowess, but his head was what made him deadly. That was the blade that needed constant sharpening and this hunger was a crack in the whetstone.

He looked up and his breath stopped in his throat. The boy with the thick, furred cap was staring right at him. His head cocked like an inquisitive dog, curious as to the snake slithering in the sand. Maun could detect firelight reflecting off his face as half of him was leaned forward away from the safety of the shadows.

The boy saw him. There was no denying that. Maun could quickly press himself against the house with the fanciful notion that the boy hadn't, but he had. Maun stared at the boy and leaned back against the house slowly, never tearing his eyes away. He was only a boy, a small child whose revelation would be discarded as a wild imagination.

The other boy next to him stood and walked over to the girl with black hair across the field. The boy with the cap then stood, and lifted a few pieces of meat into his pelted pocket. He walked towards Maun with those light, bird-like footsteps. Maun sunk deeper into the shadows and lifted his cloak around his head. The moonlight only revealed the tip of his nose and the reflection of his intense, blue eyes.

The boy stopped just outside of the shadow Maun hid within, blonde curls peeking from beneath his cap. He was no taller than Maun's hip. His face was still fat with childhood, rosy cheeks spread in a friendly grin that showed a gap in-between his teeth.

"Are you hungry?" the boy said, guileless.

Maun remained as silent and still as the wall he leaned against. The boy shuffled his feet in the snow, turning his head to glance at those in the clearing. None were paying any attention to where the boy was or that he was talking with a stranger.

"My name is Maysom. If you tell me your name, I could introduce you to everyone. There is plenty of food. You could come eat."

The boy was so sincere. His blue eyes matched his own, making Maun wonder if he had ever been that innocent once? The boy had no idea who he was speaking with, no inkling as to how much danger he was in.

Still, Maun said nothing. Saiya touched his mind with a questioning curiosity as to if she should return to him. She was somewhere overhead, circling the village with her black wings. She was better at disappearing than he was. In fact, she was a master at deception. In the night sky she was invisible to everyone, including himself.

He returned her query, asking her to be patient, but to stay close. He and Saiya had conversations that didn't use words. It was more of an exchange of images and feelings. They'd worked their whole lives to attain that level of understanding and trust as all Reticent do. He fought the urge to touch the scars on his face. He had painfully paid the price for their bond. He felt her satisfaction and she continued to circle in the sky.

Maysom nodded his head, trying to encourage Maun to speak with him. Little did he know that Maun couldn't do what he wanted, no matter how hungry he was. He stared at the boy's pockets where the meat was and looked back into the child's blue eyes. He did that a few times before Maysom opened his mouth, revealing the gap in his teeth.

"Oh yes. I brought you some if you want it." He reached into his pockets.

The meat glistened in the firelight. There were some pieces of the fur from Maysom's coat that stuck to the meat, but Maun didn't mind. He reached for the food in one swoop and the boy retreated his hand as though he were feeding a wild animal.

Maun tore into the meat and chewed loudly. He'd forgotten the taste of food long ago and couldn't miss what he couldn't remember. His mouth moved in an awkward way to keep the meat between his teeth. It was curious how much the tongue helped in chewing, but again, he'd been without it for so long there was no other way to him. His stomachache receded with each bite, filling his belly with warmth to combat the penetrating cold. He stared at the boy, who smiled in appreciation.

"Come, there's more. Lot's more," Maysom said as he stepped away.

Maun didn't move and kept chewing as he stared, unblinking. Maysom's smile faded, and Maun felt a modest amount of gratification as the boy's face turned from naïve incorruptibility to watchful anxiety. Maun called Saiya to return to him, but for a slightly more dramatic entrance.

This is what happened when you spoke with strangers. This is what happened when you spoke with *him*. Maysom's eyes darted upwards as Saiya's large wings flapped in the darkness. Neither of them could see her, but her presence loomed like the impending fall of a sharp blade.

Maun stood up and held his arm out, tensing his shoulder for what was to come. Saiya's enormous body landed on his arm with a silent grip. Her talons matched the rest of her, black as midnight. Her wings were spread beyond Maun's head, touching the edges of the roofs.

Her immense weight was nothing to Maun as she leaned forward towards the boy. He'd trained for years to perfect his ability to hold her steady. She blinked her golden eyes, the only splash of color on her besides her blood red tongue. She let out a single caw, black beak sharp in all the terror of a solov raptor.

Maysom sobbed a yell, his eyes growing three times their size in fear. He tried to run away, but he tripped backwards on unsteady feet. Maun smiled and threw back his hood, revealing the scars that crossed over his features. The boy gasped and threw out his hands in a feeble attempt to protect himself.

Maun then opened his lips, displaying his empty mouth. A nub of scarred and torn flesh that used to be his tongue wiggled in the back of his throat. Maysom shut his eyes and screamed a bloodcurdling cry that silenced the celebration across the field.

Maun lifted his arm and Saiya thrashed her wings, sending her into the sky. The boy was still screaming as Maun swept his cloak across the snow, wiping away his footprints before gripping the edge of the bars that supported the neighboring roof and climbing on top. A young woman, who shared Maysom's blonde hair, ran towards the boy, kneeling as she wrapped her arms around him.

"Maysom! What's wrong?" her voice was full of concern. She took off his cap and smoothed out his curls as they fell across his red, swollen face.

"Monster!" he exclaimed in a voice that shuddered with panic.

The young woman looked down the path between the two houses, finding nothing in the form of a monster. She glanced up and Maun fell onto his back, staring up at the night sky.

Smart, that one.

"Maysom. Calm down. You're safe. There's nothing there."

"But there was! I saw a monster. I fed it!"

The snow crunched beneath their feet as Maun heard the two stand. He heard another set of footprints join them.

"What happened?" a lower, older man's voice said.

"Maysom saw something. I think it was a bena wolf. He said he fed it, but I see no prints." The woman's tone underlined disbelief.

"The wild ones don't come down from the mountains," he replied as the sound of his chilled panting slowed.

"Not for some time, but I suppose it's possible for—"

"It wasn't a wolf. I saw a bird," the boy interrupted. He sounded calmer, but still wary.

"It's okay, Maysom. Come, Evelyn will be back soon. It will be her first order as Viden, how does that sound?"

The boy let out a breath that sounded more like a sob.

"I need help storing the rest of the meat, Maysom. I could use a strong lad like you," the man said with reassurance.

"Okay," he whispered.

Their footsteps retreated and only when Maun heard laughter again, did he turn over and peer over the roof. The boy was at the fire, helping the old man who had originally given him food earlier to store the meat in paper wrappings. The young woman had her arms folded and looked in Maun's direction. She couldn't see him, but was staring into the shadowed space in between the houses.

Her face matched perfectly to the boy's. She was a few years younger than Maun and much too young to have a son as old as Maysom. He figured they were siblings. For a few moments more, she continued to look in his direction until she grew tired of the position. She turned her back to him, watching Maysom with a furrowed brow of concern.

Maun propped himself up on his elbows and crouched further down the roof, jumping off behind the house. He leaned against the wall and widened his eyes at the knowledge he'd just gained.

Viden. A living Viden was here. He would never have believed it if it hadn't come from the mouth of a villager. That's what the celebration was for. The Oathbearing.

The dragon he was searching for was closer than he thought.

He grew up with stories of the great mountain dragon that had died in the Eshe Willow Wood, coloring the forest floor with his boiling blood, absorbed inside the Crimson Willow. As with most legends the ending changed from time to time. Some claimed the red dragon succumbed to his severe injuries during the Evandis. Others told the tale of his grief. That in the wake of the decimation of his race, he had tore out his own heart.

Maun heard all these versions and more, but what most intrigued him was a tale that flowed from the mouth of his own father as a child. He was inquisitive at a young age, leaning against the walls of his room to better hear the conversations of the meetings his father forbade him from attending.

He recalled the smell of blood heavy in the air, metallic and rustic.

"I doubt he speaks the truth. The man is mad, Ethen," a voice Maun recognized as Tacet Devu said.

Devu and Ethen were two of the few remaining Reticent's that hadn't earned their raptors yet. Which meant they were still able to talk to one another. The Tacet's Maun saw everyday with the great birds upon their arms never spoke a word and he was still unsure as to why at the time. There was a shuffling of chairs and the hard sound of metal upon wood. His mother was serving drinks as she normally did when Tacet Devu paid them a visit. Maun recognized the pattern of her footsteps, light and dancer-like, although he'd never seen her dance.

"After what you've done to him, surely, he shall remain so. Why? After all these years, why would he suddenly make such a claim? There's nothing in the Bena Mountains but snow and rock." His father's voice echoed with the turmoil of someone's authority being questioned. The tone made Maun flinch as if the back of Ethen's hand had already fallen upon him.

"His claim remained the same even after I took his eyes. He laughed as I ripped them from the sockets," Devu said with a snort, as if amused by the memory. "He lapped up the blood from his cheeks like a dog and repeated the same story of the great, red dragon residing within the depths of the mountains behind the Crimson Willow's legend."

"I've already received reports of those we sent to search. Of the ten we sent three returned, one insisting that if a dragon hid, the beast would've lost its way long ago in the tunnels as the others did. They claim that Isla's Reach burrows deep into those peaks."

There was a long pause as Ethen lifted his cup, the sound of his breath intake matching the steady, swallowing gulps of ale.

"I've never met a man that wouldn't change his story under the pain I inflict. A man would bare his back and flay his own skin if I told him to be a shedding reptile. A man would become the shape I mold him to be, but this one—" Maun imagined Devu shaking her head, dark eyes intense. "This one's been molded already. Cinaed might've given him his life for what he'd done to shape our order, but the life he spared is hollowed out by delusions and stories that will be forgotten in the new age to come. A storyteller he truly is, for they are but stories."

Ethen huffed and grunted as the sound of his chair shrieked across the floor, Ovia's gasp accompanied the soft brushes of clothes against each other.

"What do you think, love? Has the last mountain dragon escaped us?" Ethen growled low in the back of his throat. Maun's mother hummed a returning growl as Ethen gasped in pain. She probably pulled his head back by his hair. She always did that in preparation of a strike from him.

"We have enough wind and water dragons to satisfy all the blood hunger you have, *love*," Ovia spoke the word back at him with playful contempt. "This is a tale for children like Maun. I am surprised you've allowed it to go so far. Do you think Cinaed will appreciate his Falconer eyeless?"

"Cinaed's thoughts are bent on the Evandis. He's not got one to spare for the broken man. He's been mad for so long we can claim he'd done it to himself. We are needed, Ovia, and he'll not abandon us." Devu spoke with the true fortitude of a seasoned Reticent, even if unpaired with a raptor. Maun admired the way she spoke of Cinaed the Decayed, the man who would provide free will to all in Iona. Although it sent a shiver down his spine to imagine this Falconer sitting in some dark corner, eyeless and laughing.

He listened for a while longer, but sleep soon claimed him and he fell into darkness with the fading image of blind dragons, gnawing at their own hides.

Maun never forgot that night. He even attempted to find the eyeless man in between lessons and meals. He never found him, nor heard any mention of him from that point on. Eventually, he grew to accept that the man had died in the years that followed, but Maun carried that story with him to the day he sat on a roof, listening to a woman unknowingly betray the only person who could protect her.

Maun had found that willow, picking up Celosia's Glare in between the twisted roots. It was true the great tree had a crimson look about it. He stared through the forest, past the weeping branches and eventually set his sights on the high peaks of the Bena Mountains. Their monolithic heights scattering the clouds to create their own weather, promising blistering cold and misery. He decided on his path then, and the surge of vengeance lit so hot he thought the snow he traveled into might melt before him. There was but one choice for him —to find those he could exact his retribution upon. Someone to focus the heat of anger and to burn them screaming within it. He had to get there before Evelyn, this Viden, bonded herself to the dragon.

His chance for vengeance would be lost if she bonded before he could make his request to glance into the past. To the day his father died. He shot out a thought to Saiya to fly into the mountains. To search for any signs of travel through the passes. She sent him an acknowledgement and Maun darted in-between the houses, heading for the Bena Mountains that surrounded the village.

It was unwise to have caused such a scene with the boy, but Maun couldn't help the smile that crossed his face as he remembered his terrified screams. Had he not given into temptation, he never would've found out about the Viden. He had Maysom to thank for the pleasure Maun would feel as he slit her throat. After all, that's what his order did once upon a time. The Reticent weren't always assassins for hire. They were still the most feared killers in all of Iona. The ones responsible for the demise of countless Videns.

Saiya sent him an image of three people entering a cave, high up in the trail beyond where Maun had previously made camp. He narrowed his eyes as he ran along the path imagining his blade in the chest of the one who caused him so much pain. The one that the dragon would show him, even if it meant the death of everyone in that cave.

CHAPTER 7

OATHBEARING

For what seemed like an immeasurable amount of time all Evelyn could see was what the torch allowed, which was hardly more than a few feet in front of her. The cave was silent, the only sound being the tap of Alen's cane resonating into the void beyond them. By its echo, she could tell the tunnel was enormous. Evelyn knew Isla's Reach —the labyrinthine grottos that burrowed underground from the boiling waters of Elm Lake throughout all of Iona, stretched far into the mountains, but she hadn't known just how large the caverns would be. The poem of Isla's Reach was a song well known to her, having been her favorite when she was a child. As the tune goes, Isla had become the great elm tree in the middle of Elm Lake. She created the tunnels with her roots, searching for her lost love, who had been killed by her Unnamed Sister. Evelyn had always been drawn to the most tragic of tales. Though the poem was merely a legend to explain the elm and Isla's Reach, Evelyn wondered how strong a grief it would take to transform into something as stoic as an elm.

As she continued forward, the torchlight revealed the tunnel's end into a massive holding, revealing the heart of the cave. Alen's cane struck like thunder within the cavern, leveling Evelyn's breath that was suddenly so loud. The air in the room was heavy and warm, sticky with heat. She flung the sides of her cloak over her shoulders and looked at Tansey, who was mesmerized by her surroundings. The old woman's eyes darted back and forth, trying to find something solid to hold onto. Evelyn turned around and saw Alen pressing forward. She walked lightly after, stepping over rocks and thickets of broken roots. Then Alen stopped, staring ahead into the endless blackness. Evelyn tried to follow his line of sight, but couldn't make something out of nothing.

"Old friend, it is good to see you again." Alen's voice was powerful in the rocky tomb.

He didn't hold out his arms or bow his head. His expression was that of one greeting an old acquaintance, lost in the space of many years. The winkles around his eyes burrowed deeper, the torch's flicker revealing the severity of his old age. Moments passed and nothing happened. Evelyn was about to speak when she felt a shift in the air. A warm breeze that shouldn't have been so deep in the cave passed over her, smelling of burnt wood and smoke. Iona's Breath was old and worn as if its current had never been outside.

A deep rumbling shook the floor, causing Evelyn to spread her legs in an instinctive defense stance. Tansey did the same beside her. Alen was as tranquil as the Omya, without even a twitch to indicate discomfort. A deep growl shattered through the darkness, matching the vibrations of Evelyn's heart. It centered her soul, wrapping her from foot to head with a melodic hum. While it was loud and mighty, it was also delicate and smooth, somewhere in between a rising song and a bellowing storm. Every bone in her body sang with it.

A bright light forced her eyes shut as an intense heat filled the ceiling of the cave. She dropped her torch in surprise, crouching to the floor with Tansey. Alen remained standing, his face a mask of joy. He swayed in the waves of heat, white hair blowing behind his shoulders. His scarf flew off, landing at the entrance to the tunnel, but he didn't spare it a glance. The old man was bathed in light, mesmerized by what had created it.

Evelyn stood, awestruck as she gazed about the cavern. Throughout the ceiling were blazing roots, hanging to illuminate the entire cave. The bark cracked and hissed as flecks of ash floated above her head. Glowing embers twinkled, creating a star-filled sky under the mountain. Throughout the cavern were dozens of tunnels, leading in different directions deeper into the mountains. Isla's Reach beckoned, and she was sure if she were to travel any of them, she'd never see the sun again.

In the middle of the cave was a giant rock glistening in the light. It shimmered, reflecting the flames around it. The grooves were split as if shattered by a hammer blow and fused back together, illuminating another entrance to a tunnel that burned with an intense fire. Evelyn moved to walk towards it when the tunnel blinked, revealing itself to be a giant, glowing, red eye. Evelyn gasped. The iris was surrounded in black pigments of red veins pulsating with life. The center narrowed itself into a diamond shaped cats' pupil, dilating its curiosity. Through the rumble of lethargic movements and resounding vibrations, the rock became a dragon.

Oretem was larger than Evelyn could've ever imagined. His thick legs were grounded by ebony claws, cracking the floor beneath him as he righted. Red scales glowed bright in the firelight like blood on the snow. His jaw was short and muscled with crooked fangs as long as her arm and as thick as the sail post on Sou's ship. His neck curved with regality as the spikes on the top of his head touched the burning roots so high above her. The dragon could swallow them whole without the mercy of skewering them between his fangs first. This powerful predator was a mountain dragon. Only a mountain would be capable of housing a creature of his size. How the Vagu were ever able to create the first bonds she'd never know. Alen stepped forward; his head turned up as far as it could go.

"Oretem, it's been so long, my friend. I have brought you a bondsmate. Evelyn is her name." Alen held out his hand towards Evelyn, who hadn't taken her eyes away from the dragon.

She knew to earn respect she had to maintain eye contact. Oretem followed in suit, lowering his head to meet her gaze. The urge to flinch rose within her, tightening her muscles as she fought her body's natural response to cower before a predator. For she was most certainly prey. His single, glistening eye bore into her as though he could see into the core of her being; she shivered despite the cave's rising heat.

WHO SPEAKS FOR THE WISP?

Oretem's voice trembled with the scraping of rocks, quaking the ground with a soft thunder. Evelyn forced herself to keep her eyes open, fighting against the roar his voice pounded into her head. She nearly turned away as panic flooded her heart.

Speak for me? Who would speak for me?

"I do," Tansey spoke in an equally authoritative tone. Evelyn exhaled in relief and huffed a quiet chuckle to hear Tansey take on the challenge of a dragon with such confidence. She shouldn't have expected anything else from the stubborn woman.

MY LINEAGE IS LONG AND MY CLAWS ARE SHARP. MY FANGS HAVE TASTED BLOOD AND MY WINGS HAVE BATTLED STORMS. MY BONDS HAVE BEEN MANY AND ALL FEARSOME WARRIORS. THE PAST REMEMBERS THEM, AS I DO. FOR WHAT REASON SHALL I ACCEPT THIS WISP OF TWIG AS MY BONDSMATE?

His languid tone was slow, but still demanding in its authority. The burden of her grandmother's safety gravitated into Evelyn's chest, making it harder to breath as Tansey stepped forward. The great eye of Oretem still watched over Evelyn, unblinking as stone.

"My granddaughter is swift with the knife and a friend to the wolf. Her dreams travel from the sleeping world to the waking one. Her great-grandmother, Arlisa, was bonded to Noha the Cunning, the Bright Fanged." Oretem shifted his head to the side in recognition as Tansey continued. "She possesses an inquisitive mind shared with an open heart. She is young and insightful, stubborn but tenacious, and above all, kind to her very core. There is unyielding strength in her as adaptable as a river, yet immovable as this mountain. For her, I vouch."

Evelyn struggled to control the roiling emotions threatening to burst from her chest. Tansey had always been hard on her, but never once had she given up. She had formed Evelyn into the woman she was now, and she felt she hadn't thanked her enough. The love that radiated within her matched the heat of the flames above, bright and everlasting. Evelyn wanted to look at her, to see that same love reflected, but kept her gaze on Oretem, refusing to give him any reason to deny her. She'd worked too hard for this. Her hair tangled in a gust of the dragon's hot breath. He blinked then raised his head, turning towards Tansey.

Evelyn let out a breath and Alen waved his hand in the air with excitement. She looked back at Tansey, who remained still as a statue. Oretem towered over her and somehow, the old woman still seemed to be the mightiest creature in the room.

THE BOND IS RECEIVED, AND THE WORDS ACCEPTED. His long, thick neck turned towards Alen in a methodic motion. YOU'VE SHRUNK, OLD FRIEND.

Alen laughed, his mirth filling the firelit cave.

"'Tis the weight of not seeing you. I'll grow ten spans after this."

The dragon released a sound that resembled a rockslide, tumbling into glass and breaking through ice. Evelyn smiled as she realized Oretem was laughing—she didn't know dragons could laugh.

Alen nodded his head and turned towards Evelyn. She met his eyes, knowing what would happen. She'd known all her life and the time was now. She took in a deep breath, surprised to realize her hands weren't shaking, yet she was breathless with fear. It wasn't for the dragon before her, white teeth glistening and red hide burning. She was afraid of how much the bond would change her. Would she leave this cave as the Evelyn she'd always been or a stranger to everyone she'd known her whole life?

"In honor of Eteris, the first bonded dragon, we perform the Eteris Oathbearing between Oretem and Evelyn. The oath is of your own making." He gestured to Evelyn. "Monia, the first bondsmate, had no witnesses. No lavish ceremony. She spoke what couldn't be written and thus your words will not be recorded."

Tansey glanced sideways at Oretem as though cautious of a sudden attack. Alen was undeterred and looked in between Evelyn and the great mountain dragon as if performing a marriage. In a way, they would be bonded as though they had entered one. She and Oretem would break, souls shared to become parts of a whole.

"Evelyn is ready to receive her gift," Alen concluded as he touched her shoulder, stepping away to allow Oretem to approach.

The dragon lifted a claw to his neck and a snap echoed in the cave. The crackle of fire overhead soothed the room with its repetitive pitch, diming to a low glow. Oretem lowered his claw and held out a single scale the size of her palm. Gem-like it glowed red in the shadows as though a single drop of blood had landed on his obsidian claw.

We shall share a soul, you and I. Leave the scale if there be any doubt. Once touched our bond is set.

Oretem's graveled voice was firm, but held a compassion that spoke to years of experienced wisdom. He was old, much older than any being in Iona. She stared at the scale, wondering if it would feel as heavy as it looked. It represented all the years of study and practice, her thoughts and insecurities. There could be no room for doubt. She fell inward, passing through all she thought to be and all she could be. Oretem kept her gaze, eyes impenetrable. This was her choice, and he would not influence it. Evelyn couldn't remember what Nakesha looked like, but she imagined her mother standing next to her, strong and unbent. She had made a choice and Evelyn realized how hard it must've been for her to make it.

When life leads to a split path, more than often the right way is the one we'd do anything not to take.

She lifted the scale from Oretem's claw, feeling its smooth surface radiating a soft heat. It didn't burn, but the air above her hand steamed, wisps of vapor swirling about her fingers. The heat ran through her arm into her stomach, down her legs and inside her chest. Iona's Breath twisted about her, chaotic streams of glowing, blue tendrils. She tried to follow the wisps, but the ringlets moved too fast. She could see the air around her as if Iona's Breath were a living being, embracing her as a moth in its cocoon. The wind caressed her skin, running through her as easily as sunlit snow. Within a moment it dissipated, blue tendrils disappearing as the embers hanging above returned with their light. The scale in her hand throbbed, pulsating with radiant, red veins.

THE OATH, WISP, Oretem said, but this time it was different.

His graveled voice echoed in her head as though she were its source. She looked at Tansey and Alen, wondering if they'd heard Oretem, but their blank expressions confirmed his words were for her only. She faced the red dragon, who had folded his legs beneath himself. She wasn't sure what she was supposed say, only that the words were for Oretem and him alone.

I am a woman of no extravagance. I have no great battles to boast of, nor difficult feats I've conquered. I only have my little village and the simple people who reside there. Each one of them is an entire world, possessing the love and pain of what makes life so sweet. Together, they create a universe of utterly ordinary people whom I could not love more were I to rip out my own beating heart. I have bonded for them, to live for them, and to one day die among them. Evelyn breathed out and the dragon blinked, his scaled features expressionless.

Her fingers clutched the throbbing scale, feeling his indifference to a creature so small as she, but also a deep respect for what she had said. He thought she was brave. She kept her eyes locked on his, refusing to lose the regard he'd placed in her. Oretem lowered his head, baring his teeth into a low growl. Tansey tensed beside her, but Evelyn knew the dragon wasn't threatening her. He was impressed, pride breaking through the indifference.

A WISP YOU MAY BE, BUT THERE IS A GREAT STORM ROILING WITHIN YOU. I CAN FEEL IT. IT HAS BEEN SOME TIME SINCE I HAVE HAD SUCH A TEMPEST TO CLAIM. MY WINGS ARE YOURS AND MY PAST IS YOURS. TOOTH AND CLAW, WE WILL BLEED FOR EACH OTHER.

Oretem opened his mind and Evelyn's joints buckled as her head snapped back, gasping against the cosmic weight of his age and memory. She broke and the pain was incredible. She groaned as the vacuous space was replaced with fire, burning her as one cauterizes the flesh. She fell back, losing her balance. Tansey gasped, catching her before she had hit the ground. Alen shuffled over and placed a hand over her brow, his fingers cold against her searing skin. He said something to Tansey, and she gripped Evelyn's arm, pulling her up. She was half carried out of the cave, the winters chill greeting her like a blanket to her fever. Darkness separated from the light, retreating from the other as though fleeing from a battle lost. Evelyn blinked, slowly regaining her breath as her fever dissipated. Oretem's voice echoed in her mind as though from a distance.

PEACE, WISP. LET IT GO. WE ARE ONE.

Evelyn pried her fingers off Oretem's scale, letting it fall to the snow at her feet. Immediately, her thoughts were her own and she rested a hand on her chest, staring into Tansey's worried expression. The old woman's brown eyes were sharp, wandering over Evelyn's features.

"Are you alright? Can you speak?" she asked.

"Yes, I'm fine. I just need a moment," Evelyn sat on a boulder, watching the spectacle of Iona's Breath surrounding her. She could see it. The air that surrounded them all. It was everywhere. She summoned it to her hand and watched the blue strands dance along her fingers. It was the first time she had called the wind in front of someone other than Nakesha and the relief she felt at revealing herself was immense. She glanced up at Alen and Tansey, but their eyes remained focused on her, not Iona's Breath. They could not see it.

The red scale's glowing veins had disappeared when she had dropped it, but its brilliance was not lost. Evelyn lowered her hand to pick it up, but stopped just before doing so. The bond was directly linked to that scale, and she didn't want to lose consciousness again. She had to get used to the feeling, but at the top of the mountain wasn't the best place to practice. She wrapped a hand in her cloak and lifted the scale. The necklace Sou had given her fell from the confines of the fabric, swinging before her. She fingered the space where the brass coils surrounded the empty vessel. It was the perfect size for a dragon's scale. She placed it in that space and the coils wrapped around it entirely like a jeweled piece. She allowed the necklace to hang over her cloak to avoid contact with the skin.

Tansey stared at the necklace with wide eyes as if recognizing the craftsmanship. She reached out to touch it, but lowered her hand, meeting Evelyn's eyes as though she had caught her in a lie. The look was gone in a moment, and she smiled.

"Well, we've avoided seeing the inside of a dragon's belly. Let's celebrate that." The old woman blinked several times, clearing a thought. "I'm going to have to get used to that."

Tansey pointed at her face and Evelyn averted her gaze in remembrance. The color of her eyes would change to the color of her bonded dragon. They would be a deep shade of red now, the whites overtaken by crimson. The thought was unexpectedly unsettling. Everyone who looked upon her would know what she was. Evelyn ran a finger over her brow, unsure how to feel about the physical change the bond had required.

"Why did you not tell me I would need to be vouched for?"

Tansey shrugged, grimacing an apologetic smile.

"Not every Viden bonded to a dragon before the war. There were too many of them and not enough dragons. The creatures are notoriously selective. Though it was unlikely, Oretem might've rejected your bond. I could say that I did not want to worry you with such an improbable outcome, but honestly, it slipped my mind."

Evelyn rolled her eyes, attempting to reign in her frustration and slow her beating heart. The simple thought of not being able to accomplish what she'd spent her entire life training for weighed heavily on her. Tansey gripped Alen's hand, helping him climb down the pass. Everything seemed brighter to Evelyn. The sounds of the mountains were sharper, and the darkness was less daunting. Her feet were better planted, able to avoid tripping in places she had before. She caught up to Tansey and Alen, lost in her own thoughts as they talked amongst themselves.

They approached the edge of a cliff, seeing the distant flicker of the bonfire burning in the middle of Verbena. Evelyn heard the soft sounds of celebration, nothing more than a whisper, but more than what she had been able to hear before. She smiled and gazed up at the stars above, alight with the Iona's Breath. She was Viden. So much was going to change, and she greeted the prospect like it was Sou's boat ready for her departure into a new world.

CHAPTER 8

THE SETTLING OF GRIEVANCES

The air was hot with the scent of sweat and laughter. Evelyn's hands were in the air as she spun around the bonfire. Her dress billowed around her as if it would soar her into the air, and the faces of her neighbors dancing blurred with her movement, making them as unformed as the wind. Their elation mixed with her own and she was wholly herself under the night sky. The chilled night would've stilled her dancing, but her leggings beneath the thick dress kept the warmth in. Combined with her exuberant leaping and the fire she circled; it was almost too warm. She stepped to the side, trying to maneuver from the path of a running child. She was suddenly halted by a soft body, cushioned instead of beaten by hardened muscle.

"Sorry," she said as she faced a plump, middle-aged woman, her dark skin lit golden in the fire's light. Izel waved her hand with a laugh, lifting skirts that were normally covered by her baker's apron.

"Keep dancing, my girl! The Breaths and Depths know your knees won't be young forever," Izel said as she limped a slow trot to the edges of the fire, away from the celebrating villagers. Evelyn caught up with her, linking her arm through the baker's.

"My knees can spare a few moments."

Izel stared at her feet with careful consideration, leaning on her arm for support. Once she'd placed the baker on one of the many benches, Evelyn turned towards the fire, absorbing its heat.

"Always been a kind one, you have. Even if you were once a wee girl running and stealing my best bread. How you have —oh!" she exclaimed as Evelyn looked down on her. The surprise was unmistakable in Izel's tone, but what Evelyn found most disheartening was the hint of fear she'd heard. It snaked itself around the woman's kind words and twisted them, smothering them to nothing more than what Izel saw reflected in Evelyn's red eyes: a stranger.

"I hope I can make up for my mischievous childhood for my favorite sweet baker," she said, choosing to ignore and mask the hurt Izel had unintendedly bestowed upon her. Izel nodded with a forced smile, averting her gaze to the fire with an uncomfortable shift in her seat.

"Thank you, my dear. I will be well enough on my own now. Run along. I believe your friend is in need of a steady hand as well." Izel's light tone returned with a chuckle as Birdie stumbled from the dancing circle towards her, swaying as she did so. Evelyn left the baker, glad to be in the company of one who wouldn't care about the color of her eyes.

When she stood in front of her friend, Evelyn couldn't stop the laugh that sprung from her lungs as Birdie grabbed her hand, spinning in circles until she lost her grip, dropping to the ground. She continued to laugh as Birdie slipped and sunk deeper into the snow. She held out a hand to her friend. Birdie tried to swipe it away but missed, nearly falling on her back again. Her long braid was half undone, whisked in swirling golden strands that looked as if she'd just woken from a long sleep. Evelyn held her hand out again, confident Birdie was incapable of standing on her own.

"I don't need—Depths—I can stand," she stuttered.

"Of course, you can. You could probably balance on the tip of a babi's tusk," Evelyn said, her voice exaggerated with sarcasm. She grasped her friend's hand and led her away from the dancing circle. They sat down far enough where they'd be out of the way, but close enough to watch and clap if they wanted to.

"This is what I was afraid of," Birdie said as she pouted her lips in mock disappointment.

"Afraid of what, exactly?" Evelyn goaded, wanting to collect as many weapons to use against her friend as she could for a well-deserved teasing.

"You..." she pointed at Evelyn between the eyes, "You can't tell me what to do. I will—will not allow it."

The blue lengths of air that floated all around them matched the color of Birdie's eyes. They were also just as disjointed and chaotic, spinning around her with no pattern at all.

"I have no intention of telling you what to do, Birdie. When has that ever worked out for me?"

Evelyn made a point to always let Birdie do what Birdie does. When they were children, Birdie wanted to climb one of the cliffs. Evelyn knew, even then, that her friend would do it with or without her. She agreed only if Birdie consented to watch her cross the Omya on Nakesha's back. She'd always wanted to see the other side of the river. At the time the wolf was no larger than a common dog and she quickly succumbed to the churning ice water before Sou pulled them out. Although, as Evelyn remembered, she had almost made it. The following day Evelyn climbed the cliff anyway, as Birdie considered the bargain fulfilled. It was the way Birdie went about everything in life.

"That's right. Never!" she shouted much too loud before lowering her voice into a slurred child-like tone, "I want to dance again."

Evelyn chuckled as Birdie stared at her own two feet, as though willing them with nothing but a look to transport her to the dancing circle. When nothing happened, she huffed a disappointed sigh.

"My feet aren't working!" she said with a panicked shriek.

Drunk Birdie overexaggerated simple tasks and underexaggerated larger issues.

Evelyn kicked Birdie's foot but still, her friend wouldn't stand. She gasped with her hands on either side of her jaw.

"You're trying to help. Thank you!" she wrapped an arm around Evelyn's shoulder and almost knock her flat.

"Birdie, just get up. You are so drunk," Evelyn said while laughing.

As Evelyn's eyes were downcast, a pair of leather-strapped boots came into view. She looked up and met the brown eyes of Adel. He was the grandson of Alen and one of the few young men who hadn't left for adventures. He was a few years older than Birdie and had an eye for her best friend since childhood. Now that they were both of age their previously platonic relationship was eagerly forming into one of a more serious and late night one.

His hair was bright red with ringlets that resembled the tight coils in some metal work she'd seen when one wanted a door to spring open. The freckles that spread across his round face gave him youthful features that would last for his entire life. He was so much taller than all the men in Verbena that the widowed women would call him to their house to reach a particular pan or wipe the snow off their roofs.

He smiled at Evelyn and raised an eyebrow at Birdie, who mirrored his expression with a questioning smirk.

"I wonder, did the mead never arrive or did you drink it all?" his voice mocking.

"I poured it down your waste hole. Enjoy the smell of shite and alcohol." Birdie leaned back on her hands, seemingly proud of her clever retort.

The village was alight with music. The sound of snow crunching beneath those dancing was an awkward backdrop to the current conversation. Instead of taking offense, Adel laughed, long and loud. He swayed just a bit in the moonlight, and Evelyn thought not all the mead was gone. His earnest expression lifted her heart as he spoke.

"Did you really?"

Birdie leaned forward and shrugged with a nonchalant attitude.

"I bet I could dance it out of you," he said while holding out his hand.

Birdies eyes shone in just a moment of soberness, and she smiled, raising her hand to allow him to bring her to her feet.

"Who knows what you could dance me out of," she said, and left him for the dancing circle, her stride surprisingly steady and straight.

Alen looked at Evelyn with astonished eyes. It appeared Birdie was courting him back in her own way.

"Well, go get her." Evelyn waved her hand at Adel, who, with a start, jogged after Birdie.

The two linked hands and spun around each other in a clumsy mess of inebriated joy. Evelyn knew Birdie truly liked Adel and hoped for the best outcome of their new courtship. She watched the couple dance for a while, then decided she wanted to join. She stood up, but as she took a step towards the bonfire Tansey came up from behind her. Birdie looked in Evelyn's direction and pointed beyond her, mouthing *behind you.*

Evelyn nodded in feigned thanks for her delayed warning and turned around to meet her grandmother. The night had been so pleasant. Everything had gone according to plan, and she had finally fulfilled her mother's sacrifice. She wanted to enjoy the evening with Tansey, but she knew the conversation they were about to have would not be easy.

"You slew a meaty boar. Eleri had his work cut out for him," she pointed at the cook, who was finally resting on the bench beside his wife, Izel. The paper wrappings filled with the meat he and Maysom had stored together laid steaming in the cold. They clapped in synch with one another, watching the festivities with contented smiles. She wondered if they knew how their movements mirrored each other as if an invisible string tied them together.

"He went out fighting," she agreed.

The necklace Sou gave her rested on her chest, shimmering its glow across Tansey's face.

"Who gave you that necklace?" Evelyn could hear the strangled control in the old woman's voice.

"I think you know who. The same person who can't come to this feast because you refuse to see him." Evelyn wasn't planning on cutting with a sharpened edge of the blade, but there it was.

"Evelyn, there's much you don't—"

"Apparently not. I suppose I'll find out tomorrow when I see Sou."

Evelyn felt a guilty satisfaction at her grandmother's wary expression. She folded her arms and lined her lips as if preparing for battle.

"Anything that man has to say he can say in front of me." Her voice ringed in betrayal.

"That was the original plan, was it not?" Her grandmother huffed as Evelyn continued. "He said he wanted you there, but that he'd tell me whatever it is with or without you," she said, softening her voice.

"I don't know what he is talking about." Tansey looked away stubborn as ever.

Evelyn sighed as she reigned in her frustration and gripped the old woman's tense hand.

"Gran," she said gently, "Please. I've been a grown woman for some time now—" she paused at the disbelieving look Tansey shot her, "Notwithstanding this evening's childish escape." The old woman relaxed at Evelyn's admission, and she continued, "It's time I've learned everything there is to know about Nakesha. She's my mother." Tansey's furrowed brow was all the confirmation Evelyn needed to know about what would be said in tomorrow's conversation.

She upturned her hand and returned Evelyn's grip. Her fingers were strong and thin.

"I know." Tansey's voice cracked in regret. "I've been protecting you for so long that I lose sight of what is I think I'm shielding you from. Make no mistake," she held out a finger, "I stand by my decision to withhold what we will discuss tomorrow until you were bonded."

Evelyn nodded her head. "Sou said much of the same."

"On that we agree."

"Again, the same," she said a little exasperated.

Mind your tone.

Evelyn blinked away the sudden breeze that had accompanied Tansey's voice, the tone mindful and direct.

"What?" Evelyn asked even though she hadn't seen Tansey's mouth open.

"I said nothing," she responded with confusion.

"I know you said nothing, but I heard you."

"What did you hear?" Tansey cocked her head with interest.

Evelyn told her and waited as Tansey touched her hand to her chin, thinking. Just when she was about to ask what the old woman was doing, she spoke.

"Did you hear that?"

"What? No." Evelyn was confused.

"Hmm," she paused, "You didn't hear that either, huh?"

"Gran, you're not helping," Evelyn said as she tried to keep the irritation out of her voice. Tansey continued speaking as though she hadn't heard her.

"Good thing too. You would not have liked that thought. No one wants to think of their grandmother that way."

Evelyn slapped her hands on either side of her hips. "Thought? Think of you in what way?"

She gestured towards Birdie and Adel dancing close and slow.

"I don't mind—" she paused as she recognized the raised eyebrows on Tansey's face as a woman who knew what it was like to be caught in compromising positions. Evelyn grimaced.

"Oh, gran," she exclaimed as she tried to force the image out of her head.

I'm as desirable as you. Tansey's voiced flew through the air, blue light traveling with the speed of a needle through fabric.

"Yes, but—" Evelyn stopped talking as she opened her mouth in a wide shocked expression.

"That's what it is!" Tansey clapped her hands in triumph. "You can hear the voices of those around you, their thoughts."

"I can hear your thoughts?" Evelyn wanted to immediately practice this new ability, but when she tried to connect with Tansey's mind there was nothing to hear. She saw no tendrils of Iona's Breath as before.

"Not exactly. I was thinking thoughts for you to hear like *eat yellow snow, love of my life.*" Evelyn rolled her eyes. "But you couldn't hear them. Then I tried to send them to you like a message and still nothing. It was only when I allowed you to hear them that you could listen."

Tansey's smile broke into countless wrinkles of a life lived.

"So, only when you want me to hear them." It made sense to Evelyn the more she thought of it. Especially since it had been an accident when hearing Tansey's thoughts. She really did want Evelyn to watch her tone.

"It's Oretem's gift," Tansey said.

"I thought dragons only bestowed one gift?"

"They do, have you more abilities?" Tansey leaned in, confused.

"I can see Iona's Breath." She waved her hands at the blue strands all around her even if Tansey couldn't see it.

"Oh, all Videns can see the wind. Us mere common folk cannot although some of the Videns powers were visible to us. I was witness to a great many times Arlisa breathed her healing into another. How she glowed." Tansey paused, lost in memory before continuing. "Seeing the wind makes it easier to control. Iona's Breath is what gives dragons their flight and so once bonded you've a special connection with it as they do. I've taught you that."

Evelyn couldn't remember a time when Tansey had spoken of it, but she decided not to argue the point. She knew now and that was what mattered. Tansey smiled and held her arm out. Evelyn nestled her shoulder in Tansey's embrace and closed her eyes at its perfect warmth. It was moments like this that cemented their relationship. Here, within the muscled arms of an old warrior, was where Evelyn felt most safe. The closest embrace she had to a mother's touch and a love to last through the coldest of winters. They stood like that, with the cold at their backs and the fire in front of them before Tansey spoke again.

"That necklace you're wearing, it was your great grand-mother's."

Evelyn straightened out of Tansey's arms, looking down at the necklace resting on her chest.

"Arlisa." Evelyn was stunned that such a fragile piece of jewelry had lasted so long. "How did Sou come by it?"

It wasn't a difficult question and as soon as she asked it Evelyn knew the answer. What she didn't know was why he would take it from her dying mother, keep it and not give it to Tansey.

Tansey's words echoed with the deep ache of a wound that had never fully healed. "I gave it to him. He was more deserving of its possession than I."

Evelyn was shocked. Tansey never spoken of Sou with such kindness. The old woman could hardly stand to hear the man's name and she had gifted him something that had belonged to her dead daughter? Evelyn disagreed wholeheart-edly with her words, but she knew that once Tansey had spoken there was no convincing her otherwise. In the dancing circle, Birdie shooed away Maysom, who had tried to trip her as she danced.

"So, you will come?"

Tansey revealed the barest hint of a smile, a crack in her stone-like appearance.

"I will come."

Birdie broke away from the circle to collect Evelyn, grip-ping her arms hard and pulling her away, but not before Evelyn mouthed *thank you* to her grandmother.

As nervous as she was at the outcome of tomorrow, she only had what she could control today. She was surrounded by loved ones and dear friends. Birdie released her hold on

Evelyn and wrapped her arms around Adel's neck, who was singing off key with the music.

Maysom was quiet on the sidelines, eyeing a space in between the houses as if waiting for something to come out of the shadows. She turned around to see Tansey resting a hand against her heart, a somber smile creasing her beautifully aged features. Alen stood beside her, clapping as the beat of the drums and strings sped up in tempo. Eleri appeared behind Evelyn with Izel in his arms, holding her above the ground as he spun. He lowered her until her feet rested on top of his, allowing her to dance through the weakness of her knees. The baker and cook met her eyes, their smiles infectious and wholesome. The past offence was forgotten as Izel kissed her husband's cheek, joining in the celebration as if she were just as young as the rest of them.

CHAPTER 9

THE DECAY OF ALL LIVING

"Maysom? Oh, there you are," Birdie said as her little brother's small stature made itself known beside her.

Evelyn walked behind Birdie and Adel as they stood in front of her friend's home. Maysom shifted closer to his sister, periodically glancing into the surrounding darkness. Birdie had a much better hold of her mental faculties after Evelyn brought food and water to her. She still, however, wanted to make sure her friend made it back safely. It wouldn't be the first time someone had indulged themselves in mead far enough to lose their way home, freezing to death but a few strides from their warm hearth.

"Birdie, I'm tired," Maysom said, tugging at her dress.

His sister noticed, but gave him a stern look as she gazed back at Adel who couldn't take his eyes off her. Now that they were home Evelyn thought she'd help her friend in her wooing endeavors.

"Come with me, Maysom. I'll get you ready for bed. Birdie will be in shortly." She held out her hand for the boy to take.

He looked at Birdie once more, who was lost in conversation about hunting strategies. Adel was keenly interested in how the words were forming on her friends' lips. Maysom took Evelyn's hand as she led him beyond the door and into the house. The home was divided into three separate areas. The kitchen, living space, and a hallway leading to two rooms for Birdie and Maysom. Birdie's room used to be their parents. It took her a long time to occupy it after they had died.

Dirty dishes soaked in a bucket under a film of ice and soap. The wooden cupboards were closed and cracked with age. Her eye followed a fissure reaching towards the ceiling, hairline thin but stretching across the central pillar that kept the roof together. It, combined with dozens of more splits, threatened to become a crevasse in a few years if left unattended. The home had belonged to their family for generations and hadn't seen a carpenter in just as long. Adel was only a baker's apprentice, but in a small village like theirs everyone had more than one vocation. She made a mental note to ask the man to have a look around the house and see what he could fix.

"Go clean yourself up and climb into bed I'll be there in a moment," she said as she took off his cap.

His messy hair stuck out in all directions of golden spirals, springing to life around his plump features. The blue in his eyes shone of fatigue and he smiled just a touch. His little feet ran to the hallway, and he disappeared behind the door of his room.

Evelyn went into the kitchen and broke the ice from the bucket. It rang in the room with a loud crack as pieces of wooden utensils floated to the surface. She grabbed a towel that hung from the window and dried the washed plates and bowls. She set them in their assigned cupboards and ventured into the hallway, knocking on Maysom's door. When he didn't answer she called out his name.

"I'm in here," his voice called out from Birdie's bedroom.

She opened the door across from her and underneath the woolen blanket of babi fur was Maysom. The little boy in danger of being mistaken for a small, straw-filled pillow. The room was empty except for the bed and a meager vanity with an attached mirror. It was Birdie's mother's and Evelyn could recall the woman sitting in front of it while combing her golden hair her children had inherited. Mirrors were rare. Birdie had one of three that existed in their village. Not even Evelyn owned one.

She saw, for the first time, her face since the Oathbearing. Most of her features were unchanged. Her mouth was still pursed and full. The lines of her cheekbones were pleasing enough, and her brown hair was a light shade that made her think of spring. Her figure was still curved in all the places it should have been. She was pretty in her own way and quite ordinary in others, but her eyes — her eyes were not the same.

Below her slightly curved Vagu brows were light crimson irises, the color of dusk. The white was completely gone, replaced with a deep shade of blood red that glowed in the darkness. She found herself chilled by them. They were the eyes of a deadly creature. The eyes of a dragon.

She tore her gaze away and wondered how anyone was able to look at her. She suddenly held no resentment at Izel's reaction to her gaze. She let out a heavy breath and touched her cheek as if she might be able to wipe away the color from her eyes.

"I can't see," Maysom said in the dark.

Evelyn shook her head and walked over to the vanity, where a candle was held in a small metal candlestick. She forgot that she now could see in the dark better than those around her. She flicked the match and lit the candle. The light was small, her shadow covering the wall opposite of them.

"Why are you not in your own bed?" she said as Maysom clutched the blanket closer.

He looked frightened, his mouth trembling with the effort to hold back tears. She furrowed her brow and sat on the edge of the bed. She placed a hand on his forehead, wiping away strands of his blond hair.

"I don't want to see the bird again." His voice quivered in the cold.

"What bird? You've never feared birds before."

Maysom blinked and then closed his eyes as though he were trying to banish a terrible memory.

"I've never seen a bird like that. It was a monster."

"Whatever you saw, I'm sure it was not a bird."

The birds they did have were small sparrows that Maysom and the children chased in the fields. The biggest birds that they had were eagles that migrated from the south to nest in the mountains during spring and even they were small by comparison.

"Why does no one believe me?" He sat up with a raised voice, huffing in frustration.

Evelyn held her hands up and heard the front door open to the sound of Birdie laughing. She bid Adel goodnight before the door shut again. Evelyn put her hands on Maysom's shoulders and met his eyes.

"Be still, I believe you. Just tell me what you saw."

She listened as he told her of the man with scars and an empty mouth. Then about the giant bird that almost ate him before Birdie heard him scream. The story was disjointed, and he changed details several times as he tried to recall the memory.

She wondered if the boy had gotten into the mead again and drank more than his fill. It wouldn't be the first time Birdie had caught him trying to drink with the adults. Evelyn didn't want him to feel worse than he already did and understood how he'd be afraid to confess the truth. She figured if he had that bad of an experience with alcohol, then he would think twice before trying it again. It would be a lesson, she thought.

"How about this? I will investigate this matter. As a Viden, it is my duty." She straightened her shoulders and lifted her chin. "And you'll sleep in your own bed tomorrow knowing you'll be safe as long as your sister is here to protect you."

His posture relaxed and his innocent features returned to being that of the child he was. She smoothed out his hair again before standing. She was about to walk out when Maysom righted himself into a sitting position.

"And you will protect all of us, yes?"

Evelyn smiled at him to hide her anxiety at such a responsibility.

"Of course, now lie down. I'll say goodbye to Birdie, and she'll come to bed." She waved her hand for him to relax. Shutting the door behind her, Evelyn closed her eyes and leaned against it.

It wasn't that she didn't think she couldn't protect them. She could, but from what? A bad winter storm, fewer babis to hunt, the children stealing bread from Izel's simple bakery? It was still a daunting responsibility that she was happy to undertake. She only wished she was born with the knowledge of everything. Then she would have the right solution to any problem she was faced with. For a ten-year-old boy to have such faith in her abilities was heartening. He hadn't flinched at her new eyes, and he spoke to her as the Evelyn of a few hours ago. The Evelyn who wasn't bonded. It gave her the fortitude to challenge the unknown and face her duties with determination.

She walked into the kitchen to see Birdie sitting on a stool with her elbows propping up her head with her hands. She was smiling to herself. Evelyn had caught the same look on her grandmother when mentioning Jaspar.

"I see you are still clothed, thank the Breaths," Evelyn said, teasing as she sat on the opposite stool across from Birdie.

"Only barely. He was wonderful tonight, wasn't he?" She was still a little free from the drink, but at least she could speak in complete sentences.

"Oh yes, I recall him stepping on your toes only five times tonight."

Birdie chuckled and lifted her head from the table. "Well, I can't fault him for not being able to hold his alcohol."

"You're just as terrible, you know this right?"

"Oh, quiet you," she said as she rubbed her temples.

"Tomorrow is going to be a pleasure for you." Evelyn folded her arms as she looked at her friend. The woman was a walking hangover before the sun had even risen.

"I have to take Izel's bread to the breakfast feast tomorrow." Birdie's voiced pitched into a whine as she rubbed her eyes.

"Why do you have to do that? Isn't Adel apprenticing with her?" Adel was a wonderful baker that made the most delicious sweets in the village. He wanted to work in the shop, but needed to gain more experience before Izel would let him take over her bakery.

"I told him I would," she groaned.

"Why would you do that?"

"Because I love him." Birdie spoke into her hands.

Evelyn didn't say anything for a few moments, letting the words sink into the air as she tried to absorb what was just said. It was the first time Birdie had confessed such a declaration. She was unsure if it was the lingering drink.

"You love him?" Evelyn asked.

"Haven't I told you?" She tore her hands away from her face, and seeing Evelyn shaking her head Birdie continued, "Oh, yes well, I love him."

Her friend buried her face back into her hands. This was drunk Birdie. Larger issues were of no consequence to her. Evelyn laughed and grabbed her hands, lowering them to the table.

"Birdie, that's wonderful. I can see he feels the same."

Her friend's blue eyes sparkled with a smile, suddenly realizing what it was she had confessed. She shrugged her shoulders and released a short, inebriated giggle before righting herself.

I want the same to happen for you. Birdie's thoughts trailed to Evelyn in a stream of blue light, swaying as she did.

Evelyn almost responded before she caught herself. She would tell Birdie eventually, but thought that conversation would be better reserved for when her friend was sober. She smiled at Birdie's kind thought, remembering the way Adel looked her at her. The way his gaze lingered on her lips and hair with an expression that told the world he was taken, and none shall dissuade him. He loved Birdie; she was sure of it, and Evelyn couldn't be happier for her finding companionship in him. Birdie's blue eyes dimmed in the candlelight, and she rubbed Evelyn's hands in appreciation.

"I think it's time to retire. Izel will surely give me a tongue lashing in the morning. I know I will be late." Birdie lifted herself from the stool and walked Evelyn to the front door.

"Maysom is in your bed tonight," Evelyn said before stepping out into the cold.

Birdie nodded her head as though she expected as much. "Did he tell you what happened?" she squinted one eye as she yawned.

"He did. He's frightened, but I think he'll be well by morning."

"Scared me, he did. He screamed so loud." She expressed worry in the curve of her mouth as she frowned. "I'm sure he stole some mead from the feast."

Evelyn nodded her head in agreement and stepped away from the door.

"Goodnight."

She wrapped her cloak closer to her as the night's chill streamed past her in twinkling blue strands of light. It was a faded color that blended with the darkness. Her hood billowed around her head as she approached her home. When she stepped inside, she stomped her shoes free of the snow.

Tansey was sitting where she always did, next to the fire in her rocking chair. She held a cup of tea, steam lifting around her nose.

"Would you like some?" she asked, staring into the flames.

"No, I'm going to bed. It's been a long night." Evelyn thought she might be too exhausted to sleep, but wanted to lie down anyway.

"It has. Happy name day, my love. I hope it was everything you wanted it to be."

Evelyn could tell Tansey was still struggling with the thought of the morrow. The old woman's smile was feigned in mock happiness that she had a hard time concealing. While Evelyn was defeated in the thought that Sou and Tansey would become cordial with one another, she was glad that her grandmother was trying. As slight as it might be.

"It was. Thank you." She leveled her gaze at Tansey so she could see the seriousness in her words, "Thank you for being there for me. I couldn't have done it without you. I know we have our moments of strife, but you do know that I love you with all my heart?"

Tansey lowered her tea and lifted her hand to Evelyn's face, stroking her cheek. She looked at her granddaughter's features, and familiarity crossed her expression.

"I know," her conviction radiant, "I'm going to miss your mothers' eyes."

Evelyn cast her gaze downwards in shame. She kept forgetting about them. She was going to miss them too. She couldn't help feeling that she'd lost a part of herself. Tansey lifted her chin.

"Do not look away. Be proud. You may no longer have your mother's eyes, but you've earned those." She leaned her head closer to hers. "And they are beautiful."

Evelyn couldn't stop the swell of tears that threatened to spill over. Tansey kissed her cheek and then lifted her cup again. Evelyn took control her emotions and sniffed the tears away. They said goodnight to each other, and she closed the door to her room.

She undressed and braided her hair before climbing into bed. When she shifted to her side, she noticed the necklace Sou had given her was still around her neck. She lifted it above her head and examined the red scale in the center of it.

She grasped the scale in her hand and gasped as Oretem's vast mind filled her own. He had such memory. There was nothing she could distinguish; it was just too much. It was a never-ending tunnel that led to nowhere but time itself.

WISP OF A TWIG. His graveled voice rose in her mind, feeling as though he were within the room. It was impending and somber, as though she had intruded on him grieving.

Are you alright? She asked.

WERE I TO DIE BEFORE I WAKE, IT WOULD BE A BLESSING TO ALL.

She could almost see his massive eye blinking in the darkness.

I don't understand. She leaned her head towards the window, looking up into the sky, thinking she might see him flying above her. His emotions were torrential and weak as if he were drained of all fight. The Oathbearing must've taken a toll on him.

DO NOT FEAR THE DARK, WISP. IT IS WHERE YOU'LL FIND MONSTERS TO SLAY. HE WHO IS THE DECAY OF ALL LIVING.

Oretem wasn't making any sense, but he was a dragon. From what she was told they didn't tend to speak in complete thoughts. He had that in common with Alen.

Decay?

There was a flash of unease in the dragon's demeanor and then, just as fast, it was gone. His thoughts clouded and she began to lose his train of speech. He was just as exhausted as she was.

MONSTERS TO SLAY, he repeated, but the sound was low and far away. Evelyn knew of the creeping madness that came with being Viden. It was not well known of exactly the conditions of this ailment except that it manifested in each Viden differently. Arlisa, in the years that followed her bond, spoke less and less, eventually abandoning all speech except with the words she exchanged with her dragon. Tansey had warned her of this. Evelyn supposed it was the price to pay when seeing the future and for her village, she'd give all she had. This was what he must be speaking of, reassuring her that he'd remain by her side. No fear.

I'll not fear the dark, Oretem. We will fly above it, together, she thought confidently.

She felt the rise of promise in the dragon. A single emotion that lifted him from his fogged fatigue: hope. With that, he disappeared from her mind. She let go of the scale, hanging it from the bedpost, suddenly drained from the effort. The veins of glowing light upon the scale faded into a soft throb, cooling into a deep shade of red. Evelyn was keenly aware of the scale's presence, as though it were a limb separated from her flesh. She felt its phantom company drawing her in, reminding her that it was a part of her.

He who is the decay of all living. She could spend the entire night thinking about it, but her eyes were so heavy. The more she repeated the words, the more into sleep she fell, until there was nothing more to think and nothing more to fall into.

CHAPTER 10

THE LAST TIME HE FELT FEAR

Maun made his way into the mouth of the cave. Its silence made him think of Solov and its desolate stillness. The memory of wind stirring grains of sand at his feet filled his chest with an unfamiliar ache. No matter the pain of where he came from, it would always be home.

It had taken many caves to find the right one. He had a clear image in his head from Saiya, but it wasn't an exact location. He'd tracked the Viden and her companions to find its general area, but it was difficult to follow their signs when, like sand, the snow refused to remain still. He trailed them as far as the tundra allowed then, by process of elimination, ventured into the caves. The one he sought had a distinct darkness within that consumed all light.

This was the one.

Saiya was not fond of the underground, so he allowed her to remain outside the cave. He sent her flying overhead, waiting for his summons should he need her. He had no light and so he relied on his other senses to guide him. He felt no fear or depression in the dark; he'd come too far for that. It was a simple process of trusting the smell of burnt air and the slopes beneath his feet. He could hear movement ahead—it was slight, but apparent in the stillness.

He turned a corner and a faded light appeared ahead, flickering like candlelight. It signaled the end of the tunnel. He didn't run or press forward with haste. He was patient. He was always patient. With one step in front of the other the light became brighter, until he could see the outline of flames. They rose around the edge, peeking through like the beaks of infant birds, lighting the way into a gigantic cavern alight with fire. The ceiling was blazing with flames, shifting the air around him. He batted his eyes against the intense heat. In the middle of the cavern was a massive rock, jutting out in jagged spikes and then smoothing out like marble. Maun wiped the sweat from his brow and squinted at it. It wasn't a trick of the rippling air. He could distinctly see the sides of the boulder moving in and out, breathing.

He followed the groves to discover folded wings, curving into the slope of a neck that connected to a terrifying jaw of sharp fangs. Maun had found himself in the presence of a dragon. The weight of it made him step back as his legs weakened. He placed a hand on the wall and inhaled a pained breath. He tore his hand away and examined the red, burnt skin of his palm.

Saiya contacted him with concern, and he pushed her away, impassioned. This was what he'd been searching for. He thought of his mother, Ovia. The sound of her screaming. He touched the stones in his pocket and stepped forward towards the beast.

"What sort of man tempts the wrath of a dragon?" A soft, lilting, baritone voice encroached the cavern. It echoed against the walls as though coming from all sides, melting down to where he stood.

Maun cocked his head and searched for the voice. All he saw were flames.

"Are you a man of no fear?" The voice paused, and a rueful chuckle vibrated in the air.

Maun contacted Saiya to return to him and with a hesitant lapse, she flew inside the tunnel. It would be a few minutes until she reached him. Until then, he only had to wait.

"Have you nothing to say, intruder? Does your mouth remember the taste of words?"

Maun searched the flames, peering around the sleeping dragon for the voice. A guttural growl rose within his throat. He'd been too late. The dragon had already been claimed. How much did this voice know about him? His facial scars revealed his life as a Reticent, but what troubled Maun was that this person could see him, while he was blind to it. His anger grew, and he sent Saiya a sense of urgency. He needed her to speak. He was going to kill the voice.

"I can see I nicked a nerve. Quite a lot of blood spilt." It was mocking in its deep cadence. "I have something you want. I have something you *need*."

The voice lingered on the last word as though a serpent were speaking and even Maun found himself unsettled by its tone. "It is with little regret that I must inform you that I have very little need of silent strangers."

The dragon stirred, its barbed tail unfurling as the flames danced on its red hide.

It opened its eye and bore into Maun as though he were a pest not worthy of becoming a meal, but of extermination. On its back was a man shrouded in a black cloak. The hood was pulled up, shadowing his face from the fire's light.

From the tunnel behind him, Maun heard the flap of Saiya's wings. He held out his arm and she entered the cavern with a loud screech that made his ears hurt in the confined space. Her talons gripped his arm, red tongue gleaming as he spoke through her.

"You shall be the one to regret that I am not silent." Through her beak, his voice overlapped with her own raptor vocal cords. They echoed each other in a haunting, ghostly moan that spoke like a corpse from beyond the grave. Sometimes it was all he needed when hunting a down a target. People were so frightened of it they froze where they stood, making it that much easier to slit their throats.

"Reticent! You've earned your raptor. I had hoped…" The man trailed off in a delighted accent. It did not suit his low tone. "Oh, Breaths and Depths, the hourglass has been turned."

Maun didn't feel as if the man were speaking to him. He climbed down the side of the dragon, who laid its head back down on the stone ground, its entire body language speaking to extreme weariness. The man, still hooded, stood at the base of the dragon's head. He caressed its snout and the dragon recoiled, but didn't retaliate.

"You are not the Viden," Maun said. Saiya dipped her head forward, mirroring his interest.

"How do you know what I am not?" the shadowed man replied, his hand steady on the dragon's head.

"I know you are not to leave this cave alive," Maun snarled as his voice flowed from Saiya. He pulled out a dagger from his belt and held it before the hooded man. The raptor's golden eyes gleamed in the firelight as she towered over his head.

The man's laugh was delicate and silky. It enraged Maun to the edges of his control. He was able to keep his temper in check as he always was, but this man was testing his patience.

"Tell me, can you still hear your mother screaming?" The hooded man bent his head and Maun's legs buckled beneath him. Saiya lifted from his arm as his head hit stone.

HE WAS SEVEN YEARS OLD. THE SCENT OF CHICKEN ROASTING IN the fireplace filled the room with its mouthwatering scent. His mother would want him to eat the beets she stewed for him, but all he wanted was the chicken. He was sitting in front of the fireplace, watching the juice run down the side of the dead bird's crispy skin.

"Maun, back away from the fire. You'll fall in," his mother said from the kitchen.

Ovia stirred a wooden spoon in a metal pot of beets above a small brick fire. In the Waste they couldn't grow much and therefore couldn't keep much, but roots were hardy. Maun and his mother survived on a diet almost exclusively of roots. The chicken was a gift that Tacet Devu had given them from her travels. He'd never had one before.

97

Tacet Devu paid special mind to his family. She was good friends with his father. During meetings they'd often supper together and although Devu recently lost her voice, just as his father had, there was a certain link of communication between the two. As if they could tell what the other was thinking with blinks and facial tics.

Her honorary title of Tacet was given to all who joined them. Maun's father, Ethen, was given it a few days before he left for battle. Devu had remained within Soleil Citade to train the children left behind, including Maun. Ethen never spoke again after his initiation, his face still healing from the ordeal. The wounds across his face were left open to make certain they healed jagged and cruel. His parents thought Maun couldn't hear their conversations, but he was always listening, always learning. His intelligence separated him from the other children, he knew more than any of them thought. He knew how Ethen gained his scars.

"When will the chicken be ready?" Maun asked her.

He sat cross-legged as Ovia put down the wooden spoon and walked over to the fireplace. She lifted a tong and poked the chicken as it oozed liquid onto the fire, sending out sparks of flame.

"It's nearly ready, love," she said as she sat next to him.

When Ethen left, he hadn't said goodbye or hugged his son. He looked at Maun with an expression of indifference and touched his wife's cheek. It might've been tender had he not caused the bruise that welled under her eye. He was always leaving her like that. But what could Maun do? He knew his father's temper and decided he had to grow. He had to wait—wait to become taller, older, and stronger. Then he could leave and take his mother, if she would go with him.

He wasn't sure she would.

The day he left, Ethen had grazed the bruise under Ovia's eye. She flinched and clutched at the grey stone around her neck, hanging from a simple leather band. He lifted a similar one resting against his chest, Celosia's Glare binding the two of them. Ethen's dark eyes burrowed into Ovia's, and she stuck out her chin in defiance. She lifted her hand to a cut on his lip. Her touch lingered on the split skin, pulling on the cut until blood welled over the dried scab. A similar cut appeared on her own lip, her breath catching as the skin broke. She nodded, accepting the pain with a sense of odd relief. Ethen stole a quick glance at Maun, his scarred face showing as much emotion as when his skin was perfect. He left in silence, disappearing from their home for war without farewell. It had been three days since then and still there was no word of his wellbeing.

"I'm hungry," Maun said, looking at her.

Ovia had light green eyes and strawberry red hair. At least that's what his father called the color of her hair before he stopped talking altogether. Maun had never seen a strawberry. Her jaw was square and strong from abuse, baring small scars on her cheeks like the embroidery of a worn tapestry. Still, Maun found her to be the prettiest person in Solov. All the others were so serious and silent. Ethen was always distant and avoided conversing with his son whenever possible. So, it was no great change to have his silence be so permanent.

"One more word and you'll get nothing but beet stew," she said, wrapping her arms around him and holding him close. Her skin was warm, and he nestled into the crook of her arm as though the spot was meant for him.

"Mother, will father return?"

He wasn't sure if he wanted him to return. It was a complicated mess of emotions that called for a more mature mind than his own. Ethen was still his father, no matter the harm he caused.

"He will. We are incomplete without him." Ovia spoke confidently and with hope.

She stared into the fire, and he could see by the gleam in her eyes that she meant it. The stone walls of Soleil Citade were tall around him. Red banners hung from the ceiling, baring the mark of the Reticent with large black wings.

They wanted for nothing and were well cared for by the Tacet's that checked in on them. Their plates were made of silver and their furniture was of the finest fabric. Maun hadn't known poverty. He only knew his family and the Order they belonged to—the leader they served. Cinaed the Decayed was terrible and mighty. His vision of a unified Iona, free of Viden sorcery was of the upmost importance in their household.

But Maun wanted more. What was beyond these stone walls and that scorching Waste? Was there anything softer than sand? Was there a place where he couldn't hear his parents fighting and screaming?

"What if he doesn't return?" Maun asked.

Ovia turned her head slightly, like a cat noticing a fly.

"What did you say?"

He repeated the question and suddenly, he found himself across the floor, his cheek burning as if placed against a hot iron. The crown of his head scraped against the stone wall of the fireplace, his skull throbbing from the impact.

"Say it again." She spoke in a calmed voice, her hand lifted in the air, palm red.

He sat up across from her. He knew he shouldn't repeat it.

"What if he doesn't return?"

Another hard slap seared his other cheek. Had the skin split? He couldn't tell.

"Again."

"Mother, please —"

His head veered backwards as Ovia landed another blow across his face, his small shoulders shaking from the weight of its sting. His head felt so heavy.

"Again," she said, calm as before. Her unblinking green eyes reflected the fire behind him.

"I don't —"

She struck him again, hard enough for him to see black spots clouding his vision. He fell onto his side, whimpering as tears flowed onto the rug beneath him.

"What if he doesn't return?" he whispered, his jaw sore and pulsating.

He braced himself for the whip of her hand, but instead felt her soft lips against his throbbing cheek. She grasped his shoulders and with hands on either side of his face, kissed the tears that fell from his jaw. She gathered him up in her arms again and he clung to her.

"Don't you miss him?" she said against his hair.

He nodded fervently into her shoulder.

"Yes, more than anything," he said in-between gasps of sobs.

She lifted him out of her lap and leaned forward to look into his eyes. The bruise under her eye beamed purple and yellow in the firelight.

"He loves you as do I, my sweet darling, since the day you came into our world." She combed her hand through his black hair. "But we mustn't harbor doubts. We must beat them out, yes?"

Maun nodded again as a sweet grin spread across her face. She was the only one who smiled at him that way. She stood and left him sitting on the floor, drying the leftover tears he shed by the fire. She paused on her way into the kitchen, her back to him. He looked at her, wondering what made her stop.

"Mother?" he said, still trembling with pain.

She gasped and fell backwards clutching at her neck. Maun backed away at her sudden movement. She was breathing heavily and gripped the stone around her neck. He thought she must've been choking so he reached for the necklace. She turned away from his hands and arched her back in pain.

"No! Don't touch it!" she yelled, then screamed so loud he felt the ground tremble from her raw agony.

A loud crack emanated from her face as her jaw unhinged in an angle that was unnatural. Maun cried out and clutched his mother's hand as she writhed on the floor.

"What do I do? Mother! What do I do?" he screamed at her, vision blurring as the tears reformed stronger than before.

"I'm sorry!" he shouted as if it would keep her from harm. As if he had caused it somehow. He must have.

She continued to wail as her cheek with the bruise caved in, green eye mangled in-between bone and flesh. Blood poured from her face as another piercing shriek escaped from her.

A cacophony of bones splintering, and flesh tearing combined to create a foul song accompanied by Ovia's relentless, soul-rendering screams. They grew less human the more her face broke at invisible hands. Maun could see nothing causing her pain yet looked around the room with the fervor of an insect blindly following flame to its death.

The crunch of her bones ceased, and her flailing halted to a sporadic tremble. She was unrecognizable, her face a fleshy pulp of sinew and muscle that was turned inside out. Her teeth fell out of a contorted mouth like a broken porcelain doll, scattered around her strawberry hair.

Worst of all, she was still breathing.

Her breath came in ragged, short rasps through a lacerated nasal cavity collapsed in on itself. Maun was terrified. He huddled next to her, watching the rise and fall of her chest. The struggle of her clinging to life. It was his fault. What he had said caused this to happen.

She was mumbling, but it sounded like air escaping through thick tar. He leaned in close and saw bubbles of spit and blood leaking from what used to be her mouth. Her fingers twitched within his palm. She had no strength, barely holding onto him. She tried to speak, but with no face her voice was incoherent.

He placed his ear closer to her, feeling the mixture of blood and brain matter splattering on his cheek. Still, he could not make out what she was trying to say. She let out another short-bubbled gasp and then laid still. Her chest stopped moving and she sunk lower to the stone floor, dead.

Time was nonexistent as he remained by her side, frozen in his tears. His mouth opened into a frigid gasp, limbs refusing to move. He didn't know how long he sat in his mother's blood, but the fire had gone out when Tacet Devu had discovered them. Maun was carried away in silence as they cleaned up her mutilated body and he knew he would never taste that chicken.

MAUN WOKE WITHIN THE CAVERN AS SAIYA LOOMED OVER him, large black wings flapping in concern. Her elation at seeing his eyes open flowed through him, and helped as he tried to collect himself. The hooded man was kneeling next to him, still unrecognizable beneath the cloak.

"What did you do to me?" Maun said through Saiya, his voice a torrent of grief.

"I reminded you of your purpose," the man's voice slithered across the space between them.

The memory had been burned into his mind since it happened, but reliving it was a nightmare Maun cared not to revisit. He was there. It felt so real. His mother's face—the torn flesh and concaved features. The man was right. Experiencing it again revived an old hate. He recalled Tacet Devu explaining to him Celosia's Glare and the consequences of those who wear the twin stones. His father had met a foul fate and so, whoever had killed his father, killed his mother.

He felt the stones in his pocket. They were still there. They weren't the ones that his parents had. He couldn't have taken those without cursing himself. He traveled all the way into the depths of the Eshe Willow Wood for the ones he possessed. The rhyme echoed in his mind as he thought of the curse that every Reticent memorized.

In the Willow Wood she sees with stones,
take one and leave your bones.
Her eyes are black, she's many to spare,
take two and keep her Glare.

It was an essential step in the Reticent initiation to obtain Celosia's Glare, but to never take only one. One would curse the possessor of death, but two would enable the thief to leave the forest unharmed. The stones were usually exchanged between Reticent couples to ensure devotion. Precious few used it for other purposes such as Maun. He'd always planned to gift it to the person who ruined his life. To have them die in the way of the person they loved most as the stones' intended purpose. Maun stood and looked down at the man, who was still crouched before him.

"Who are you?" he asked.

The man stood, walking towards the dragon with a heavy limp in his leg. Maun's eyes widened as he remembered the stranger in the woods. The one he let get away.

"You?" Maun said as Saiya's red tongue stretched out with his voice.

The man lifted his hood to reveal a scared face of burnt flesh. One eyebrow was gone, replaced with strings of overlapping healed scars that looked like he'd been doused in oil and set alight. It reached across his left cheek and down his neck, disappearing beneath his black cloak. The other side of his face was untouched, the skin smooth and tan with one bright red eye and the other, pale as a light crimson fog. Despite the man's scars, he looked familiar. Like an older version of a man he knew years ago. A thought came to Maun, and he blinked, unbelieving.

It couldn't be.

"I know who killed your father," the man smiled as the fire from the walls displayed illusions of shadowed demons across the floor.

He took a hobbled step back with an arm outstretched towards the dragon. The beast lifted his head and with a great, flaming eye, he stared at Maun. The world fell away and all that was left was that great, flaming eye. Colors swirled as his mind tore at itself, splitting him as he fought the pull of his body. The effort was too great, and the pain receded once Maun gave into its groping travel.

He was somewhere else. A place he ought not to have been. He was on to a metal, wooden ship. A woman sat in the middle of the hull, holding a glowing, white scale in her hand. Blood rained down on them as screams echoed from above.

CHAPTER 11

CATASTROPHE

Something was wrong. She couldn't wake. Fire kindled across Evelyn's skin, burning and searing her flesh in a frenzy of brutal pain. A flash of red rushed across her mind's eye.

A wing?

It swirled in black smoke against a dawning sky. Then darkness and the pain of flames scorching her body consumed all else. She was dreaming. A scream formed in her throat—a release she was denied as the phantom flames burned her in her paralyzed state.

She could feel the bed beneath her. The sheets bundled around her torso, but still, she could not move. The bright light of snow blinded her as blood spilled onto its frosted surface in a motion too slow for reality, the droplets resting in a patterned coil like rubies against a woman's white throat. She was dreaming. She knew it, so why could she not wake?

Bodies of soot and shadow laid in heaps across the pureness of the ice. A single hooded figure stood in its carnage, fire blazing on every collapsed household. She was running—running towards a frozen campfire, where an unattended cart stood as if a relic from another time.

She fell as the pain returned. Writhing on the floor, she burrowed her fingernails into the tundra. She wasn't injured, but her chest burned in agony. A deep hole was forming inside her, pulling everything she was into its black abyss. She was going to die if she did not wake.

Wake!

Evelyn's eyes opened, frozen in her posture, unable to move a single finger. She gasped in ragged intakes of air through her nose; her mouth unable to open. It felt as if there was an invisible figure sitting on her chest, pressing against the rise and fall of her breath. Her arms and legs were stuck to the bed. No matter how much she commanded them, they would not move. A tear rolled down her cheek as she stared at the ceiling.

Shadowed figures crept from the sides of her vision, but she could not turn her head. She knew they weren't real. Her body still slept as her mind played out imaginary people. They climbed the walls and stared at her from the top of the ceiling. They were human in shape, but slid and crept like oil atop water. They dripped down from the awning, dangling just above her face, staring at her with piercing, black human eyes. Although they had mouths, they seemed unable to speak, using their all too human eyes to pierce the barrier of Evelyn's soul. She tried to scream, but only managed a muffled sob. With all her might she willed her fingers to move. They did. She wiggled one, then two, until finally, she could twist them in the sheets.

The shadowed figures faded as she regained control of her body. In one swift jolt all the strength she poured into herself burst. She sat up, nearly falling off the bed as she stifled her scream into the blanket she'd wrapped around her hands. Her room was filled with twilight as morning sprung from the window. The shadows were gone, and she was left in her own terror.

She searched the room, finding nothing that resembled the tar creatures that plagued her waking dreams. She'd never experienced anything like that before. The dream was fractured and so impossibly real. The inherent nature of it felt wrong. She had been paralyzed. In everything she knew about the bond between Viden and dragon this was something else entirely.

She had a growing sense of foreboding the more she thought of it. Was this the effect of her visions? Was this the price of madness? She remembered the blood and fire. The cart. Out of everything she saw, she recognized the cart. The one she and Birdie spotted the other day while hunting. She couldn't piece everything she saw together, but she could start there. Evelyn collected her thoughts, trying to mend a broken puzzle.

She could speak with Oretem. The dragon may be able to help her gather the disjointed images into a cohesive story. She grabbed the necklace by the leather strap, placing the red scale in her hand and watched it glow, golden veins pulsating.

She expected the mind of Oretem to be crushing, for his vast knowledge to overwhelm her as it did before. The strength she had received from the scale had consumed her, invigorating her limbs and dashing fear from her heart, but she felt nothing. The weight of his consciousness was little more than an empty vessel. When she tried to reach out to him, she was met with an invisible wall, a mental block she could not penetrate. Every fear of misfortune she had was exasperated by her inability to contact him.

She dressed herself in black trousers and a thick long-sleeved tan tunic. Her boots hugged her feet as she lifted her cloak around her shoulders, Oretem's scale swaying across her chest as she reached into the pouch. Her daggers were where she left them, the hilts smooth on her fingertips. She bundled the scarf-like material of her cloak around her neck and opened her door slowly as not to wake Tansey.

She had to see Oretem. On her way, she'd stop at the campsite where she'd seen the cart. The outsider would prob-ably be long gone, but she had to check. Her hair fell around her shoulders as she crept past Tansey's room, the old woman's snoring slipping through the doorway.

As she exited the house, she walked across the field where the night before the whole village sang and danced. The snow still held the imprints of feet bouncing and kicking, a dark tinge of blue lighting the snow as the moon sunk. The village was quiet with the silence of sleep. She made her way to the mountain pass and whistled.

She didn't know if Nakesha would answer her call, but the journey would be faster with her. Evelyn waited a few minutes, then saw the outlined shape of the white wolf's figure glowing in the twinkling light. Nakesha crept towards Evelyn, dragging her paws in protest to being woken up so early.

"I'm sorry, vain one," she whispered, caressing the wolf's shoulder, "but I need your help." Nakesha blinked in acceptance.

She climbed on the wolf's back and, with a quick whistle, was whisked away higher into the mountain. She gripped the white pelt in between her fingers, urging Nakesha to move faster. They reached the spot where she first saw the cart on the edge of the cliff overseeing the village. Evelyn could make out its general shape in the darkness, her dragon eyes detailing its outline. It was still there. Halfway buried in snow with the campfire gone under the ice.

She grew nervous at the sight of it. It hadn't moved since she last saw it. The owner may have gotten lost in the mountains. They might've found a tunnel to shelter from the cold and ventured too far, losing themselves within Isla's Reach. Or maybe they abandoned their belongings, the weight too much for them. It didn't make sense either way. The village was clearly visible and if there was any trouble, they would've sought help there.

Evelyn patted Nakesha to continue, and they made their way across the boulders and paths to arrive at the campsite. The wolf rested on her hind legs as Evelyn dismounted. The sun was low on the horizon as light spilled across the land, the snow reflecting orange and red.

She went to the cart and opened the compartments to find spices and perfumes. There were cabinets filled with dresses and blankets, metal pans and iron skillets. These were all the possessions of a peddler. They would never abandon their livelihood. From what she remembered of Jaspar, he always kept an eye on his cart. This was similar if not the exact same as his, but he wasn't due back in the village until the end of winter. That was still a month away—unless he decided to return early.

Evelyn thought of Tansey and him laughing together. All the nights her gran spent out late and returned flushed. Their heartfelt farewell as he departed the village. Tansey hadn't cried—she was too strong for that even if Evelyn could see how much she wanted to. Yes, he could've returned early for her grandmother, but if so, where was he?

She stepped away from the cart to walk back to Nakesha. It might not be too late to find him if he were lost. It had only been a day as far as she knew. As she took another step, something cracked beneath her foot, shattering apart from the frost.

She kneeled and swept the snow away to reveal a red stain that traveled upwards away from the cart. Evelyn held her breath. She'd killed enough babi to know the sight of frozen blood.

No. Breaths and Depths, please no.

She uncovered the trail of blood, growing wider and leading where she had last seen that dark shape over a pile of snow. Her chest tightened as her hand came across something rigid. This wasn't ice. Her hands trembled as she removed the remaining snow to reveal a nose peaking beneath the sleet. She sank lower to the ground, the weight of what she knew was under the snow crushing her.

Evelyn gasped as she uncovered Jaspar's mutilated face. One eye was shut with permafrost clinging to his brows and grey beard, the other was missing. The entire left side of his face was stripped of skin and flesh. The ragged ends of muscle and veins hung in frozen icicles where his teeth jutted out, exposed to the cold. Evelyn stared in horror as she followed the carnage to the clean deep slit in Jaspar's throat, blood frozen around the gaping wound. It was done fast and with expert skill. It was a small comfort that he hadn't lived long after being cut. The damage to his face looked to be from an animal, but she'd never seen such marks on a body before. She knew what a babi or bena wolf could do to a human, but this was entirely different. It looked as though a sharp pointed tool, like that of a farrier, tore and scooped Jaspar's flesh in long strips, almost in a medial pattern.

Evelyn covered her mouth as she tried to assess what she was seeing. Jaspar was murdered. That much was clear. There was someone in the mountains, someone dangerous, that came across the peddler. Evelyn stifled an involuntary cry as she realized the smoke from the doused fire was most likely from the murderer. That pile of snow was Jaspar, already dead. The dark shape above it, the animal consuming his flesh as she watched.

She noticed a glimmer by her leg and pulled from the snow a long chain with a wooden compartment. She opened it and found a lock of brown, greyed hair. She bit her lip to keep it from trembling.

How was will I tell Tansey? Has she not suffered enough?

She placed the locket into the pouch of her cloak, feeling as though she'd just placed a block of ice there. Two men in this life had died on her grandmother. She couldn't imagine such pain. Finding love only to lose it and when the Breaths granted a second chance, that too was taken. Evelyn felt an uncontrollable anger at the spirits of Iona for asking Tansey to bear such a burden. How much could one person stand to endure? Nakesha rose and walked over to Evelyn, touching her snout to the top of her head. She licked her forehead, sensing her distress. Evelyn leaned away and patted the wolf's nose.

She tried to swipe the rest of the snow away, but the ice had hardened. She couldn't turn Jaspar over to face Iona as was custom for burials. If left faceup she risked his soul losing its way, wandering the land in search of his unmade grave. She tried to turn him over, but his frozen body refused to move.

Evelyn...

She started at the sudden voice. It was small and traveled as though wearied from a long journey.

Evelyn...

She stood and searched her surroundings. It wasn't a thought. It was a voice. Nakesha sniffed the air, whining. A small tendril of light made its way to Evelyn. At the end was a small globe, glowing with wisps of mist surrounding it.

Run, it said, breathy and feminine. *Run to Reva. Find Meric.*

The globe pulsed, then faded as the words waned into oblivion. Evelyn brought her hand to her chest, reaching into the pocket where her daggers laid, eager to be used.

"Who are you? Who is Meric?" she said into the empty air. Nobody answered and she was left more unsettled than ever.

There was so much she didn't understand. It was time to find Oretem. She'd come back for Jaspar.

Evelyn! Where are you?

The thought vibrated in her head, tearing from within her skull and Evelyn nearly fell at the magnitude of it. Was that Birdie? She sounded frightened. Then a cluster of thoughts echoed inside her mind, overlapping each other with impossible volume.

Does Evelyn ride upon his shoulders?

There is something wrong. Celosia's Depths! Evelyn... has she abandoned us?

Breaths preserve us! She's left us! He will kill us all!

The thoughts grew in fear, screaming over one another. It was a garbled concoction of the masses. Evelyn covered her ears, falling to her knees with a groan.

Nakesha whimpered and looked towards the village. Something had gone horribly wrong. She could hear everyone, and they were terrified. Strings of blue light whirled around her in chaotic fashion as she was bombarded with their petrified cries. The wolf lowered her head beneath Evelyn and lifted her with her snout across her back. Evelyn gripped her mane as the voices became more panicked. They shouted her name and screamed for her whereabouts.

Nakesha approached the edge of the cliff and what Evelyn saw silenced the voices. Oretem flew above her village. The air stilled, the wind ceased to move, and the echoes of life in the mountains all at once quelled as if smothered. Oretem's massive wings beat with the sound of a thousand drums. It was all she could hear. They thundered to the pounding of blood in her ears.

He opened his maw and a jet of red and orange flames detonated across her village. The roofs of houses exploded, sending spears of jagged, flaming wood through snow and escaping figures. Some caught fire and laid on the ground, writhing and burning, while others stood awkwardly, skewered by flaming wooden projectiles. Evelyn's mouth opened in a deafening scream. She gripped her necklace and the scale pulsed.

"STOP! STOP IT!" she yelled with her mind and body. Oretem dipped in the air and closed his jaw to the flames. His neck arched as if fighting off an invisible opponent.

The unseen barrier crumbled under the gravity of her plea and instead of lucidity, Evelyn found madness. Oretem's mind was a deranged wreck of scattered thoughts. He couldn't focus on one for very long. He was splintered. Stretched too far as the cracks in his mind broke deeper and deeper.

All he could see was red and all he craved was blood. It had been so long since he had tasted blood. His wings were strong at his back, his legs muscled, taut with the new faux freedom he found himself in. All should tremble before him. He was the last, his kind murdered and forgotten. He would remind the humans of his fury. The ire of a mountain dragon.

He could feel her. His once bondsmate. Still his bondsmate. Wasn't she? No, there was another, the Decayed. He broke Oretem. Fractured him. Oh, if only he died with the rest of his kind. He saw a man running from a burning building. His weakened limbs limping with the help of a long wooden cane. Hadn't he known him? Something tickled in the back of his mind with the recognition of friendship, but it was quickly overpowered by his unstated bloodlust.

The man looked up as Oretem dived towards him. The old man's robe swayed in the gust his wings created. The dread in his features drove Oretem to savageness and he roared as his fangs stabbed into aged muscle and thin limbs. He chomped with the sound of the human's bones grinding against his teeth, blood trickling down his jaw as he swallowed.

There was something wrong with this. He couldn't see through the red. He felt her. She was in torment. Terrible torment. She begged him to stop. He couldn't. The Decayed split him.

FORGIVE ME. He growled as he lost himself in the red and gave into the madness.

Evelyn fell from Nakesha's back, crumpling to the ground with the taste of Alen's blood still on her tongue. Oretem's scale dangled from her chest as she heaved, but nothing came up. Sobbing, she gasped in rented breaths.

Alen.

She wiped her mouth, trying to rid the phantom taste of his flesh against her teeth. What possessed Oretem so that he savaged a dear friend and the home he knew meant so much to her? The Decayed? The murderer in the mountain? It couldn't be. The man had been dead for years. Still nauseous, she climbed back onto Nakesha's back, who growled for violence.

In a spray of upturned snow, she bolted down the mountain. The voices returned to Evelyn as they descended, but the closer she got the more they faded, until she heard nothing at all. The beats of Oretem's wings disappeared, smoke darkening the sky as she appeared from the mountain pass.

The only sound was the deep crackle of burning homes. It hissed like hot coal doused in ice water. Burnt flesh and soot permeated the air. Nakesha carried her forward, fur catching the ash as she dismounted. Evelyn's stomach churned as she walked the grounds of her village. With each step, she walked closer towards all she knew to be lost—a familiar blizzard of black snow corrupting what was once her home.

Chapter 12

One Final Kindness

There's a specific kind of silence amongst the dead. Its stillness allowed the snowfall to scream as loud as a rockslide and the grate of ice beneath a boot to cause an avalanche. The air was devoid of breath, dead as the villagers that scattered the burning ruin. The only true sound was the crackling of wood burning as Evelyn passed the destroyed homes. The ground was black with soot, only revealing the pure snow underneath with her passing boot prints.

Bodies littered the empty field where they had all once linked arms, dancing only the night before. She followed the contorted faces and reaching limbs, finding those she recognized and those too burnt to know for sure. Izel laid face down in the snow, her body blistered and boiled. Evelyn recognized her by the apron about her waist that still held a layer of flour. Her clawed fingers reached for another body across from her, the face blackened and oozing. The body was far too seared to know for any certainty, but Evelyn knew in her heart Izel reached for Eleri. She stared down at the baker and cook, numb before the tragedy and terror at their end. Her hand hovered over Izel's face, trembling with the urge to touch the baker's cheek. She couldn't. She lifted her hand to her mouth and stifled a sob, her cheeks wet with tears.

They surrounded her. The bodies of those she swore to protect stared through open lids, horrific grimaces directed at her. Even those whose eyes were closed, Evelyn could feel their unrest, condemning her for failing them. She couldn't break. Not yet. There had to be others. She couldn't be the only one left with breath still within her.

She walked away from Izel and checked the others. Their faces melted into their hands, screaming with open mouths. Evelyn's palms were black with ash and singed skin. She wiped them on her pants and in her peripheral vision caught the sight of blood.

She recognized the pattern, coiling in a specific way that overwhelmed her with a sense of dread. She'd seen the same one in her vision. Her breath stilled as she ran around the corner. Her heart dropped and she fell to her knees beside the body of Adel. His chest was caved in, revealing splintered ribs jutting from his torso like spears. Surrounded by blood and spilled organs, Adel laid within the imprint of a giant dragon claw print. He'd been crushed. Evelyn longed to turn her head, to banish the image from her mind. It was not how she remembered him — it was not how she *wanted* to remember him. But her gaze was fixed, involuntarily committing the scene to memory for future nightmares. She stared, wide-eyed at the ruby-like droplets of blood that surrounded his body. The perfect rendition of what she'd seen.

Evelyn gripped the edges of her cloak until her hands went white. She couldn't contain her tears any longer. They fell, unbound by restraint or control, plummeting down her cheeks like raging rivers within a storm. If she were to be driven mad, knowing she could've prevented such a death was a sure way to break her mind. Adel had been a childhood friend. She'd watched him grow into a man. A man who had plans.

Birdie.

Evelyn suddenly realized an intense heat burning along one side of her body. She turned around, eyes darting across the flames that engulfed her best friend's home. The front door was blown inwards as the blaze licked upwards towards the roof. She staggered to her feet and without a moment's hesitation, entered the flames.

The heat was intense and smoldering. Evelyn blinked as the waves burned her eyes.

"Birdie!" she yelled into the inferno. The roof had collapsed, pieces of wood and furniture laid broken across the floor. She called out her friend's name again before hearing a soft moan from a pile of wood right beneath the open roof. Light blue tendrils of wind gathered above the pile like soft breath.

Evelyn pulled wood that was alight with fire from the pile and felt the skin on her hands singe. She ignored the pain and kept calling out Birdie's name. Evelyn gasped as she finally reached her friend.

Birdie's hair was wet with blood. Her arm bent behind her back in a way that left no doubt to its uselessness. The pillar that held the roof together had fallen on her, crushing her pelvis and legs. Evelyn stared at the pillar, following the thin fractures that had split into grand splinters of jagged wood. How was she ever going to lift it?

Birdie's neck was arched to the side, pinned by one of the legs of a wooden stool. It was only when Evelyn tried to lift her head did, she realize the leg was through Birdie's neck. The splintered end peeked from the other side, dripping blood that sizzled in the heated air. Birdie moaned in pain, blood spurting from her mouth as she lifted her hand over Evelyn's to stop her from moving her.

"Birdie, I need to get you out. I must lift this." Evelyn smoothed out her blood-soaked blonde hair.

"Man—there was a man. Grabbed Maysom—roof collapsed," Birdie's blue eyes were wide and insistent as she gurgled out her words. "Maysom... find Maysom."

The flow of blood increased as Birdie spoke, pooling into a boiling puddle that was much too large. Evelyn tried to stop the bleeding with her hand, but could only watch as it slipped through her fingers. Frustrated, Birdie lifted Evelyn's hand away from her neck as she repeated her command with more urgency.

"I'll find him," Evelyn said, holding her hand, but when she tried to leave Birdie only held on tighter.

She turned around, searching the shifting air but only found fire. She turned to look behind her and saw a small figure laying in the remnants of a cabinet. Maysom's little hand was outstretched towards his sister in a last desperate attempt to reach her. His blue eyes were wide open in the shock of death, staring at her as though his soul were trapped within the corpse. A long slit colored his neck in crimson blood.

Evelyn fought the compulsion to scream at the sight of his young innocence extinguished. His death was not of the dragon or the collapse of the house. He'd been murdered, deliberately and callously so, by the fear that was trapped in those empty eyes. The cut in his throat was of the same exper-tise that ended Jaspar's life. Evelyn shut her eyes, swallowing her guilt as she turned to Birdie who was dying before her. Her heart raged against that reality, the two battling for dominion over her common sense. Birdie was dying and there was nothing Evelyn could do to stop it.

She had one final kindness she could bestow upon her friend. She had no other way to ease her passing and telling her the truth of her brother was a pain worse than death.

"He's fine. He's unconscious, but he's alive," Evelyn said while smiling. The corners of her mouth trembled in the lie. Her chest ached as she wiped Birdie's face of soot, smearing blood across her cheek.

Birdie smiled with bloody teeth and her body jerked rigid as she tried to speak again.

"Take care... of him. He will not... underst—" She shut her eyes then opened them again, bulging as she gasped to take in air. "Man in... black. Looking—you. I told... him. I'm sorry."

The last word grinded against her teeth as though she was forcing it out. Birdie's hand gripped Evelyn's in a tight hold, her last bit of strength powerful in its attempt to remain alive as long as possible.

"Shh, you did nothing wrong. I'll take care of Maysom," Evelyn choked on the empty words. Birdie tightened her fingers around her hand, digging her nails into Evelyn's skin. She gritted her teeth, spraying blood as she spoke one last time.

"Adel."

The light in Birdie's eyes faded with his name upon her lips, rolling to the back of her head. She jerked once more before the blood from her neck stopped bubbling. Her chest rested without movement and her hand slipped from Evelyn's. She was gone, her features displaying a passing in death that had not been peaceful.

Evelyn sat there for a moment, staring at Birdie's contorted expression, unable to comprehend she no longer lived. The body a husk of a person she once knew best. Her mind raged against that knowledge. It couldn't be. They'd spoken only the night before. Danced and drank together. How could she be gone? There was never a moment without her and for the first time Evelyn breathed air that Birdie no longer shared.

She looked behind her, watching as the flames crept closer to Maysom's body like scavengers reaping the rewards of a predator's leftovers. He caught fire, his skin searing and blackening under the starving blaze. She was horrified, but couldn't look away. She was stuck in time and captured by a type of darkness that was only spoken of in the dead of night where nothing living could hear of it. She hardly felt the blisters that appeared on her skin as the heat burned. She lived for her village. There was nothing left of it. What more was there to continue for?

Tansey. Her grandmother's name enveloped Evelyn like a cold breeze, chilling her against the ravenous flames that threatened to eat her alive. She felt the lick of the fire around her, and gasped at the sudden pain in her hands that burnt in the flames. She stood and panted as she realized she was surrounded by the inferno. The entrance of the blown-in door was blocked by a wall of orange and red. She could hardly breathe. The smoke and heat burned her lungs with each breath.

Evelyn gathered what was left of her strength and lifted her red hands to the door. She pulled her grief and sorrow into her hands, trying to bundle it into a torrent of wind to ease the passing through the fire. It wasn't working. She felt a wall inside herself. Some kind of barrier that only let a tendril of power seep through.

She gathered the droplets like sifted, wet flour as blue light swirled around her fingertips. It was hot, but powerful and yet, she could not grasp it. She leaned forward as Oretem's scale swung from her neck, brushing against her bare arm. The droplets became a river, pulsating in her veins with a rush of energy. She slammed her arms down and a gust of hot air tore its way through the flames as she ran into it.

Her body slammed into the snow, and she heard the soft sizzle of her hands in ice. Pain exploded from her fingers which were peeling skin in black and red clumps. She coughed for what felt like hours, inhaling the crisp, clean air with difficulty. A spray of sparks floated around her as Birdie's house collapsed in on itself, crumbling to ash and embers. What was once a home of family and friendship had become nothing more than a fiery pyre. Evelyn was exhausted, her body slumping against the weight of all she'd seen. The burst of Iona's Breath she forced from herself left her empty and incapable of conjuring it again. She tried as she sat there, gasping fresh air into her smoke riddled chest. It was a pitiful small whistle of air that couldn't move the drifting ash. Why couldn't she control it?

This was her fault. She was Viden. She should've protected them. She saw it coming and yet, she did nothing. She'd failed. Her mother died in vain and everything she'd accomplished was for naught. Birdie's pleading voice echoed in her mind as Maysom's eyes stared at her while he burned. She hadn't done enough; she had never been enough. Adel stared at her with empty eyes that seemed to beg, *where were you*? Evelyn felt a part of her disintegrate, withering as though rotten away. All she had been before putrefied into the image of Birdie and Maysom burning.

Tansey.

Birdie had told a black, cloaked man where to find her. Sensation returned to her limbs, and she regained her sense of self, if only a little. She took one last look at Adel's broken body and ran.

CHAPTER 13

THE DUEL OF GRIEF AND INDIFFERENCE

Maun stood in the shadows of a hallway in the Viden's home. Evelyn's house was small, smoking in the light snowfall of ash. It was one of the few houses that hadn't burned. Instead, it had caved in from the stomp of Oretem's massive claw. A large hole in the ceiling gave way to light and cold, wood scattering the floor among the disarray of melted ice.

Maun arrived at the village before Oretem. He was given the chance to find the Viden before the great, red dragon decimated Verbena. He didn't know where to find her, so he did what he did best. He found someone who could tell him: the boy and his sister from the feast last night. He had looked through a window and saw them sleeping together in peace. He was silent as he broke into the house. It wasn't difficult. Their primitive homes provided nothing to keep them safe from intruders.

It was quiet in the village. A sound Maun was all too familiar with. It echoed like the thunder of a great storm. He recalled the smooth feel of his dagger as he held it against the boy's throat. He had used Saiya to ask where the Viden was. The sister begged him, pleading for the life of her little brother. Had she not known what pleas meant to him? Absolutely nothing, but he loved them all the same.

She gave the Viden up. The pained look of betrayal etched in her freckled face smothered the remaining spark of her defiance. She knew what she had done. In everything that satisfied him, he was most pleased to see that she had regretted it. Stuck between two stones and she found herself crushed either way. It wasn't long after that, Maun heard the panicked shrieks of the villagers.

Fire and smoke rained down on Verbena. Oretem's roars vibrated the ground and within a few seconds the ceiling collapsed on the woman, burying her beneath the wood and snow. The boy cried in his arms. He called out for his sister and for Evelyn. Maun glided the knife across his throat. He made sure to make it deep and quick. He felt nothing as the boy gasped against him. He fell from his arms inside of what used to be a cabinet that blew away from the wall. Maun left the siblings to their fate as he walked among the dead to the Viden's home.

He turned away from the hole in the ceiling, walking across the threshold towards an open door. Inside the room was a makeshift bed, spilling hay through the gashes in the fabric. It covered the floor, mixing with an array of possessions. Under a pile of wood was the figure of a woman. Maun crouched a few paces away and watched the lumbar lift and fall as she breathed.

Her nose bled a small puddle under her aged face. This couldn't be the Viden. She couldn't have been in hiding for so long. If she did then she was a coward who didn't help her fellow people during the war. There was only one way to be sure. He hopped a few steps forward, still crouched, and lifted the old woman's eyelid. They were a light brown with the whites still intact. No, Evelyn must be of some relation to the unconscious woman. Her mother perhaps? She seemed too old for that.

The woman's features were lean, but her skin sagged in wrinkles. Speckled grey hair hung loose around her shoulders. The corners of her mouth were absent of laugh lines and thin as though she rarely smiled. He concluded she was either a mere guardian or the Viden's grandmother. In any case, she wouldn't leave her behind. Evelyn was absent from the bodies he inspected after the attack. She would return. He only needed to wait.

He stood and placed himself back in the shadowed hallway beyond the hole in the ceiling. The light forced the perspective from the hallway into blackness. He could stand in the middle of the room and not be seen.

This is what he most enjoyed about his profession. No, not profession. He didn't exactly choose this. After the death of his parents, he had nothing else. He recalled the child who had never seen a strawberry; how little he knew. Reliving his worst memory concluded he didn't have much else before either. But it was his life. He entombed himself inside the Order brick by brick. It was either that or face the winds of the Waste. He chose to kill himself slowly.

Saiya flew over the house and sent him a sense of awareness. Someone was coming. He gripped the hilt of his dagger, making sure to keep it within the folds of his cloak. Whoever came in would be able to see the glint of its silver surface in the light. The woman panted as she entered the home, wearing a green cloak that billowed around her knees, boots tracking in soot and ice. Her pale face was stained in ash and streaks of blood, brown hair wisping around her blood red eyes.

Those eyes. They were Viden eyes, but more than that. They had the hint of a glow in the shadows. It wasn't disconcerting, but it was unusual. Was Oretem still bonded with her? It made sense. That would account for why the dragon was now mad. His soul split between two people. What the dragon showed him was a gift. Maun finally knew the name of the one he was searching for: Meric. His parents were slain in the battle of Elm Lake, but he still carried the burden of his family's mistake.

He didn't know where to find the man, but a name was more than what he had before. He touched the pocket where the stones sat, caressing the curved outlines of their shape. There was a sense of satisfaction in knowing after killing the

Viden, he would embark on the journey to kill another. His true target.

Evelyn entered the room where the old woman laid.

"Gran," she said in a hushed voice.

She lifted the wood from around the old woman's body and shook her shoulders. The unconscious woman groaned, and her eyes flitted open. She lifted a hand to her nose and flinched in pain as she wiped blood from her face.

"Evelyn, are you alright? I heard screaming and when I went to check on you the roof caved in. I... I don't remember..." the old woman looked around the disarrayed room as though she were in a place unfamiliar to her. "What happened?"

The Viden helped her stand and held onto her arms as she up righted a turned over chair. She settled her grandmother down onto it and crouched down to her knees, looking into her eyes, red irises running with tears as she smiled.

"You're alive," the Viden's voice pitched in a controlled sob. "Is... everyone..."

Evelyn's grandmother didn't finish her sentence as the Viden's smile disappeared into a frown that writhed in grief.

"No one, not even — ?"

"Birdie, Maysom, Alen. They're gone. All of them." Evelyn straightened her back as though trying to push against the weight of what she was saying. Her eyes hardened and he could see a smoldering anger in those blood-filled eyes.

"Someone found you. I failed." The old woman bowed her head in shame.

Evelyn gripped her withered fingers into a tight hold.

"No, this was my fault. I didn't realize what it was I saw. He killed him. I thought I was doing the right thing going to find the cart..." she trailed off, realizing she said something she should not have.

Maun held his breath. She found the peddler in the woods. She knew there was an intruder in their midst.

"Killed who? What cart?"

Evelyn's frown deepened as she reached inside her cloak,

pulling out the wooden locket Maun had left behind with the peddler. She placed it into the old woman's hand, who trembled at the sight of it. Her fingers shook as she opened it to reveal a lock of hair that matched her own. This was who he belonged to. The old woman snapped the locket shut, holding it to her chest.

"How?" she said, her eyes dry, but straining in a conscious effort not to weep.

"There's no time. We must leave," Evelyn said, her expression urgent, but gentle as though she could see the grief that Maun couldn't within the old woman.

"Leave? We can't leave. This is my home. I'll not run from the face of a coward who thinks they can take my granddaughter from me." She tore her hand from Evelyn's grip, standing with the posture that Maun recognized as a defensive form. She was trained in the fighting arts.

"Gran, *everyone* is dead. There's nothing left for us here. Oretem…" she paused, trying to find the right words to say. "He isn't well. Something is wrong with the bond. I haven't the time to explain now. *We must leave*." The Viden spoke each syllable as if she were speaking to a whining child.

The old woman's shoulders relaxed, and she sighed, defeated. She looked at the locket, running a finger over its carved surface before placing it over her head. It hung low on her chest, swinging as she met the Viden's piercing gaze.

"Where do you suppose we go?"

"Reva," Evelyn answered quickly.

"That was fast. What's in Reva?"

"A name."

Her grandmother leaned forward, letting her granddaughter know she wouldn't take another step unless she shared more. The old woman was a stubborn creature. Maun was curious about her past. She seemed as hard and immovable as Ovia, but the calluses on the old woman's hands were not from hitting her granddaughter.

That kind of stubbornness was what would kill her. Maun gripped his dagger tighter and stepped forward, placing his heavy boots methodically on the floor. Every creak was accounted for. He released his breath with every step, becoming the silence he was trained to be. The thrill of creeping forward towards the unsuspecting women filled him with excitement. The last Viden to die by his blade. It was an honor bestowed upon him by the Decayed, assuring Maun that should he complete this task he would do all that was within his power to aid Maun in his search for Meric. Maun cared not for being in the debt of anyone—especially a man whose insanity claimed dominion over any say he could possibly have. Maun wasn't naïve to think he was anything more than a means to an end for the Cinaed, but he had little choice in the matter. It wasn't for the Decayed's pleasure that he would complete this task. He would feel Evelyn's blood on his hands for his own amusement. Evelyn sighed deeply and stopped trying to push her grandmother out of the house.

"I need to find someone named Meric."

Maun's feet froze to the ground as if ice had encircled his ankles. A chill rose through his neck and that old familiar rage boiled in his blood. Depths damn the Order. Damn the dragon and his bondsmate. Powerful as the Decayed was, the man couldn't give him what Evelyn just did. A clear path to his purpose. She was a map.

The Decayed may have created the Order and under normal circumstances Maun might've followed him as Tacet Devu and his father had. But Maun left the Order. He may still be Reticent, but he had his own plans. A surge of vengeance swirled inside him like a storm, and he felt Saiya soar higher into the sky as his emotions mixed with hers. He breathed in and kept the name locked within his chest where it became a burning ember, waiting to spark into an inferno. Shadows still cast themselves about Maun as the Viden's grandmother stared at Evelyn with a confused expression.

"Meric? Who told you this?"

Evelyn wiped a hand across her face and rubbed her tired eyes.

"I don't know. I heard it in the woods from a globe of light."

"Light? But how—"

Evelyn gripped her grandmother's shoulders hard. The look in her red eyes contained fury and anguish. Maun thought she might slap the old woman.

"I don't know. This is the problem, you see. I should, and I don't. We are leaving. Now. We need to find Sou." She walked past the old woman, turning back to speak again. "Sou will take us to Reva." Evelyn pulled her grandmother's arm.

"Does he live?" the words sounded oddly hopeful, but reserved as though the old woman couldn't decide which manner of way she'd prefer to find whoever this Sou was.

Evelyn turned with the tired determination that Maun thought might've had the power to move a boulder. She'd inherited that from her grandmother.

"He lives. I didn't find him amongst the…" she trailed off, not wanting to say the word. "He must live," she whispered.

Evelyn handed her grandmother a cloak and blade, laying underneath slabs of splintered wood. She and the old woman left the house as Maun crossed the room to follow them. They walked through the snow away from the burning village. Maun crept in between the homes, stepping inside their footprints to mask the sound of his own.

Evelyn paused and looked behind her as he waited behind a burning collapsed roof. He watched her in-between the groves of broken wood, her eyes wandering the air as if following a moving light. What was she looking at? There was nothing there as far as he could see. She followed whatever it was to where he was waiting.

It was then that realization came upon him. His cloak rustled in the wind, creating a small breeze around him. He clutched the folds of the fabric, but it was too late. The Videns of the past could see Iona's Breath. It made easier to control and it was helpful when discovering people who waited, such as himself, with dangerous intentions.

Celosia's bloody Depths! He should've remembered that,

but he'd never hunted a Viden before. It was a time before his training when it was the Order's sole purpose.

Her footsteps encroached closer, snow crackling beneath boots. He would be discovered. He wanted to follow her all the way to Reva unnoticed. She'd be more inclined to lead him to Meric without knowing of his presence, but even uninclined Maun had ways to make her comply. He called out to Saiya who dived in from the sky. He felt the beat of her wings and the excitement that flowed through the wind around her.

He stepped out from behind the burning roof. Evelyn's red eyes widened as she froze then backed away, her focus shifting about the black cloak that billowed around him. He knew the boding presence he exhibited, the dread that seemed to emanate from his being. It was as though she recognized him. Her eyes darted around his posture and the bodies littering the ashen ground, looking upon him as if she'd seen him in this exact spot, standing exactly as he was. She reached inside the scarf of her cloak—for a weapon no doubt. He cocked his head to the side, careful to show no emotion. He lifted his arm as Saiya's black wings hovered above his head. Her immense weight fell onto his arm, and he watched without expression as Evelyn's mouth opened in silent shock.

She stumbled as she backed away, never taking her eyes off Saiya and her shadowed presence. Evelyn's grandmother ran to her side, gripping her arm as she looked into Maun's eyes, refusing to be intimidated. Maun wondered again what the woman was like in her youth. She'd have made a good Reticent.

Evelyn glanced behind her, contemplating running. She could try. She would fail. She then turned back around and whistled. It was a unique tune from a song Maun had never heard.

"Evelyn." Saiya's voice mixed with his own, melding together into a horrific animalistic growl.

He enjoyed the crack in the old woman's stone expression as she heard his voice. It was enough to place fear in the bravest of people. Evelyn flinched as if slapped. She covered her mouth, horrified by what was before her. She was speech-less. He could tell she'd never seen a solov raptor before, but her grandmother had. Her glare was still set on him.

"Tongueless vermin. I should've known," she said, pushing Evelyn behind her. She pulled a long, black dagger from her cloak. It was thin, the hilt spiraled in iron, curving inwards into her wrist. It was a beautiful weapon. He would have it.

Evelyn looked the old woman up and down in confusion. Then glanced back at Maun, wondering how the two knew each other. Maun had never seen this woman in his life. But that didn't mean she didn't have experience with his Order.

"Yes, you should have. You have something I need." He allowed a small smile to cross his lips as he glanced back at the terrified Viden.

"I don't know you. If you came for me why not end it with me? These people — " she threw out her arm to the corpses that cackled in the flames. "Meant nothing to you. Birdie and Maysom meant *nothing* to you!" Evelyn's voice traveled across the village into the ears of the murdered who laid in heaps around him. Were those the names of the boy and his sister? He couldn't recall. He grinned.

"Yes."

Evelyn inhaled in a sharp intake of breath, stunned at his callous response. The red in her eyes shone brighter as anger overruled her fear.

"What could warrant such barbarism?" she spat at him.

"A name," he repeated her words back. Her anger trans-formed to confusion then fear as realization swept over her.

"Evelyn, run. Go. You are no match for his kind," her grandmother said in hushed urgency. Evelyn didn't move. She shut her mouth, her expression turning hard. She reached inside her cloak and pulled out a small throwing knife. It was short, only a hand's span. There was the Viden. His smile widened.

He uncovered his dagger from beneath his cloak and stepped towards them. His feet made no sound as he walked. Evelyn's eyes darted behind him and the glint of something spiteful shined within them. Maun's smile disappeared as he was thrown to the ground. Pain exploded in his shoulder, tearing and ripping with the cruelty of a dozen knives. His opened his mouth in a choked howl as a cloud of white fur brushed across his face. Fangs sawed into his muscle, blood spraying onto the snow. Saiya shrieked above him as he stabbed his dagger at the mass of fur. After many attempts, he finally met flesh and a loud whimper echoed in his ear. He was released, vision blurring as he gathered himself onto his hands and knees. The muddy shapes of Evelyn and the old woman came into focus as he stood.

The Viden rode on the back of a giant wolf, its body stained in blood around the shoulder. She gripped her grandmother's hand trying to lift her onto the creature's back, as it was much too tall for the woman to climb onto herself. The wolf noticed him running towards them and growled. Its maw and teeth were stained in his own blood. Maun ignored the anguish in his shoulder and lifted his dagger.

"Tansey!" Evelyn yelled.

The old woman, with more speed than he thought capable, released her granddaughters' hand and met his blade with her own. Their breaths mingled as she bared her teeth at him.

"You'll not have her," she spat at him. The sloppy drool went into his eyes and he grimaced as she kicked his feet out from beneath him. "Go!" she screamed and slapped the hide of the wolf, who ran away from the village.

No! She couldn't get away. Maun commanded Saiya to chase the Viden down and retrieve her. The raptor cawed, following the pair towards the direction Omya River. He would make sure she saw the dead body of her grandmother before he was done with her.

He lifted himself to his feet and threw down his dagger at the old woman who parried under the movement. She spun and landed on her knees, meeting his blade with arms raised. Breaths and Depths, she was fast! With a series of quick jabs, she stabbed at his gut as she stood, forcing him backwards. Blood from his shoulder dripped onto the ice, leaving a trail as she pushed him back. She leaped, clashing into him with her shoulder. Pain erupted from the contact, and Maun shut his eyes against the agony. He staggered back, his arm dangling almost useless in the fight.

Fool! You've grown arrogant. He imagined Tacet Devu's voice berating him within his head. The woman who raised and trained him would be disappointed to see the array of superficial cuts the old woman was able to land upon him. It had been some time since he'd fought someone worthy to cross blades with. This woman was more worthy than all of those who'd died by it.

"I know of your kind," Tansey sneered at him. "You killed my daughter. You killed Jaspar, didn't you? He was coming for me!" She bellowed as she brought down the dagger. He swiped it away with his own, ducking under a panel of broken wood that had tumbled from a collapsed roof.

The past he had wondered about had come back to taunt this woman. It drove her against him and, if used correctly, might overpower him. She might be faster, but he was smarter. He revealed himself from behind the panel of wood and walked to the middle of the village. Flames glowed around him in random lumps of soot and cinders. Tansey met his eyes, experienced hands curled into fists. He could practically see steam floating above her as she stared him down with anger. He could use that.

Come for me. In these final moments, live in your hate.

As though hearing him, she screamed, running towards him. He lifted his dagger and, with a clear mind, met hers with a swiftness he'd trained for years to accomplish. In the fury of her anger, he didn't know where the steel ended and he began. The two were one and he felt his own body move without pain as he receded into a state of absolute annihilation.

She twisted the dagger with the hilt out and threw her weight into the jab at his gut. He caught the old woman's wrist, using his other hand to clip her jaw. She gasped at the loss of breath as he used her weight to swipe her own blade across the inside of her leg, severing a large vein that poured like the well of a fountain. She clutched the wound, realization spreading across her features like the blood seeping through her fingers. The cut was deep, and she winced as she tried to put pressure on it. Maun flipped his dagger and without hesitation brought wrath upon her. She was slower, but still met his blade as he lunged. She grunted in pain and staggered as he pushed her back, jumping over the charred bodies of her fellow villagers. He felt nothing as their fingers cracked under his boot. They had always been beneath him. Why should he avert his stride even in death? Tansey panted as they looked each other over the body of a woman holding a half-burnt child in her arms. Snow smoldered underneath the two, creating wisps of smoke that drifted about them. She lifted her gaze, meeting his eyes again. Her leg trembled and she raised her hand, blood dripping from her fingertips.

"I'll not survive this," she said, simply and without fear. Odd, this one. She didn't seem the kind to beg, but still Maun had hoped. He liked it when they begged. Disappointed, he shook his head. "She stronger than you. She's stronger than me. May you die upturned."

A curse. Quite a curse to be spoken out loud. She risked her own soul just by speaking it. The victor may choose to keep the other upturned in retaliation. Not that he believed in such ridiculous superstitions. The Order burned their dead. Life was life and death gave into blackness. There was nothing after.

He pursed his lips as she lifted her dagger. Tansey would not die without it in her hand. What an opponent she'd have been in her youth. He almost regretted wounding her. They could've had a spar that lasted through the day. She would've still died, but what a glorious death it could've been.

He pressed forward as mists of snow tossed around them. It was a thing of beauty, her hate and his indifference. They fed off each other, bringing out a manifestation of pain that life was nothing but a terrible cycle of who could last the longest. Tansey lifted her steel and the sound of it clanged against his own. She swiped it to the side and tried to pierce it into his ribs. He blocked the attempt with a punch to her leg, leaving her gasping. She crumpled against him and like shifting sand, the flesh of her chest split as his dagger buried itself there.

She exhaled sharply, clinging to his shoulders with ferocity. He winced as her fingernails dug into the bloodied lesion on his shoulder. Her bright, brown eyes fluttered as she tried to speak, reaching for the necklace at her throat. She clutched it with the same fervor as its previous owner. Tansey fell from his grasp, her body upturned below him. Blood pooled beneath her as her eyes stared outwards among the dead, joining them with a last quick fall of her chest.

Maun leaned over her and grabbed the iron dagger from her limp hand. It was heavy but as he tossed it in the air, he found it to suit him quite well. Her hand stretched away from her; the wooden necklace laced in between her fingers. He kicked her hand, the locket clattering far from the old woman's body, disappearing under the snow and ash. He breathed in a heavy breath and walked away, clutching at his shoulder. His stamina invigorated by the fight. Would her granddaughter be the same? He would soon find out.

Chapter 14

The Departure from a Place so Beautiful

It was him.

How was it possible for one to move with such silence? Had she not noticed the change in the wind she would have continued onward, unaware of his steeled, murderous glare behind her. She'd never seen his like, expressionless yet burning with hatred. She would've been chilled by his emptiness had she not felt scorched by his intense animosity. How long had he been following her? The image of the outsider's black cloak swirling around him like his eagles' wings throbbed in her mind like a festering wound. She'd seen him, seen what he'd caused. She splintered apart, recognizing the pieces of her vision falling into place. Maysom knew. Why hadn't she listened? Why hadn't she said anything? The voice in the back of her mind tormented her with the possibilities of what she could have done different. What she should be doing different now.

"We have to go back!" her voice was overpowered by Nakesha, panting beneath her.

The wolf would simply not listen. She kept glancing up, sniffing the air as if worried something would attack from above. The injury in her shoulder seeped with blood, but it didn't seem to bother the animal. Evelyn ran her hand over the wound and was relieved to realize the cut was not so deep as she feared. Her mind wandered to the cloaked man and his dark bird companion.

Could such a creature be called a bird? She'd never seen anything like it. Maysom was right, the eagle was monstrous. The blackness of its wings was a personification of Celosia's Depths. Its yellow eyes held an intelligence never meant to be in a creature so malicious. It was far too human, reflecting the hatred of its master. She'd seen eagles before, but never that large and never with such stark human understanding.

She tried pulling on Nakesha's pelt to steer her back to the village, but the wolf remained fixated on her course. Tansey was alone, fighting that wretched man. She shivered at the memory of his scarred face, the sound of his voice through the eagle. He hadn't moved his lips at all. How was that possible? Was it similar to her bond with Oretem? It couldn't be. There was so much *wrong* with it. She couldn't explain it to herself. Tansey seemed to recognize the man although she was certain her grandmother had never met him before. The old woman avoided all talk of the war she'd fought in before Evelyn was born but now, she wondered if a piece of that life had returned in the form of the outsider.

"Nakesha! Take me back!" she screamed. Again, the wolf ignored her. Evelyn's thoughts turned to Sou.

Will I find him burnt? His hut turned to ash in Iona's Breath? No...

She couldn't bear the thought. Yet she was bearing it all the same. Birdie, Adel, Maysom.... Tansey. She stared at her blistered hands gripping the wolf's fur. The grief crushed her from the inside out, pressing against her with such force she feared she'd never breathe properly again. She had to go back for Tansey. Once they reached Sou, he would take her back. He had to.

She saw the outline of his home. It was untouched and his figure grew as he ran towards her. He carried a pack over his shoulder, a panicked look consuming his kind features. He pointed towards the sky, yelling words she could not hear over the roar of the wind. A swooping gust of air swept over Evelyn, throwing her from Nakesha back. Her body couldn't bend to the shape of the tundra, and she tumbled before landing on her back, gasping. The cold air cut into her lungs like knives as she regained her bearings, trying to lift herself from the ground. When she placed pressure on her hand it crumpled under her weight. She cried out and landed on her back again, clutching her broken wrist. White spots clouded her vision as she sat up, blinking into focus. She held her hand to her chest, realizing the white spots were snow being hurtled in all directions. Nakesha was growling and snapping at a black shadow pinning her down.

"No!"

The giant eagle was on top of the wolf, digging its claws into her belly. Blood sprayed onto the ice in chaotic patterns, encircling the two like a foul ritual. Evelyn ran, halting just before the battling creatures as she lifted a hand. Iona's Breath thrashed about Nakesha and the eagle in a torrent of blue light that should've been easy to control. Evelyn groaned in frustration as that same light escaped her grasp. The eagle shrieked, black beak dripping with blood.

Nakesha turned over, sinking her fangs into the eagle's wing. It screeched in pain as it flailed around, kicking up snow with its talons. The wolf was larger than the bird, but its claws were longer and sharper. Evelyn sprinted up to the side, holding her broken hand to her chest and unsheathed one of her throwing daggers. Tansey had made sure to train her using both hands, but her broken one had always been her strongest. She held the blade out, franticly searching for an opening. The beasts were tangled, and Evelyn was just as likely to stab Nakesha as the creature attacking her. She was about to get closer when strong fingers grip her arms, pulling her backwards. She turned to attack but stopped, recognizing the familiar head scarf resting on Sou's forehead.

"No! This is a battle of fang and claw. Neither of which you have," he said as he dragged her away.

"I can't leave her! Tansey is still out there," she struggled against his grip, but he was too strong. He spun her around, baring his panicked gaze into her own.

"We must." Sou's green eyes were wide, urgent but brimming with grief. He knew the pain she was grappling with. "You cannot help them."

No. She had to. This is what she was supposed to do. What good was running when everything she loved was behind her? She had feared bonding to Oretem would change her as quakes change the earth, but what had happened was far worse. This was her fault, and she could not leave without doing everything she could for those left. Evelyn bared her teeth, pushing Sou away. He fell onto the snow in a hard swirl of white mist. She ran towards the fighting animals, leaving Sou in the echo of her name.

Nakesha was growing tired. Her body lagged against its own will to survive, tongue hanging heavily from her jaw. She'd lost so much blood. It dripped down her legs as her paws dragged red prints across the ice. The eagle's talons paced the snow, crouching to lift into the sky. The two had ventured further away as they fought. Evelyn growled, knowing she was too far to throw her dagger. She forced her legs further, muscles burning as she tested their endurance. The eagle flapped its wings, lifted, and hovered overhead. Nakesha staggered, trying to get out from under its shadow. Her predatory expression waned as she ran, limping with her tail tucked between her legs.

Evelyn was almost within range. The eagle dived; its wings angled in line with its arrow-like body. Evelyn held out her dagger, throwing her arm forward as the blade left her hand. It flew straight, gaining altitude with a little less speed than if she'd thrown it with her broken hand. The eagle spotted the glint of steel and lowered a wing, flying beneath the dagger. She missed. Evelyn held her breath as the eagle spun in the air, the steel of her knife sinking into the snow, abandoned.

The world went still as massive wings enveloped Nakesha, the bird's shadow swallowing the bright snow in a patch of complete darkness. The wolf whimpered, yelping as the bird's claws sank into the back of her neck, crimson dancing across the sky like spilled paint. She writhed on the floor and a sickening crunch echoed across the space in between them. Evelyn's feet became ice, staked to the ground. She gasped, her chest splitting open. The sound of Nakesha's neck breaking reverberated in the distance that separated them, echoing for eternity in a place where happiness did not exist. The dagger she threw was only a few feet from her, the brightness of its edge reflecting in the sunlight. The black eagle stood over Nakesha and with its great golden eye, stared at Evelyn as if to say, *you are nothing but meat.* Blind with rage, she glared at the vicious beast, tears streaking down her sooty cheeks. She'd lost everything. Her home, friends, family and now her bena wolf. Nakesha was hers, her beauty, her vain one. Her companion of the hunt and of her heart. Stolen from her, taken. Murdered. Evelyn ran, lifting the dagger from the snow, bellowing an anguished cry.

I will rip your tongue out with my bare teeth.

Evelyn's inner voice was so foreign, so violent, she thought it couldn't have been hers. It echoed in her mind, growling with the ferocity of a dragon. The eagle lifted itself from Nakesha's body, flying rapidly towards her. She tightened her grip on the dagger, the curved hilt burrowing into her skin. Sou called out to her. She hardly heard him. She only heard her own animalistic growls and the wind rising with the creatures' wings. The turning of time halted, suspended in the air with the glint of steel in her hand. The eagle cried out, reaching out with sharpened talons and Evelyn threw her blade.

The bird swirled in the sky, screeching as her knife reached its target. Red burst from its shoulder, showering the snow in its gore. Its wings folded in as it fell from the sky, struggling on the ground as it tried to lift its bulk into the air. Waves of snow and feathers scattered about the ground as it tried unsuccessfully to take flight.

A grim smile grew on Evelyn's face as she neared the animal. She would kill it. It deserved to die. She thought of her people. Their burnt bodies and broken flesh. Nakesha laid in a bloody heap never to howl again.

The bird uprighted itself, thrashing its talons across the ice. They were long enough to skewer a wild babi boar. Just as Evelyn was within a few paces, she reached into her cloak, fingering the hilt of a dagger, ready to die in trying to kill this creature of death. A gust of wind threw Evelyn from her feet, pulling her backwards and catapulting the eagle far from where it once was. She landed in strong arms gripping her waist. Had she done that? She hadn't been able to conjure the Iona's Breath when it mattered. So why now? Her arms trembled, trying to tear herself away from Sou's arms as the eagle attempted to take flight. She beat her hands against his grasp, ignoring the pain in her hand.

Sou said nothing. He took the beating and rested his head on the back of her neck. She screamed, falling to her knees as red colored her vision in grief and anger. He rocked her back and forth as she cried. It was too much. She'd lost too much. She stared at the eagle. It continued to jump into the air, flying away in bursts back to the village.

Emptiness grew within her like a parasite, feeding on the void in her chest, expanding it. She stopped crying, stopped screaming. She had nothing and therefore, had given up herself to feel nothing as darkness consumed her. The bruises covering her body faded to a dull ache. She looked to where Nakesha laid and lost herself in the blood that pooled beneath her beloved friend. Too much. It was all too much.

Hands gripped her shoulders, shaking her into awareness. Sou kneeled before her, mouth open in a frenzied array of movement. How long had she been sitting here?

"Get up! Get up!" his voice clashed against the emptiness. Sou glanced behind him in panic. The crow's feet at the corners of his eyes pronounced. "Now, lass!" He grabbed her arm and lifted her.

There was a dark figure in the distance, growing closer. A billowing darkness around the figure bent its shape like a shifting shadow. A cloak? She snapped into reality. The outsider. Tansey. She knew what his presence meant. There was no time. No time to mourn. Evelyn ran alongside Sou, matching the speed of his feet. His pack thumped against his back as they got closer to the dock. She almost tripped in the transition from snow to wood. Sou balanced her with a quick grab of her arm and pulled her inside the boat.

She sat on the wooden bench behind the helm, numb to everything around her. Sou untied the rope, pushing against the dock. The ship rocked, then balanced itself out as they ventured into the middle of the river. A fog of cold water drifted, clouding the fading dock with a wash of mist.

Evelyn watched the dock as it grew smaller. The thickening mist turning into a wall, shutting her out forever. Just before the white mist covered the dock, the outsider appeared, holding his black eagle. His silhouette shifted with his cloak, making it difficult to see him as human. Like his eagle, he was a black rip in the landscape, a dark, brandishing portal to a place of pain. Smoke rose from what remained of Verbena. It was almost peaceful. Her mountains stood strong, unaffected by the catastrophe below it. Evelyn hadn't realized how magnificent they were.

Birdie was right. How could she leave a place so beautiful?

PART TWO

INTERLUDE

MOTHERLESS

20 YEARS AGO...

If there was ever an emotion that couldn't be tolerated it would be her own misery. Tansey felt it within her, sparking and crackling to life as she sat by the fire, a cup of tea in her hand. Her mind was a stagnate muscle of thought, lost to the flames in the hearth. The more she watched the colors, the more they formed into the shades of her daughter's face. Ten years it had been. She hadn't seen the features of Nakesha for ten years.

There were days she was afraid she'd forgotten them. The shape of her nose or the color of her eyes. Then she sat in front of the flames, and they all came back to her. Nakesha never took after herself. She was her father's daughter.

"Depths damn you, Kalen. You were always better at everything," she said with a fond smile. She often spoke with him. She knew he listened; she just couldn't hear him.

Her husband died much too soon and she was unprepared for facing life without him. She'd always been sure of herself. She knew the clash of the world and how to resist its scars. His death was the only one that hadn't healed properly. It was a scab she constantly picked at, allowing the pain to remind her of what she had lost. The blood swelled, but she was willing to peel back the skin again and again to make sure she never forgot. She was so afraid of forgetting.

"Where is she, Kalen? Where is our daughter?"

There was no answer. There never was. Ten years ago, Nakesha—against her mother's wishes—left Verbena. It was such a time ago that Tansey had forgotten the exact words exchanged between them. There was yelling. She was sure of that.

Nakesha had met someone. A Vagu man who promised everything that men do when smitten by first love. What was his name? She couldn't remember. Tansey sighed. Now, ten years too late she supposed it wasn't so awful that Nakesha wanted to leave Verbena.

Tansey was unfortunate enough to have traveled with her mother. Arlisa could never have been described as affectionate. Sometimes, Tansey felt as if she wasn't born of her womb but of a strange beggar from a distant city. She'd asked that once. Arlisa kissed her forehead and never answered. She almost never spoke. The woman withdrew into herself the older she got. Those who knew her before Tansey was born spoke of a vibrant woman who often talked herself into trouble rather than out of it. It wasn't until she bonded and received visions had she sought the words of her dragon more than the people around her. While it was not spoken of, Tansey knew it was the visions. She recalled hearing her soft weeping in the night when she woke from a dream, seeking her dragon for comfort and leaving Tansey in her worry.

Noha had been slender dragon that had a mane of green and blue membrane hanging from her neck the way horses did. It blew in the wind, bright and majestic when she took flight. She had the same membrane trailing from her tail. The most beautiful of all dragons, a wind dragon in her element. When she flew it was as if the earth tipped and the ocean became the sky. Her mother never looked happier than when she was in the air with Noha.

She'd taught Tansey how to be a warrior, training her with little words, glares, and hand gestures. It was brutal work. Tansey flexed her fingers, feeling the ache in her joints when the weather was especially cold. During these training sessions, she resolved to close her mind to the pains of her body to better perform and please her mother. In doing so, she included her emotions as well, locking them away for when she had the time and energy to deal with them. It worked for the most part, but there were some memories too painful to unlock. If freed Tansey feared not to survive such an onslaught of pain after all the years they had laid dormant. The screams. The blood. They echoed from within, but Tansey gripped her cup, ignoring their quiet calls. Noha was the only creature to have understood her mother. Tansey held much resentment for that. If Arlisa hadn't dreamt, hadn't bonded to Noha, would Nakesha had ever left? Would Kalen had died? Would they had ever met? It was the same, endless circle of questioning she'd had over the past ten years and she was still no closer to an answer. She only knew Arlisa had failed her as a mother and so Tansey had failed her own daughter. The only difference was that she admitted her fault and should she ever see Nakesha again, she'd tell her.

As with many children then, and now, she'd grown up never having known her father. The war took the men more often than the women. Until there wasn't a choice anymore. Cinaed was no discerner of genders. He killed men, women, and children alike without thought of mercy. Tansey had fought the assassins who raided villages and took children for the Order. There wasn't much known about the Reticent but in the height of their power they were the most feared cult in all of Iona—still were. Mothers saved all they owned to hire a Venandi just for the slim chance they might be able to track their kidnapped child. Tansey had never heard of any successful rescues.

She'd heard of a great battle over the burning waters of Elm Lake. News traveled to Verbena slowly and with different endings. Some said the battle was won and Caia reigned triumphant, while others claimed Chao was burning his way down the south. But not to worry, since Verbena did not exist in the outside world. The villagers were kind and compassionate but had little experience with war. The Breaths and

Depths help them if they succumbed to the horrors of what she'd witnessed in her years fighting alongside her mother. The village wouldn't stand a chance. Tansey sipped her tea and grimaced as the cold flavor shivered down her throat. As usual, she had been too lost in her thoughts for too long.

"You always told me I could warm a fireless hearth. I can't even keep my tea warm," she said as she stood.

The ache in her chest apparently had room not only for the pain of her daughter's absence, but also for the grief her husband left behind almost thirty years later. The worst of it was that Kalen had been taken so casually. There was no great battle. He hadn't fallen upon a sword or been skewered by the claws of raptors. He fell from a roof and slowly perished in their bed, raving and screaming in terror at images his mind was too damaged to heal. It was a slow death, a painful one. She trembled to recall the sorrow of his passing.

She poured the remaining tea from her cup in a bucket of dirty soap water, then grabbed the kettle from the counter, placing it on the hook above the fire, careful not to burn her hand on the handle. She sat down in her chair, waiting for the water and leaves to boil. She watched the flames cast shadows across the room, traveling shades dancing upon her hands.

She lifted them from her lap and twisted them in the air. The lines of her palms were more pronounced, and age spots multiplied on the tops of her hands. When had those appeared? She couldn't tell if they were shadows created by the flames or of her weathered years. She swore off marriage to remain young and even without her husband she was succumbing to the ailment.

She traced the shallow wrinkles of her hands and thought that if Nakesha were to return in the morning, would she even recognize her own mother? The brightness of Tansey's brown hair had faded and there were wisps of grey that had begun to show from the roots. It was the beginning of her transformation. The quiet life she had built after a childhood of war was the loneliest she'd ever been.

She fought against a tear that teetered on the precipice of

her eye, but to no avail. It fell like the snow outside, cold, formless, and enduring. The kettle shook as the water evaporated, whistling as it escaped from its neck.

A heavy, repeating strike vibrated through Tansey's home.

She started at the sound, lifting a hand to her chest. It was well past midnight, and she couldn't think of a reason for any of the villagers to come to her door. She took the cloth she hung on the side of her chair and grabbed the kettle.

The pounding was insistent and much too hard for the knuckles of a hand. The door frame shook as if straining to keep whatever force beyond it from entering. She thought it must be a boot. She stilled herself, locking away her debilitating thoughts of the past. She placed the kettle on the counter and walked to the closet. The knocking still shook the door, demanding entry. She opened the closet and unsheathed a dark iron dagger. The hilt felt cold against her fingers. It was her mother's.

Arlisa didn't speak when she died. She only placed the dagger in Tansey's hand as she bled out on the cobblestoned streets of Reva. She was thrown off Noha's back during a battle for the city. Tansey remembered the raw teeth marks on her mother's body, a sickening confirmation that Noha had reached behind and flung her rider with no more emotion than swatting a fly. Arlisa faded to the wind as she fell away from the mortal world. Noha died soon after one too many raptors tore her wings to shreds, but not before she killed as many Reticent as her own. Tansey remembered the burnt and crushed remains of the people they were meant to protect, killed by foe and friend alike. It rained blood that day. The beautiful wind dragon broke her neck in a crash just outside of the city. It was after that battle that Tansey moved to Verbena. She couldn't see the use of fighting a war with an enemy on both sides. Their only protectors unable to protect their charges from themselves. She'd never forgotten the howls of those dying on the battlefield. Turning her mother towards Iona was a memory as hurtful as her husband dying.

She fingered the hilt and felt a familiarity. As if Arlisa were a spirit within the blade, guiding her in a way she couldn't in life. The striking of the door grew as she wrapped her hand over the lock. She lifted the latch and with a single pound of the person on the opposite side, the door burst open. Tansey lifted the dagger, then froze. The bitter cold filled the house with flurries, but she couldn't feel them. The ground could've opened beneath her, and she wouldn't have noticed. She dropped the dagger. It clattered to the floor with a steel song.

A man in a heavy cloak held Nakesha in his arms. His black hair was long under a red headband that covered his forehead. He held Nakesha close and with pleading green eyes shivered in front of her.

"Please," he said, breaking the shock Tansey was trapped in.

Her control shattered and all at once she felt ten years worth of heartache. Ten years worth of worry and uncertainty. The nights she'd spent by the hearth, wondering if Nakesha were alive. She was here in this man's arms, breathing and beautiful. All those nights imagining her daughter's face in the fire, and she'd still forgotten how beautiful she was. Unable to speak she moved aside and let the man enter.

His boots were thick with ice, and he spun in the room before he noticed the hearth. He kicked the chair Tansey had sat in, toppling it on its side. He knelt and placed her daughter on the floor in front of the fire. He threw from his shoulder the burlap cloak over her, and Tansey gasped.

A child was strapped to his back. Her fat cheeks huddled against the man's neck, asleep. She didn't look older than two years of age. The child sucked on her thumb, lips plump and wet. Her brown hair curled in waves under a woolen cap that rested above eyebrows that slanted upwards just a touch. Through all the nights Tansey had imagined her daughter's face she found similar features in the child's.

Oh, Kalen. What have I done?

The man stood and she found herself surprised at his true figure. He was thin and much older than she previously thought. As old as she was by a year or two. Much too old to be the father of the child, or so she thought. His clear eyes were tired, exhausted by whatever he'd gone through to make it to her door. He had an open wound that sliced just below his collar—she hadn't noticed before because his shoulders were covered by the cloak. He sighed as he righted the chair and sat down. What ever happened to the young man she left with? Had the relationship gone sour? Is that why she'd returned?

Tansey kneeled next to Nakesha and touched her cheek. She was cold, her skin like stone in the mountains. Her slender nose bore a cut on the bridge and a line of blood from her nostril. She'd been attacked. Tansey's hand drifted downward, and she felt something thick and wet slick over her fingertips. She lowered the cloak and choked back a gasp as she saw the deep gash that ran across her daughter's belly. The inside of her body peeking from the wound, ripe flesh glistening in the shadows. There was nothing needle and thread could do for a wound so dreadful.

"Nakesha. It's mother. You are home," she said, but Nakesha only shivered in response.

Her daughter's face was just as she remembered. Her dark hair and defined cheekbones complimented her thin lips. She looked so much like her father that Taney's heart ached, but her brown hair, covered in snow, was exactly like her own. She was older. Her laugh lines were deeper around her mouth and eyes. As if she'd spent the last ten years in a state of complete happiness.

"You're going to live, my love," Tansey whispered, wiping away tears. She had to live. There was no other option, but the blood-soaked cloak argued that point. She stood, suddenly aware of the stranger who brought her daughter bleeding to her doorstep.

"Who are you? What happened to my daughter? Why is she…" she couldn't say *dying*. She wasn't *dying*, only injured. She'd recover.

"My name is Sou. We were attacked." His head righted itself as if she'd woken him from a deep sleep. The headwrap on his brow flowed over his shoulder, stained in blood. She didn't know if it was his or Nakesha's. There was so much of it.

"Attacked? By whom? Where has she been?" She raised her voice. The urgency of it leaking into the anguish she couldn't bury. No control—she had nowhere to put the memories being created.

"I know this is difficult—"

She cut him off with a scoff. "Difficult? You know this is *difficult*?" She tightened her hands into fists. "You know nothing. You've no womb. How can you possibly know? Ten years! It's been *ten years*!" Tears dripped from her jaw. She crossed the room where her dagger laid on the floor. She heard Sou stand from the chair, following in her wake. She spun around, holding out the dagger. The tip breadths from the base of his throat.

He only stood there. He didn't raised his hands or beg for his life. There was a kindness in his eyes that spoke to a type of grief she knew. The torment of war, the misery of memory. Only those who had known its pain could see it in others, and she saw it in him. Still, she pointed the dagger at him.

"Tell me everything you know. Or I swear by Celosia's bottomless Depths, I will *kill* you." She meant it. Her hand didn't shake or falter. She would strike and she wouldn't regret it.

"The child is all that matters," he said as he reached for the strap at his waist.

She'd forgotten about the girl. Tansey blinked as he unwrapped the cloth and cradled the small girl in his arms.

"Evelyn, this is your grandmother." The girl slept unaware as he held her out to Tansey, whose eyes glistened at the sight of the child. She shook the dagger as her lips trembled. Only Nakesha mattered right now.

"What *happened* to my daughter? I will not ask again." She couldn't think of anything else. Her eyes wandered to the hearth where Nakesha laid. The cloak lifted and fell with her irregular breaths.

"The battle at Elm Lake is won. Cinaed and Chao are dead,

but at a great cost. Caia and her dragon fell." His voice was strong, but his eyes fought tears.

The last Viden was dead. An overwhelming sense of despair settled over Tansey. When Noha died there were still so many. As the war raged on more and more returned to Iona until all their hope rested on a poor street urchin turned Viden. Caia. An entire generation of dragons lost. Even if Chao had gone mad with his bondsmate, it was still a devastating loss. The pain of losing her mother was similar and Tansey was shocked to have felt the extermination of dragons so comparable.

"The last gone?" she whispered.

Sou shook his head, then looked at the child.

"Not the last."

Tansey glanced at the girl as she sucked her thumb. The innocence of her age brought a calmness to Tansey's rage. Could it be possible? She had never showed signs of being Viden and neither did Nakesha. Despite the power skipping them, it was possible this girl possessed the ancient potential.

"She dreams?" Tansey watched the movement of the girl's eyes under her lids. They were rapid in their flow, darting left and right as if following a firefly.

"She does," he said with a smile. "She's only started sharing her dreams, but still, there are those who know of her existence. Caia sent a message that she couldn't protect her anymore. That she did what she could and to hide the child. We knew then she was lost." He frowned as his finger brushed the red cheek of the sleeping girl. She fidgeted in his arms, then settled again into sleep.

"We left Birny as soon as the message was received." His brow furrowed as if the memory were distasteful.

Birny? She was in Birny all this time. Tansey's heart broke at the knowledge her daughter was less than two weeks ride away.

"But I received word of the battle's end a month ago. It doesn't take that long to travel from Birny to Verbena." She was surprised to not have heard the great Decayed was dead.

At least from a trustworthy source. She thought that news would've traveled much faster. She'd have celebrated if she'd found out under different circumstances. The knowledge didn't seem important now.

"Nakesha was captured by Reticent a week into our journey. I was searching for her the rest of the time."

Tansey covered her mouth with her hand. So long. She'd been their captive for so long. The pain she must've suffered. A boiling anger took hold of Tansey, building new strength into her tired arm holding the dagger. Those bond desecraters had taken her mother and now, she was in danger of losing her daughter to them. Had sheer will been enough to heal her, Nakesha would already be conscious and sipping tea by the fire. But as was her fate to be, Tansey wasn't strong enough.

"Why didn't you protect her? How could you not find her?" She knew the hatred was misplaced. If anyone was to blame, she was. If she were a kinder mother, Nakesha would never have left, or perhaps if she'd have let her go, she'd have visited. Tansey might've been a part of her granddaughter's life. She'd missed so much. But to face that blame was too much for her to accept. She needed to blame someone else. And by the look of it, he didn't disagree with her.

"It is my great regret. Had I not cared for the girl I might've found her sooner." He looked at Evelyn with fondness in his aged eyes.

"Surely you cannot blame the child for your ineptitude," she spat the words as she circled him, lowering the dagger.

She walked to the hearth and sat next to Nakesha, who breathed as if a rock were lodged in her throat. Sou lowered himself in the chair, the girl resting in the crook of his elbow. Tansey placed her knife on the floor, but kept the blade by her hand, ready to strike if needed.

"The blame lies with me. I am deeply sorry."

He meant it. His voice cracked at the apology, eyes glistening as he gazed at Nakesha. They were full of love. Perhaps he was her lover. It had been known to happen between the young and old. Not that it was any concern of hers. She couldn't think of anything else that she cared for less.

"Your words mean nothing. You've failed her." This was her fault, and the words were to herself. But Sou didn't have to know that.

"My words may be hollow, but rest assured your daughter has been avenged."

Tansey glanced up at the man, looking upon the deep slit in his collar with new eyes. A darkness settled about him, and she itched to reach for her dagger. He withheld a vengeful blackness in those eyes that Tansey hadn't seen previously. She resigned to its presence, comforted by the knowledge he'd punished those responsible for hurting her child, imagining with grim satisfaction their demise.

"She will die," she whispered as Nakesha's breath became more infrequent. She caressed her cheek with the backs of her fingers. She was much too young. Children were supposed to outlive their parents.

"Aye," Sou said, his words exact but edged in sharp misery. "Her daughter needs you. She is Viden. The last remnant of an ancient pact that has protected our lands for centuries. The fight isn't over. Iona will need a Viden again, and Evelyn is the only one."

Tansey removed her hand from Nakesha's chest and held out her arms to the child. Sou's mouth curved up in a small smile as he handed her over. In her arms, the girl was small and so warm. Her feet wiggled as she dreamt. She had spat out her thumb, which was wet with spit.

"Evelyn," Tansey whispered in awe. Such a beautiful child. She glanced at Sou and tried to find any resemblance but found nothing. How could a father leave his child? But the question Tansey most feared was what if he tried to take her? Evelyn twitched in Tansey's arms as if she knew someone else held her.

"You will abandon your daughter?"

Sou lowered his head in a spent chuckle. The anger grew again. What could be so amusing?

"Wrong on both counts. I am not her father, and I will not abandon her."

Tansey stiffened and tightened her hold on her grand-daughter. He would take her away. The only piece of Nakesha she'd have left. She wondered again what had become of the young man, but she could live without that information. She had to focus on what was in front of her.

"Who are you to her then?"

He rubbed his cheeks, and she could see grey strands of hair that peeked beneath his head scarf. "I know Nakesha's husband," he said with the clear intention of not revealing more.

So, they'd remained together all these years. Why hadn't they traveled together?

"Why isn't he with you?" Sou looked at Nakesha with tired eyes. Tansey knew the answer. "She told him to stay, didn't she?"

Sou nodded. "Your daughter has been happy, Tansey. She's loved and his heart broke to stay behind. But he knew it was the right thing to do. They both did."

She wanted nothing to do with him. Happy? Loved? Nakesha could've been just as loved and just as happy with her mother. Evelyn would never know the truth of this man. She had to be protected. Whatever the cost would be Tansey would pay it. She may be Viden, but she would never need to act upon it.

"Get out," she whispered, grimacing against the burning hate behind her eyes.

"What?"

"Get out!" she screamed, standing abruptly, and holding the dagger out at him.

Evelyn stirred in her arms and her eyes fluttered open, woken by the sudden movement. Tansey smiled as she looked into her dark brown eyes. So much like her own.

"Hello, little one," she said, clutching her small hand.

The girl recoiled in horror. She squirmed in Tansey's arms and slapped her across the face.

"Soup!" Evelyn cried out, terror engulfing her once peaceful features.

He leaned forward in the chair and enveloped her in his arms. Tansey dropped the dagger as she held her cheek, rubbing the sting of the slap. It hadn't hurt physically, but emotionally, she felt as if she's been bludgeoned with a hammer.

Sou rubbed the girl's back and comforted her with soothing words. Words that Tansey was at a loss for. Evelyn didn't know her. Hadn't known she existed. Nakesha never spoke of her and that hurt more than any physical pain. Sou stood from the chair with Evelyn in his arms.

"I will leave you, but as I said before, I will not abandon her," he patted Evelyn's hair as her cries quieted. "I made a promise to her mother. A promise that applies to you as well. To protect her."

Tansey cast her eyes downward, unable to bear the thought of him seeing her shame. She would not show him more weakness than she had to.

"There is an abandoned ferry hut on the Omya River. We stayed there for a few days waiting for Nakesha to be well enough to travel. When it became apparent she wasn't healing..." he stopped speaking for a moment, his silence an apology for not coming sooner. "That is where I'll stay. Away from the village, but close enough to watch. The river needs a ferryman anyway, and I can repair the abandoned ship there."

Evelyn was quiet again as she buried her head into Sou's neck. She probably thought she had a nightmare. The comfort she felt in his embrace was obvious and Tansey envied the contentment she had in his arms.

"She may be Viden, but without a dragon there's nothing she can offer to the rest of the world. Nakesha is *my daughter*. That girl is all I'll have left of her." She sobbed out the truth with a crack in her voice.

Tansey hated herself for what she hoped. She prayed to the Breaths and Depths that Nakesha would die in the night. Her pain ended and her voice joined with the wind. She listened to

155

the agonizing sounds of her daughter fighting for breath. Blood oozed from the fabric, staining the wood beneath her. There was no surviving that and there was no painless way to die from it.

"No, it is not."

Tansey started. Who else was left behind when Nakesha left Birny?

"What use is a Viden without a dragon? She'll never need to grow into that role," she said, his smile irritating her. The last dragon was killed on the burning lake. Chao and Varsha were gone.

Weren't they?

"Your daughter and granddaughter are not all I brought with me. There is another dragon. An old one that lives in your mountains. He waits for the day she comes of age."

Tansey's shoulders slumped as she remembered the stories she'd heard from the villagers when she first arrived in Verbena. An old beast, a dragon by the name of Oretem. He'd left to fight in the war, finding places to rest in the Eshe Willow Wood. The story ended with his death under a giant willow that soaked his blood. That tree was known as the Crimson Willow.

"He died. He died years ago." She placed her hand back on Nakesha, feeling the rise of her chest. The act comforted Tansey in the face of everything she was learning. Truths she hadn't felt capable of accepting.

"You don't have to believe now. It doesn't change that it's true. Once you've had time, you and the rest of the village will know. His protection requires the silence of the entire town. As well as hers." He inclined his head at Evelyn, who had fallen back to sleep. "Surprises harbor unexpected reactions and we'll need to control those."

She nodded. She had time. Her mind was too numb to absorb what he required of her. Her thoughts clouded and all she could think of was Nakesha. Sou stood from the chair and Tansey clutched the dagger. He didn't flinch at her movement.

"Be with your daughter. I am sorry I couldn't protect her.

She is precious to me too. I will take Evelyn — " he paused at her distraught expression. "I will bring her back, this I swear. I will begin explaining things to her and to you. There is much to decide. She will come to know you. She will love you." He smiled at her.

Tansey glared in return. She would have to be reminded of this day for as long as he lived here. For the rest of her days, she'd look upon his face and see the dying eyes of her daughter. Her remorse and guilt would be his burden. She could not shoulder it alone no matter how faultless he might've been.

Sou moved towards the door then turned back, reaching into his cloak. He pulled out a necklace, brass coils curled around an empty space where Noha's scale used to be. Tansey had gifted Arlisa's necklace to Nakesha when she was just a girl. A time when Kalen was alive, and Nakesha couldn't sleep without a song. When Tansey had finally found her peace.

"For what it's worth, I never saw her without it," Sou said, his green eyes comforting. Tansey turned away, staring into the fire as she clutched her daughter's hand. The necklace was a symbol of her failure, an emblem to show how much like Arlisa she turned out to be.

"Keep it. I never want to see it again," Tansey said, refusing to look at him.

"I will return in the morning."

Without another word he left, the door closing softly against the night wind. Tansey stared at the floor and felt all she held back. She clutched Nakesha to her chest, cradling her in her arms as she wept. A soft whimper spread through the air like the helpless call of an abandoned kitten. Tansey sat up and stared into the open eyes of her daughter. She blinked, unseeing and unfocused.

"Don't... bastards. Long... gone," Nakesha said, murmuring her words as if she were still asleep. She didn't seem to realize she was in the arms of her mother. Tansey held her close and kissed her forehead.

"Nakesha, it's ma. You're safe. I'm going to take care of you." Tansey smiled despite her daughter's pale features.

Nakesha's head leaned into Tansey's arm, confusion then realization returning to her dark eyes.

"Ma…" she whispered. Tansey nodded and held her hand to her cheek, kissing Nakesha's fingertips. She tried to say more, but her tongue only peeked from between her lips as if it were too big for her mouth.

"Evelyn is safe. She is with Sou. They're both safe." Nakesha relaxed at that, and her taut muscles limped in Tansey's arms. "You've done well. So very well." Tansey's lip quivered as she spoke.

All her defenses were laid bare in the presence of her dying daughter. Nakesha continued to mumble in her arms, unable to stay lucid. She would moan in pain and cry out for mercy from an unseen hand. Then, just as quickly, chuckle and ask someone named Louve to wait for her tomatoes to ripen just a season longer. She was trapped in a constant state of delusion that crushed Tansey from within. This would take hours, even days. Tansey closed her eyes, feeling tears run down her cheeks. How could she bare it?

"Kill… me…"

Tansey opened her eyes, disbelieving. Nakesha had been able to pick up the dagger. The dark iron held close to her chest as her brown eyes bore into Tansey's. She shook her head with a fury. No, she couldn't. This was her daughter's delusion speaking. She wasn't thinking.

"You bastard… kill me," Nakesha said through clenched teeth. Tansey knew her daughter couldn't see her. She saw a Reticent. A soulless man who tortured her for the location of the last Viden. She still thought she was with him. "I'll tell you… nothing."

Tansey felt a pang of pride. She was a far better mother than Tansey ever was. A fire lit in Nakesha's expression, as though she had sprung up clean from muddy water. She returned, free from the hallucinations her waking eyes plagued her with. This vibrant, intelligent woman was her daughter.

"Help… me," she whispered, gritting her teeth as she groaned in pain.

"Do not ask me," Tansey said, hardly able to speak the words.

"Ma..." Nakesha moved a single finger over the back of her hand, using all her strength in the effort. "It is done."

Tansey shook with grief. Nakesha knew her fate and was asking her mother to help her meet it with swiftness and dignity. Tansey thought of Kalen, his once handsome features contorted in sweat and pain. Had she not seen her husband die so slowly, she might've refused this horrific burden. But she had and she couldn't bear to watch it again.

"I was wrong, Nakesha. So wrong. I loved you poorly and for that I am so sorry." She rested her forehead on Nakesha's and willed the words to sink into her daughter's skin. To spread, multiply, and grow into something she could hold onto as Tansey took the dagger from her fingers. She buried the blade into Nakesha's chest, guiding it to the center of her heart, breaking her own in its journey. It slid there more easily than she would've thought. She'd forgotten how easily steel made flesh its sheath.

Nakesha gasped and let out a deep, satisfied sigh. Her slack form rested against Tansey's chest, no longer moving with Iona's Breath. She was gone. Tansey kept her eyes forward towards the fire as she turned her body over. Releasing Nakesha's soul back to Iona to join the wind. She was in pain no longer.

"Take care of her, Kalen," she brushed the back of Nakesha's hair as she soaked in the warmth of the fire. "I never deserved either of you."

There are those who become stronger through their hardships. Trials that test the will and hearts of warriors to be more than what they are. Tansey had reached her potential long ago and driving that blade into her daughter's chest didn't make her strong. It broke her. She lifted the dagger; its cold hilt burning her skin. This was what her life had come to. The pinnacle of her misery. She wanted to follow the dark path into the void. To see her husband again, laugh with her daughter, and dance among the wind where nothing could confine her.

Evelyn's small, plump features filled her mind as she dropped the dagger, still wet with Nakesha's blood. She'd made a promise and until that promise was fulfilled, she would continue as she'd always done. Motherless in every way possible.

CHAPTER 15

THE TRACKING OF A LADY

T he day was bright but beneath his cloak, hidden in an alleyway, Meric was a shadow. He stood apart from the hustle of Reva, teetering on the edge of society and exile. It was a sharp ledge to balance upon, but that was what it meant to be Venandi. He scanned the crowd, searching for his target, hooded eyes rifling through the masses of elegant apparel he thought ridiculous for everyday wear. It looked exhausting to be in such finery day in and day out. His eye caught the movement of a familiar gait, flowing with the grace of a spring breeze. The woman across the city street rhythmically looked over her shoulder, eyes exploring every dark corner she passed. Her blonde hair crossed in intricate braids, giving the illusion of a golden crown upon her head. Her dress was fine with delicate green silk that look far more suited for a nightgown than a day dress.

Given what he'd been hired to prevent her from doing, he figured it was intentional on her part. She was eloping, and it seemed her choice of companionship wasn't what her family approved of. The scandal alone was enough to not only ruin her reputation, but that of her father, City Lord Fallon. The man controlled the city with impunity, and seldom had he given second chances to those who broke the law. Including, it seemed, his own daughter. Meric wondered if this was just the girl's desperate attempt to break free of society's expectations of her. He wasn't privy to the discussions between the wealthy, but he knew enough to know he wanted no part in it.

Grae had more experience with that part of society, even if he had forsaken it. Meric had a home once, though he'd forgotten it. All he had were moments, flashes of recollection and strange feelings. He found it best to not dwell on the past unless he had access to what made the absence of his memories easier to bear. His tongue felt fat inside his mouth as he licked his lips, craving the taste of ale.

Later, he thought, pushing the urge from his mind.

The silver chain that ran from his earlobe to the tip of his ear brushed against the back of his neck. He pulled his hood further over his head, keeping the silver from reflecting the day's light. If anyone saw his ear, they'd immediately know he was Venandi. He needed to follow Juna until she arrived at her final destination without arising the suspicion of his profession.

He exited the alleyway and snapped his fingers to signal Grae and Anya to move. The bow at his back moved with his stride, quivers brushing the back of his head. His fellow Venandi kept a reasonable distance in case Juna noticed his pursuit. His people often ran in pairs. For years it was just him and Grae, until his friend had gotten himself wrapped up in the race for a jewel thief from a wealthy heiress. The woman hired several Venandi to ensure the heirloom's safe return. Anya alone, mere minutes before them, brought down the thief. The culprit was a small man, who was half starved and ragged with sleeplessness. Meric felt a pang of remorse as he unsuccessfully tried to recall his name.

There was usually a fight when multiple Venandi were hired for the same task, each claiming the other stole from them. Profits vanished, bones were broken, and some lost their lives. There was a time during the war when they worked together. Instead of losing their lives at the hands of each other, they sacrificed themselves for their fellow Venandi. But that was before Meric's time. Grae was older. He could remember what it was like then, though he rarely spoke it.

He had been certain they'd be able to take on the unpaired Venandi. He recalled preparing for a fight, anticipating the spill of blood. Instead, Grae invited her into their ranks. He claimed he was impressed by her tracking skills, which was entirely true. However, Meric remembered the gleam in his friend's eye as she looked upon him for the first time. A bit of life that was previously missing suddenly appeared and hadn't left since Anya had joined them. Meric was wary of her for the first few months, searching for deceit, but all he found was a woman much too angry at the world to be bothered with lies. She'd been a part of their group for a few years now and it was hard to remember what it had been like without her. She was a valuable member.

Grae, while dense in some ways, was an excellent Venandi partner. He saw the best in others when it came to skill and talent. He recruited Meric off the street and Anya from solitude. If he had stepped into the role of leadership, Meric wouldn't question it, but Grae never fit into the mold. Often, it was Meric who took the lead on missions, but any final say was a group decision.

The street was busy with people in carriages, pointing at the ragged clothes of the less fortunate. Their gloved hands remained inside the vehicles as if just sticking their fingers outside might stain their precious clothes. Men wore vests of designed fabric that expressed their station. The more loops in the design the richer you were. Meric looked at the shirt beneath his cloak, not a loop to be found. There were quite a lot of rich folk out today.

The sky was clear, allowing the sun to cut through the cool breeze of oncoming spring. But the air still chilled most people and so, Meric's cloak didn't stand out in a crowd of them. Juna was one of the few who didn't wear one, which made it easier for him to follow. Her thin dress trailed behind her like flowing water. She *did* look stunning. She turned around and he ducked behind a cart of fruit, inspecting the oranges as if he was just another buyer.

She craned her neck for one last look, then darted up the stairs of a nearby building. The door slammed shut behind her, losing its echo in the volume of the crowd. He knew that building. Its run-down wooden walls and alcohol-stained floors brought some interesting memories. But what was she doing there?

Two people in similar cloaks walked next to him, hooded with their heads bowed slightly. Grae stood on the opposite side of the cart and picked up a lemon with a leather glove. His thin nose peeked beneath the shadow of his light, blue eyes, capped by thick, dark eyebrows. One was higher than the other and slightly curved at the end, but it was never noticeable under his sandy hair. At thirty-eight he still had the stamina, youthful features, and build of someone Meric's own age, although he couldn't be sure of the exact years he had. Grae and Anya figured him to be in his mid-twenties, but it hardly mattered.

"She's meeting him at Decorum. Clever, but strange," Grae said, inspecting the lemon.

Decorum was a well-known brothel. Grae, Anya, and he would frequent the establishment often. They had some of the best ale in Reva. The women were quite good at conversation, although Meric thought most of them just wanted a chance to be introduced to Grae. His friend was aware of the women who sought for the chance to bed him, but he simply liked talking with them. He'd pay them for a kiss saying, *I'm looking for a different sort of tongue lashing*, then begin hour-long conversations. Meric suspected there was another, larger reason hidden behind wild yellow eyes, but he never breathed a word of his suspicions. Anya was far more willing to do more than converse with the women and men alike. It wasn't uncommon for her to disappear on the arm of anyone who caught her yellow gaze.

"Even I wouldn't have thought of looking there," Anya said beside him.

She fingered an orange before sticking it in the pocket of her cloak. They'd had to resort to occasionally stealing food in the past few weeks. They'd managed to keep up their strength with the occasional fruit and bread, but Meric could feel his muscles straining for the vitality of meat. They couldn't survive on scraps for much longer. Jobs were in short supply, so the success of this mission was paramount if they wanted to have a decent meal in their bellies tonight. Meric's stomach growled as he inhaled the scent of fowl cooking from a nearby cart. Anya's hand remained in her cloak, as though she were afraid someone would take the orange from her pocket. As if someone would be mad enough to steal from a Venandi.

There was only one thing that frightened Meric and those empty, scarred faces scared everyone. The Reticent were everything the Venandi were. As master trackers they— though not as common as his people—were often hired by the same high lords and ladies as he was. While Meric brought his captures back alive, it wasn't the same for those speechless animals. They were more hated then the Venandi but, like the rich with their tattooed eyes, it had become a trivial game of who could survive and outmaneuver their wealthier opponents. Anya had helped them on more than one occasion to avert their paths from crossing with a Reticent. How she had such knowledge Meric didn't know, but from the look in her eyes he knew it would be an unpleasant explanation.

Anya's black hair contrasted her fully yellow eyes. She'd had them tattooed a few months ago. Her once blue irises now only held a small trace of the color. Most of the women in Reva tattooed their eyes. It was a dangerous and fashionable trend that had gained traction in recent years. Meric had known a lady or two that had gone blind from the procedure.

It had started as a way to honor the fallen Videns, a permeant way to remember their sacrifice for ending the war. Despite the good intentions of honest folk, people still forgot, and it turned into a game with high stakes. The darker the color the more you risked blindness and it soon became a painful beauty standard. Yellow was hardly perilous, but

Anya's new eyes held a spark of mischief in them. She was more than just a beauty. Her cleverness resulted in a sharp tongue that could cut more deeply than her daggers, which were deadly in their own right. More than often, he or Grae had to step in to prevent Anya from going too far. It was common for her to lose herself in the fight, almost as if she were in another place, fighting another person. It was most likely the reason she was alone for so long, but it was because of her that their bounties were so successful, if infrequent. She regularly complained that when she was alone she ate better, but would always follow the insult with a smile. She'd grown just as fond of them as they were of her.

"We go in together. We don't want to frighten her. We're merely taking her back home to her father," Grae said, eyeing the both of them.

"But why a brothel? I understand it's a good cover for her escape, but it doesn't feel right," Meric said. He was always asking questions. Always trying to make sense of situations that often didn't have to make sense for them to be paid. He questioned anyway, it felt wrong to do otherwise.

From the corner of his vision, a hooded man in an old cloak that was stained and tattered circled them. Meric didn't have to see the man's face to know he was a beggar. Reva was full of them. It was an epidemic in which no one felt its symptoms until you were on the streets. Thanks to Grae, Meric had survived the disease, but it didn't make him sympathetic to their plight. If he consumed himself with the trouble of others, he'd lose what made him survive in the first place. He'd only so much room for compassion. Despite what was right, he had his limits.

"Why does it matter? We scare off the boy, take her home, and collect our payment," Anya said with a frustrated wave of her hand. She hated his questions. As long as she had money in her pockets, it was work well done as far as she was concerned.

"It matters because it could affect the outcome of the job." Meric turned towards her, abandoning the need for stealth since Juna was inside. Anya rolled her yellow eyes and folded her arms. The beggar held out his arm to Meric, fingers trembling. He still couldn't see the man's face. "I have nothing. Begone," he said, his voice as sharp as the point of his blades at the ends of his bow. Still, the beggar persisted, arm outstretched for mercy.

"So, she's either whoring on the side—which is unlikely given her station—or she's meeting Endri. I don't see how either of those options interferes with our job."

"Do you know how many of those women come from wealthy families?" Meric furrowed his brow in frustration. Anya was brilliant, but she also displayed more than a thimble's worth of ignorance due to her impulsive nature. She sighed as if he were in the middle of the world's most boring topic.

"I could not care less. All I know is I've got a job to do and questioning it just makes everything harder." She spoke with venom, but her expression conveyed experience. She was a little younger than Grae with a past she'd shared with little detail and vague emotions. Grae tried to speak, but Meric spoke over him.

"You do know these are actual people?" Meric waved off the beggar beside him, still holding out his hand. "They're not just missions and coin. What we do can alter someone's entire life."

The beggar grabbed Meric's cloak with stiff fingers, creeping like worms through the dirt. Meric took in a quick breath as his instinct took over. He seized the man's hand and bent it to the side. Not enough to break his wrist, but enough to cause him pain. The man inhaled sharply, but made no sound and twisted his hand with a swift yank as his other hand fell upon Meric's wrist. The sudden move startled Meric and he released the beggar immediately. The man walked away, holding his arm against his chest. The move was calculated and learned. He must've been a solider in his life before the street welcomed him.

The faces of the downtrodden he'd delivered to the affluent

people who'd hired their services flashed through Meric's mind. Men who wanted out from under an abusive father's belt. Young women, like Juna, who wanted the simple right to marry who they wished. Criminals who needed bread to feed their starving children. He'd delivered them all and collected on his payments. Then drank them away at Decorum.

There were people who deserved their capture, but they were few, much too few to make the money worth more than a couple of ales. Anya smiled the kind of grin she does when she's about to end the conversation with a sentence that deserves a good thrashing.

"How many lives have you *altered?* The way I see it many are overdue for a change. Why should I be the only one whose life hasn't turned out the way I once planned? It is the way of the world and I'll take what pleasure I can from what little I am given." Her bright eyes glowed beneath her hood as Meric's face grew red. She was right, of course, but he wasn't going to let her know that. He was about to speak when he staggered to the side, pain radiating just over his temple and down his neck. An orange split on the ground at his feet as he straightened, his hand rubbing the side of his face. Grae's teeth bared in a disappointed grin that showed all his teeth.

"That's enough," his voice was calm, but there was no disobeying it. "If the both of you don't quiet yourselves, I'll use the last of our coin to pay Due to keep you outside where she may do whatever she pleases with you."

Due was the bartender and Madam of Decorum and the most horrid drunk Meric had ever met. She was almost two heads taller than he was, with a slender build that deceived every man who thought he could harass her. With the strength of five blacksmiths, she could make any man beg for mercy against the power of her blows. She was someone neither Anya nor Meric wanted to face. He knew Grae was serious, and he knew Due would take the money. Anya and Meric stepped away from each other, abashed they got so carried away. It wasn't a conversation they hadn't had before and Meric was disappointed in himself for letting Anya bait him.

"Good choice," Grae looked in-between the two, "I admit that this doesn't quite fit. There's something Fallon hasn't told us, but it is not our place to question it," he said, satisfying them both. Grae had always been a good balance. "Anya stays by the entrance in case Juna slips past Meric and I. I'll talk with her. Meric, have you got my back?"

"I think Decorum is the last place anyone would stick a knife in you, but yes. I'll defend you from the wiles of all the broken-hearted women you won't bed." Meric said with a half-smile. Even Anya chuckled and Grae's mirrored her with a soft grin. The mood lightened and Meric sensed that feeling of comradery he was so familiar with between the three of them. They had their differences, but they were still a team, still a family. Meric hadn't known any other.

He followed Grae as he led them to the entrance of the brothel. Anya rested her back on the wall next to the door, surveying the crowd, her yellow eyes apt and focused. When Meric crossed the threshold after Grae, his senses overloaded at once. Men and women crowded together in laughter and drink. The wooden floor glistened with the burning smell of heavy ale, sticky and old.

The bar was long, with bone goblets lining cracked walls along with decorations of swords and paintings of suggestive positions no proper citizen would be caught in. It looked like a menu of sorts. However, Due only claimed to have appreciated the artistry. She stood within the bar, pouring a drink for a gentleman with a decent number of golden loops in his vest. His combed hair and clean boots suggested a life of luxury. Not to mention the silver wedding band around his wrist.

Meric lowered his hood, revealing the bright Venandi earring that brushed against his neck. Grae did the same, but no one blinked. Decorum was one of the few places where the room didn't go silent at the sight of them. The presence of Venandi usually meant a great possibility of violence, and Decorum was no stranger to a fight. In fact, Meric had started a few just to forget what the drink couldn't wash down.

Grae made his way to the bar, where Due was washing a

goblet with a rag. Her massive fingers made the mug look little more than a wine glass. Her brown hair was tied in a braid that fell over her shoulders and rested in-between her small chest. She cocked her head to the side as she saw Grae and Meric approach. Her stature loomed over their heads like the lookout on a ship. She rested her elbows on the bar and half lidded her dark eyes in a failed attempt to appear sober.

"Grae," she said, slurring a bit at the end. "Haven't seen a man like you yet. How's a kiss for a pint?"

Grae smiled and covered her hand with his. She sighed and was about to speak again, when the man with the wedding band spilled his drink over the table and on Due's feet. She stood upright as though she hadn't a sip of alcohol.

"Oy! Hold your drink. You've got fingers, haven't you?" she said, leaning over him. He seemed unperturbed—no doubt from the ale. He stretched his neck up with a sly smile.

"I do and I can show you how I use them." His light eyes held no fear and Meric smiled as he saw what the man couldn't. Under the bar, Due still clutched the bone goblet. She lifted it and with an unreasonable amount of strength, squeezed the mug until the metal bands popped off with a loud pinch. The bone cracked into several splintered pieces while the screws flew across the room, one hitting the man in the forehead. He leaned back with a newfound panic in his drunken demeanor.

"Or I can show you mine. I know your wife, Lamac." The man blinked in surprise at the sound of his name. "Soil my floors again and I'll tell her just what you like doing with those fingers of yours." Her lips pursed, challenging him. Lamac stumbled off his stool and walked out of the brothel on unsteady feet.

"I would probably tell his wife anyway," Meric said as Due turned her attention towards them. It didn't have much to do with being the right course of action but more of making Lamac suffer for not being content with what he had. Greed was an abhorrent emotion that Meric knew all too well. He saw it every day and the days he felt it himself were the ones he drank the most.

"Celosia's Depths drown him. I've no inkling who his wife is," she said with a frown. Meric and Grae chuckled as she leaned over the bar again. "You don't have to be Vagu to trick people. You've only got to listen. With enough ale in him there's nothing he hasn't vomited about his so-called dreadful existence."

"Your cleverness is alluring as ever," Meric said with a nod of his head. Due only snorted and slapped her hand on the bar, shaking all the drinks that rested upon it.

"So, is it to be pleasure or business? The two aren't exclusive," she said with a wink to Grae.

"We're here on business. We're looking for a girl—" Grae began before Due interrupted him.

"Well, finally. Took you ages, but I can find one to your liking," she said, lightly touching the collar of her chest. Meric rolled his eyes, but Grae continued with a soft expression.

"Temping, but no. She was wearing an emerald dress, long blonde hair in braids. She came in not too long ago." Grae only ever gave out the bare minimum of information when looking for someone. It seemed counterproductive when in actuality it protected the individual from other eyes who may be looking for them. Well, protection to be found by them and no other Venandi.

Due straightened from the bar, averting her eyes to the dirty goblet that she began to clean with vigor. Her demeanor changed drastically from obvious flirtation to avoidance. Meric looked at Grae, who shared the same expression. She knew the girl.

"I haven't seen one like that. Sounds too pretty for our fine establishment," she said, raising her eyebrows.

"We're only returning her to her father. She has a reputation he's trying to protect," Grae said, revealing more than he normally did. Due only shrugged and set down the mug.

"Were that we all had fathers to protect our reputations," she replied with bitterness. Her eyes scanned the inhabitants of the brothel, resting on the countless women in lowcut dresses that worked for her.

"Due, he didn't—" Meric started to say before Due slammed the goblet down on the bar with a loud bang.

"Can I get you something to drink or must I ask you to kindly leave?" Her voice was low, but on the brink of a darker, more brutal emotion. Grae opened his mouth, but Meric was quicker.

"Two please. Thank you, Due."

She poured the ale from a metal vase, took his coin, and left them to attend other customers. Grae lifted the mugs, while Meric cleared a space on a table nearby. They sat in between a red-haired woman with a pinned up blue dress and a mustached man who was far too old to engage with such a young person.

"I don't see her among us here. She must be upstairs. Anya would have come in if she left," Meric said as he sipped from his cup—which was more gulp-like then he intended.

Grae did the same, glancing at Due behind the bar, roaring with laughter at some obscene joke. She watched them from the corner of her eye.

"She's hiding her. Probably smuggling her out with the boy," Grae said, forming a fake smile.

"I knew this was different. What would prompt Due of all people to help someone like her?" Meric scooted in towards the table as a woman passed by him, running a hand over his shoulders. Grae shook his head as he looked up the stairs. Meric took another drag of his ale, a familiar, tingling, numbness making its first appearance. He fought the urge to close his eyes at the sensation, not wanting to alert Grae to his indulgence.

"We could always let her," Grae said.

Meric sighed and rubbed a hand over his face, wiping beads of ale that had escaped his mouth. The stubble on his jaw scratched his palm. It wasn't an order. Grae was only thinking out loud. He wanted to agree with Grae, but there was always an excuse. Always a reason to continue. They needed the City Lord's money if they were to eat. He'd given the last of it to Due. "It's not as if we're hunting a murderer," Grae continued, fingering the hilt of his mug.

"Yes, but Anya would surely kill us. She's eaten less than you or I. We need the coin, Grae."

His friend's blonde hair covered his eyes as he lowered his head. When he lifted himself, Meric could see the Venandi within him. A tracker with one purpose: to hunt. He mirrored that expression and pushed down the guilt rising in his chest. He could drink it away with the money they earned after. There was no other way to live. It was all Meric knew and to his dismay he was Depths-damn good at it.

He lifted his goblet, prepared to consume whatever ale was left when Grae gripped his wrist. His friend glanced at the mug, which was already empty, and stared at Meric with pitying eyes. Meric looked away, too sober to confront what he knew to be worry in Grae's knowing glare. Grae sighed and shook his head before redirecting his attention to the rest of the room.

"Well," Grae lifted his goblet in a salute and swallowed a small drag, the mug still nearly full. "I'll miss this place."

Meric nodded with understanding. He knew they would never be allowed in the brothel again after today. Grae smiled and clapped his hands as he stood. The man with the mustache next to him ran his decrepit fingers through the red hair of the girl on his lap. Grae picked up the girl and placed her on the lap of an older woman with deep red lips across from her. The red lipped woman gasped and clasped her hands around the young woman in a protective embrace, but relaxed when she saw it was Grae.

"Breaths be denied, I'll spill your guts for that. Who the Depths are you?" The old man stood and revealed a large stature that must've been from working iron. His veined, grimed skin was taut over burn scars and soot that suggested a professional relationship with a forge. Grae didn't seem apprehensive as he leaned his head to the side. "Well man, you think that earring makes you some kind of Lord? I see no design in your vest." Spittle flew from the blacksmith's mouth.

Grae's smile disappeared and in less than a blink, the old man was thrown across the bar. Dishes and goblets smashed onto the floor as people stumbled over the body of the blacksmith. Due's face contorted into a vicious growl that was drowned out by men and women who joined in the brawl. Meric didn't look at Grae, although he knew his friend to be in the middle of the fight. He slipped past the punches and received a kick or two in his attempt to reach the stairs.

When he did, he gripped the handrails and pulled himself up as if escaping a roaring sea of heat and sweat. His mind settled into a calm that reached to the tips of his fingers. He left behind the shouts and mayhem, purging the world around him until he found his true self. The feral boy who couldn't have known that in order to stave off starving on the street, he'd have to slowly fall to his death to the bottom of a bottle.

When will the glass break, I wonder? To think I had any choice at all unveils how much the fool I still am.

CHAPTER 16

WHERE IT ALL WENT WRONG

When Meric reached the top of the stairs, the large, open space of the chaotic dining room narrowed to a single hallway lined with doors. Each were closed, but the shadows under the door frames flickered like candlelight. The sounds of drunken brawling gave way to the soft grunts and moans of the many rooms occupants. A floral scent flowed through the doorways in a clash for the senses. The permanent ale stench beat the delicate smell into submission, creating a mixture that was not kind on the nose. The hinges of the doors were rusted and bent from the overuse of slamming and battering. The wood held scratch marks and splintered cracks, where force had been used to either keep the door shut or pry it open. Meric thought both outcomes told a tale he'd rather not hear.

He inspected each door, listening to the voices within. The one he wanted would be silent; Juna wouldn't want to be found. She'd equate silence as hiding, when in fact, it was a beacon to her location. He pressed his ear to the door third from the last and heard nothing. He peered at his feet, watching the shadows of figures from within shift involuntarily. The motions of the living always betrayed those trying to hide. In his experience, only in death was true secrecy achieved, although not ideal for the one escaping.

He gripped the knob and turned, but it refused to move. He heard a quick shuffle and a stifled gasp. He backed away from the door and kicked the edge where the knob was. The brittle wood gave way into splinters and opened with a brief swing. As soon as he entered the room, he knew the uneasy pit he felt deep in his stomach was validated.

Juna stood with a young man in the center of the room next to a large, padded bed. The green dress flowed from her frame, encircling her small feet. Her shoulders hunched over a bundle in her arms. A baby rested against her chest, squirming in its mother's arms. Its tiny fist was raised in the air as if in protest to being woken. Endri stood behind Juna with a protective arm around her waist. His chest lifted in an obvious front for bravery.

Juna said nothing. She only stared at Meric, her deep, brown eyes defiant. This was what Fallon wanted her away from. This is what he hoped to entomb from the peering eyes of society.

A baby.

"Please, let us go," Endri said. He was a tall young man, a few years younger than Meric with dark hair falling over his shoulders. His features were handsome enough—a good strong jaw and bright green eyes under heavy brows, but his lip was wrong. It ended at the left nostril as if he'd been cut with a blade in his childhood.

Meric had seen such conditions before. Usually, the infant didn't survive the first few months of birth as the babe couldn't suckle properly. It would either starve to death or drown in its mother's milk before even starting life. The ones who did survive would wish for death. The poor souls were looked upon as bad luck and were often shunned into beggars. If they were so fortunate, they might obtain scattered work from the few who sympathized with their plight.

This man hadn't the haunted, starved look of those who begged so he must have the compassion of someone who granted him work—work away from the eyes of others.

Meric ignored him.

"Juna, your father awaits your return. Please, come with me." Meric held out his hand, though he knew Juna wouldn't take it. She backed further into Endri's arms.

"I will not," she said with the ferocity of an entitled woman who was accustomed to being obeyed. She clutched her child closer and raised her chin. Meric stifled a fond sigh; Juna's attempt to intimidate him was almost endearing. It wouldn't work. He squared his shoulders, deflecting the regret he knew he'd feel when this was all over. She was certainly not going to come with him. Not willingly, at least.

"Do not assume this is a request, Juna. You will be returned to your father."

Juna's hard features cracked at Meric's unapologetic tone, revealing the small, inexperienced high Lady she was. He cringed inward at the prospect of separating a child and mother. Not having known either of his parents, Meric understood what it was like to grow without one. Just when he thought he reached the bottom of the bottle he found a deeper chasm to fall into. This was why Due hid them. The child brought it all together, showcasing an ugly painting as to what the wealthy were capable of when their reputations were in jeopardy.

Endri pulled Juna to the side and stepped in front of her. The young man was thin, wispy with narrow shoulders that made the blue tunic and black trousers he wore sway with his movements, unfit to his leanness. He balled his hands into fists at his side with an awkward stance. The boy had never fought in his life. The sight would've been humorous if the situation were not so disheartening. Meric made a conscious effort not to glance at the baby cooing just behind Endri.

"I have money," Endri said. Confident—he had expected the situation he found himself in. Juna grabbed his arm, delicate fingers pulling at the sleeve of his tunic.

"It's all we have," she whispered. He placed a hand over hers, staring at the floor, then into her eyes.

"If that's what it takes to get you and I out, then so be it. I can make more."

Her fingers relaxed at his words and the corner of her lip upturned into a loving smile. Meric could tell she didn't believe he could, but was proud of him nonetheless. Meric felt as if he were intruding between the two, looking in as an outsider on an intimacy he had no inkling to understanding, but knowing it was something he wanted for himself. The chasm deepened; his tongue dried.

"How much have you?" He stepped forward, his earring brushing against his neck, reminding him of who he was.

This could be the solution. If Endri's silver pieces had decent value, he could let them go. He could claim to Fallon that they simply couldn't find his daughter. Reva was a massive city with a large population. The docks were an open door, bidding welcome and farewell to a few precious, but the gates were littered with hundreds of those who walked for thousands of paces to trade in the city. It was a simple matter of blending into the crowd. It wasn't too difficult to slip under the nose of the city guards, but the Venandi were more observant than that. Fallon knew what he was purchasing with their services, a guaranteed restoration of merchandise he'd invested in. Juna was nothing more than cargo. Meric thought of the consequences, weighing them. If what Endri offered was heavy, enough it could adequately tip the scale to benefit them both. Grae would agree with his decision and Anya wouldn't care as long as she received her share.

Endri and Juna backed away from him. It had never been Meric's intention to have people fear him. When he'd lived in the alleys, he remembered his body shaking against the cold, baring his teeth at people who gawked while he ate stolen bread with the feral nature of a dog. Every day was a day to fear, until Grae had seen the humanity in his wildness. He had no wish to harm anyone and avoided violence if he could. Although, more than often, the savage boy within him woke, reminding him how one never forgot the past. He blinked away the memories he could remember and shoved the ones he couldn't further from his mind as he brought his gaze upon the couple in front of him.

"I have twelve silver pieces," Endri proclaimed, proud of his accomplishment, fingering the straps of the leather pouch at his belt.

For someone with a face such as his, Endri certainly should have felt proud. It was far more than Meric expected. But not enough to cover what Fallon had promised—forty-five pieces. It was enough to last his whole group months of food and lodging. Twelve pieces would cover a few weeks at the most. Less, if Meric wanted to keep up his habit.

"Is that all?" he said, raising his eyebrows. Endri's proud expression vanished, and he looked around the room as though trying to find some coin that may had fallen on the floor.

"Take this," Juna held out a necklace that was hidden in her bodice.

Meric grabbed the necklace from her hand, and she flinched. Meric ignored her response, inspecting the gem. It was smooth to the touch, apart from the ridges of clear stone surrounding the opal gem at the center. It shimmered in the dim candlelight, reflecting its surface inside his palm. He was no jeweler, but he could see its authenticity with his own eyes. The gem offered far more than what Fallon had. The baby cooed in Juna's arms as Endri wrapped an arm around her shoulders. Meric glanced in-between the couple, deciding on his next course of action.

They seemed genuine and the way Juna's fingers dug into the baby's blanket pulled at the orphan boy who lived in the alleys. That boy lived inside Meric, drowning in ale that couldn't kill him. If he took the jewel, would he be leaving them in poverty? Would they abandon the child to a life on the street to sleep with their eyes open and their bellies empty, as he was? The questions were like the pinprick of a needle, inconsequential but irritable enough to make him uncomfortable. He had to take the jewel; Grae and Anya needed it. Knowing what might become of Endri and Juna didn't put him at ease. It tortured him, but he could remember them when no one else would. It was his curse and also all he could offer.

"What is this to you?" he asked, placing the necklace into the pocket of his cloak.

"Nothing more than a past life," Juna said, kissing the top of her baby's head.

"What do you do? How did you come across the silver?" Meric pointed at the pouch tied to Endri's belt.

"I am a seamstress's assistant. I complete alterations and design family vests." He bent his head in a show of shame. It was a woman's occupation but a valuable trade. Meric nodded his head, feeling the length of chain hanging from his ear. It made no difference to him the gender roles society assigned to certain jobs, but society wasn't filled with people like him. Thank the Breaths and Depths for that.

"How did this happen?" he gestured to the baby.

"What does it matter to you?" Juna stepped forward, voice raised. "The conventional way, if you must know. Or do you think babies just appear?" Endri rubbed her shoulders to calm her, but she shrugged him off, her face narrow with fury. "How did she *happen*? She happened...and I chose. I chose her and I chose him." She glanced at Endri with devoted eyes, then turned back to Meric. Her expression was hard and worn. "Why I cannot live a life I choose is beyond the comprehension of one brute such as yourself, but you are what will define the rest of my life. Will you destroy the only happiness I have ever known, or will you *let us go*?"

Meric kept his face expressionless, but her words struck him as deep as a blade. They lodged themselves there, grinding and tearing. He nodded. The money from the necklace would be enough. There was always another job even if they were far in-between. He could afford to let them escape.

Her relieved expression turned to rage as she looked beyond Meric. Endri shook his head in dismay, a tear rolling down his cheek. Juna tightened her arms around the bundle, the baby cried out in an embrace too constricted for her comfort.

"Your companion doesn't seem to agree. Celosia's Depths drown you." She leaned forward and spit at his feet.

Meric turned, expecting to find Grae. He wasn't sure how much his friend heard, but it was surely not the entire conversation. Once he explained, he was confident Grae would agree with him. A familiar figure stood in the doorway, but it was not his fellow Venandi. The tattered cloak that had begged for food in the square below loomed before Meric without the hint of any infirmity. His previously hunched over body was erect with the stance of a man stronger than he looked. No, not a man—a woman. The belt at her hip carried a sheathed dagger and a short whip that tailed small, sharpened bones. Leather straps laced up her legs, keeping in place curved plates of dark metal over her knees, imbedded and scratched from what looked like teeth. Her face was shadowed in the cloak, staring down at the couple behind Meric, gaze fixed on the baby with a kind of hardened silence that could cut stone.

There was no time to think. He knew without thought who this woman was and what she was after. Fallon had sent another Venandi, one with an entirely different purpose. That meant her partner was not far behind. He thought of Anya and Grae, sudden worry overcoming his concentration. Meric banished the intrusive thought. His friends were more than capable of defending themselves should they need to, but Juna and Endri could not. He thought of nothing but the escape of the young woman and the innocent babe she carried.

Meric lunged at the cloaked woman. She leaned to the side and dodged Meric's oncoming fist, passing by him with as much effort as wind through blades of grass. She ran towards Juna who screamed as she fell to her knees, shielding her baby with her body. Endri, to Meric's amazement, stepped in front of Juna, landing a blow onto the Venandi. His fist cracked into the side of the woman's ribs. She doubled over and released a short gasp before straightening up a full head taller than the inexperienced seamstress's assistant.

The Venandi gripped Endri by the back of the head and lifted her knee, crushing it against his face. The sound of Endri's teeth shattering against metal reverberated in the small room. His nose exploded, snot and blood trailing into his ruined mouth. His eyes rolled to the back of his head as he swayed, teetering on the unconscious. He stepped towards Juna, who cried out in horror at the sight of her lover's pulverized features, and fell faceup on the ground in front of her. Meric grabbed the Venandi from behind, but with unbelievable strength, she jerked her body forward and Meric went tumbling over her head. Meric cursed himself for his overindulgence below. Before he could catch his breath the Venandi gripped the back of his head and slammed his forehead onto the floor. The cloaked woman continued to use Meric's head as a battering ram until he saw white and red cloud his vision.

He reached a hand to the pack on his back, holding his quivers. The Venandi must've realized what he was doing because Meric felt his scalp tear as he was lifted and pressed against the wall. Juna had crawled to the space between the wall and bed, huddled over her baby, weeping and shaking.

"Go!" Meric said through clenched teeth. The taste of blood was hot in his mouth, eyes batting away more blood that fell from his forehead. She glanced in-between Endri and Meric, as though struggling to decide on who to run to. She screamed a wretched sob and stood, running past Endri to the open door. She was able to take two strides before the Venandi reached out her hand, gripping Juna's hair the same way she had with Endri. Meric struggled against the Venandi's grip, but the crushing pressure of his head against the wall was a pain like none he'd ever felt.

Juna howled in pain and lifted one hand to her head in instinct. The woman took advantage of the distraction, slamming her knee against the side of Juna's head, rendering her limp and silent as she dropped her child. The babe wailed as the Venandi released her mother's hair, letting Juna land with a thud on the hard wood floor. She bent, the leather straps on her arm stretching as she picked up the screaming child. Meric breathed heavily under the weight of the woman's hold, but the more he tried to tear himself away, the more she pressed his head against the wall. His skull was going to crack like thin ice if he couldn't escape.

Meric lowered his hand to the bottom end of his bow. It was more than a simple archer's weapon. On the ends were blades that could be twisted off and used as daggers for close combat such as the situation he found himself in. The problem was that the Venandi held him out at arm's reach, making it impossible for him to use her weight against her to twist out of the position he was held in.

Meric gritted his teeth, deciding he'd have to improvise. He threw all his strength into one side of his body and launched himself to the side while pushing off the wall, angling his bow and slashing it across the Venandi as he twisted. The skin on the side of his head ripped; pain like the burning of a hot iron spreading down his temple to his cheek. He heard the slash of fabric as the pressure in his head lessened. The woman stood still as Meric blinked away blood to see a long cut across the Venandi's shoulder, ending in the middle of her chest, just above the small white bundle in her arms. Meric had come dangerously close to slicing Juna's baby in half. He blinked repeatedly, trying to adjust his vision to the release of pressure in his head.

The Venandi's hidden face turned downwards at the wound, and she shifted the baby as though fearing red would stain her blankets. Blood dripped from her black attire to join the couple at her feet. Endri and Juna laid together in a colorful display of crimson and silk. The ends of her grown were stained in the spreading layer, pooling beneath Endri's head, blood in his mouth bubbling.

The Venandi held the screaming baby with one arm and darted out of the room. Meric stumbled, gripping the frame of the door before glancing at the bleeding lovers. From the start of the Venandi making her appearance, to the sound of her receding footsteps took all but precious few minutes. It happened all too fast and Meric found it hard to catch up with the time he was left with. He growled deep in his throat and shook his head, focusing and forcing himself to push back the pain in his skull. He left Juna and Endri in the room, knowing Juna would've wanted him to pursue the kidnapper. The filthy black cloak ran down the stairs just as Meric exited the room. He had been hired to find Juna. This woman was hired to find her baby. Meric's fury fueled him as he jumped down the stairs, skipping several steps.

The fight had died down to a low rumble of groans and prostrated bodies of unconscious drunks. He came across Grae held flat against a table by Due, her bloodied fist up, teeth bared into a vicious snarl. Grae's smile was red stained which only seemed to antagonize Due. The Venandi sprinted to the front door and Meric had no time to help his friend.

"Upstairs, now!" He screamed as he passed them.

Due caught a glance of Meric and her enraged expression transformed into horror. She looked up the stairs and released Grae, almost throwing him off the table. Meric thought he must've looked terrible because Grae immediately grew wide-eyed and pushed Due out of his way up the stairs. Meric stumbled out of the dark brothel and into the light. His head pounded with new vigor as though receiving strength from the sun.

He looked through the crowd and spotted the white blanket in the sea of dark cloaks. Anya ran up beside him, her yellow eyes sweeping over his beaten features.

"What happened? Your face…" she said, her tone strained and angry. Her gaze followed his, locking onto the kidnapper.

He didn't answer her. He didn't have to. He knew Anya would follow him as he chased down the false beggar. He ran into the crowd and Anya was close behind, her breathing even. People gasped, moving out of the street as they gave chase, catching the sight of his earring gleaming in the sunlight. They knew better than to get in the way of pursuing Venandi.

The cloaked woman turned hard down a corridor between the stone buildings. Anya was the first to follow with Meric just behind her. When they turned the corner, Anya cried out as a black shape lifted her from the ground and threw her against the side of the building. Meric looked up in time to see dagger-like claws reaching to tear his head from his neck. He pulled his engraved bow from his back, the Venandi's blood still staining the bottom blade, nocked an arrow and released.

He heard a screech that pierced the flesh of his bones as the animal fell to the ground. With its massive form upturned, Meric could see its full shape. A solov raptor stood before him with faded black wings spread to the length of two full grown men. The creature dipped its head towards the arrow that was little more than a splinter in the raptor's wing and pulled it out, snapping it in two with its sharp beak. Meric's chest tightened with rage.

Reticent.

The false beggar stood at the end of the corridor, her hood down, revealing not the expected silver chain of a Venandi, but a mass of scars across her face like deep caverns of blood. She was far older than Meric would've guessed by her strength — or perhaps the scars only made her look older. Her white hair was cropped short against her scalp and held its own array of scars separate from the ones on her face. Her lip upturned with the slightest menacing curve.

Meric stepped forward and nocked another arrow, aiming for the scarred woman's chest. The raptor placed its claws over Anya's unconscious face, rhythmically stretching its talons like the retracting claws of a cat. He stopped walking, but still pointed his weapon at the Reticent. Meric growled, taking a step back as the raptor lifted its talons higher, still hovering over his friend's face. There was no doubt the Reticent would command her raptor to kill Anya, but the baby's loud cries seemed to absorb the scared woman's attention. Meric, again, was stuck in the in-betweens of decisions. But there was no choice, and he was a fool to believe he had one.

"Such a small thing. There is no need to worry. I'll not drop her," the raptor said in a voice that was inhuman.

Meric hated this city and the people in it. He hated himself and all the pain he'd caused in his life. But he cursed the Reticent. There were unspoken rules between the races of men and the Reticent broke every one of them. They were traitors, deserters to their Venandi partners. The sharpened blade to Cinaed himself, responsible for the Viden's and dragon's extinction and now reduced to hired men and women to kill those Meric was charged with capturing.

Before Meric could retort, the scarred woman leaped from the ground and climbed the stone wall of the adjacent building. Her agility amazed him, legs and arms reaching farther than he would've thought possible. The wails of the child grew soft as she ascended, running along the rooftops, and disappearing.

He switched his focus onto the raptor, holding the point of the arrow breadths from the animal's large golden eye. Its claws pulsated as if fighting against the urge to set Anya free.

"Release her," Meric said low in his throat.

His fingers shook with a violent temper that threatened to banish logic from his thoughts. He couldn't overpower a solov raptor, but his heightened fury was telling him otherwise. He'd failed in every way possible. Those golden eyes bore into Meric, challenging him to a welcomed fight.

Just when he thought he'd have to lose his life to the creature to save Anya, the raptor lifted its claw and threw down its grey tipped wings, lifting itself into the air. Meric raised his arms against the strong draft the raptor's wings created. It circled above them then turned to the direction of its master, following her in a sickening bond that left death in its passing.

Meric lowered his bow, breathing in heavy gulps of air as he crouched next to Anya. She stirred as he shook her shoulder, groaning when he lifted her into a sitting position. Her yellow eyes fluttered open, and realization came upon her in an instant. Her arms gripped Meric's as she turned towards the sky.

"They're gone," he said, reassuring her.

He expected her to respond with an array of foul-mouthed curses, but instead, she rested her back against the wall, dread and misery contorting her features. Her mouth quivered as she tried to speak. Meric watched her with concern as this display of unguarded emotions was highly unusual for his friend.

"I heard a baby," she whispered, looking where the Reticent once stood.

Meric lowered his head and sat next to her, resting the bow in his lap. He fingered the carved engravings of dragon wings on the body of the weapon, its smooth journey reaching to the curved blades on the ends, shining in the sunlight. In the phase of transitioning Anya into their group, Meric had a difficult time adjusting to her presence. It had always been him and Grae for years and Meric remained distrustful of the new Venandi. She'd been with them for nearly a year when she returned from a night of drinking with the carved, bladed bow.

"I missed your name day," Anya had said, placing the bow into his hands. Her blue eyes were untattooed and bright beneath her dark brows.

He was so stunned by the beauty of the weapon that he stood silent, admiring the bow before turning back to her.

"I do not have a name day," he responded the way he told Grae years ago during one of their conversations in the alley. When his friend was teaching him how to be human again.

"Yes, you do. It was yesterday and I missed it." She raised her brows, urging him to accept the obvious lie. She had spoken to Grae and upon learning that he didn't know when his name day was, Anya resolved to make the first day of summer, which had been the previous day. It was a gesture so foreign to him at the time, that Meric thought the simplest way to understand it was to accept it.

"Then I thank you for the gift."

"You'll find it hard to be grateful after I've finished training you with it. I am not a kind teacher." Her voice was hard, but her eyes shone with anticipation, as though she'd been waiting for such an opportunity to tend to something that might grow.

Anya tucked a strand of black hair over her ear and gave up an involuntary grin. That night and every night for the next few years they'd met in the Dattadri Greens by the Unnamed Dragon and practiced. Anya was true to her word and brutally educated him on how to read the direction of the wind and how the stance of his legs mattered. She drove him to madness at times, making him crouch in the tall grass, blindfolded to train his ears as well as his eyes to aim. He'd once asked her how she knew such knowledge of the bow.

"You and Grae are not the only Venandi I've traveled with," she replied with no intention on sating his curiosity.

He treasured the weapon now as he treasured no other possession. He could no sooner leave his arm or leg behind, and his back felt weak without the weight of the blades and quiver.

The bow had become an extension of himself and her training, while demanding, solidified her in his mind as an irreplaceable member of their group.

Meric was brought back into the alley with Anya as she stood, searching for an abandoned child. He remained seated for a moment, but was soon implored by the responsibility to return to Decorum

"We must go back," he said, lifting himself off the ground and placing the arrow and bow onto his back. He held his hand out, but Anya still stared into the empty space of the alleyway. "Grae needs our help, Anya. We must go."

At the mention of Grae her demeanor changed, a worried frown replacing the despondency. She swept her black hair across one shoulder.

"It all went wrong, didn't it?" The finality in her tone was only surpassed by the trembling apprehension of what the answer to her question was.

Meric lined his lips into a regretful frown. It couldn't have gone more wrong and yet, it was about to get worse. He had to face Juna and reveal the fate of her child. A fate that would've been kinder had he returned with her baby dead in his arms.

CHAPTER 17

BLISS IS A FAR-OFF WORLD

Evelyn closed her eyes against the wind that twisted around her. It curl over her arms, joining together at her hip only to break apart, then come together again in the soft rustling of the sail above her. The small ship bent and bobbed with the will of the water below. The Omya River was a calm presence, but she could find no comfort in her lullaby.

She opened her lids and saw the ever-changing landscape. Gone were the white-tipped mountains. Smooth grass-filled plains laid before her with a small hill cresting upward every so often. The transition from winter to spring was jarring, as though she had entered another world. She'd never seen so much green in her life.

As she looked upon the landscape, it withheld its awe-inspiring majesty. Where were her mountains, the frail beauty of the ice-tipped peaks? The whistle of frozen air and the crisp grate of crushed frost? She was lost in a world unlike the one she grew up in, foreign and strange. Evelyn sat on the edge of the boat, leaning over the railing with her hand grazing the river below. The ripples widened, dripping from her fingertips. She was mesmerized by the shapes in the river, gliding and flowing without the care of what lurked above. She envied the river and its carefree nature, abiding by the laws of Iona to be as unbound as it wished.

Sou stood at the helm of the ship, his clothes swaying in a constant wind, blowing into the sails above. Sometimes, it seemed as if the air circled only about the sails, but she wasn't in a state to judge reality. If she looked too closely into the water below, the eyes of Tansey, Birdie, and Maysom would stare back at her. Their faces contorted with pain, begging for her to save them.

She's been silent for long enough. Speech may yet help her. Sou's thought trailed around her in a wisp of wind that seemed to dance with anxiety.

This wasn't the first time she'd heard his thoughts. The past week he'd expressed his concern for her well-being, and she ignored them all. The pain was too near, far too raw for her to do anything but to sit in her own dark thoughts. Yet, every time she thought she'd numbed herself to her grief, Sou's voice brought her back, aching in her loss. It was the flash of lighting, followed by the booming sound of thunder, lighting the way back to her senses.

"Where are we?" she said before he could speak. Whenever she felt that he'd try to bring her out of the fog, she'd ask of their whereabouts, although she hadn't the slightest desire to know.

A timid grin spread across his lips as he stepped down from the helm, leaning against the railing next to her. She rested her head on the wooden rail, not meeting his eyes.

"Towards the end of the Omya. See those patches of shrubbery?" He pointed to a cluster of bushes lining the banks of the river. She glanced up without raising her head. "Those only grow with a steady supply of rain, which Reva has. If the wind stays as it is, we should see the horizon light up the city within a few days."

Had they been on the river so long? She mulled over the loss of her sense of time and found there was a sliver of who she used to be pulsating and writhing in the grief of all she'd lost. It begged her to see the brightness of nature around her and the wind that tousled her hair, but she felt nothing. There was nothing left to feel.

"What is this place called?" Evelyn lowered her hand into the Omya, nothing. She craved the touch of something beautiful, pure, and bright. Sou nodded with enthusiasm, pleased that she was speaking with him. She would, for now.

"Well, this is Dattadri Greens," he said, lifting his hands towards the empty grassland. She lifted her head then, taking in the view as if it were a painting to be interpreted. "It is said to be a land of contemplation and peace. I've stepped on the grass, and it is as soft as it looks. Would you care to feel it?"

Evelyn turned toward him; her crimson eyes glazed over as she tried to comprehend what he was asking of her. Her body was a husk of her former self, sinking lower into a pit, daylight dimming overhead. Sou's eyes wandered from her empty stare; even he couldn't look into her dragon gaze for long. She was marked for the unfortunate, fated to remain in misery. Such misery.

"Feel?" she whispered, looking at her blistered palms, remembering the sound of Birdie's dying breath and Maysom's crumpled corpse.

Her wrist pained her beneath the tight fabric Sou had bound her with, palms stinging with the slightest brush of air. It all paled in comparison to the invisible open wound within her, but she was present enough to know it wasn't right. Being Viden, she should've been able to restore herself faster and without much effort. There was so much she should've been able to do and couldn't.

Sou reached into a compartment on the side of the ship, pulling out a long hook with a serrated edge and a pole with a net attached to the tip. He walked over to Evelyn and gently moved her to her feet so he could reach over the railing. Long patches of grass dangled into the water, within reach of his hook.

With a grunt, he stretched it out and cut the grass, leaving a hollowed space in between the foliage. The clips landed in the net he held below. He pulled both in, resting the hook on the floor and lifting long strands of greenery from the net. He bunched them together, holding them out for Evelyn.

She stared at the plant a moment before grasping it in her hand, running her fingers from root to stem as though the grass were someone's hair. Its grated surface rubbed uncomfortably against the blisters of her palm, the edges gliding between her fingers. She could feel the plant, feel her palm, the wind at her back and the spray of the river. She could *feel* again.

"What do you think, lass?" he said, sitting on the edge of the ship.

"I can feel it. I haven't been able to feel anything," she whispered with a small smile. He leaned forward, his arms folded in concern.

"Is that how you knew something was wrong?"

"No," she said, shaking her head, "I mean, I could feel the wind and the water, but I couldn't *feel* the wind or the water. It doesn't make much sense. I couldn't feel what the water was or how Iona's Breath blows. But this," she fingered the grass, lifting it to her face and closing her eyes to the touch, "I can feel what this plant is and how it changes me. Iona's Breath feels different, like it did before."

The breeze washed over her, embracing its wisps across her face and arms in what felt like a caress, a confirmation that it knew her and missed her.

Sou's grin widened and he patted her shoulder before jumping off the railing. The fog was beginning to lift, the dead eyes of Birdie and Maysom fading into the background of her mind. They still watched her, their sorrowful expressions taunting, but she could no longer see them with her waking eyes.

"It is the small things that create bliss such as this," he said, feeling the length of cloth around his head.

"Bliss is a far-off world I fear will never collide with mine again." Evelyn still held the grass, sitting on the bench at the bow of the ship. Sou followed, resting next to her, his frown deepening as she looked down.

"What happened, lass?" he asked.

Her face contorted into a heavy frown, lip quivering. Memories replayed in her mind with ruthless force, threatening to bind her in her grief again. Sou held her hands, smoothing out the hardened blisters with his fingertips. She fingered the grass held firm in her hands. This small patch of grass was in constant danger of drowning at the edge of the Omya, yet it persevered. It seemed foolish to take such strength from a plant, but she did. She pushed back tears, telling Sou everything that happened.

He listened in silence as she spoke of her vision, the discovery of Jaspar, the death of Birdie, the appearance of the man in the black cloak, and Tansey's bravery.

"You can no longer control Iona's Breath, but you can still see it?" he said, inclining his head, expressive and thoughtful.

She disengaged her hand from his and spun her fingers through the air. She focused on the space above and with a strain, failed in conjuring a breeze. The wall that barred her from power loomed inside her with the strength of iron. She couldn't break through, except for the slow drip that flowed from its cracked surface.

"It's like the trinkle of water from a crack in the mountain. I feel as if I've been pushed into a small crevasse where I can only breath in the smallest of gasps. I know it's there. I can *sense* it. But I can't take it."

He grasped his chin, lip pouting in contemplation.

"You've been cut off from Oretem somehow, but are still connected with him. Like the last strand in a ripped cloak, you are apart, but still linked. I know not why you can no longer control Iona's Breath. This is a thing I hope we can uncover in Birny. What is most surprising is that you heard the wind. *That* is your gift," he said, wonder encircling his last words. She stared back at him, bewildered at the revelation. She'd only heard of such things happening in stories.

"The wind told me to find Meric? Like a Vagu?" she said, looking at the strands of wind twisting in the air around them.

He chuckled as he ran a hand across the long fabric hanging over his shoulder from his headband.

"Not quite. The Vagu are more in tune with Iona to hear the impressions of the wind, of those who have passed on. But they cannot actually *hear* voices. In that regard, and in many others, they are just as ordinary as you or me." He paused with a small knowing smile. "There was only one person I know of who had this gift. The first Viden, Monia."

Her curiosity piqued at the mention of the first Viden. She didn't know much of the history behind her people; the name was familiar, but she couldn't recall how or why. Sou lined his lips with a disappointed frown, but it wasn't directed at her. It felt more like the frustration of a dedicated teacher having failed a bright student.

"Monia was a Vagu. One skilled with the talent for understanding the wind. Now, most Vagu are experienced with this gift. It is within their nature, and it comes naturally to them from the time they are born. But Monia, her legacy lies in her ability to *listen*."

Evelyn breathed in, taking a moment to listen to the way the Omya bubbled, and the grass rustled.

"She heard them all," Sou continued, "The ants marching to their favorite tree, the bark hardening in the winter and the kick of a babe in its mother's womb. One day, she heard a voice across the forest. The speaker has been lost as time has passed. Some say it was her long dead lover, but there are no such songs of a great love. Others claim she heard it from the Crimson Willow, but that willow was named after she was long dead. Most believe she was contacted by the first dragon which even then would've been unknown.

"She was told to venture from her keep in Edewor and climb the tallest tree in the Eshe Willow Wood to find the destiny she longed for: a soul matched for her own for listening and hearing. That is when she met the wind dragon, Eteris. It was said his tail was the longest in living memory. Its colorful membrane covered many acres."

Evelyn smiled and lifted her head towards the sun, imagining the historical event as if it were being played out in front of her. The story wove into what she pictured Monia and Eteris to have felt and how frightening it might've been to be so different.

"He gave her his bright scale and her eyes changed. To what color it was varies on which version you listen to. I like to believe her eyes turned as green as the grass in your hand." Evelyn tightened her hold on the plant with a gentleness that respected the reverence Sou told the story with. "She and Eteris traveled to the ends of the known world serving Iona and creating the Videns. She conversed with the Iona's Breath to match those who dreamt with dragons who were open to bonding. After all, they had more to gain than the Videns did."

Evelyn lowered her head with a questioning look.

"What did they gain? That has always been a question in my mind, but there was never a definitive answer."

That disappointed despondency returned as he thought upon the question. It was obvious she knew much less than she should've. Shame was a companionable friend to her grief; together they crushed her confidence.

"Dragons are not immortal, lass. Not naturally, anyway."

Her mouth opened, and she looked away, pondering for a moment. "I just assumed—I mean, I always heard of them dying in stories of battle, never of age or sickness."

"Oh, they were as mortal as you or me, but the bond granted them immortality. They could still fall by blade or poison, but if either could be avoided then aye, they could not die. We gained many powers such as control of the wind and other gifts the bond granted, but what are those compared to immortality?"

"You know so much. Why didn't you teach me?" Her red eyes brimmed in tears.

She regretted the accusation as soon as she spoke it. He was not to blame for her shortcomings. She only wanted to be free of the pain, if only for a moment. Place the blame elsewhere so she could take in a breath, fill her lungs with air that wasn't mocking her survival. Her chest heaved, heavy with regret. She could see he harbored no ill will, and worse, he seemed to agree with her, nodding his head with arms opened.

She fell into his embrace, weeping against his chest as her resolve crumbled to dust. She'd lost everyone. They were gone and it was her fault. She left a mad dragon within a mountain and a murderer wandering the desolated snow. Either now had the opportunity to leave the frosted desert and release their fury upon innocent people she was supposed to protect.

"I'm so sorry, lass. None of this should ever have happened."

Evelyn remained in his embrace until her tears quieted. She withdrew from him, wiping her eyes. As much as the moment pained her, she felt better for it. She cleared her throat, having no wish to dwell on that which she could not control.

"So, the orb I heard, it was someone who'd joined the wind? Passed on?" she said, talking to distract herself. "Could it have been mother?"

The thought had immediately entered her mind when he first suggested she'd heard the voices of those joined with Iona.

"It's possible, but unless they reveal themselves or you recognize —" Sou paused at that, knowing Evelyn had never heard her own mother's voice. She looked to the water, understanding his meaning, a quiet sadness seeping into what she already knew. "It's never certain. A long-lost dragon from centuries beyond could've spoken to you, like one might've with Monia. It's more likely someone who knows you."

Evelyn swayed with the ship, rocking with the lull of the river. Sou breathed in a sigh as though gathering the courage to ask her a difficult question. He lowered his eyes to meet hers. "That man in the black cloak. Did you know him?"

Her red eyes gleamed in the sunlight as she looked at him. Anger boiled within her, remembering the silence the man walked with, the great bird that murdered Nakesha.

"I saw him in my vision," Evelyn said, voice ripe with bitterness. "But I've never seen him before in my life. That eagle," she looked up, expecting the bird to descend. "I've never seen an eagle like that."

"That was no mere eagle. Have you heard of Solov?" he said. The sails above them clattered against the ropes that held them. The wind was picking up as she felt the ship move quicker down the river.

"The desert to the south. I've heard of it." Tansey had taught Evelyn the lay of the land. She couldn't navigate her way through Iona, but she knew her geography well enough.

"Those beasts from the Waste are called solov raptors. They live and die in the sand, but when the Reticent came about during the Evandis, Cinaed the Decayed had them capture the creatures, attempting to create a bond similar to what the dragons had with Videns."

Decayed. She recalled Oretem speaking the name and when she reiterated what the dragon had spoken Sou's eyes grew grave but certain. "That's impossible. Cinaed fell during the Battle of Lake. The poor creature's madness is clouding what is present and past. It is more likely that he is reminded of the Decayed by this Reticent."

Evelyn felt a twinge of doubt scratch the back of her mind, but she resigned to trusting Sou's judgment. She nodded her acceptance and motioned him to continue.

"They were successful, but at a great cost. Their cult required a sacrifice. The raptors, under torture and misery, claimed speech as their boon from torment, and the only way to do so was to have them eat the inductee's tongue."

Evelyn grimaced, recalling how silent he'd been, the grotesque voice that emitted from the raptor on his arm.

"He never spoke. The raptor spoke for him. That was why I couldn't hear him following me," she said. Sou nodded with a rare gleam in his eyes.

"He claimed he wanted you for a name?" he whispered to himself. Evelyn adjusted her posture to answer as the ship rocked.

"At the time I was too frightened to think about what that meant, but now the only explanation must be Meric. I told

Tansey almost those exact same words. He must've been listening to our conversation before he attacked."

Sou shook his head in agreement, coming to the same conclusion as she.

"I hadn't known such creatures as he existed. Reticent. An apt name for one so silent," she whispered. Evelyn's body shook, hands trembling with overflowing rage. "I wondered if Tansey knew him, this Reticent. The way she looked when she saw him..." Evelyn clenched her jaw. Guilt festered in her chest, sickly and growing. "I should've aided her."

"You might expect me to say he'd have killed you, but the truth is far worse. He'd have captured you, lass. Tortured you. I've seen the fruits of their labor and trust me, it's no labor when ripping flesh from bone is relished as sport." He leveled his eyes to meet with hers, hardening to emphasize his seriousness. "He didn't kill your mother. One from his Order did, but he's long since been dead."

Evelyn could see from his expression that he'd talk no more on the subject. She leaned back, curious as to how Sou knew so much. His knowledge was vast for a simple ferryman, but she didn't want to discourage what she was already learning. So, she would remain silent for the time being, even if it went against her nature.

"The Reticent were originally Venandi that sided with Cinaed. Do you know what the Venandi are?" he continued with a lighter tone and a half smile.

Evelyn huffed and slapped the side of his arm. His smile warmed her heart. Even at her worst, he was able to bring her into the light.

"Of course I know the Venandi. Go on," she insisted.

"Their ability to track dragons and Videns alike was unmatched by no one other than their abandoned Venandi companions. The Reticent are the reason for most of the deaths during the Evandis, although why dragon turned against rider is still a mystery. Dragons gathered in their hundreds to confront Cinaed and within the span of minutes half were ripping their own riders from their backs. Forcing their sane kin to battle not only the Reticent, but their mad brothers and sisters. I'm sure I do not have to explain to you the horror of such acts," Sou paused, allowing the gravity of the history Evelyn barely knew to sink like a stone in the river. "The Reticent created their own organization, a cult with the purpose of gaining true power. Power over others. They are still active today if not rarer than before. Except instead of occupying an army, they use their deadly talents for hire. This man is the first I've seen since the war." He looked at Evelyn and she matched his gaze. The seriousness of the matter was always present in her mind, but now it dawned with an understanding that she should've realized sooner.

"He'll find me. He knows where I'm going," she said simply, the knowledge like a rock in her stomach.

"Aye, which is why we cannot remain in Reva for long. I'm taking you to Birny. I have friends in the city who can help figure out what is happening to you. To lose a Reticent you need a guide who thinks like them. We need—"

Evelyn cut him off already knowing.

"We need a Venandi."

CHAPTER 18

BURIED ALIVE

Meric and Anya had returned to Decorum only to be thrown out by Due. When they had entered the brothel there were only a few women in the building. The only evidence of the previous chaos being the broken legs of upturned tables and the speckled blood coloring the floor.

When Due spotted them behind the bar Anya immediately ducked as a blade flew over her head and buried itself into the wall behind her.

"Get out!" Due bellowed, "If you ever show your faces again, I'll cut them off and use your pretty eyes as ice for my drink!" Her eyes were red with not only anger, but grief. She'd been crying at her perceived failure, but to Meric it appeared to be something deeper. Her entire body shook with a pain akin to sorrow, but Meric said nothing as he and Anya left the brothel that had once been a haven to them.

His chest grew hollow as he stepped away. Decorum wasn't exactly welcoming, but he felt comfortable there. The company was satisfying, and the ale was exceptional. Due, while hard around the edges, never failed to make him laugh. He was going to miss her, even if she despised all that he was. He couldn't blame her. They surmised that Grae had taken Juna back to her father and so Meric stared at the ground, numbing himself for what was to come.

The townhome of City Lord Fallon was a tall building that stood erect in-between homes of lesser wealth, but was by no means poor. Its marble walls were of the smoothest stone and seemed to radiate with a brightness that surpassed its equally stunning neighbors. The frame of the door was built of the same stone, but engraved with golden designs of circles and ovals. They overlapped each other so that the arraignment became one large ring, glimmering in the sunlight. Vines gripped the walls surrounding the City Lord's mansion, clinging to the stone. The foliage was beautiful, but beauty would not stop a trespasser from climbing over the walls. Meric noticed guards patrolling the grounds of Fallon's estate, keeping his land secure and protected. He supposed that was well enough protection, but he wouldn't bet his life on it.

A familiar tall man with a large, brown beard stood at the foot of the marbled door. His purple vest was adorned with an elaborate design only surpassed by the engravings on the entrance of the mansion. He held a gold-tipped spear in his hand that towered over his head and looked to be more suited for style rather than actual combat.

His eyes traveled up and down Anya with a small envious lip. It was only then that Meric recognized the man. Kiev was a frequent customer at Decorum, using the City Lord's coin he earned for women and ale. He wore the same uniform at the brothel, but with the dim lighting and Meric, usually having a few drinks in him, hadn't connected the two until he saw Kiev's sly bloodless smile. The man would always, sooner or later, end the night with a bloody smile. He often complained about the number of cups Meric had and pursued Anya as if she were some sort of animal head to be mounted on the wall.

"I don't reckon I've ever seen you out of Decorum," Kiev said, leaning his head against the spear. Meric didn't answer, knowing the man wasn't talking to him and not trusting the words that would slip past his bruised mouth.

"I'm glad I can say the same about you. Although, perhaps

I may have seen you once or twice." Anya brought a hand to her chin in mocked puzzlement. "I thought that might've been you on the street the other night, sleeping in your own piss. I understand that drunkards have a hard time knowing which way to point it," she spoke without looking in Kiev's direction.

The guard opened his mouth in feigned offense, and he twisted an imaginary knife in his chest.

"Bloody hurts, it does, but no matter. You think about where I point it." His voice was gritty in the back of his throat, and he gripped the spear with both hands in a way that was both suggestive and far too generous.

Meric steeled his gaze and tossed his head to the side with an annoyed glance.

"Let us pass, Kiev. We're expected." Meric crossed his arms to prevent his hands from becoming fists.

Kiev ran a hand over his beard and looked at Meric as if he'd just noticed he was present. He nodded with a shrug and knocked on the door with the heavy metal ring at the center.

"What does the other man look like?" Kiev said, pointing at his bruised face. "I'd like cross fists with him."

She would skin you living, Kiev. And I think the world would be better for it.

Meric tensed his shoulders and felt his fingers curl into his palms, despite his crossed arms. Under normal circumstances, he was able to ignore Kiev's attempts to rise him to rage, but today was anything but normal. He itched to reach for his bow. The guard had always wanted to fight him. When deep in drink he boasted of his strength and soldier's prowess, strutting, and calling like an overtly colorful bird. The nights when Kiev managed to kindle his anger into flame were nights Meric could hardly remember. He'd wake to the hazy memories of flashing, bloodied fists and more than a few new pains that would make it hard to move for days after. Grae would recall the night to him with an exasperated sigh and a lecture on his overindulgence. It never needed to be said but, while he fared better than most of Kiev's drunken brawlers, he knew he never won a fight with the man. Perhaps Meric could turn the tables today and show him exactly what a sober Venandi was capable of.

Just as Meric was about to respond, a woman with tattooed blue eyes answered the door. Her dark hair was pinned up, braids wrapped around the back of her head with long flowing locks, spilling over her shoulders. She wore a necklace that held a vial of clear liquid. What the vial held he had no idea.

"Ah, yes. Your partner arrived sometime before you. They are waiting," she said in a low rasping voice. She sounded like she smoked willow, which was common among her kind.

She wasn't a servant as most of the rich people in Reva had. She was Vagu. Her slanted eyebrows, like his earring, gave away her occupation. If one could call a race an occupation. They were no different than he, except that they could tell the future—or so they claimed—and commanded power over the wind. He found the entire notion ridiculous. But who was he to question the righteous ideals of his betters? He'd never seen either claim with his own eyes.

It was common for affluent citizens to house a Vagu. It was a symbol of power and people thought twice in trying to undermine their neighbors if they knew a Vagu was in their service. Their feline features unsettled Meric, emitting a superiority only surpassed by the people they served. He supposed that was why they were able to fool so many.

The woman, Dianai, ushered them inside. Kiev stood upright to his original position with the spear gleaming against the blue sky as the door closed. The brightness of the marble walls and floors matched the elegance of the townhome's outward appearance.

Embedded along the corners of the pristine rooms were pillars of red wood that crisscrossed the ceiling in a beautiful illusion of what a forest might look like. It was astonishing. Meric hadn't stepped inside the home when Fallon had hired them. Grae took on that role and met with Dianai. As the City Lord's representative, she related Fallon's terms before officially employing them.

The Vagu's green dress was similar to Juna's in that it flowed like silk from her slim frame. It was a tad more antiquated than the current fashion, which showed quite a bit more skin. Her entire upper body was covered by the dress with long sleeves that pointed just above the middle fingers of her hands.

She cascaded instead of walked, while cutting corners and opening doors. The townhome was so large Meric had to keep a mental note of where they were in case they needed a quick escape. He knew with each step there would be nothing quick about it. Finally, just as Anya huffed beside him in impatience Dianai turned around with her cat-like blue eyes.

"I'll know should you require anything," she smiled, pointing to the elaborate door in front of them and ebbed down the hallway into an adjacent room.

Anya's gaze followed the Vagu until she was gone from their sight. She turned to Meric and brought her thumb to her mouth. Before he could protest, she gripped his cheek and pressed her wet thumb to the edge of his scalp cracked with dried blood. He shrunk from her touch and looked at her with bewilderment. She hadn't done that in years.

"It's been some time since you've bled that much. I've forgotten the sight," she said, shrugging. It almost sounded like a slant, but he could hear the concern in her voice.

"I'm fine." He sighed and Anya nodded in encouragement as he pushed the door open.

The room was as bright as the rest of the home, but was clearly a space that was rarely used. The sunlight that peered through the high-walled ceilings was speckled in floating pieces of dust, while the furniture laid immaculate as the day Fallon had purchased them. The opposite wall was filled with books and scrolls. A clear line of sift hugged the outside of the scripts, except for a few that had been used regularly.

Books on finances and biographies of past City Lords looked to have been disturbed. A scroll rested on the desk that was titled *The Decay of Isla Om*, the author a Vagu man long since believed to be dead. It was a controversial poem that many claimed was the story of Iona herself—though few believed that to be true since Iona was more of an ideal than a divinity of flesh. According to the poem, Isla and the Nameless Sister created the land and, as with many poems, their story ended in tragedy. In any case, it was a common enough song he'd heard in the taverns, although he couldn't remember the words at the moment. He often found the mournful tune playing in his mind with a familiarity that confounded him, since it wasn't a song he paid much attention to.

City Lord Fallon stood behind the desk with his hand near the scroll. His vest fit tight around a large chest. The golden design upon it was indiscernible to follow. His wealth surpassed every living soul in Reva. In the past, it was Meric's opinion that Fallon wasn't an unreasonable man—but he wasn't a good man. And now with the knowledge that Fallon sent a Reticent to take away his grandchild, Meric felt disgust rise in his belly.

The man's athletic build and strong chin were matched in the features of Juna, who sat on the chair closest to the library's wall. Her bloodied emerald dress was gone, replaced with a more suitable attire for her station. She was still considered young, even if she had obviously reached womanhood, and so her pale, red dress covered her shoulders down to her elbows. The color had not the same allure as her previous dress and accented her swollen eyes that wept with stoic tears. A bruise formed above her temple where her head had collided with the Reticent's knee. Her golden hair had been pinned back into neat braids without any memory of its ragged past attack. She stared at Meric with a deep hatred that he felt from across the room.

Grae stood next to Fallon with his hands behind his back. His jaw was colored purple from Due, no doubt. His face expressed no emotion as Anya and Meric stood next to him. Meric watched for any signs of grievance, but only could see a Venandi's mask.

"Unharmed, I said." Fallon gestured towards his daughter, who turned away with a quivering lip. "Is that too large a word for you lot?" he said in a low, growling voice. It commanded respect and obedience without question.

"There were complications. As I mentioned, it was not us who injured Juna," Grae said with as much authority. Even though he wasn't present during her attack, Grae knew Meric better than anyone. There was no situation in which Meric would've inflicted so much damage upon an individual who wasn't threatening his life. "Had we been aware of certain... changes," he paused, leveling his blue eyes at Fallon, who seethed beneath his glare. "Events may have played out differently."

"I told you what your price demanded. Anything more wasn't worth my breath—least of all my coin."

Meric's hand tightened into a fist, but he remained silent. If anyone was to lose control, it was best for it not to be them. Fallon would make it impossible for them to find work in Reva, if he hadn't already decided on that outcome. They'd have to move to another city to survive.

"Is that the value you place on your grandchild?" Anya muttered loud enough for Fallon to incline his head towards her in a way that was predatory.

"Anya," Grae said through his teeth.

Meric nudged her elbow, surprised at her outburst. She was normally silent and did everything in her power to make sure they were paid the coin they deserved.

"What is the value of your tongue? I assure you, I can find a prolific use for one so sharp," Fallon said, his eyes lingering on her lips. She lifted her head for a retort, but before she could Meric walked across the room.

Grae uncrossed his arms and Fallon spun to watch Meric walk towards his daughter. Juna's hostility amplified at his closeness, but her eyes pled for knowledge. She wanted to know what happened to her baby. Meric steeled himself as he reached into his cloak pocket and pulled out the golden necklace. The opal gemstone glittered in the dust-filled sunlight.

"This is yours." He placed the necklace into her hand that rested on her lap.

"Tell me she is dead," she whispered. "Tell me my girl has passed to the wind."

Meric's heart broke as rot filled his chest. It infested every part of him until there was nothing left to feel. He stared at her with blank eyes certain there was no comfort in the world he could gift her. She looked up, finding no relief in his dead expression. Her body seemed to crumble as she leaned forward, crouching over empty arms that craved her child.

"I am sorry I could not stop her," he said in earnest, but his monotone voice couldn't express his regret properly.

Her moist eyes lingered on his, then slid to her father. She bared her teeth and stood, running towards him. Meric thought she was eager for an embrace, some small comfort from the man who was supposed to protect her. Instead, she slapped him, hard and loud. It echoed in the room and an enduring silence followed. Meric held breath in suspension.

"Why?" she whispered, tired and spent. As if every bit of her misery resided in that slap.

Fallon wiped his mouth of spit, features expressing neither love nor compassion. Instead, he raised his eyebrows as though her blow were nothing more than the inconvenient backhand of a child.

"Such small creatures you are. So beautiful and poised." Fallon ran the back of his hand across her cheek, wiping a tear away. "How well you hide that smell between your legs. The lure of weaker men." He gripped her chin with force. Anya inched forward, but Grae gripped her wrist, pleading with his eyes for her to not interfere. "What proper man will have you now that it's stretched out from the head of your bastard child? I did what I had to do for the standing of this house — for the honor of your name. Strike me again and I'll sell you to the whorehouse your crippled lover died in."

Fallon released Juna's chin with a thrust to the side. She gripped the edge of the desk to keep herself from falling, heaving in a heavy sob with a hand over her mouth in a failed attempt to stifle her cries.

Endri was dead. Meric's open mouth closed as he peered at

Grae, who grimly nodded in confirmation. When the Reticent hit him, she must've collapsed Endri's nasal cavity. With the split in his lip the blood would've pooled in his mouth making it impossible for him to breathe. He drowned in his own blood and Meric did nothing to stop it. He should've turned him over, he knew better. He saw the blood bubbling in the man's mouth, suffocating him as he left Endri to pursue the Reticent. It would've only taken a moment.

But it's within moments that egregious mistakes are made and solidified into regretfully memories.

Meric found himself with a phantom grip on a bottle of ale. He lifted his arm to pour it into his mouth, but instead, it fell upon Fallon. The man gasped and, with a crack, his head snapped to the side against Meric's fist.

Before he realized the monumental mistake, Meric had landed several more blows across the head of the City Lord. Grae and Anya shouted behind him, pulling him away from the wretched man. Meric fought against them, dark hair clouding his vision as he was pinned against the bookshelf by Anya.

"Stop!" she said into his ear. "Do you realize what you've done?" Her voice wavered in terror and anger.

"A child! He condemned a child to those animals. His own flesh!" Meric boiled in his outrage. He didn't need a drink—he needed a barrel.

"Forget the child. Do you realize what you've just done, Meric?" she repeated each word as if they were the last ones, she'd ever speak to him. The break in her voice brought him out of the fog and he relaxed against her grip.

Depths drown me, I've killed myself.

She released him and he turned around to see Fallon wiping the side of his mouth with a blood-soaked handkerchief. There was a cut below his right eye and his styled, slick hair frayed in all directions. Grae's limbs were taut with the anticipation of violence. He was ready to leap to Meric's rescue, but as he turned to Anya, his expression changed to uncertainty. They both knew such an attempt would prove unfruitful. Meric was a dead man.

Fallon straightened from the desk he leaned on to his full height. Two heads taller than anyone in the room, he towered over Meric.

"Death will be a mercy," he said through bloodied teeth. "No one will hear you beg for it." His baritone voice clung to the back of his throat like rocks in a sea storm. Fallon turned to Anya and Grae who—to their credit—stood their ground as he loomed above them. "I'll make sure the only coin you'll receive are the ones you earn from the filthy street walkers who need a quick pull and tug."

Anya glanced at Meric, but he couldn't meet her eye. His gaze was fixed on Juna, who stood near the desk, tracing the lines of the scroll she looked to have been reading.

"I never wanted this," Meric whispered, the words clawing their way out of him like a snared beast from a hunter's trap. Was he speaking to Juna or to himself?

She turned from the scroll to look at him, lifting her face close enough for their breaths to mingle. Meric noticed flecks of Endri's blood marbled in her perfect braids. The look in Juna's eyes was an ocean of grief. Its vastness surpassed any attempt for understanding. He knew in losing himself in their depths that she'd never recover. She still had the golden necklace in her hand. She lifted it and placed the jeweled chain around her neck. Looking down at the scroll, she recited with a bitterness that would only ripen with age.

"He did not see it, the pit so deep, she buried him alive for hers to keep."

She lifted her gaze, expression empty of everything that had once filled it. Endri and her child were gone and all she had left was pain. She glanced at her father and nodded slightly, as though he needed her permission for what was to happen next.

Fallon gripped Meric's cloak, tearing him from Juna's steeled eyes. He didn't feel the tight grip of the City Lord's meaty fingers around his neck or hear the protests of Grae and Anya as he was dragged outside. He couldn't taste the blood on his tongue as the guards kicked his face or the cold of the irons placed around his wrists. He thought he heard Kiev laughing and perhaps the bite of the brute's fist connecting with his mouth.

The City Lord owned his own prisons beneath the town-home, a remnant to the fear of a dragon attack during the war. He was dragged across sharpened stairs and graveled ground, thrown against bars that rattled in the darkness. It wasn't until Meric was within the cell, had he realized what had happened. He beat the City Lord. Attacked the most powerful man in Reva. He heard the click of the lock and the resistance of his friends from above as they were banned from the grounds.

The air was stale and wet beneath the world. He had no light nor warmth, no bed or chamber pot. Worst of all, he had no ale. Nothing to wash down the torment and shame. He lifted his hand to his ear and found it torn and bloody. The earring missing, and his back bare of his bow and quivers. They must've ripped it off him in the struggle. He hoped Anya and Grae had picked it up. Anya could find use for it, but it would be far more valuable as coin. If they sold the weapon, his friends would have more than enough funds to start over somewhere else. He knew they would have to. There was no other choice.

Meric wasn't alone under the ground. Singing—a woman was singing. He couldn't see so far down the line of cells, but he knew she was there. There was no shuffling of bare feet or the erratic clattering of chains. Only a pulsing blue light emanating from the furthest cell. Perhaps she had a window? The light reminded him of clouds passing across the moon. Had he been under the ground for so long? Had the day given way to its darker companion?

The woman's soft, lilting voice floated with the humid air through the iron bars. The lyrics settled upon Meric like an incurable pain he was desperate to be rid of. Over and over the woman sang. Her grief-stricken lyrics brought comfort to his raw sorrow. He begged her to cease so he might wallow in his penance. No amount of pleading swayed the prisoner to remain quiet.

In fairest words, there is no say, the heart's torment of Isla's Decay. Found, she did, a man of blue. In love, if love were ever true…

Meric could only listen as he soon found himself joining in the music, if only to remember he had once heard it before.

CHAPTER 19

ALONE IN THE WORLD

Although the silence between Sou and Evelyn had broken, they often remained in long bouts of muteness. The stillness of the Greens made Evelyn feel like if she were to speak anything above a whisper the earth might crumble beneath her. She stood at the helm, gazing upon the shifting grassland before turning to Sou, pulling tight the mast rope.

"What about Meric?" she asked. The memory of the voice in the mountain had echoed in her mind the past few days, imploring her with desperation. She had to find him; it was almost as if she'd made a promise without speaking. She just knew he needed her somehow.

"Find him if you can, but I'll not risk your life for someone we don't know. We'll leave as soon as I can find a Venandi pair to take our coin—with or without Meric. We'll not spend days in the city if I can help it." He spoke with conviction and wouldn't be challenged on the subject.

A determination enveloped Evelyn as she let his words settle. Barring her from a task only made her that much more committed to the end goal. He wouldn't keep her from finding this unknown man and she let him know that with the glare she returned. He shook his head with a sigh, but said no more.

There was more she needed to tell him, and she struggled

whether she should share the information but, in the end, decided it was the right course of action.

"I can hear all voices of the wind, Sou, even thoughts," she said, noticing the stems of grass the ferryman had given to her days ago resting on the taffrail. The shoots had withered, becoming brittle to the touch and when she tried to grasp them, they fell to pieces between her fingers.

Sou widened his eyes with panic, his irises darting back and forth. He involuntarily leaned back as if she would strike him. The sight was jarring, and Evelyn grew worried that he feared her. She lifted her hands in a display of peace.

"I can't hear everything. Only what you want me to hear. I can't listen to anything you haven't wished for me to know."

She relaxed as his shoulders lowered, expression reposed as he settled into his original position. He had the look of a man who had barely prevented a dark secret from escaping to the ears of an enemy. "Well, that might've been good to know before," he said, frowning. She continued to bare a melancholy grin.

"You only thought of my welfare. It was all I had to wake up to each day. You took my sorrow along with yours and I cannot begin to express my gratitude."

It was true she had lost her home, but so had he, and she had been remised to have forgotten that he grieved as well.

"Lass, there is something I have to tell you." He seemed to struggle as he spoke, the words leaving his mouth as if being forced. He was a man of the dirt. The strength of his bones and the toil of his hands were what Sou relied upon. Evelyn knew him to be a man of action and wisdom, even if his advice came at the expense of your own shortcomings. He was always understanding and kind to a fault, so to see him fumble was a sight unfamiliar to her. "Verbena may have been where your mother was born, but Birny was her home."

Evelyn felt her body tense, unprepared for whatever Sou was about to say. She leaned back, craving to know but frightened to death of how the answer to her question would change her. She had changed so much already.

"What's in Birny?"

Sou furrowed his brow in an attempt to keep tears from falling. He looked over her with a pleading expression, as if he were standing before an avalanche begging for it not to crush him to splinters.

"Your father."

Evelyn leaned back; her lips parted against what was just said. Her father? He lived? Her mind raged against what Sou revealed. She laughed, shaking her head, but it soon dissipated as Sou's distraught eyes bore into hers. Was this what Sou and Tansey had meant to speak to her about? He had kept this from her—him, and her gran. Her entire life, Evelyn had known herself to be alone in the world, looking upon the families in her village with mothers and fathers. She'd been content with her emptiness—an emptiness formed by lies.

Sou looked away, unable to meet the betrayal she couldn't help but express. How could they have kept this from her? He turned back to her, a focus in his eyes that revealed he held no regrets. He thought he was protecting her. Evelyn didn't want to think about protection. What good had it done? She braced herself as he opened his mouth to speak, but she couldn't have been prepared for what he said next.

"Your sister too."

CHAPTER 20

THE DEATH OF CALIAN

If fear was a being of living tissue, eating its way through the world, Maun thought it might've been the darkness of Oretem's cave. The concept intrigued him. He almost opened his mouth to try to speak with the vast emptiness, but remembered Saiya flying overhead. Maun never felt fear. It was purged long ago with the death of his mother, but he remembered its ravenous hunger, the feel of its teeth gnawing at his bones and pulling his soul from a body much too young to understand the implications of its absence. He stared down that darkness, letting the void merge with his own hollowness.

It had been a little less than a fortnight since the destruction of the village. He'd spent that time tending to Saiya's wounds. Her right wing had dislocated when she fell from the Viden's knife stab. The cut itself was shallow for her size, but the fall had severely damaged the integrity of her wing. The various bites and scratches from the wolf were significant, but treatable. It was her wing that was the most problematic. When he tried to set it, she bit and clawed at him. Eventually, he'd been forced to strike her across the beak, knocking her out cold.

Without flight she was useless. He wouldn't have been able to carry her across Iona and a raptor that cannot fly is a dead raptor, especially in this endless winter. But he wasn't through with her usefulness yet. He set the wing and bound her with rope he'd taken from the peddler's cart. He needed to tend to his own wounds as well. He'd been able to lift his arm, but the shoulder that the wolf bit would fester if not properly tended. While Saiya slept off her injuries in between meals, Maun suffered through his. They remained that way for days as they consumed the body of the wolf.

It wasn't from a need to make use of the animal's body in a way that was respectful to Iona—to Celosia's Depths with Iona. Saiya deserved to feast on the enemy she defeated. He ate the wolf's meat, not just out of necessity, but for the same reason. They were alive and the beast was not.

The hollowed-out home of the Viden was better than most shelters he had in the past. It did him well for the days he and Saiya had to heal. She woke near the end of the week, cawing and reaping her talons through the wooden floor. He felt her resentment and ire at not being able to spread her wings. The compulsion was so strong, he grew troubled that she might dislocate the wing again, so he released her.

The sight of her disappearing into the air through the hole in the roof was as close to contentment as Maun could feel. The bond demanded a certain level of shared understanding. It was inevitable for them to claim a kind of responsibility for the other, but it never overshadowed his commitment. Saiya was a part of the Reticent and a Reticent can always be replaced. They meant nothing. Nothing at all. Still, he displayed a small smile as he turned his head from the cave and heard her screeching call.

Maun knew he had to face him. His sect demanded him to pay his respect to the one who had created them, but it was not to bow to his will. Cinaed may have been the leader the Reticent followed, but Maun was no longer part of the Order. His own path hadn't changed. If anything, the road to his revenge was clearer, smoother than before. He'd already spent too much time in the repugnant village. The people were beginning to rot. The flames, days after the attack, kept the small town warm and thawed. The snow did nothing to stop the natural course bodies underwent when empty and spoiled.

He reached out to Saiya and she dived without a sound, landing on his unharmed arm. She was a tad slower than before her injury, but was recovering quickly. He suspected her to be fully restored within the next few days. Her heavy weight pushed against his muscles, tightening them with her claws. The injury his shoulder sustained had faded down to a dull ache, exasperated by the cold climate.

He stepped into the darkness, swallowed by the mouth of the cave. There was an outlandish feel to the tunnel. As if once followed through, it would spit him out into a world so unlike the one he left, it would be impossible to escape. Of course, he knew that to be false. However, it didn't make the journey any less haunting. As he entered the chamber, he smelled warm soot drifting from the burnt roots above. The flames had extinguished to soft ember glows that reminded him of stars lingering in the dawn, red and persistent. Oretem laid where he was before in the middle of the crater-like room. His deep rumble vibrated the pebbles at Maun's feet and sent a pulse through his body. His large, glowing red eye was open and watchful. Cinaed stood at the edge of the chamber near a fire he'd built with fallen roots. The shadows of the flames glittered off Oretem's scales in a corrupted crimson glare.

Saiya nervously ruffled her black feathers, attempting to look bigger. Her anxiety flowed through him as she stared at the dragon, black plumes brushing his cheek. He pulled on her beak in a way that reassured her. She nipped at his fingers with a calmer demeanor.

"Ah, she lives," Cinaed said, turning from the fire. His clouded eye glowed in the shadows as he grinned at Saiya.

His father had spoken of this man as if he were a legend come to life. Maun never met Cinaed as a child. He'd only seen portraits or heard descriptions of their great leader and none of them accurately portrayed the older man before him. This rider, who brought purpose into the world. In a time when men and women bloodied the other in epic battles he'd only heard of in song. He wondered what it was to be in the heat of combat, the rush of hundreds of those whose only goal was to kill you. It brought a slight fever to his blood and Saiya opened her beak in a short caw, feeling it too.

Now, the great legend limped as his scarred face contorted under discomfort. It was known Cinaed wandered the Solov Waste in his youth, perfecting the way of the Reticent. He founded Soleil Citade where Maun grew up, learning how to tame solov raptors. It was also rumored he went mad from the heat, but that madness was necessary to bring about choice to all within Iona.

Cinaed's strength waned even as he tried to hide it under his silken voice.

"I wondered. The visions aren't as clear as they should be." His burnt face stretched against a bitter laugh. "It's fitting, isn't it? That I should grasp for what I wish to never have possessed, to rid myself of what most people seek to know." Maun's mind bent against the confusing words as he met Cinaed's clouded gaze. Madness simmered as deeply as any grave in those eyes and, just as quickly, disappeared to assert flashes of sanity.

"I can assume the Viden escaped." It wasn't a question. Cinaed's slithering voice crept along the walls, surrounding the chamber.

"I've come to bid you farewell. This is where we part ways," Maun said, speaking through Saiya, her tongue blood red in the flame light.

"No." The authority in Cinaed's voice was absolute.

Maun hadn't heard that word often, and when he did, it stirred his darker impulses. He scanned the room for other exits, but found that his only way out was where he had come in. There wasn't much he could do with a dragon to protect the Decayed. He decided to talk and to wait.

"Are your visions clear enough to see that we have more to do together?"

"Did you know that when a dragon and Viden bond, they share a soul?" Cinaed said, ignoring his question. He walked up to Oretem, who closed his eye under Cinaed's touch. The dragon's long tail dragged across the cave floor, scraping massive boulders across the cavern. "That is perhaps the reason why compatibility was so paramount during the rise of Videns."

Maun furrowed his brow, watching Cinaed run his fingers over the red dragons' scales. It wasn't a comforting touch. It was a malicious and conspiratorial caress. He lifted his hand and turned to Maun, scarred features puckering in the shadowed firelight. He gave the appearance of a man in flames. It was an awe-inspiring visage. It was no wonder this man led the charge against would-be fortune tellers and lesser beings.

"I did know this. I am Reticent." Saiya displayed her black wings with pride.

"This other Viden shares a part of Oretem's soul. He cannot serve two masters, no matter the hold I have against him. We are... incompatible. As Chao and I never were," he said with a slick whisper as though the dragon might turn on him. The beast growled as the floor rumbled under Maun's feet. "She must die. If it were as easy as dying then I would've long ago, but breath is sweet, and I've developed a taste for it. So, she must die. There is still no silence in my sleep. She will grant me silence if I take her protectors. She must."

Maun folded his arms so that his hand rested on his ribs, near the old woman's dagger that hung at his side.

"Evelyn is going to Reva, but she is not what I pursue."

"Yes, the young man, Meric. Tell me, you saw my grand death, did you not?"

Maun recalled the vision of Caia and her dragon. Her husband beating his father to death and so his mother. He clenched his fist, jaw twitching as enmity grew within him. He nodded, looking towards the rock wall to hide his emotions that were so plain to see.

"That was in the pursuit of a kind of vengeance. An attempt for the ultimate power. The death of another and the satisfaction of their downfall for the thing that you take for granted. Silence," he whispered the word as though he'd never known its meaning. "I failed. A lustful craving for dominance blinded me from my true goal, but Iona weakened all the same. I killed all of her champions, broke every shield but one." He held out his hand with a single scared finger. "All but one."

Maun had no idea what the man was speaking of. It seemed the rumors were true, and falling into a boiling lake hadn't helped his sanity. The urge to leave grew ever stronger the longer Cinaed spoke. Reasoning with insanity was like screaming into a sandstorm. The torrent winds drowned out your cries and you only ended up flayed.

"Your failure is not mine." Maun bared his teeth. He fulfilled his purpose in conversing with Cinaed and now, it was time for the conversation to end. "I will leave, and you will let me."

"Will I, now? By which goddess do you believe will allow that to be so? Iona or Celosia?" Cinaed wrapped his hand around the hilt of a sword at his side. His snake-like movements might've once fooled his enemies, but Maun saw the flow. Maun saw everything. "Iona was always merciful, but murder?" He pursed his lips, thoughtful. "How many have you murdered?"

Maun wouldn't answer. How many was all his life?

"Celosia, she was ever vengeful and ornery. Perhaps she is your goddess? The better of the two for one in your position, but inevitably less powerful. That was unfortunately of her own doing. So, I ask again, by which goddess would you care to pray too if you should try to leave my services? Should I turn you over or leave you upturned? Important questions, Maun."

Saiya stared down at Cinaed, baring her golden eye with a sightless terror that remained unfounded in the old leader. He chuckled and patted Oretem who stirred under his touch.

"Neither. I choose myself, as I always have. What position I die in is of little consequence to me. I serve nothing greater than what I am capable of, and I am capable of a great many things," Maun gripped his blade with steady fingers. The anticipation of a fight was as desirable as the smell of blood. It called for the starved with the promise of renewed vitality, the feeling of victory.

"As am I, Reticent. You wish to exact your vengeance? You shall have it. The whole truth of it. I shall force it upon you." His mouth curled with harsh lines, making his scars seem like serrated blades. "I have not survived the boiling lake to be squealed at by an orphaned shoat who thinks himself the butcher. I hold the blade, Reticent."

So much talk. Maun felt his cut-out tongue in the space where it used to reside. Sometimes it was a phantom in his mouth that thought it could speak. He didn't care for conversation, and he'd indulged the old man long enough.

Saiya took to the air as Maun unsheathed the dagger, shoulder still sore from the bite of the wolf. His features remained impassive even as his dagger hand stilled in delight. He ached to thrust the blade into the old man's chest. He may admire him for his past deeds, but they were as crippled as his lame leg. The Videns were gone. Only one remained and he needed her.

"So, you have chosen. Here is your vengeance."

Maun opened his mouth in a wordless scream. Saiya shriek bellowed within the walls of the cave. It joined with Oretem's roar as he lifted himself from his prostrated position. Cinaed hadn't moved. He only lifted his hand and Maun felt the push of his mind as blackness overtook his vision. He tried to fight it, but the overwhelming pressure threatened to tear his skull apart. He gave into memory.

HIS MOTHER EMBRACED MAUN IN A TIGHT HOLD. HER EYES WERE blue like his, gleaming in the darkness. They huddled together under the floorboards, her breathing slow and quiet. He was barely a toddler, just having found the balance of his feet. He peered in between the wooden panels, hearing the shuffling of feet and the clanging of furniture.

She placed a hand over his brow and kissed his forehead, closing her eyes as a pair of boots hovered above them.

221

"Where is the boy?" a feminine voice said, cruelty lacing the edges of her words.

There was another shadow, taller and thicker than the other, casting itself across from the one above them. The woman chuckled at the silence with deep amusement, but Maun found no humor in the insidious sound.

"Send in the young Reticent. Perhaps he can find them," another deeper voice said, a man this time.

"I live alone, there is no one else," Aunt Yaya said, courageous but trembling.

"Do you take us for fools?" the woman said, boots leaping forward, melding into the shadow of Aunt Yaya. The sound of metal clanging echoed through the air, and Aunt Yaya cried out as her knees hit the floor.

Maun's mother bit her lip and clutched him tighter in her arms, fighting against a sudden urge to stand.

"I don't know this boy you speak of," Aunt Yaya panted, "I live alone."

The shadow jerked and she gasped in pain. When he and his mother climbed under the floorboards, Maun hadn't known why Aunt Yaya wouldn't hide with them. He barely understood why they had to hide at all. He tried to turn his head to ask his mother, but she held him so tight he couldn't move.

"You'll get nothing from this one. It's clear she'd rather die," the man said, stepping forward.

"Perhaps we should grant her request?" the woman replied.

"Perhaps you should do as I said and send in the Reticent." His graveled voice was tinged in impatience.

"They're gone! They're not here!" Aunt Yaya said in desperation. "Kill me if you came for blood and die upturned while you're at it!"

The woman chuckled again, leaving Maun chilled. His mother's lip quivered, and a small whimper escaped her before she clasped a hand over her mouth.

"You've heard tales of what we do and what we take. You've prepared. Fascinating. Cinaed was right. Love is the death of free will. I shall cut your bonds." Her shape seemed to rise, and a sharp sweeping movement dashed across the floor.

Aunt Yaya grunted and fell with a small gasp. Maun's mother released a quiet sob and buried her face into his messy hair.

"It's incredible how many of them offer their own lives. We're not killing their children. We aren't barbarians," the woman said, her shadow drifting towards the man.

"They've lived their entire lives without truly living, Devu. Sacrificing oneself for another is the doctrine of the Videns. They've poisoned the minds of everyone to abandon their own basic instincts. Once Cinaed defeats them, free will and choice will once again be available to all with Celosia's rule."

The one above them, Devu, huffed in response, stepped outside the home, and returned with the sound of another pair of boots. They crept in silence as if walking on soft grass. Maun, too young to understand danger, lifted his head against the wooden floor to get a better look. His eyes fell upon a man cloaked in black, his face riddled in open cuts. They cracked with fresh blood, seeping out of the wounds. He recoiled at the sight, his stomach clenching against the bile that traveled up his throat. It couldn't be real. He buried his face into his mother's chest, clinging to what felt safe.

She pushed him aside and dug her fingernails into the dirt outlining a small door that laid beneath them. He remembered Aunt Yaya and Mother creating the tunnel, claiming it to be a way to the heart of Iona, but he was always told it was only to be used when home wasn't safe anymore.

Maun whimpered as she pulled on the wood, the metal latch catching on the corrosive rust. She grunted and pulled again, baring her teeth in a tear-stained snarl. Maun found her features frightening and whimpered again, but louder.

"Shh," she whispered, kissing his forehead. She tore at the rust with her fingernails, trying with hurried panic to open the door.

He tried to stifle his cries, but the tears kept flowing. Emotions that he'd never felt coursed through his veins, unbidden and without explanation. How was he to control what he didn't know? Why were they hiding? Who were these men in their home? Maun had not the capability of understanding these questions let alone the answers he might receive.

His mother allowed a soft frustrated grunt and ran her fingers through his hair as she held him tighter. She begged him to remain silent, but he couldn't control the depth of his fear. Maun heard the soft steps of the scarred man standing over them. Then he heard laughter from the other two. It only made him cry louder. His mother's tears fall on his head as she sunk further into the floor where no space remained but the tunnel below—the tunnel they couldn't reach.

"I suppose we only needed your presence," Devu said, her voice deep.

There was a snapping of wood and cracking of boards as light filled the dim space where Maun and his mother hid. He peeked over her arm and saw two men and a woman looking over them, giants to his child's eye. The woman and man, who were but shadows before, stared at him with hard eyes. Free of scars they looked human, but the emptiness in their eyes reflected the monsters Maun feared that lived under his bed. He'd never been more frightened. He was frozen in it, gripped in the claws of fear as it ruptured his view of what good life held.

Another man knelt above him, scarred, dark eyes absent of any kindness. He never spoke a word as he pried Maun from his mother's arms.

"No, no, no," she muttered, clinging to his small body.

She crushed him against her as she attempted to postpone the inevitable. Maun tried to stay with her, but his young strength was no match for the brutality of bigger men. He screamed for her. She sobbed as her arms were forced open, fighting against the scarred man. She bit his hand and still no sound escaped his lips. He jerked his hand free, dark with blood and struck her across the face. Still, she held on. Maun's cries filled the room, echoing through the floor and out of the home.

The scarred man took out a dagger and held it aloft. Her bright eyes widened at the blade, dark hair billowing around her panicked features. The man looped an arm around Maun's waist, lifting him from his mother's grasp. He wailed with arms outstretched, watching his mother reach for him, despite fear reflecting in her eyes. The scarred man held the blade to her throat. She pressed against it; her throat split as she screamed.

"Calian! Remember me!"

Blood swelled over her chest and spread beneath the floor. It wasn't quick. She spat and choked, blood bubbling from the slit in her throat *like the pressurized crack between two river stones, struggling to stop the rage of a strong current. Maun watched it rain across the scarred man's boots. He flinched, but the man who held him remained as stone. His mother writhed on the floor, gasping and spewing, spasming and convulsing until she just... ceased. Her eyes were left open, red-rimmed tears falling across her smooth cheek. Her arm rested against the boards, still reaching out for him.*

Maun struggled in the stone embrace of the scarred man. His mind as splintered as the floorboards. He stared at his mother's corpse, unable to comprehend the reason for it all. What had the scarred man done to her? Why wasn't she moving? What would happen to him?

The scarred man handed him to the tall man standing by Devu almost throwing the boy into his reluctant arms. Maun caught a glimpse of Aunt Yaya laying on the ground, her arms over her head as though she had tried to block the weapon that had struck her. Her long black hair fell away from a face displaying young features that looked similar to his mother's. Blood trickled from her jaw that was open at an awkward angle, like a serpent eating a rat. He turned away, wondering why she wouldn't rise.

"What am I to do with this?" the man said, raising his voice over Maun's increasingly growing cries. The scarred man didn't answer. He only stared then turned away, exiting the home.

"You know they can't answer, Ethen," Devu said once the man was gone. Her short dark hair silhouetted angular features that ended in sharp corners. She gripped Maun's head and shoved him into Ethen's shoulder, quieting his sobs against the man's neck.

"I thought this would be his Child of Fortune," Ethen said, leaning his head away from Maun as much as possible. His grip was hard on Maun, hurting his arms as he bobbed him up and down in a failed attempt to calm him.

"Apparently, your time is up, my friend. It's time to join the cause. Ovia will be pleased. She's been waiting for this."

Maun's throat hurt as his cries quieted. He had no inkling as to what was occurring. He only knew the man who held him was not his mother. He wanted his mother. Why hadn't she stood to come to get him? Had he done something wrong? Was this punishment?

"Ovia will train the little pup. I suppose it is time. Will you accom-

*pany me to the Eshe Willow Wood? Celosia's Glare is the first step, is it
not?" Ethen released one arm from Maun who almost fell from his grip
as he was let go.*

"It would honor me," Devu said, shaking the man's hand.

*Ethen wrapped his arm around Maun again as they moved to exit
the home. His home.*

*"Let's meet your mother, shall we?" he said with an underlining tone
of resentment.*

*The last image Maun saw as he was carried out of the house was
Aunt Yaya's twitching fingers, and his mother's pale arm reaching out
of the floorboards, stretching for what seemed like a hand to lift her out.*

WHEN MAUN CAME TO, HIS BACK WAS LEANING AGAINST THE
cave wall. His vision blurred, then cleared as he focused on the
swaying black shapes before him. Saiya hovered just above the
ground in front of him, her talons splayed out before her. She
screeched at Cinaed who brandished a water-stained blade in
his hand.

The Decayed parried around the raptor, but was held back
at every turn. He limped as the sword grew heavy in his grip.
Oretem growled and he lifted his head, long neck coiled for
striking. Maun groaned and reached into his pocket. The
stones felt smooth against his skin. Their purpose was obsolete
in the face of what was about to happen. He was going to die.
He was surprised to realize he was angry. As a Reticent he was
irrelevant, replaceable, but his vengeance was not.

He took out the stones from his pocket, twisting them in
between his fingers. He connected with Saiya to escape
through the tunnel, but she refused with a loud caw. Maun
stared into the face of the monstrous dragon, lifting his chin in
a resigned nod. He knew this was the likely outcome of his
actions and yet, he found himself regretful.

He closed his eyes waiting for the pain, the feel of flesh
melting off his bones, but nothing happened. Instead, he felt
the pull of another consciousness, not Saiya, but one of pain

and woe. It was old, an age he'd never imagined. He heard a deafening roar from Oretem. Maun opened his eyes, covering his ears as the sound penetrated through every conceivable barrier. The dragon writhed on the floor of the cave, his claws curled in an unseen agony.

Cinaed stared at Maun's hand with violence such as he had never seen in a man before. The sight chilled him as he listened to the anguished growls of Oretem.

"How is it you come to know the truth of Celosia's Glare? That knowledge... only I—of course. *Of course!*" His tone expressed unhinged madness. "He lives then, still? Ah, to think he knew and still thought to change me. A friend he always was." Maun grimaced as he stood with Saiya flying above him, poised to dive when ready.

His father, reviling man that he was, allowed Maun to be present at some meetings he held with the other inductees. The Tacet's remained silent as their raptors spoke for them. It was during this time he discovered the truth of their silence. Ethen thought Maun too dim witted to understand what was happening. What he hadn't known, or rather what he refused to acknowledge, was how eager Maun was to please him. So, he listened. Maun learned all he could, but this? He turned to the dragon whose soul was splitting. He never heard of this.

He had wondered how Cinaed was able to get Oretem to bond with him. How two people could share the same dragon. It was unheard of. He thought it was his power of memory. He tortured the beast with his worst memories to force him to bond, but that wasn't it. Cinaed didn't have a dragon scale, he'd checked. Celosia's Glare wasn't just a token between Reticent couples to ensure devotion or against enemies to grant them the death of their most beloved. No, they had the power to control dragons. Maun continued to rub the stones, watching Cinaed's features try to mask the fear. Fear he tried to instill in Maun. Hadn't he known? Maun couldn't feel fear.

"This was how you did it." Saiya combined her voice with his in a harsh whisper that cut through the heated air. "Why dragons fought each other and killed their own riders."

He couldn't contain the admiration in his tone. Celosia's Glare was dangerous. Anyone who didn't understand the legend risked their own life when pursuing the stones. But the risk was necessary, essential to prove their dedication. Maun sought his as was his right, but not for the fealty the Order expected. Instead of taking a bride and exchanging the stones, he planned to put them to use. He never suspected the value of that use. Taut scars stretched his mouth into a threatening grin.

"The Order has truly lost its way if the likes of you are leading its front." Cinaed's hand trembled as he lifted his sword. "An army of cutthroats and men for hire. A wasted use of the gifts you were given. Don't you know you do not matter?"

"I do not lead them. I left them. I don't matter, but there was once a time that I did. What am I to do with that?" Maun said, tasting bitterness without a tongue. Cinaed met his gaze, his smile ever present with the knowledge that he'd done something irreparable to Maun. Where did fire find the callousness to burn flesh? Maun's rage scorched through him, and he didn't know where it came from. He had the advantage and Cinaed knew it. He was younger, faster, and now with Oretem on the ground senseless, he was stronger. He flicked his head to the side, motioning Saiya just enough for Cinaed to understand the moment he'd lost.

She curled her wings inward and dove with her talons out, gripping Cinaed by the shoulder and pinning him to the ground. He howled in pain as her talons buried deep into his skin, scraping against bones. Oretem's head pounded against the cave's wall, ripping out the roots from the ceiling and tearing apart rock. The whole mountain seemed to quake under his suffering.

Maun felt the dragon split inside as he stretched out his mind towards him. The creature was a shell of what he used to be. He was now filled with unbridled hate and misery; a madness Maun could control and use.

"Will you be the one to finally free me?" The Decayed

whispered through bloodied teeth. "I took her name! I took her warriors! Falconer told me that fire would color the sky—" he stopped speaking with a screamed as blood oozed from his shoulder. "I made the Reticent. I *am* Reticent," he said, his clouded eye watering.

Saiya burrowed her claws deeper and Cinaed winced, still gripping his sword. The blade wouldn't lift from the ground. He was weak, a fossil to his former glory. Maun owed no allegiance to a man such as he, and neither did the Reticent. He leaned over the Decayed and picked up the sword, weighing it in his hands. The pommel held two stones similar to his own. He checked the placement of his fingers, careful not to touch Celosia's Glare. The sword was much too unbalanced for him. He preferred daggers, but this weapon suited the occasion.

"You were," Maun spoke through Saiya who leaned in breadths from Cinaed's face. "And Reticent are replaceable. We need only steal another child from their mother's cold, dead arms. Fortunate for you, one stands before you. Now, tell me, in which goddess do you believe?"

Cinaed growled with a tortured, scarred glare, his eyes reflecting a madness long since waiting for death. Maun lifted the blade and brought it down on his head. Cinaed's eyes rolled as his skull split in two, spraying blood across Saiya's wings and Maun's face. He licked his lips, tasting the blood of the Decayed. Saiya shrieked, pecking Cinaed's clouded red eye, empty of light as his life's blood seeped from the fissure in his scalp.

Maun felt passion when fighting the Viden's grandmother. The memory excited him, but the sight of Cinaed's own blade sticking from his skull was as dull as watching soup cool. The creator of the Reticent, rider of the Cursed Blood Tooth Chao, Tormentor of Memory, and Bondbreaker was dead, and Maun felt nothing.

He turned from the fallen old leader and made his way to Oretem. The dragon breathed heavily on the floor with withered, tired eyes. His limbs trembled as he leaned his massive head to the side, looking upon Maun.

THREE TIMES. I'VE BEEN SPLIT THREE TIMES.

The dragon's voice was as thunder beneath the ground. It spoke with strength, but also delirium. He was on the cusp of derangement and if Maun hadn't control, he thought the dragon would tear the mountain asunder in his rage. He smiled to himself. For the first time in his life, he could direct his thoughts, his speech, to another being. He had no need for Saiya to speak for him. It was liberating even if he could feel Saiya's begrudged acceptance of the new addition into their relationship.

You've a new master. I'll not be kinder. In fact, I expect you won't know the difference.

It was odd hearing his own voice flow between him and Oretem. It was foreign and he was surprised to find it so hollow and empty even if it came from his mind. He preferred it combined with Saiya's. She tore at Cinaed's corpse, contented with his conclusion.

THREE TIMES. THREE TIMES. THREE TIMES, Oretem repeated. The dragon was like its old master, a relic of the past.

Maun lifted Celosia's Glare where Oretem couldn't turn away from the stones. The dragon raked his claws across the graveled floor with a loud scrape and sighed a heavy growl, yielding to Maun. He thought of Evelyn and Meric, of Ovia and the mother he couldn't remember. He felt the ghost of Devu's hand on the back of his neck, squeezing with such brutal force. Who was Calian? Who was he before Maun was born? He turned to Oretem, determination in his gaze.

He saw his reflection in the dragon's pupil. His scars were crisscrossed with Cinaed's blood hardening against his neck and cheeks. His dark hair was familiar and waved the same way the woman's had in his memory. They were alike in every way he and Ovia were different. The edges of his eyes bordered crimson and grew from the edges until the color engulfed his irises. Only a faint lighter red appeared where the blue once dwelled.

He frowned, taking in his emotions. He tried to replace his despondency with indifference, but the memory of his true mother was... clouding his focus. He needed to find out more. Why had Cinaed returned? What was all that talk about goddesses? Celosia and Iona were ideals, not goddesses.

He couldn't leave, not yet. For the first time, he had access to the answers, but he couldn't just abandon his task. No, he had to do something he swore he wouldn't. The oath he made was easily broken by the unexpected turn of events he found himself in. He had Oretem. That single fact upturned every preordained decision he had. His aim remained the same, just a few thousand feet higher than before, on the back of a dragon.

He turned away from Oretem and looked upon Saiya, who had a mouthful of Cinaed's cheek. She tilted her head up as the flesh dripped blood across her feathers. She swallowed and met his eyes. Maun impressed upon her what his plan was and her role in it. She ruffled her feathers, spraying red over the stones. Her golden eyes gleamed in protest, but Maun brought down his iron will over her and she relented.

He wouldn't admit it, but he was apprehensive about being separated from her. They'd never been apart so far a distance, but this was a task only she could do, and it had to be done. She flew and landed on his arm, staring into his eyes. Maun relayed his message, imploring her to repeat it exactly as he thought it. She blinked with understanding and dipped her head towards him. He lifted a finger and touched the tip of her beak. This was as close to affection as he could be without breaking his vow. Love nothing. Wearing Celosia's Glare ensured that, but there were Reticent in the past who had broken this most sacred covenant and died for it. His parents. They were foolish enough to love one another, however wretched that love was.

Saiya displayed her wings with a loud shriek and lifted herself into the air. She circled over him for a moment, then disappeared down the tunnel. Her consciousness grew dimmer the farther she flew, until after a few minutes he only had the faint whisper of her presence.

He was left to himself and the chaotic mind of a deranged dragon. It took him a long time to grow accustomed to the absence of his raptor, but soon enough he was able to come to terms with its hollowness. She was still there, gnawing at the back of his mind, even if it was harder to notice. He looked forward to hearing her recollection of traveling to Reva, the look on Tacet Devu's face when Saiya gave her his message, and the prisoner she'd bring back to him.

Maun turned back to Oretem whose red eye glinted in the darkness as though weeping. He watched his reflection shade and warp in the fire's light.

Show me everything.

CHAPTER 21

REASONABLE MEN AND
CHARITABLE ACTS

"I'll wait here," Evelyn said as she reached the end of Farron Port.

Sou nodded in appreciation, turning around to meet a thin man in a large vest that displayed a simplistic design of golden loops. His combed hair and pristine fingernails spoke to the nonexistent labor his subordinates seemed to be abundant in. Men and women toiled at various ships docking into the port. They called to one another in sailor's language that Evelyn had a hard time deciphering.

She stood in the middle of the dock, then made her way to the side and leaned against one of the wooden posts, concentrating on the chaotic wisps of blue tendrils dancing around the ship workers. She opened herself to listening, curious as to what they were thinking. But the silence was as mild as the river stirring beneath her. She hadn't decided whether she preferred the conditions to her power or if it was frustratingly inconvenient. The people she heard had to *want* her to hear them. The entire purpose of thoughts was so that one could judge in silence, regardless of intentions. Most people never spoke the whole truth of their ponderings and so, Evelyn knew most, if not all thoughts were kept closely guarded.

The more time she spent watching the workers, the more she realized just how cut off she was in Verbena. She was still dressed warmly in her winter clothes, while so many others were in loose, thin garments for the hotter southern climate. Many glanced at her attire with curiosity, judging her silently. Most hadn't spared her a single glance, working too hard to notice. She was just another incomer into a city that swallowed and spit out dozens of people everyday. Who were they to pay attention to her? It was a startling clash to the watchful, close-knit community she'd grown up in.

The man Sou was arguing with—Bron, his name was— pointed at their little ship with a grudging twitch in his eye. They stood on the edge of the pier, Bron's back to a table littered with documents. A large bag rested on the corner that looked to contain a few personal items, such as a spyglass, ink for quills, and an extra vest that looked similar to the one Bron wore, but was richer in color and vintage. Sou shook his head and lifted four fingers, while Bron displayed all his digits. Evelyn knew nothing of haggling, but she could tell Sou had lost. The old man nodded his head, handing over the coin to Bron. The well-dressed man motioned for a woman in a plain vest over a ragged, green shirt to write in a book the finance exchange. She tore off a page and handed it to Sou, who stuffed the paper into his pocket with some irritation.

Evelyn motioned herself off the post, but was pushed to the side by a passing sailor. She tried to convey her apologies, but the man continued, ignoring her presence. She looked up to find Sou stuffing something into his pack. It was probably some last-minute supplies from the ship. He muttered to himself as she followed him down the wooden path to a dirt road, leading away from the port. His pack shifted on his back, collapsing against empty space. They carried so little with them.

The path was downtrodden in horse, wagon, and footprints of varying shapes. Sou, in his frustration, kept a fast pace that Evelyn had difficulty keeping up with. When he didn't slow down, she placed a hand on his shoulder, forcing him to abate.

"What's the matter?" she asked with little patience.

"I've been charged a pretty silver piece for my claim on the dock, but five pieces?" he raised his voice, shaking a hand in the direction of the distant ships. "That's enough for food and board for four days in the city. Bron is never generous, but I had thought him to be a reasonable man."

Evelyn sighed and peered at the road ahead. The grass plains drifted into rolling hills, but there was no city. Reva was a long walk ahead and she agreed that they shouldn't remain in the city for long. So, they needed to get there as soon as possible. It would bode ill for them to still be on the road come nightfall.

"And here I thought the world was full of reasonable men."

Sou's crimped brow relaxed, and he chuckled. Evelyn allowed herself a small smile, even if she was still angry at him. When he revealed the existence of her sister and father, Evelyn was too shocked to speak. The conversation ended with her leaving him on the other side of the ship, unable to speak with him until they docked in Reva the next afternoon.

All the questions she had sat in her mind like an infected wound. The more she picked at them the more they bled. Why had they never come for her? Why couldn't Sou and Tansey have told her before her Oathbearing? Did they even know she was alive? All those conversations of seclusion and longing to discover what laid outside of Verbena, none of them even tempted Tansey to tell the truth? Or Sou, for that matter.

How was it that in discovering the survival of members of her own family—in the wake of all she had lost—she was the loneliest she'd ever felt? Evelyn wasn't a fool. She was curious as to how Sou knew so much about the Reticent and the Vagu. His knowledge of Videns seemed much too vast for a simple ferryman. There were stories yet to be heard from him and Evelyn was determined to know them. All of them, but for now she had to focus on getting to Reva.

"Reasonable men and charitable acts," Sou said with a half-smile.

He turned and they walked in silence as they continued down the road. It was an hour later before Evelyn's feet ached with each step. The other travelers who'd been walking for days without a ship to aid their journey strutted past them as if Evelyn were a lame horse. Her tightened calves burned as they trudged up the hill, temples dripping with sweat. The day was already warm, but the trek made the heat unbearable. Evelyn fiddled with the wooden clasp at her neck and threw the fabric over one shoulder.

Her chest constricted as she remembered the smoke and the heat of the flames. She could smell her people burning. Evelyn shook her head and grunted as she leaped forward, passing Sou who raised a slow fist in the air.

"Aye, there's a good lass. Show the old how it's done," he said, breathless and weary.

With each exhale she whispered the names of her fallen friends. Birdie, Alen, Maysom... Tansey. She failed them in life, but perhaps for the remainder of hers, she could find the reason for their demise. Madness wasn't an embrace to transform into chains in one night. If Oretem could destroy an entire village that harbored and loved him, then Evelyn could only imagine what he'd do to a city like Reva. She had to find out what went so wrong to prevent it from happening again.

She reached the top of the hill and gasped. The landscape shifted into a wide, flat plain of shifting tall grass. Evelyn had never seen the sea, but from the stories Tansey had told her she imagined this sight to resemble a green ocean, ebbing with the wind. Further down the road, not too far a distance, was a massive city on the side of two hills, blended in a way that looked like a small version of her mountains. The greenery ended where the city began, transforming into rock and stone. She could see the faint flow of people walking with vibrant colors. The city was alighted in figures, reminding her of fireflies flashing in communication to one another. But that wasn't what initially captured her attention.

Just outside of the city, towering over the grass was the skeleton of a dragon. Its thin snout opened to reveal fangs stained with white patches of sun rot and claws as wide as the largest home in Verbena. Its ribs were coated in long grass, stretching over the bones as though trying to lose itself in the plain's many hills. In between the greenery was the tail, its soaring spikes perches for small birds chirping in the distance. She continued to stare at the bones, her mind wandering to stories of fallen dragons, trying to decide if she recognized any description from the corpse displayed before her.

Evelyn's heart ached for her bondsmate. Even in the wake of his destruction, she'd known Oretem's mind. She shivered to remember the chaos of his madness. Something or someone had driven him to that. He couldn't enter into such mania without callous prodding. It had to have been the outsider, the Reticent. Somehow, he'd driven her dragon mad, but without talking with the murderer himself she had no way to know. It all started with Meric. She had to find him.

"To think once there had been many," Sou said beside her. She started at his presence, not noticing he'd caught up with her. "She's known as the Unnamed Dragon. She probably fought for this city, and they don't remember her name. Neither do I."

Sou cast his eyes downward in a small bow of respect, thoughtful and sad.

"How do you know it was a she?"

"The males were hardier with brutish limbs." Evelyn nodded, remembering the sheer immensity of Oretem's body. "The females were leaner, but much more agile. During the Evandis, they were the best warriors in the sky while the males fought on the ground. It was folly for a male dragon to fight a female in the air, and by the height of her tail bones I'd say she was a wind dragon. The best flyers of their species."

She glanced at the body of the dragon again and mimicked Sou's respectful bow. Then she turned away, continuing down the road to the city, picturing what the Unnamed Dragon may have looked like in her prime.

Once inside Reva, Evelyn remained close to Sou. Not out of fear but because the city was so crowded. Shops lined the roads with signs of inventive names such as Mirror My Steps for shoes and slippers, and Cattle Ware for leather belts and satchels. The ladies on the street wore fine fabrics Evelyn had never seen before, donning dresses that looked as thin as bedsheets and as smooth as crystal ice. The men's cropped hair was usually covered by a hat, and they all wore vests with varying designs of loops embroidered along the surface. Their attire seemed to wear them instead of the other way around. The elegance of the citizens matched the grandeur of every building, colorful and bright with sturdy confidence.

Evelyn noticed people glancing at her dirtied trousers and furred babi boots. Her cloak did little to mask the smell of her long journey and she realized many of them had moved to the other side of the street to avoid crossing her path. She ran a hand through her tangled hair and met the eyes of those who dared to look upon her. She wouldn't be shamed. No matter how insignificant she felt among these beautiful people.

It was incredible to think she'd dreamt of visiting the city for so long and how circumstances could drastically change the experience. She blinked and saw a woman in a carriage, bundled in layers of thick scarves that draped through the window, flowing as her vehicle passed them. Her horse's hooves clattered on the stone with trained determination. As she got closer, Evelyn held her breath, discovering the fine woman had bright green eyes—fully green eyes.

Evelyn turned to Sou, lifting her hood in panic. She'd forgotten about her eyes; everyone would know she was Viden. Her mind raced to understand what she saw. Sou patted her shoulder and lowered her hood as she gaped at him, shocked.

"There's no need to worry about your eyes. You will find the practice quite common here." He pointed to a shop just ahead with a sign that rocked in the breeze, Behold the Eye.

She looked through the glass and watched as a young woman in a violet dress sat on a padded chair. Her black hair fell in boxed braids over her shoulders as she gripped the chairs handholds with tight fingers. The man that stood over her held a small device connected to a lever at his foot. He pressed the lever and the device sputtered to life in his hand, the tip vibrating at an invisible speed, but to her dragon eyes Evelyn could see the tip sharp with the point of a needle.

She continued to watch, confused as he dipped the machine into a cup of purple paint, the color matching the darkness of the woman's dress. Then as he lifted the device over the woman's eye, Evelyn grimaced as every muscle in her body fought against what was happening in the room. She glanced back at Sou in horror. He shrugged as if sticking a needle in someone's eye was as common as piercing a woman's ear.

"She will go blind," Evelyn said, aghast.

"Few do in fact, but what is the saying? Beauty is pain."

"I've never heard such a thing."

"In any case, you won't be recognizable by the color of your eyes. Red is among the rarer colors, but not unheard of. I wouldn't have risked coming here if I didn't think you wouldn't be able to blend in. Now, we must find you something to wear. That above all will draw unwanted attention."

Evelyn scanned her clothes, knowing just how apart she was from the rest of the migrants. Even the travelers on the road had looked cleaner than her. Her fingernails were black with dirt, soot still staining her skin. Her tunic was splattered in blood, but those portions were hidden under her cloak.

She nodded and Sou led her to a shop a few down from Behold the Eye called Rings and Riches. She half expected it to be a jewelry boutique, but was pleased to see an array of attire for both men and women. Some of the dresses were so fine, Evelyn couldn't possibly imagine herself draped in one. There was the standard golden embroidery across the hem of the dresses, varying in design and complexity. The vests that most of the men wore were much of the same. She wondered what was so fashionable about loops and circles.

A plump woman with a large bust came from around the desk she was writing at. Her red dress was dark and formfitting. She had light pale slippers that shown just below her golden hem, displaying an easy-to-follow pattern of coils.

"Good afternoon. How may I help you?" she said with a

bright smile that faded as soon as she laid her fully blue eyes on Evelyn.

What a foul creature.

Evelyn almost laughed at the sudden thought that traveled down a blue line of wind, quick and penetrating. She'd become so used to the silence of the past week that the woman's sudden and loud voice would be a relief if it wasn't so rude.

"Yes, we are in need of a new wardrobe," Sou said with authority in an accent Evelyn had never heard him in speak before. As if he'd all the coin in the world.

"I see," she cast a suspicious glance. "I will need to see your family vest."

"Madam, I am weary. I'd come across trouble on the Dattadri Greens—vagabonds and such. Thieves who stole most of my property I was transporting. Including," he pointed to his torn cloak. "All my clothes."

"And her?" The woman raised judgmental eyebrows in her direction. Her brows were quite crooked, Evelyn thought. Sou glanced at Evelyn with disinterested eyes.

"What about her?" he said without any attempt at hiding his irritation.

She's polluting my shop with those pitiful clothes. Look at her boots. The woman glanced down at Evelyn's shoes with lined lips, wrinkling her nose. *What sort of animal is she wearing and why does it smell so?*

"Is she not in need of clothes as well?"

Evelyn covered her mouth with her hand to stay the smile that threatened to show.

"Her?" he laughed as the woman looked on, mistrustful. "I suspect she was born in her tatters. No, she is but my house servant that traveled with me. I would've left her outside the shop, but she is the size of my granddaughter who is resting at home. I'll need you to size her up."

The woman straightened with less defiance, but glared leerily. She laced her fingers in front of her and faced Sou who hadn't changed his expression.

"I will still need to see that family vest, sir. People try to jump stations all the time. I'm sure you understand my position as a Lady of Riches."

"Riches indeed, there are other shops I could acquire what I need. But no matter, as you wish." Sou reached into his pack and took out a dark vest worn with fraying edges. The golden ends surrounded in ovals and loops that surpassed many of the current clothes already in the shop. The woman took the vest and ran a hand over the design, her mouth opening in slight astonishment. Evelyn quickly masked her surprise. Where had he gotten that? She was sure it wasn't with them as they traveled.

The woman inclined her head and motioned for Evelyn to step forward. She took her to the back room and with a series of violent needle jabs and coiled tape, the woman measured her.

Upon my word, she is filthy. There should be a wall around this city so people such as she cannot enter. I'd sooner throw her out with the rest of the beggars had I not such a heart. At least her master is a respectable man otherwise I could not put so little value on my standards. Celosia's Depths, child, close your mouth! I can barely breathe with that stench —

The woman continued with her excessive thoughts for some time during the fitting process. She was just as unkind with her hands as she was with her thoughts. At first, Evelyn found the humor in her situation, but soon tired of the seamstress's relentless ill-temperament. Just as she was about to voice her irritation, the woman left her naked in the room.

She looked for her clothes, but was surprised to find them nowhere in the dressing room. With nothing to cover herself, Evelyn waited. A few moments later, the woman came back with a fresh set of black trousers, a thin pale tunic and lean underclothes.

"I couldn't let you leave in such terrible apparel. Bad for business. Your master shall be charged," she said with a disgusted frown.

There was only one item Evelyn cared about and she couldn't begin to dress until she knew its whereabouts.

"The cloak. What did you do with the cloak?" She stepped towards the woman, who lifted her hands, fingers curled inwards as if she feared Evelyn would somehow taint her.

"I wanted to discard the dreadful garb, but your master insisted on keeping it. Everything else was tossed. Dress now, he is waiting," she said before slamming the door.

Relieved, Evelyn donned her new clothes. They fit well, even if her skin was still layered in dirt and sweat. Her furred boots bulged out of place, but once she put on her cloak it wouldn't be noticeable.

She exited the room and met Sou in the middle of the shop, who was now dressed in a sophisticated black vest and white tunic. The design in the fabric traveled all the way down the sides of his black trousers. The shoes he wore were bright and were in no shape to travel long distances. A red headband still rested on his forehead above his familiar eyes, although his expression was that of a complete stranger. She wondered how he learned to switch roles so well. The pack he wore at his back was gorged and stretched with the new clothes he'd purchased from the crooked-browed woman.

"Well now, it won't be so unseemly to have you at my side," he said with forceful meanness. "Thank you, Lady of Riches. Have a pleasant day."

The woman nodded and turned her head at Evelyn with a twirl of her red dress. They exited the shop and continued down the road, deeper into the city. When they'd gotten a reasonable distance and the crowds had grown less congested, she stepped beside Sou.

"What a gracious woman." Evelyn peeked beneath her brows at the ferryman, who gave her an apologetic glance. "What was that all about?"

"The ways of Reva are of a different world, lass. It is far from what you've come to know in Verbena. Silver and coin are all that matter here, and the rich are the only people that thrive. She'd have turned me away if I hadn't assumed that role."

Evelyn shook her head in disbelief. She had some concept

of money, the little the villagers had they gave to Sou for providing goods. Most of the coin they obtained were from lost travelers who were grateful to have found shelter from the cold blizzards. But she could hardly imagine turning away someone in need because they were unable to pay for what was necessary to live. She glanced at the people on the streets in torn clothing, absent of any design, reaching out their hands to the elegant people walking past them without a care.

The city was everything and nothing how she thought it to be. It was polished and grand, but with a center that smelled of corruption. One only had to look past the flowing dresses and lovely faces to see what crawled beneath.

"Why should that matter?" she said, knowing it was a pointless question.

"It shouldn't, but it does, lass. At least here. Once we get to Cronies Inn you can bathe, and we'll find something to eat. There are places of beauty here, away from the in-between slums of the rich and the unfortunate which we now walk. You can explore while I search for a Venandi pair. Perhaps you'll find your Meric. Hopefully by this time tomorrow we'll be on our way out of this wretched city."

Evelyn agreed and retrieved her cloak from Sou. She covered her shoulders, but let the attached scarf hang to her knees. It was still quite warm, and she wasn't used to the southern weather. She figured because the city was near Solov Waste to the east, the heat traveled with fiery intent.

"How did you come by so much coin and where did you find that vest?" she asked eventually. "I imagine that stunt in the shop was improvised."

Sou shrugged and scratched the side of his stubbled face in a nonchalant manner.

"It's actually your coin. I had been saving it for your Oath-bearing. It's being used for its intended purpose. I planned on using it to take you home." He showed her a small, wearied smile, but she didn't return it. She was still hurt by his secrecy and Sou cleared his throat before continuing. "As for Bron, he can buy a new vest with my five pieces. Well, maybe not a *family* vest. Those are harder to replace, but I don't see how he couldn't manage it. The world being full of reasonable men and charitable acts, after all."

An involuntary grin spread across her face, forcing her ire to relent. It was the exact thing she expected Sou to have done. They'd fallen back into their old banter and companionship. The looming knowledge of what he had kept from her remained a cloud-like shadow over them, but she could see the sunlight peeking through.

Evelyn's stomach rumbled, but the call of a bath was stronger as she imagined cool water rinsing away the troubles of her journey. It wouldn't be enough. Whether she bathed in the freezing waters of the northern Omya or the vapors of Elm Lake, nothing would ever lessen the strain of her experiences. At least she'd made it to the city, and it was as magnificent as she thought it to be. But it was also a city of specific tastes she found to be sour in her mouth. She remembered the dragon's corpse laying beyond in the sea of grass. The Unnamed Dragon. She thought it a fitting representation of what laid within Reva: thoughtlessness, and macabre fascination.

Chapter 22

A Simple Ferryman

S team drifted in the air around Evelyn, dancing in its suspended form until finally dissipating. She rested within the tub, savoring the transitioning coolness of the water as it lost its warmth. When she closed her eyes, she could almost picture the white tips of the Bena Mountains and if she ran her arms over the surface, it mirrored the feel of the cold winter breeze. Then she would open her eyes and be reminded by the commotion of the street below her that she was far from home.

She couldn't remember much of the escape from Verbena. She recalled Sou wrapping her in a blanket and the sun rising then falling again. She was aware of the sun's journey, and the light of the moon, but she was fastened to her misery until Sou pulled her out of it. She could still feel it. The widening cavern of her grief suddenly shook, cracking and crumbling.

Her mind flashed red with the memory of Nakesha, bloodied and broken. Her wrist throbbed in the memory of falling from the wolf's back, failing to protect her. Evelyn closed her eyes, but Maysom stared back at her, burning. She opened them again to a room so empty it only amplified the feeling that she was entirely alone in the world. She couldn't breathe. Her chest rose and fell, but the air seemed to take little heed to her demands.

Panicked, Evelyn gripped the edges of the tub, trying to pull herself out. Why wouldn't her legs work? She slipped and her head submerged under water. Instead of lifting herself, she remained. There was quiet in the bath. She could hear the beat of her heart, reminding her she still had one. It drummed to the rhythm of Iona, pleading for its continued existence.

It took a few moments, but her stampeding heart slowed to its normal cadence. Eventually, her lungs ached for air, and she rose from the water. Gasping, she rested her head on the back of the tub, letting herself breathe. Her body welcomed breath even as her soul resented its company. She curled in on herself, covering her face with her hands, fingers pressed against her cheeks. Tears fell from her like rainwater through a canopy of leaves, uninhibited by barriers and indifferent to their surroundings. She became utterly lost in the haze of water within and around her.

How had it come to this? For what purpose had all she loved suffered so horribly? She thought back to all the times she'd challenged Tansey, running away from lessons, and speaking ill of her to Sou. All those moments she could never recapture and the time she'd spent with her taken for granted. Evelyn lifted her head and sniffed, wiping her tears. She shouldn't be alone. She wanted nothing more than to sit in the water for eternity until she was nothing more than a drowned corpse. A corpse couldn't remember, couldn't regret, and she regretted so much.

"Enough," she said to herself. "They're dead and Tansey never wept."

The cavern in her chest ceased its trembling, but it never filled. It was there, in the deepest corner of her heart, waiting for her to come and look down its bottomless pit. Wake it to life so she would descend into the false welcome of nothingness. There was more to be done. She hadn't the faintest idea of what the future held for her, but she would pursue it nonetheless. Her people deserved more from her, but it was all she could offer.

Evelyn turned her head to look about the simple room Sou

had rented for her. The walls were a deep red, reminding her of the sapling willow trees that boarded on the edge of her mountains. There was a dresser in the corner that preceded another smaller room where her chamber pot was located. The bed was large, much larger than the simplistic hay-filled cot she slept on for most of her life. Its lush sheets covered what had to be a goose feathered mattress, beckoning her with the promise of a softly embraced sleep. There was an open window beside the bed, allowing the setting sun to dim her room. She wished to succumb to a dreamless slumber, but remembered the oiled figures of her waking nightmare. Evelyn pushed the thought of sleep away and glanced at Oretem's scale on the dresser, nestled in the compartment of Arlisa's necklace. Red reflected the orange of oncoming night, making it bright against its brass coils. Sou didn't have to tell her not to touch the dragon scale as she was competent enough to understand what that could mean.

The few times she'd touched it before the attack, she could enter Oretem's mind. There was a sense of oneness, a conversion of their selves in a way that was as intimate as her knowing the skin of her own flesh. When she begged him to stop the ravaging of her village, she'd lost herself to the oppression of his madness and the muscles of his flight. For that time, she was the dragon, inhabiting his body as if it were her own and he knew her. Down to the core of her being, he knew her. If she were to touch it again, he'd know exactly where she was and there was no knowing who had his enraged confidence. She couldn't risk even the slightest touch, or she'd endanger a city that had already known the destruction of dragon fire. She'd keep the scale close, but stowed away on her person where contact with her skin would be less likely if near impossible.

She sighed and lifted herself from the tub, the faint tinging of droplets following her as she made her way to the bed. Sou was downstairs drinking at the tavern below, waiting for her to accompany him. She hadn't meant to spend so much time washing, but she was truly filthy. The servant girl who had shown her to the room had waited outside her door. Evelyn had puzzled over this as she wasn't used to having people wait on her. Once she began to bathe the water had darkened significantly and soon, she found herself repulsed by the grime she'd waded in. She realized the servant's presence wasn't a normality, the girl only knew by the look of her she'd need to drain and refill the tub. Only after she had done this, had Evelyn heard the receding steps of the girl down the hall. She walked to the bed where she placed two cloth covered packages on the sheets.

She opened one to reveal clothes of varying uses, laying them out one beside the other. Three dresses of the same cut laid before her. One was blood red and tighter around the bust, while another was a pale blue, covering the wearer up to the neck. The last one was a rich green that left the top of the shoulders bare, flowing down into longer sleeves. Each was made of the same thin fabric she'd seen on most of the women. What troubled her was the lack of covering on the back of the dresses. Each of them left little to the imagination as to what Evelyn would look like from behind. She'd never worn anything so fine or so revealing. She recalled many women wearing shawl-like cloaks to cover themselves and was relieved to see Sou had purchased one of neutral color to match each dress.

She opened the other package and found a wardrobe much more to her liking. Three sets of black trousers, four earth-toned tunics, two short-sleeved and two long-sleeved, and an acceptable amount of underclothing. The outfits seemed to be fitted for a small man, but as she held them up to her body for size, she determined they'd do.

Evelyn stared longingly at the trousers, but resigned herself to pick up the long-sleeved dress, finding that it covered her in a way that felt less revealing than the other two. If she was to blend in, then she must dress the part. The fabric was a little looser around her hips than what she was used to and when she walked to the opposite wall to hang her towel, she recoiled at the feel of her thighs rubbing together. When she'd worn dresses in the past, they were drab and thick for the snow-covered landscape she lived in. Her wardrobe was never about elegance and always favored practicality. She would wear pants beneath her dresses for extra warmth and hadn't experienced what it felt like to have her skin stick and chafe together.

She could suffer quite a few discomforts, but she wasn't about to suffer this. She lifted her dress and pushed one leg through the trousers, pulling it over her hips, feeling much more comfortable. The loose fabric around her waist hid the extra layer. Still, she smoothed out the front of it to make sure.

She glanced at her babi boots in the corner, but realized they were about as fashionable as a necklace made of moldy bones. Just as she was about to exit the room barefoot there was a knock on her door.

"Yes."

"Are you decent?" Sou's voice was cautious as well as insistent.

She opened the door and still cocked her head at his usual attire. The second outfit he'd bought at Rings and Riches accented the lean muscles under the slender fabric, making him appear fit instead of simply thin. The black headband across his forehead looked like a mismatched earring with the attire, but Sou's wide smile distracted most of the oddness. In his hand, he held a pair of small white slippers, plain, without any of the adornments found on most of the women's feet. The ends of his hair were damp as he looked her up and down.

"What a horrifying visage," he said, looking at her dress as he stepped inside. Evelyn closed the door behind him. She ran her hands over her arms, feeling the fine fabric catch on her hardened blisters. She raised her brows and pointed at Bron's family vest, hanging over Sou's tunic like a poorly fitted boot. He smiled at that and nodded with a pursed lip. "I've made do. I suspect you have as well."

It never irritated her before how well he knew her, but then again, he also hadn't thought to know her well enough to confess to the survival of her father and sister. She rolled her eyes and lifted the dress to her ankles to show him the trousers she wore underneath. He barked a laugh, presenting the slippers in his hand like an improv gift.

"You're going to loathe these." His tone suggested humor, but his mouth turn downward into a heavy grimace.

Despite the anger, she felt a small sense of comfort at Sou finding her so predictable. She felt much changed since Oretem's attack and it was a relief to think she might've retained some little sense of who she used to be. She took the shoes from his hand, the material hard and unyielding against her fingers, and slipped them on. Her toes bunched together at the tip, forcing her to place her weight on the balls of her feet. The blisters she obtained from walking for hours on the road into the city were going to pale in comparison to the ones she was sure she'd receive from these monstrosities.

"Loath?" she shifted her weight without the relief of comfort. "No. Abhor or detest feels more accurate."

Sou huffed a chuckle before striding across the room to peer out the window.

"I purchased you footwear more suitable for travel for when we are ready to leave this city. You may choose then to toss what you now wear. I rented the room across from yours. It's a bit smaller, but you can't hear much of the street should you prefer a quieter room."

Evelyn was indeed startled by the bustle and volume of the city, but she preferred it to the bellowing of her thoughts should the quiet endure too long.

"I don't mind the noise. Did you bargain for the second room?" she asked, remembering the haggle on the docks.

"Rooms are set prices. I paid what it costs, but like I said before, we'll not be here long. Inns are one of the least expensive luxuries in Reva. This a city where trade and commerce prosper so they must accommodate all sorts of classes, rich or poor." His tone was sarcastic as he clicked his tongue.

"Which is this?" Evelyn gestured to the large bed and spacious room. It was much finer than anything she'd had in Verbena. The room smelled of willow, and her cloak swayed in the breeze from the open window, nearly dry from its recent wash.

"A happy medium," Sou replied. Her forehead creased at what she once might've drunk in with excited furor, but now only added to the pressure of not understanding everything so foreign to her. Her eyes lingered on the bed, the way the sunset painted colors across the smooth walls, the soft swirl of the water in the porcelain tub. This luxury was a *happy medium*?

"The daylight is fading, and I must go out. Will you be alright here?"

She came back to herself, shaking all thoughts inconsequential to what she knew she must do. Without looking at Sou, Evelyn walked over to the window and donned her dry cloak. She thought about wearing one of the shawls, but decided she could no sooner part with her grandmother's gift than her grandmother herself and she'd already had no choice in the latter. She reached into the pocket, pulling out her set of throwing knives. They glinted in the light, as if heaving in the breath they were denied when hidden. She tucked them into the back of her sash wrapped around her waist, comforted by the easy reach and familiar weight.

"I'll be safe wherever I am," she said, staring into him with the blaze of her red eyes, hoping he couldn't stand the baring of her gaze. He couldn't make her stay and she wasn't going to lie to him by telling him she would. If something were to happen, she didn't want him thinking she was safe asleep in her bed. He sighed and turned away, but not with the sigh of defeat that she had hoped.

"I did agree for you to explore, but it's sunset now. I don't like the thought of you going where I cannot see, never mind where the sun is not shining."

She gripped the leather straps of Oretem's scale and hung it to her sash next to her knives. She used the end of the fabric to grip the scale and tucked it into the sash, hiding it from anyone who might mistake its reflective surface for a gem. Her anger spiked. She was not a child to be told that she couldn't be out after dark. She was a woman grown with more than enough skill to defend herself in darkness or sunlight.

"Oretem attacked in the daylight. I have no reason to believe I am any safer here in the height of day than out there in the depths of night. You must make use of the little time we have here and so must I. Shall we go together?"

She would prefer to travel on her own. Sou had never in truth agreed with her stance on finding Meric. If they should wander the city together, she feared Sou would overpower her errand with his own. His sole focus was on finding Venandi and from the look in his green eyes that hadn't changed. Then again, he knew the city. He knew the streets and the people. He had traded in the city for years while running supplies to and from Verbena. She ached for the familiarity of her mountains. The crisp air of stone and snow. There she could find her way, get lost, and find it again. Here, in this land of narrow streets, heat, and wood, she was less confident. Sou had connections with which she might be able to ask about the whereabouts of Meric. He shook his head.

"No, if I am to hire a Venandi they'll be more inclined to enter my service if I were to come alone."

"Is it because I am a woman?" Evelyn said without accusation, but curiosity.

She knew it wasn't Sou's stance that women were any less capable than men, but she wasn't sure of the people he was planning on meeting with. She wasn't ignorant to the plights of being underestimated because she was a woman. Even in her small village she'd had to unnecessarily prove men wrong when completing tasks that anyone with a capable mind was able to accomplish. Once she saw Reva and her citizens, she prepared herself for that eventuality.

"No lass, it is because you are a Lady." She raised her eyebrows and he smiled. "Well, you look like one. The difference is significant. A woman can be anything. A spy or assassin. I've met many Venandi women, but a Lady—or a Lord for that matter—is a conspirator, a plotter. Venandi are distrustful folk, but if I ask around for one with you at my side, especially in your fine dress…" He grimaced. "They'd sooner bring a knife to my throat to inquire about ulterior motives."

"I can change," she said, gripping the side of her dress. "The difference doesn't sound as significant as you claim."

"No. It's not. But for your protection you must assume this role. Venandi may be a suspicious lot, but they're keen of mind. A woman is predictable while a Lady is less so. Just like any man, a woman may end the conversation with the swift swipe of her own sword hand. A Lady is not one to soil her own palms with such vulgarity." Evelyn suppressed the smile that threatened to form at Sou's sarcastic tone before his voice turned serious again. "The rich will hide behind the scars of a Reticent, waiting for you behind the door of your own home. Venandi will choose the path they can see most clearly, but will divert to one laid with the most coin. Now, in my experience these bounty hunters can be fooled by either man or woman, Lord or Lady. I've seen them die at the hands of one of their own, but as I've said before, things are very different here, lass. Trust is as hard to come by as willow flowers in the harsh winter."

Evelyn sighed and rubbed her fingers against the palms of her hands. The blisters had healed, but the new, scarred skin itched something fearsome.

"How much truth can we spare to tell them? What is to stop them from abandoning us before we ever get to Birny?"

He patted the pouch at his belt, the coins he had saved clinking together in unison.

"It's a simple matter of deciding at what point we pay them. Obviously, only once we are safely in Birny will I give them any payment. At least this is what I will tell them before I allow for them to think they've haggled me into sparing a few coins in advance, but the larger portion I will dangle before them like a twine of thread before a cat. On the leash of a thread, they will stay with us through the entire journey for the promise of the entire twine. As for how much truth to tell them, I will say we are in need of protection from another Venandi. Which is closer to the truth than we'll ever have to tell them. Their kind were once a tight knit family of brothers and sisters. Now, after the war it's as though they are fighting one another for the wealth of their dead, rich father. Work is scarce for them and the chance to undermine another Venandi only strengthens their opportunities at better food and finer beds. As for you, I'll tell them the truth of what they'll see. A prosperous woman who will pay a high price for her safety. No woman of your rank would hire protection herself. I represent that wealth well enough and can speak for you."

"And you will speak as my what?" she asked a little irritated at the idea of him making decisions for her.

She couldn't fathom why any powerful woman or man would want anyone speaking on their behalf. There was much power lost in that and although she understood the reason for it, she would drive that idea from the Venandi's mind once they were outside of the city. If they wished to speak with her then they shall do so, without the go-between Sou insisted acting as.

Sou's eyes softened and he hesitated a moment. A faint blue strand of light pulsed, as if unsure of announcing its presence. As soon as she admitted her gift, she'd heard no more thoughts from the ferryman. Evelyn regretted that decision even if she felt it was the right one. There was something he wasn't telling her, and she could see he was thinking of it at that very moment. He still hadn't answered her, his eyes searching hers.

"What are you not saying, Sou?" she tried to be firm with her voice, but she only sounded tired. She was so very tired of secrets.

Whatever he was grappling with seemed to age him before her eyes. Sou's forehead creased under the band and the lines around his eyes deepened into cracks like that of an egg under the slow weight of a boot. The man before her suddenly wasn't the one who dragged her half broken from her burning village. He didn't have the confidence of the actor who looked down upon the Lady of Riches, bargaining and outspoken without a care for the less fortunate. He was Sou, the ferryman. The old man with wise crack for every wise word, diminished with uncertainty. She'd forgotten him, thought him dead with everyone else that was left burning, including her.

"Every wealthy household has a Vagu within their service. It is a sign of their affluence as well as a spokesperson for the household." His voice was low as if spoken through a narrow tunnel.

"Then you'll disguise yourself as one? What if they ask you to prove it?"

"I will show them."

He lifted his fingers to the back of his head and untied the straps of his headband. Evelyn blinked in confusion. She tried remembering a time when she'd seen the man without the band. She couldn't. In her earliest memory of Sou, she could recall resting, bundled with the absolute surety of safety. She could suddenly not recall a time when she'd ever felt more safe. She remembered the feel of his warmth against her cheek and the soft fabric of his headband brushing the top of her head. She remembered lifting her head, trying to shift her position. Cold. She was suddenly miserably cold, and she couldn't move. She was bundled too tight. He said something to her. Something about being quiet. Evelyn shook her head, losing sight of the old memory as the cloth slipped from Sou's face.

She stepped back in shock at the sight of his crinkled forehead over a pair of slanted dark eyebrows. He tore his gaze away from her and lifted his hand towards the open window. His long fingers extended, floating as if to catch a butterfly. The tips met, clasping the trap shut. A sharp breeze bent the wind, but not the air around her. No. A flux of Iona's Breath converged at the tips of Sou's fingers, bursting with blue, like the crack of ice under the summer sun. Shapeless and free it bent under the bed, through the covers and across the thin curtains. It escaped through the window, closing it with a rough shake. The stillness of its absence filled the space between her and the ferryman.

Vagu.

The word erupted in her mind, leaving her lungs without

breath. The silence was so absolute she felt the empty air crushing her. It hurt. Why did it hurt so much?

Evelyn closed her eyes against the assault of tears. Her body betrayed her, and she grimaced as they fell hot and acidic down her cheeks. She could hardly see Sou in the heat of her anger, the blur of her tears. The shape of an outstretched hand appeared before her, and she recoiled. Her hands fists at her sides, refusing to wipe away the weakness that poured from her malformed dragon eyes.

"Do not touch me," she snapped, her voice a hardened whisper. "You knew. You *knew* the whole of it. Everything. Birny and my family... that I could control Iona's Breath and you said nothing. You did *nothing*." She should've opened the door and pushed him through. She would have if she didn't need him so. If Sou wasn't the only Depths-damned person she had left in a world she couldn't possibly navigate on her own. A world where her family were either dead or strangers to her. It was all so backwards, so convoluted with deception.

"Once we reach Birny, you won't have to bear me as a burden to the memories of what you've lost and what I've kept from you. All of what I did not do was to protect you. That has always been my purpose. Forgive me." His voice broke as he finished.

"Stop that," Evelyn whispered, trying, and failing to control the betrayal in her voice.

"Stop what?" his voice echoed in uncertainty and hope. She wanted to crush it, tear it to pieces between her teeth like the wolf she'd lost.

"You *lied* to me. You are as much a stranger to me as my own father. So do not speak to me with such sincerity, as if you deserve my pity. You do not know me; you only know what the dead tell you. Have you heard my mother's voice? Does she speak to you? Can you hear the voices of our village? Adel and Birdie? Tansey?" she gasped, suddenly realizing she had not been breathing.

"I am alone." Her voice was the crack in the mountain that preceded an avalanche, the rumble before the earth split, a fissure in a steeled blade. She was the thing that broke, catalyzing calamity.

"You know that is not true," Sou stepped forward, his voice adamant, but earnest. "There was only one who could hear the dead and I've told you her tale. It is you who can hear voices on the wind, lass."

Evelyn met his eyes, their green color glistening in fought tears.

"They do not speak to me. I have heard nothing beyond what I was told in the mountains. I am too broken." She heard herself as if from afar and felt pity for the poor creature she had become. How insignificant and small, hollowed out by what had happened to her.

"Then *mend* yourself." His voice was quick and quiet as if spoken from the lips of a dying man. "The broken things of this world are not rebuilt by the memory of what they used to be. They must become something new. Stone cannot shape itself; wood cannot carve its own skin. The crack in stone is smoothed out by the wind and water that rages against its surface. The gaping slits of a dying branch rent and tear from the burrowing roots of new seeds. If you are to heal yourself, you must do what hurts the most. You must wake up; eat the food you cannot stomach and walk the ground you cannot tread. Then you do it again. The next day, and the day after that and the day after that, until your hardships are victories, and your hollowness is fulfillment. You are not made to be broken. You are made to transform."

"I am so tired, Sou."

He moved to embrace her, but she stepped away. "Did Tansey know?" The question hardly needed answering. Sou nodded only once, running a hand through his hair. "I always thought it was because of my mother's death she despised you."

"She was within her rights as a mother to hate me for that. Although being Vagu didn't thaw her contempt over the years."

"Is that why you never came to the village? Because of Tansey's hatred?"

There were so many questions left unanswered. So many normalities in her life where she just assumed the answer or never thought to ask. She had enough of assumptions. Sou's mouth turned downwards, slanted brows drawn inward in thought.

"In part. I do not hear the voices of the dead, but I feel their impressions. As you know, every Vagu is capable of this. What you may not know is that we hone our ability towards a specific interest. Some train their skill towards the growth of plants, listening to the shape of their needs. Others make a profession from their ability, such as midwives who center their power towards a mother's body and the infant she carries, feeling the guidance of our lost loved ones to tell us the best path to take."

"For what purpose do they guide you?"

Despite herself, Evelyn felt anxiety rise in her chest. She couldn't keep the tension from her voice as she remembered Tansey's fear and trepidation when speaking of the Vagu. Their sly tendency to predict false futures and unnatural abilities. Her old friend had most certainly lied. What other use of the wind did he have that she couldn't shield herself from? Sou looked into her red eyes and turned away, unable to keep her gaze.

"I listen for those around me. I practiced in the art of human emotions. That is more the reason why I didn't go into the village. It is difficult to ignore those impressions. Especially when a single person's animosity can drown out the whole of a village."

He sighed; his shoulders remained taut as if stretched by invisible strings. Evelyn took in a deep breath, calming her thoughts.

"Can you feel me?"

"Aye."

He met her eyes at last, straining to maintain the contact.

She realized he was forcing himself to listen to her emotions. His body shook slightly, fingers trembling at his sides.

"What do you hear?"

"A dragon's wrath, and a friend's betrayal. You are rife with it." Sou's voice trembled, tears skimming the rims of his eyes. "I am sorry, lass. I only ever wanted to protect you."

Evelyn bit the inside of her cheek to keep herself from screaming. Protect. It was an empty and useless word that had no place in their world, yet it was what she aimed for. It was what brought her to Reva. What was she to do once she found Meric? Protect him? Was she not traveling to Birny to discover how to stop Oretem from releasing his anger on the world? She was the cracked stone, the splintered wood. She was the thing that broke, but could she do as Sou said? Could she transform?

"Do you know how to block out the noise? The impressions of the Iona's Breath?" Sou furrowed his brow, surprised at her questions, nodding. "Shield yourself," she continued, "My animosity will not cauterize this space between us and you forcing yourself to it will only keep it bleeding." Sou's lids fluttered in relief as his body relaxed, but his eyes held tight to the grief of her anger. She ignored the rising guilt in her belly at the sight. "Teach me how to do that. The thoughts of others can be... overwhelming. We can lessen both of our burdens if you teach me to shield myself."

"I can do that."

"Good." She met his gaze again. "Why emotions?"

Sou sighed, looking at her through his slanted brows. It was strange to see him without the headband, not in the sense that he was exposed, displayed for belittlement. The physical features of his Vagu heritage were more like a reveal, a hidden passageway or compartment. Something that was always there, only uncovered to those who were searching for it.

"Evelyn." He'd spoken her name.

She'd only ever heard Sou speak her name on a handful of occasions. Once when that Vagu girl had paid for passage on his ferry. Evelyn had wanted to remain and play with the stranger, but he sent her off with her name sharp on his lips, almost a rebuke. Another was when he pulled her out of the river when Birdie had challenged her to swim across. Again, he'd said her name, berating her for her foolishness. Now though, he didn't sound angry. He was begging, his feet planted on the edge of a cliff, her name a plea to not thrust him into empty air. She pushed.

"Why, Sou?" she was unapologetic with her tone, but the deepening darkness around his eyes made her heart constrict.

He let out a long breath as if it were his last one and stood up in a way she'd never seen before. His shoulders lifted, chest bared and tumid as if bulked by manual labor. His lean form was still spare, but proliferated as though he were purposely hiding his true form under his clothes. They no longer seemed too large for him and the darkness around his eyes shifted into his gaze. The kindness of those green irises disappeared into a deadening forest of rotten leaves, reminiscing the beauty it had lost.

"To hurt people."

Chapter 23

A Gambler's Game

Maun pulled his black cloak closer, fingers clawed in the bitter breeze. He was more than comfortable with his own physical silence, but the emptiness that inhabited his mind was beginning to weigh on him. It was exacerbated by the frosted wasteland of the mountain he stood on.

He'd woken from the most recent memories Oretem had provided and decided it was time to see the sky again. There was much to think about, and he couldn't risk having the dragon's muddled thoughts influence his own. Cinaed had truly broken the beast. He was a half-living creature, a walking corpse of disjointed awareness that had no purpose in life.

Maun hated this mountain and the snow that fell upon it. He missed the sand and the sweat at his brow from trudging in the heated sun. He longed for warm nights and blistering days when his eyes burned in the brightness of a cloudless sky. He looked over the valley where the village once laid. Up on the mountain, he was above the blizzard that obliterated the once burning town. From where he stood the winds were calm, serene even, but below that he could hear the faint scream of the frostbitten storm. Within an hour the village would be gone, and the bodies buried to be forgotten. Ice was as much a devastation as fire, and he knew which he'd prefer. He hadn't given it much thought, but found it curious that there were only a few people in the whole of Iona to carry the memory of those below.

He shook his head and pushed the thought to the back of his mind. He had to be cautious. Gaining the memories of his past life was a tool, not a reward. At first, he thought to use it as a weapon, commanding Oretem to show him glimpses of his former life. In truth, it was simple curiosity.

The image of his mother's cut throat flashed across his mind and an unfamiliar pain thrust against his chest like a carpenter's screw burrowing into his flesh. He learned that his father died of fever before he was born, leaving his mother, Eli, and another woman, her sister, Aunt Yaya, to raise him in a small city by the name of Ciar. It was a wayward town, but had a larger population than Reva, housing transients and incomers. It was a resting point for travelers and traders to larger cities.

He could remember what her arms felt like around his small frame, and the tear-soaked softness of her cheek against his forehead. He couldn't expect to feel what he had never experienced but now... now he knew. He was loved. The word was foreign, the feeling unwonted like a needle underneath the nail or a pus-leaking wound. It needed to be removed, severed from him as swiftly as a gangrenous limb. But he didn't know how. He crouched onto a boulder at the mouth of the cave and sat with his head in his hands.

There was nothing in the world more important than the task at hand. He'd built his whole life around the one who murdered Ovia and Ethen, but what Cinaed did to him muddled the past and present in a way that left him... unsettled. He had no experience with such disorder. The Reticent were incorruptible with the single mindset of absolute superiority. Love nothing. He loved *nothing*.

He reached out to Saiya, binding his mind and fastening his thoughts away from everything that made him weak. She accepted his presence with a sense of relief. It was difficult to communicate over so long a distance but not impossible. It took practice and they'd perfected the skill over the years. He was a part of her. He imagined his formless tongue still wagging inside her belly, always with her.

When this is over, we'll return to Solov.

He closed his eyes against the feel of the sun on her wings.

She shared her elation at being in the clouds over Reva, the warm air curling around her feathers as she dove. He could only see flashes and impressions of what she saw. Their bond wasn't like the Viden's, no matter how hard the Reticent tried to replicate it.

He had limitations the dragon riders didn't. Their combined power could easily overcome them, but they had their own flaws. The dragon scale was where their bond originated. If they were separated then they couldn't communicate. The Reticent and their raptors could, which was an advantage that led to the death of several Videns and dragons alike. Sometimes it was a simple matter of separating the scale from the dragon's bondsmate — its absence accelerated the madness that came with being Viden. A far more effective route to this would've been to shatter the dragon scale altogether. Death was quickly followed after this soul-shattering sundering, usually by the Viden's own hand. The bond between a dragon and its rider was more than physical, and the Reticent had failed in that regard. Saiya and he didn't share a soul, although at times it felt as if she had unwittingly merged her own with his.

Maun reached into his pocket, feeling the smooth surfaces of Celosia's Glare. It bewildered him to know how so small a thing could wield such power. There was but one person who fought in the war beside the Decayed alive and she made Maun the man he was today. Did the Tacet know the true purpose of Celosia's Glare? He wondered how a stone the size of his thumb nail could bend the will of dragons.

He sat upright as Saiya's consciousness tapped against his mind. He closed his eyes, concentrating on the feel of her presence, until he was able to shift in between his own mind and hers.

Devu's bright, clear eyes flashed across Maun's mind. Her white hair was short, brilliant against the light skin of her middle-aged features. The scars at her cheeks rose into her scalp where more lines of puckered, hairless skin crossed in remembrance of her own raptor's talons. An'gan's black form towered over Saiya with as much age as his Reticent. His flight feathers dimmed from pitch black to grey at the ends.

"You are not in Soleil Citade, I assume," An'gan's voice was guttural and light, almost playful as Devu spoke through him. Maun concentrated and felt Saiya's voice combine with his own.

"You knew I would not stay. You know the burden I bear —what I seek."

Maun was brought back to the cold and wind as the storm below grew louder. He tightened his fists, focusing back on Saiya. Devu's swaying form appeared within his mind, cocking her head to the side.

"It's a burden only to you. A Reticent doesn't feel guilt or pain. There is only instinct, and instinct bears no vengeance," she said, An'gan's red tongue stretching.

Maun sighed at the common lecture he was given by Devu, but at least the woman used her words and not fists. He had come to realize though that bruises healed—words did not.

"He is there in the city. I've discovered his name, and I know who he is." Saiya conveyed no inflection, no emotion, and he enjoyed watching Devu's features contort in the same vindictive glare that was so familiar in the old Reticent.

"If you are so sure, why have you not come yourself?"

Maun hesitated. He couldn't tell Devu about Oretem, not yet. He wasn't ready. He'd been so occupied in recovering his lost memories that he'd forgotten about Cinaed and his grand plan for the world in the wake of his return. Maun cared little for the Order and its rigid rules. If he told Devu, he'd risk his freedom. He only wanted the vengeance that had been denied to him for so long. Once that was completed, then perhaps, he'd consider sharing his discoveries with the Order.

"I'm in the Bena Mountains. They could be long gone by

the time I arrive. I ask you, in the memory of my father, to bring me the man who killed him. Alive, so that I may watch him die in the way of his most beloved," Maun said, twisting Celosia's Glare in his hand, feeling the rage well inside and spill over as Saiya snapped at the air.

"Who is it he loves most?" An'gan whispered as Devu traced a scar on her chin. Maun repressed a growl as the image of the Tacet standing over his mother's corpse filled his mind.

"I don't know. Observe him, Devu. Find out, and kill everyone else," he said, feeling blood boiling in his veins, remembering Evelyn and the threat she posed.

As a Viden, she still had a connection to Oretem, frayed as it was it was still a threat. Evelyn had served her purpose and led him to Meric. The sooner she was disposed of, the better.

The old Reticent's shape twisted and blurred as Maun found it harder to maintain the connection. Devu stood and walked over to Saiya who backed away with raised wings.

"It will be assured, but know this—I accept this task not in the memory of your father, but for the freedom you may gain in this murderer's death." Her voice was harsh, an animalistic sneer twisting the scars that had maimed her face. "Give me his name and retribution shall be yours, my Child of Fortune."

Devu had always called Maun her Child of Fortune after the death of his parents, for that was what he had become. But he was a Child of Fortune before she had claimed him and simply a child before that—a son to a woman who called him Calian. He was there, suddenly, hearing her gurgle his name through the slit in her throat. He blinked, repelling the memory, and returning to the blistering cold that numbed his fingertips.

Maun was rent between abysmal hatred and rooted respect. Devu wasn't kind, but she wasn't cruel to Maun as his parents were. It wasn't until he regained the memories of this child called Calian that he had realized there was something different. A way of life that hadn't embraced the abuse of a small child and degrees to which he had experienced that abuse. It was a life he had not known could be any different. It simply was. Maun tried to remain the man he was before the memories, but he could feel the change. The creep of emotions that laid beneath the surface of his Reticent training. He had to remain indifferent. He did not matter.

"His name is Meric, and he'll be traveling with a woman, Evelyn. She'd have just arrived in the city, perhaps a few days ago. She has Vagu blood." The lie rolled easily off Saiya's tongue.

He couldn't tell Devu she was Viden, but she had to know Evelyn possessed similar qualities to avoid detection. He recalled how she was able to follow the wind his cloak created to his location.

Devu leaned back and rubbed her hand across her chest, grimacing as if experiencing the pain of an old battle wound. An'gan flapped his wings in the darkness, his massive form making Saiya look like a sparrow.

"Meric..." she said, a look of recognition passing across her thoughtful features. "And a Vagu, interesting. I believe we know where to find him. I shall remain observant for the time being."

"Saiya will remain with you and send me word of your progress. She is to aid you in whatever capacity she is capable of. Bring her back to me unharmed," he spoke with fervor knowing that, though Devu was calculating, she respected the bond between raptor and Reticent.

"Of course. Do not linger so long in the cold when your blood was born with the sun's desert heat. I'll see you soon, my Child of Fortune." The words ought to have been kind, but were filled with a kind of disappointed malice.

Maun breathed in deeply as he released his hold on Saiya's mind. Her emotions clung to him as he withdrew, her mind pecking at the back of his own. He lent her a sense of pride in her accomplishment, and she drunk that rare emotion up as if she'd been deprived of water.

He stood from the boulder, his eyes searching the raging storm below the mountain. He stood above it all. Is this what Cinaed felt at the height of his reign? Atop the chaos of people, looking over events he'd caused and moved like the pieces of a gambler's game?

There was still more to discover regarding the Decayed. There was an insect in the back of Maun's mind, biting him. Cinaed's talk of the goddesses was nonsense to his ears, but he knew one word. One single word that had the power to make him hesitate even for a moment before the killing blow. Falconer. The name of the eyeless man, the one whose stories brought about a reality that no one had believed. Cinaed had too much conviction in his own beliefs, as if he were trying to convert Maun before he killed him. It was time to look into that past and discover what the old leader had in store before Maun placed that blade in his skull.

CHAPTER 24

VAGU

Once when Evelyn was in her twelfth name year, she had managed to break out of a particularly boring lesson on the length of a dragon's memories to Sou's little hut. The ferryman held a fishing rod under his arm, hook in one hand and a small minnow in the other. The little creature's mouth gasped in the frigid air, eyes wide, unblinking, and helpless. It thrashed against his hand, as if knowing its inevitable fate. He lifted the hook to its pulsating mouth and slowly, with precision, pierced the minnows' jaw through to the top of its head. She remembered hearing the hard, popping sound of the fish's skin as the hook made its way through the flesh. It suddenly went slack, the body limp in Sou's hand, but its mouth still moved against the hook. The fish lived, gasping with a metal pin skewering its head. Evelyn felt like that fish, speared by the echoing words of Sou's confession.

He walked to the window and peered out into the twilight of the setting sun. His back to her, blocking her from whatever his features might reveal.

"As you have obviously realized I am not the simple ferryman you thought you knew." There was a corrosion to his voice, slick with regret and shame. A yoke carried for far too long in the muddy shallows of past memories. "I was an angry young man. My family had suffered under the oppression that most Vagu do in cities like this one. I spent my childhood here, surviving and hiding while my parents searched for budding Videns. I was nearly a man when they were killed by a drunken mob. Before I could understand the hatred, I mirrored it, absorbed it, and fed it back to the people who sold it to me. I thought I could be exactly what they accused me of. I promised grieving women that their dead fathers said they would never bear another child. I assured children that their departed parents foretold a life empty of great deeds. I caused the wind to stir and objects to levitate, to threaten and trick the world I thought to have treated me so wrongly."

Evelyn gripped the post on the side of the bed to balance herself. Sou had begged her not to push him, pled with her name. Now that she had done the deed she felt as if she were staring into the long drop, suddenly realizing and regretting what she'd done in her anger. Tears caught in her eyelashes as she stared at the back of the man she'd known all her life. She glanced down at her own steady hands, suddenly realizing it was not only he that was a stranger to her.

"I lied and I relished in those lies. I told false fortunes until it was too dangerous for me to stay. It took time, but when my predictions proved less than truthful people began to gather and plot. It was apparent I had not long to live if I stayed. I traveled to the Eshe Willow Wood and lived on the outskirts of Edewor in a hollow willow tree. People who dreamt made the trek to the city to receive answers, an explanation to their visons. Many were accepted by dragons. I stopped them on the road and gave them false witness to their hopes. I told them their loved ones wanted them to sell silk in Ciar or find peace on the beaches of the Celosia Sea. I once sent a man to the Waste to die. I still wonder how many potential Viden's I strayed from that path. Had I not, would there have been enough to thwart the destruction of the dragons?" Sou lowered his head, lifting a hand to his face. She couldn't tell whether he covered his mouth in consternation or was wiping tears from his cheek. "A young woman came to my willow. She didn't come for fortunes; she came for a broken man's garden."

His voice softened, and Evelyn knew the young woman he spoke of.

"Lyn," she said, imagining what a woman who had captured Sou's heart had looked like. The old man tuned around, his face a mask of memory. He was lost in it, drowning in the words unspoken for so long.

"My wife," he gasped the words, as if the title were a rope tethering him to shore, his one and only way to survive the churning current. "She'd been visiting friends in Birny, traveling back to Edewor and stopped to admire my garden. She was unimpressed and told me exactly the spot where my flowers could receive the most sun and when to cover them in the upcoming frost. She'd trained her ability to listen to the weather. She knew precisely when it was the right time to plant and when draught would occur. It was for the love of all growing things she lived for. She tended to me as much as my garden, pruning and cutting away the things that hindered my flourishing. She loved me. I did not deserve that love, but she loved me all the same and I found that my existence within the willow wasn't enough anymore. I left the Willow Wood and she left Edewor and we made our life in Birny. The city was so close to Edewor we had no need to fear the prejudice of others. Our neighbors knew us a friends and life was simple. We built an inn, named it Mire after my mother, and enjoyed the company of people from all walks of life.

"Then Cinaed and his legions of Reticent swept through the land. Dragons were falling and Videns were murdered. Children were kidnapped and everything was fire and death. We stayed in Birny. It was close enough to the Vagu capitol to be relatively safe from the Reticent, but that did not stop disease. Many people from cities all over the country migrated to the Eshe Willow Wood, stopping in Birny to rest before continuing to Edewor. Lyn and I did our part in housing them. Including, people from Ciar."

He swallowed, but the muscles in his neck strained as if refusing the act. Evelyn remained quiet, lowering her head to rest her forehead on the bedpost. She knew the plague that had savaged the city. It had lasted for years, until a quarantine had been put in place and the sickness died with those who caught it. Even as a small child, she remembered Tansey cleaning the supplies she received from Sou with vinegar for fear the disease would spread to their small village.

"She died in my arms that winter." Sou looked at his hands, eyes glaring at the wrinkled skin as if they carried the disease that killed his wife. "I left the city, gave the inn to the Vagu to do with as they would. Everything was grown and I had not the talent she had for maintaining growing things. I joined the effort against the Reticent, using my ability to sense the emotions around me. I interrogated and spied, fought and killed. I did this for years, reporting to various Videns including Caia, although I never met the woman. It was a long time before I felt the impression to return home. I was on the border of Elm Lake and the Solov Waste when a tempestuous wave of heated wind knocked me nearly unconscious. I think Lyn wanted to be sure I knew it was she who was sending me home." He chuckled, a brief moment of levity before his frown returned. "When I returned my home was occupied by your mother and father and their two daughters. You were but a babe, and they were kind. Your mother would not see me turned from my home and offered me to stay in the spare room. Their eldest daughter, your sister, had seen her eighth name day and doted on you as if you were her own child. Your parents had resumed ownership of the inn Lyn and I built, and I helped where I could." He stopped speaking, studying her features for any kind of response. Evelyn wasn't sure if she was masking herself or was too wearied to express her emotions properly. They boiled inside her with the strength of Celosia's Depths.

"You chose not to leave again. Why?" She pushed herself away from the bed, determined to stand on her own feet again. Sou had stayed in Birny because he felt obligated to return the favor of her father's and mother's generosity. He'd ensconced himself too far into their family, knowing it was the only one he had left. She was a burden. She had always been a burden.

Sou met her gaze and smiled. For the duration of his tale, Evelyn felt like she was in Oretem's cave without a torch. The darkness was overwhelming, and she could only navigate by the reach of her fingers and the echo of her staggering breath. The slight corner of Sou's upturned lip was the soft flicker of a single candle in the void. The old man's smile gravitated into his eyes, and Evelyn nearly choked with the relief of a light that could lead her way out.

"You are truly Tansey's granddaughter. Lass, you know why I stayed, and you know why I remain. There is nothing in this world that would ever make me part with the little girl who used to call me Soup."

She took in a breath, arms across her chest to keep her body from collapsing.

"You... you took me away. You took me away from them." She was sobbing, horrible gut-wrenching sobs, that threatened to fold her in half. Sou stepped forward, both hands cradling her face. He crouched down at eye level with her and wiped her tears with his thumbs. His expression one of immense pain.

"We had to. Your mother and I had to keep you safe. I was supposed to protect her on that journey. I was meant to protect the both of you and I shall carry that shame for the rest of my life." The corners of his eyes crinkled with tears as he smoothed out the hair from her face. "I'm taking you home. We are going home."

Evelyn didn't collapse into his arms; she was resolved to never need the strength of his embrace ever again. She touched his hand on her face, slowly withdrawing it. She held it for a moment, staring into those green eyes that she could never fully trust again. She mourned for the people they used to be, the relationship they once had. They had to forge a new one, but time was not on their side.

"Not yet," she said, tightening the clasp of her cloak around her shoulders. She dared him with the burning of her eyes to try and stop her. Sou simply nodded and reached into his tunic, pulling out the small glass vial she'd periodically seen around his neck. He pulled the stopper and raised it to his cheeks, collecting the tears that fell. She furrowed her brow, rubbing her hands together as she faced him.

"What are you doing?"

He stoppered the vial and tucked it in underneath his tunic, tapping his chest before letting his arms fall at his sides.

"True Tears."

She waited for him to explain further, but he said nothing.

"Is it some kind of Vagu magic?"

He sighed, his shoulders slack against what looked like an incredible invisible weight. He shook his head, thin wisps of blue light trailing around him as if he had hundreds of thoughts.

"What is magic to you is natural for another. I don't have the time to explain the properties of True Tears at the moment, but ask me again and I will tell you another time."

She exchanged a quick subtle nod with him, reaching for the handle of the door. She felt the weight of his hand on her shoulder, turning her gently towards him.

"Will you promise to be safe?" Sou squeezed his fingers when he saw her mouth open to protest. "I have the greatest confidence in your ability to defend yourself. What I fear is your involvement in the affairs of others. The ground may open, and the world may die, but every stone is a gem in your eyes."

"What is that supposed to mean?" She was impatient to leave the room. She stared at his hand on her shoulder, and he removed it. Evelyn could almost taste his remorse on the air. It was bitter.

"You've changed much, lass, but not that much. You are kind and, in this place, kindness is dangerous." He paused, baring into her gaze for a moment before shifting it beyond her. "You cannot save everyone." He spoke the words knowing she'd resent him for it.

"Is that what the wind tells you?"

She watched his expression for the hurt, prepared herself to grit her teeth to spite it all, but the smile that formed on his face was anything but hurtful. He huffed a chuckle and shook his head. He looked into her eyes, searching, and finding whatever it was he was looking for. Her frown faltered, softening at what she didn't want to admit. Despite the rift between them, he still thought he knew her best. She hated how it soothed her sharpness, dulled her revolve.

"Can we agree to return in two hours' time?" His tone was light, as if they were off to the market to prepare a meal.

"Two hours," she agreed.

Sou stepped around her, opening the door. Evelyn followed him out, gripping the handrail as they made their way down the stairs. Cronies Inn roared with loud conversation and hearty meals. The scent of boiled chicken and fresh vegetables cooked in broth permeated the air around her. A few incomers' thoughts speared their way to her, wondering who she was and how striking her eyes were. They exited the inn, and she unwrapped the scarf around her neck, wondering how the air could be so warm when the sun was gone. Sou's footsteps began to retreat and she turned around. Before he disappeared into the darkness of the night, Evelyn felt the press of an unanswered question in her chest.

"Sou."

He turned back, his cheeks sunken and eyes blazing. He was exhausted and so was she. She wanted nothing more than to wrap herself in the fine blankets of her soft bed and drift into oblivion. There was so much to do. To enter oblivion was to forget Sou's betrayal, Nakesha's bleeding corpse. It also meant forgetting Birdie's laugh and Tansey's callused hand holding her own.

"What are their names? My father and my sister."

Sou sighed an apologetic breath.

"Your father is Ranvir, and your sister is Era."

Evelyn thought once she knew their names, she might know them. That some secret, hidden part of her would recall the color of her father's eyes or whether her sister preferred strawberries to raspberries. All she could do was conjure in her mind, as she had done throughout her life, what imaginary traits they might have. Knowing their names resolved nothing. She realized she had been silent for some time, staring down the cobblestones. She glanced back at Sou who returned her stare with concern.

"Do you feel something?"

She knew he meant through the wind. Had Tansey or her mother spoken to her? Had they enveloped her in an embrace of comfort and reassurance? Were they impressing upon her the love of strangers half a world away, waiting for their long-lost relative? Evelyn lifted her head and stared down the glittering torchlight of the street, listening to the soft chatter of the occupants inside the inn behind her. The air was musty, heavy with moisture from the river in the north and the sea further south. The night was silent and dark and empty.

"I feel nothing."

She turned from Sou and walked away without turning back.

Chapter 25

Decorum

Feeling the cobblestones beneath her feet, Evelyn looked to the night sky, following the strings of candlelight that hung from the rooftops over the street. The flames were small, but just rich enough to light the main road. She couldn't see the stars in Reva, but the candlelight reminded her of them. The corners of her lip upturned, thinking she was only seeing a different kind of starlight, a closer human version of the sky's quiet brilliance. Off to the sides, in the alleyways, was darkness. Evelyn glanced into the in between streets and decided she wasn't desperate enough to venture there.

The street she walked was a busy road with groups of men and women laughing and stumbling by. They never mingled, but walked with their own gender, calling to the other when passing. It was a concoction of what looked to be wealthy and poor alike. While passing the taverns, Evelyn saw a mix of robust and hardy working men, clanging mugs of alcohol with those whose appearances suggested light if any labor.

The women were of the same class. Their hems were absent of complex designs, and she saw a few who wore trousers. Most of the women had attire she hadn't thought was appropriate for Reva's polite society. In the time Sou had allotted her, Evelyn had ventured into those taverns without much success. The servers and barkeeps were as drunk as their patrons. They referred her to other taverns, which in turn, directed her to more pickled establishments until she thought it was some sort of communitive immature witticism of the inebriated. The last tavern she visited was of the same disposition and Evelyn's patience had run its course. She grew weary of the barman's leering smile and refusal to be of any help. Just when she thought she may have to spill a bit blood to sober her relentless humorists, a seated drunkard on the stool next to her by the name of Lamac told her of a brothel called Decorum having said, "If your Meric isn't pissing in the alley he'll he sticking it somewhere there. The Breaths and Depths know I did and to my great and abysmal misfortune so does my wife. Celosia's bottomless Depths would drown me if I wasn't already."

Evelyn had left Lamac to his self-pitying drinking and made her way down the street, reading each sign for the tavern the drunkard had spoken of. She had spotted the decorative sign and now stood in from of the tavern or what might've been a brothel. Peering into the window she saw through glaring light, men and women tangled together in drink and lust. The thought of their wandering hands touching any part of her sent a chill of outrage down her spine. It was far more likely that she'd break those hands and that wasn't the sort of attention she needed to draw. Evelyn was glad she wore the cloak Tansey gave her in place of the shawl. It covered the ornate dress she had believed would help her blend in when it only made her stand out in the night crowd. The commotion from the brothel was loud and echoing. She decided she was going to have to abate her hesitation. She might not have control of Iona's Breath, but she never needed to rely on that anyway. She was trained well, and the lessons Tansey taught her echoed in her mind. She fared fine in the other taverns and this one would be no different.

Down the alleyway next to her, she heard the clanging of metal and the shuffling of feet. Evelyn started at the sudden noise, hand reaching for her daggers. Her fingers grazed the hilt of a blade as she stepped closer. A hooded figure appeared hunched in the darkness, arms deep into the rancid remains of discarded food. The floor of the alleyway was littered with broken plates, spoiled vegetables, and an array of rotten meat. At first the beggar didn't seem to notice Evelyn's approach, lost in their hunt for anything salvageable. She got within a few paces before the beggar straightened, glaring at her through the shadow of their hood with yellow wolf-like eyes. That stare bore into Evelyn with a hunger and desperation she had come to know very well. What struck her was the intensity of those wolf eyes. They looked as ready to devour Evelyn as much as the spoiled food around them. Whoever this beggar was, they were starving.

Evelyn had no coin, but she stepped forward and upturned her palm in a peaceful manner. She could find a way to help, bring the person to Cronies Inn where Sou could buy them food. She could go search for Meric afterwards. When she took another step, the yellow eyes narrowed. If she could see the rest of their face, she imagined the beggars' teeth would be borne into a snarl. Those distrustful yellow eyes blinked, then disappeared into the darkness of the side street.

Evelyn sighed. It wasn't as if the hooded figure was the first person she'd seen starving. She'd seen plenty on her way in, but there were so many it wasn't possible for her to help them all. Yellow eyes was one person out of a multitude she could do nothing for. It didn't stop her from trying.

The ground may open, and the world may die, but every stone is a gem in your eyes.

Sou's words echoed in her mind, and she thrust them from her thoughts. She didn't want to think about Sou. She didn't want to think about how even with so much dividing them, he was still the one who knew her best in this world. It hadn't mattered in the end. Yellow eyes was gone and Evelyn was left in front of a brothel, searching for a man she didn't know in a place she had no idea how to act.

She suppressed a laugh, thinking how she never could've imagined that this would be her life. She could tell herself she had no idea how much she had until she lost it all, but she knew, and it sat like a hot coal in her chest. Evelyn took in a breath, released it, and stepped inside.

The brothel was large with open spaces in between packed tables. A bar reached from one side to the other with light colored wood, stained muddy from spilled ale. The ceiling bridged in thick oak and tall candles that burned bright, casting shadows across the room. Wax dripped from the chandeliers, creating piles of slick oil across the floor.

Loud laughter emanated from those within the tavern. Men and women clutched their bone goblets and kissed the necks of the working women in their laps. Evelyn made her way to the bar, avoiding eye contact with the many occupants who had certainly noticed her. A few gripped the hem of her cloak, but she walked on, pulling the fabric out of their hands.

When she reached the bar, she sat on the stool and placed her hands on the countertop before lifting them with a grimace. The wood was sticky with dried ale, spit, and whatever else she couldn't imagine. The barman's back was turned as she knocked on the wood. He turned and her eyes widened to discover the man was, in fact, not a man. The woman's green eyes were uncolored, and she pursed her lips curiously, as though Evelyn had arrived early for a previously set appointment. She was the largest woman Evelyn had ever seen. The barmaid's massive fingers gripped a towel in her hand, making it look more like an infant's rag.

"Looking for work, darling?" her breath was husky and smelled of heavy ale.

Evelyn shook her head and glanced at a woman close to her age take a man's hand, whose youth had passed many years ago, up the stairs at the opposite end of the tavern.

"It's not what most would call honest work. But to the Depths with that," the barmaid said, lifting a bone goblet from the highest hook on the wall. "You'll have a bed and food. It's more than most of us started out with. Those eyes of yours will fetch a pretty silver piece. You've got a nice face—perhaps a

Lord will take a liking to you." She laughed as if it were the pun at the end of a joke.

"I told you, that's not what I'm here for. I'm looking for someone," Evelyn said asserting her voice with a bit more force. The barmaid seemed to respond well to her tone, raising her eyebrows in appreciation.

"I see. Just who might be this wayward man?"

Evelyn narrowed her eyes and leaned away. She had to be careful how she asked. She didn't want to seem eager, and she didn't want to give away how little she knew. All she had was a name, but she had to give the impression she knew what she was doing.

"I never said it was a man."

The woman chuckled and filled the goblet she held with ale. It added to the excessive booze aroma that seemed to permeate her skin. The silver rings on the woman's fingers glistened with what might've been rust or dried blood.

"Oh, for you, darling, it'll be a man. I'm not usually mistaken about my patrons... desires. What did he do? Take your precious jewels?" She glanced at Evelyn's chest and smiled. "If that's the case, either find another to fill the empty position, or if he really *did* just steal your jewels, hire a Venandi," she spat the word as if she bit into a rotten apple. "If that's who you're looking for you'll find none here. Their kind is not welcomed."

Evelyn watched the woman's expression writhe under a bitter storm, promising violence. She had some foul play with Venandi that much was certain. It was a good thing Sou was in search for one and not her.

"I'm not looking for a Venandi," the barmaid's shoulders relaxed as Evelyn continued. "I'm in search of a friend. I just entered the city earlier and he wasn't where we agreed to meet."

It was a believable enough story without revealing too much. The woman seemed to have taken a liking to Evelyn in a strange, tight-fisted way. As if she would just as soon throw her out as she would house her. The woman placed the ale-filled goblet in front of Evelyn and inclined her head towards it. Her blonde braid falling over one shoulder.

"Drink it," she said without any room for question. Evelyn did anyway.

"What for? I have no coin to give."

"It's on the house. One can tell a lot about another by how they hold their drink."

Evelyn doubted such an experiment was worthy of credence. But the barmaid was just as drunk as her customers. She swayed on her feet even as she stood there with the bar as her balance. There was a hidden intelligence in the woman that Evelyn hadn't failed to notice, but even drunken cleverness could be capable of insightful judgement. She decided to proceed, but with caution. She reached her hand for the goblet when a loud man from behind slammed his shoulder into her, nearly knocking her off the stool. His drink overflowed onto the bar, splattering his trimmed beard.

"Due! On the house? On top! I'm in the house, I am. Why might I not have a complimentary beverage?" The man's breath reeked of drink, and Evelyn hardly understood him he was slurring so much. His vest was a dark purple with many designs that looped down and up his back.

"Kiev! To the Depths with you, imbecile!" Due leaned across the bar, gripping the man's shirt in her claw-like fingers. Her hand was so much larger than his face that Evelyn wondered how she was able to fit the rings she wore on her fingers. She must've had them specially made.

"Had you not the face of a mangy dog I might provide said *complimentary beverage*. Seeing as you are, I'll charge you extra for the simple act of showing it here."

She released her hold, and the man just lifted his goblet, drinking in the last of its contents. He reached into his pocket and pulled out a silver piece that was larger than most Evelyn had seen. Due nodded and placed the money in her dress pocket. She picked up a pitcher below the counter and refilled the man's cup.

"I'll accept that charge now that there's bloody ale for the rest of us since that brooding, dark-haired Venandi is gone. Hmm, I'm in need of a fight." He burped, then turned to Evelyn as if she knew of someone he could spar with.

His body was screaming his drunken attitude, but his eyes were alert, lustful for anything that might bleed. She held his eyes and didn't like at all what she saw in them. When confronting a wild bena wolf, one does not turn away and run. It is best to maintain eye contact while backing away. She couldn't leave, but she would be damned if she relinquished dominance to this man. When she didn't answer he gave her a leering smile and faced the tall woman. "For what it's worth. I'm sorry about your nephew, he was an ugly sort, but a good lad," he said with a shrug. Nothing in his tone suggested he was apologetic and Due glared at him. He flashed his teeth in a smile, took down another gulp and walked away to the table he'd come from. Due's lips lined into an oppressed frown that hid a quivering chin.

Due crossed her elbows on the bar top, her expression tight, thin, looming frame making the wood creek under the pressure of her weight. Her stricken look faded as she gestured to the goblet, then back at Evelyn, still expecting her to drink. Evelyn gripped the goblet; the bone was smooth, an iron hilt surrounding her hand.

She swung her head back and while holding her breath, let the ale travel uninhibited down her throat. The drink was smoother than the kind she had in Verbena, but stronger— much stronger. She pulled her head forward with a grimace and pushed the mug away from her. It was strange how sudden the drink took effect. The shadow that seemed to be a constant canopy surrounding her relented somewhat. The gloom rose and floated above her, still tethered, drifting along to her movements, but she was surprised to realize her despair dissipating like morning mist. She could feel the alcohol in her stomach twist and turn as if uncomfortable in bed. Finally, it decided to rest, and she released her breath. A little lighter headed, but more like herself, like she was before. She touched her chest, holding in a hiccup as Due picked up the goblet with a satisfied smile.

"I see you now, darling. Who is it you're looking for?" Her green eyes held an openness that Evelyn thought was rare for a woman such as she. Even her tone of voice changed from hostility to one of guarded sympathy. It was a slight change, but a change, nonetheless.

"His name is Meric." No sooner than the name escaped her lips Due slammed the goblet onto the bar, crushing the bone into pieces. The look of sympathy in her disappeared into a glare Evelyn had only seen in Nakesha when she was disturbed while eating.

"Get out," she whispered. "I'll not hear that name uttered here and I will not suffer any of his kind."

She'd heard Due use that term before. That look in her eyes mirrored the same tormented stare when Kiev mentioned her nephew. The two were connected. Her confidence grew as blood raced to her limbs, calling to action or perhaps it was the ale.

"His kind? Then he is Venandi? Was he involved with what happened to your nephew?" Evelyn leaned forward, unperturbed by Due's shaking hands gripping the bar.

"You'll not speak of Endri, you know not —" She paused, her mouth open in confusion. "*Is he Venandi?*" she said, exasperated.

Evelyn could see realization cross Due's face as she ascertained that Evelyn wasn't who she claimed to be. It was a dangerous position, but she held her ground, determined to get as much information as she could from the woman.

"I need to find him."

"Celosia's Depths," Due swore as she furrowed her eyebrows, regretful. "I need to stop drinking so much."

"Please, Due, I don't have much time. Just tell me where he is and I'll —"

Evelyn caught Due's wrist that was halfway on its journey to striking her. The woman's green eyes widened at the speed of

Evelyn's reaction. She was just as surprised. Though her bond was frayed, she hadn't lost her Viden reflexes. The barmaid's startled expression molded to that of a hardened combatant, and she lifted her other arm for a blow. Evelyn spun and used her weight to slam Due's arm onto the bar's edge. She screamed a low bellow, hugging her arm, still standing. All Evelyn could think was if Due couldn't stand, she couldn't fight.

She gripped the stool, lifting it over the bar and breaking it against Due's skull. The barmaid moaned and stumbled, falling out of sight behind the bar. The tavern grew quiet as all eyes stared at her. The escalation of the situation felt as if it were placed outside of time. Evelyn had difficulty realizing she was in the present, acting out in front of dozens of people who would remember her. Her eyes searched the faces of the crowd, frantic for an explanation that wasn't there. Why had she done that? *How* had she done that?

She'd always excelled in her lessons with Tansey when it came to combat, but this was different. Due was a woman of incredible strength and muscle. When Evelyn caught her hand, she could feel how her jaw would've broken under the weight of the barmaid's fist, yet it was no more effort for her than lifting firewood. It was heavy, but if held in the correct position, easy to carry. She hadn't meant to fight back so impulsively.

She remembered Verbana. A Reticent running after her with black wings soaring overhead to rip her spine from her back. Due stood with teeth exposed into an angry snarl. The drunk man, Kiev, raised his cup and cheered. Others joined in and clapped, but she never took her eyes off the seething woman.

Kiev stood from his table and stumbled to her, placing an arm around her shoulder. He pointed at Due with his mug.

"I think this would be a good time to run, girl. She's going to kill you!" he yelled into her face, laughing in his drunken manner. His musky ale breath made her gag, arm creeping from her shoulders around her waist, fingers looping where Oretem's scale hid.

She ripped away from his arm and punched him in the nose. His drink crashed to the ground as his hands covered his face, bending over with a shout.

"Me bloody nose! Celosia—Celosia's bloody—*Depths*," he sputtered through clenched teeth as Evelyn backed away, fingers throbbing. The crowd kept cheering, ignoring Kiev's barks of pain.

She ran out of the tavern and down the street until she was out of breath. She stumbled around the corner of a closed carpenter's shop, gripping the stones for support. Her chest lifted and fell as she rested her back against the edge of the wall. She let her head fall back and laughed at the absurdity of what she'd just experienced. Evelyn wondered if that might've been the ale's doing, but what was there to be done except laugh? So far, she'd done everything that Sou told her not to and somehow still managed to find out more than what she knew before. She thought, had she not mentioned Meric, that she and Due might actually get on. The barmaid seemed to have good reason for not particularly liking Venandi. Despite what harm Due might've done to her, Evelyn liked the woman. She closed her eyes.

There is good. It's not all ash and blood. There is good.

It was something she had to remember, assimilate into the core of her being. The words felt more like parasites, little worms eating her alive, knowing they weren't a part of her. She couldn't think of it now. Evelyn replayed the confrontation in her mind, searching for anything that might point her in the right direction.

Sou had asked her to stay safe. She had in the sense that she'd not shed a single drop of blood, her own blood that is, but she'd failed miserably in not drawing attention to herself.

She hadn't learned much, but it was more than what she previously knew. Kiev spoke of a brooding man with dark hair. From Due's reaction to the name, she surmised Meric was Venandi. A hated Venandi, by the sound of it, and involved in the presumed death of the barmaid's nephew, Endri. That kind of information must be known to someone who wouldn't crush her head like a berry. She pushed herself from the side of the shop and turned the corner, determined to spend what was left of her two hours between taverns.

Her steps were halted as her body was crushed against the grip of a large man. She struggled against him, but he pinned her arms to her sides in a nefarious embrace. She looked up to find a familiar brown beard tickling her cheek, blood drying on its trimmed ends.

Chapter 26

Mad Beneath the Earth

The only way Meric was able to find water was to follow the sound of it dripping in the darkness. He crawled across the damp floor to where the sound echoed and ran his tongue across the rough stone, his lips and tongue raw from the sharp edges of the wall.

There was no way to tell how long he'd been below ground. The moonlight he saw his first night had disappeared, along with the company of the woman who was singing. He'd tried speaking with her, but never received a response. Fallon's men must've heard them and blocked the window that was in her cell. For all he knew she died, and he was in the dark alone.

The dripping continued as it always did. Without it he would've died a long time ago and yet, he damned its life-giving properties. Even though he was starving, stomach knotting in painful growls against his thinning frame, the thirst was worse. He tried to go without it, to let his body crumble into mud and waste, but the ache was just too great. He'd become a slave to the water, listening to its fall with anticipation and relishing in the relief he felt when sopped up like a pig at the trough.

He leaned back, watching the endlessness that was the blackness of his cell. From the glimpse he got when the window was open it was a small cell, with horizontal bars that left no room for even a rat to squeeze through. He couldn't stand upright, having to crawl from one point to the other. He wasn't sure he could stand even if he wanted to. His legs had been bent for so long, he feared they may remain so were he ever freed. Although that fear was nearly gone. It was hard to remember that there was anything beyond this blackness, a world above that shined of sunlight and color.

The only sense of time he had was the rate his facial hair grew. He'd never thought to time it, but by the feel of it he estimated he'd been down there for months, perhaps more. It felt like so much more.

"Good morning, Cass," Meric said in no particular direction. He'd named the woman after a little girl he and Grae had been hired to rescue in one of the first missions he had been assigned before officially joining the Venandi.

The girl had been kidnapped by her father who had a reputation for using his fists instead of his words. It was the job that convinced him to join Grae and one of the few that ended with rightful justice for everyone involved. Cass was reunited with her mother, while her father perhaps once sat in the very cell Meric resided in. That was its own ironic justice.

"It feels like morning, does it not? Listen." He paused, letting the drip of the water fill the prison with its echo. "It's raining."

He was certain that she was dead. Meric kept waiting for that familiar smell, the foul odor that came with rotting flesh, but it hadn't come. She might not have had the strength to speak anymore but even then, he would hope to hear a sigh or even a grunt, anything that told him she was there. It disgusted him to think that he couldn't notice the smell because he'd grown used to it. He'd been under the ground for so long that there was no more fresh air to breath. The ravenous murk that surrounded him swallowed it up, leaving only the invisible stench of death.

He hadn't known such darkness before, but the sense that he was utterly alone was a feeling all too recognizable. The memories of his bare feet roaming the twisting roads of the back alleys were brought to the forefront of his mind. Usually, the ale he'd consume kept those images from his recollection along with the various people he'd captured and delivered to their death, but without the alcohol he couldn't stop the flashbacks.

When the guards blocked the window, leaving him in darkness, he screamed until his throat was raw. He writhed on the floor like an animal, begging for light. His agonized cries were the only voices he heard in response. Once he'd spent himself, he slept, then woke to vomit and shake, muscles bursting in uncontrollable ticks and cramps. Then slept again, only to wake and endure the same torture over and over. He might've endured the spasms and retching for days, he had no way of knowing. Meric only knew that after an eternity of being ill, he woke once again and thirsted for more than just ale. That was when he began his service groveling at the steady drip of water.

"I hope you have a good life with your mother. From what I remember she was a good woman," he said, raising his hand in front of his face, the shape of his fingers lost to his sight. He thought of Juna and saw her haunted expression as he told her of her baby's fate. He shut his eyes and still saw her, staring at him. Darkness against darkness and he couldn't escape those pits of grief.

Although he knew his cellmate to most likely be dead, it was helpful to talk with her. He knew it to be impossible for her to be Cass. The mother and girl left the city shortly after their reunion. Where they went, he didn't know, but he hoped it was a place far and opposite to Reva. It was comforting to speak what was on his mind to a possibly decaying corpse instead of abandoning himself to his most inner thoughts.

"I never knew my mother," he said, his mind wandering where it frequently did when he spoke to her. "I remember glimpses, shapes and… songs."

He furrowed his brow at the unconscious thought. She used to sing to him. He could remember her voice, but not the tune. The faint melody of it brought about mixed emotions he was in no condition to untangle. He just remembered loving her more than anything, even now. Even as he struggled to remember what she looked like, the thought of her caused an incredible pang of absence. Meric sniffed and hit himself on the forehead with the chains surrounding his wrists. The pain was a distraction to the more intense agony within him, but his thoughts only continued. They spun and condensed like ripples in water, growing bigger until they engulfed the lake of his mind.

He remembered more of his mother than he did his father. Meric could only dredge up feelings of being safe when he searched his memories of him. There was no face to connect the thought, nothing to grasp as an image. Only a pinprick, a needle-thin sting of emotion that said he was once safe. Was that not that the epitome of fatherhood? Did that mean he was a good father? Meric would never know. They left him. That he could vividly recall, the encompassing fear of abandonment and uncertainty. The emptiness of it all hollowed him and he hit himself again—and again, and again, metal clawing his forehead, blood welling above his brow. He forced himself to push those early memories to the back of his mind, certain that he couldn't bear living through them under the ground so far from everything that reminded him he was alive.

CHAPTER 27

THE CROSSING OF PATHS

"You bloodied my vest, girl. I'm going to need payment." Kiev's hot breath whispered against her ear. Her thoughts ventured to the most horrible form of payment he might force upon her. "I'll take that—"

She leaned her head back and slammed her forehead into his face, his already bent nose cracking under the force. The skin of her brow split against his front teeth. He released her with a howl, blood pouring on the stone street.

Evelyn fell to her knees, losing her balance in her attempt to run. The one cup of ale she had inhibited her equilibrium. She stood to escape, but as soon as she'd taken one step, Kiev grabbed the back of her hair, undoing her loose braid. Her scalp rip as she screamed against the pain. She kicked him in the gut, but his grip held firm as he bent over, pulling her to the ground.

Her head bounced against the stone. She moaned her pain as her vision blurred and her head rang with one high-pitched note. Kiev said something, but Evelyn couldn't understand the garbled mess of words. He lifted her from the ground as she grew conscious again, reaching for her daggers. He saw what she was doing and gripped her arm, pulling it up against her back, and she cried out as her barely healed wrist twisted in pain. Tansey used to tell her to never underestimate the element of surprise, and Kiev had surprised her. She was able to overcome Due because she saw what was coming and Due only had brute strength. Kiev seemed to have that and a competent knowledge of combat skills.

"You've got something pretty I want," he said, and he yanked her arm further up her back, slamming her against the side of the carpenter's shop. Evelyn heard a pop, and her arm went limp. She gasped at the agony of her shoulder separated from her arm, pain radiating like stinging needles in her veins.

She screamed at the passing drunkards, but they simply ignored her. Her cheek throbbed against the cold stone and her throat croaked in her failed attempt to call for help. Kiev pulled her deeper into the adjacent alley, away from the eyes of those who would do nothing to help her. He lifted her cloak and ran his hands across her waist. She growled through the flaying pain in her arm and raked her fingernails across the top of his hand.

He muttered a curse and his grip loosened. It was only a fraction, but it was enough. She tore herself from his hold and spun, unsheathing a dagger in the process with her other hand. The man had more to drink than she, but his body was far more used to the strong ale than she was. He caught her wrist as she moved to stab him in the neck.

Horrified, she berated herself for being so foolish to have drunk on a night she was supposed to have been on her guard. It was one cup, but it was enough to make her slower, even with her Viden reflexes. Kiev showed a victorious smile and punched her. Evelyn gasped and raised her hand to strike him back, but she was seeing double. She missed and he punched her again, her ear ringing with the sound of an echoing crack. She couldn't see out of one eye.

Her legs buckled, then turned limp. His grip on her arm was the only brace she had to keep herself from collapsing. He pushed her against the wall, the cold stone soothing the deep forming bruises on her back. She dropped the dagger, finding no strength in her fingers. Evelyn lifted her head and with her last bit of energy, tried to hit him again. He laughed at her exhausted attempt, kicking her legs out from beneath her. She fell with a quiet moan as her other eye began to lose vision from the swelling.

"What sort of woman are you? It hadn't needed to come to this. Depths, girl, you're a bloody fighter, that's for sure! And *fast*," he said with an appreciative nod as he wiped his lips of blood. He kneeled and lifted her hips, fingers running under the sash at her waist.

"No, no," she mumbled, trying to crawl away, but he pulled her back.

She stared further down the alleyway, watching the darkness as it swirled like thick tar. She couldn't tell if it was the darkness itself or something else moving. She couldn't survive this, could she? After all that's happened, she'd lose something else too. Something she hadn't thought to lose.

"Stay still," his voice graveled in irritation.

His hands went to her hips, untying the sash around her waist. A light metallic click reverberated off the stone and his bearded mouth displayed a full row of bright teeth. He held up Oretem's scale, inspecting the necklace. He lifted himself to the tips of his feet, still crouched. He looked down and recoiled at her confused expression.

"Celosia's Depths girl, I'm not opposed to hitting a woman, but I've no need to force myself upon them." He patted his bloodied vest that showed the complicated design of golden loops. They overlapped as Evelyn blinked, Kiev's shape blurring and shifting with the surrounding darkness. "I've more than enough to have them come willingly. I saw your jewel when I bumped you in Decorum. I tried to slip it off you before you broke my face, figured you bloody owed me for this," he pointed to his nose that was bent to the side.

"Please," Evelyn said, bringing herself up on one elbow. Her head pounded as she fought the urge to close her eyes. "I need that. It's mine."

He couldn't take it. She'd earned it. It was more than her connection to Oretem. That scale represented all that was sacrificed, everything her mother died for and the people she failed. He couldn't take it. Kiev laughed again, cocking his head to the side as if pitying a horse with a broken leg.

"Not anymore. As I said, you bloody owe me, twice over," he spoke with venom as he stood.

Evelyn pushed herself to her knees and swayed as she rose, her dislocated arm swinging. She eyed the necklace, Oretem's scale glinting in the torchlight from above. Kiev had no idea what it was he held in his hand. All of Iona thought dragons to be extinct. He didn't know he was in the presence of a Viden. If her bond were not fractured, he wouldn't have dared to assault her in the corners of the alleyways. She lifted her hand, her fingertips grazing the edge of the scale. He chuckled at her weakness, thinking he could afford for her to be close.

She reached into her power, felt the trickle of her potential. The stream that led to the dam that blocked the wind from her. Evelyn pounded against that invisible shield, letting all the emotions that she subdued surface to be her hammer. All that consumed her mind were the faces of those buried in the snow, turned to ash, and left to memory. Something cracked, then splintered, and she reached inside with one last blow.

It broke.

Her sore limbs flooded with strength as her eyes cleared with perfect vision. Her shoulder straightened and mended with snapped muscles connecting and reforming. Blue lines of Iona's Breath whirled around her, hair twisting across her face.

Why do her eyes glow so? Sorcery! What kind of trickery is this? Kiev's thoughts came to her across one of the blue tendrils, dripping with fear. Her jaw clenched with fury as she curled her fingers around the glowing scale with a tight fist. He pulled against her grip, but there was nothing Kiev could do against the power she held.

"This is no trick," she said, her voice soft, but sharpened with burning emotions, too many to identify. She was all the wind was with nothing that remained of what made her weak, what made her Evelyn.

Kiev froze, his eyes growing twice their size, stunned that she'd answered a question he hadn't asked. He let the necklace go with a shaking hand, but his expression was hard with resentment.

"Take it. Vagu witch or whatever unnatural creature you are."

So much power. There was so much in her that she felt as if she could destroy the city, then rebuild it with the magnitude of her will. She stared at the scale in her hand, felt its pulsating warmth, the distant echo of a mind older than her mountains. Oretem was resting, curling in the cavern of her beloved snowed peaks, the air hot and burning from his fiery breath. She felt the potential of what she could be if she could rebuild her soul, reunite with Oretem. It could be hers.

Evelyn glared into Kiev's eyes as the wind tossed her hair in every direction. Her cloak billowed about her body, giving her the impression of dark cascading wings. Dragon wings. Her voice traveled with a growl, unrecognizable and fierce.

"I am Viden."

She lifted her hand and the torrent of wind left her. She imagined an edged knife arrowing its way through the blackened mist, condensing and spinning. Kiev's expression flashed with sudden regret before the side of his head popped—no, not popped. His head racked backwards as though Iona's Breath were a brick of solid force, dragging his scalp across it, breaking through skin, skull, and brain with its momentum. He fell onto his back, laying on a bed of blood and viscera. Evelyn dropped the scale as she felt the dam rebuild, losing grip on her power.

Panting, she stood over Kiev and placed a hand over her mouth to keep herself from screaming. One empty eye stared at her while the other drooped in the vacuous space where part of his forehead should've been. What had she done? The man was despicable, who knew if anything he said was true and even if he hadn't planned to rape her, he still assaulted her. She touched her healed face, stunned at how fast she was renewed after being beaten. She glanced at her palms which were perfect and absent of the red, irritable, scarred skin.

She'd defended herself. She had to kill him, hadn't she?

No, he was giving her the necklace back. She'd frightened him enough to make the exchange, and she hadn't taken it. Evelyn remembered the heat in her veins, the surge of might she felt as the wind she'd spun into existence had burrowed into Kiev's skull.

She clutched her chest, appalled at what she'd done, even to one as brutal as he. Her heart thundered inside her chest, beating against her lungs as if defying the murderous body it resided in. Had Oretem felt her? She certainly felt him. She rolled her shoulders at the phantom ache of his folded wings. Perhaps fortune had been with her, perhaps not. She stared at the corpse of the man who attacked her and felt everything that disgusted her. Her adrenaline was fading, and her sudden burst of power left her teetering on the edge of unconsciousness. The world was growing dark.

Footsteps. Someone was approaching from behind. The daggers had fallen from her person when Kiev untied the sash. Evelyn spotted them a few paces from Kiev's body, spattered in crimson. She lifted the pouch, pulled a blade from its sheath, and swallowed the bile in her throat at the slick feel of Kiev's blood on the hilt. Her heart steadied and she turned, blade outstretched to the endless alley. Obstructing her view of the darkness was a hooded man. His blonde hair fell flat against his temples, jaw angular and squared with mature age. His eyes were sunken as if he'd spent the last few days with little sleep, skin clinging to his cheeks, giving him a gaunt appearance. He was probably fifteen years older than her, but she couldn't say for certain. His ear flashed with an earring, hanging close to his neck with a silver chain.

Behind him was another cloaked figure, smaller, in the shape of a woman under the blacks of her cloak. She held a bow drawn with an arrow pointed at Evelyn's chest. The bow was artful with carved designs of dragon wings and flowing wind. On the tips of the bow were curved blades embedded into the wood. They coiled inward then twisted out at the tip in a spiraled hook that fitted a blade for disembowelment. Evelyn glanced at her blade, wondering if she could throw it before the woman could loose her arrow.

The archer was familiar; Evelyn could see the glint of yellow eyes behind the darkness of the cloak. The archer stepped closer, and Evelyn could see in the faint moonlight the woman's features. She was about the same age as the man, with black hair and tattooed yellow eyes, staring at her with that same wolf's fierce wariness as she had outside the brothel. Her cheeks were as hollowed as her companion's, skin stretched over bone. She held the bow with precision, but her fingers shook with the effort. A similar earring glinted on her ear, swaying with her movements.

"What in the Depths happened here?" the man said, looking at Kiev, his brows knit together.

Evelyn held out the blade, unwilling to let her guard down. This could be another surprise attack. She bared her teeth, fighting against the exertion of what she'd done creeping into her legs. Her body was exhausted, burned out by her healing and emotional turmoil.

She'd killed someone.

"You saw what she did," the woman said behind him, her voice laced in caution.

Evelyn gripped her dagger tighter and took a stumbled step forward. The blue-eyed man raised his hands, showing that he held no weapon.

"No, I didn't Anya. *You* saw something on a stomach that hasn't had food in nearly a fortnight and ran off. I merely followed."

The yellow-eyed woman, Anya, stretched the bow tighter at Evelyn with an accusing stare.

"Grae, see if she has any coin," Anya said, dipping her arrow.

As Grae moved towards Evelyn, she cut the air with her dagger and lifted her other hand to balance as she swayed. She knew there was no chance she'd be strong enough to fight them off if they chose to attack, but she'd fight, nonetheless.

"You *will not* touch me," she said through her teeth. She

meant it to be a threat, but it was made weak by her trembling voice.

Grae continued to walk towards her with a knowing eye. He could tell she was drained, that she would collapse at any moment. She stood for as long as she could, her legs aching with the effort. The world spun and fell. Evelyn braced herself for the stone to hit her hard, creating new bruises where the old ones had healed, but gentle arms caught her and lowered her to the ground as though she were being tucked into bed. She fought to keep her eyes open. If she could see, she could remain conscious, but it was getting harder. She blinked repeatedly, forcing her eyes open.

"Breaths and Depths, Grae. That's Kiev. I'd been following him, hoping he might say something about Fallon's prisons, before he went into Decorum. What could've done *that* to him?" she stole a glance at Evelyn, eyes edged in unease. She stepped closer to Grae, whispering, "I know what I saw. You felt that wind as I did all the way across the alley and that light... you saw it. It led us here. I thought I heard…"

Anya stood above Kiev, inspecting his body sprawled on the ground. Grae crouched and picked up the dagger she'd let go of during the fight. The one in her hand gleamed in the darkness as if calling out for its fallen comrade.

"Look at the wall. It's covered in his blood. In the height of the fight, she likely struck him repeatedly against it."

Anya returned his gaze with one of utter disbelief.

"Look at his head, Grae. There is not much left of it. I have seen men with crushed skulls, but I have never seen anything like this."

He stood from his crouch, lifting the pouch of daggers, and sheathing the one in his hand.

"We've been surviving on scraps, and less so on sleep. You cannot trust your eyes, Anya. The light we followed was moonlight, nothing more. It was fortunate that we did. Who knows what might've happened to her if we hadn't?"

"Happened to her? Look what she did to him! We can't

help this girl. She's not one of us, look at her dress. Are those trousers?"

Evelyn felt her cloak being opened to reveal her fine green dress lifted at her ankles, showing the dark trousers she wore underneath. It was muddied by the attack, but it still showed her forged wealth that was supposed to protect her in the city. From what she'd experienced it did little in that regard.

"What is she doing out here?" Grae said. She could feel his fingers closing the cloak around her again.

"It doesn't matter anymore, look," Anya said, a delighted lilt to her voice.

She held out Oretem's scale in front of Grae, whose blue eyes brightened in the darkness. Evelyn stirred on the ground, but she couldn't move her limbs. She was entirely spent and now was helpless to keep the strangers from taking her necklace. She tried to speak, mumbling into the ground to tell them to leave her alone. To give the necklace back and let her sleep on the ground in peace.

"Where do you live?" Grae bent over her, shaking her shoulder with a gentle tug. The movement jolted her awareness as she spoke.

"Give it to me," she whispered. "Mine."

"Grae, this will give us time. We can survive long enough with this to figure out how to rescue Meric. I'm sure she's more than enough jewels to sustain her." Her tone harsh and filled with resentment.

"You don't think I know that? You forget. I once wore a vest, too," he said with frustration. The woman refused to look away from his weighty stare. Evelyn mumbled again, but couldn't form words.

Meric. They knew Meric.

Anya lined her lips in an irritated frown like a child who'd been reprimanded by a parent. Evelyn was so tired, arms aching with phantom bruises. She wanted to sleep and wake in the mountain air, myriad with the hot scent of Tansey's morning tea—Nakesha's howls echoing in the distance, and Birdie's laugh as she danced with Adel.

"Lady, where do you live? We'll take you home," Grae said, one brow raised under his blonde hair. Anya groaned behind him, and he silenced her with a glare.

Evelyn was disappearing. Her consciousness fading into blackness. It wouldn't be very long until she was gone, and they would leave her. She wasn't certain if she'd wake. She wasn't certain she wanted to. She thought of joining Tansey in the wind. What would she tell her? That she died in the alley of a city for the simple pleasure of not having to face the following day? No. Tansey would never accept such an end. Evelyn couldn't join the wind with her loved ones without the knowledge of why they died. She couldn't face the shame of it. When the time came for her to finally rest in the embrace of Iona's Breath she would do so with answers.

"Cronies Inn," she said with a rasped gasp, forcing it out.

"She's an incomer. No one will notice her absence, but she will remember us when she's coherent tomorrow. We'll have every Venandi after us by morning," Anya said, placing Evelyn's necklace in a pouch inside her cloak. Her hood rustled in the wind, releasing strands of her straight black hair.

"Perhaps. Perhaps not. Could you fathom the possibility that she'll be grateful we saved her life instead?" Grae retorted, lifting Evelyn off the ground.

Her head rested against his chest, his breathing lulling her eyes to close. She had to stay awake, she had to fight. They'd hurt her. She had to find out what they knew about Meric. They could help her. Her mind battled against opposite ideas, making it harder to stay present.

"Of course! Grateful. As grateful as she will be when she remembers we stole from her. You have about as much wit to make a decision as a farmer has to fight a seasoned thief," Anya said, footsteps quick.

"I wonder out of the two who has the most to lose. The farmer or the thief?" Anya remained quiet, her steps in sync with her partner. "It's my decision to make," Grae continued, holding Evelyn tighter as if Anya might tear her away from him. "It's what Meric would've done, and he never claimed to have his wits about him."

The silence endured until Anya let out a sigh, presumably tired of arguing.

"We have to get him out," her voice was soft, gentle as if she were speaking about a child.

"We will. We just…" he paused as if remembering an unpleasant memory. "I *can't* leave her behind."

Evelyn felt herself lifting, floating on the air as they walked. She couldn't make out the rest of the conversation as they exited the alley. Her eyes remained closed and from behind them, she sensed the darkness of the alley transform to the human starlight that she knew to be the torches from above. She gave into a sleep so deep, she forgot the faces of the people she lost. All she knew was a silent slumber that could keep the dead in their graves and the living remedied of their cries.

CHAPTER 28

THE WHOLE OF THE WORLD

When Evelyn woke, she rubbed her eyes, wondering how late she'd slept in. The light from her window was bright with sun, but unusually warm. Why was it so warm? She tried to sit up, but her head ached with too much sleep.

"Not so fast. It's alright, you're safe." The voice was deep and kind. She knew that voice. Her eyes went in and out of focus as she lifted her head, feeling a hand on her shoulder helping her upright.

"Soup?" It had been years since she'd called him that.

The shifting shape in front of her changed and bent until all colors stood still and formed a cohesive line of sight. Sou sat next to her on the bed, his cheek an ugly painting of purple and yellow. There was a tear on the collar of his tunic, the fabric stretched to expose part of his shoulder. A long, raised scar stretched across his skin, disappearing beneath the rest of his clothing. It had the look of an old battle wound and she wondered how he had gotten it.

"It's a fine meal to be," he said, smiling. There was something different about him. His headband was gone.

Evelyn shook her head and suddenly it all returned. The fire and screaming, Birdie dying in her arms. Sou's confession of his true self, the betrayal and hurt. She remembered the brothel and Due, Kiev and the gelatinous way his brain patterned the alley. She recalled being carried. Anya and Grae. Meric. Her hand flew to her chest, gripping only fabric.

"Sou, I lost it. They took it," she said, placing her hand over her forehead, feeling the perspiration gather on her scalp.

"I know, lass. I was on my way back when I saw the thieves placing you on the steps of the inn," he grazed his thumb over a bruised cheek. "Two against one was not ideal, but I'd fought against worse odds. The man was easily subdued." He fingered his torn shirt. "This was the extent of his damage, but the woman with him managed to remind me of my age. They fled and I carried you inside. When I couldn't wake you, I searched you. Oretem's scale was gone along with your daggers." He inclined his head, concerned.

Evelyn threw the covers off and stumbled away from the bed. She was still wearing her dirtied gown, the sash swaying in the breeze from the open window.

"I said not so fast. Find your feet before you run." He gripped her arm to keep her from falling.

"How long have I been asleep?" she said, watching the sky turn orange from the setting sun. It was nighttime when the attack happened, surely, she hadn't slept the whole day.

"We're only an hour from the moon's shift. You've been in bed all day. What happened? I searched you for wounds, but..." he paused, weighing his words. "You're perfect. Not a scratch on you. Your wrist is no longer enflamed, even your palms are as they once were."

Evelyn took in a shuddering breath and found her balance, disengaging herself from Sou's grip. She couldn't believe how thoughtless she'd been. She knew nothing of the world, nothing of Reva. Why had she thought she could find a single man in a city of thousands all by herself? She could've died — would've if Grae and Anya hadn't found her.

She looked back at Sou who was waiting for an explanation. She could lie, but where would that get her? So, she told him. She lightened the brutality of her beating, and the fear she'd suffered. There wasn't any need for him to know the extent of how close she'd come to death. She left out the portions concerning Meric. After telling Sou of the desperation and malnourishment of Anya and Grae, to confess that they sought a way to free their friend from whatever prison he currently sat in was one too many variables that threatened her safety. So Evelyn resigned to keep the knowledge close on hand if she had any hope of finding Meric. When she finished, he gripped her shoulders, his fingers digging tunnels into her flesh.

"Does the Reticent know? Did Oretem feel you?" she shook her head.

"No. I don't believe so. I felt him but he was deep in sleep. Fortune—in her strange humor—seems to smile upon me at odd times."

"Fortune cannot smile, and she certainly has no sense of humor. Otherwise, I would've courted her long ago for some Depths-damned peace and quiet."

He released her with a sigh, rubbing a finger across his chin with relief. Sou stared at her for a moment, contemplating what she'd said.

"I never should've let you go alone," he said, his voice fraught with blame. She sat back on the bed, lowering her head to her hands.

"It would've happened either way. If you forbade me to leave, I would've sowed the same path. It's my fault, I shouldn't have made such a scene at the brothel." She hesitated before she spoke again. "You warned me."

He'd been right. She hated that he was right. She expected a low blowing jest to her pride, but she only heard regret as Sou spoke again. "Aye, but you were defending yourself. An animal shows that kind of response. It's not the issue that you went out, it's that I should've been there."

Next to her, Sou's fingers twisted into fists. He wouldn't look at her and she hadn't the words to comfort him. After a few moments of silence, Sou scratched the tip of his nose and faced her, his eyes blazing with questions. "Those two that found you. Were they wearing silver earrings?"

Evelyn remembered the glint of metal swaying on their ears. She nodded, and Sou lined his lips with a frustrated frown.

"What does that mean?" she said, brow furrowed.

"They were Venandi. I thought I saw something shining in the depths of their hoods. I should have—" he stopped speaking when Evelyn lifted a hand to silence him.

"Enough. What's done is done. I was a fool for thinking I could venture into a city I knew nothing about, and you were neglectful in watching over me. I'm alive and what matters most is that we get Oretem's scale back." It wasn't until after the words were out of her mouth that she realized she'd spoken with less tact than she meant to.

Sou stared at her for a moment, then nodded his agreement.

"What's done is done," he repeated, granting her a sympathetic glance. "This city is large, lass. I think you might've seen the last of those two. They likely sold the scale to a jeweler already if they are in great need of coin."

Evelyn had thought that, but the reality of being separated from the scale was akin to sawing her own arm off. She needed to find it. There was a pull within her chest that gravitated outside the inn, as if she could sense the scale's presence. She thought that if she followed it, she might be able to find the scale again. She wasn't sure if there was any value in it, seeing as she couldn't conjure up a breeze that would knock a glass over.

She remembered the swell of power she was able to grasp last night. The dam within her breaking and washing over her with everything that told her she was Viden. The scale was the key to her power. She reached inside herself and found that trickle, the little sliver of Iona, beckoning her to take what was hers. It was torture to be half of who she truly was and if she remained separated from the scale, she feared that she'd become even less so.

She thought of Kiev and the feel of his fist against her cheek. Evelyn grimaced at the memory and raised her hand to her face, rubbing at the phantom pain. That dark alley summoned her with the faint drip of blood from Kiev's shattered skull to the floor beneath him. No matter how much she was justified in claiming his life, she still regretted her part in it. As if she's only woken up moments before committing the deed, her heart quickened, and her breath stopped in her throat.

"I killed him," she whispered.

Sou placed gentle fingers on her chin, lifting her face so she had to look into his eyes.

"You did what you had to do. Killing is nothing like the songs of battle sung around the fire amongst friends. You'll find no comfort in dwelling upon questioning your motives or that of the dead ones. All you can do is keep moving forward with the hope that there was no other choice."

His words were forceful in their vehemence, spoken as if from experience, but she detected the hint of compassion that was inherit in every piece of advice Sou gave. She gave him a quick nod, and he released her chin, placing a strand of her hair behind her ear.

"I hope you had more luck than I last night. Were you successful in hiring Venandi?"

Sou rolled his eyes and leaned over his knees with his head in his hands. He rubbed his forehead with a groan before sitting upright again.

"I'd forgotten how feared Vagu are in this city. Living all these years as Sou the ferryman has left me... unpracticed in dealing with such hatred. I hadn't expected it to have disappeared, but I had hoped people might've outgrown fearing what they do not understand. After how I lived among them all those years ago, I suppose I cannot fault them. I fear we may have to take our chances ourselves."

"Perhaps not," Evelyn said, determined to stay in the city as long as she could.

Sou looked at her with a skeptical frown. She could see that he knew what she was going to propose.

"No. No, we are not doing that. If what you saw and overheard is as dire as you claim, then they are near death as it is. How would they be able to prevent your demise if they cannot prevent their own? Never mind escort us across Iona. They might've saved you, lass, but only because there was a profit in it for them."

Evelyn stood again, but this time she held her ground. Her feet became weights that refused to move until he at least considered her idea. "Everything that everyone does in this Depths-damned city is for a profit. The woman wanted to leave me, but her partner wouldn't allow it. They had their prize and he helped me anyway. If we find them, then whether they sold Oretem's scale or not, they are still our best chance at obtaining it. How am I to prevent what happened from happening again without it?" She hadn't meant to shout, but the question struck between them like a roaring avalanche.

"Is that what you think you have to do?" Sou said, leaning forward, pity heavy in his eyes.

She turned away; she didn't want to see that. She wasn't deserving of pity.

"Oretem is mad, Sou. Completely mad. It's only a matter of time before he'll leave those mountains, those beautiful mountains..." Evelyn paused, breath catching. "And do what he did there somewhere else. Somewhere with families. People who have daughters and sons, friends, and lovers. I can't let that happen. I won't. I need that scale. We must find a way to stop him."

Her body was still with conviction. She was surprised by how liberating the confession felt, as if she'd broken a vow of silence she'd kept for years. She breathed easier even if she was still weighed down by the memory of it. Sou sat in silence, contemplating his response. She thought he was going to argue, but he cast his eyes downward with a sharp nod, conceding, but not necessarily agreeing.

"Very well. How do you suppose we start?" he said, lacing his fingers together.

She could see that he was still doubtful, but was relieved that he was giving her a chance anyway.

"Simply. Let's walk."

EVELYN WAS CERTAIN THAT SHE HAD NO SUPERNATURAL connection to the location of Oretem's scale. She and Sou had been wandering around the city for hours with nothing but her intuition. Darkness had fallen again and the floating candles that hung overhead mocked her as she peered into the alleyways.

"I had hoped that in light of last night's unfortunate dilemma you'd show more caution when it came to these dark corridors," Sou said, his tone reproachful.

"I am." She patted the long dagger at her hip that Sou lent her. "I'll carry it in my hand now."

She took out the blade with a soft metallic song. The handle was curved against her palm like her throwing daggers, but it was heavier than what she was used to. She twisted it in the air finding its balance, so it rested with a comfortable grip in her hand.

"Hmm," he murmured, staring into the darkness. "These alleyways are connected. They might lead us deeper into the city. They're more of a road for the less... amiable of people, but you already knew that."

"It wasn't the *less amiable* that attacked me. We've avoided them this far and have come up with nothing. We must at least try," she said, stepping further from the lights of the main road.

"Breaths and Depths lass, your gran would be disappointed. I can imagine her knocking both our heads together before stating we'd half the brain of a stone for not venturing in sooner," he said with a chuckle.

Evelyn didn't turn to face him, but she couldn't help to crack a half smile. Together they ventured into the swirling mist of black and blood-stained cobblestones.

Even with the dagger at her side Evelyn was glad Sou was with her. The people they'd passed by were certainly not people she'd have liked to face alone. They wore grins of missing teeth, huddling around makeshift fires of broken wood and old shoes. She wondered how any of them could be cold in this heat. One of the corridors ended with a flat wall, barring them from continuing. When they turned around, they'd been greeted by a wandering street walker, brandishing a thin blade and raving about skies that were falling and shadows that turned back time. She saw a woman huddled in a corner nursing a small babe in a tattered blanket, only to discover upon closer inspection that it was a muddied doll at her breast.

The sights filled her with more sadness than fear. These people were lost in their own minds, tormented by what life had brought down upon them. It was a side of Reva that was indeed lost to the glamour that was presented outside of these forgotten halls.

They'd come across another opening that led to a main road. Sou stepped aside to allow Evelyn to escape the darkness and enter the candlelight, casting shadows across the massive mansions lining the even cobblestones.

She glanced back at the famished faces and pitched corners of crouched cripples, her eyes lingering on the woman who smiled at the doll against her chest.

"There's nothing to be done, lass." Sou said, his voice sorrowful, but firm.

"I know. I just..." she couldn't find the words.

What could she possibly have said that would make a broken mother see the face of a child's toy? Would it be kinder to allow her to continue living in the fantasy the doll provided her? There was no solution that left the mother healed.

"They're beyond the help of one person, no matter how much your heart may ache."

Evelyn glanced at Sou. He returned a sad smile and patted her shoulder. She turned the dagger in her hand, sheathing it and stepped out of the alleyway. She wasn't sure where the back streets had led them, but they were definitely not where they were before.

Large homes shinned in the darkness, their smooth-stoned walls giving off their own light. Windows glowed with the warm flicker of hearth-filled fires. All of them had gates guarded by men in different kinds of uniform. Some had the obvious tailoring of wealthier fabrics, while others dimmed in comparison, but were still finer than anything Evelyn had seen closer to the inn.

The streets were silent and empty of people. It was a drastic change from what she'd experienced last night. Her very breath seemed too loud for these streets. She wondered who lived in these grand homes. Standing among them made her think of the little house she and Tansey shared. It was so small in comparison, the entire home being the size of a single room in one of these massive mansions. As she and Sou continued, the guards watched their movements. Her long cloak masked the trousers she wore, and the night shadowed her boots. She refused to wear another dress after last night. Evelyn gripped Sou's arm as she had seen ladies do while walking.

Sou accepted her touch, nodding at the guards they passed. Their suspicious eyes softened as they inclined their heads with an appreciative look. They were probably used to being ignored and although Sou was probably only conveying simple human kindness, he made it possible for them to walk about without questionable glances. There was but one home that hadn't any guards outside.

The building was massive. Its marble walls were decorated with vines and golden loops of varying designs. The wall that enclosed the mansion hid whatever activity was held within. Evelyn could hear the murmur of voices, but they were too muddled to make anything out.

Once they appeared at the entrance, she saw through the gated iron bars a path that led to the far-off looming doorway. Its marbled front adorned in a large oval that looped in what she could only describe as a spider web of circles. It was a beautiful engraving that reflected the moon in dazzling bright shadows, dancing on the gardened landscape.

Lining the pathway of flowers and bushes were men in familiar violet vests, gathered in greater numbers than their neighbors. Some stood at attention on the path while others walked in pairs, marching the grounds with watchful eyes. The embellishment of their designed clothes surpassed anything she'd seen thus far, except one. She remembered Kiev and how ornate his vest had been. She pulled Sou to a stop and stared at the uniforms. There was no mistaking the fine fabric and deep coloring.

"We cannot stay here. This is no place for Venandi and frankly neither for us. I cannot believe I am saying this, but we should return to the alleys." Sou's voice was a quiet whisper.

"This is where we'll find them," she said, not taking her eyes off the company of guards. A group closest to the gate looked up at her voice, the rest knocking their heads in curiosity.

Sou huffed a disbelieving chuckle. "In the prisons, perhaps, but not just idly walking around as you or I."

"That man I—" she cut herself off as the red of Kiev's blood flashed across her vision. She pulled Sou's arm, eyes on the guards. "He wore the same uniform. Anya and Grae called him by name. The woman was following him."

"He wore *that* uniform? That—" Evelyn shushed him before his tone echoed through the whole street. His brows pinched into his forehead, green gaze frantically searching their whereabouts as if he were frightened of an attack. She wasn't sure why he was suddenly so fearful.

What did it matter if Kiev were part of this particular group of guards? There were so many of them that it was likely they hadn't noticed his absence. In any case, he died far from here and it had only been a day. What could've happened in a single day?

"Celosia's Depth's, lass. I wish you told me before we came here," he said, looking back at the neighboring guards with a more wariness.

Evelyn hadn't told Sou about how the Venandi were searching for Meric. She knew he'd never have agreed in her pursuit for a man neither of them knew, but she had to keep him in the dark a while longer. At least until they found the pair, then she could move forward with what she had in mind. As far as Sou was concerned, they were going to find Oretem's scale, perhaps hire the two Venandi, but he knew nothing about what else she was shaping.

"I hadn't known who he was until I saw the uniforms," she said, squeezing his arm. Sou shook his head, trying to lead her away, but she stood firm.

"We must go, lass. We must go *now*." His voice shook with urgency.

A group of guards thumped their hands across their chests, the echo eerily similar to the sound of Kiev backhanding Evelyn as she fought helplessly for her life. She held onto Sou tighter, and he flinched. She loosened her grip, suddenly aware that she hadn't died in that alley. Sou's eyes lingered on her hand, then back at her and a heartbreaking realization grew across his features.

"It wasn't just a rough scuffle, was it? He nearly killed you," Sou's tone was low and filled with anger. She'd rarely seen the emotion within him, and he was angry with her. It was a sight she was uncomfortable with, and she glanced away unable to meet his eye. It wasn't long ago that she was the one to throw such indignation at him. "How did you—"

"This is exactly where we need to be," she said, cutting him off.

She couldn't leave, not when they were closer than they'd ever been. Meric was on the other side of those gates. Grae and Anya would be nearby. It was at that moment she understood Sou's stance on her compulsion to find Meric. She was set on a course to find Venandi who argued about leaving her to die the night before, retrieve Oretem's stolen scale without knowing whether the pair had sold it or not, break into a heavily guarded affluential home and rescue a man she'd never met. It was insanity and Sou didn't even know most of it. She was about to suggest for them to continue walking around the outside of the property, looking for the Venandi pair in the dark corners of the adjacent alleys, when a deep forceful voice echoed behind her.

"Lady, the hour is late, and the moon is full. One should not be out alone, even in these heavily patrolled streets."

Evelyn turned to find herself facing a tall man whose unyielding features stared at her through the bars. His uniform hugged his form as if it were specially made to accommodate the bulk of his arms and legs. His dark eyes gave off no light in the darkness and his mouth was turned down not in anger, but duty. He gripped a golden spear in his hand that glowed with the same brilliance as the home behind him. She gave what she thought was a convincing smile and pulled Sou closer to her side.

"I am not alone, sir. I was just enjoying the warmth of the air tonight," she said, her voice leveled even if she felt her heart pounding in her chest. His dark eyes relented somewhat into a confused expression. He withdrew from his structured stance, leaning slightly on the spear.

"Have you not heard?" he said with genuine shock.

Evelyn held in a breath and smiled again, hoping that her bright teeth would distract that she hadn't the faintest clue what he was talking about. Sou cleared his throat and eyed her with an amused glance.

"Of course, officer. That is why I insisted upon accompanying her. She is not one to be told no," the ferryman patted the dagger on his belt.

"Then allow me. A man who can murder City Lord Fallon's head of security is not one to be dismissed as a common street walker. As someone who knew the man personally, I can say that even a Vagu," the guard peered at Sou with an unapologetic look of disgust. "Would've had a difficult time getting the better of him. I must insist that you return home until the culprit is in irons."

Evelyn felt her stomach knot and twist as the words settled around her. She knew the brute was skilled, but *head guard*? She killed a man of reputation and her confidence dimmed in light of that. If she couldn't find the Venandi pair they might turn her in for the return of their friend, and here she was speaking with the very people looking for her.

"Have you any idea as to how long I should be confined to my home?" she said, feigning annoyance.

The guards stood straighter, gripping the spear in his hand tighter. He pulled his vest down and smoothed it out over his chest. Evelyn thought it was similar to an animal showing superiority to a rival.

"Not long, Lady," he said with a fixed glare. "I am sure the reward money is incentive enough for those who saw something to come forward. It's a big city, but City Lord Fallon's pockets are... monolithic. Now, please go home."

Evelyn inclined her head and gestured for Sou to press forward. Once they were out of sight of the guards within Fallon's estate, she led him to a corner at the edge of an alley. It was shadowed from the rest of the men who stood watch. Sou tried to continue onward into the dark hall, but Evelyn remained with her back against the wall.

"Depths drown us all, Evelyn!" he said through his teeth. There was her name again; she'd grown tired of hearing it on his lips. "You killed a man in the service of Fallon. Breaths and Depths preserve us. I know you did not mean to, but that makes our situation much more complicated. Damn the Venandi and damn the scale, I must get you out of the city. Tonight." He ran a hand across his stubbled chin and rubbed his eyes.

"I am not leaving," she said, feeling the cold at her back. She soaked in the chill of the stones with a small sigh, letting it give her courage.

"Aye, you are. Even if I must bind your limbs and drag you out." Sou shook his finger at her, slanted eyebrows animated with fiery indignation. She watched a trail of blue wind swirled around his hands, lifting strands of his hair with a small breeze.

You'll die, and I'll have failed.

She heard his thoughts as clearly as though he had spoken the words himself. What affection his voice lacked was abundant in the thought he let slip. She didn't think he meant it, but the reality of her in such immediate danger was enough for him to forget to shield himself. Just as soon as it had come, he was walled from her again.

She lifted her hands and gripped either side of his face. The crow's feet at the corners of his eyes smoothed at her touch. He lifted a hand to hers and rubbed the back of her hand with his thumb. She was still so angry. She wondered if the fire of her wrath would ever dissipate, but the urgency to have someone near her, close to her was greater. Sou and she shared a history, a bond she should've had with her own father. It was broken, but she clung to the scraps, hoping that they could reforge whatever was left.

"Everyone dies, Sou. You can't prevent it. Help me."

"Don't you want to see your father? Meet your sister?" He pulled her hands away and they fell at her sides. "You say I can't prevent death, but neither can you. This notion you have that every life in Iona is in danger, it's too much. You're one person, Evelyn. Oretem has been in the mountains for decades and he'll stay for decades more. There are people in Birny who can help in trying to find out what went wrong, but to fix it? I hadn't the heart to tell you before, but no. I know of no one who can mend the bond. I am taking you to your family so that you may live, lass. *Live*. The longer we stay here the more likely that Reticent will find you and now even that isn't the most pressing concern. Think of your mother, think of what she would've wanted for you."

Evelyn stood quiet for a moment, recalling everything she'd done in her life and who she'd done it for. There was never a time she had simply *been*. She tore her eyes from Sou, anger pumping through her heart, scouring every memory she had. She only had what she'd lost and the directionless mad fury of a dragon, nothing more.

"I think of her every day. She is in my every thought. Will I never be rid of her?" Evelyn's voice was a chasm of truth, deep and unwelcoming. When would she be only Evelyn and cast from the shadow her mother's death left behind? Sou took a step back, shock written in his tired eyes.

"I have no way of knowing what she would've wanted. I

never knew her. You didn't feel what I felt. You didn't share a mind with Oretem as he drank the blood of our people." She licked her lips, remembering the taste of Alen, the feel of his flesh crushing against her teeth. "I can still taste their blood. I can still smell their bodies burning. I can still feel the beat of his wings at my back." She felt the trickle of her power flow easier into her. A small crack in the dam fractured then mended, over and over until she closed her eyes with a blinding pain in her head. She thought she had imagined the pull of direction throughout the night, considering it to be nothing more than her stubbornness. Now, as she recalled her merging with Oretem, that small pull became unbearable, splitting her towards whatever was dragging her apart. It was as if half of her resided in some long-distance land and her other half was trapped in trying to return to it.

She looked up, pushing Sou away and ignoring his concerned expression. His green eyes troubled with what he saw was happening to her.

"Are you well?" he reached for her, but she'd already left his breadth.

She moved where her body was pulling her—no, not her body. It was deeper than that. It wasn't her organs and veins straining against the confines of her mortal flesh. It was the essence of her being, ripping in a way that felt like her mind might split, physically implode. The pain took her in the direction of an alley across from Fallon's mansion. She knew without understanding that a part of her was there—in the darkness it called to her. A piece of her soul she hadn't known was missing.

"I can feel you," she whispered, speaking to Oretem. She knew he couldn't hear her unless she were touching the dragon's scale, but it felt like reassuring an old friend.

"Lass, what are you doing? I know you don't—"

She ran before he could finish his sentence. She thought again of Oretem and the feel of his claws with the wind at his back. The pain redoubled and she nearly fell at the magnitude of it. She grunted, fighting through the sensation, wondering how long she could maintain her sanity. The closer she came to the alley the less her pain erupted like a boiling geyser, until it nearly vanished when she pressed herself against the wall.

There in the blackened mist, wrapped in a dark cloak, was a figure crouched in the darkness, watching the City Lord's mansion, a familiar bladed bow at their back. Evelyn glanced behind her and saw Sou rushing towards her, his feet growing louder with every step. She knew in a few moments the figure across from her would hear him and run into the labyrinth of the alleyways. She'd lose them and her single chance at survival. She unsheathed her dagger and revealed herself from the edge of the wall.

Anya stood with a startled gasp and turned, yellow eyes ravenous. Evelyn's mouth opened as she took in the sight of the skeletal woman before her. Her eyes were even more sunken than the previous night and below her left cheek, a black bruise swelled down her jaw. The woman was draped in a thick cloak, but Evelyn could see her shivering in the warm air. She raised her dagger with open palms to show she had no intention of harming her. Anya's vacant stare turned icy, and she took a few steps back into the alley. She seemed unsettled that Evelyn had snuck up on her.

"I won't hurt you. I've come to help," Evelyn said as Sou caught up with her, breath heavy at her side.

He followed her gaze to the haggard woman and sighed as though he knew that this would end badly. "Hello again. Where's your friend?" he said, hands folded against his chest with no more worry than he would have when gardening.

"I don't see him," Evelyn said, looking down the alley and seeing only black mist.

"He has a name, incomer." The woman's voice was tired.

"I remember. It's Grae, yes? And you're Anya." She stepped closer. "You saved me, thank you. Let me return the favor, you're hurt. We can feed you and Grae too."

Anya, with a wearied hand, reached over her shoulder and unsheathed the blade at the top of the bow. The blade quivered in her grasp as she pointed it at both Sou and Evelyn.

"That was Grae. I'd have left you, but perhaps I was too quick to judge. I can be fickle," she cocked her head like a wolf deciding whether or not to attack. Evelyn gripped her dagger tighter. "I wonder what Fallon will do with those pretty eyes once I turn you in. He's quite upset, so much that he might grant me more than silver."

Evelyn shook her head. This is what she had feared.

"I know what it feels like to be helpless when one that you love is in danger. We can help you." Evelyn ignored Sou's sharp exhale. Anya chuckled, but there was no amusement in the act.

"Help? You, a Lady, wants to help?" She lifted the blade higher with the tip pointed down. "I wouldn't ask for the molded bread you discarded."

"We've a job for you. From what Evelyn has told me you are in need of silver. We can pay you for services rendered," Sou said with a hint of doubt in his voice. Anya didn't seem capable of protecting herself let alone them.

"Why would I accept your offer when the answer to everything I need is at the tip of my blade?" Anya stepped forward, prowling.

"Because I can get Meric out," Evelyn said, the insanity of her plan being put into reality. Sou looked at her with surprised and disapproving eyes. She'd have to answer for that later, but at the moment she couldn't falter.

Anya stopped moving and lowered her blade with the slightest twitch. She narrowed her bright eyes, wind tousling her straight, black hair across an emaciated face. Her hood bent to the breeze, cloak shifting above the hesitation her body betrayed in her.

"How do you know his name?" Her voice was soft and pleading.

"I was conscious when you took me from the alley. I heard many things, but do not mistake this as a charitable act. If you and Grae enter our services, only then will I agree to help you rescue Meric."

Sou took a step closer to Evelyn, aged features taut with

irritation and worry. It was an expression she was growing used to, a parental glare that spoke of disappointment.

"Lass, this is madness. A voice in the wind told you to find this man, but there's nothing to suggest he'd know anything about what happened in Verbena. Going down this road will only lead to violence. What do you hope to accomplish in doing this?"

She looked into his eyes, trying to mask her own doubt, deciding it was useless. She embraced the doubt, let the fear set in, then trapped it. The thing writhed and screamed inside her, and she smothered it, squeezing until it submitted. Fear wasn't a thing meant for dying, but she could train it, break it to do her bidding.

"I haven't a clue, Sou." She smiled, mirthlessly. "What would've happened if Monia ignored the voice she heard? You claim I am but one person—so was she. I need you to believe in me. I can't do this alone, but I will if I must." Her voice broke at the end, but only slightly. She kept one eye on Anya who craned her neck to listen, but she knew the woman wouldn't understand even if she heard anything.

"You are not alone. It just seems like no matter where we go, I end up having to fight in the dark. I can't see what may lay in wait," Sou said with a shiver. The wind blew light around his body, shimmering in the darkness as if he were its master.

"Neither can I, at least not in the way I'm supposed to. This isn't just about Meric. Whether she knows it or not, she needs our help. Help me help her. They need to get out of the city just as much we do."

Sou nodded and stepped to the side of Anya, watching her with cautious eyes.

"My offer stands. Enter our services and I'll make sure Meric will be rescued." Evelyn felt her tone rise in impatience.

Anya sniffed and took another step forward her blade still raised. "You need to get out of the city."

"Yes, we need to travel to Birny, but obviously in considering recent events we need protection on the road. As you said, I've pretty eyes that need to stay in my head."

The woman chuckled again, but this time there was a hint of humor to it. Her eyes relaxed into a glance that looked to be admiring Evelyn's tenacity. She hadn't thought she was being brash, but Evelyn thought if the Venandi saw her that way then it benefited her.

"I don't think I've ever met a Lady so unladylike." Anya pointed the tip of her knife at the bruise on her jaw. "I tried selling your jewel. The owner beat me once he inspected the gem. He accused me of trying to pawn a fake. Said there was no stone in existence as pure as the one I took from you. The lot of you are liars and I'll die upturned before striking a deal with you." Her voice was venomous and full of hatred.

Evelyn's shoulders fell in dismay. She needed this plan to work. Where was her partner? He might listen to her.

"Anya, please I only—" the woman cut her off with a low, dark hiss.

"I don't know how you killed Kiev. The Breaths know he deserved it, but whatever you did, it wasn't natural. And this —" She pulled out the necklace, Oretem's red scale gleaming in the misty shadows. "This is worthless."

She threw the necklace at Evelyn who, without thinking, caught it in her hand. She gasped as the scale rippled with pulsing light. It grew hot in her hand as she felt Oretem's claws crunch the stone beneath his feet. His eye bore into the face of the black-haired human who twitched against the wall. The man's eyes rolled to the back of his head as the memories he commanded Oretem to share with him took over his mind.

Such torment he experienced through those memories. It was almost enough to make the dragon pity the Reticent, but then again, pity was a human emotion. He thought he could feel... he thought... he *thought*!

Oretem raised his massive head from the ground and shook it. He could feel her, she was in Reva. Pain. Such *pain*. He remembered his havoc and the lives he took. Remorse flowed through his brief clarity. He had tried to protect her, built a wall in between their souls to save her. But she had broken through it, shattered it with her anguish. The grief and sorrow buried inside such a small creature as she was enough to fill the vast memories he experienced through his thousands of lives. She was trying to find someone, someone the Reticent was looking for.

No! He couldn't know, he wasn't in control. Maun would make him confess, command him to betray his oaths. He'd already made him do so much. His mind was muddled and his thoughts were scattered. An old and mighty dragon indeed, to succumb to Celosia's Glare.

WISP. STOP ME. YOU MUST STOP ME.

His mind fractured like glass beneath a pool of water, distorting his vision and skewering his lucidity. The world was as red as the embers overhead. The darkness that was his cave deserved to be free, to spread and collect ash.

He felt his wings disappear, his claws gripping a blade with small fingers, such fragile and rounded nails.

How? How do I help you? His bondsmate begged. Such compassion. He'd forgotten what that felt like.

KILL ME.

Evelyn's back arched in pain as Oretem's neck stretched out in a great roar. She clawed the street, feeling the ground tremble at his might. His agony was as potent as the hot sting of boiling water. There was another presence, another consciousness. It bore down upon her like a cloud of black smoke, smothering her with deep apathy. It echoed with emptiness so vast she was filled with it.

I see you... it whispered with red eyes that shone in darkness.

She recognized those eyes, though they'd been blue before. She screamed and fell backwards where the void swallowed her.

CHAPTER 29

A BARGAIN STRUCK

The high-pitched ring of metal on metal reverberated through the alley, its echo confined to the hall as though the black mist absorbed all sound. Evelyn pushed herself off the ground with a hand to her head, rubbing the base of her aching temple. Oretem's scale laid beside her. She bent and gripped the leather straps, placing the necklace into her cloak pouch.

Looking up, she saw Sou and Anya tangled in swift combat, their blades meeting in brilliant white sparks. The Venandi woman seemed far too weak to put up any resistance, but if her will to survive were a weapon it would have killed them all. Anya parried around Sou with the subtlety of a cornered beast. She made no attempt to hide her motions or strikes, knowing she wasn't strong enough to evade the blows Sou delivered. Had Sou wished to he could've killed the woman ten times over, but his movements suggested he only wanted to incapacitate her.

Evelyn stood and out of the corner of her eye she detected more movement. A darkened figure was darting through the swirling fog of the alley, making its way to Sou's turned back. She unsheathed her dagger and leaped in front of the oncoming stranger. Their blades met with a heavy clang. She almost lost her stance from the power behind the blow.

Beneath his deep hood, Grae's clear blue eyes stared into her own with a stunned, opened mouth. He quickly closed it and pushed against her blade with a grunt. Evelyn was thrown back and knocked into Sou, who stumbled from the contact.

Anya took that distraction and lifted her curved blade, its black hilt like glistening oil. Evelyn leaned backwards over Sou and blocked the blade from entering his chest. The old man let out a heavy breath before turning towards Grae's oncoming assault, his rapier thin and needle sharp.

"Oh aye," Sou said, meeting the Venandi's sword with a wide smile. "This is a fine negotiation."

Evelyn chuckled with the familiar rush of adrenaline she'd felt when sparring with Tansey, only this time it was real. Evelyn realized they had moved deeper into the alley, the hall becoming narrower and darker. She struck high at Anya, who blocked her blade, but left her midsection exposed just as had Evelyn intended. She drove her fist into the woman's stomach and she collapse at the sudden loss of breath.

Evelyn heard Sou's blade continuing to sing its song against Grae's. She was tempted to look behind her, but Tansey's voice echoed in her mind. *You've only two eyes and to keep both you must always restrain them from distraction when fighting.*

Anya recovered and thrust her blade across the air like a net she was casting over a river. Evelyn jumped back, barely missing the sharp edge of each thrust. On the final stab, she pushed her dagger through the curved point of the blade, catching its hooked tip. Anya growled and tried to disentangle the blade, but Evelyn lifted her arm and twisted so that she was behind the Venandi with her arm and blade pinned across the woman's chest.

Anya grunted and lifted her chin up as the edge of both blades caressed the skin of her neck, hood falling as she tried to throw head back to break Evelyn's nose. She felt the edges of the blades digging into the Venandi's skin with each thrust.

"Stop! You'll kill yourself," she said, trying to hold the woman still. Anya managed one last attempt to break free, then moaned and collapsed into Evelyn, her legs falling from beneath her.

Evelyn turned around, holding Anya as she lowered herself to the ground, the Venandi limp in her arms. Grae had Sou's blade pinned against his, sneering at the ferryman. Under his eye was a colored bruise, freshly made. Evelyn thought it was from when Sou had attacked them, thinking they meant her harm last night. Sou's shoulders fell with a sigh as if he were growing tired of a game he'd already mastered. He took in a breath and blue streaks of Iona's Breath escaped his mouth, flowing like daggers into Grae's eyes. The Venandi cried out and dropped his blade as if he'd received an eyeful of sand. Sou lifted his elbow and rammed it into the man's face. Grae groaned and backed into the wall, holding his jaw.

Sou held the ragged man's own rapier at his throat, the blade reflecting the red spots in his glaring blue eyes. Blood flowed from the corner of his mouth; his teeth stained in crimson, sallow skin gaunt from hunger and sleeplessness. Evelyn marveled at how well the two were able to fight given their physical conditions.

She looked down at Anya, who was conscious, but with little strength to lift her own head. She glared at Evelyn, her yellow eyes defiant and with no fear, as though she had been waiting years to die. The sight filled Evelyn with a sense of profound sadness. She was relieved to see that the cut on the woman's neck was superficial. She dropped the tangled weapons and wiped the blood that dripped across Anya's collarbone, inspecting the wound. It would heal with no indication it was ever there within a few days.

Grae's panicked eyes darted from the blood, then back to Evelyn as he wiped his mouth.

"Anya, are you alright? I've been looking for you," he said, his voice deep with concern.

"I'm fine. I've been avoiding you," she replied, still glaring at Evelyn. "What kind of Lady wields a blade?"

"The kind that has needed it in the past," she said, choosing to continue hiding her identity. If this was their response to experiencing the little they'd seen of her true nature, she could only imagine what reaction they'd have to the truth.

"Do you not remember? Anya and I found you in the alley last night. We brought you back to the inn," he spared a passing glance at Sou. "Let her go. A life for a life." He stepped forward, allowing the rapier Sou held at his throat to pierce the skin, blood welling beneath the blade.

"I've no intention of harming either of you. As I told Anya, I want to help," she said, eyeing the Venandi in her arms. Anya tried to wiggle out of her grasp, but her attempts were little more than an annoyance. Strapped to her back, Anya reached for the second blade at the end of the bow, but Evelyn gripped her wrist and held it. Anya growled her discontent.

"Your help comes with conditions. I don't accept them. I don't believe you," the woman snarled, then spat in her face.

Evelyn flinched, but didn't retaliate. She wiped the spittle from her cheek and looked at Grae whose eyes rolled with a frustrated gleam as if this wasn't the first time Anya spat in someone's face.

"What are your terms?" he said, meeting Sou's gaze. The ferryman hadn't taken his eyes from the Venandi, observing him with the experience that, up until recently, Evelyn had no idea he possessed.

"Sou," she said, her voice stern. The old man murmured his acknowledgement and lowered the blade, still poised to defend.

Evelyn repeated the same deal she had told Anya, imploring Grae that she was genuine. There were a few times Anya interrupted with an insult, but she ignored the woman. Once she was finished Grae remained silent for a moment, thinking upon the terms.

"How much?" he said, his fingers tapping against his chin. Anya turned her head, gritting her teeth at her partner in disbelief.

"You cannot be considering—"

"Shut up, Anya!" the force in his tone matched the blazing

contempt in his exhausted eyes. "Had you not gone out on your own, we might've avoided this entire situation."

Evelyn felt a tinge of sympathy for Anya as the woman's bearing faltered slightly at her partner's harsh words. It was obvious the Venandi cared for one another; their searing exchanges were undertoned by fear and worry. Anya wasn't despondent for long, focusing her fury and resentment at Evelyn.

"Had you left this one in the street last night I need not have left. One of us needs to do what must be done. I took it upon myself to bear whatever burden that might be."

Evelyn matched Anya's hostile stare and looked back at Grae. He opened his mouth to reply another useless retort, but she'd had enough. This was going nowhere and there wasn't much time. She shoved Anya from her arms. The Venandi cried out as her head hit the stone floor, hand slowly reaching to rub the back of her skull. Evelyn stood and looked over Anya with her hands at her hips.

"Stand then if you've the strength to carry such a burden. Go on, show us how much stronger you are."

Grae huffed and flared his nostrils at her, but she ignored him. Sou glanced at Evelyn, brow arched in approval. Anya struggled to lift herself to her elbows, but she kept falling onto her back. Evelyn sighed and gripped the sides of Anya's cloak —not too gently—and lifted her so that she was sitting upright against the alley wall. She separated their blades and bent over her, sheathing the weapon back into the bow and her own at her belt. She stared into those tired yellow eyes, defiant yet close to shattering. The woman was spent and still, she continued to look at Evelyn as if she were Celosia personified. She admired that, but if Grae's reactions were of any indication, it was also her greatest fault.

"What does it matter how Kiev was killed?" She turned to Grae. "Or how much we will pay you?" She faced Anya. Whether the woman's lips quivered in anger or fear she couldn't know. "You have the chance to save someone you love. Most might be willing to die upturned just to be gifted the choice you have right now. It's only when you've lost someone to the wind forever do you realize what you would be willing to do given this exact opportunity."

No tears rose to Evelyn's eyes. She was calm, but the ache in her heart was as sharp as the day she watched her village burn. If she could, she'd cleave herself bloody into the wind to bring back all those she had lost. Their faces flashed across her mind, and she made sure that Grae could see she meant what she said. He narrowed his eyes, uncertain he could believe her.

"Trust isn't a trait that comes easily to us." Grae folded his arms, rubbing the corner of his bruising jaw.

"Trust is a face that masquerades as a mask. It is alluring and seemingly too inconceivable to behold. You can never truly know whether the one who wears it is genuine until the facade and the face become one, and you realize it was never a mask to begin with. It takes time," Sou said, his tone cautious, but tolerant.

He lowered the sword and flipped it in the air so that the hilt was pointed towards Grae. The Venandi glanced between the rapier and Sou for a few heartbeats, then slowly wrapped his hand around the weapon, its small handguard covering his fingers. He held it a moment, then lowered the blade when it was clear Sou wouldn't attack him.

Grae glanced at his companion with an expression of preparedness. He reached into his cloak pocket.

"I have something that you might want," he said with a smirk that Evelyn found laughable. She knew exactly what he had and his admitting it felt like an agreement between them of sorts.

"I know, so please kindly return my daggers." She stepped forward, palm out.

Grae hesitated a moment as though surprised that she knew he had taken them. The blue-eyed Venandi sighed and shifted his hand into a different pocket, pulling out her daggers, their dark hilts curved and all accounted for. She felt the familiar metal against her fingers as he handed them to her.

She pocketed them in the front pouch of her cloak where

they were easily accessible. She inclined her head in thanks at him as he turned away, looking down the end of the alley, his true face covered by the mask Sou had spoken of. Just because they'd decided to not kill one another didn't mean they trusted each other.

"How do you propose we spring Meric from the clutches of our benevolent City Lord?" Grae said, his face twisting in disgust at the mention of Fallon.

Anya grunted her disagreement as she looked down the alley. Evelyn pointed at her and smiled; the woman wouldn't appreciate what she had in mind. "She will stay here." When Anya opened her mouth to protest Evelyn spoke over her. "She needs rest and food. Once we have Meric we'll come back for her."

Grae nodded his agreement, even if he showed a little conflict at the thought of leaving his partner behind.

"Grae, you can't—" Anya started before Grae kneeled beside her, hand on her shoulder.

"I'm doing what you want me to do. I'm bearing the burden of what needs to be done to get him out. You will only drag us further down. I'm sorry. I *will* come back for you." His words were kind, absent of all the resentment he'd bludgeoned her with before and fierce in his promise.

"Your Vagu will stay with her," Grae said, standing from his crouch. Evelyn raised her eyebrows, ready to bite the head off that particular snake. He was not in charge, and she was surprised by the anger that rose to boil at his dismissal of Sou. His tone when he'd said *your Vagu* was ripe with prejudice and Evelyn, despite her own complicated feelings on Sou's past, was quite put out with it.

"His name is Sou, and he will come with us. We won't be able to get Meric out without him." She met Grae's watchful stare until he broke the contact.

"What can a Vagu do that we cannot?" He looked at the ferryman with a skeptical expression, as though he'd personally experienced some sort of trickery at his hands.

Sou wasn't exaggerating when he told her that the Vagu

were hated in the city. She'd known they were disliked even in her small village. Tansey hadn't liked them, but the look in Grae's eyes was a deeply indoctrinated suspicion.

"I don't suppose you've ever heard of a diversion?" she said, turning her head to a meet Sou's relaxed expression.

He raised his slanted brows and pursed his lips like he'd tasted an especially sweet apple. She quirked a small smile at his quizzical demeanor, even after a brawl in the middle of a dark alley where he might've met a more permeant fate, the ferryman continued to remain lighthearted. As if Grae's prejudice were as inconvenient as the drizzle of a light rain.

"Oh, a little havoc here, a splash of unexplainable occurrences there, and you've a fine recipe for distractions."

He winked and Evelyn relayed her plan. It was simple, but simplicity was often the best option in dire situations. Grae questioned some, while Anya protested most of it, but in the end, Anya resigned to staying behind with a silent, begrudging animosity and Grae agreed with a few adjustments.

Sou conveyed his opinion through expressions that were a secret to no one among them. It was evident that he had no desire to remain in the company of these particular Venandi and least of all carry out the role he assumed in Evelyn's plan, though he hadn't said a word to undermine her. She was grateful for that, even if she felt that, given all he had kept from her, she was justified in what she withheld from him.

As they exited the alleyway she reached in-between the folds of her cloak, feeling the shape of Oretem's scale. Her relief at being reunited with it was overpowered by the memory of touching it. *Kill me*, Oretem had said. It was his madness speaking, devouring him from rational thought. There had to be another way. She hadn't lost the hope that she and Oretem could become one again. Even if she had no other choice, what force on Iona could kill a dragon? She didn't want to think about what that meant.

She hadn't exhausted all her options yet, despite what Sou told her. He hadn't been to Birny in twenty years, even longer from Edewor. A lot could change in that time. The Vagu must know how she might reclaim Iona's Breath. Why her bond with Oretem had fractured.

She'd find a way to save him, she had to. She remembered the Reticent—Maun, the red dragon had called him. Seeing him unconscious and seemingly dreaming left her with a rock in her stomach. Oretem wasn't afraid of this man, he was bound to him. How? What did Maun want from Meric? How had he discovered who she was? His voice echoed in her head with such dejected coldness, like all emotion were purged and nothing was left but the silence of pain.

For the first time she felt the level of danger she placed herself in. She understood why Sou was so adamant to leave the city. The man who slaughtered her people was someone who not only found enjoyment in the act of killing, but also the thrill of the hunt. He was coming for her now and her heart hammered in her chest, imagining the beautiful buildings burning, the street walkers screaming. Like her vision in Verbena, she had tipped the hourglass and just watched as the sand ran out.

Chapter 30

Resurfacing

As a child, Meric had ventured into the labyrinth of alleys that was home to the forgotten and mindless. He survived by stealing and begging, never talking to anyone and running from all those who approached him. He was feral when had Grae found him. He'd weathered starvation and mutilation from his fellow street walkers for eight years. He remembered the hunger and the loneliness; perhaps that was why his current lack of food hadn't bothered him as much as an average prisoner. He'd known what it was like to starve. After some failed speeches and unconvincing arguments Meric took a leap, something he'd never thought he was capable of. The years spent on the streets taught him that people were never who they appeared to be and to always keep what you knew close at hand.

Grae was everything Meric taught himself to stay away from. He had the look of those who shunned him, beat him, and starved him. He recalled the glimmer of fear in Grae's eyes when they first met. It was probably due to the fact that Meric threatened him with his rusted dagger for whatever coin laid within his fine pockets. But all the same, it felt more like Grae saw the ghost of another within Meric's frayed and wild appearance. He gave up his coin without hesitation and an uncertain wonder in his fair expression. Even as Meric threat-

ened his future friend with death, in the days after the robbery
he kept coming back, usually with food and clean clothes. In
time, they were able to hold a conversation that hadn't ended
at the tip of a knife.

Thinking of his friend clouded Meric's mind with apprehension. He hoped that Grae and Anya had started a new life
away from Reva. Breaths and Depths know they deserved a
start fresh, especially Anya. Much of her history was left
unsaid, but he caught glimpses of what she might've lived
through by her actions and the way she treated him. He didn't
want to think about them anymore, didn't want to think about
what he had lost.

"Can you sing that song again?" he said, knowing Cass
wouldn't answer. "Please?"

Meric turned his head to where he thought she might've
been. He'd been alone with his voice for so long that it scraped
against his mind like screeching metal. His thoughts were so
loud that he needed something other than his own voice to
drown out the emptiness.

"Cass, I need you to say something," he whispered, low and
beseeching. His skull throbbed, scalp hardened with blood.

He gripped the bars with tight fingers, the metal damp and
cold against his skin. He shook the bars, pulling with what
little strength he had. His teeth grinded into a snarl as he
punched the irons, chains clattering against the metal. He was
so alert, so focused, and so sober. His tongue craved the warm
drink. He could almost feel it, slipping down his dry throat. He
wanted to forget again.

He could hear Juna's baby crying in the arms of the
escaping Reticent. It was confined to Meric's cell like the
infant was there screaming at him. He covered his ears as he
pictured Endri's broken face, blood pooling beneath him as he
drowned in his own blood. He was going mad. He was going
to die in the way he began, in the dark, talking to the dead. An
old woman sat across from him, her withered skin drooping,
spilling from her skull. She stared at him, decaying, rotting
before his blind eyes.

"Speak, damn you! Depths drown you and Breaths be denied, *speak*!" he screamed across the cell. He knew it was pointless, but what else was he to have done? If he was going mad, it was best to jump in with both feet. Fortunately, with his bound limbs he'd drown quickly.

He was about to scream more obscenities when the words stuck in his throat. Was that a voice? His chains rattled as he fell on his hands and knees, holding his breath to better listen. The old woman was gone, only blackness remained where she once sat. There was the shuffle of feet and the creak of a door hinge. He was suddenly bathed in light, so bright he lifted his hands and huddled in the farthest corner of his cell.

What sort of hallucination was this? His eyes burned from the glare; he couldn't see.

"Meric," the light beckoned. There was a shape shadowing its illumination, the outline of a body. He squinted his eyes and forced them to focus. Was this Cass? Had he finally joined with Iona's Breath?

The blurred shape came into focus and Meric stared into the features of an unknown woman. Her forest green hood covered a long braid of dark hair, flowing over her shoulder like a reaching branch. The brightness behind her illuminated pale skin and full lips, beaming as if in moonlight. Her slightly slanted brows creased as though she were looking upon a creature writhing in a foothold trap. He thought that he'd like to smooth out her worry with a caress, but he couldn't lift his arms. She was saying his name, the words slow and far. He was speechless against the radiance of her beauty, the glamour of her burning irises. She glowed with ethereal fire, and he thought if he could stare into her ruby eyes for eternity, he might be forgiven of everything he'd ever regretted.

There was a sudden force gripping his shoulders, shaking him into coherence. He glanced about his cell and noticed the arms that ensnared him. Grae crouched beside him, his face a mask of tension and colored with bruises, a cut splitting his lip. Had he been fighting? Meric blinked and stared into the blue eyes of his friend. Was this real? Was he really there? He must've spoken out loud because Grae nodded with impatience.

"Yes, we're truly here. We've come for you. Can you stand? You must," Grae said, pulling on his arms. The woman bent over his wrists, using a small throwing knife to pull the pins from his chains. They clattered to the ground in a heap.

Meric groaned, using Grae to balance himself. He still couldn't stand straight inside the cell and when he took a step he fell, but before he hit the floor someone else caught him. It was the woman with the ruby eyes. She looped his arm around her shoulder and with Grae on his other side, half carried him out of the cell. Meric straightened from his crouch and disengaged himself, leaning on his friend as he pointed down the hall.

"There's someone else here. A woman… down there." He couldn't leave Cass. He wouldn't have survived this long without her.

"Meric, there's no—Oy!" Grae called out as the woman ran past them down where Meric pointed.

"Which cell?" she echoed back.

"A window—the one with the window," Meric's voice croaked, raw from screaming.

She was gone for only a few moments, glancing into each cell before returning to his side, footsteps splashing in pools of water. She pulled his arm back over her shoulder and with a strength that he thought strange for her small frame, continued to carry his weight on her own.

"Wait," he tried to turn around. She kept moving forward towards the small staircase that led to the surface, Grae leading in front of them.

"There's no one there," she said, huffing from the effort of pulling him up the stairs.

"Yes, she had a window. She sang to me." Meric lifted his bobbing head. "Cass!" he yelled.

She pulled his arm with a strong tug, and he winced at the sudden pain.

"Quiet! There is no window. You were hallucinating." Her

tone was harsh with impatience. Then, with more kindness, "This sort of darkness can make you see things, especially if you're alone."

He couldn't have imagined her, could he? He heard her immediately after he was thrown into the cell. The more he thought of it the more muddled and bizarre the entire experience had been. He was in no position to turn around himself and look for her.

They stopped just outside the door, Grae peering around the corner as if waiting for a signal. He heard metal clattering against belts, and boots marching past the prison entrance.

"I've secured the family, sir. There doesn't seem to be any intruders on the grounds, and no one was harmed by the glass. Some of the men described falling stars, but all I found were a few stray silver coins. It's more likely their boredom got the better of them and one may have accidentally hit the window," said a voice that sounded much too eager to please.

There was a murmur of some more guards passing by, buckled boots snapping in formation.

"It wouldn't be the first time that's happened," said another voice, obviously the commander by his authoritative tone. Meric was surprised the men weren't reporting to Kiev. He was probably spilling some poor drunks' blood at Decorum. "But given our unique situation, place more guards within the house and take a patrol once more around—"

A roaring clamor of broken metal and earsplitting iron shook the ground with a slight tremor. Meric gripped the woman at his side tighter, peering at the crook of her slight smile. Grae turned to her as though waiting for permission to continue—Meric thought that strange. Why was Grae following her direction? He glanced at her ear and found nothing to suggest she was Venandi. So, who was she?

She nodded her approval and pulled at Meric to continue climbing. He shied his gaze away from the light as it grew brighter, lifting his arm to shade his eyes. Once they surfaced Meric was shocked to discover it wasn't the sun he was peering at, but the moon. How could the moon be so bright? How long had he spent in that cell?

He blinked several times to adjust his eyesight and when he did, he stared with an open mouth. The pathway that led to Fallon's mansion was in ruin. The irons of the gate that once barred the entrance were broken and scattered throughout the grounds. Flowers and bushes were turned over and rooted with stems that spilled dirt like blood over the once pristine gardens.

It looked like a storm had swept through the path, but he'd only heard of such storms in Solov, where spirals of blistering sand could strip the skin off flesh. He'd never in his entire life seen one of those in Reva. A few unconscious guards bent over the shattered gate, some had their legs skewered by the irons, staked to the ground, and groaning their pain. The rest of the company had their golden spears lifted, yelling orders and shouting for explanations.

"Evelyn, this way," Grae whispered, gesturing them to move away from the chaotic scene.

She turned and led Meric to a section of the wall that was covered in thick vines. He had always thought these plants were a safety hazard for one as prominent as Fallon. But like most of his kind the display of his wealth was far more important that his wellbeing, which was fortunate for Meric.

"Can you climb?" Grae said, placing a hand on his shoulder.

"Don't suppose I have much choice." He looked up, measuring his ability. The wall seemed much taller than he remembered.

"I'll follow behind in case you need a boost," the woman said behind him, her shoulders tense with urgency. Her hood rustled in the breeze and her eyes followed the wind in a strange way. She continued to look behind her at the distracted guards with a worried expression.

Grae nodded and jumped, pulling himself several spans with only a few steps. Once he reached the top, he beckoned Meric to follow. Meric gripped the largest vine and pulled with great effort. His shoes had molded from the damp air in the prison, and he slipped as he climbed. The woman ascended; he could feel her presence beneath him. He was so much slower than he should've been, but it couldn't be helped. The few times he fell, her halting reach was all that held his ground. He arrived at the top, gripping Grae's outstretched arm. He turned around to help the woman, holding out his hand. Their fingertips touched when he noticed two men approaching the wall, their violet vests glinting in the moonlight.

She watched his expression and met his eyes. Her gaze steeled and her form went stiff, fingers still grazing his own. He thought that if they remained perfectly still, their presence might go unnoticed.

Meric knew they were finished when the guards looked up, their breath halting in their throats to scream for their superiors. He couldn't go back. He would fall on their swords before being dragged to that void where the dead haunted the living. Evelyn reacted faster than he did, pulling something out of the folds of her cloak. The small throwing knife glinted in the darkness, slicing through the air as she thrust it from her hand. The guard gurgled, straining to stop the flow of blood with a blade piercing his neck. He choked, falling to his knees, looking at Meric in a way that reminded him of Endri before collapsing. The other looked at his dead comrade, opening his mouth to scream when a shadow appeared behind him, hands twisting his head with a sickening snap of bone and muscle. The man released the guard, the body falling limp beside his comrade. He ventured over to the other, pulling out the blade from the guard's neck with a short, sick, sucking sound.

The woman turned back to Meric, her burning eyes red with regret. She stared at his outstretched hand a moment and moved passed it, crouching over the top of the wall then leaping over it, landing on her feet like a cat on the street.

Who is this woman?

The man who broke the neck of the guard reached the top, hurling himself to the opposite side. Grae jumped and stumbled, while Meric failed altogether and bruised his knees on the cobblestones. His friend helped him to his feet, allowing Meric to lean against him while his legs remembered what it felt like to stand on his own.

The woman—Evelyn, he thought he heard Grae call her— breathed in a sigh, listening to the noise of the guards being discovered. The commotion of the murdered men grew louder, and she stepped closer to the shadowed man that had helped in his escape. In the moonlight, Meric could see his face more clearly. He was an old man, but walked with the gait of experience and certainty. His aged features were angular, as if his skin were fighting against the force that insisted he grow old. The wind tousled his greyed, brown hair down the back of his neck, curved eyebrows raised over alert green eyes. He lifted the bloody knife, wiping it on the edges of his cloak before handing it back to Evelyn.

A Vagu! What is Grae doing with a Vagu?

"We must not linger," the old man said, his eyes roaming over the wall before meeting his own. His stare crept through Meric for a moment, as though he were listening to a distant whisper. It made his skin crawl remembering the rumors of the Vagu hearing the voices of the dead. There was never any indication that the rumors promised validity, but this man was different. He wasn't housed in the great mansions of the Lords and Ladies of Reva, he was wild. A free Vagu, undomesticated by the societal hierarchy of a broken system. Meric wasn't sure if he was keeping the Vagu's gaze out of admiration or consternation. The old man withdrew his stare, sighing with a deep breath.

"Who are you?" Meric said, turning to Evelyn. Before they could answer a panicked guard's voice trailed over the wall, disappearing with shouts for a search.

"There is no time. This isn't the place for these questions," Grae said, tugging at his arm towards a dark alleyway.

Meric allowed his friend to lead him, although he hardly needed a guide. The clammy air smelled familiar, enveloping him in the black mist he would always know so well. He recognized the standing figure, resting her hand on the narrow wall, yellow eyes beaming with relief.

"Anya!" he couldn't believe he hadn't thought to ask of her.

She was so thin, arms dangling at her sides like twigs, too weak to keep a hold on the thick branch of an oak. Her skin clung to the ridges of her neck, displaying a long but shallow cut. Shades of purple and yellow colored across her skeletal jaw, making her sunken eyes bright with exhaustion.

Fallon had indeed made it impossible for them to continue their profession within the city. The City Lord was powerful, but not so much that a pair of seasoned Venandi couldn't slip out of Reva unnoticed. Shame spread in his heart at what his friends sacrificed to rescue him.

Grae left his side and looped Anya's arm around his shoulder. She resisted, but almost fell from the effort.

"You should've left me," Meric said, reaching out with a hand to steady her.

She gripped his fingers, rubbing her thumb against his palm. "Yes."

To anyone else her tone would sound cruel, but he could hear the solace in her voice. He smiled and she responded with a nod, still clutching his hand as though she feared someone would come and take him away.

Though he and Grae had known each other longer, Meric felt just as deep a friendship with Anya. He assumed she was the driving force in his rescue, preferring to starve than leave him to rot beneath the ground. There were times when she looked at him—as she was now—with that maternal glint in her yellow eyes. He glowed with the warmth of what it might've felt like to have a mother.

"Can you walk?" Evelyn said from behind them, cutting through Meric's thoughts.

Anya glared at the woman, took a step, and immediately tripped—almost bringing Grae down with her. Meric had little strength to help and Grae was struggling to hold her up. The Vagu appeared around them, gripping Anya by the waist and cradling her like a child in his arms. She struggled in the embrace, but he held her firm and continued through the mist of crossing alleyways.

Grae winced as he ran a hand over his bruised jaw.

"I'm glad you're alive. The kindest thing would've been to kill her if you had died." Grae's lips curved slightly, but his eyes spoke of how lost they'd been without him. The sight of it left Meric without the words to express how mutual the feeling was. He pat his friend's back and Grae left him behind to follow the Vagu.

Evelyn's green hood appeared beside Meric; her head turned towards him, an intense silence between them. She stared at him as though waiting for some magic, a warding to cure the stillness. The vehemence of their first meeting was still fresh in his mind. She looked to be no older than he and though she was beautiful, she was ordinary without the supernatural radiance his hallucination provided. But her eyes... they were the same. That ruby blaze incinerated everything she laid her gaze upon and the longer she looked at him the less he could tear his own eyes away. Whoever tattooed them was the finest artist he'd ever seen.

She had the features of a high Lady, but the attire of an incomer. She took each moment with skill and ease, as if she'd spent her whole life training for the times when aim mattered the most. Yet there was the shadow of guilt in her flaming eyes, an abysmal hollow he knew all too well when one had innocent blood on their hands. He had so many questions, but the silence of the alley was broken by the clatter of steel and whispered shouts of approaching guards.

He spared a single moment analyzing what she might've been thinking, wondering if the answers laid in the way the breeze swept across her hair or the twitch of her mouth. He wanted to thank her. He was cautious of her intentions and shuddered to think what she was promised in return for his freedom, but he wanted her to know the depth of his gratitude. He wasn't sure he'd have survived much longer in that underground world. He tried to form the words, but they stuck in his throat, unaccustomed to be spoken.

Breaths and Depths, I would've died down there were it not for you.

Her eyes glinted with some appreciation as though he'd spoken out loud. She inclined her head in acknowledgement, then ran into the darkness of the alley. He sucked in a sharp breath, tossing away the strange exchange and left behind the confused and chaotic voices of those who had imprisoned him.

CHAPTER 31

TRUE TEARS

Meric stared at the mug of ale before him, its hilt glistening like sweat. The shape of the cup bent like the curve of a woman's back and beckoned with just as much sensuality. When he took a sip, the ale slipped as easily between his lips as a tongue, warm and carnal. He sighed, closing his eyes a moment to savor the slow spread of numbness he so missed. His eyes snapped open at the sound of water dripping. He never left. He was still buried in the dark, undying, and mad beneath the earth. Grae had lifted his mug to his mouth. Holding it just above his lips, he met Meric's wide stare.

"Are you well?"

Meric breathed in sharply, watching the condensation on Grae's cup drop to the table. His chest loosened, releasing his heart to beat in its normal rhythm. How quickly he'd been transported back to his tomb with nothing more than a sound. His tongue remembered the grime in the water he'd lapped up on the prison wall, commingled with every foul thing he couldn't see in that all-consuming darkness. He pushed away the ale with sudden disgust, reaching for the pitcher of water in the center of the table.

"I'm only thirsty," he said, pouring the water into another mug. He drank its contents and refilled the cup again and again. Grae finally drank from his cup, watching him with a thoughtful expression.

"Should you feel the need to reach for something stronger during my tale, I won't stop you."

Grae began to tell of what happened during their separation, his weariness threaded through the tale. Meric was shocked to discover he'd been in the City Lord's prison only a fortnight. What he had thought was months in captivity was only a fraction of the time. He was more surprised to hear about how the mystery woman, Evelyn, came to be a part of the rescue. Grae reiterated finding her near death in the streets next to a dead Kiev, the guard's head a burst fruit. Meric stared at the mug of ale, wondering what he was supposed to be without it.

Cronies Inn contained a light crowd, mostly consisting of old men reminiscing on past deeds with other older men. The hour was late, too late to have even the most drunk customer awake. They were only a few hours away from daylight and each passing moment made it harder for them to remain in Reva, but they had to rest. Anya was in no condition to travel in her current state.

Evelyn's Vagu companion, Sou, had been rather insistent upon following the alleys to the edge of the city to escape the same hour they rescued him. But before Grae or he could protest the red-eyed woman asserted that they would return to the inn where Anya could gather her strength. He'd never seen a Vagu glare at their betters so intensely, nor a woman of means to be so familiar. It was a strange relationship he wasn't sure to make of.

When they had arrived, Sou allowed them to wash and granted them fresh clothes. Evelyn purchased some food from the kitchen and gave Grae and him a bowl of chicken and broth. She carried more of the same for the rest of the company in a room on the second floor. She had disappeared into the upstairs hall, leaving him and Grae to catch up on what had happened.

Meric ripped his gaze from the ale and picked up a leg of

chicken, soaking it in the broth. Grae reach for his own share, the voracity of his consumption matching his own. His friend glanced up while hunched over the broth, his gaze grateful to Meric for withholding his questions until they'd eaten. The strong flavors of herbs and salted stock warmed his belly as he ate, slick juices running down his chin. They didn't speak for some time, enjoying the taste of food so long denied them. In time, the broth and chicken were nothing but a shallow pool and a few strands of crispy skin.

Meric ran a hand across his cheek, wiping bits of chicken from his beard. His fingers grazed his earlobe, still hard with blood from when his earring had been ripped from the skin. Grae opened his mouth, raising a finger before reaching into his cloak and pulled out the glimmering silver earring, swinging with its looped chains.

Meric wrapped his fingers around the earring, surprised by how thrilled he was that Grae had managed to hold onto it. He ran his thumb over the silver, rubbing the dried blood away until it gleamed in the torchlight.

"Kiev is a damn brute—well, a dead damn brute now, but I was able to take it from him before he threw us out." Grae shuffled his feet nervously below the table. Meric nodded appreciatively, wrapping the earring around his opposite ear when Grae looked up the stairs.

"When you returned Evelyn here, is that when Anya left you?" Meric said, wiping the side of his mouth.

Grae rolled his eyes and did the same, licking his fingers.

"At first, we were only separated. That Vagu thought we had done his Lady harm." He touched the bruise under his eye. "We escaped through different alleys, and she didn't return to our usual meet point that night. I checked some other safe areas we'd claimed, but she was still nowhere to be found. So, I returned the next night here, thinking she might have been hurt." Grae looked down and Meric could only imagine what it must have felt like for him to think he might've lost another he cared for. "I didn't find her, but I saw Evelyn and her Vagu leave. I thought to find Anya I needed to think of what she would want me to do. I—" he turned around at the sound of a door slamming upstairs, his hand inching towards the edge of the table to the rapier hanging at his belt.

"What's wrong?" he said, looking up as Grae did, but finding nothing of concern.

"Nothing," his friend answered, turning back to him. "I'm just waiting."

"For what?"

Just as he was about to answer Sou appeared from the hall, meeting Grae's eyes from atop the stairs, his arched brows stitched together with fury. He made his way down the steps and within a few strides he was leaning over the table, his hands white knuckled.

"Where is it?" The old man's voice was low, almost a growl in the back of his throat.

Meric glanced at Grae, who formed a prideful smile, similar to the one he had when Due was beating him.

"You realize it's nonsense that you should have such regard for superstition," Grae said, tapping the table with his finger.

Sou sighed and released the table, running a hand over his face. The man was exhausted, his eyes sagging with sleeplessness. Meric started when Sou patted his shoulder to encourage him to make room at the table for him. He shifted to the side for the old man, advertent to being so close to someone who had broken a man's neck with his bare hands only hours earlier. Sou reached over him and grabbed a stray piece of uneaten chicken skin, placing it in between his teeth.

Grae furrowed his brow, appearing to be surprised by how casual the old man was. His blue eyes burrowed into Sou as if the Vagu could conjure a blade from thin air.

"You realize *you* stole that nonsense. If it means so little, then give it back," Sou said, wiping his hands on his trousers.

"It matters not what I believe. It's your superstition. You're right. It does mean very little to me but not to you, which makes it valuable. I'll give it back if you release us from our bond," Grae said, his blonde hair falling over his intense stare.

"The deal was struck. A man is made of many things and

his word is what holds it all together, good men and cruel men alike. Remember what I said about trust." Sou wasn't harsh with his words. In fact, he seemed almost parental, as if he were attempting to pass on a life skill.

"I can see the edges of your mask. You haven't told us everything."

"Give me my vial. I've told you everything there is to know about getting us to Birny safely." Sou held out his hand with a patient stare.

"I've heard that before from a man who charged us with the protection of one he seemingly *cared* for. He lied and the family I made for myself was nearly destroyed."

"Grae, give it back," Meric said, noticing the tremble in Sou's hand. Whatever Grae had stolen it was valuable indeed, enough to send a shudder through the hands of a man who killed with such ease.

"Meric, we aren't bound to this man. What I hold he will trade for," Grae said, speaking as if Sou weren't present. "I had to get you back and now I need to keep you. I didn't spring you from prison just to throw you into another. This collateral I hold can break the cell he holds us in."

"Oh, Celosia's Depths, lad! You were fortunate enough to take my True Tears from my person, but that doesn't guarantee you freedom, which incidentally, you already possess, from me at least. True Tears are difficult to obtain, but not impossible. Give me the vial or not. It's hardly collateral that I will trade tooth and nail for. Leave—I will not stop you, but then I cannot help you," Sou said leaning forward, his eyes kind. Meric ignored the old man's tone, trying to focus on Grae.

"This entire city is a cell. Return it," he said, a little more forceful.

"Why?"

Meric had the sudden feeling that the roles were reversed. Before his imprisonment, he'd been the one asking endless questions—he still did, but it came with a little more restraint. Had he thought more before acting he might've avoided the entire situation he found himself in. Looking at Grae's withdrawn features and tired eyes was like looking into a mirror from his childhood. His friend had never been without food and security. Coming from a family of wealth and being a successful Venandi, he'd known nothing of surviving the streets. He'd never known hunger like what he'd experienced these weeks, not like Meric.

"I'm an escaped criminal. Tell me, how are we supposed to leave Reva with every guard on the hunt for me? How many Venandi would love to be the one to collect on the reward money? Sou brought down the gates of Fallon's estate with a furious wind, something we thought to be nothing more than a story."

"Furious? Aye, I suppose it was." The old man interrupted with a shrug.

"We need him to get out." Meric continued, side glancing the Vagu who rolled his eyes, probably frustrated at being talked about as if he weren't in the room.

"We will manage," Grae said, using a tone Meric found unfamiliar, as if whatever he demanded required swift results. He sounded like someone who wore a decorated vest. Meric hesitated then decided he couldn't run into the void blind. He had stared into utter blackness, and he was resolved to not experience that again, no matter its form.

"No," he said in a quiet, but firm voice. "Anya cannot stand, and you've just had your first full meal since we last met. We aren't up to the task of handling ourselves, let alone what we've been hired to do." He shot a glare at Sou who seemed unaffected by the look. "And if what you've told me about Kiev is true, then they need us as much as we need them. Return that vial or you'll be underground alone because I will not go back."

Grae's eyes widened, alarmed by what Meric threatened and glanced in between the two of them as though he and Sou were complete strangers. He reached into his cloak and pulled out the clear vial, shaking it in his hand, taunting Sou by pretending to have it slip from his fingers.

"You lot care for Anya?" Sou said, his voice suddenly loud with her name.

Meric stood at the same time Grae did, pushing their benches askew as they reached for their weapons. Grae's hand clasped the hilt of his rapier, while Meric clung to the knife that came with his dinner. Sou let out a barking chuckle, leaning back with a smile, his hand raised in supplication. Meric exchanged a look with Grae, who lowered his hand a fraction of an inch.

"I probably should have phrased that differently, forgot who I was speaking with. All I meant was you lads want her well again, aye?" he said, leaning forward again.

Meric nodded, sitting back down. Grae remained standing, hand hovering above his blade. It was so rare to see such an open display of authenticity. It made Meric turn his body to the side so he could better see behind him, cautious that ulterior motives were in play. No one was this sincere, not without expecting something in return.

"If a man lived his whole life without ever seeing a mountain, he'd say it was a fallacy that one could explode with fire. Return my True Tears and feel the ground rumble." Sou's green eyes glinted with the passing shadows. It was illogical to think the man was anything but a deceitful Vagu, but for some unexplained reason, Sou's words pressed into his mind, a strange challenge of some kind.

Grae seemed to come to the same conclusion as the hard line of his mouth softened and he placed the vial in Sou's hand. The man curled his long fingers around it and nodded in thanks. He stood and gestured for them to follow.

Meric stepped to Grae's side, who still watched the Vagu with a guarded frown. They climbed the stairs and Meric felt the muscles in his legs tremble from the effort. He rubbed his temple trying to lessen the ache in his head from when he had hit himself with the shackles. The pain was getting worse. He felt the chicken and broth swirl in his stomach and thought for a moment it would all come back up. Anya may have been in worse condition than he or Grae but in feeling how much strain the climb was, made him reconsider how far any of them could go on without rest.

"What is in the vial?" Meric said under his breath when they had reached the top. He leaned against the wall, trying to level out his breathing. Grae seemed to be unaffected, but Meric saw the slight tremor in his friend's legs.

"I've only heard rumors. It can supposedly cause pain and suffering, depending on its potency of course," Grae said in the same low breath, but with an air of skepticism.

"Potency?"

Grae turned his head to answer when Sou's voice echoed in front of them.

"How sincere you were when the tears were collected. The more ferocious and genuine the emotions the better they can take effect. However, you are lacking the most important aspect to True Tears. To heal."

"You are saying that through pain and suffering, your tears can heal a person?"

"Aye! You listen very well," Sou jibed, but Grae's glare wasn't amused. "To splint a leg, we must set the bone, to cauterize a wound, we must burn it shut. For True Tears to mend the body, we must suffer its effects."

"What effects? How much pain?" Meric stepped forward, pushing himself from the wall. He stared at the vial peeking in between the old man's shrewd fingers, suddenly teeming with the urge to break it across the floor.

"As your friend said, it depends on its potency. The stronger the emotions the more pain, but the faster you will heal. As to its effects it is not so much a physical pain as an emotional one. True Tears remind the soul to tend to the body, a flint to set a burning blaze. In this inferno one is consumed with who they truly are. It is a painful thing for everyone, to be forcefully shown what we've broken within ourselves, but it is fleeting. Soon forgotten once the fire is doused."

The old man leaned towards the door then turned around, glancing in between him and Grae. He seemed to be in search of a hidden motive, as if he were trying to come up with a reason to deny them entry to the room.

"I was saving this vial for the journey, just in case, but my Lady insists we use it now. I do not have the same confidence in you that she does. You will abandon us as soon as we leave the city. No, do not interrupt," Sou said, raising his hand at Meric, who had opened his mouth to disagree.

Grae may have given off that impression, but Meric was determined to get out of this wretched city. There was no drinking away the dark corners of his deeds anymore. Leaving Reva was not only necessary to save his life, but those of his friends. They could start anew, perhaps find meaning in being Venandi again. Birny felt like as good a place to start as any.

"You will leave us," he glanced at Grae before returning his gaze to Meric. "Perhaps not right away, but you will. When we cross the Idris or in the middle of the Dattadri Greens. So, to prevent that I will give you a portion of your payment now. Twenty pieces out of a total of ninety-two."

Meric almost lost his footing again, leaning a hand against the wall. He'd never seen that much coin in his life. Grae hadn't moved, but from the way his jaw tightened it had been some time since he had either.

"Half. You will give us half the coin now and the rest when we've completed the bargain." Grae dipped his chin in a show of authority, but Meric knew he'd do it for the twenty pieces. Celosia's Depths! He would do it for even less. The corner of Sou's mouth turned, and he shook his head.

"Thirty. I am no fool, Venandi."

"Thirty-five and consider the matter closed," Grae said, his voice hitched in desperation. Meric knew this was Grae's pride speaking, and Sou's knowing eyes flickered with the same conclusion. He hoped Sou wouldn't force Grae to concede what little power he had in having to accept thirty pieces should the old man stand his ground.

"Fair enough. Thirty-five now and the rest when you've delivered us to Birny. I will also, at my Lady's command, share my True Tears," he continued to speak to Grae, his tone gentle.

"If springing your friend from his cell was not reason enough to establish the simple *thought* of trust then perhaps a smaller, more impactful demonstration will." He twisted the clear vial in his hand, fingering the lid.

Grae huffed as he lowered his shoulders in annoyance. The three of them were of similar height, with Sou being slightly taller. While the Vagu was closer to a grandfather in comparison to Meric's age—to Grae, the old man could've been his father. It was probably why Grae disliked the man so much. He didn't care for being spoken to like a child. Although Meric thought it to be more than that. His friend acted as if Sou had wronged him in a past life.

"Will it help her?" Meric said, his fingers stretching out with anxiety at his sides.

Meric hadn't the time to think about the repercussions of trusting these people. Time wasn't on their side and the sooner they established a line of understanding the better. All that mattered now was Anya's well-being and leaving the city.

Sou tore his gaze away from Grae, a generous amount of sympathy passing through his green eyes. "Aye, it will help."

Meric closed the door behind them once they entered. As he turned the world grew dim, the only light emanating from a few candles passing shadows over Anya's withdrawn features. She looked terrible. She laid on the bed, her cheeks sunken as though her head had the skin tailored to display every jagged line of her skull. The bones looked ready to split the skin. Grae took in a sharp breath and Meric didn't hear him exhale.

Evelyn was sitting on the bed next to Anya and stood when she noticed their presence. Her cloak rested on the back of a chair near the open window, a cool breeze circulating the room. He hadn't noticed with the cloak on just how much smaller she was beside Sou. Her hair was loose around her shoulders, falling in waves of dark curls. He had no objection to a woman in trousers, but a Lady in them was a strange sight.

"How is she?" Grae said, finally taking a breath, his eyes fixed on the sick woman.

"I have done all I can for her. She won't take more than a few sips and it is not enough." She gestured to the full bowl of broth on the nightstand, steaming still with warmth. "She is in no condition to leave tonight, and I've heard more guards patrolling the street below. It will not be long before they check the inns."

Anya's bruised face was turned into the pillow, her chest rising and falling with deep sleep. Her skin had a bit more color than before, but she was so thin it was a wonder she had the strength to breath at all.

"We are not leaving her," Grae said, his hands balled in fists. "Your Vagu claims he has some magic that can cure her."

Evelyn walked up to Grae, who leaned back at the sudden movement. Her red eyes narrowed, and she glared at him with every intention of being heard.

"I'll not tell you this again. His name is Sou, and he saved your life tonight." Her voice was calloused. She had long since grown tired of repeating herself. Evelyn had the bearing of every strong-willed Lady Meric had ever met, but without the mask of superiority.

Grae met her glare and Evelyn kept it as though she had practiced for years staring at others larger than he into submission.

"I will *not* leave her," Grae repeated with the same impact, but quieter.

"I would not ask that of you," she said, her expression insistent. She glanced up and down his face like Sou did before, searching, but for what Meric could only guess.

"You both saved my life. I'll never forget that. If you would stop fighting me at every turn you might see that I am trying to return the favor."

Grae relaxed his shoulders and nodded, blue eyes traveling to the bed where Anya slept. His walled expression gave way to concern the longer he looked at her, his bearing crumbling in whatever horrific scenarios he had created within his imagination.

"Make her well," he said, not taking his eyes away from her.

The old man brushed Anya's black hair from her face and hovered the vial just above her mouth. He dipped the cylinder and a few drops poured into her parted lips.

Meric leaned forward and gripped the foot of the bed, Evelyn watched beside him as Grae held his breath. Anya grimaced as if experiencing a nightmare, her eyes darting beneath her lids in frantic jerks. She relaxed a moment, remaining still and for a time Meric had never been more miserable. He dared to hope and once again he was forced to relive the consequences of believing in what the world never had—good people.

Grae kept his focus on Anya as though his determination alone were enough to make her well again. His voice tangled through his teeth, not daring to look at Sou, who remained calm. "You are a cruel liar, Vagu. Did you expect—"

Meric jumped back from the bed as Anya arched her back, her mouth opened in a painful gasp. Grae leaped to her side, gripping her hand as she convulsed, yellow eyes wide and frightened.

"No... no," she groaned, meeting Grae's eyes, but not truly seeing him. "She is here. Away... go away. It hurts!"

She shut her eyes, limbs trembling. Grae rounded on Sou, but the old man placed a hand on the side of his face. The touch was so surprising that Grae lowered his fists, blue eyes gleaming in the candlelight with tears.

"Wait," Sou whispered, moving his hand to Grae's shoulder, squeezing in the way a father might to his son.

Meric looked over at Evelyn, her brows lowered in concern. Her fingers next to his, holding the bed frame with knuckles as white as his own. She released her grip, letting her hands fall to her sides and an expression of awe came about her features. Meric turned back to Anya, expecting to be met with a face marbled in black and yellow, but instead stared into the features of a woman whose body knew no violence. Her bruises were gone, skin smoothed by some unseen force. The sharp angle of her boney jaw filled with healthy muscle and her cheeks rounded, pink with vitality. Even her hair shone darker in color, discarding its bitter frailty at not being washed for weeks.

Evelyn sighed beside him in amazement, walking to Anya's bedside. Grae stared at Sou, refusing to turn around.

"Look," the old man said, nodding over his shoulder. Grae shook his head, a tear running down his cheek.

"No. No, you have tricked us." His words were meant to be harsh, but Grae's voice leaked from his throat like a thirsting man denied water.

Meric gripped his friend's shoulder. Grae spun around as if he had forgotten he were there, and his eyes immediately traveled to Anya. He lowered himself onto the bed, entwining his fingers through hers, expression one of disbelief. He lifted his other hand to her perfect cheek, and she opened her eyes. They shone with the brightness of the sun at its burning peak. Meric shook his head, running his hand across his face, thinking on the only word that echoed in his mind to explain what had just happened. Miracle. He'd never seen one and he wasn't sure what to do with the knowledge that they existed.

"How?" Meric said as Anya stirred, drifting between wakefulness and sleep.

Sou twirled the vial in his hand, the remaining liquid conforming to its prison.

"The Vagu have been a part of Iona since Isla and the Nameless Sister first created the land. We are part of the dirt and the growth. This is but one aspect of that companionship. It's said that Isla herself was the first Vagu. Whether you believe in such fables is entirely up to you, but it's the only explanation I have to offer."

"I did not know that this would truly work," Evelyn's voice was gentle as she faced both he and Grae, expression one of genuine compassion. "Please, take what is left."

He glanced away with a furrowed brow, trying to sort through the addled emotions that came along with one showing unexpected kindness. There had to be more to it, a hidden motive he was unaware of or expectation of compensation. She already had what she wanted, a band of protectors to take her to Birny. Was this a ploy to ensure more favors in the future? What did she want in return? He opened his mouth to voice his mistrust, but stopped when she held his gaze. Her gem-like eyes never left his and through their gleam he knew the thought of payment had never crossed her mind.

They all had little experience with it, truth and kindness. He thought back to what Grae had told him about her killing Kiev, the disgust she exhibited when she had stabbed the guard during their escape. Whatever it was she was after, she and Sou hadn't told them the whole truth of it. They killed with ease yet took it upon themselves to heal them. If she wanted a Venandi escort there were dozens in the city that could've done the job better than his band. Many would decline the position because of Sou, but he didn't know any of his kind that would turn down ninety-two pieces of coin. So why go through the trouble of breaking him out of Fallon's prison, spending the time they could have escaped nursing them back to health? Why had she chosen them?

Sou held out the cylinder to Grae. His friend stood from the bed, releasing Anya's hand who slipped in and out of consciousness. Meric met Grae's stare and nodded, knowing despite all that they did not know about each other, Evelyn and Sou were their best chance at surviving whatever may come.

"Cheers, my lads," Sou said with a tired smile. It was clear he did not want to share his True Tears, his green eyes dark with some hidden grief when he watched Grae take it from him.

Grae tilted the vial, his throat muscles tightening as he swallowed. Meric stretched his hand out to Grae when he had finished, gripping the vial with tight fingers. He leaned his head back and emptied the cylinder before he could convince himself otherwise. The droplets were exactly how he expected them to taste, salty and dry as if taken from the sea.

At first, he feared it was a trick, some bending of the fading moon that made the room shine brighter. The candles in the room grew, pulsating with radiating light until he could see no more. He was blind and empty. So empty. He cried out, but his voice was lost in the void, swallowed by the darkness. He was alone, crawling in the nothingness, abandoned, and forgotten. They'd left him. His parents had condemned him to despair. It lived inside him, this emptiness, growing and extinguishing any light he may use to find his way out. How could he not feel this creature within him, eating him? How could another bear to look upon him? This thing wearing the black shroud of oncoming death gnawed at his bones, prolonging his suffering. The shroud within him lifted and he saw the face beneath it.

"No more... please. Let me die."

As quickly as he had spoken the thought, it was over. He opened his eyes, and he was staring at the floor on his hands and knees, Evelyn's hand on his shoulder. Panting, he looked up and Sou was on the floor, Grae in his arms, his back against the old man's chest, staring into nothing. Already, the memory of that endless tomb was retreating from his mind.

"Can you stand?" Evelyn whispered beside him. He nodded, pushing himself from the floor.

It was remarkable. His body was healed. He flexed the muscles of his legs and rubbed the spot on his head where the chains had broken the skin. Nothing. His forehead was smooth, and his mind was free of the pulsating agony he'd struggled with since the rescue. He touched his ear and the flesh bore no scars. No pain. He was shocked by how feeble he'd been. He knew now that he had been a breath away from toppling over into a sleep. One he wasn't sure he'd have been able to wake from.

"How do you feel?" Evelyn said, her voice underlining a quiet nervosity.

Before he could answer Grae took in a large breath and groaned, peeling himself out of Sou's arms. They stood together, Sou's hand out in case the Venandi fell. Meric let out a relieved breath at seeing his friend's bruises gone and his complexion returned to its alabaster hue. They looked each other over, their silence creating a vacuum of uneasiness. Neither knew what to say of what had happened. Although he could barely recall the experience, he couldn't bear to attempt to speak of it in fear the memory would return somehow.

"You and I should spar again sometime. It was an unfair fight, Vagu," Grae said, pointing at Sou, still catching his breath.

Meric saw Evelyn's furious expression that shone through her red eyes. She was about to speak when Sou chuckled and grabbed Grae's hand in an unexpected shake. He flinched slightly at the contact.

"It will be a pleasure to best you again, Venandi," Sou said, before pushing Grae away with a rough step, blonde hair falling over his blue eyes.

"We feel ready to leave," Meric said, answering Evelyn as she turned towards the bed.

Anya's eyes fluttered open with a sigh then she burst from the bed, almost falling when she saw them all gathered around her. She stood with fists raised, eyes wandering to Grae and Meric, her pack. She relaxed for a moment, recollecting recent events before turning towards Evelyn.

"I remember you. What did you do to me?" she said, pointing at her. Evelyn lifted her hands as though she'd come upon a growling dog.

Sou explained in short words what he did. Once he was finished Anya was quiet for some time trying, as Meric was, to process the generosity she'd received.

"Next time let my body heal on its own. Whatever magic that was, it is unkind." Her voice trembled against the fading memory of whatever it was she saw "You. I still would've left you," she said, staring at Evelyn with harsh yellow eyes, but her lips turned upright at the last moment.

Instead of being offended, Evelyn inclined her head and grinned as if some secret had passed between the two. She had a beautiful smile that was only beautiful because she meant it. He tore his gaze away from her and cleared his throat.

"Since we are all in fine spirits, I suggest our immediate

departure. The road to Birny is long and it'll be longer still from behind iron bars."

"I need food first," Anya said, jumping in place and laughing as if she were a child that just discovered a puddle.

"We do not have the time," Meric said, gripping her arm as she tried to walk past.

"You will make the time until I am sated or at the very least until I forget the feel of my ribs straining to rip through my skin." She pulled her arm from his grip, shuddering.

He had to remind himself that out of the three of them, he was the only one who had lived on the streets and fought off starvation not just for weeks, but eight years. The door opened, then closed behind him with Anya leaving the room in an awkward silence. It was broken by the sound of Sou picking up scattered items into a pack for their journey.

"Aid an old man. Moving around will help your renewed strength," he said, waving a hand at Grae to accompany him. His friend raised an eyebrow and walked over to the Vagu, talking with him but not assisting in any way.

Evelyn had made her way to the window, taking her cloak from the chair before kneeling beside the bed. She pulled out a pack, stood and placed both the pack and cloak on the tangled sheets. Meric strode over to her as she reached into a pocket of the cloak, inspecting a row of throwing daggers.

"Thank you," he said simply.

She placed the daggers back into the folds of the cloak as she turned towards him, brown hair falling across her face. She pulled a strand behind her ear and nodded; the corners of her lips turned up. It was the kind smile that one gave to a persistent merchant, appreciative but had no interest in any of their wares.

"Of course."

"You've not been to Reva, have you?"

She shook her head and returned to packing. "I've come to know it though the little time I've spent here."

"Then you may understand why the others may never voice their gratitude. This place will break you." His voice was low, and he felt as though an explanation of some kind was in order.

"Our voices rarely speak the truth of what we feel. I do not need them to speak of it. I know, and it's not their gratitude I want."

"What do you want?" The question was a nocked arrow in the dark. She lifted her face, those red eyes burning a hole into his own.

"I want what was agreed upon. Safe passage to Birny." She reached into the pack, fumbling within a pocket, the sound of silver clinking like wind chimes. "You've been officially hired."

She placed a few silver coins of varying sizes in his palm. Many of the pieces were much larger than the rest, worth a week's stay at the inn with food to spare. When Sou had promised ninety-two pieces, Meric had assumed they would be of the same size and therefore of the same value. Staring at the differing proportions of the coin in his hand he realized that the ninety-two pieces could be worth a lot more. If Evelyn was a Lady—having any concept of how money worked—she would've realized this and only given him coins of similar shapes. He looked up from his palm, meeting her gaze through the hood of his brow. Her mouth was set, eyes focused but too strained as though through force of will.

She was afraid he'd refuse. He could see her mind running with ceaseless arguments she'd prepared for that possible outcome. The visage she displayed was a woman of modest fortune who was accustomed to giving orders, but he could see through that. She was taking every step by the moment, not knowing when the floor would give out beneath her. She was like him, and he felt an involuntary sliver of connection thread through him to her.

"Then I suggest we drag Anya from the kitchen and leave," he said, pocketing the coins. Her entire body eased, as if invisible chains had released her. She walked past him towards the door then turned back, brows furrowed with that familiar crease he wanted to smooth away.

"Cass," she spoke the same as though she were speaking of

the dead. "Whether she was real or not, she was real enough for you that had I found her, I would've taken her with us. I want you to know that."

He was still wary of Evelyn's hidden intentions, but he remembered how she immediately acted at the prospect of another human in that desolate prison. He could at least conclude that she wasn't the sort of person to abandon another to a fate so dark. He nodded and she seemed to accept that as an understanding between them.

The door suddenly swung open; Anya swiftly latched the lock. Grae strode to her side, his face serious. Meric stepped closer to Evelyn, taking his place beside her as was his duty now.

"There are guards downstairs asking about him," she gestured to Meric, her tattooed eyes darting between them all. "They're questioning the innkeeper as we speak. We don't have much time. I think they saw me listening."

Evelyn darted to the bed and threw on her cloak, placing the pack over her shoulder. The rest of them did the same, Anya racing to the corner of the room where Meric's bladed bow and quivers hid in the darkness. She handed it to him, and he gave her a nod of appreciation. She'd kept his weapon safe. He strapped it in its rightful place across his back, feeling the weight like the embrace of an old friend.

"We can't go downstairs, they'll see him," Grae said as they formed a circle.

Evelyn glanced at the disheveled sheets on the bed and held them in her hands. Sou pursed his lips and looked out the window.

"Ah to be young and resourceful," he said as Evelyn raised her brow in surprise. Sou opened his mouth as though offended and took the sheets from her hand, tying them together as he spoke. "I was young once, Lady. Many a times I used this very tactic to escape the bonds of a parental house-hold that would forbid me from pursuing adventures."

"Can we take the alleys to Farron Port?" Evelyn said, helping Sou tie the knots.

If they came here on a ship, the journey would certainly be easier, but Fallon would have the docks watched. No one would exit or enter the city through the ports until they were caught.

Sou shook his head, apparently thinking the same thoughts.

"They'll have shut down the docks. We might as well lock ourselves in the cells we found Meric in if we try to take the ship." The old man sounded regretful, morose to leave his ship behind. He glanced at Grae whose arms folded with contemplation.

"The alleys are still our best chance. The main entrance will be too heavily patrolled." Grae leaned his head towards Meric. "But this one can guide us through to an exit less obvious."

He agreed with a slight nod, turning his head as he listened for the heavy sound of footsteps. The same ones he'd heard for hours on end while in Fallon's prison.

Once Sou finished the makeshift rope, he tied it to the bed post and tossed it through the open window. Meric led as they climbed their way down, while Sou remained to make sure everyone was safely out of the room before he followed the rest of them. Once he had his feet planted on the cobblestones, the air above them echoed with loud knocks and shouts before a splintering crack reverberated through the window. Meric led everyone into the closest alley, fading into the black mist that, though he was eager to escape, felt like home.

CHAPTER 32

THE ALLEYS

E velyn followed Meric through the thick fog, blue tinges of wind mingling with the blackness of the mist. She felt the presence of the others behind her, hearing their footsteps and Grae's breath at her back. She peered through her hood, glancing back to see Sou at the rear, turning around to watch for pursuers.

Meric took a quick right and then another, veering through the darkness with the ease of one born into it. He seemed to know the halls intimately, as though he'd spent years mapping them in his mind. She expected to hear his Venandi companions voice their opinions on which path to take, but they seemed to have full confidence in him.

Anya blew a soft whistle that sounded like the chirp of a bird. Meric stopped at once, eyes searching, and expression voided of emotion. Evelyn stepped closer to him, leaning against the wall. In the swirling mist she saw shapes—the shadows of street walkers. But that wasn't what the Venandi were watching. Their gazes were locked at the end of the alley, shaded in darkness that not even her dragon eyes could pierce.

"Are we being followed?" she whispered.

He nodded without glancing in her direction. Blue wisps of Iona's Breath mingled with the fog, turning black with corruption.

She couldn't tell if there was anyone coming. Meric lifted his head to the sky where the tops of the wall reached out into the starless night. That's when she saw it. A shadow going against the black mist that swirled at the tops of the wall. It was faint and she was impressed that the Venandi could see it. Whoever was following them was gaining and using the walls to run them down.

Grae sucked on his teeth and motioned his head forward. Meric grabbed her hand, his fingers enveloping hers with a grip that had the power to break every one of her fingers. He pulled her forward.

"Stay close. Don't lose me," he whispered, looking into her eyes.

Evelyn stared at his shadowed face, his honey-colored eyes bright within the dark. Ever since her eyes changed, she'd grown used to people not being able to look at her for long. Even Sou couldn't keep his discomfort a secret. Meric's ability to look into her flaming irises and hold them was a kindness he couldn't know he'd just given her.

"I won't," she said, returning his gaze with the same boldness.

He turned and bolted into an adjacent alley that wasn't the one she thought he'd go down. She spun with him, her hand still gripped in his, the others close behind. Meric's feet were light in their cantor, his breath the quietest of them all. It reminded Evelyn of Nakesha's light trot before she burst into a run while hunting. It was obvious that he knew the alleys better than even the street walkers they passed. Most were sleeping against the walls, while some curled inside divots where the wall had split or broken into a small crevasse. It was where they'd be less likely to be seen and disturbed by others. They didn't stir as she passed.

Meric turned a corner and Grae made his way alongside Evelyn, matching the speed of her steps. She noticed Anya and Sou taking the rear, their breathing even and calm. At first, Evelyn thought they'd just gotten into the rhythm of the chase, but soon realized they'd formed a circle around her, keeping her within the reach of their hands and weapons in case whoever was tailing them caught up.

While she was grateful that they assumed their job without hesitation, she was surprised to discover she was ill at ease with the arrangement. She and Sou had helped the Venandi rise from Celosia's Depths only to resurface to a storm.

She continued after Meric, sliding around corners and looping in what appeared to be circles to her. She thought it might've been a ploy to confuse the shadow that still followed above them. He took a left, shifting closer to the wall, following a crack in the surface that led to a small open hole, only large enough to crawl through. She assumed that it routed to the other side, but she couldn't tell in the darkness. A gust of wind passed over Evelyn's head and instinctively, she looked up to see what had caused it. Before she could, the force of a body left her gasping on the floor. Anya was laying on top of her. The woman's yellow eyes were downcast, her arms covering Evelyn's head, protecting her from whatever had ventured into the alley from above. Evelyn twisted out from beneath the Venandi, casting her vison about her and seeing nothing to warrant knocking her to the ground.

"What did you see?" she asked.

"I don't know, but I felt it." Anya looked to the sky, her yellow eyes narrowed, scouring the darkness above. She turned back around, staring at Meric. If Evelyn could light a fire from Anya's enraged features, the entire city would've burned.

Meric's back was against the wall, hand gripping his shoulder. He looked down and showed a blood-stained palm. Evelyn froze in the alley, looking at the long cut that made its way from the back of his shoulder to the tip of his collarbone. The cut wasn't deep, but neither was it smooth and straight like the cut of a throwing knife. Instead, it curved as though a being of flesh and blood guided the blade... or claw.

Anya met Meric's eyes and Evelyn knew she'd lost them. Grae glanced at the wound, staring at it for a moment, his mouth turning into a hard frown. He rounded on Evelyn, and she placed a hand in the pocket of her cloak, fingers gripping the handle of one of her throwing knives.

"Who are you?" His tone was abrasive, the question sandpaper in her ears. He thought the raptor had been aiming for her.

Sou stood at her side, hand hovering above the hilt of his dagger. She glanced in between the Venandi, straining to keep her head above the churning water of her choices. She grasped the only tether she had, meeting Meric's eyes that bore into her with the ferocity of a man trying to decide between two impossible choices. Stay and die in the alley by the sharp talons of a shadow or perish in the darkness of a cell with his eventual capture should he leave her behind.

"Let us be gone and part ways. I think we'll all be the better for it," Sou said, an under toned threat in his voice. Grae unsheathed his rapier, pointing it at the leather pack on her back.

"You will give us your coin. If you refuse, your life will suffice. Payment for your deceit. Whatever secrets you possess we will not die for them." Although he stared at Evelyn, he spoke to Sou, his voice a low rumble before the storm.

"Depths drown us, and Breaths be denied, boy! There is no time for this! We are not the only ones on the run. What makes you believe Evelyn and not Meric was the target?"

Grae showed not the slightest touch of hesitation. Instead, he shifted his gaze to Sou, tightening his grip on the rapier.

"You *are* a sly one, Vagu. Is this your refusal?"

Anya spared a glance with Meric, who placed a hand on his friend's shoulder, opening his mouth to speak with him. He shook it off and stepped forward. Sou moved in front of Evelyn, Grae's sword point resting on the ferryman's chest. She unsheathed her dagger, pulling it from the confines of her cloak and prepared herself to fight the Venandi, all of them if needs be, but Sou lifted a placating hand.

"Grae, my lad, you lie to yourself," his voice was soothing, the voice she'd heard so many times throughout her life, teaching her the error of her ways when she was too stubborn to see it. "I am not a gateway. Your guilt is far stronger than my demise. It is insatiable, and I can only feed it. There is but one way to starve it unto death. You know what you must do."

Grae's hand trembled, sword lowering in between the stagger of his breath. Evelyn glanced between the two men, wondering what it was that Sou felt through the wind to make Grae hesitate. The silence in that moment stretched into the night, echoing back a sinister laugh, animalistic and human all at once. Gooseflesh rippled across Evelyn's arms and her breath caught in her throat with the memory of black wings and a tongueless man. Meric nocked an arrow in his bow, aiming it towards the sky. Grae turned his back from Sou, peering upwards as Anya did, her dagger gleaming in the fog.

Meric caught Evelyn's gaze, looking down towards the opening in the wall.

"Go," he said through his teeth.

The tension rose to the narrow point of a knife, teetering on panic. She stood still, refusing to leave any of them to the fate of what laid within the black mist. There was a sudden emptiness in the air, the silence mocking them with its longevity. She felt the whooshing of wings overhead and crouched, but couldn't see anything when she looked up. The Venandi did the same, Meric trying to aim at what was invisible to all of them. Sou flexed his fingers, hands collecting blue wisps of Iona's Breath.

Evelyn searched within herself, reaching for the only gift her father had ever given her. But every time she had a solid grip on the wind, it slipped just as easily from her control. It was so close. She could feel it, but she couldn't hold it the way she did before she was bonded. She ran her fingers over the scarf of her cloak, feeling the shape of Oretem's scale within the pouch. Did she dare to touch it? Would it help save them, or only bring about death faster?

She looked to Sou who was watching her with a tremulant mouth hardened with anxiety. He motioned for her to escape, but she shook her head. She wouldn't leave him — she wouldn't leave any of them. The shadow was circling them as though creating a beam with the darkness that warped in the alley, announcing their location to its caliginous master. The shadow shifted, growing larger, diving with a speed she couldn't measure.

Meric lowered his bow and gripped Evelyn's hand. He pulled himself and her through the opening, his breath uneven and quick. It was far from the calmed confidence he had displayed before. As she and Meric reached the other side, Grae and Anya appeared from the wall behind them. Sou was nowhere to be seen. Panic gripped her and Evelyn suddenly realized how much further the black cavern of her losses could collapse should anything happen to Sou. Meric still held her hand, his grasp as tight as a line of fishing string against a strong current. She tugged against him, ripping her hand from his with enough force to leave her fingers throbbing.

She turned towards the wall, a thundering rumble vibrating through the stone and beneath her feet. Sou was using Iona's Breath. He was being attacked. She crouched to enter the hole again when Meric grabbed her wrist. She was pulled up, her trapped hand pressed against his chest. She brought her dagger up, shoving the sharp edge against the skin of his neck. His eyes stared her down with the severity of someone who'd known the bite of steel and was unafraid of its cold purpose.

"Leave him," Meric's voice was calloused, angry at the situation he'd found himself in.

If they survived the night, he and his companions would be gone by morning. It didn't matter. None of it mattered if the only person she cared for in the world were to die only a wall's distance away from her.

"I didn't ask it of you. Do not ask it of me," she whispered, hearing the roar of the wind grow and feeling precious time slip once again through her hands.

She glared at him, her hand steady on the blade, defying his command. She stared down the burning irises of a mountain dragon—his hazel gaze was no match for her. He endured her stare for another moment before an understanding glimmer passed through his features. He groaned and released her, shoving her away and freeing his neck from the edge of her dagger. He made his way to the opening. She followed, determined not to be left behind when a troop of guards burst from the adjacent alley.

Evelyn was struck with the blunt end of a spear across her back. She staggered and spun around, slashing her dagger through the air that diverted a spear thrust. In her peripheral, she caught sight of a massive guard, running towards her with giant fists gripping his spear horizontally. Meric stepped in beside her, pushing her out of the way. The guard rammed his weapon into Meric's chest before he had any chance to avoid the blow. He was thrown onto his back, heaving for lost breath. The guard straddled Meric, the spears length choking him as he flailed below the man.

The guard that had struck Evelyn across the back bared his teeth, holding the weapon with the point leveled at her chest. This was the same man she had spoken to earlier in the night at Fallon's estate. She sensed no recognition in his eyes.

"Alive! Fallon wants them living." The man shouted at the guard choking Meric. The heavy man relented and lifted the spear just a touch. Meric heaved below him, wheezing with violent coughs.

Three guards had pinned Grae to the ground, using their knees to incapacitate the Venandi. Grae gasped against the cobblestones, straining against the weight of the men. Anya leapt onto the back of one of the guards, sliding her blade across his throat. Blood sprayed over the designed vests of his companions. As she released the dead man, another guard came from behind and thrust the opposite end of his spear across her legs. Anya fell to the ground with a cry of pain. She quickly stood and raised her weapon to strike, but stopped when the man aimed the spear point at Grae's throat.

Evelyn raised her hand to grip Oretem's scale, but the guard before her lifted his spear, the smooth edge resting against her cheek. He narrowed his gaze, brow furrowing as he met her glare.

"We've met," he said before turning to look at Meric—a hateful gleam in his autumn eyes. "You look well. Far too well."

"Let us show you how well we are. I'll have you pissing blood!" Anya said, pacing like a caged animal. The woman was breathing heavily, eyes mad for violence. The guard sighed, rolling his eyes.

"Bind them tight, especially that Venandi woman," the man's dark eyes roamed through the alley, searching. He turned back to Evelyn, mouth tight with irritation. "Where is your Vagu?"

Evelyn held her silence, refusing to avert her gaze. Her body trembled with fear, but not of the guard before her. The wind still raged beyond the wall. How much longer could Sou fight before she would have to bear the silence of his defeat?

"Men, take the Venandi back to the estate. The Lady and I will be having a chat on the company she keeps."

Meric grunted as he was pulled onto his feet. The large guard's weighty fingers closed around the back of his neck as he was pushed forward. The Venandi struggled as they were dragged away—Anya spitting, cursing and thrashing as they tried to bind her. Evelyn could only think of all the ways she could kill the man in front of her before Fallon's guards took the Venandi out of sight. The spilling of blood was a storm that still wept above her, but she'd grown used to standing in the rain. The guard stepped towards her, spear glowing golden in the moonlight. Suddenly, the ground shook and the wall behind her exploded into large, ragged pieces of rock.

She threw herself to the floor, covering her head as stone crashed around her, the sharp edges cutting into her arms. Screams filled the air as the guards were pummeled onto the floor. She heard the hard sound of a body crashing and the feral howl of pain. Whether it was human or not, she couldn't tell. Something lifted, soared, and disappeared into the sky. When the dust settled, she rose to see the small opening in the wall had expanded to empty space, obliterating that there had ever been a barrier in the first place.

The guard that had stood before Evelyn was buried under a pile of rubble, bloodied hand still gripping a gleaming spear. The other guards were either unconscious or dead. Some had their limbs bent in awkward angles, while many had their heads split open, blood pooling the alleyway in rivulets.

Anya stood, helping Grae out from under the body of a guard. The two of them displayed scratches on their cheeks from the debris. They reached for their blades, squinting through the darkness to find the rest of their company. Meric was on his hands and knees, holding his injured shoulder, but was otherwise unharmed. Evelyn turned, twisting to find the body she heard fall, desperate in her search for it to not be Sou. She couldn't breathe, her heart raging against the reality of what her mind was telling her had happened to him.

She faced the broken wall and Sou walked through the black fog, standing firm with his arm outstretched, wisps of wind trailing around his entire body. The blue trails of his power faded into the night as he withdrew his hold on the gust, slanted brows furrowed with enraged intent, mingled with exhaustion. Relief flooded through Evelyn's veins, and she fought the urge to throw her arms around him. To tell him she was sorry, and that the damage they had inflicted upon the other could heal.

Forgiveness is a sacrifice, but death is everlasting. Once gone, it will always be too late.

Despite the sudden realization, she stood frozen in her relief, unable to speak the words she knew needed speaking. Tansey always told her she was too stubborn. Sou's chest heaved with heavy breath, and he stepped over the broken stone, catching his foot a few times. The ferryman passed over the bodies of the guards, making an effort not to look down at the blood staining his boots. He strode over to Meric, gripping the man by the arm and hauling him to his feet.

Evelyn spotted a glimmer in the rubble, her dagger a few paces from where she had landed. She strode over and picked it up, holding it in her hand, unsure if she would need it. Before she joined the others, she noticed a feather strewn across a piece of the blasted wall, nearly invisible had it not been for the black color fading into a dark grey at the tip.

It belonged to a raptor, but not the one that attacked her in Verbena. That one had been coal black, with no trace of color beside its golden eyes. She allowed herself to breathe again and felt the numbing horror that possessed her fade into a more manageable kind of fear. When she last held Oretem's scale she'd known he was still in the Bena Mountains. This entire time, she'd thought the only way Maun would be able to get to Reva so quickly was on Oretem's back. Now, she knew it was someone else, most likely another Reticent. But she wondered why he wouldn't come himself.

The gutting fear of her own demise ran rampant within her, but the city would stand come sunrise and the lives of those within it. The relief was powerful, but fleeting. It was soon overcome by the need for escape. Meric. The raptor hadn't been aiming for her, it had caught Meric. Maun had a fellow Reticent in the city, doing the work he was too far away to complete. She didn't know how he had gotten word to another so fast, but it hardly mattered. She needed to get Meric out of the city before this assassin could find him.

She left the feather where she found it and made her way to the others. The moans of the waking guards grew louder with each passing moment. Many began to scream their pain as they woke. Evelyn wilted listening to their cries.

"This way," Meric said, running towards the end of the alley.

Without faltering, Grae and Anya took up their position at Evelyn's side and together, with Sou behind her, they ran after Meric. She peered at Sou, who wouldn't look at her. He kept his focus forward, glancing upwards with those unfamiliar dead eyes.

They reached the end of the alley that emptied onto an abandoned town square. In the middle of the square was a shattered well, surrounded by the stones that used to make up its shape. The road was similar to the one they took when entering the city, but overgrown with grass the height of her knees. The growth and cobblestones melded, making the terrain appear forsaken, uneven, and dirty. The deserted shops were falling apart, the overgrowth finding purchase in cracked stones. Most of the structures still held the scorch marks of dragon fire, remembering what the rest of the city had forgotten. It was the first time Evelyn had seen the scars of the Evandis, the destruction fastened to a darker era. It was a time before she was born, but even in her small village she'd heard the stories of Chao's horrific attack on Reva.

Grae withheld his breath beside her, looking over the shattered well with hard eyes. Evelyn couldn't be sure, but she thought she noticed a quiver upon his mouth before the Venandi turned away. Sharply, he sprinted forward with no regard for those he left behind. With no torchlight to light the road, they followed him into darkness. Evelyn immediately felt relief as she ran into the open air, fog dissipating from her sight as blue tendrils of light reappeared above with the breeze.

They left the desolate town square until the stone at their feet turned to dirt, the grass growing longer with each step. Before long the foliage was above her head, reaching towards the night as if to join it. Having their vision blocked by its thickness didn't seem to faze the Venandi. They continued onward, using their hands instead of their blades to make their way through.

Evelyn trailed after them, shoving away the grass that had sprung back to its original position. She lifted her hand to reposition more when her fingers grazed against something hard and thick. She touched it, thinking it was the trunk of a tree but recalled seeing no forests outside the city. She gazed upwards and saw several white pillars jutting from the ground, connecting to a ridge as thick as the largest willow.

She gasped, realizing where it was she stood. Residing in the skeletal remains of the Unnamed Dragon, Evelyn imagined what it might've been like to be the prey of a beast so mighty. The tall grass reached around the dragoness's spine as though imitating the green hide she might've had in life. Her bones glowed in the moonlight, casting shifting shadows of the surrounding grassland. Evelyn stood in wonder and couldn't help the sense of amazement that this incredible beast had once lived. She lowered her head, forcing herself not to gawk at the Unnamed Dragon's remains. She felt unworthy of soaking in the wisdom her bones might've left behind.

The Venandi led on for what seemed like hours when they came upon a clearing. Iona's Breath flew across the plains, ages upon ages of green stretched as far as the twilight of the oncoming sun allowed her to see.

Anya, ran a hand through her hair, resting a palm on her forehead. "Bloody Depths drown us all," she cursed softly, sighing with a heavy breath in Grae's direction.

The Venandi came forward, strands of hair falling over his angry blue eyes.

"We never should have bound ourselves to these people," Grae said, staring straight at Sou.

Meric met her gaze, coldness spreading through Evelyn's body like she'd been thrown into the Omya. She implored him with her eyes that she had no choice. Whether he could detect that, she couldn't tell. A faint, thin line of blue ran over his shoulder towards her, his thought accusing.

Who wants you dead?

She kept his stare, unwilling to say she knew what he asked, unable to give voice to his question. *Not I. You. He wants you dead, and I wish I knew for what reason.*

She'd used them. She hadn't a choice, but that didn't make what she did taste any less bitter. The fruit of her choices were rotten, but she found that she regretted nothing. She did what she had to do. They'd escaped the city and Meric was safe, at least for the time being. Meric approached her, his companions poised to flee or attack, waiting on the result of his actions. He glared at her, then through her as though she were a spirit wandering in search of her grave.

"We cannot linger," he said, looking back at his fellow Venandi. "More of Fallon's men are likely not far behind, and they cannot search the entirety of the plains. They will stop here and report back to the bastard to discuss their next course of action. By the time they've convened we should be days into the Dattadri Greens."

Evelyn met Sou's glance; he was just as puzzled as to Meric's continued attachment to their contract. He had more than enough reason to break it. She had been so sure once they'd escaped the city, he and the protection his profession offered would be far beyond their reach. Grae's brow creased, and he opened his mouth to argue but Anya gripped his hand, speaking with her eyes for him to be silent. Meric turned back to Evelyn, his mouth hardened into a sardonic grin.

"Plenty of time for a Lady to share why a Reticent will kill us all."

PART THREE

INTERLUDE

The Decay of Isla Om

The sand stirred beneath Cinaed's feet like gelatinous waves, threatening to pull him under, his lungs half full of the grainy rocks. He couldn't decide which might be a better death, suffocation or dehydration? He hadn't brought nearly enough water and it had only been a few hours since he ran out. The heat was relentless, breaching the thin layers of cloth covering his skin and scorching the uncovered portions of his face. Had he any skin beneath his eyes left? Were his cheeks raw muscle, baking in the wide inferno that was Solov Waste?

The sun was high in the sky, beaming rays of hazy illusions that looked like pools of water, but would disappear into the bright horizon with each step he took. Cinaed was certain that this was no place for him to die. He'd received no impression from the Vagu he'd met in the Eshe Willow Wood that the young man would be sending him to his death, but who knew the true intentions of a people so influenced by superstition.

I listened to that superstition and now here I am. Always the fool.

What was his name? It was an odd name that reminded him of a meal. The sun seemed to burn brighter as he tried to remember. It didn't matter anyway.

He'd spoken with the young Vagu because he had no other choice. He'd begun dreaming and that above everything had to be prevented. He couldn't sleep, fearing what he might see and what he might do should the dreams prove true. He'd seen so much, far too much. He knew dreaming could manifest at any age, but why now? Why him?

The Videns were regarded as humanity's greatest warriors and peacekeepers, but he was a simple cobbler. He had not the desire to do more than what he had been doing all his life, making shoes. He wasn't the *finest* cobbler, but he was content with his success. Perhaps it was due to his service to the street walkers. Once a month he selected a day for the souls living in the dark alleyways to visit his shop, providing repairs and replacements to cover their sore and callused feet. He'd done it for years, finding value in the smiles on their weathered faces. That had all ended when the dreams came. He couldn't focus on his tasks. He made mistakes, and the value of his materials were inconsequential when handled improperly. Everything reminded him of his dreams. Shadows cast a familiar shape or the simple act of sewing a needle through leather brought on a sense of cognizance, as though he'd lived the experience before.

At first, he could explain it away. Of course the needle in his hand felt familiar, he worked with it every day. It was natural to fear a shadow, the absence of light had always been the enemy to mankind. It is a simple thing to cast away doubts in the daylight but once the sun set, they crept back through the darkness to plague his dreams. They'd evolved from everyday tasks and the familiar faces of his customers to disasters and strangers. People laying in their own blood, battles with the echoing screams of the dying, and great winged beasts tearing bodies apart in ways he'd never thought was possible. He woke seeing enemies where there were none, haunted by what he saw. Sinking into a madness that would eventually consume him, creating no difference between him and a shoe without its matching pair. Useless. Why had this happened to him? Why couldn't his silent slumbers be just that: blackness and escape.

He hadn't meant to leave his shop. The paranoia had made

him careless to what truly mattered in his life. He'd owned a leather belt to strap his apron on when cobbling. It became a living being, staring at him as he worked the leather, tightening around his neck and threatening to suffocate him. He'd seen it in a dream, killing him. He abandoned the shop, left it open for anyone to walk in. He'd spent the night facing the corner of his room, a whimpering child in the form of a man, fearing the dark. He went back to the shop the next day and found it had been ransacked. When he stepped inside, he discovered a dead street walker among the scattered remains of what had made up his life. The man had shoes of his making, though they were old and tattered. Around his neck was the leather belt, eyes bulging, tongue swollen. Killed by his fellow street walkers for a hole of molded leather to place their feet in. It was all gone. His entire life, shattered and stolen. He left the city that same day and traveled to the forests of the Vagu to be told how to stop dreaming, not to bond. It had brought him nothing but misery and death.

He closed his eyes against the reflection of the still and barren landscape, his mind poisoned by the number of dead eyes staring back at him through the grains of sand. Countless. They were countless. They stared at him as if he were the one wielding the blade that had cut them out. Men with scarred faces and wild winged monsters flew into a battlefield, their howls and screams lusting for blood. Children being carried away from the broken bodies of their parents and dragons lighting the sky with fire. It was there before him. Had the heat finally driven him mad, or were his dreams as sleepless as he was?

Cinaed wiped the sweat dripping down his brow, trying to walk straight, but knowing his feet were leaning in circles. His vision was getting worse. The sands turned into an ocean of blood, falling through the horizon as it melded with the sea before him.

The sea?

He could see the sea. The sun cast a red shade on the sand, making it only seem like blood. He stumbled and wiped a hand over his face, bits of sand clinging to sweat. He couldn't tell what was real anymore. It may be another hallucination, disappearing just as the phantom pools of water had. But with each step the blue of the ocean grew brighter. Crashing waves beat the rock formations along the beach, thundering across the Waste.

He was told he'd find his answers by the driest ocean, and no water was more arid than the Celosia Sea. Her water was more salt than liquid that made drinking inconceivable, but then again everything that lived within Solov Waste was a marvel of the unbelievable. His own journey here should've been impossible, yet here he was, dying at the edge of impossibilities.

"You seek an answer. The Waste will be swift in its response. Edewor is not the place for you. Solov is," the Vagu man had said, his green eyes burrowing deep into his own. He knew, Cinaed suddenly realized too late. He knew exactly how frightened he was and how he sought an end to his torment. He'd sent him to die. It was the only way to be rid of the dreams.

Cinaed shuffled closer to the sea, doubting its blinding reflection until his feet touched the water. He took off his ragged boots, the last remnants of his past life, and buried his toes in the clay-like mold the soles of his feet created. He sat on the wet sand, lifting a hand to his lips that were cracked and bloody with thirst. His tongue felt fat against his cheek as he ran it along the caverns of his dry mouth. Death it was then. He had hoped for something more, but remaining in the Waste meant he'd never see the fruition of the horrors he'd seen. Given the choice, any choice, he'd do anything, and it seemed that meant dying.

He continued to gaze out into the sea, its sparkling waves gentle and rolling like his home within the Dattadri Greens. He felt the sun at his back abate, as though setting. He turned with the expectation of fading light, but instead realized he sat in the shadow of an eclipse in the shape of a man. Cinaed squinted his eyes against the bright illumination of black against the sky. The man-shaped eclipse reached out, holding a canteen of water. Any thought of death flew and escaped Cinaed's mind as he snatched the canteen, throwing his head back as the water flowed to the back of his throat. Only when his body shook with the urge for breath did he stop and gasp, lifting himself to his knees.

"What in Isla's Reach are you doing here?" the eclipse said, its man-shape bright against the glaring sun. A speaking eclipse. If Cinaed could laugh he would've, finally convinced he'd gone mad after all.

He tried to speak, but found that his throat was raw and too dry to soak up the water he just drank. He needed more. He gripped the eclipse's human hand, pulling him down as he tried to beg for more. The sky reached down and grabbed his shoulders, hoisting him up with a grunt. It led him to the side of a dune littered with sea rock and coated with a thin layer of salt. The sandbank was large, providing the much-needed shade that Cinaed required to gain his bearings.

The eclipse sat him on a rock and turned its brilliance towards a ship that wasn't exactly a ship. Beneath the bow were long paddles that seemed to keep the entire structure from sinking into the sand. The stern was a buried wheel, connected by a long slab of wood, creating a handle to pump the wheel. By lifting and lowering the handle, one could propel the vehicle forward using its captain's body weight to steer, very similar to a small sailing vessel. On top were giant pitchers of water. The eclipse, still bathed in light, opened one and refilled the canteen.

It walked back to the shadows, dropping from the sky to reveal its true form. Cinaed was amazed to see what was standing across him. His eclipse was a large man covered in layers of thick clothing; every bit of his skin covered. A scarf hugged his head, wrapping around his face to where only his dark brown eyes were visible under slanted brows.

Cinaed groaned inwardly as he felt his relief turn into disappointment. The Vagu he saw in the Willow Wood sent him across the Waste only to find *another* Vagu. The man handed Cinaed the filled canteen and took a seat on a rock across from him as he drank its contents.

He pulled down his scarf to reveal dark skin and a long scar that ran from the tip of his temple to the bottom of his jaw. The wound looked old and worn, as if it had been sanded down by years in the heat. The stranger was weary and wrinkled, stoic in his gaze that shifted everywhere but on Cinaed. His expression was scarcely readable, as though he'd forgotten how to behave socially.

"What is your name?" Cinaed asked, taking another gulp, his throat moist enough for speech.

"I left my name a long time ago. You may call me Falconer," he said, seemingly more interested in the way a brief breeze swayed the sand at his feet.

Cinaed thought it odd to leave a name. It wasn't a physical object that one could just abandon, it followed you throughout your existence, whether you chose to acknowledge it or not.

"Falconer, it seems I am in your debt," Cinaed said, although he had no intention of repaying a deed that came from a Vagu. He might as well have been conversing with a Viden, and that was the very thing he was trying to avoid.

"As far as I know I am the only one who calls Solov home. There are quicker ways to die, you understand?" Falconer said, puzzlement etched in his features.

"I did not come here to die."

"No? Then may I ask what you are here for?"

Cinaed hesitated, unsure of what to say. It wasn't his intention to die when he started the journey. What had it been before?

"An end."

Falconer raised an eyebrow, meeting his gaze before averting it again. He furrowed his crowed eyes and reached out his hand for the canteen. As Falconer drank, he spilled some onto the ground, sand darkening with the damp moisture.

"Aye, you'll find that here. An end to all things."

They didn't speak again for some time as Cinaed regained

his energy. The ache in his limbs lessened as the effects of the water began to bring strength back to his body. Soon, he felt well enough to stand, but stayed where he sat, watching the scar on the older man shift against his jaw muscles.

"I don't suppose you know who I am?" Cinaed said, breaking through the sound of crashing waves. Their meeting couldn't be a coincidence. He had thought the young man in the willow had sent him to die, but perhaps it was to meet this man. Could he know how to stop the dreams?

Falconer eyed him with curiosity as if seriously searching through his memory for any familiarity. He looked down, shaking his head.

"Should I? I've not spoken to another soul for..." he trailed off, inclining his head to the side, chuckling. "You know, I've lost track. Imagine that?"

Falconer continued to chuckle to himself as if he'd heard the joke of the century. Cinaed leaned forward, curious as to why he'd been sent to meet this man. He felt the breath in his lungs, the burnt skin on his cheeks. Alive. He'd teetered on the edge of death, thrusted back into the world of the living and it had never tasted so sweet. He wanted an end to his visions, but not at the cost of this feeling.

"Why are you out here?" he asked, feeling the sand shifting beneath his bare feet.

Falconer rubbed his chin and rested his face in his hand as he looked out to the sea. He was the perfect painting of contemplation.

"When you've seen everything, there is only nothing left. And what a beautiful nothingness this is," he said, his dark eyes reflecting the blue of the sea.

Cinaed hung his head, thinking that he was going to get nothing coherent from this man. He'd lost his cobbler shop, left Reva to take the word of an untrustworthy Vagu to wander the Waste in search of a madman. It was more than sunlight that addled his mind.

"If only the whole world could be as nothing as this," Cinaed said, at least agreeing with the beauty of what laid before him. He wasn't immune to the allure of seclusion and isolation the Waste offered. If an end was what he was searching for, he'd certainly found it here.

"Oh, it could," Falconer said, standing with excitement. The motion was startlingly quick for one who was so calm just moments before. "It once was, long ago in the time of Isla Om."

Cinaed felt a tickle in the back of his mind as he thought of the name. He'd heard it before, but as a child.

"I'm not sure I remember the story," Cinaed mumbled, shifting further from the changeable man with an air of caution. Falconer gasped and smiled, his teeth dark and over-lapped from malnourishment.

"Then I will remind you. I hope you will appreciate the manner of its telling more than Onyx. I was, after all, a story-teller among my people."

Falconer made his way to the sand bank, skipping with the step of an excitable child. Cinaed searched the beach for anything that could be given that name, but they were the only ones there. Who Falconer was speaking of, Cinaed hadn't the faintest idea.

The scared man stood with hands outstretched, seeming to concentrate on the blistering sand beneath his feet. Cinaed raised his hand to his mouth, tracing the cracks in his lips as he contemplated how much madness had gripped the man before him. He eyed the sand ship and wondered if he could operate it on his own. He turned back to Falconer and gasped as a powerful wind scooped up the sand at the man's feet, twisting into formless shapes around him. The man was lifting the Waste with his Iona's Breath.

Cinaed stood, wondering if he should run, but knew he wouldn't last the rest of the day without water. He remained, watching the bits of sand form into figures, their humanoid shapes flowing with Falconer's expert hand.

There were two women standing next to him, their shapes curved with flowing, gritty hair. Their forms lacked detail as though Falconer couldn't remember what the women looked

like. He smiled at Cinaed, looking for approval. He gave the
conjurer a wry grin, hoping he wouldn't see how uncomfortable he was. The Vagu controlled the nature of Iona and therefore made themselves unnatural. Their conversations with the
dead were universally abhorred, but it was their control of the
wind that Cinaed detested the most. What could he do against
such an attack? What could anyone who wasn't Vagu or Viden
do? He wanted no part of that power.

"Isla Om was an island who wished to be human. She
ached to see those visiting her beaches, then would weep at
their departure. For millennia, she begged Iona for this gift,"
the sand figure of one of the women waned in volume until
Cinaed could almost see through her. A twisted, malformed
heart appeared in the center of her chest, pulsating into cracks.
"Her heart was breaking to see the joys of human existence
and so her beaches soiled in dead fish and her trees poisoned
wells of fresh water. As the only spit of land, she became unin-
habitable, and we began to die."

The other woman rose from the dune, taller and thinner
than the other, but with hair that curled in every direction,
twisting like fire. Mists of sand looped and swirled around her
head as though she were steaming in the heat of the
baking sun.

"Her sister, nameless as she's always been, lived beneath
her in the form of a volcano. She was content in her form,
causing eruptions to form more earth for the humans Isla so
loved, but it laid dead beneath the sea. Her fire couldn't breech
the surface where Isla resided alone. She spoke with Iona,
beseeching the world's spirit to give into her sister's wishes.
Iona agreed, but only if she would abandon her form as a
volcano and become human as well.

"For the love of her sister, she agreed. Iona granted Isla's
wish and they rose from the sea together holding the hand of
the other for the first time." The two women embraced as Isla's
figure mended into a solid form, her heart pulsing with vigor
within her sand body. "They both retained their powers. Isla
and her sister created land together, forming the Waste we

walk upon, the mountains to the north and the plains to the west. Her sister lit the flames for the earth to rise and Isla brought the bounty of forests and rivers, beast, and fowl."

The sand thundered as Falconer lifted his hands, Iona's Breath creating mountain peaks and individual blades of grass, trees, and banks. Cinaed stood with his mouth open, stunned at what the old man spawned from bits of rock and dust. This was beyond what he thought a Vagu capable of.

"For years they lived this way. Isla thrived among the humans, never having been happier in her existence. Isla's sister found happiness in hers, but her heart burned for her volcanic form. She missed the sea and its enveloping warmth. There was no more earth to create, and she ached to implode, fragment into creation. It was only through the love of Isla that the Nameless Sister resisted her nature. As time passed Isla met a man—a man of blue eyes. The same color of the sky she long stared into as an island, imagining the life she could have among his own kind."

Falconer lifted a finger and the figure of a man with a lean build grew in between the embracing sisters, his arms holding Isla's waist. The Nameless Sister's form stirred, as though only now realizing the empty space she held.

"Isla decided to depart from where she lived with her sister and go with her lover. She couldn't have known how this would break her sister. How the raging river of fire would flow across what she had thought was a life living in contentment. Her sister tried to quell the flames within herself, knowing it was the way of humans. But she wasn't human—she was never meant to be human and the thought of being human *alone* was enough to crack the hardened surface of her boiling rage."

More wind blew from Falconer's fingertips, surrounding the three figures in what seemed to be a combination of clouds and waves flowing and ebbing in between them all. Cinaed was captured by the spectacle. He was sure he'd heard the tale before, but having it played out before him in this fashion, it became an entirely new story.

"All she had given up and she would be alone still, trapped

in a form she felt half alive in. She took Isla's lover to the center of Iona, where she and Isla first emerged from the sea. She begged the man of blue, pleading for the love of her sister. She implored him to stay, to love Isla—but stay."

The Nameless Sister dimmed in beauty as the man turned his head, looking upon Isla's figure with a radiance Cinaed thought impossible. The figures had no faces, but he could see the depth of the man's love through the eyes that Falconer gave him. His slits were an open window to the sky.

"It was the pity in his blue eyes that drove her to understanding," Falconer whispered with what appeared to be a deep sadness. "It was not their absence she feared, but their love. It was enduring and she realized she would never again return beneath the sea. She would have to destroy it all, drag it down with her to be who she once was."

Balls of sand flew from the woman's hands, trailing dust like fire as they crashed into the surrounding dunes. Cinaed felt the rocks shake beneath him from the impact.

"Isla's love was bound by something else, something stronger, and her sister could not bear her human form a moment longer. The ground cracked beneath her and she devoured, sinking back to whence she came, making sure to bring everything she and Isla created with her. The man of blue tried to run, but was caught between the shifting earth. He raged and fought, but the earth was hungry, and the Nameless Sister swallowed him living."

The man devolved into the sand, reaching for the sky. Cinaed could almost hear his nonexistent bones crushing under the weight of the ground, lungs gasping for air as his light eyes grew dark. He couldn't looked away, captivated by the man's gruesome fate.

"Isla felt her sister's rage and raced to meet her. She arrived in time to see the blue eyes of the man she loved disappear beneath the ground. She could not save him."

Isla's hands dug into the sand, screaming without a mouth for her beloved. Cinaed thought he saw a tear running down the length of Falconer's scar, but it could've been the sweat.

"She reached and reached, but she was only human. The depth of his death was too far for her and so, she stood alone in the hollowed hole of his grave, decaying as the world crumbled around her." Isla fell to her knees, sand billowing, her form falling apart. Then she placed her hands into the sand where branch-like arms grew from her body, burying deep into the ground.

"Grief and pain were all that the sisters became. To save the world she loved, Isla willed her arms to embrace the land. She grew roots, searching for the man of blue, hoping beyond hope that she'd find him and, in her desperation, hold the world from sinking."

Isla's sister rose into the air, her fire curls drifting about her head as though she were under water.

"Her sister diminished to the bottom of the sea, bringing with her everything but the land that Isla held with her rooted arms. She remains there, waiting for Isla's roots to rot and break, her rage still boiling the water surrounding her. Isla grew and grew until there was no place left to grow, no place left to look. She couldn't leave; she was bound to the place where the two halves of her heart died. Her sister smolders beneath her, waiting to take back all she'd helped create. Time lost the name of her sister and the man of blue, but Isla never forgot. She continues as she began, as a spit of land mourning the life she couldn't have."

The sisters had their backs to each other, but Cinaed could feel the connection that bound the two together. Falconer's hands lowered and their forms dissipated with slow intent as if wanting to remain, but knowing that they couldn't, until they disappeared completely.

"Thus ends the tale of the Nameless Sister," Cinaed said, recognizing the name he knew the story by. The way Falconer told the tale was more metaphorical than he remembered, but he knew it was the legend of how the elm was created. The great tree standing solemn in the middle of the burning lake. As well as Isla's Reach, the mythical tunnels rumored to be beneath the land.

"Thus ends the tale of The Decay of Isla Om," Falconer corrected with a cautious eye. "It's been some time since I've told it. Is it not curious how villains create their own demises? Although I hesitate to refer to the Nameless Sister as a villain. Were the tale in her perspective would it not be a tragedy as well? Ah. Such is the burden of all storytellers. We are cursed with vision that sees through such eyes for those who cannot see themselves." he continued with an inquisitive nod.

"I'm not sure I follow," Cinaed pinched the brim of his nose.

"As a storyteller I must understand the motivations of those within the tale. Otherwise the telling would be as droll as dry spit. When I speak of cursed vision I mean that, despite my own moral reservations, I see what lies beneath ones amoral conduct that others would cease to acknowledge due to their reprehensible actions. Think of it like — "

"That is not what I meant," Cinaed said, losing his patience.

"Aye. I see. Only from great rage can a creature such as a dragon be born and in time Videns. It's fitting, isn't it? That the Nameless Sister should create that which could stop her," Falconer's tone suggested he thought long on the subject.

Cinaed bent to pick up the canteen and took another long sip, closing his eyes at the feel of its coolness collecting in his belly. He thought it curious that Falconer would think that the Videns were protecting Isla when in every story he'd ever heard they defended Iona. Meaning the land and everyone who lived in it, but he supposed that could include the elm tree. He had a hard time believing that when being forced to witness visions of horrible happenings. It didn't seem the future held the peace that they so preached.

"What does it matter if what is seen cannot be stopped?" Cinaed said, looking out to the ocean, remembering the bloated eyes of the strangled street walker. "Madness is the fate of the Videns and to that I say, *what more could we expect?* The Videns cannot protect themselves, by what incentive do I have to believe they can protect us all?"

Falconer took the canteen from him with a fast grip as though afraid Cinaed might run off with it. He stared at him for a moment, his scar twitching in agitation. "They must. Without Isla, the world will fall. Fire will color the sky with blood and ash, and there will be nothing left to dream of," Falconer said with eyes that seemed to see something that Cinaed could not.

He had thought the man simple for believing in a story told to children before bedtime, but he was intrigued by what he said last. *There will be nothing left to dream of.* He shifted his gaze back to the sea where stillness and beauty were abundant without the burden of life. This was what it was like before Isla and her sister rose from the Depths.

He couldn't be the only one who was so against the influence of the Videns and their dreams. Were there others such as he who wanted to build a life on a beach such as this? Away from the oppression their visions beat upon them like waking nightmares? Men and women who craved power over being told what they should be?

Cinaed felt a rush of wind, but instead of it coming from the ocean it blew behind him. He turned around to see a massive eagle landing on the sand ship. Its wings were black as night and painful to look at in the brightness of the dunes. Once Cinaed's vision adjusted he could see long talons gripping the handle of the ships steering. In one claw it held a large lizard, dripping blood onto the sand. His eyes widened as he recognized the eagle. He'd seen them in his dreams, tearing apart bone and flesh. Instead of being frightened, Cinaed was fascinated—he'd never imagined seeing a solov raptor in person, let alone being able to remember them in a future that hadn't existed yet. The thought would've made him sick had he not admired the raptor so.

Falconer dipped his head and walked to the creature, speaking soft words Cinaed couldn't hear. The man lifted his hand and stroked the eagle on its head as the beast snapped its beak. He stood amazed that Falconer could touch the raptor without losing a finger, however he could now guess how he'd gotten his scar and the bearing of the name Onyx.

"So, is Falconer your name or your livelihood?" Cinaed said, taking a cautious step forward. Falconer displayed a half grin and continued to stroke the raptor as he grabbed the lizard from its talons.

"Aye," he said simply. "If an end is what you seek, then I believe Onyx and I can accommodate that wish. There is an end in endlessness." He gestured to the sea and the horizonless Waste. "We've been alone for a long time. You and I could find it together."

Falconer hadn't taken his eyes off his raptor, but Cinaed could hear the hope in his voice. The man seemed useful enough and he'd given Cinaed just enough incentive to remain with him. At least until he uncovered the reason the Vagu in the willow had sent him to a sun-worn wanderer whose only companion for who knows how many years was a bird that couldn't talk back.

He wasn't promised dreamless nights, but there were things Falconer could teach him. He only endeavored to free his mind of the torment. He would hear more about a time where there would be nothing left to dream of. He felt the visions gnawing at the sanity he clung to, it was chipping away at him. He had to find a way to make it stop. Whatever it took, he would do it.

Cinaed lifted his head towards the sun as it baked the ground beneath him. Its relentless heat already taking a toll on his sense of logic, but it was of no consequence. He thought about the man who cobbled for the street walkers, sacrificing his profits for the smile of a grateful stranger. That man was dead, murdered in his sleep and all that was left was a nightmare reanimated in his empty corpse. He knew what to do and how to get there, all he had left was to wake up.

"Falconer, help me find the end to it all."

CHAPTER 33

A DRAGON'S MEMORY

Maun felt his way through the fog, his crimson eyes fluttering open from the memory Oretem had showed him. He sat upright, feeling the warmth of the dimming fire overhead tickle the stubble at his jaw. He grabbed his chin, wondering how long it had been since he'd shaved. He'd always kept a clean jaw; it was proper to do so, like scouting an unknown area or keeping a blade within reach.

He'd commanded Oretem to show him the most important memory Cinaed had, and he ended up in the Waste, listening to a story he'd heard a hundred times before, sung in taverns all across Iona. He remembered the peddler humming the tune before he killed him. It was difficult to believe that had been only a little more than fortnight ago. How short a time it took for everything in his life to have changed. There was much in the memory that he didn't understand, but what perturbed him was how insignificant Cinaed seemed.

A cobbler? The great Decayed who rode the Scaled Windstorm was a cobbler from Reva? The man was... naïve, too simple to have been the one who led the charge for the Battle of Elm Lake, whose slithering voice still permeated across the cave walls, his blood yet staining the ground where Maun had thrust the man's sword through his skull. Cinaed the Decayed, who created the Reticent, convincing hundreds of Venandi to abandon their brothers and sisters to a cause that resulted in their own tongues being ripped from their mouths. That broken man wandering the Waste couldn't be him, yet Maun knew it was. There was nothing memorable about him. He was so ordinary, so young. The only thought that occupied his mind was to rid himself of his dreams. Cinaed had foreseen the coming of his own destruction, the blank stares of the men and women he would eventually kill, and it drove him mad. Maun couldn't be sure whether it was the Waste's heat or the assailing dreams that had turned Cinaed the Cobbler into Cinaed the Decayed. All he knew was that one had died so the other might live and as Maun recalled the hollowness in those pleading eyes before he brought down the sword, he wondered if Cinaed might've always longed to have never been born at all.

Most disturbing was how human Falconer seemed. As a child, he imagined the man running after him, screaming as streams of blood poured from his eyeless face. He'd built up this monstrous form within his mind, creating a foul persona that was barely recognizable as a man and yet, that was all he was. It was clear that Falconer had mastered the skill of taming solov raptors. Was that the contribution his father and Devu had spoken of? Had he fought against the torture required for the bond between raptor and Reticent? It was always told that the man who taught Cinaed how to bind a raptor perished in the Waste when he founded Soleil Citade. Not much else was known beyond that. For a moment that lasted no longer than the brief gust of a sparrow's wings, Maun wondered exactly what Saiya thought of before she was forced to eat his tongue.

YOU KNOW LITTLE OF THE ANGUISH A CREATURE OF THE SKY SUFFERS WHEN CAGED. SHE, LIKE YOU, HAS KNOWN NOTHING BUT HER PRISON. Oretem's voice was a whisper of graveled rock.

Maun crossed his legs and gazed upon the beast. The spikes across his spine were short, but thicker than the bodies of most trees. Flames flickered across his scales, fabricating an illusion in the shadows that rubies hid, buried within the cave walls. His head rested on his front claws; lids closed as though he were asleep. The dragon's large eye opened, surprisingly reflective in the darkness. Maun could see his entire person in the pupil.

It was the most he'd spoken in two days. The dragon had moments when his mind seemed to settle into who he used to be, but would soon be lost, falling through the split in his soul between him and Evelyn.

You're right. It's a shame you sit so comfortably in your own. I've never known such weakness.

The dragon blew out a heavy breath that threatened to blow Maun from his sitting position, but he managed to hold his stance.

No. IT WAS BEATEN OUT OF YOU. THEY CUT YOUR FLIGHT FEATHERS, GROUND YOUR TALONS TO THE BONE. HOW WERE YOU TO DO WHAT YOU WERE BORN TO DO? WHERE HAD YOU LEFT TO GO BUT BEHIND THE IRON BARS THEY MADE FOR YOU?

Maun's chest tightened; he was unaccustomed to being so exposed with anyone. Not even Saiya had seen him so transparently. He tried to block the dragon from his mind, but his presence was so looming, so astounding that Maun couldn't bar the magnitude of Oretem's presence.

I am what I am.

THIS IS THE MINDSET OF PREY AND VERMIN TOO SIMPLEMINDED TO KNOW BETTER. WE, WHO SEE THE WORLD FROM ABOVE, KNOW WHAT IS, IS NOT WHAT WILL ALWAYS BE.

Oretem hummed and the ground vibrated with its echo. Maun could feel that the beast was trying to be comforting, his head inching forward. For a moment, Maun was engulfed in the sound, overcome with the feeling as though experiencing the closeness of a kind embrace for the first time. He had the sudden recollection of being held in his mother's arms, her hand rubbing his back. Eli was humming and he felt the vibrato of her song through his small body, reminding him of the sound her heart made when in the womb. He stood, baring his teeth, hands curled into fists on either side of his head, banishing the memory as though it were a striking vapor serpent.

I AM WHAT I AM! He screamed in his mind, directing all his rage at the mountain dragon. Oretem silenced his humming and shrunk to the corner of madness where he belonged.

She should be honored that I grew to be the man I am. She shouldn't have resisted.

Even as the thought traveled from him to Oretem, Maun felt the sting of regret in his heart. The image of Eli's pale hand hanging limp from under the floor passed over his memory like a black cloud, suffocating his anger into empty grief. Amazing, how similar and excruciating the two felt in comparison to one another.

He needed to focus on the task at hand.

Cinaed and he were more alike than Maun had realized. They each had a single goal that hadn't included what the rest of the world wanted from them. The Decayed as a young man, not too far from the age Maun was now, wanted nothing but to live the life he was always meant to have. His fear that the visions were poisoning him against his own nature, his free will, was as sharp as the blade at Maun's hip.

It was the design of the Order to free those who wanted nothing to do with the Videns and their teachings, at least in the beginning. He knew better than to share that viewpoint now. The Videns were gone, yet the Reticent still sought Children of Fortune. The Reticent had indeed become hired assassins to murders and highborn miscreants.

What was so important about this memory? What had impressed Cinaed so radically? He recalled the man's words as Saiya held him down, *Falconer told me that fire would color the sky.* The desert man had spoken of dreamless days and that is what the former cobbler had clung to, white knuckled against the death he thought he'd been sent to Solov for. Maun's mind wandered to a thought, a question he'd never thought to ask or imagined thinking of.

What if the Evandis was a lie?

LIES, LIES, LIES. LIVES AND LIARS, LIARS AND LIVES. BURN THEM ALL...

Oretem's thoughts continued to rant mindlessly, rage boiling under every word. His emotional endurance waned under the weight of his changeable moods. One moment he was lucid and the next it took every bit of control Celosia's Glare gave Maun to keep the great dragon inside the cave. He thought back to the memory of Caia and her dragon Varsha battling Chao. Was that what Cinaed was after that night? The elm? For what purpose?

Maun's mind ran wild with the possibilities. If the war were but a front for a madman to regain his sanity, could he have stumbled upon the end to all things? If the legend of Isla's Decay were but a story, why would the last Viden die protecting a fable?

Oretem growled and shifted his legs, the ground rumbling under his immense bulk. Maun stumbled then regained his balance, still thinking through the theory.

HER BURDEN IS GREAT, TO HOLD THAT WHICH FIGHTS HER EMBRACE.

The dragon spoke as though he were reciting an old poem, his demeanor respectful and sorrowful. His voice was distant as though he'd forgotten he was not alone. Maun gripped the hilt of Tansey's iron dagger with firm fingers. It was all theoretical, the hopes of a dead madman and the ravings of a touched dragon. But at the very least, Maun knew the elm was revered and worthy of guarding. Devu would deliver Meric and Maun would kill the man, but what about after? What was to become of him once his vengeance was sated? He knew he'd have to deal with Devu, decide what was to be done with the woman who had set him on this path. He wasn't sure what the future held, but he had Oretem. Who could deny him anything? Who could oppose him? It was worth another trip into the past to see what could be. He turned towards Oretem, the dragon muttering more nonsense Maun had no idea what to make of.

Show me the birth of this world.

I CANNOT.

Maun inclined his head, letting the dragon's answer linger in the air as he reached into his pocket. Celosia's Glare was small, but its influence changed the world, far more than Maun had ever known. He brushed his fingertips over the smooth black stones.

Show me the birth of this world, he repeated, the voice in his mind resolute and merciless.

He knew the moment the effects of Celosia's Glare reached Oretem by the dilating of his crimson pupil. Maun's reflection was cut in half, severed as quick as his own tongue. The dragon's wide eye begged for release, growling as his body shook from the effort of denying him. Maun's own body trembled at the rip in Oretem's soul. He shuddered and opened his mouth in a silent cry of pain as the split traveled from Oretem through him, continuing to rip into Maun as though he were being pulled underground while the rest of him remained on the surface.

He'd always felt a small inkling of what Oretem did, but never like this. He was being torn apart. Maun pulled his hand from his pocket and fell to his hands and knees, gasping for breath. As soon as he released Celosia's Glare his body was whole again. The pain throbbed like an old battle wound, but he no longer felt like he would die from it. Oretem raised his head with heavy hot breath.

You keep it from me! Why do you hide it? Maun's thoughts seemed to bounce from the walls, his anger fueling the fire above his head. He walked to the dragon; his steps furious with determination.

The old beast was fighting him. He would break him again, bend the creature to his will. He was Reticent. He took out Celosia's Glare and held them in his palm, holding the small black stones within a finger's breadth of Oretem's quivering eye.

The dragon squirmed on the floor, writhing in an agony that Maun felt in his blood, dousing the fury he'd felt before.

He fought through the pain, his fingers shaking from the effort. He did not matter. He *did not* matter!

WE...DID...NOT...EXIST...

For the first time the dragon sounded old, his voice like the deathbed confession of a regretful man. Maun fell to the floor, his hand still holding the stones. Sweat dripped from his brow to the edge of his jaw. The darkness surrounding him grew dim, shadowed with the loss of his strength.

That isn't possible. Dragons... he paused, closing his eyes, then reopening them with better sight, *Dragons have always been a part of this world, created as Celosia sunk to the Depths. Through the birth...of this world.* Maun stubbled through the revelation, working within his mind to fit the pieces of what he knew to be true.

APART. TORN APART THEY WERE BY HATE. PAIN AND GRIEF FIGHTS FIRE AND PAIN. OH, ISLA'S BANE! Oretem snarled and snapped the song, bringing fear into its melody with graveled anger.

Maun recalled Cinaed's memory of Falconer, the eager man hoping for Cinaed's companionship. *That she should create that which could destroy her,* he'd said. Dragons. Dragons were born of Celosia, of the Nameless Sister. The two were the same. In returning to her volcanic form, Celosia—the Nameless Sister—created dragons. The world had already been born. Dragons... had been a mistake.

Oretem, is Celosia within the lake? Are the sisters real?

EATER OF TONGUES! BUTCHER OF THE INNOCENT! YOU MAY BE RETICENT, BUT I AM A DRAGON! His thoughts bellowed within the cave, threatening to shatter rocks upon the floor. *WOULD YOU HAVE ME BREAK AS EASILY AS A MOUSE BENEATH MY CLAW?*

I find that in breaking things we are all the same. What spills from our shatterings contains neither honor nor bravery. Only oblivion. You and I are no exception. So, mouse or dragon, I will see you break.

He let his anger return with a passion that could've made him exhale flame and ash. He fixed his eyes upon Oretem and bore into him every horrible thought he'd ever had. The agonized screams of the people he'd murdered and the glee of blood on his hands. The dragon arched his neck as he roared his pain, the mountain shaking as his mind broke yet again. Maun gasped and clutched his chest as the connection between him and Oretem cracked within his own body. Physically he was unharmed, but the phantom ache hurt like nothing he'd ever experienced. Was Oretem's madness becoming his?

The dragon expelled his energy and fell to stone floor, his thoughts flowing like molten lava, too hot to contain but continuously restrained by impassible barriers of rock.

GONE IS THE NAME OF A MAN SO WARM. BUT ISLA KNOWS... SHE KNOWS... SHE KNOWS...

Oretem spoke with the calm tone of a fragmented creature, forced to live when he would've otherwise chosen death. Maun felt the rise of an unknown emotion encase the lining of his heart, crushing it with... shame. He was repulsed by the feeling, taking an involuntary step back as he stumbled from its powerful force. He was never supposed to feel this. With effort, he brushed aside his discomfort and felt the trickle of Oretem fading beside him.

The dragon's mind fogged with tar, sticking to random memories and old resentments. He kept reciting the poem, out of order and with no voice for song. Maun had broken him again. He felt the smallest pull of regret, but not out of pity. No, he wished he'd not given into anger so quickly and instead of slowly lifting the scales from Oretem's hide with deliberation, he'd bludgeoned the dragon with the ferocity of a red-hot poker into a forge. Even then, he knew it wouldn't have worked. He'd been fortunate to wake when he did when Evelyn had spoken with the mad dragon. Oretem hadn't the capacity to reveal much of what he and Maun had been doing deep in the mountains, but he wasn't foolish enough to think it couldn't happen again. If Oretem had revealed his plan to involve his old mentor, then all could've been lost.

Maun understood now. It all made sense as to why Oretem couldn't show him the memory. Dragons had the ability to look as far back into the past as the oldest of dragons. Oretem and the rest of his kind were not alive during the making of the world. He wasn't baring Maun from accessing the memory—he physically did not have it.

Maun had never given much thought to Celosia. Like Iona, the name was a way of being. He never considered the possibility that the names were anything more than ideals. Celosia was the antithesis to Iona, being of darkness and depth, while Iona was breath and light. Now, as Maun had come to realize, it was not Iona, but Isla who claimed these attributes. It never mattered to Maun. The Order believed there was no wind to join them with their loved ones, as they loved nothing. Was he mad enough to consider the possibility that Iona—Isla—lived in the elm? That her roots truly kept Celosia from dragging the whole of the land back beneath the sea? Cinaed hadn't sought just for the destruction of dragons and Videns. The madman had started a decades-long war in the pursuit of his own suicide, detached to the fact that he'd have killed the whole world too.

He glanced at Oretem whose expressionless eye stared into a void only he could see. It was foolish to keep a beast so unhinged. It was only a matter of time before Maun would suffer through the same visions Cinaed had been plagued with. It could happen any day, its unpredictability setting Maun's teeth on edge. Oretem had to die, but with his size and strength only another dragon could kill him. Even if there was another dragon to do the deed, he wasn't sure Oretem could lose. Therefore, he had to discover another way to rid himself of the beast before he began dreaming. So far, his slumber had been silent and dark, but he knew time was running short.

There was nothing in him that desired to possess such power. He had more trust in the skills he'd earned through years of brutality and practice, than those obtained by unnatural means. He wouldn't fall to the same madness the Decayed suffered from.

Maun turned his back to the dragon, ash falling before his eyes from the embers of the ceiling's firelight. His arms shook as he thought of everything that had changed in his life. He used to be a simple assassin, searching for the man who murdered his family. He wasn't so simple, so insignificant anymore. He was still Reticent, but more and more it felt like the life of another man, one who was fighting to stay alive.

He reached out to Saiya, desperate to feel something familiar. She opened her mind to him over the plains of the Dattadri Greens, wings soaring above lush grasslands. She felt his discontent and flowed into him who she saw him to be: a fierce hunter, companion, and speech-bringer. Maun's mouth curve upwards as she was the one who made speech possible for him.

Maun had never doubted so much in his life, but with Saiya to guide him he would always be led back to who he was. She released a loud caw into the sky, enjoying the sun at her back. He asked her through sensations how went their pursuit. She answered through images and senses, such as the endlessness to the wide plains and the small figure of Devu running below her with An'gan flying just above, his lighter feathers rustling in the wind.

Maun nodded and reluctantly separated his mind from hers, deciding this was the last time he'd ever send her away. While he had always known their relationship to be useful and mostly out of necessity, it could no longer be denied that they were a part of each other. The thought of her absence used to make no more difference to him than the begging of dying men, but now he would sooner spend the rest of his life in this barren land of snow and ice than be parted from her again.

Once Meric was brought to him along with the news of the Viden's death, he'd finally leave the darkness of the cave, stray into the light and be relived of the burden to feel.

CHAPTER 34

TO PROVE THEM WRONG

E velyn looked upon the wide plains, herds of onni deer grazing in the near distance. Their antlers spread from their heads in what looked to be an extension of their long twitching ears, watching their passing with a cautious glare. Her legs ached, but far less than they had the first day. It had been three days since they left Reva—three days since the escape that had almost seen them all dead. Evelyn was no stranger to traversing hard terrain. In truth, she found the flat grassland easier to tread than the uneven, rocky ground she grew up climbing.

She recalled the times she and Nakesha would be gone for days in the mountains, hunting babi. But they had ample time to rest throughout the day, having little urgency in their pursuit. The extent of repose the Venandi allowed were intermediate brisk sprints before taking a brief stop, a few minutes to catch one's breath, chew on some onni jerky to wash down with stale water before the run began again. It was exhausting, but Evelyn knew the importance of maintaining their speed. When the first night fell, she thought it best if they continued through the moon's dominion, thinking they'd wanted to put as much distance as they could between them and the city. When she had said as much, Grae had given her a hard look, condemnation in his wearied eyes.

"The night hides more than just the path, even more so from above. But please speak to me more about how to best do my job," he'd said before turning his back to take the first watch. He hadn't spoken much more to her since then.

Without further argument, they stopped that night and every night since. Finding refuge within the Greens, its high-reaching foliage a living shield against prying eyes. Evelyn hadn't pressed the issue, although she had to physically bite her tongue to keep herself from doing so, reminding herself that while there was no trust between them, the Venandi had stayed. She recalled waking the next day, frightened but expecting to find herself and Sou alone in their makeshift camp. When she managed to come to terms with their absence, she turned and looked to the brightening horizon through the forest of grass, surprised to see the three Venandi standing just outside the foliage. Their shapes were silhouetted in light, watching the sun rise as though it were a custom unique to them. Now, three days later they were still together, a spiteful silence between them that she had difficulty adjusting to.

If she spoke, they'd ask her about the Reticent chasing them and she'd have to lie. Evelyn didn't want to lie, but as much as the silence protected her, she knew it would eventually incapacitate their ability to work together should the worst happen. She recalled the times she and Birdie had been at odds and every time their hunts resulted in missed opportunities and angry words. It was only after they reconciled that they found the ease to be content with their success or failure. Though she'd only known the Venandi for a short while, they had distinct personalities she was able to identify.

Anya was the most thick-headed person she'd ever met, but she reminded her of Tansey. Her grandmother's resilience and strength glowed from the woman as if her spirit were guiding the Venandi. Grae's prejudice against Sou spoke to a deeper hatred that she suspected had nothing to do with the ferryman personally. She couldn't trace that man to the one who refused to leave her to die in the alley and she wondered who it was that Grae truly hated. He had a single purpose and that was to keep his Venandi family together, whatever the cost. His own decisiveness was only outmatched by Meric, who was abundant in the kind of empathy that was detrimental to his own wellbeing. He hid it well, but not well enough. It was as if Fallon's prison wasn't the only cell he'd been locked in, and this new secondary freedom was one he didn't know what to do with.

They'd traveled off the main road, closer to the Greens in case a quick escape was needed; the tall grass was an ocean of green that was easy to get lost in. Neither she nor Sou were to enter the forest without one of the Venandi unless, as Anya had said a few days back, "You care to be a raised skull on the tip of a shoot. It would take that long for someone to find you."

They'd also been warned against venturing too close to the onni deer who were inclined to stab their horns into the gut of whatever approached them. In seeing the onni, one was to keep a watchful lookout on the shifting Greens, which more than likely concealed an elosi cat who were the onni's main predator, although the big felines had no qualms against attacking passing humans.

The day had been long, and Evelyn slowed herself to a brisk walk, the rest of the company following the ritual of the past few days. Anya's pace brought her beside Evelyn, slowing her breath as Grae and Meric walked into the Greens, scouting ahead for a place to make camp. Sou remained behind her, as quiet as the rest of them. The most he'd spoken to her were of a few breathing exercises to help her block out the thoughts of others. She practiced the lessons before she slept each night, but it was hardly worth doing when everyone's thoughts were just as mute as their voices. It was impossible to know if it worked or not. The last time she heard a thought was Meric's when he'd ask who was trying to kill her.

Breaths and Depths, how am I to protect him if he doesn't know he is the one in danger?

"Stop that."

Evelyn started, turning her head towards Anya, who was chewing on a thick strip of jerky. "Stop what?"

The woman took another bite, grimaced, and spit out whatever half-chewed onni she found unpalatable, then bit into the strip again.

"Thinking. It makes you look like you're ready to squat in the Greens for a long overdue shite." Anya stuck her pinky into her mouth, running a nail across a back tooth.

"Feeling the sudden urge to squat, are we?" Evelyn said with a sarcastic smile. Through the many days of their travels, she and Anya had several times ventured into the grass together to relieve themselves. Anya was a poor traveling companion and even worse company during a time that was so private. The only good thing was that Anya also suffered the indignity so she could hardly mock Evelyn without being mocked herself.

"I truly hope you step in it one of these days." Her yellow eyes gleamed in the setting sun, reflecting an annoyance Evelyn found to be comical. She afforded her a single nod, pursing her lips as if in approval.

"It's good to have realistic hopes in a situation like ours. I'll build on yours and say I hope the Reticent pursuing us is up to the knees in it. At least we'd be able to smell their approach."

That had been enough to make the Venandi woman smile, if only a little. She released a soft chuckle, a look of contentment overcoming her annoyance. A silence took over the mood as Grae and Meric continued in their search of a decent place to rest. Evelyn felt the air between her and Anya thin, not exactly a path to friendship, but at least one of mutual tolerance. She'd felt something similar in Cronies Inn when the Venandi had first woken from her healing. A faint, wispy tendril of wind had flowed to Evelyn, her thought sharp but graceful.

I suppose Grae was right about you that night.

At the time it was the most affection she'd ever heard from the woman, gifting her a sense of ease that they could, in time, come to an understanding. At least until the raptor had shown up in the alley. Now as she returned Anya's smile, she thought this might be the only opportunity she'd gain to ask the questions that had been keeping her up at night.

"Why are you here?"

Anya turned towards her, the strip of onni sticking out from her mouth as she chewed. She took out the meat, her eyes reflecting that familiar annoyance.

"I think you could answer that question better than I could."

Evelyn shook her head and sighed, trying to think of a better way to ask.

"I mean why are you here *still*? You could have left, but you're still here. Why?"

The Venandi placed the jerky back in her mouth, shoving the entire strip into her cheek with loud, obnoxious chewing before finally closing her lips to swallow.

"Grae wanted to leave, but I wouldn't. Meric neither. I can't speak to their motives, but I have my own reasons." She continued to walk, face forward as though she didn't want Evelyn reading her expression.

She wasn't going to ask what Anya's reasons were. She knew she'd only answer with silence, but she remembered the hungry glare in her eyes when in the alley. There are those who flee from the pursuit of danger and those who fight it. Then there was Anya, who likely provoked it with a stick just to see if she could rise it to anger. The woman reminded her so much of Tansey. The fire that burned deep in her grandmother and the loss that fed those same flames blazed within Anya. Evelyn reminded herself that the Reticent were a cult of assassins that brought about the end to the Videns not more than two decades ago; their path of destruction had not focused solely on the destruction of Verbena. Grae, Anya, and Meric probably had, in some way, experienced a loss at their hands.

"Whatever those reasons are I thank you, nonetheless. I would be dead more than likely, but I would've understood," Evelyn said, reaching into her pack for the jerky she and the rest of their company had been surviving on since the start of their journey. The taste was similar to the babi strips she'd had in Verbena, but the onni meat was old and thick, making the texture closer to shoe leather than food.

"Is that an apology?" Anya raised her eyebrows with feigned shock.

Evelyn smiled. They were silent for a time as Evelyn ate, imagining she swallowed Izel's warm bread instead of the stale meat that traveled like a stone into her stomach.

"I am sorry, Anya. Would you have taken the job had you known a Reticent hunted me?"

Anya scoffed and shook her head, black hair rolling over her shoulders in waves.

"If you recall, I wouldn't have taken it for the reasons you gave us back in Reva. But here we are, so I suppose it doesn't matter anymore. If we can make it across Idris Stream, we stand a much better chance at losing the Reticent, although it's unlikely." Anya sounded much too eager for the later, almost as if she were overcompensating through her cavalier attitude.

Idris Stream? They were taking her back in the direction of Verbena, only a day's ride away from Oretem and Maun. She couldn't go back there. It was much too close and although she couldn't prove it, she felt confident that Oretem would somehow sense she was near.

"Is there no faster way?" she said, trying not to sound as nervous as she felt.

Anya shook her head and pointed southwest.

"That way is Solov Waste and the only people who can cross it are the Reticent themselves. We can't cross Elm Lake without a proper metal ship, so it's a shame I left mine back in Reva," Evelyn rolled her eyes at Anya's sarcastic tone. "We face the same problem with the Omya. The river is far too wide for us to swim and although it's warmed by the Idris, we still risk a cold, sleeping death should we attempt it. Idris Stream is the only choice in an otherwise impenetrable wall of hot and bone-chilling options. It's narrow enough for us to cross and warmed by Elm Lake to feel like no more than a warm bath. From there we'll venture into the Eshe Willow Wood where it'll be far harder for the Reticent to track us with their raptor. These Depths-damned open plains are the perfect hunting ground for those winged demons. The closer we get to Birny the closer we'll be to Edewor and not even the Reticent will hazard themselves against the Vagu capital."

"Are there no paths in between the cliffs of Elm Lake? Does Isla's Reach not tunnel through the rock?" Evelyn asked without optimism, seeing that her options were indeed limited.

Anya hesitated, staring at her as though she were working through the decision to speak the truth or lie. She opened her mouth to speak when Meric appeared from the Greens, walking up beside her.

"Isla's Reach is a story. There are no tunnels, but there are paths that lead down into the lake. Unfortunately, it'll feel like standing next to a blacksmith's forge in the height of summer. Many who have ventured too close to the cliff's edge have fainted from the heat just to fall to a burning death. Even if one were to make it to the other side, the Rya River falls into the lake, and I doubt her flow provides any footholds. I'm not saying it can't be done, but Idris Stream has as much chance of killing us as an irate flea. Whereas Elm Lake is the angry boar that can't help its nature," he said, the quivers at his back clanging together softly.

Anya's lined her lips into a tight line, looking away as if uncomfortable with the subject.

"It's time, wind whisperer. Let's be on with it," she said, walking towards Sou. Meric led Evelyn into the Greens, followed by Anya who guided Sou behind her.

The foliage was thick and many times Evelyn was hit in the face by a passing shoot, but she'd grown so used to it that it hardly deterred her. Her conversation with Anya brought about a confidence she decided to embrace and hurried her step next to Meric.

"It is real, you know," she said, not meeting his eyes. In her peripheral vision she felt him glance in her direction, moving a shoot of grass out of his way.

"What is?"

"Isla's Reach. Her hands burrowed deep into the mountains to the north."

"Is that where you are from?"

She looked at him then, his honey-colored eyes fixed on her own.

"A Lord might ask you to forgive him for asking a question wrought with such doubt, but I'm not a Lord and you're not a Lady," his voice wasn't cruel, only resigned, as though he didn't expect her to answer the question at all.

She felt her chest burn with the willfulness she'd experience whenever Tansey forbade her from visiting Sou. Her stubbornness had gotten her into trouble more times than she cared to recall but, in this instant, she found some use for it. To gain his trust she would need to trickle in the truth, to protect him she must prove him wrong.

"I was born in Verbena. It was a little village at the base of the Bena Mountains," she said, watching as his eyes widen with surprise. He turned his head to the sky, nodding in affirmation, before bringing his gaze forward towards the endless green.

"Well, that explains much," he said, pursing his lips. "Living in mountains and feeding off raw babi meat has left you feral."

Evelyn smiled, a true smile that left the corners of her lips up for longer than she could recall in recent memory.

"Quite feral, I'm afraid," she said, allowing herself a soft chuckle.

"Why are you running?" he asked, seemingly thinking she would answer whatever question he asked. Again, she had to prove him wrong.

"I told you before, I don't have to answer that," she said, thinking of all the ways the Reticent could kill her if Meric should discover the truth of her being Viden. She was ignorant as to the reasons Maun wanted Meric but she had no trouble knowing why he wanted her dead.

"You have. It won't stop me from asking. We've a long journey and I'm persistent."

From the side of her vision, she detected a small smile; she enjoyed that. She felt like she saw a rare bird, brightly colored but hidden within the golden leaves of a thick tree.

"Anya said you had decided to stay. Why?" she said, looking up at him.

The stubble on Meric's jaw had grown into a modest brown beard, blending into the corners of his temples where dark, wavy hair swooped over his thick brows. He was a tall man compared to her; shoulders set wide, but lean like there was never a time in his life when he stopped moving. He glanced through her, an inquisitive glint in those hazel eyes that poured over her question like it was a fork in the road.

"You avoid my questions yet ask some of me? What is the rule of a bargain? Never to ask a subordinate what you wouldn't be willing to do yourself." He clicked his tongue as Anya and Sou continued talking in low tones behind them. Something about a more efficient way to slice the throat of an enemy. From Anya's minimal interruptions she seemed to take a liking to the topic.

"If everyone took that to heart, then there would be no need to hire anybody and I've never struck a bargain before, so you can't expect me to know or follow the rules. Besides, I believe you just made that up."

Meric lowered his head and chuckled. Evelyn parried around a thick barrier of grass, leaning her head up at the darkening sky. It was getting difficult to see her way through the foliage. Her dragon eyes weren't hindered by the dark, but the Green's endlessness presented a challenging hike, becoming nearly impossible to gauge where she was without the position of the sun. She stepped closer to Meric, who hadn't lost his stride despite the rising moon.

"Never struck a bargain, have you? For someone who hasn't hired services before, you don't seem like a novice." His eyes traveled to hers and she was curious by the friendliness in them.

"Was that a compliment?" she said, straightening the scarf of her cloak about her shoulders.

"An observation, I assure you."

"A complimentary observation, I gather." He shrugged as she continued. "I come from a place where a person's word was worth more than the coin in their pocket."

"No such place exists." His tone was stoic.

Evelyn felt her stomach sink and all at once the pleasant conversation sunk into the ashes of her people, the fire and blood, staining and burning what had once been her home.

"No, it doesn't," she said in a soft voice.

He spared a glance at her, a question burning a hole on his tongue. He opened his mouth to speak but closed it, evidently deciding it wasn't worth asking. A question burned on her own tongue and before she could stop herself, she spoke it into being.

"Why have you not asked me why a Reticent pursues me?"

He raised his brow, dark hair caressing the temples of his face like wind-blown branches. He was silent for a moment, his jaw clenching in thought.

"I thought I did when I asked why you were running but admittedly, I haven't directly asked because it does not matter. What's done is done and there's nothing left to do but try not to die, and I've been doing that for as long as I can remember. So, in truth, this is nothing I haven't done before."

The look he gave her was frightening, as though he hadn't a care of whether he met his end today or the next. She wondered what it was that plagued him that he thought his life so meaningless. He granted her another small smile, the rare bird making its presence known with a passing glimpse.

"So, to answer both of your questions, I stay and I do not ask what you've done to awaken the ire of a Reticent because alive is how I would like to end this business contract. For all of us. In the end, that is all that matters." He met her gaze and for a moment she allowed herself to believe him. She felt the urge to grip his hand, to feel his fingers in the touch of friendship she hadn't felt in so long. She resisted, instead looking away as they finally entered a small clearing. Grae stood in the middle, blankets already strewn across the ground with tall shoots of grass covering most of the sky in a dome-like veil in case a raptor flew over.

"This clearing is more befitting a Lady than the last. There are far less elosi droppings than before," Grae said, his tone mocking. Anya walked up to him, pinching the side of his arm. The man winced, furrowing his brows, and rubbing the spot she twisted.

"Enough of your bellyaching. I've grown tired of hearing it," Anya said, glancing at Evelyn with a tolerant eye. Evelyn hid her smile as she laid out a blanket in between Meric's and Sou's.

Grae reached into his pack, pulling out two bright apples, layers of red and green skin overlapping to make its surface glow like a forest in the fall. Sou clapped him on the shoulder and laughed. Grae didn't respond with the same enthusiasm, but he was obviously happy to be eating something other than onni.

"Well done, lad. Where did you find these?" Sou said, grabbing both. Grae handed him a small hand knife from his boot to cut the fruit into even sections, dividing out the slices to each of them. Evelyn, Anya and Meric wasted no time in partaking, the juicy flesh running along the sides of their mouths. Evelyn closed her eyes and groaned, savoring the tang of the green while enjoying the sweetness of the red.

"I found them on the edge of the Greens. They probably fell from a farmer's cart who may be looking to sell in Ciar. Once we arrive in the city we can purchase some more for the rest of the journey," Grae said, picking at his teeth where bits of the apple skin stuck.

"A whole bushel, I say," Meric said, his words muddled by the apple he chewed.

"Shouldn't we continue through the city?" Anya asked.

"It'll be the last place we can replenish our supplies before reaching Birny. It's not as grand as Reva, but it's largely populated. We can blend in easily without fear of detection. If we arrive during the morning hours as I've planned, then we should be stocked and supplied before noon. We won't stay in the city overnight," Grae said. Anya nodded with some relief.

Evelyn understood why she wouldn't want to stop, but they were already almost through the little they were able to gather from Reva. There was no way they'd make it to Birny without more.

Evelyn finished her share, her stomach content even if it growled for more. Sou smacked his lips and handed Grae his knife back, the Venandi sheathing the blade in his boot. Anya brought the final slice she'd cut with her knife to her mouth, the skins of her apple surrounding her feet.

"I'm too weary for more conversation. The lot of you will keep your voices low or you'll be speaking through a hole in your throats. Then it's onwards to Ciar!" Anya's exclamation should've been encouraging, but her tone sounded like a drunkard being forced to leave the tavern with no place left to go.

It wasn't long after that Sou, Grae, and Anya were all asleep, leaving Meric to take the first watch. Evelyn curled inside her cloak, the spring wind a more bearable temperature than the humid air she'd experienced in Reva. She fell into a light slumber, half waking every so often at the sound of a bird's flight or the soft rustle of Sou's cloak as he twitched in his sleep.

She was suddenly pulled from the darkness of sleep by the sound of steel unsheathing. She sat upright, her hand inside the pocket of her cloak, curling around the curved hilt of a throwing dagger.

Meric crouched beside her, a finger over his lips as he stared into the twilight of the purple sky. Grae and he had taken the watch this night, allowing Anya a full night of rest. The previous nights had been Grae's and Anya's. Their company slept soundlessly around them, unbothered by the tension that gripped the early morning. It brought Evelyn back to the dawning day Oretem had burned her village.

The Greens rustled, circling their camp in a way that left Evelyn's heart in her stomach. She stared at the elosi droppings on the edge of their camp. She'd never seen the fierce cats with her own eyes, but could imagine long fangs ripping into her throat. The foliage rustled once more, then parted to reveal a small rodent, no larger than her hand, inching its way towards the apple skins Anya had left. Evelyn sighed and lowered her hand from her pocket, watching as Meric did the same with his blade.

"Not as fearsome as a Reticent, but it's best to be overcautious when dealing with their kind," he said, his voice bitter, but heavy with relief.

There was that phrase again, *their kind*. Due said it, Grae said it, and even Sou had spoken those words. It wasn't just used in describing the Reticent, but the Vagu and the Venandi as well. It aggravated her that each of them thought themselves separate from the other. Did any of them bleed differently than the other? She recalled how otherworldly Maun had seemed, his horrific presence looming over all the carnage he'd caused. Yet, when Nakesha raked her fangs across his flesh, he bled all the same. He was only a man.

"They were once Venandi. One of *your kind*," she said, her irritation apparent in her tone.

Meric seemed surprised that she knew that, and his frown deepened as he faced her. She fought the urge to reach for the dagger at her hip; the blade sung to her.

"It makes no difference. They haven't been Venandi for a long time. I doubt they remember they ever were." Meric's voice was low, graveled in the silent air. She'd never heard him raise his voice, but she couldn't help feeling the heat in his tone. Whatever the Reticent did to him, he carried it like a weighted chain around his neck.

"Everything makes a difference, Meric. Like Isla's Reach, all actions impact others in ways we can't see. I'm not claiming the Reticent are worthy of forgiveness." She met his gaze, feeling the burn of her own red eyes. "I could never forgive. All I am saying is that perhaps, in the beginning, they may have been good people who lost their way." She pulled her cloak closer around her shoulders as the breeze blew tendrils of Iona's Breath around the both of them.

Her words seemed to have no impact on him as he leaned in close. His eyes set on hers with an intensity that she was growing familiar with.

"The last Reticent I ran into killed a man with one blow and tore his child from her screaming mother's embrace. She survived, but the child was lost to the Order, and I ended up in the blackest prison to ever exist below the ground. There are no good people. There never were."

Evelyn sat in silence. So that was the reason he was placed in prison. He hadn't killed Due's nephew, but it was clear he blamed himself all the same. He'd been trying to protect them and failed. She knew better than anyone the wounds of guilt that refused to heal—they still seeped within her.

It was awful and the pit of her stomach lurched at what she knew was an honest response from him. She was sympathetic to his experience, but she had suffered too much to be told there was no goodness in the world. If she stopped believing in that, was there any point to the breath in her lungs or the feel of the wind? She thought of Anya and Grae, their stubborn animosity and their commitment to see her to Birny alive. Sou, who would sooner die than see her harmed.

"If that were true, then you would not be standing here," she said, refusing to allow his sour mood to deter her core beliefs.

Meric leaned back, folding his arms with a quizzical expression as though she were a puzzle he couldn't solve.

"You seem to have a high opinion of yourself."

Evelyn scoffed as she adjusted her cloak around her body. She glanced at Sou's sleeping form, his long hair spilling over his nose and blowing in and out of his open mouth. The ferryman was the best person she knew. His claims that she still held within her the person she used to be was all she had to keep her moving.

"No, just the opinion of one better than I," she said, watching the wind dance through the Greens. The silence of the rising sun endured between them, and Evelyn savored the peace of its stillness. Meric stood, preparing to wake the others when he turned back towards her.

"When this is all over, will you stay in Birny?"

There wasn't any way to know for certain. Sou insisted it would be safe enough and she wasn't sure how meeting her sister and father would alter her course. At the moment, she was resolute in healing Oretem and breaking the hold Maun had over the dragon. It was a bond much too dangerous to be continued. She had a plan, but she wasn't going to tell him that.

"I don't know," she said, standing with the weight of another day of uncertainty. Would they make it to Ciar or would today be the day a raptor tore them limb from limb?

Meric nodded and scratched the side of his beard.

"What about you?" the question hung in the air like a broken rope, she wasn't sure why.

"I don't know," he replied in a whisper. A thin tendril of wind twirled around his head, reaching for her as though the broken rope were remade.

I need to see you safe.

His thought surprised her, the voice tender and overwhelmed with responsibility. He stepped towards her, his hand flexing at his side as though he fought the desire to reach out. He stared into her eyes, holding them as no other had been able to do.

"I know nothing of whatever it is that led you here. I can only protect you from what follows, but I hope that should we live through this, you might find some peace. It seems we are both in need of it," he said, letting the words float among the wind as she gripped the hilt of her blade, reminding her how deep a beautiful thing could cut.

She tore her gaze away, an unsettled stirring writhing in the center of her chest. A need to connect, an ache to be touched, held in an embrace where she didn't have to be strong. She turned her back, fighting the tears that she refused to let fall. She heard Meric wake the others when a scream, loud and panicked, cut through the camp like a scythe cutting wheat. Evelyn lifted her head and, without thought, ran through the Greens towards the direction the sound came.

"Evelyn!" Meric shouted through his teeth, trying to keep his voice low.

He ran after her, his breath quick and heavy behind her. She heard the footfall of the others giving chase, but she didn't slow her stride. She ran for a heartbeat more then stopped, unsure of which direction to take. The grass blocked all view of the plains and she'd lost the way the scream had come. Meric stepped in beside her, having caught up, his eyes angry pools of honey.

"Stop. We don't know what—" Another scream pierced the air, this one lower, plainly male and frightened. She turned right and followed the screaming, Meric jogging beside her without argument, his expression concerned and determined.

They reached the edge of the Greens with a clear view of the main road. A wain was overturned, apples littering the plains down the hill. The black horse dragging the wagon was neighing wildly, its body tied to the crippled cart. The pack animal reared on its hind legs, beating its hooves at a large crouched cat. The feline hissed, cutting the air with claws that could disembowel a boar. A man stood beside the horse, holding a whip while his family, a woman and small girl, huddled behind the capsized cart. The child held a small dog in her hands; the animal was barking and thrashing in her grasp. The cat's muscles twitched with power, its bulky form more than a match for both man and horse. Grae, Anya, and Sou emerged from the grass forest staring at the spectacle, gasping from the chase.

"It's an elosi," Grae said, his voice despairing as though there was nothing he could do to help the family.

"Finally, some fun. You've all grown so dull," Anya said, her wolf eyes gleaming with a hunger that could only be satisfied by the hunt.

Grae moved to say more but she turned around, silencing him with a quick, light palm slap to his forehead before clasping her hand in his. She smiled at him as though she were a child persistent in getting exactly what she wanted. Grae released a deep sigh and though he tried his hardest not to, returned her smile. "Wait, let's think about —"

Evelyn didn't hear what else he had to say, sprinting forward with her dagger in one hand and a throwing blade in the other. She glanced beside her to see Meric had bolted the same moment she had; his bow in hand, fingers curled around the riser. Together they rushed into the plains towards the danger she knew neither of them should interfere with.

CHAPTER 35

TO STAY FOR SO SMALL A THING

I'm far too sober to be this stupid, Meric thought as the form of the elosi grew closer. The great cat's muscles bulged from powerful legs, mighty fangs reaching past its snapping jaw, dripping with thick spittle. When Meric began his futile run towards the attacked family, he hadn't expected Evelyn to be by his side. Her arms swayed close to her chest, gripping her blades with a fierce gentleness that could only be achieved with years of training. Her red eyes focused on the growling cat lunging as the man with the whip snapped his weapon.

"See to the woman and child," she said, pointing at the huddled forms at the end of the wagon. The woman was around his age, young and frightened. Her arms wrapped around a little girl who had her mother's dark hair and bright grey eyes. Meric brought his gaze up to the toppled wagon and saw a vantage point where he could properly shoot from. He nodded at Evelyn, splitting their path to opposite ends of the wagon.

Evelyn stood at the man's side, her feet set apart with a slight bend in her knees, ready to leap in any direction she needed to go. By the stance of her feet, it was clear she spoke true of her home in the mountains. Her back stood straight, eyes locked on the hissing feline with the intensity of a huntress. If she looked small next to Sou than she was a child in comparison to the man. His long thick legs held a body of solid muscle, broad shoulders curving into a neck as wide as a wooden beam. The man held up a blocky arm, cracking the whip in the air.

Meric bent over the woman, her eyes growing wide at the sight of his silver earring. She scooted away, trying to bring herself to her feet, but he held his hand up, pointing his bow away from their terrified expressions.

"Don't run," he said, knowing that the elosi would make quick work chasing the woman and her child down, tripping them before ripping their tongues through their throats. She hugged the girl closer, breathing heavily with anxiety, but staying seated on the ground. He turned around to see Grae had followed him to the family. Anya stood beside Evelyn, her blade twisting within eager fingers. Sou approached the man with the whip, placing a hand on his shoulder and pushing him behind the women until his back hit the cart.

"My horse!" the man screamed, a grieving terror in his voice. By the sound of it the animal was obviously more than just a means of transporting goods for him. The black mare whinnied as though she understood the distress in her master's voice, kicking up dirt with her hooves in a front of intimidation.

The cat hissed and struck out a paw, missing the horse's bowed neck by breadths. Evelyn bent her arm next to her ear, breathed in, and released the throwing dagger with a rapid flick of her wrist. The elosi hunched its shoulders, sliding across the ground as though its paws were mere extensions of the grass beneath them and howled as the blade sunk into its shoulder. The knife fell from the cat's flesh when it launched itself at Evelyn, blood coating its fur in crimson. Anya vaulted towards the mass of claws and fangs, swinging her blade at the growling animal. Meric moved to climb the cart, his bow arm aching to be of use. The woman grabbed his cloak, clutching the fabric with white-knuckled fingers.

"Don't leave us," she said, panic brimming in her voice. He stared at her a moment, startled by the conviction in her words. Her eyes kept darting to the girl in her arms, crying into her chest with milky fluid running down her nose. He recalled the pleas of those he'd been sent to capture, their cries for him to leave them be, to forget he had ever found them, but he couldn't remember a time when they'd begged him to stay. The feeling was unfamiliar, and he sensed a rising warmth in his chest at the thought of easing someone's fear instead of causing it.

"What are your names?" he said, trying to keep his urgency as mild as he could, given the circumstances. She stuttered a moment, panic twisting her tongue before she gained control of her fear.

"Lian," she said, then looked down at her daughter. "She is Retia. My brother, Isaad, help him!" Her voice pitched with anguish.

Meric leveled his gaze to the small girl, only one grey eye peering from between the folds of her mother's cloak. The dog growled in her arms, baring its teeth.

"Stay with your mother, Retia." He pried Lian's fingers from the fabric of his cloak, turning around slightly to look at Grae. "Keep them out of the way," Meric said before leaping onto the cart, bow drawn and aimed.

The cat lashed out at the women, claws raking the ground beneath it in heaps of dirt. Anya jumped up and down, screaming and swaying her arms to appear larger than she was. The elosi was undeterred and crouched further into the grass, its hind legs slightly lifted in preparation for a swift pounce. Evelyn bellowed and leaped in front of the cat, slashing its muzzle with her dagger. The elosi yowled and sneezed, blood spraying across its face, red staining its bared teeth. Evelyn moved to strike again when the cat swiped a massive paw at her ankle, ripping the fabric of her trousers and throwing her onto her back.

Meric leaned in to shoot, but the cat rose above Evelyn, straddling her with its lithe form and rippling muscles. Anya leaped onto the cat's back, pulling its round ears up and stabbing her blade into the skin of its neck. The elosi bucked, trying to dislodge Anya while attempting to tear Evelyn's throat out with its thick, sharp fangs. Evelyn wedged the blade of her dagger into the elosi's maw, sawing into the cat's sizable mouth as flagons of blood poured over her like a red bath. Meric growled his frustration, unable to see a clean shot that didn't threaten Anya or Evelyn.

"Kill it!" Evelyn screamed, blood coloring her teeth as she grimaced. The cat's maw was nearly split to the ears, its eyes wild with rage.

"Die, you stupid beast!" Anya yelled, bringing her blade down with each word. The elosi's neck was riddled in punctures, but its muscles were so thick that Anya's dagger could find no purchase on a main artery. She looked down and bent to the side, thrusting her blade into the softness of the elosi's thin belly. The cat lifted its head in a growling howl and spun off Evelyn, throwing Anya off its back with a hard clash. Its jaw hung low, saturated in its own foul bodily fluids.

The elosi set its predatory eyes on Sou and Isaad, the man's red hair swirling around freckled cheeks. The whip in his hand cracked in the air, its snap echoing across the plains. The cat growled and, faster than Meric thought possible, struck Isaad across the chest, leaving long ragged cuts from collar to waist. The horse neighed and fought against its restraints, hearing her master scream. The big man bellowed his pain, back arching as he fell to the ground, writhing. Upon hearing her brother's cries of pain, Lian stood from behind the cart, dark hair shifting across her face with the expression of one who would stop at nothing to protect those she loved. She released an anguished cry and ran from her hiding place, gripping an apple she lifted from the ground. Grae sprang after her, gathering her up in his arms by the waist before she could reach the man. Sou crouched over Isaad, hands outstretched over his chest, blood trickling through his fingers. Lian threw the apple, hitting the cat on the head. It growled and turned away from Sou. Its ears pricked back and its shoulders hunched as it looked past Lian, moving with a savage purpose.

Silence. Iona seemed to withdraw her Breath, leaving the plains in utter silence. Retia appeared from behind Grae, holding her dog against a tear-stained cheek. She was so small, lip quivering as she gaped at her uncle. The cat stared at the child, an empty gleam in its predatory eyes, as though it knew its life were at an end and would drink whatever blood it could before joining the wind.

"Isa," the girl said, sniffing and oblivious to her own mortality. Lian turned, glancing in between her child and the elosi. She screamed, thrashing against Grae, who held her in a firm grip. He glanced up at Meric, knowing that she would only hinder his aim should she interfere. As dire as the situation had become, the child was bait. Meric stretched the string of his bow, exhaled, and released the arrow. The shaft buried itself into the cat's side, near where the heart would've been. The elosi stumbled, more blood pouring from its useless mouth, although he couldn't be sure whether that was a result of his arrow or Evelyn's blade.

The elosi continued its path, limping from its many wounds. Time seemed to slow, moving without sound or urgency. Retia's mother flailed in Grae's hold, her cries silent to his ears. Isaad clutched his bloodied chest, failing to stand as Sou tried to stop his bleeding. From his peripheral Meric caught Evelyn running towards the elosi, covered in blood, a throwing knife in her hand. She threw it, the blade burying itself into the cat's hind leg. The animal didn't flinch, dragging the useless limb as it continued its path towards the frightened child. He always knew elosi were the strongest and hardest to kill of the plains cats, but this animal was something else entirely. Any other beast would've fallen from wounds so grievous long ago. He nocked another arrow and released, this time through the elosi's throat. It burst through to the other side in an explosion of blood, the cat gurgling, but not slowing down.

Meric pulled the string against his cheek, the feathers on the end tickling his ear. Iona's Breath returned to the plains, assaulting him with the deafening sound of all the pain surrounding him. Meric bared his teeth and stood, thundering a cry as he leapt from the wagon. The cat looked up and lifted its claws to disembowel him in the air. He released the string, the arrow burying itself into the cat's black eye. He rolled as he landed, turning around to see the elosi falling to the ground. Its tongue hung out of a limp jaw, blood flowing from its burst pupil. He panted, standing over the cat, its dark fur matted in blood and dirt.

Grae released Lian, his sight set on the dead elosi with a look of astonishment. Retia ran into her mother's arms, sobbing for her uncle with a repetition that left Meric's heart in his throat. He glanced at the fallen man, whose teeth were bared in pain as Sou ripped strips of his tunic, pressing them over his seeping wounds. Lian carried her daughter to her brother, hand outstretched for his. He caught it and she squeezed it fiercely.

"You stupid man. It would be just like you to die on this empty plain and leave me with nothing but that Depths-damned horse to remind me of your endless idiocy."

Isaad grimaced a smile.

"Beau!" the big man yelled, lifting his chin in the mare's direction. "You'll not be elosi chow this day." The horse nickered with a worried head shake. "She has a lot more sense than I and clearly a tougher hide—ah," he winced, meeting Sou's eyes. "Well, stranger, will I live?"

The old man leaned back on his knee, looking over Isaad with a sigh, both hands pressing the cloth against his chest. Blood spread through the fabric like flames over grass, the skin of Isaad's face growing pale. Sou turned to Lian, green eyes bright with calm logic.

"Have you needle and thread? These wounds must be closed or he will bleed to death."

She shook her head, tears falling from her chin onto her

brother's face, his eyes fluttering closed. Evelyn crouched beside Sou, favoring her right leg that wept with blood. Her arms and face were splattered with gore, giving her the appearance of one who'd been thrust into the bloody bowels of Celosia's Depths only to be spit back out just before death.

"I need a fire, lass. Build me one," the old man said, gesturing to the tongue of the wagon that had been broken by the horse's hysteria. She moved to gather the wood, her injured leg becoming less of a hindrance the more she used it. Grae came up behind Sou, whispering with a hand on his shoulder.

"We cannot make a fire."

The old man rolled his eyes, hands straining to contain Isaad's blood. He turned his face to Grae, curved brows furrowed in mock confusion.

"I should think Venandi would know a task so essential to surviving the wild. It's fortunate we have Evelyn, who is excellent at it." Sou's voice was rife with sarcasm and if it weren't for the red-haired man dying before him, Meric might've laughed. Grae didn't seem offended by the jab, looking at Isaad's pale features with a pitying frown.

"It will draw far too much attention. Is there no other way to stop the bleeding? Have you no more True Tears?"

"I do not. It will be a small fire, Grae. Would you have this man die?" Sou whispered back, his question an honest one. Grae met the old man's eyes and, for the first time, Meric thought he caught an agreement between the two, a kind of truce.

"Do what you must," he said, squeezing Sou's shoulder in what looked like hopeful assurance.

Evelyn set up the wood next to Sou, gathering a handful of grass in her hand. Lian settled Retia next to her uncle and made her way to kneel beside Evelyn, reaching into her pocket. She pulled out flint and stone, striking the two in a flurry of sparks that eventually caught, the grass smoking with red embers. Evelyn cupped her hands over the grass and blew into it, nursing the smoke until it smoldered into a small flame. She placed it into the tower of wood, continuing to breathe into the flames until it burst with height. Sou held out his hand to Grae, who stared at his open palm with perplexity.

"Give me your rapier, it's blade is sufficiently flat enough to cauterize his wounds."

Meric thought Grae would object, but his friend seemed to have no thought of argument as he unsheathed his blade, placing the tip into the flames. Within minutes, the point of Grae's rapier glowed as brightly as Evelyn's eyes, though hers more resembled blood-colored gems. He handed the blade to Sou, who lifted the soaked tunic. Blood ran down Isaad's torso in rivulets of crimson. It was fortunate Isaad was a large man; his broad chest absorbed the impact of the elosi's claws that would've left most men eviscerated.

"Hold him," Sou said, emotionless, as though he were purposefully distancing himself from what he was about to do. Lian gripped her brother's wrist and shoulder while Evelyn held the other. Meric knelt opposite of Anya, each pressing down on Isaad's legs. Grae picked up a small piece of the wagon's broken tongue, placing the wood in between the man's teeth. He cradled Isaad's head on his shoulder, wrapping an arm around his brow to keep him still. Isaad groaned, mumbling against the wood in his mouth. Retia held her dog tight, staring with horrified confusion as Sou pressed the red, hot rapier onto the broken skin of her uncle's chest.

Isaac writhed against their hold, screaming through the pain, biting the wood between his teeth with a strength Meric hoped the man would maintain until he was fully healed. Even with five people holding him down, Isaad tested the strength of all pinning him. It took several attempts to cauterize a single cut, but Sou was persistent and, in the end, Meric was nearly sitting on the man to keep him still. The smell of burnt flesh permeated the air and he saw Evelyn stare at the searing skin, her eyes intense. Her fingers tightened on Isaad's twitching hand. His skin sizzled, blackening under the glowing blade and stopping the flow of blood. Sou continued the procedure, his hands steady in cauterizing the open flesh. Finally, after much screaming and tears, Sou had finished and Isaad fell unconscious. Grae moved to allow Lian to hold her brother, her hand resting above his burns as through she could take his pain through her touch.

Retia stared at her uncle, tears flowing from eyes incapable of understanding what was happening around her. She ventured over to Grae's side, pressing her small body into the crook of his shoulder. His friend's eyes widened at the unexpected gesture, and he placed a hand on her back, patting softly. The dog squirmed in her arms, twisting until finally the girl released it, wrapping her arms around Grae's neck. The canine sniffed its surroundings, venturing over to the dead cat and relieving itself on its corpse.

"How far are we from Ciar?" Evelyn asked, trying to wipe the elosi blood from her face, but only managing to spread it further across her skin.

"A day and a half at the most," Grae said, placing Retia in the hole of his crossed legs, her head resting against his chest. The girl's cries had quieted, and she looked to be nearing sleep from the exertion of the morning's events.

"We will stay," Anya said, answering the unspoken question they all were thinking. "At least, until the wagon is repaired, and you are able to reach Ciar unimpeded."

"That is if you would welcome our aid, lady traveler," Sou added as he inclined his head towards Lian, who was fixated on the sleeping form of her daughter in Grae's arms. She looked up at Sou, her gaze traveling to each of them with an exhaustion that was more than physical. Her body yielded at the relief of not having to bear the burden of her troubles alone.

"I would. Thank you." Lian pressed her cheek against Isaad's hair, seemingly wanting to say more, but hadn't the strength to do so.

Evelyn made her way to the agitated mare, reaching out a hand to calm it. The animal backed away, nickering its worry. She placed a hand on the mare's nose, gently caressing up in between her eyes. The mare calmed, allowing Evelyn to untangle the ropes on the remaining tongue of the wagon.

"Come help me right the wain," Sou spoke to Anya. She followed him to the wagon.

Grae stood with Retia in his arms, her head resting in the curve of his neck. He looked across the plains, his eyes searching for what Meric knew would be impossible to find. The Reticent. If the assassin had seen their fire, they would redouble their efforts in the chase, perhaps send their raptor to scout ahead. If the Reticent had already caught up, they would wait in the Greens for the cover of night to attack.

"We should not be here," Grae said to Meric as he approached.

"No," he replied simply. It was true. If they had any sense, they would've left Lian and her family to the mercy of the elosi. There was the possibility that the Reticent hadn't seen the fire or heard the cries of Isaad's pain across the Greens. It was doubtful, but not entirely implausible that should they leave now, the Reticent may merely pass by the family. It was also more likely that in helping them escape the jaws of one snare, they'd led the family into the path of a more dangerous trap.

"How is she?" Meric said, adjusting the position of his bow slung across his back. The girl's arms were curled into her chest, fingers tight in the fabric of Grae's tunic.

Grae looked down at the rise of Retia's back, her breath flowing even and calm.

"Sleeping. I don't think I've ever held a thing so small," he said, his arm cradling her as though she might break in his grasp. Meric could hear the concern in his friend's voice.

They all knew staying went against every Venandi instinct. In Reva, it was a matter of survival, concerned only with the self. Compassion was for the weak and altruism was the ideology of dead fools. But here, so far from the city, in the great plains of the never-ending Greens, it felt like the creed of an ancient way of thinking that no longer applied to the present when, during a time of old, it was necessary to have been so callous.

I feel more myself than I ever have.

He looked at Grae and there were no words that needed to be spoken between them. His blue eyes held the worried gleam of one who wasn't frightened for his own well-being, but of one who remained so small a thing he'd never before held.

CHAPTER 36

HECTOR THE SWALLOW

The day had been spent collecting fallen apples from the plains and fixing the wain to work with one tongue. Meric had helped Sou tie the opposite side of the mares' reigns to a latch beneath the wagon. Beau nickered in annoyance at the unbalanced feel of the wain, but she hauled without too much complaint. The cart wobbled when pulled, but it was no longer in immediate danger of collapse. Lian offered a small pail of drinking water for Evelyn and Anya to wash the elosi blood from their bodies. Sou tended to their superficial wounds, including Evelyn's ankle which he bound in clean linen, and provided spare clothes for her. Her current garb was soaked in blood, and she buried the ruined clothes when she had finished washing. Lian offered a simply made blue linen shirt to Anya, who wore it with appreciation.

They abandoned the corpse of the elosi, leaving it for the crows. There was no sense in dragging it along for food. The animal was far too large and Isaad was in no condition to walk. The weight of the apples, Isaad, and the elosi would've been too much for the hobbled wain. Meric couldn't suppress the feeling that the cat's remains acted like a kind of marker to their path. They had retrieved their weapons, but anyone with a mind for combat would know the injuries the elosi sustained were of steel and shaft. He could only hope that should the

Reticent find the body, they would conclude that anyone traveling the road could've felled the animal.

It was growing dark and hiding the wain in the long grass was not an option. The wagon was far too unstable, and it would leave a path of broken grass in its path to make the effort meaningless. They hadn't made it far, lengthening their journey to arrive at Ciar far below the time frame Grae had predicted. At the rate they were going, it would take another day, perhaps two to reach the city. They had agreed that they would stay to ensure Lian and her family could travel on their own, but the more they traveled together, the harder it was to speak of departing. The wain was as mended as it could be, slowly taking its time but taking it, nonetheless. Isaad had been drifting in and out of consciousness, mumbling and groaning quietly in the wain. Retia spent most of her time at Grae's side, her mother either having to bolster the cart over a rock or tend to her brother. The little girl was quiet and would grab his friend's hand if she saw the wind move the Greens in a way she found frightening.

Grae spoke to her often, showing her the difference between the wind rustling the grass and a potential predator stalking within them. It was an unusual lesson for a child who hadn't seen her eighth name day, but Meric supposed Grae thought if she was going to remain with him, she might as well learn something useful. It reminded him of the way Grae had taught him to act in a society he hadn't lived among in years. She never spoke, but seemed curious and nodded when he asked her if she understood him.

They stopped on the side of the main road, partially hidden behind a hill Anya had scouted. Lian brought out a wax-coated, leather hide that covered them from the elements, held up by two poles staked into the ground. She brought her brother out from the roofless wain and under the covering, laying him on a blanket and wrapping him with a fur that looked to be onni pelt.

"Bloody useless muscles. I'd rather you were fat. At least

then I could blame you for being so Depths-damn heavy," Lian said, wiping sweat from her brow.

No one mentioned lighting a fire and Meric was grateful for that. The weather hadn't required one and Lian had offered them as many apples as they wanted.

They each settled onto a spot under the leather roof with Grae leaning against the wheel of the wagon. Retia laid near him, eyes open, her small dog curled in her arms. The canine had a golden, muddy appearance with long hair that fell from its floppy ears and short snout. Lian sat on the ground with her brother's head in her lap. She combed her fingers through his red hair as though it were as instinctual as breathing. Meric didn't think she realized she was doing it.

"My sweet. Would you like a story? I know Isa tells them best, but I can try," she said, hope gleaming from her grey eyes. The girl continued to stare into the darkness without sight. Lian sighed, looking at Grae with features made older by what she'd gone through.

"Has she spoken to you?" she asked, her voice almost a whisper.

"She has not," he said, leaning forward towards the girl. "Will you tell me the name of your dog? This is the third time I've asked you and I'd really like to know."

The girl curled tighter around the animal who fidgeted with a quiet groan at being constrained. Lian flashed an encouraging smile at her daughter.

"Go on. Tell him the name you chose."

Retia ran a hand through the dog's long hair, lifting its chops to reveal a line of spit along the dog's hairy lip. She bit her mouth shut, looking at her uncle with those innocent eyes that knew so much violence in so short a time.

"His name is Drool," Lian said, trying to keep the worry out of her voice. "Isaad had purchased him thinking he was the puppy of a large breed. Beau is well enough at sensing trouble on the road and Isaad dotes on her as though she is his own child, but he wanted a creature with sharper teeth for added protection. It wasn't until we had him for over a month that we realized the little tyke was fully grown. We thought of returning him, but Retia wouldn't hear of it. They're quite taken with each other, and I thought as long as he protects her then that is enough for me. He was the one who had sensed the elosi before any of us, even Beau."

Anya propped herself on one elbow, glancing in between Retia and Grae.

"I've traveled the plains before and never have I come across an elosi so wildly intent on killing. She was Depths-possessed to take us all to the grave with her," Anya said, revealing more of her past than Meric had previously known. By the look Grae exchanged with Anya, he hadn't known she'd journeyed the Greens before either.

Lian chuckled, but the sound held no humor.

"That elosi was male. To someone who has little experience with them it's easy to mistake a starving male for a female. They do not appear to be malnourished which is how most people die by their claws. It is why he attacked us with such ferocity. Normally, Isaad is able to scare away the cats with his whip, but this one was desperate. The beast was after Beau and Isaad, the ginger fool that he is, would sink to Celosia's Depths for that horse."

"This ginger fool would appreciate some silence," Isaad spoke from his sister's lap. Lian pursed her lips into an angry frown, eyes wide with the color of storm clouds.

"You bastard son of a pig! How long have you been awake?" Her previously thoughtful caress turned aggressive as she pulled his red hair with a hard tug. He grimaced and pouted his lips with the expression of an especially annoyed sibling.

"Would you insult our mam so? She was the finest sow of her brood." He hovered a hand over his chest, wincing as he shifted his position in an attempt to lay more comfortably. "I think I can recall that foul mouth of yours cursing a few thousand paces back when the wain had been stuck a second time."

Meric thought it was fortunate that the elosi had injured Isaad so badly, as Lian couldn't do much more to him without killing him. Her mouth formed into a hard line, fingers shaking with a fury that might've rivaled the cats.

"The next time the wain gets stuck I'll be using you as a wedge beneath the wheel." She crossed her arms over her chest, refusing to look at him. He reached over his head and grabbed her wrist, prying it from her twisted arm. Lian's mouth quivered, eyes watering as she stared into the darkness.

"Lian," he said, his tone begging for forgiveness.

"I thought you would die," she whispered, her voice broken in a soft sob.

"Of course you would. An apple could fall on your head and you'd scream that the sky was falling."

"Celosia's bloody Depths! If the Breaths will not deny you, I will. One time, Isaad. We were children! Will you never let me forget it?"

"Never," the man said with a smirk.

Lian's looked down on her brother, enraged features softening into a surrendering chuckle. She tugged on his head once more, ruffling her hands through his red hair in a way that left no doubt of her forgiveness. Meric had never seen anything so uncorrupted, beautiful in its simplicity. He averted his eyes, meeting Evelyn's, whose ruby gaze glowed in the surrounding darkness. Before he would find it impossible to look away, he turned his head back to the siblings. Lian helped Isaad sit up next to her with his back leaning against the wain.

"You're still a pig's bastard. Mam would've agreed. Come any closer to death again and that elosi will seem like a common house cat compared to what I will do to you." The corner of her mouth curved, and he chuckled as he winced. Retia sat up, Drool's tail wagging as she brought herself to her feet. Her little hands were curled into fists at her side, her entire body taut as though she were fighting every instinct to run into Isaad's arms.

"Ah come here, little bird. Your uncle needs strong arms like yours to hold him up." He reached out for her, and she released a strangled sob before crashing into his chest. The man gasped, eyes bulging as though he were thrown against a stone wall. He gritted his teeth, but didn't cry out, holding his niece as though her love caused him no pain.

In watching Isaad hold Retia, Meric was mournfully aware that he never knew his father. Had he ever been held in such an embrace? Did his father, like Isaad before him, take with him to the grave the pain that would've burdened him as a child, knowing he was the one who had caused it? He must have. Meric thought of all the children who were separated from their parents due to his actions. Juna's baby girl screamed in his mind. Meric blinked away the phantom wail, his tongue suddenly dry. There had been many things he was much too sober to act upon and thinking of his childhood was one he hadn't the strength to face yet. Instead, he looked away from the family, staring at the grass in his hand as he tore it to shreds.

The next hour passed with Isaad and Sou exchanging questions. Where were Sou and his company going? How they came to be on the Greens when the elosi attacked? What were their occupations and lives? Sou was quick with his responses, giving Isaad a tale to fit what he saw: hired Venandi escorting him and Evelyn to Ciar. Meric was impressed by how casually Sou had been able to avert answering questions, redirecting the conversation in ways that had Isaad revealing more of his life than theirs. It only proved to Meric that his suspicions were warranted.

The journey, up until now, had been relatively quiet; their mutual silence was a collective choice. Meric wouldn't ask questions he knew wouldn't be answered, and Sou and Evelyn would pay them when they reached Birny. They could keep their secrets, but Meric knew they were frightened by those same secrets. He sensed no malice from either of them, their natures becoming familiar to him the more time he spent with them. Sou was the most patient man he'd ever met, enduring Grae's backhanded retorts and delivering quick-witted japs that lightened the entire company. Evelyn was quiet, but not silent. Her actions spoke to a woman who knew her own mind and would not allow others to deter her from doing what she believed to be right. But her eyes glowed with a fire, lit by grief and an anger that he didn't think she herself fully knew. He wondered if that was the source of her strength and thought how much longer it could burn before it collapsed into cold embers.

Isaad told of their lives toiling at the earth—he and his sister being the last members of a multi-generational family of apple farmers. After the death of their parents, Lian and Isaad shared the apple grove, journeying together to sell in Ciar and splitting the profits of their earnings. Retia's father had been a wayward traveler, looking for work to pay for his wanderings. He stayed on the farm for a time, employed by the siblings until the man's meandering spirit grew too strong to ignore. It was a quick liaison, neither believing they'd ever see the other again. Lian spoke of it fondly and without regret.

"Home is a place of your making and I see a structure built with stone," Sou said, his green eyes bright with genuine gladness.

Lian's mouth spread into a wide grin.

"You are kind," she said, her dark hair flowing over one shoulder as a breeze swept under the leather roof. Retia's head nestled into the crook of uncle's arm, looking up at him with her mother's eyes.

"A story, Isa?" she said, her voice as small as she was. Lian sighed in relief upon hearing her daughter's voice.

Isaad looked down and tightened his hold on Retia, resting his cheek against the top of her head. He glanced in between his audience; his dark eyes mischievous.

"My girl loves a good story. Has anyone got a request?"

"I think we would be happy to hear whatever Retia would like," Evelyn said, a gentle grin spreading across her tired features.

"You hear that, little bird? What story would you like to hear?"

Retia glanced over at Grae; the corner of her lip curved. She sat up, looking into her uncle's eyes with an intensity that was far too mature to be in a girl as young as she.

"Grae taught me how to look for elosi in the Greens. I can protect you now." She spoke in such earnest, that Meric thought he could hear Isaad's heart break. The man's eyes grew moist, and he kissed the top of her head.

"Little bird, that is my duty and one that you should not worry yourself for."

"I will teach you, Isa. Then we can protect each other." She looked back at Grae, whose blue eyes radiated with something akin to pride. He nodded at her in approval, and she nestled back into her uncle's arm. "Tell me something new."

Isaad wrapped his other arm around his sister. He winced in pain, but it seemed that holding them was worth it. "Very well. I heard this tale when I was your age. Grandfather heard it as a younger man in a tavern when selling apples to the Vagu in Edewor. Your favorite storyteller, Falconer, was the one he heard it from."

Retia's eyes widened in anticipation. Meric had heard tales of Falconer, a Vagu man who had run out of stories to tell and so disappeared into the Solov Waste. Never to be heard from again. Isaad cocked his head, trying to remember how the story started and then spoke in a low, but dramatic voice.

"Hector the swallow was a young bird. He was born in the Eshe, singing to the willows to aid their growth. It was what his kind did, serenading the vines to grow long and strong, their bark thick and unyielding. I'm sure Sou could attest to that."

Retia glanced up at Sou who raised his curved brows, spreading his arms to show the length of an imaginary vine. "The birds sing all through the day and into the night. As a boy I would wake to willows that had grown twice their height overnight," he said, his tone low in the way one would when exaggerating a tale. Evelyn glanced at Sou with a somber smile, as though she knew something the rest of them had not.

Retia's grin spread wide, her small teeth like little white beads. Isaad nodded gratefully and continued.

"Hector had never been outside of the Eshe and wondered what it would be like to spread his wings in a sky free of trees.

He decided it was time to sate his curiosity and only told his mother of his departure. She was the oldest of the sparrows with silver wings and the only one who'd been singing since the Eshe was but a collection of seedlings. She gave him a stone to take with him to the outside world. She sang to him — as sparrows do not speak, they sing. *Think of this stone as my eye,* she sang, *and I shall watch and keep you safe.* So, he carried it within his beak and flew beyond the canopy of willows into the great blue sea that lives in the sky. Can you imagine, little bird, what that might've been like for him?"

Retia looked beyond the awning of their covering and into the star-filled sky. She shook her head, grey eyes sparkling in what Meric thought was her wild imaginings of flying into those stars.

"He fell in love. Not with another sparrow, but with the wind coursing through his feathers and the sun warming his back. The empty sky was so peaceful, he thought there was nothing in the world that would harm him in a place so wonderful. The stone had become a burden, heavy in his beak and seemingly without use. So, he dropped it. It fell and disappeared into the Eshe. As it fell, he couldn't tell whether it was his mother's or Celosia's glare that he saw staring at him through its reflection."

Evelyn, who had been listening to the story with interest, furrowed her brow, leaning forward slightly as though she recognized the name of someone she'd known long ago.

"What happened to the stone?" she asked.

"We'll come around to that," he said, chuckling and raising one brow in amusement that his story should captivate not only a child, but one as old as Evelyn as well. Although Meric doubted she had any real interest in the story itself, her question had the tone of someone in search of information — not the fanciful curiosity accompanied with a story being told.

"It wasn't long after he discarded the stone that he noticed a shape forming on the horizon, black and growing larger as he flew. Do you know what had come?"

"A dragon," Retia murmured, her eyes beginning to close.

"Aye, a great black dragon. He was so large he blotted out the sun and Hector was enslaved in the shadow. He couldn't find his way back to the Eshe and the only bits of light he could see were the gnashing of the dragon's white fangs. Just when he thought the end had come, there was a flash of silver in the darkness, fluttering to and fro until the sea in the sky was blue once more. His mother had come and in her beak was the stone had he let go. The dragon retreated and she led Hector back home into the Eshe. When they perched on a branch, he turned to her and sang, *I let go of the stone. How could you know where to find me?* She sang back, *This stone holds not only my sight, but the gaze of the Eshe. It is heavy and I knew you would let it go. You are my son. I will always find you and bring that which have you lost.* From that moment on, Hector flew above the canopy of willows, but always returned to the Eshe when the stone he carried grew too heavy to carry."

A collective sigh echoed through the camp, aside from Grae who had fallen asleep in the middle of the tale. Retia had followed his example, eyes shut, breathing softly in her uncle's embrace. Sou leaned his head to the side, a questioning look in his eyes.

"I myself have heard this tale. It is common among my people, although you've changed the ending. Which under the circumstances can be forgiven."

Isaad opened his mouth to speak, but Meric spoke before he could.

"How does the tale truly end?" he asked, glancing in between the two men. Isaad looked down at his niece, making sure her slumber was genuine before nodding to Sou. The old man turned to Meric, his grey streaked hair tousling in the breeze.

"The essence of the tale is the same. A child must explore the world and bring with them all their parents have taught. The parent's duty to the child is never ended, aiding them for the entirety of their lives." Sou's gaze became somber, glancing at Evelyn, who had succumbed to exhausted sleep soon after Isaad had stopped speaking. "When Hector dropped the stone, he was eaten by the dragon. His mother caught the stone at the moment of his death."

"Well then, I'd say she failed in her duty." Anya said, turning herself away from them and towards the darkness of the plains for the first watch. Meric ignored her, laying himself down to sleep, but not before another question bit at the back of his mind like the prick of a thorn.

"What became of her? Hector's mother."

Sou laid on his back, staring out from beyond the canopy in the direction of Ciar. "She loved him more than anything in the world. She died."

———

MERIC WOKE SOME HOURS LATER TO RELIEVE ANYA OF HER watch. He'd sat in silence, listening to the breeze stir the Greens. He always enjoyed the last watch, observing the sunrise bathe the land in light. It felt cleansing somehow, as though daybreak was the moment when he had no past, and no future. He simply was.

He watched the horizon, still dark but growing lighter. He was lost to the sky when he heard breathing, heavy and thick as though one were being suffocated. He sat up, hand hovering over the blade at the tip of his bow. Isaad laid asleep next to Lian, her dark hair covering most of her face. Retia slept in her mother's arms, Drool belly up next to her. Grae and Anya were soundless in their slumber, the rise and fall of their chests in sync with the other. Sou laid still with an arm across his face, snoring softly with his mouth open. Behind him, Meric heard Beau snort, the sound of her ropes brushing the wain as she shook her head. He noticed Evelyn at the edge of the camp, laying on her back and staring into the roof of their leather covering.

He stood, making his way towards her, realizing she was the one who was breathing so hard. Her red eyes were wide, unblinking, and frightened beyond comprehension. Her mouth trembled, tears running down the sides of her face.

"Evelyn. What's wrong?" he said, clutching her shoulder. A sudden terror reached into his chest, holding him hostage in the dread that lived in her gaze. She shuddered, lids twitching as though she were fighting with all her might to close them. He looked up and saw nothing but the shine of the leather's wax coating. He grabbed her hand, expecting her fingers to close around his, but she was as limp as the dead. As a child he'd known a street walker who suffered from a condition in which certain smells or weather changes caused his lungs to constrict, making it hard to breathe. When panic overtook him, the man placed a hand on his chest leveling out his breathing and riding out the episode. Evelyn's body didn't mirror the man in his memory exactly, but it was all he had to help her with. Evelyn's mouth was closed tight, gasping through her nose in small, ragged breaths. Meric leaned over her, turning her head towards him. He met her eyes and kept them, the terror that engulfed them abating somewhat.

"Breathe with me," he said, placing her hand on his chest. He took a deep breath in and out, and she did the same. He repeated the process until her inhales grew deeper and her exhales longer.

Eventually her fingers curled against his chest, gripping his tunic in a way that pulled him closer to her. She closed her eyes and sighed, turning onto her side with a quiet groan. She released her grip on his tunic and sat up, looking over the sleeping forms of their company until stopping on Lian, Isaad, and Retia. The fear he saw in her eyes before returned with a vengeance, and she turned her gaze to the plains.

"We need to leave." Her voice was almost a whisper, barely contained in its urgency. She stood, placing her belongings in a pack. He stood next to her, hearing Sou, Anya, and Grae stir to wake. Confusion replaced the relief he felt at her being well again.

"Wait," he tried reaching for her arm, but she pulled away. "What was that?"

"Please," she pleaded, voice hard against her throat. "These people... the longer we stay the more danger we place them in. A danger they know nothing of. We must leave. Now."

Meric knew she was avoiding his question, but he couldn't argue with her words. He had been planning to speak with them that morning of leaving.

"Very well," he said, and the relief in her expression was palpable.

"Don't wake them," Evelyn's eyes rested on the family, their features serene as they slept. "Let them keep their peace."

Meric afforded her a quick nod and strode to Anya and Grae, explaining what Evelyn said but left out the condition he had helped her through.

"It's past time we'd left, but to leave without a word?" Grae said, glancing at Retia. Her arm resting over the length of Drool's belly.

"She has her uncle, Grae, and a strong mother," Anya said, creasing her brow, yellow eyes companionate. Grae took one last look at Retia, and hope kindled in his eyes that she would continue in her happiness. He turned and picked up his rapier, swinging his pack over a muscular shoulder and striding towards Evelyn who was speaking with Sou. The old man's features were weighed with worry, the lines in his face more pronounced.

"Grae will miss them," Anya said, refusing to look at the family. Although she would never admit it, Meric knew she spoke for herself as well.

"As will I," he said, meeting her gaze.

They walked out from beneath the leather canopy, entering the tall Greens without looking back.

CHAPTER 37

HARP STRINGS

Evelyn's heart pounded in her chest, breath catching and limbs aching. She ran alongside the Venandi, hard and fast. She was doing everything she could to forget what she had seen, battling the need to go back to Lian and her family. Sou was behind her, heaving with heavy breath, but keeping up. Anya ran at arm's length, with Grae and Meric taking the lead. Evelyn shook her head and urged her feet forward, leaping in her strides. The images of her dream filled her mind, merciless in their assault.

There had been a pale light, radiant against a fog of dust and rock. It beaconed the end of a tunnel, its walls branched in twisted roots, narrow and wet with a slickly condensation. It was so hot she felt she might die from it. She ran as fast as she could towards the light, but her limbs were sluggish, and she fell. It seemed that she would fall for eternity, and then she landed with a terrible rock-tumbling force, the walls crumbing around her. She couldn't breathe, the air knocked from her lungs. She reached over the edge of a slanted cliff, the jagged end of rocks cutting into her flesh. A form writhed in the water below, boiling, burning, and screaming. She managed to stand and found herself in a village, small sailing boats riding the river on waves of fire. Her vision flashed red and orange, heat burning her eyes closed.

When she opened them, the ground she walked on was covered in ash, flaming embers rained down from a black sky. Grae held a small child in his arms. Retia. He wept over her, and Evelyn couldn't tell if the small girl was dead. The ground shook and Lian stood before her, dark hair cascading around her like a cloak. Her wain overturned, apples scattering and transforming into blood. It spread across the Greens, sloshing at the woman's feet as though she waded in a red river. Evelyn tried to call out, but her voice wouldn't work. She clutched her throat and when she tried to scream again what came from her was more animalistic than human. She knew that voice. She turned around and a hooded man wearing a black cloak advanced on her, holding out Tansey's iron dagger. Meric's honey-hazel eyes stared into her own, blocking the view of the hooded man. The iron dagger slashed between them, blood splattering his pained features and she screamed, pain erupting deep within her chest.

That was the moment she woke, paralyzed and staring into the empty eyes of those black-oiled figures. Their forms hovered above her, slick and dripping thick, tar-like fluid. She couldn't breathe, her chest constricted with the familiar heaviness from before. She tried to move, to scream, but she couldn't. The figures crept closer, and Evelyn saw something had changed. Their eyes. They were black no longer, but blue. She recognized those eyes. Birdie's eyes. The dead woman's irises gleamed raw with animosity as though accusing Evelyn of letting her die. Evelyn recalled feeling tears running down her cheek, powerless to stop the horrific images her sleeping mind showed her waking mind.

Then Meric was there. His hand clutching her own, turning her head away from Birdie's dead glare. She could still feel the warmth of his chest against the palm of her hand, breathing with her—for her, until she could do so on her own. She remembered the fear, the knowledge that she was being hunted. She grew angry at herself for having been so lax as to put Isaad, Lian and her daughter in danger. If she had seen Grae holding Retia, then she needed to get them as far from the family as possible. To protect them she had to abandon them. The guilt was overwhelming, bringing her back to when she'd left her village and how it burned in her absence. Evelyn ran faster, the ground beneath her feet bending to the strength of her stride.

She felt a hand on her arm, slowing her down to a walk.

"Where was this enthusiasm days ago?" Grae said, his chest heaving, brow slick with sweat. Evelyn was suddenly tired, lungs expanding inside her chest with the thundering of her heart.

"I'm starting to like the feeling. Clears the mind," she said, out of breath.

"Well, you've a lot to think on then. You've hired us to protect you and that's difficult to do when you run out of sight."

She turned around and saw in the distance the rest of their group hurrying to catch up. She'd been so lost in her own thoughts she hadn't known she passed them.

"I am capable of looking after myself for a moment of solitude." She tried to hide the annoyance in her tone, but he was right. She had a lot on her mind and had no patience to command her frustration.

Grae placed a hand on the hilt of his rapier, walking alongside her with the gait of someone walking for the simple pleasure of it.

"Of that I have no doubt. But that elosi was no Reticent," he said, squinting against the sun.

"Have you fought one before?" she asked.

"An elosi?"

"No, a Reticent."

Grae leaned his head back and laughed, looking down at her as though she'd asked if snow could fall upwards. She frowned, not appreciating his reaction and rolled her eyes as his laughter abated.

"No, of course not," he said, his voice breaking with a residual chuckle. "I'm alive, aren't I?"

Evelyn scoffed, lengthening her strides to walk past him.

He quickened his pace, walking backwards to continue their conversation.

"Oh, and you have?" The smug smile that spread across his lips was both annoying and disarming. Evelyn could see why Anya liked Grae; his demeanor had a cavalier charm. Despite them being older than she by a decade, Anya and Grae were both equally immature in different ways, making up for the others faults and building on their strengths. They suited one another. She wasn't sure why the two of them hadn't admitted their feelings. It was so obvious to her she had thought they'd been bound to each other already.

"No, but I think I could make them sweat. If only a drip," she said, refusing to give him the satisfaction of being right.

"Very well. I'll give you that. A drip." He turned around as Meric, Anya and Sou made their way beside them.

"Where was this enthusiasm days ago?" Anya said, echoing Grae's exact words.

"We've discussed that already," he told her, flashing a smile in her direction. She raised a brow, wiping strands of black hair from her slick brow.

"Care to share the highlights?"

Grae shrugged, looking through the plains that rolled with grass covered hills. "Running is good for the mind and there's no one among us who's fought a Reticent."

Anya cocked her head to the side, nodding. "Well, we're all alive, aren't we?"

Evelyn bit her lip to keep herself from commenting on the exchange. How could they not see it? She glanced at Meric whose stoic features bent into a grin.

They walked for some minutes more and broke into a run again. No matter how hard or how fast she pushed herself, she couldn't unsee what she had seen. The dream haunted her, and she wondered how the Videns before her could've stood to wait for what may or may not have been averted. The day had grown long, and they decided to make camp early, traveling deeper into the Greens for good measure.

Evelyn settled onto her blanket, swallowing the last bits of her onni jerky. A cool breeze swirled through the Greens, wisps of blue light twisting and dancing among the foliage as though it were the grass that created the wind. Grae had said they should arrive in Ciar by midmorning the next day and she realized she would miss the plains. The open landscape was the most peace she'd felt since leaving Verbena. Even in fighting the elosi, she'd felt the rush of hunting in the mountains, stalking with Nakasha's calm breath beneath her. She thought of her wolf, large paws pressing soft snow into a compact sheet of ice for her to step in. Nakesha would've loved running through the grass, hunting onni and giving the elosi a reason to fear. She missed her.

"What are you thinking about?" Sou said, leaning forward to wrap his arms around his knees. Evelyn raised her head, running her hands through the folds of her blanket.

"Nothing. Just what might happen tomorrow." She hadn't lied to him entirely. She was worried about what was to come. Nothing ever stayed the same. She was forced to leave Reva just as she was beginning to understand its rubrics. She'd journeyed the Greens for nearly a week and just as she was growing to appreciate it, she would be thrust into a place she'd never been with new customs she'd have no time to learn.

She recalled sitting with Birdie at the top of the mountain, gazing upon her small village after their last hunt. It felt like so long ago. She remembered longing to see beyond that frozen horizon. She'd understood herself well enough to know that eventually, she'd yearn for the simplicity of the snowfall. She yearned for it now, her heart aching for a home she could never return to.

"There's nothing to it. A few hours to replenish our supplies and we'll be gone," Sou said, taking out his dagger and dragging a cloth over the steel. Evelyn had told him of her dream, and though Sou tried to hide it, he was worried. She noticed Grae unsheathe his rapier, taking a stand on the edge of their camp and thrusting it into the air. It was the first time she'd seen him practice and she watched in approval at the balance of his form. It was good, legs spaced out and back

447

straight. His wrist turned, gutting an imaginary foe, and twisted to thrust out again. The blade cut through the air only to be stopped by another, Sou. The old man held his dagger with a lazy hand, a curious look in his green eyes.

"You demanded another spar, if I remember correctly," he said, his voice challenging. Grae's lip curved up into a wry grin, blue eyes steeled with confidence.

"I did."

Without another word Grae swiped his rapier in a circle, guiding Sou's blade with its movement until he broke the contact with a wide sweep. Sou backed away, features taut with an excited smile, stepping aside Grae's broad lunge. The Venandi brought the sword up attempting to use his own weight against Sou's weaker form, but the old man was quick, catching the rapier close to the hilt. He pushed it aside and stabbed for Grae's belly, which he easily blocked.

The duel continued and each man was able to bring the other to a yield many times over. Evelyn thought that Sou might've been fighting a younger version of himself in the prime of his youth. Grae fought with skill and youthful creativity, while Sou battled with experience and dexterity. The times Grae was able to defeat Sou was in circumventing conventional sword stances, tricking the old man into thinking he would go one way and drive his blade home into a different direction. Sou combated that with remembering Grae's idiosyncrasies, how he lunged and when he stabbed, the tells his body would betray before making a move.

Evelyn wasn't the only one entertained by the sparing session. Meric and Anya watched with interest, and occasionally would add their own unhelpful counsel.

"His feet! Kick his feet!" Anya said, causing Grae to lose his focus and land on his back as Sou took her advice.

"Whose side are you on?" he demanded, glaring at her from the ground. She laughed, shrugging as she chewed onni meat with an open mouth.

"I've never seen someone as good as you with a blade," Meric said, smiling. "How does the dirt taste?"

Evelyn chuckled as Sou flipped his dagger with the blade resting against his forearm. He reached out with his other hand and Grae clasped it, grunting as he was hauled to his feet. Sou patted the Venandi on the back, looking at the rapier in Grae's hand.

"I quite enjoy seeing you look up from the flat of your back," the old man said, chuckling before his expression transformed from one of humor to pride. "A weapon is only as good as the one who wields it and you've an excellent blade. Well done."

Grae wiped dirt from his cheek and blinked at Sou, his expression one of surprised appreciation.

"I think there are still more angles from which you could see me from the flat of *your* back, Vagu," he said. His tone was abrasive, but the blue in his eyes shone with hope. Sou lined his lips, sheathing the dagger at his belt.

"I should like for you to try, Venandi. Tomorrow evening?"

Grae accepted the appointment with a hard nod, turning his back, but not before Evelyn detected the hint of an ardent smile. Sou placed his hands on his hips, watching the young man walk away with a parental gaze gleaming in his green eyes. Evelyn suspected to see many more evenings filled with the two sparing.

As evening fell, Meric sat up to take the first watch, Anya and Grae laying on blankets near him. Sou sat beside her on his own covering, staring into the night with his hands behind his head. As Evelyn settled into a comfortable position a thin trail of blue light tousled the hood of her cloak carrying Sou's voice.

Block my thoughts.

They'd done this each night and each time she had failed. He told her it was all in the breathing, the calm release of air to clear the mind and wall out all distractions. It was the opposite of all she'd ever trained for. Tansey taught her to embrace the chaos and let it fuel her limbs to action. She closed her eyes as Sou recited a song, something about a young woman waiting for the return of her wife from war. It pierced into her mind like the strike of a viper, quick and loud. She had no choice but to wall it out or she'd never sleep.

She concentrated on her breathing, inhaling through her nose and exhaling through her mouth. The song still thrummed in her mind, off-key in Sou's terrible tone-deaf voice. Evelyn shook her head and opened her eyes, glaring at Sou who laid in silence, his eyes closed as though he were asleep. She saw wisps of thin light bending to the pattern of his song. It reminded her of a harp's strings, and she reached out with her mind, grasping with imaginary fingers the cords of his thoughts.

The world fell silent, limiting itself to the Greens brushing against one another. Sou's eyes snapped open, and he tugged against her, his thoughts writhing in her grasp. She felt all that he was, his pain and fears. The love he bore for her was almost too much to comprehend. How could someone hold this much love within them and not shatter? She was transfixed by it. There was something else, too. Something he wasn't ready for her to know. A voice echoed in the back of her mind—Sou's voice. He was screaming, but it sounded so far away. Suddenly it was all around her and she was shoved into the dominion of his command.

LET ME GO!

She did and he was gone. Sou was propped on his elbow, breathing heavily and looking at her with green eyes that had turned dark in the shadows. She tried to speak, her apology making its way up her throat, but he held a hand up.

"That's enough for tonight. We'll try again tomorrow, but I think you've discovered your own way," he said, a tremble in his voice. He tried to console her with a half-smile, but she could see she had unsettled him. He laid back down, but this time turned his back on her, the slow rise and fall of his body giving into sleep.

Evelyn curled into herself, clutching the folds of her cloak beneath her chin. She was afraid to sleep, dreading what she might see. The soft murmur of the Venandi talking was not enough to distract her. She thought of Lian and her family,

Isaad, Retia, even Drool and Beau. She had the smallest hope to see them again in Ciar, entering the city soon after they did, but it was unlikely they would ever meet again. She couldn't stop thinking. Sou's frightened eyes stared back at her through closed lids, flashes of her dream crossing her memory with relentless fervor.

Out of everything she saw — the river of fire and the mysterious tunnel collapsing around her — it was the body that fell, burning in a boiling lake, that haunted her most. Although they were not taking the cliffs along Elm Lake, she couldn't help the feeling that this was an event she had to do everything in her power to stop. The image was foreboding, and she could still hear them screaming. Her lids fluttered, and her final thought was of Meric's rough features covered in blood, and the terrible fear that whispered in her ear the truth she could not accept: that no matter what she did, Meric would die.

CHAPTER 38

THE LIFTING OF MASKS

The sky was swimming in starlight. Meric laid on his back, watching the twinkling of the night through the awning of grass. The sky above Reva was much too bright to see stars, but in the middle of the Dattadri Greens their brilliance covered the night in crystal-like gems, breaking through the veil of darkness. He was once told that the world was a cave, and only when the way was shut could the jewels, trapped in the walls enclosing them, be seen. He couldn't remember who had told him that. He hadn't recalled it until now and was suddenly unsettled by its opaque origin. He pushed the thought away, thinking on the morrow.

He was looking forward to sitting in a chair, perhaps reclining in a tavern, eating a meal that didn't threaten to break his teeth and a soothing bath to wash away the grime of their trek. But he knew a chair and a meal was all he would hope to get in Ciar. He longed for a bed, a place to rest where he didn't have to scrape rodent droppings from his clothes.

"We need to talk," Anya whispered beside him.

He turned his head to see her lying next to him, her hands folded together on her cheek. It was growing late in his shift, and he'd known Anya wouldn't need to be woken up. She was always ready to take over as though she had some second sense her watch was approaching. Beside her Grae propped himself on an elbow, glancing at Evelyn. By the cadence of her breathing, she was asleep, although her back was turned from them. Sou laid with his back to Evelyn, seeming to slumber with the same depth.

"About what?" he said, although he knew this was coming. They were reaching the halfway point in their journey and the mystery surrounding Sou and Evelyn had reached its tipping point.

"Our generous benefactors," Grae said, eyeing Meric with the same look he'd given him when he'd been too deep in drink. Meric glanced in between his friends, realizing suddenly this conversation was specific to him. He leaned forward, clasping his hand together.

"Yes?" he said, a challenge seeping through his tone.

Anya rolled her eyes, sitting up with her legs crossed.

"You know as well as I that I don't say things of this nature lightly, but..." she hesitated, sighing.

"Depths, Anya. You'd find confessing to murder easier. Just say it," Grae said, nudging her arm with his hand.

"I like them," she said, staring at Meric with steeled yellow eyes.

It wasn't the confession he was expecting. He blinked, cocking his head to the side, trying to determine if the real Anya were sitting before him. Her jaw clenched and he almost laughed to realize she was being serious.

"You like them? You don't like anyone. You don't even like me."

"Of course I don't like you. You're an impulsive, braying mule who bit the hand that fed you." Her voice traveled as a whisper, but her tone was loud with accusation.

"You?" he pointed at her; his lips spread in an incredulous smile. "You're calling *me* impulsive?"

"I didn't beat a City Lord."

"Only because I was closer."

"Enough," Grae hissed through his teeth. "I think what Anya is meaning to say and failing terribly at it is this: we want to see them safe across the Iris and into Birny as badly as you do."

Meric felt the crease in his brow deepen, confusion obscuring what he thought this conversation would be. "I don't understand. Speak it plainly."

"We need to remain objective," Grae said, glancing at Anya who kept her eyes on Meric. "We cannot protect them both if one of us is... distracted."

"Distracted?" Meric repeated, growing frustrated. Anya groaned, rolling her eyes again.

"You've both heaps of dung for brains," she said, leaning forward and ignoring Grae's offended expression. "I like them, but you like *her.*"

Meric's chest constricted, and he felt all arguments stick in his throat, choking him with a stutter. Anya leaned back with a satisfied grin. The smile transformed to a pitying one as she looked in between him and Evelyn.

"Meric," she whispered, her voice gentle. "Don't do that to yourself. Our paths have merged for the time being, but they will eventually part. Our duty is to guide and protect —"

"I think she's capable of protecting herself," he said, interrupting her. Even as he spoke the words, he felt the hypocrisy in them. He saw what she was capable of and yet, he knew in his heart of hearts there was a reason he pulled her through the alleys, ran after her in the Greens, drawing his weapon beside her as she confronted the elosi.

"That she is," Grae agreed, sitting up on his blanket now. "But we don't know what else she may be capable of. I am of the same mind as Anya. I've grown... tolerant of their company."

Anya scoffed, placing her hands behind her, and leaning against them.

"He likes them too. Especially Sou." She flopped her head to the side, looking at Grae with a mischievous grin. "What is it you said about your spar with him? *An extraordinary display of prowess from which I could learn much from.* Give two men a blade and they will either kill each other or forge a lifelong friendship. It's difficult to tell which as both involve the shedding of blood."

"My feelings have nothing to do with my duty. I'm not hindered by them," Meric said. There was no point in denying his fondness for Evelyn. He was a brute and a drunk, but Depths drown him if he wasn't an honest brute and drunk. He wasn't sure what it was he felt, but they were right. But whatever it was he saw in her ruby eyes had no claim to his heart. At least that's what he told himself.

"Not in its current state, but eventually they will have everything to do with your duty. My eyes have not been tattooed into blindness," Anya said, wind blowing loose hair about her face. "That is why we wanted to speak with you about it now. Once we deliver her to Birny, it is unlikely we shall ever meet again. Reva is no place for us, and I doubt Birny can maintain us. To find work we will need to travel. And Grae is right, we've no idea what else she is capable of."

Evelyn sighed and turned around; her features relaxed in sleep deep in her green hood. Meric gazed at her, thinking on how she carried herself, how different she was from anyone he'd ever met. The way she had attacked the elosi and the fierce look in her eyes as she held her blade to his throat in the alley. He recalled her smile when he'd called her feral. The compassion in her expression as she offered Sou's True Tears to heal him. How could he see so much and know so little? Whatever it was that Evelyn was or was not capable of, he believed she was no more able to inflict malicious harm than he was. It didn't make either of them honorable, but it didn't make them monsters either. Meric recalled an echo of Evelyn's words from the day before about good people losing their way.

"We know what she *isn't* capable of and that is convincing us she is a Lady," he said, trying to change the course of the conversation. He plucked a small shoot of grass in his hand, breaking it apart in his fingers as he told Grae and Anya of where Evelyn claimed she'd been born.

"Verbena? I've never heard of it," Anya said, wrinkling her

brow. Grae looked into the Greens, deep in thought, but having no recollection of the village either.

"Neither have I," Meric said, watching a breeze tousle Evelyn's hair across her nose. "It's somewhere further north, in the Bena Mountains. She spoke of it as though she could never go back."

Anya inclined her head towards Sou, whose breathing had grown quiet.

"I'm not sure what to make of him. It's obvious he cares a great deal for her. I suspect he might be a relative or at the very least her guardian. If you hadn't noticed, her brows are slightly slanted."

Meric had noticed, but that only meant she had Vagu ancestry. Grae had a slanted brow, but he never emitted any supernatural power over the wind and through his observations neither had Evelyn. It didn't prove Sou had any relation to her.

"Before we broke you out, I met that man's blade in the alley," Grae whispered, his tone still with remembrance. "His dagger has feasted on enemy blood before. He fought like they did when Chao attacked Reva."

Grae seldom spoke of the Evandis. Meric knew his friend was young when Chao had descended upon the city, nearly destroying it and all those who lived within. It was only by the Videns resilience that the city survived. The battle had been won, but the cost claimed far too many lives, both civilian, Viden, and dragon. Though Meric had yet to be born, he still heard tale of the day the sky wept blood. The blue in Grae's eyes darkened, the memories of what he'd experienced a burden he hadn't let go of.

"You speak as though you were there."

Meric started as Sou lifted himself from his prostrate position, shadows creeping over his features, moonlight bending in the clouds above. Anya squared her shoulders and sat straighter than before as though she wore armor beneath the linen shirt Lian had gifted her. Grae remained still, his eyes trailing to the edge of his blanket where his rapier laid.

"I was," he said quietly, meeting the old man's eyes. "Were you?"

"No." Sou shook his head. "But rest assured that I did my part in fighting that war."

"What part?" Meric asked, half expecting the man to dismiss the question. He did, staring at him with a deep sadness in his green eyes.

"More silence. More lies," Grae said, the wind stirring the surrounding grass behind him.

"Silence does not always equal falsehood. In my experience, it is within that silence that truth screams the loudest. If you would only listen to it, that absence of sound, you might begin to understand why I hold my tongue. But perhaps old age has made me cynical." Sou smiled, his grin infectious. "You've discovered the obvious. Aye, Evelyn is not a Lady. You have the right of that. And as she seemed to have already told you," He met Meric's eye with a disapproving stare, clearly upset she had shared something of herself with him, "She grew up in the mountains under my watchful eye and after some… ill-fated circumstances I am returning her to the remaining family she has left."

His voice held nothing that enticed happiness. Meric rubbed his chin as Anya leaned forward with a curious look in her yellow eyes.

"What ill-fated circumstance?"

A small breeze blew about Sou, rustling his cloak across the ground. He tilted his head, peering to the side as though he were eavesdropping on a private conversation. He turned back to Anya, a debilitating kindness in his eyes that made Meric look away, afraid of what those eyes could make him tell.

"I'll answer that if you tell me what it is you saw when my True Tears touched your soul," Sou said, his voice driving the compulsion to unburden. Meric kept his gaze on Anya, wondering if she felt the same pull to put down the yolk of her life's monolithic weight. Her jaw twitched and the muscles in her neck tightened as though she were trying her hardest not to scream.

457

"I saw the dead," she whispered, so quiet Meric wasn't sure she spoke. "And the ones who had made them so. They beat me, and I was left for dead, among the dead, with nothing but the absence of what I lost."

Grae blinked in surprise then cast his eyes downward, placing his hand over hers. Instead of recoiling, she gripped his fingers, holding him as though she were lost in a raging river, and he the only tether she had.

Meric was at a loss for words. Sou leaned his head to the side, frowning in a way that old men do when hearing a sad story. The Vagu had a power about him that Meric had never heard of before. There was nothing notable about his kindness. Meric had come to realize that that was simply how Sou was made, unfailingly kind—but it was not the sum of his parts. Sou possessed both a natural and supernatural ability that made those around him feel like they were not only being listened to, but understood. There was no coercion in the act, only the naked feeling of being seen entirely.

Anya exhaled a heavy breath, relaxing her posture, the armor she had donned gone. She sniffed and released Grae's hand, staring at Sou with astonished eyes.

"How did you do that? How did you... know?" she said, stunned.

Sou shrugged and rubbed the side of his stubbled face.

"There is more to the Iona's Breath than cool air. I am Vagu. I listen and with listening comes understanding," he said, a half-smile spreading across his aged features.

"Vagu magic," Grae murmured. The old man faced Grae, a brisk wind curling through the loose strands of his hair.

"If it pleases you," Sou said, his voice weary. "Or perhaps it is but a trait of my people. As tracking is of yours, a skill honed for generations. Perhaps if you asked, I might relieve you of what you most fear."

Grae stiffened, locking eyes with Sou as though challenging him.

"Do you hear the voices of the dead?"

"No," Sou's tone was absolute. "I only feel the impressions

of my departed loved ones as all Vagu can. Once more, it is a skill. One that I have focused on to better understand those around me. What others are feeling, their happiness and sorrows. That is all. You are free. Ever free to be silent or to speak. The decision has been and always will be yours. I hold no dominion over choice. Nor can I tell the future—that is a burden long believed to be dead."

Meric's shoulders slumped in relief. Truth and trust were what he sought, and what he believed Sou had just given them. There was still much unknown, but it was a start. He was amazed by what Anya had confessed. He glanced at Grae, whose posture remained fixated in place, but the tension in his muscles loosened with a quiet exhale.

"Is it so simple as that? To listen?" Meric said, breaking the silence.

"To listen takes a great deal of practice," Sou said, gesturing towards Evelyn. "She's a good lass, but as stubborn as tundra in spring. I am ever a student to the wind. You three are nothing compared to her."

"Well?" Anya said, brows raised in expectation. "You promised."

Sou nodded and smacked his lips as though he were trying to decide on what to have for supper. "I should stop doing that. Very well. You've lost someone. The lot of you look like you've lost someone. Am I correct in assuming that?"

Meric thought of his parents and the scattered memories of his mother singing him to sleep. No one spoke, and Meric understood what Sou had been speaking of when it came to silence.

"Then the truth is far less complex than you think. She's lost people too and all at once. There is a reason I cannot tell you how it happened or why. It is not only for her protection we keep our secrets."

Meric wondered how a life could change in so short a time. Little less than a month ago he'd been drinking in Decorum, capturing innocents to fill his cups. Now, he was eluding a Reticent, fighting elosi, and traveling with a Vagu—something he would've scoffed to discover weeks ago. Meric noticed Evelyn as she moved her hand so that her finger was pulling on the corner of her mouth, displaying her teeth. If there was anything that could argue she wasn't a Lady, the small glint of drool running down her chin was certainly the most convincing. He smiled and suddenly could not envision his life not having met her.

"Grae," Sou said, pulling Meric away from his reminiscing. "How old were you when Chao came to Reva?"

Grae shook his head and held his hands together as though gripping a ledge and refusing to let go for fear of falling.

"It is common knowledge that Chao assaulted the city, but that doesn't mean you have the right to ask about it. No matter the *impression* you might feel," Grae spat his response with the venom of a cornered vapor serpent. Meric had never seen his friend so uncomfortable, and he nearly told Sou to hold his tongue, but the old man said not a word. Sou let the silence flow, its ebb softening the air instead of sharpening it. He inclined his head without the expectation of a response, unveiling the look of a man with only an ear with which to listen. A tear rolled down Grae's cheek as his body seemed to yield before such an offer.

"I was thirteen," he said, his voice a whisper.

"That must've been difficult. Being on the cusp of manhood, but still looked upon as a child." Sou's compassion was unbearably loud, ramming its way through every barrier Meric had built over the years. He could only imagine how Grae must feel, hearing such words directed towards him.

"The dragon wasn't the worst of it. It was the people, our neighbors. Panic and fear will turn family into strangers and friends to enemies." Grae ran a hand through his blonde hair and laughed without any mirth to it. "There was a boy I grew up with. Jean, his name was. He looked a lot like you." He glanced at Meric, who was too somber to speak.

"Best friends we were. Chao had come in the daylight, spitting his fire for days. I hid under the ground with my family, enduring the rumblings of the buildings above us collapsing. It seemed endless, days upon days with the senseless fear of burnt-out candles and darkness. I was so frightened of the dark then. The fighting was constant. I grew used to the screams, eventually I'd come to rely on them to get to sleep." He bowed his head shamefully. "We had our underground shelter, but we never truly believed Reva would be attacked. Our supplies were minimal, but we'd managed to ration our food. However, we'd gone through the water. There was a well in the middle of the square, where my family home was."

Meric remembered the collapsed well where they'd all escaped Reva. He'd chosen that route because that part of the city never recovered from Chao's ravaging. It remained an empty, desolate place that still bore the scars of the Evandis. Meric thought it mustn't have been easy for Grae to have gone back there.

"Everyone was too weak to make the trek to the surface. It was a choice of who had the best chance of making it back and that was me. Before I left, Abhi, our house Vagu, gripped me by the arm, her fingers peeled from the hot stones she helped move to keep the entrance to the surface clear. She'd begun seeing shapes in the darkness, forgetting the battle above. The constant darkness of being below the ground was too much for her mind. My mother kept as close an eye on her as she could, but she disappeared one night, and we found her among the dead when Chao had his fill of blood. She held onto me and whispered with the fervor of madness, *Go back, they whisper. Always, they whisper. Go back.* I shook her off, afraid she'd drag me into a corner where my parents wouldn't find me beyond the candlelight.

"I grabbed a pail and my father's butcher knife and through the fire, rubble, and buried limbs I found my way to the well. Jean was there, collecting water for his family. We hardly recognized each other we were so sooty." He laughed at the memory, a fond smile forming, then disappearing with a gradual heaviness. "He looked at me, then through me, as though I were mist. We'd both been buried by flames, and I knew this boy had risen from the ashes my friend no more. He struck my jaw with his fist and took my pail. I didn't hesitate. I cut him as he ran from me."

Grae swept the air with his hand as his voice wavered. Anya stared at the ground transfixed on the crushed grass beneath her blanket.

"You killed him," she wasn't asking a question. Grae shook his head, wiping a tear from his cheek.

"No. I severed his heel. He fell hard, his leg collapsing beneath him. I took both pails, filled them with water and left him there screaming my name. Which I suppose is just the same. When I returned, Abhi, crouched in the corner, stared at me in silence, but I knew what she would ask. Did I go back? She left us before she had the mind to speak to me. When the city guards found us beneath the rubble, it took them hours to convince us it was safe to surface. Once we did, I saw Jean. He was still there and by the look of him I'd figured we'd parted ways no less than a week." Grae's eyes were dark with memory, as if he saw his dead friend instead of the old man before him. His expression was haunted by the horrible, distorted features of rotting flesh that tickled the back of Meric's memory with horror. Grae's reservations regarding Sou suddenly fell into place. The woman had been driven mad by the attack—her words could've meant anything, but to a young man, barely more than a child, they predicted what he could not do.

"It was war," Meric said, trying to wrap his head around that kind of trauma. "You can't be blamed for what you had to do."

"Yes. Yes, I can," his friend said, clenching his hands together into a large white-knuckled fist.

As Meric's gaze traveled back to Sou he was struck by gleaming ruby eyes. Those crimson irises brought him back beneath the ground, into that dark prison, where Evelyn had first stood before him, shining with the brightness of the moon he had mistaken for the radiance of the sun. How brightly she'd burned then, and yet, she glowed still. He didn't know how much Evelyn heard, but by her forlorn expression, she'd heard enough. She stood, hair wild around her shoulders and made her way to Grae.

Anya and Sou remained silent as she kneeled by Grae's side and placed a hand on his shoulder. That seemed to rouse him, and he flinched, looking at her with violence behind his blue eyes. She cupped his cheek, and Grae inhaled sharply, fighting the tears that threatened to break his resolve.

"Someone once told me that we are all but one catastrophe away from being different people. As someone who's only living because you chose *not* leave me behind, allow me to say you turned out not so terrible a man."

Grae stared at her a moment longer, lip trembling, breaking. He leaned his head onto her shoulder, shaking with sobs. She rested her head against his and stroked the back of his hair with tender fingers. Meric had never seen his friend in such a state, weeping without reserve, but it wasn't a sorrowful cry. It was the relief of a man whose burden fell from broken shoulders. The weight of it had cut deep and with its freeing, blood flowed back with the indication that healing was possible. Grae seemed relieved and as he lifted his head, Meric could hardly recognize his friend. His features were the same, his body lean as it had always been, but his presence changed.

Meric imagined that Grae could feel Jean's raspy breath against the back of his neck, screaming in his ears all these years. Evelyn had helped him place the dead boy back into the grave. Grae met Anya's bright yellow eyes. She placed her hand in his, stoically embracing her tears with the ferocity of a stubborn stone. Anya stared at Grae with a tenderness not often seen in the woman, blazing into life the love Meric knew she bore for Grae, but had not yet spoken of.

Sou remained cross-legged on his patch of grass, turning towards Meric with a thoughtful expression

"If your silence could speak, what would it say?" Sou's eyes bore into Meric, coursing as though the old man's gaze were a green river.

Meric couldn't imagine what secrets his silence could reveal. How foolish he'd been for ever thinking he'd been alone in his pain or had a reason to drink. He hadn't one sip of ale since that night at the inn, but he still craved the elixir. He had thought to pour himself cups of it when they'd reached Ciar. Now that desire left him empty in the face of all that Grae and Anya had endured. What Evelyn had said was true. In the aftermath of their catastrophes, they'd lost their way.

He had lost his way.

"That there is nothing to say to those who have suffered far more than I ever have," he said, glancing at his companions who met his gaze with expressions that seemed to disagree.

"Where is it written that suffering only belongs to those who've worn its shroud the most? How would you measure that? Is the gardener not worthy of sadness because his flowers failed to bloom in the spring? Or the mother who hasn't slept for a week due to her baby's cries? To be sorrowful is an indication that you've experienced joy. Fear is the precursor to courage. Embrace it for its ability to help you grow."

They were only words, a concoction of sound and cadence to allow communication, and yet Meric had never heard such truth. How could a man he'd known for such a small amount of time know him so intimately? See to the core of his fears, his faults, and want to help him still? A breeze swirled around Meric, encircling his body in what felt like the warmth of an embrace. He closed his eyes, listening to his silence as he felt Sou's compassion reach him through whatever it was the wind had impressed upon the old man.

"I know little of my childhood. I cannot remember the faces of my parents. All I have is the sound of my mother's singing and the strong presence of my father's strength. If my mother and father had ever embraced me, the feel of their arms has long since left my memory. They left me in the care of a neighbor, an old woman whose name I cannot recall. I have but one memory and that is the bloated, rotting face of that old woman. She died, you see. I suppose it was age that had killed her. In the evening, she had sent me off to bed and that morning I'd found her on the floor. I thought she was asleep. I, being a child, waited for her to wake up, for days and then weeks. I ate her food, drank her water, all the while smelling her body turn to slop, but not understanding that she was dead."

Meric shuddered, closing his lids, and visualizing the old woman's melting skin and swollen gaze, staring at him with eyes that, no matter how many times he tried, would not shut. It was when her eyes bulged from the bloating that he had finally realized something was wrong.

"It was so hot, and I had to tread the floor carefully as not to step into the sludge she had turned into. I had soon run out of food and water, holding out as long as I could, but eventually I knew I had to leave. I was so hungry, so thirsty. The old woman was no longer recognizable as human, her bones draped in the thick tar that had once been her drab dress." He paused, a humorless chuckle escaping his lips. "It's incredible. I can recall the simple stitching of her dress's hem, how it looked like the coils of spiral grass that grew in her garden, but I cannot even conjure a line of my own father's face. I fell into what remained of her when I tried to leave. I remember reeking of the dead for weeks after. I stayed close to the house, hoping my parents would return. When they didn't, I ventured into the alleys, stealing where I could, fighting when I had to, and surviving by whatever means necessary. Then I met Grae."

Meric spoke of Juna and the theft of her baby, what he heard and felt in Fallon's prisons. He spoke of the black hole he'd been living in far before he was ever placed in the underground cells. All the regret he'd gathered over the years in failing the people he was hired to find and sentenced to the life they'd been running from. The vast emptiness that had always been so present in his life. He suddenly recalled what he had seen when he'd drunk Sou's True Tears. The shroud of darkness lifted its mask and Meric had been confronted with his own hollowed face.

When he was finished, Meric stared into that dark precipice and realized that it wasn't as deep as it once was.

Evelyn placed her hand next to his, the wind caressing their bodies as though trying to bring them closer. Her hand radiated heat with its closeness. He touched her fingers with his own, and all at once duty became something more, something stronger.

"What in the Depths just happened?" Grae said, his voice risen in confusion.

"We've lifted our masks, Venandi, and exchanged trust. I know you all the better for it and I believe that by speaking your horrors you've invited some good to replace their vacancy." Sou smiled, laying back down with his hands behind his head, closing his eyes as though he'd only woken to reposition himself and not change the fabric of the lives he traveled with.

Grae and Anya exchanged a look of exhaustion, but Anya remained upright as Grae laid back down. She raised an eyebrow at Meric and leaned forward.

"We still have a few hours before daylight. Get some sleep," she said, patting his chest, her hand lingering a moment before dropping.

Evelyn's red eyes glinted in the moonlight, glancing at him with a tired smile. She stood and returned to her patch of grass, staring at the sky. Meric was about to lay down when he noticed Evelyn's eyes darting from side to side as if she were following a shooting star.

She raised her head, a panicked look distorting her once relaxed features. He glanced up and saw a pale shape circling above them. It was too large to be a star traveling across the sky and too round to be a bird. Meric was about to ask Evelyn what she thought it to be when the shape descended, falling from the sky to land at his feet with a sick squelch, like the sound of a boot sinking into thick mud. Evelyn screamed and Meric shouted his horror as a head lolled to the side, mouth open, pale features splattered in blood below a familiar unruly mop of red hair.

Chapter 39

Almost

M eric stared into the empty eyes of Isaad, the man's once stubborn gaze hollowed by a death that had been a surprise. His thoughts immediately turned to Lian and Retia. He scanned the night, wondering if the blood from their severed heads would rain down from above. Grae stood, his blue eyes horrified as he followed the blood that spread beneath Isaad's head.

"Retia!" he screamed, his gaze shifting to the Greens surrounding them as if the girl were hiding in them.

Anya unsheathed the blade at her hip, staring into the sky with Meric. He could see nothing, only stars that seemed too beautiful to have spit out something so monstrous.

Evelyn stared at Isaad, her cheeks glistening with tears. She looked up, her ruby gaze darting back and forth as though she was following a light invisible to the rest of them. She furrowed her brow, eyes circling and then resting above Meric. She gasped and threw herself at him, crashing into his chest and falling to the ground. Meric heaved in a heavy breath, feeling his back ache at the impact. When he sat up, black talons ripped the soil from where he had stood, wings beating, a dark beak opened in a loud shriek. The solov raptor turned, talons lashing out towards all that moved.

Meric crawled across the ground, reaching for his bow

when those same talons appeared before him. He leaped to his feet his mind racing against the impossibility of what was before him. This raptor was old, its feathers losing color at the tips, its tongue a pale crimson. He knew this raptor. Meric breathed in sharply, searching for Evelyn. He shifted his head and realized she was behind him, looking at Sou, who raised his palms towards the raptor. The wind seemed to rise from the ground, screaming its defiance and lifted the beast in the air, tossing it into the night. Its scream echoed across the stars, sounding more human than animal. Grae and Anya turned their attention towards Evelyn, turning their backs on her with their weapons out.

Meric looked towards her and she met his gaze, a strange fear in her eyes. As though there was something she needed to confess, but was too late in speaking it. The raptor dove back down, beating its wings. Their blankets and packs lifted and tumbled, grass uprooting and spraying dirt. Meric squinted to keep specks of soil from his vision. He dodged the raptor's snapping beak, nearly losing a score of flesh from his neck.

Anya gripped her dagger and slashed at the raptor, grunting with each thrust, but the blade couldn't land true. The creature was quick, flapping a wing to unbalance Anya as she continued her attack. She stumbled and the raptor wrapped a long claw around her arm, lifting her into the air. Meric reached for her, but the raptor shrieked, biting and missing his hand by a breadth. Anya struggled against its tight grip but with her weapon trapped in the raptor's claw, she had no hope of escaping. The animal opened its beak to tear out Anya's throat when a short blade pierced its shoulder, causing the raptor to scream in pain. It released Anya to the earth where she fell with a grunt.

Grae gripped Anya by the arm, pulling her out of the reach of the screeching bird. Evelyn gripped another one of her throwing daggers. She took a moment to aim and flung her arm forward, the air whistling around the blade. The raptor spread its wings, leaping into the air as the blade cut through the raptor's leg instead of its neck.

"Run!" Sou yelled, his voice guttural with wrath. The raptor ascended, disappearing into the sky. "We cannot fight what we cannot see!"

Grae lifted one of the packs that had been thrown towards them, tossing it onto his back before dashing into the Greens, Anya at his side. Meric spun in place, picking up his quivers, but unable to find his bow. Panic crept into his heart at the thought of being weaponless. He turned and saw Evelyn at the edge of the Greens holding out the bow, blades gleaming in the moonlight. He snatched it from her hand, throwing the quivers onto his back and running with her and Sou into the endless grass. The surrounding forest of green coiled in the darkness as though trying to trap them, to hold them hostage for the raptor to find. He knew their passage was leaving a trail for the creature to follow, allowing it to easily divide them within the thick foliage. They could only run so far before losing each other in the chaos, leaving each of them ripe for picking. Their best chance of survival was to stay together.

"Into the plains!" Meric shouted, knowing Anya and Grae could hear him even if he couldn't see them.

He ignored the thoughts in his mind that whispered of his failure. He felt a rush of air as they burst from the Greens and into the plains. Anya and Grae appeared beside him, breaths catching, and expressions fixed in matching determined glares. He stared into the wide plains towards the direction of Ciar, running with all the might his legs could carry him. He felt Evelyn beside him, sprinting and breathing with the echo of all he feared to lose. He sensed a presence above him, looming like the moon, but with darker intentions.

He ducked as he felt the beat of swooping wings. But Grae was not quick enough. His friend cried out and fell, gripping an arm that was slick with blood. Meric stopped running and turned back to Grae with Anya beside him. She gripped Grae's arm while Meric pushed against his back. The wound was clean and deep as though caused by a thrown blade. It was no ragged wound made by the talon of a raptor. A black throwing dagger laid buried in the ground, dripping with Grae's blood. Anya and Meric locked eyes with the same thought.

Reticent.

Grae grunted and shoved Anya, pushing her back towards Evelyn, leaving the dagger behind. They continued running as Evelyn looked towards the sky. How was she able to see them? Raptors were impossible to spot at night and she followed their flight as if it were flying in midday.

"Get down!" she screamed, throwing herself to the ground.

Without hesitation, he threw himself down, feeling the rush of wind at his back and the sound of claws scraping together. He braced himself for the pain of his skin splitting, but all he felt was a storm above him. The hood of his cloak blew about his face as he looked up, the strong wind making it hard to keep his eyes open. Sou was standing, his hands reaching towards the sky in a torrent of wind that stirred the soil. Pebbles lifted from the ground, grass twisting and breaking from the earth.

Meric blinked against the storm, shielding his eyes with his arm as he stood. Grae, Evelyn, and Anya did the same, staring at the raw power of Sou's ability. Evelyn's gaze shifted with alarm, and she reached for the long dagger at her side. Meric could make out the faint outline of a figure coalescing from the darkness as though conjured by it. The figure was donned in black. A hooded cloak billowing about them in the storm Sou created. Metal plates were strapped to the figure's knees, gleaming with rusted blood, dented with malicious use.

The silent assassin was here at last.

The Reticent's features were hidden beneath the hood, but Meric knew her. The one who had taken Juna's baby. A familiar belt of weapons hung low on her hip, the whip deco-rated with sharpened bones gripped in her hand.

Meric wanted to scream for them to flee, but where was there to go? The Reticent walked as though she had no concept of time or urgency. If she made any sound, it was drowned out by the sound of her raptor's cries.

Meric, Anya, and Grae moved as one. Anya darted around

Meric, lifting her dagger as Grae thrust his rapier forward, aiming for the Reticent's gut. Meric nocked an arrow, pulling the string to his cheek—his target, the middle of the assassin's chest. It all happened too fast. The Reticent ducked under Anya's blade, striking the blunt handle of her whip against the back of Anya's head with a sickening crunch. She fell to the ground, body still, eyes closed. Grae shouted as the Reticent lashed her short whip around the rapier, cords of thick leather refusing to break against its sharp edge. The assassin dragged the weapon back, pulling Grae into her embrace and lifting her knee. The metal clashed against Grae's skull; his head propelling back before slumping to the ground without a sound. Meric released the arrow, his aim true, but the Reticent lifted a metal plated arm, deflecting the shaft as it shattered across its dark surface. In between the time it took for one to blink, the Reticent had subdued most of her opponents. Meric stood speechless, staring at the motionless bodies of Grae and Anya, horrified that he couldn't tell whether they breathed or not.

Meric strapped the bow to his back, pulling the curved blades from the ends and twisting them in his hands. Evelyn appeared beside him, a low growl in the back of her throat. She leaped in front of Meric, her blade screeching against the bones of the Reticent's whip. The assassin was still hooded but Meric saw a flash of white hair, a puckered scar raised over a grinning mouth.

Evelyn's blade sung in the night; swift were her movements as she blocked the assassin's blows. The Reticent's whip cracked the air every time it met steel. Meric raised a blade and joined Evelyn, slashing at every open opportunity to score flesh. Evelyn thrust her blade down aiming for the Reticent's gut, but she snapped her whip across the blade and backhanded Evelyn across the face. She fell hard to the ground, clutching her jaw. Meric came up behind the assassin, trying to take advantage of the distraction but the Reticent spun, whipping her weapon and drawing blood as a piece of jagged bone opened the skin of Meric's cheek.

He bared his teeth and swept his blades apart, slashing into the air. The Reticent parried backwards as Meric stepped in front of Evelyn. She stood, blood trickling from the corner of her swollen lip. Meric glanced to the side, watching Sou stand before the bodies of Grae and Anya, wind roaring from his outstretched hands, keeping the angry raptor airborne and away from his friends. Meric felt a small sense of relief, knowing if Anya and Grae were dead, Sou wouldn't waste time on protecting them. The raptor shrieked its frustration and dived in and out of the wind. Sou's knees bent, shaking with the effort of keeping the raptor in the sky. The old man was a powerful Vagu, but not even he could outlast the stamina of a blood lusting solov raptor. Meric looked back at the Reticent and thought that if he or Evelyn could land even a single mortal wound on this woman, perhaps they stood a chance against the beast. Even if they did manage to kill the Reticent, the raptor would more than likely tear them apart for killing its master. Every outcome seemed bleak and the more scenarios Meric ran through his mind the surer he was of their own deaths.

He glanced at Evelyn, her jaw darkening purple. She met his gaze, and he knew she felt no pain, only rage in those burning eyes. He nursed that same rage, stoking it for Anya and Grae, who would die without ever having spoken of their love. For Sou, who would be ripped apart protecting them, and for Evelyn, who would perish with steel in her belly, fighting at his side. For Lian, Retia, and Isaad. Their deaths hung over him like so many he had caused. He felt his anger grow, merging with Evelyn's, wrath boiling in her eyes to the point where her irises seemed to glow with it.

She growled, turned towards the patient assassin, reaching into her cloak, and throwing a blade before Meric could take in a breath. The assassin stepped to the side and leaned, avoiding the knife which disappeared into the darkness. Evelyn ran forward, swinging her dagger across the assassin's chest. She blocked the attempt with her whip, the leather coils wrapping around the blade. Before she could pull Evelyn in the way she did with Grae, Evelyn spun beneath the blade coming up behind her, the assassin's arm trapped behind her back. Meric stabbed to eviscerate the woman, but she kicked out a leg, her boot crashing into Meric's jaw. Pain exploded across his face, black spots dotting his vision. Evelyn lifted her weapon to cut the steel across the Reticent's throat, but she heaved her head back, colliding with Evelyn's face. She cried out, but didn't let go, snarling as blood seeped in between her teeth. She struck the Reticent on the side of her head with the hilt of her blade. The assassin rolled to the side, jerking herself from Evelyn's hold, standing before them without any hint to an injury.

Meric panted, feeling his teeth throb. He thought it was merely fortune that his jaw hadn't broken from the Reticent's kick. He wondered if the assassin had a plate of metal on the tip of her boot. Meric yelled, swiping his blades into the air, but the assassin leaned backwards, missing every blow, dodging every cut. Meric felt sweat drain down the back of his tunic. He was losing this battle, his legs and arms growing heavy with exhaustion.

Evelyn's blade and the Reticent's whip met, bones shrieking across steel. She landed a fist into the Reticent's gut, plummeting her to a knee. She bent over without a grunt, but recovered, shoving her shoulder into Evelyn's chest. She fell onto her back, and the Reticent stood over her as though Evelyn were an insect beneath her boot. The assassin cracked her whip back, aiming to strike Evelyn's enraged face. She rolled, the whip missing its target by breadths. Evelyn kicked out her foot as she stood, but the assassin leaped, her motion as light as the beat of her raptor's wings. The Reticent anticipated every avenue of attack. She was too quick, too skilled, and worse—she seemed too relaxed. Almost like the fight wasn't worth the effort of her true prowess.

There were too many times Meric should've been dead. He was much too slow. Only Evelyn seemed to be able to keep up with the woman and even with her skill, every blow she managed to land, the Reticent returned to her tenfold. She kept throwing herself in front of her as though attempting to draw the Reticent's attention away from Meric. It seemed as if the assassin was trying *not* to kill him. The woman's swirling black cloak fell to her ankles, a small breeze billowing the fabric around her feet. Meric glanced behind him, and Sou was on a knee, arms shaking as his storm abated. Anya had regained consciousness, blood running from her scalp down the back of her neck. She stood, staring at the raptor in the sky, then at Grae, still unconscious.

"Meric!" Sou bellowed; his voice rasped from exhaustion. "Get Evelyn out of here!" The old man's arms fell to his side, Iona's Breath as still as a corpse and he collapsed. Evelyn screamed.

The raptor shrieked with excitement and dived towards Sou's prostrate body. Anya leaped over the old man, howling as she thrashed the air with her dagger. She wrapped her arms around the raptor's chest, moving to stab the creature, but it clamped its beak around her shoulder. She screamed in pain as the bird tossed her to the ground, rolling, blood staining the shirt Lian had gifted her.

Tears ran down Meric's face. The Reticent's hood fell from her shoulders, revealing the familiar white hair and puckered scars. She opened her mouth in a soundless scream, revealing the shapeless lump that was once her tongue in the back of her throat. Her expression showed no malice or glee. She seemed to be indifferent to Anya's cries of pain and Evelyn's strangled, angry scream. Evelyn reached into her cloak. Meric thought she was pulling out another throwing blade, but in her hand was a glowing gem. The same one from Grae's description that Anya had unsuccessfully tried to pawn. Across its surface were veins of glowing red light pulsing in the night. The Reticent's eyes grew wide and for the first time, surprise etched across her face like hidden shadows in the night.

Evelyn's cloak floated around her, brown hair surging about her face which seemed to smooth and heal. The bruise on her jaw disappeared, and her swollen lip returned to its normal shape. A storm seemed to swell from within her, wind coalescing as though upon the sea. Meric stood in awe. Evelyn's eyes were twin rubies, brilliant and terrifying. She lifted her hand, baring her teeth into a snarl as a gust of Iona's Breath tore the ground beneath the Reticent, flinging her into the air. She landed with a hard thud, eyes wide with angry disbelief. Evelyn's feet hovered above the earth, and she threw a gust of wind at the raptor, the gale throwing the beast wing over body in a tangle of violence Sou couldn't hope to match.

The air trembled as Evelyn turned her attention to the Reticent, whose impassive glare remained fixated on her with a move to strike. She hung the whip on her belt and unsheathed a dagger, the blade's bone hilt bright in the darkness. Evelyn landed on the ground, eyes still glowing, and met the assassin's weapon with her own. An echoing clang reverberated through the blades, threatening to break the steel. Meric thought he'd never seen anything more incredible or frightening.

He ran to Sou with the knowledge that Evelyn needed no protection he could offer. The man gasped for breath as Meric turned him over.

"Help… her," he said, barely audible.

"I think you know she doesn't need my help. You need to get up. She has her distracted," Meric said, helping Sou stand.

The old man grunted and as he stood, he stopped, transfixed by the fight between the Reticent and Evelyn. Her movements flowed like water as Evelyn's consumed like a blazing wildfire.

"No!" Sou said, loud and fearful. "She has to let it go. Evelyn! Let it go! He'll see!"

He tried to move past him, but Meric placed a hand on his chest. The old man was too weak to fight back.

"I've got her," Meric said. "Run into the Greens. Go!"

Anya had thrown Grae over her back, grimacing against the pain in her shoulder. She grabbed Sou's arm. Meric exchanged a look with Anya not knowing if this would be the last time he ever saw her. Her yellow eyes steeled as she turned her back on him and dragged Sou with her into the Greens.

Meric ran towards Evelyn, her glowing eyes pools of

blood. The Reticent's back was turned which gave Meric the opportunity to stab her from behind. His blade fell, but the assassin caught it with her own, turning her head slightly to sneer at Meric. Pain suddenly enveloped his face as she rammed her elbow into his cheek. Teeth cut into his lip, blood dripping from his mouth. Evelyn jumped several heads into the air, yelling as she brought her dagger down. Beaming, spiraling wisp's of wind creating needle-like spikes surrounded her. The Reticent turned, but what weapon could she use that would stop Iona's Breath? Meric grinned, hope flaring that the assassin was as good as dead.

Evelyn's glowing eyes glazed as though she suddenly lost sight and the spikes traveling towards the Reticent dissipated. She wavered as her steel met the assassin's and she closed her eyes against an unseen pain. The Reticent jerked to the side, slashing Evelyn's arm from wrist to elbow. She cried out and stumbled, the scale falling from her fingertips.

Meric tasted blood and stood beside Evelyn, whose eyes appeared to be watching something other than what was in front of her. He was so tired, so spent in what seemed like a fight lost long before it had started. He almost did it. Almost completed a mission he thought to be honorable and for someone who deserved it. He would be struck down, perhaps left face up. But it was here, in between Evelyn and the woman who would kill her, he'd gladly wander searching for his grave.

"I will die before you harm her again," he said, his mouth slick with blood.

Evelyn groaned and staggered beside him. She gripped her bleeding arm and swayed with fatigue. She was going to pass out. He had to remain standing, otherwise his promise would prove true sooner than he wanted. That, more than anything, made his stomach turn with anguish.

The Reticent cocked her head to the side, expression flat and chilling.

"No. You will watch," an inhuman voice said from above, guttural with animalistic fury.

Before Meric could act, he was thrown to the ground, his shoulder skewered with sharp talons. He bellowed in pain, blood oozing across his chest. Evelyn stepped forward, unbalanced with her dagger raised, but the assassin kicked out her feet from beneath her. She dropped her blade, collapsing to the dirt. Meric screamed her name, reaching out for her as her eyes rolled to the back of her head.

He clawed at the raptor's talons, scratching them with raw fingertips. The Reticent stood over Evelyn, dagger in hand, hovering just above her chest. Meric thrashed, pulling at the creature holding him down. He knew its claws were tearing deeper into his flesh, but all he could feel was his heart fracturing to pieces as he watched the tip of the knife slip into her chest.

Suddenly the Reticent was thrown back, several paces, in a gust of wind. The dagger clattered to the ground. Sou stepped into view, collapsing onto the ground beside Evelyn, wiping hair from her face. He gripped the cord of Evelyn's necklace, the red gem gleaming in the air. He placed it in her cloak. Anya appeared beside him, grabbing Evelyn's arms and throwing her over her shoulder. She turned to Meric and stared helplessly at the raptor who shrieked and tightened its claws into his shoulder. He moaned as his muscles contracted, blood seeping into the ground.

"Leave me," he said through clenched teeth.

"She won't kill you," Sou said, glancing at the form of the Reticent in the distance trying to stand. "Think of her. Think of Evelyn. We'll find you."

"Leave!"

Meric groaned again as the raptor shifted, snapping at Sou who shuffled away on unsteady, weak feet. Without a backwards glance, he and Anya disappeared into the surrounding forest of grass towards Ciar. A few moments passed and the Reticent stood over him. Her impenetrable eyes glared, holding nothing but the darkest of voids. She picked up his dagger and struck him in the head. Everything faded into blackness and shade.

CHAPTER 40

THE ABSENCE OF WHAT WAS LOST

eric!

Evelyn sat upright with a gasp. Her unfocused eyes struggled to make sense of the blurred shapes moving far down the wide alley. As her eyesight cleared, she glanced behind her to see Sou laying asleep on the ground next to her. His arm was outstretched in the shape of where she'd been resting. They were in another alley, leading to a large square where a market bustled with life. The overlapping conversations of bartering echoed through the empty hall. They'd made it to Ciar. The city was known for its busy trade and although she was not fully awake, she hadn't expected it to be so loud. She rubbed her eyes and shook Sou. His eyes snapped open to panic before he realized it was her.

"How do you feel?" he said, sitting up and placing a hand over hers.

She winced at the tender spot his fingers grazed over. Her arm was wrapped in cloth, stained red from the cut the Reticent had given her. The wound burned, but it wasn't so terrible that she couldn't stretch the limb. She recalled her throbbing jaw and bloodied lip. Those had healed when she held Oretem's scale, but after she had dropped it, all other pains remained. She lifted her hand to her chest, feeling the comforting shape of the scale. Her body ached and the back of her legs smarted from when the assassin had kicked her down.

"I am unharmed. Where are the others?" she said, glancing around but finding no sign of Anya or Grae. She recalled Anya leading them into the tall grass as she fought and Meric…

Her lungs tightened, breath staggering as memory returned in flashes of steel and wind. The last she saw of Meric was when he was pinned to the ground, black talons biting into flesh, groaning in pain. The wrinkles surrounding Sou's mouth deepened as he faced her.

"Anya and Grae have gone to get some provisions. Meric was…" He paused, placing a hand on her shoulder. "I am an old man, lass. My strength with Iona's Breath is not what it used to be. I couldn't get you both to safety. He was taken," he finished heavily.

Evelyn glared, but not at Sou. She kept her focus on the wall in front of her, berating herself for not protecting Meric better. She had called upon every lesson Tansey had ever taught her, working with Meric to overcome the Reticent — and still it had not been enough. Sou, Anya, and Grae were moments from death. She couldn't allow that to happen. She'd made her choice, knowing should she fail, it would weaken her. The power of Oretem's strength had coursed through her veins, obliterating all doubt that she could lose. It wasn't until she had touched the scale that she and the Reticent were evenly matched. She'd been so close to driving steel through the assassin's heart. When had the thought of killing another person become so natural to her? Evelyn remembered the feel of the wind surrounding her body and the rush of invincibility. She could've killed the assassin — would've, if Maun hadn't evaded her thoughts.

Just when she was about to strike the killing blow, Maun forced Oretem to show her the memory of Tansey in the snow, her life's blood escaping her slim frame. A woman so fierce, buried faceup beneath ash and ice. She felt Maun's dagger stab through her grandmother's body, penetrating and sharp. She lost focus, consumed in the grief of Tansey's confirmed death.

She tried to return to the battle, but she'd already dropped the scale and with it, all the remaining strength she had left. She continued to snap back and forth between reality and memory until the Reticent knocked her to the ground.

She shouldn't have used the dragon's scale, but what else could she have done? She had so little left to live for and losing anyone that night was not a choice she could fathom making. Sou read her features and moved her shoulder so that she was facing him.

"For whatever reason, Maun wants Meric. He must've sent this one in his place. We can only thank the Breaths he hasn't chosen to leave the mountains yet." Evelyn had told Sou about what she had seen when Anya had thrown Oretem's scale at her in the alley. The arrival of the raptor not long after confirmed that Oretem could see exactly where she was when she touched it. The ferryman was quite adamant that she was not to use it again. He knew why she did what she did, but she could tell he wished she hadn't. "This woman is most likely in Ciar just as we are. It's the only city on this side of the lake and she can't risk going forward without food and medical supplies if she wants to deliver Meric alive. It seems that despite being Viden you are not a priority."

His lips curved into a disheartened half smile, but she could see relief in him as well. She knew that Maun pursued Meric, and she was foolish enough to have thought she could protect him from such a foe. Her stomach felt as though it had been filled with sharp rocks, cutting with the memory of everything she should've done differently.

In fighting the Reticent, she'd noticed that she was actively trying to kill her and only attempting to incapacitate Meric. Once she realized the assassin's true motives, Evelyn had done her best to keep the Reticent's blade against her own. She'd hoped that Meric would be the one to take Sou, Anya, and Grae into the Greens, but he seemed determined to remain at her side.

"How are we to find him this time?" she said, her voice

lacking the previous confidence she had when she'd first sought him out.

She thought of Tansey and how her body must be buried beneath several feet of snow by now. She had no hope of ever finding her grandmother and turning her over towards Iona. Tansey would wander the tundra, forever in search of a grave that would never exist.

"You must listen. I told him to think of you." Sou inclined his head with the self-assurance she lacked.

Evelyn shook her head. How was she to hear his thoughts out of the cacophony of voices that surrounded her? There were only a few people she could make out as they passed the alley, thinking of why she was there or if she were dangerous, but the rest of the voices clattered in her head making it difficult to listen to her own inner thoughts. Many here were not shy of voicing their fears and opinions of the strangers in the alley.

"He doesn't even know what that means. He must *want* me to hear him. Even if he did, I don't know if I'd catch his voice in this sea of noise." Her heart sank, threatening to vanish entirely under the wave of her despair. This was all her fault. She recalled the sound of Isaad's severed head as it crashed into their camp, the glazed, horror-struck look in his dead eyes. Where were Lian and Retia? Had their heads become a home for maggots as Isaad's surely was now? She left to protect them and instead she'd sealed their fate. She felt a monster for thinking it, but it would've been kinder to have let the elosi destroy the family. Either way she was responsible for their deaths, and it drowned her to know that. A hand gripped her chin, Sou's green eyes pulling her from the Depths.

"It is your fault," he said, as though he had read her thoughts. "And it is mine. It is Grae's and Anya's fault, Meric's and Maun's. Celosia's Depths, lass. It is the fault of the elosi and Reva's city guards. Your gran's and Oretem's. We each have a claim to self-pity, and I'll not stand here and allow you to take more than your share."

Evelyn turned away from him, blinking away tears. She

had two choices. She could remain on the ground and surrender or do as she had done since leaving Verbena—get back up knowing she'd greet the ground bloody again. She turned back to Sou, prepared to fall once more.

"This will be the true test of our practice. I haven't tried blocking out the thoughts of a city yet," she said, wincing as two thoughts fought against each other for her ear. The lace-thin blue tendrils twisted around Sou with speed, tousling his hair, incoherent as they mingled.

"Each breeze is different from the next. Some flow while others tear, and some can be as familiar as rays of sun across your skin. My voice is different from Grae's, is it not? I imagine he has a much higher pitch." Sou chuckled. "Have you heard Meric's thoughts, even for a moment?"

She nodded, thinking back to the rare moments she glimpsed inside his mind. Meric's voice mirrored his thoughts. Both were low in tone, but as still as the smile he hardly showed. The wind that carried them would rise and fall, inquisitive, without boundaries. He was always questioning, and it showed with the wind. His thoughts were that of a breath caressing the trees to better feel the leaves.

"Then you shall hear him. We'll find him."

He looked past her shoulder and a wide smile spread across his face. Evelyn turned to see the Venandi making their way towards them with a burlap sack in Anya's hand. They knelt beside Sou.

"You're awake," Anya said, one brow raised. She reached forward, punching Evelyn in the arm. Pain spread to her fingertips, and she groaned, glaring at Anya who ignored her entirely. The woman seemed to be recovered from the blunt end of the Reticent's whip, but Evelyn noticed Anya stretch her neck to the side, brows furrowed in what might've been an ongoing headache. Grae looked much worse, sporting a deep black bruise under one eye that spread to the edge of his temple, and a swollen nose. She suspected it had broken when the Reticent had crashed his face into her metal plated knee.

His arm was wrapped in white linen, a light shade of red staining the fabric.

"We were able to snag some bread and sausage," Grae said, pulling out a loaf of stale bread and a long rope of meat smelling fresh with fire. He used his hands to rip an equal portion for the four of them.

"What happened?" Evelyn said, biting into the warm meat.

Anya glanced at Sou, only moving her eyes as she devoured the bread. "You didn't tell her?" she said, her voice gentler than what Evelyn was used to hearing from the woman.

"She knows about Meric, but that's as far as we've gotten," Sou replied, his teeth ripping into the sausage.

"It wasn't as exciting as you might imagine. Sou and I went back for you and Meric, but we could only escape with you." Anya's tone was filled with regret and Evelyn held no resentment for that. She wished they'd taken Meric instead of her as well. "We hid until Grae regained consciousness. I couldn't carry the both of you, and Sou, high and mighty a Vagu he may be, also couldn't carry on without rest. I truly thought we were dead." She laughed, chewing loudly with her mouth open. "I didn't much like the feeling of that. Didn't know I wasn't ready." Her eyes flashed towards Grae before meeting Evelyn's again. "Anyway, despite my gut telling me that we would all die, we didn't. The Reticent never came after us. Once Grae woke a while later, we carried you to Ciar. You're welcome."

"We couldn't risk the chance of our presence being known, so we slept here. We can't tempt a single whisper of where we are if we have any hope of getting Meric back," Grae said, looking through the veil of blonde hair that had fallen over his brow.

"This is what our lives have come to. A series of kidnappings and jailings of the person whose job it is to prevent these things from happening to you. Or so we thought," Anya said, wiping her mouth of grease, side-eyeing Evelyn with a knowing glare. They knew.

"I am sorry. I didn't know how to tell you," Evelyn said.

"I've never met a Viden before. Thought the lot of you had died," Grae said, his lips curving into a dry grin.

"Depths, if I hadn't been trying to keep this one alive," Anya inclined her head towards Grae, "I might've applauded the performance. The glowing eyes and tempest were a sight to behold. I knew I saw something when we found you with Kiev. It was no wonder I couldn't sell your dragon scale. They haven't been seen in twenty years." Anya scoffed, but her disposition was uncomfortable. She fidgeted with the edge of her cloak as though she was having a hard time sitting still.

"You're not angry?" Evelyn said, surprised by how well they'd come to terms with the truth.

"Well, I wouldn't say that, but…" Grae paused, pondering his next words. "Let's put it this way. How wrong must things go before they can go wrong no more? I've lost my best friend twice, faced death more times in the past fortnight than I have in my entire life and bled at the talons of a solov raptor. Now I'm hiding in an alley, waiting for not one Reticent, but *two* to finish the job. One waits in your mountains with a mad dragon, a creature with the capacity to kill us all, and the other aims to deliver Meric for reasons unknown. *Also* possessing the capacity to kill us all." He shrugged. "It's easier to let the anger go. Where can I place it, on you? How can I blame you for something you had no choice being born into? I could and I have, for others," he spared a glance at Sou, "But it's not right. I've come to realize that none of us deserve the things that were done to us, but we are responsible for the choices we make in spite of them, and I've wasted enough of my life trying to quench my thirst with brine."

The words came from Grae's mouth, but they sang with the wisdom of Sou's voice. How ever Sou had explained the truth, it was apparently a long discussion. She met Sou's gaze with gratitude. She turned to Anya and Grae, trying to keep her mouth from trembling. Was this what it felt like to be unveiled, freed of pretending and wholly herself without the devouring fear of abandonment? They chose to stay after escaping Reva and they chose to stay still, even after knowing the whole truth of herself. She had a hard time grasping why. Anya sighed, holding out a hand. Evelyn stared at her reaching fingers, hesitating a moment before clasping them in her own.

"You're our friend, Evelyn. That means we get to be angry with you while helping you. I am angry that Meric is gone. I am angry that it was him that needed protecting and I am angry that we don't know why. It was a thing we should've heard from your lips and not Sou's," she paused, squeezing Evelyn's hand. "I am also angry that your village was destroyed, your people murdered, and I am grateful to have met you. We might still be walking the path that leads to our deaths, but we would've reached our graves far sooner had you not found us." Anya released Evelyn, yellow eyes beaming with genuine gratitude, but also that fierce wolf gaze now so familiar.

Evelyn was speechless. She was sure that Meric's capture held Anya in place more than anything, but Evelyn envisioned the possibility that the yellow-eyed woman would've been standing exactly as she was had their places been switched. A sense of belonging spread through her heart, filling her with a feeling she thought to have been dead with the loss of her home.

"I'm assuming that Sou told you about everything I can do," she said, lifting her head at her old friend who smirked. He must've told them the rules of her gift otherwise she was sure that they'd been more averse to being around her.

"Yes, and I have a question about that. Are Anya's thoughts more annoying or mine?" Grae said, flinching as Anya slapped his arm, throwing breadcrumbs all over the street.

Evelyn chuckled and pointed in Anya's direction.

"Not that you're irritating. You're just a lot more vocal about what you want to say to me, but don't," she said, trying to ease the revelation, but it didn't seem to offend Anya. The woman shrugged while pursuing her lips, acting as though she hadn't expected any less.

"If you can find Meric then I promise to attempt to rein in my thoughts a little." She pinched her thumb and forefinger together.

Meric's name hung in the air like a broken sail, unable to catch wind. It was midday, perhaps more. They'd lost half a day while she was unconscious and since she'd been awake, Evelyn hadn't heard Meric's voice at all.

"Have you been trying?" Grae said, his eyes bright with hope.

"She hasn't had the chance yet," Sou said, placing his elbows on his lap. "With some food in your belly, you ought to try now."

Evelyn breathed in and stood, walking to the end of the alley where the thoughts of all those in the square swirled around her in wisps of light invisible to everyone but her. The city was awake with hundreds of people weaving in and out of shops. Carts of goods littered the open square, resembling wains that reminded Evelyn of Jaspar's. Everything from food, jewelry and weapons were being sold and bartered. She saw a wagon filled with apples and thought of Lian and her family, grief rising in her heart like bile. The people wore every color imaginable, from drab skirts and weathered shoes to elegant gowns and suits. It was a blacksmith's forge of different metals, alloyed together to make a new and strange multipurposed knife.

The buildings were mostly built of stone, and many of the inns bustled with incomers of every size and shape. She stretched her mind beyond the crowd, through the buildings and under the ground. She never had the chance to practice her gift or learn its limits other than what she'd done with Sou while traveling the Greens. She'd been too busy trying to stay alive. If Meric was thinking of her, he still had to want her to listen for her to hear him. There were too many probabilities, too many variables that should make this impossible.

She still had to try. Evelyn let her mind spread to the corners of the city, plunging herself into the cacophony of voices as she had that night when Sou had plagued her with his singing. The tendrils of thoughts lined up like loose harp strings, beaming with light. She reached out with invisible fingers, touching each string, knowing the person it belonged to entirely. She felt the fear of a man selling fish, wondering who the shadowed woman in the alley was and how much coin she might give him before his sickness left his children fatherless. A small girl combed the hair of a straw doll, her only worry being the strange, red-eyed woman staring at her. Evelyn closed her eyes as she felt each cord, the world becoming silent as she traveled through each one, listening for that breath of curious thought she knew to be Meric's. The same breath behind a hesitant smile, honey-colored eyes that never faltered in meeting her own. Her chest ached and she knew she reached for him with more than just her thoughts.

Evelyn...

Her eyes snapped open, watching as Iona's Breath danced around her shoulders. Fog-like it swirled, condensing into a weightless orb before her face. This was not Meric's voice. The ball of light pulsed, radiating a familiar mist she'd seen before. She reached out her hand, fingers trembling as the urge to touch the light burned in her with a pain she'd always carried with her.

"Mother?" she whispered. She thought of every moment, the seconds, and hours, days, months, and long years she'd been without Nakesha. The conversations Evelyn couldn't recall, and the embraces shared that she couldn't remember feeling. She'd been loved and it hurt knowing she had no memory of that love. She felt a loss so dear, she thought she might vanish before the shifting wind, fading away to join the blue wisps that disappeared at the end of its twisting tendrils.

Meric is where Eli died. Tell her I am sorry. The mournful voice was feminine, just like the one who spoke in the mountains.

"Is he alive?" Evelyn said, desperate to keep the voice with her. The orb pulsed again, but was beginning to fade as the mist swirled to an iridescent cloud. "Please, where is he?" she asked again, curling her fingers around the trails of light, feeling its cool mist smooth over her palm, hoping to know whose voice spoke to her.

The orb said nothing as it slipped through her fingers and vanished without a trace of where it went. Evelyn gazed over the crowd, meeting the eyes of a few whose thoughts were guarded against her, but by the look in their alert eyes, they'd witnessed what had happened. Could they see the light? She knew only Videns could see Iona's Breath so what they saw was a strange woman speaking into the air. Evelyn suddenly knew they had very little time in Ciar. She turned her back on the people who spoke amongst themselves, already spreading the rumor of her actions.

She ran back to Grae, Anya and Sou who had finished their meals.

"I heard something," she said, panting.

Sou and Anya stood while Grae rummaged through the sack, inspecting that everything was in order for a quick departure.

"Meric?" Anya said, hands fists at her sides.

"No," Evelyn shook her head, trying to make sense of what the voice said—what her mother could've said. "I heard a voice. The same one I heard in the mountains."

Sou exchanged a wearied frown with her. The worst kind of disaster had struck the last time she'd seen the orb and she could tell he was running scenarios in his mind at what could be in store for them now that she'd heard it again.

"One who has passed?" Grae's voice was rough, guarded. It was clear he still was uncomfortable with the idea of such power. After hearing what he had gone through during the Evandis, Evelyn couldn't blame him. Despite Grae accepting what he had done, forgiving himself was an entirely different mountain to climb and knowing there was a possibility that Jean could speak with him beyond the confines of his grave was a cliff with a long and dark fall.

"Yes, but I don't know who. I only know it is a woman," she said, seeing that had eased his worry. "She said Meric is where Eli died. She said that she is sorry. I don't know what it means."

Anya's head snapped up, eyes wide and disbelief etched across her features. It was like watching the light of a candle fade into the background of a darker, and deeper shade of blackness. Anya took an involuntary step backwards as though she were refusing to do something someone was forcing her to do.

"Who spoke to you?" she whispered; her voice was small, but sharp.

"I don't know, she—"

Evelyn was abruptly shoved against the wall, her back arching against the uneven stones. She cried out at as Anya held the scarf of her cloak, tightening it around her neck enough to make breathing difficult, but not impossible. It was a tactic to incapacitate, to keep her still and trapped, not to strangle. Tansey's lessons brought memory to Evelyn's muscles, and she looped her arms in between Anya's, pushing down on top of them. The Venandi grunted her pain as Evelyn gripped her wrist, pulling her arm back as she kicked a leg out from under her. Anya fell forward with a grunt as Evelyn shoved her foot into the space between the woman's head and shoulder. Anya struggled, but with her body pinned and her arm trapped in Evelyn's grasp, the woman could only growl in protest. This had only lasted moments in which Sou had blinked and Grae had taken a single step.

"Anya! What are you doing?" Grae's voice was hard with anger.

"I can't go back. I can't. Who spoke to you?" Anya said, her voice a frenzied mix of fear and hate.

"I don't know," Evelyn said through her teeth, trying to keep her anger reigned in from the unprovoked attack. Had this woman not just spoken of friendship? She was about to spit the fire of her rage when she felt Anya trembling within her grasp. The woman was terrified.

"I don't know who spoke to me," Evelyn repeated, making an effort to speak in a calm voice. "But wherever it is that you can't go back, Meric is there." At the mention of his name, Anya's trembling ceased. "I'm going to let you go. Will you attack me again?"

Anya gave a single shake of her head, her cheek pressed against the stones. Evelyn stepped back, positioned for the defense if Anya should be lying. She wasn't. Anya stood and turned, glaring at Evelyn with begrudgingly apologetic eyes. It was the most she knew she'd ever get out of the woman, but Evelyn didn't care about apologies.

"Who is Eli?" Grae said, his voice repentant as though he was sorry for asking.

Anya shook her head, but she wasn't saying no. She was denying the question's existence. Her jaw clenched, eyes glistening with tears she failed to control.

"You know where he is, don't you?" Sou said, stepping forward.

Anya's hardened features stared daggers at the three of them, as though blaming them for her tears. She swept a hand across her face so hard she left red marks on her cheeks.

"I know where he is," she said, her voice hard and weary. She turned her back and burst from the alley.

Evelyn ran after Anya into the crowd, Sou and Grae following close behind. Anya seemed to leave craters in the wake of her sprinting feet. Whatever the woman was running towards, it was a place where blood stained its floor.

Weaving through the market was no small task. People refused to move out of the way as Evelyn struggled to keep up with Anya. Sou, behind her, let out a cacophony of *pardon me* and *my apologies* as he twisted in and out of the horde. Anya was in her element, flowing with the crowd as though she were born into it. Once they reached the opposite side of the square, the people thinned out to a reasonable mob, growing less populated the closer they came to the cities edge.

They traveled this way for some time towards the cliffs, the sun losing its brightness through the veil of clouds. Anya stopped running, staring at a silhouetted shape near a cluster of rocks at the edge of a cliff. Vapors from the boiling lake misted over the drop off. The mist parted, revealing a small home with cracked boards of swollen and rotting wood making up its skeleton. The house was ominous, standing alone as though its only occupants were the spirits of those who considered company inconvenient and violence a reasonable solution.

Grae looked to Anya, who hadn't taken her eyes off the misty structure.

"What happened here?" he said, concerned. When she didn't answer he turned his attention to Evelyn. "Is he here?"

Evelyn reached out, isolating the feel of Meric's thoughts. It was much easier to focus without the combatant noise of every person in the market, but it did her little good if Meric wasn't thinking of her. She continued to listen, but there was nothing except silence.

"He might be unconscious. It doesn't mean he isn't in there," she said, glancing at Anya, who she was growing worried for. Apart from her hands, which were shaking fists, the woman had turned to stone.

"Anya, what happened here?" Evelyn said, echoing Grae's question. The Venandi ignored her, acting as though she stood alone.

Sou sighed and stood in front of Anya, blocking the view of what paralyzed her. The woman gasped, taking in a breath she'd been holding all this time.

"When we enter, we'll need a way out. You know this place. Is there a way we don't know of? It's not out here for nothing," he said, his voice firm, but gentle. Always gentle.

That seemed to rouse Anya to the present. She straightened her shoulders, sniffed, and answered with a single nod.

"That's good," Sou said, lips lined in satisfaction. "This will be a swift rescue. Whatever we do, we must do it quick. We hardly escaped unscathed last night and there's no reason why that wouldn't be the same now. Grae, have you the healing supplies? We will be needing them."

Evelyn's stomach lurched as she tried to bar her mind from imagining the state Meric could be in. Grae's brow creased as he seemed to be trying to do the same and patted the satchel that was filled with all their provisions. Sou stepped closer to Anya, lowering his gaze so that she couldn't turn away.

"You were hired Anya. It's time to honor that agreement. You *will* deliver us to Birny. All of us." Sou's voice appeared harsh, but there was a strange encouragement that interwove his words.

It was as if he knew exactly what would rise Anya to action. He spoke to her as a captain, rousing a disheartened solider to fight along his side. Evelyn felt it settle into her chest, giving her strength to combat the anxiety of what they might discover within those dark walls.

Evelyn… a soft voice traveled on the breath of a wisp. It begged for mercy, and she backed away, holding her head as she felt its intense heft.

Grae stepped forward, placing a hand on her shoulder.

"Is it Meric?" he said. Evelyn gasped, watching the vapor swirl around the abandoned home.

"He's there. He's in pain," she said, the edge in her voice unable to hide her distress.

Screams ripped through the air, two distinct voices, but agonized as though the same pain were ripping them apart. Evelyn watched recognition flash across Grae's face. His blue eyes grew wide, breath hitching before whispering a name.

"Retia."

CHAPTER 41

ISLA'S REACH

*I*n fairest words, there is no say, the heart's torment of Isla's Decay. Found, she did, a man of blue. In love, if love were ever true. Torn apart, they were by hate of her sister's love, who did wait. Born of fire, she burned alone and took his life for her own. He did not see it, the pit so deep, she buried him alive for hers to keep. Wind and grief fights fire and pain. Love binds all and that is Isla's bane. Rains fell and the ocean wept, for Isla drowned her sister and under the elm she is kept. Lost is the name of a man so warm, but Isla knows and forever mourns.

Meric woke with a groan and a sharp pain in the back of his skull. The melancholy voice of his mother's singing lingered on the edges of his waking mind, a fading blue light dissipating from his vision before it vanished entirely. He lifted his head from his chest, the muscles of his neck screaming in protest to being in one position for so long. He tried to blink away the blood that had dripped from his forehead, but it was crusted and hard over the skin. When he attempted to raise a hand, he discovered that he was bound to a chair.

His arms and legs were wrapped in rope, rubbing his skin raw. He turned his head, vision adjusting to the darkness of his prison. The room was vacant of any furniture except for the chair he sat on and his bladed bow in the corner. A hallway to another section of the house was adjacent to him, but was shadowed in darkness. It was a home, although it had been some time since anyone had lived here.

A fireless hearth rested in the corner, cold and dusty. He twisted his wrists, testing the strength of the ropes. They held firm as he rocked his chair from side to side, feeling the rope burn his ankles. The chair tapped the floor and a soft echo reverberated through the wood like it had been hollowed out.

How was he still alive? Meric's mind raced through the possibilities of why the Reticent would keep him living. The most logical conclusion would be to gain information on the whereabouts of Evelyn, or what she was. He knew it to be impossible, but in recalling everything he knew about Videns, which wasn't much, she fit into every criterion. Her eyes, the power she had with the wind, and the gem she had held in her hand.

A dragon's scale.

That was the true reason she was being hunted. He quickly understood the validity of Sou's argument about keeping his secrets, but Meric couldn't help but wonder that if he had known then perhaps he might've protected her better. Questions burned in the back of his mind, plaguing him without answers. If she were Viden then where was her dragon? What futures had she foreseen? He almost laughed at the impossibility of it all. These were questions he suspected would be presented to him.

So, it will be torture then.

He thought about the last words Sou said to him. *Think of Evelyn.* As of late she'd occupied most of his thoughts, but what difference did that make here? What had the old man seen that Meric couldn't? He cared for Evelyn, far more than he'd been able to think on. There were moments when she glanced in his direction that he lost his thoughts in the curve of her lips. But what could thinking of her do as he sat in the dark waiting for his torture to commence?

Perhaps the Vagu knew what the Reticent would do. Perhaps he was telling Meric to think of the one person that could get him through the pain. He also said that they would find him. That was unlikely. He wasn't a fool to believe that he'd get out of this alive, but as soon as he thought of those ruby eyes, he knew he wanted to see them again. He could do it. As long as she occupied his thoughts, he could stand the pain.

Meric gritted his teeth against his own imagination, running wild with ways the assassin would attempt to draw out what she needed from him. He shook his head and searched the room for anything that could be used to cut him loose. The Reticent was nowhere Meric could see, but that didn't mean she wasn't watching.

There was nothing in the room for Meric to use. Not even the rough floorboards were splintered enough for him to topple over and cut his bonds. Had Evelyn and the others made it to Ciar? Meric wasn't sure where he was, but by the moist heat in the air, he thought he was still near the lake. His shoulder burned with pain, but he was surprised to find it bandaged and cleaned. He rolled it a bit and winced at the feel of stitches pulling at the skin.

Why in the Depths would a Reticent take the time to dress his wounds? He concluded it was done to give him a false sense of hope. That the assassin could be reasoned with and, if Meric cooperated, he would be set free. Did the woman think Meric a child, with no concept to the cruelty of the Reticent? He was Venandi. Surely, the assassin knew that he would not be so easily swayed by false promises.

He jerked in his chair once more, but it was no use. There was no escaping his bonds and he felt the shadow of his own oncoming death darken his mood. If he was to die, then he would have his murderer look him in eye while doing so.

"Will you hide in the dark like the creature you control or do you just fancy being mysterious?" Meric said, his body tense as he waited for a response.

The silence endured, his own voice echoing back to him in the empty room. Just when he decided he was alone two pairs of bright, golden eyes appeared from the rafters of the ceiling. They blinked, dilating with intelligent predatory pupils. Meric retreated further into his chair as the two raptors leaned forward, revealing their black feathers in the fogged sun shining through the only window. The old raptor that had stabbed him through the shoulder cocked its head to the side, looking at its companion. The second raptor was smaller, lean with youth and darker feathers. Meric shuddered, breath catching in his throat at the thought of two raptors gnawing at his bones while living. How is it this Reticent had two raptors and why had she attacked with only one? Meric knew next to nothing about the initiations required of the Reticent cult, but he knew enough to know each assassin had but one raptor. The larger one shifted, the light catching a spread wing that had been lost in the darkness. It moved, lifting from the shadows to reveal a woman tied to a backless chair, dark, long hair falling across her shoulders. She stared past him, grey eyes vacant of emotion.

"Lian," Meric said, his voice hissing through a clenched jaw. She didn't stir. He caught sight of a wide crimson stain, splattering the front of her dress. It traveled down, soaked into the hem.

"It's not my blood," she said, monotoned. Her eyes met his then, looking far older than how he remembered her. "It flowed from him like a river, and I waded in it."

Meric lowered his gaze, remembering Isaad's head falling from the sky.

"You will look at me," Lian said, her voice a sharp whisper. Meric did, lifting his head and staring into the abyss of her grief. "I watched as my brother was split open, without reason. One moment he was there, teasing—always the insufferable teasing," she gasped, losing her breath to speak before continuing. "The next his blood was... everywhere. Depths drown her, she killed Beau and crushed Drool's little head beneath her boot." She shuddered, a sob escaping her lips.

"What can I say that will comfort you?" Meric whispered, knowing there was not a word he could utter that would make her family whole again.

"Nothing," she said, tears mingling with the blood on her

cheeks. "Words mean nothing to the dead, and I am as good as."

Meric fought his own tears, looking up at the raptors with kindled hatred. He looked back at Lian, seeing Juna reflected in her grey eyes. There was no forgiveness to be found in what he had failed to do for them. Absolution was a myth, and here at the end, he refused to die begging for its existence.

"What have you told her?" he said, steeling his gaze against the loathing she looked at him with.

Let it be the wind that stokes my anger. Hate me, Lian! Nurse your own inferno.

"Her? *She* didn't speak a word to me. It was her raptor — miserable and ugly creature!" Lian pulled against her bonds, spitting at the old raptor who looked on from above with indifference. "She has my daughter. Had her bird tell me he'd eat her alive if I didn't do as she said. She brought me here, left me in the company of that one." She leaned her head towards the smaller raptor. "Returning with *you*," she spat the word with disgust.

"You didn't answer my question," Meric said, keeping his voice low.

"Nothing," she said, exasperated. "What could I say? She asked me questions I couldn't answer. Who were you were close to, your upbringing, and parentage."

Meric's brow creased, head pounding from the ache in his skull. Why would the assassin want to know about his parents? What could she possibly be after if not Evelyn?

"Is this why the lot of you left? To save us from this?" Lian moved her elbows against the chair. Meric recalled Evelyn's frantic urgency to leave that morning, the state he had found her in. Had she seen this? Did she think in leaving them she could alter their future?

"I think so," he said.

"Well done," she scoffed.

The large raptor leaned forward, feathers hacking along its body, opening a sharp beak to speak with a voice that was neither woman nor beast, but something altogether unnatural and terrifying.

"Let us not surrender to cheap bitterness. I've long since lost the taste for it."

Lian withheld a breath, staring past Meric's shoulder with unblinking eyes. Heavy boots reverberated around him, the soft chime of bones brushing against each other. The Reticent appeared, stepping into the soft light between Meric and Lian. Retia stood at the Reticent's side; her little fingers curled around the assassin's. She looked so much like her mother. Retia was bruised, a cut splitting the edge of her scalp from where the Reticent had most likely knocked her unconscious to make Lian compliant, but she was otherwise unharmed.

"Let her go," Meric said, knowing it would be impossible to bargain for the lives of both Lian and Retia. The assassin had what she wanted. There was no further use she could have for the girl. "You have me. I will tell you what —"

Before he could finish, the assassin reached for the whip hanging on her belt, snapping it into the air. Sharp bones raked across the flesh of Meric's leg. He screamed, pain erupting like shards of glass piercing through the limb, blinding him to all other sensations. When he had caught his breath, Meric heard blood dripping onto the floor.

Darkness. I remain beneath the world.

Retia shook beside the Reticent, tears blurring the color in her eyes.

"You will tell me nothing. Which is why she will stay," the raptor said from the rafting, mimicking the cold stare of its master.

"I don't know who my parents are. I cannot remember them," he said, panting through the pain. "They abandoned me to the alleys of Reva. Who are you? What do you want of me?"

The Reticent blinked, scars shifting in the shadows. She looked up at the awning, a mysterious sorrowful glint in her eyes as her raptor leaned forward once more.

"I was but a courier, one meant to deliver you to the person who would answer that question. But circumstances have changed. I will be your death, but first you will tell me of Evelyn, the Viden."

The younger raptor shook its feathers, rumbling the growl of a new voice.

"Devu! You will bring him to me. He is mine to kill." This voice had the same inhuman qualities as the Reticent—or Devu as she was just named, but it was obviously a different person. The voice was younger, feral with anger and walking the line of control.

"You lost that right when you lied to me about the Viden. It is impossible for her to exist!" The older raptor snapped at the younger one, rearing to tower over the other. "Your petty vengeance is nothing compared to a living dragon. We must find the Viden. Kill her and take control of her dragon before they can reunite. Look at what we have become! I am a veteran of the Evandis. I fought alongside your father in cleansing Iona of her parasites. He would be ashamed to see how you allow one to slither still, all for the insignificance of one man who had no part in his death. Of all my Children of Fortune, you Maun, are my proudest achievement and my greatest disappointment."

Meric's head lolled to the side, grimacing against the tremble in his leg. He was too addled with pain to think on what Devu was saying. It was too much. He tried to focus, commit to memory what he was hearing. Although he didn't think he'd live long enough to recall any of it to another. He tried to imagine Evelyn, the ruby glint in her eyes that always seemed to see into the core of him, but she faded into pain and blood.

"You will not deny me this," the younger raptor spat, spreading its wings high into the ceiling. "Not after what you did here. Not after what you took from me."

Devu tightened her fingers around Retia's hand. The girl flinched, but didn't pull away, staring at the ground. The assassin stepped forward, black cloak rustling about her boots.

"How do you—" she stopped, tearing her eyes from the

raptor's, and looking down at Retia. "It matters not. An'gan, restrain Saiya, but do not harm her."

It was strange hearing the raptor speak its own name, but the creature obeyed, lifting a clawed talon, and bringing it down on the younger raptor's skull. Saiya flailed in An'gan's grip, feathers floating to the ground. Saiya's human and animalistic howl was cut short as An'gan closed his other talon around her beak, silencing her.

"The way of the Reticent has always been a hard way for you, my son." An'gan pruned Saiya, gently running a beak through her feathers as Devu spoke through him. The Reticent kneeled in front of Retia, placing a loose strand of dark hair behind her ear. Lian growled in her seat. "You never did learn to master your emotions. We will speak again when this is over," An'gan whispered, his grotesque voice surprisingly tender when combined with Devu's.

The Reticent turned, looking in between Retia and Lian before reaching into her pocket. She pulled out two black stones, each hanging by a leather strap.

"This one is yours," An'gan said from above, Devu holding one necklace to Retia.

Retia stared at the stone, leaning away from the necklace. Devu grinned, an ugly, soulless muscle twitch.

"Do you remember the story Isa told you, about Hector the Swallow?" Retia nodded and Meric gaped. Devu had been watching them for days, perhaps since the moment they left Reva. The assassin lifted the other necklace, dangling it in front of Lian's fisted hand. "This one is for your mother. To keep you safe." She met Lian's eyes, the threat nocked and pointed at the woman. Lian forced a smile, looking at her daughter with a helpless grin.

"Where is Isa?" Retia said, staring at the stone still held out before her. Devu wiped a tear from her jaw, rubbing a thumb against her cheek.

"I told you. He is sleeping. His head was hurting him a bit," An'gan said, sticking out a red tongue. Lian gritted her teeth, a snarl escaping her lips before she mastered herself.

Devu turned to Lian, eyes swirling in darkness. "Who is it you love most in this world?" Her merged voice lingered above them. Lian lined her lips into a hard frown, betraying herself by glancing at Retia.

Devu held the stone above Lian's fist, but she refused to open her hand, meeting the Reticent's gaze with defiance. It was a simple stone, small and black in color, but there was something else to it. Meric felt a pit form in the depths of his stomach. As simple as it may be, the assassin had pulled the stones from her belt, keeping them where she kept all her weapons. Meric recalled the true ending to Hector the Swallow. This was a trick.

"Don't touch it," Meric said. "Lian! Don't tou—" again, his voice was cut short by pain. Devu had backhanded Meric, the edge of her metal plated arm clipping him on the jaw. He bit his tongue, blood pooling inside his mouth. Meric's vision blurred, a groan escaping his lips as he drooled blood onto the floor.

Evelyn...

Retia peeped like a small bird, looking at her mother with fear in her expression. Lian exhaled a heavy breath and grasped the stone with shaky fingers. Devu wrapped the leather around Lian's wrist, making sure the stone would not be dropped. Retia leaned forward and gripped the other necklace, placing it over her head.

The Reticent stood, leaving Retia in between Meric and Lian as she moved behind her mother. Lian breathed in sharply, her chest heaving with terror. Meric watched as Devu lifted the whip from her belt. The rodent bones clinked together, echoing across the empty space. Lian gasped, a sob escaping her lips as she stared at Meric, who could only look on in horror. Retia began to cry, realizing something terrible was about to happen, but unable to understand why.

"Do not fear, little bird," Lian said, tears dripping from her jaw. "Mama will be alright."

"Where is the dragon?" Devu said through An'gan, who

tightened a talon around a thrashing Saiya. Meric blinked, opening his mouth to say something, anything.

I don't know. Breaths and Depths... I don't know.

The words wouldn't form, and Devu cocked her head to the side, raising the whip.

"No!" Meric screamed, but it made no difference. The whip fell across Lian's back, ripping through flesh and fabric. She howled, grey eyes bulging, gasping. The same moment that Lian screamed, Retia fell to the ground, shrieking as blood swelled across her back, staining her perfectly intact shirt. Meric bellowed, writhing in his restraints, feeling the ropes cut into his wrists. What evil magic was this?

"Same question," Devu said through An'gan, the raptor shook its head as though excited by Lian's and Retia's screams.

"I don't know! Depths drown you into oblivion!" he screamed, spitting blood. "She is a farmer and the girl only a child. Any pain you wish to inflict upon them I will take and more!"

The calm way Devu inclined her head stunned Meric, as though the Reticent were considering how many legs she could pull from an insect without killing it.

"You know, I think you could." Devu raised the whip again, Lian's head lolling to the side as she muttered her daughter's name. Meric screamed and suddenly his face was pressed against the floor, wind roaring into his ear. Everything was chaos, shrieking, and steel clashing. Someone stood over him, yelling his name. The ropes fell from his legs and wrists, his body slumping to the ground. He pushed himself up and Evelyn's arms were around him, pulling him up.

He groaned and stood, using her as support in place of his ruined leg. An'gan and Saiya were pressed against the ceiling, fighting against the storm Sou pushed against them. Grae untied Lian, slapping her face into wakefulness. The woman groaned, falling from the chair to kneel next to her child, who laid unconscious. She ripped the stone from Retia's neck, unwrapping the stone from her own wrist and tossing whatever foul magic they contained into the shadows of a corner.

Devu had been thrown across the room, laying on the floor as Anya stood over her, blade scraping against hers. Something flickered in Anya's eyes. Her snarl relaxed, and recognition swept across her features. Devu's mouth opened, as though she'd forgotten she couldn't speak. They knew each other.

Anya growled and lifted her dagger, stabbing it down with such ferocity Meric was sure the Reticent would choke on the blade, but she rolled as Anya's dagger hit wood, standing with a scowl. Anya screamed into the Reticent's face, taunting her with her fully functioning tongue. She sliced her blade into the air, missing the scarred woman's nose by a breadth.

"Where is he?" Anya said through her teeth, growling with bestial malignity. "Do you know my face? Or is it not bloody enough to recognize!" She advanced with another slash, catching the Reticent on the arm.

Grae picked up Retia, the girl's body as limp as a thin branch, using one arm to help Lian to her feet. Devu ignored her bleeding arm, looking up at the raptors shrieking high in the ceiling. Anya spat more hate at the Reticent, but her words were drowned out by the clash of blades and roaring wind.

Evelyn led Meric to Grae's side, stumbling the whole way with his lame leg.

"Anya!" Evelyn screamed, but was ignored as the woman continued her assault on the Reticent. "Celosia's bloody Depths—Anya! Show us!" she said, louder.

Anya met Devu's low strike, and looked back at them, gaze shifting to the floor. The yellow in her eyes burned for combat.

"Sou!" She screamed, pushing against Devu's blade with all her strength. The old man turned, swiping one hand in Devu's direction. The Reticent stumbled back, Iona's Breath lifting her from the ground and heaving her against the wall. Even through the thunderous wind, Meric could hear the sound of ribs cracking.

Anya ran over to them, falling to her knees, hands swiping the cracked wood. She reached her hand under it and the wood split, panels lifting to reveal a hole big enough for one person, perhaps two, if the second were a child. Inside the opening was a second trap door with a rusted latch poking out above it. Anya jumped in, using her fist to turn the latch, congealed rust cutting into the knuckles of her hand. After a few punches the latch turned, and she swung the door open to reveal a muddy darkness, heat rising.

Meric stared into the hole, confused as to how Anya knew of its existence.

"Follow the tunnel until you reach the end where it meets the cliffs. Then keep running. Do not stop," Anya said, staring into Evelyn's eyes. That look frightened Meric. It was the look of someone who didn't expect to see the next day.

Evelyn stared into the hole, her brow creasing as though she were trying to think of alternatives to going underground. She looked at Meric, evidently not being able to contest their only way of escape.

Anya reached out a hand, taking Lian's and lowering her by the wrists into the tunnel. She let go and Lian cried out as she fell, the fabric of her shirt falling over a shoulder, exposing the raw lacerations of Devu's whip. Lian stood, blood running down her outstretched arms. Grae handed Retia's unconscious body to Anya, and she lowered the girl into the hole, dropping her into Lian's arms. Grae and Evelyn jumped down, joining the bleeding woman in the darkness. Meric heard the raptors above shriek with ear splitting savageness. He peered over his shoulder to see Devu clutching her side, bringing herself to one elbow with a strangled howl of pain.

Meric turned back to Anya, who looked at him with that same vacant glint in her yellow eyes. She didn't expect to make it out. He wasn't about to allow that to happen. He took hold of her arm and fell into the hole, dragging her down with him. His back hit stone, slick with condensation and hot air. Anya fell on top of him, and he felt the skin on his leg tear, the stitches in his shoulder stretching further than they should. He gritted his teeth against the pain. Anya got to her feet and for a moment, it seemed like she would climb back up. Instead, she cupped her hands around her mouth.

"Sou! Get down your saggy arse down here!" Her voice

echoed down the tunnel, resulting in dust falling from the low ceiling. Meric looked around with a shuddering breath. The air in the tunnel was thick with moisture and heated air, warm water dripping down rocky walls branched with roots. The roots weaved in and out of the rocks, cradling them as though keeping them from collapsing. Many were broken or rotted through, boulders the size of Meric's head trembled with instability.

Isla's Reach. It existed. The tunnel reminded Meric of Fallon's prison and bile rose up his throat at the thought of being crushed, forever entombed in darkness.

Meric heard Sou yell, a clattering of bodies clashing together. Beast and man screaming in a mess of inhuman voices and shrieks. Sou's feet appeared out of the ceiling, gripping the trapdoor, and closing it as he clashed to the floor. In his hand, he held Meric's bow, the quivers strung across his back.

"Am I the only one with any Depth-damned sense? Run!" the old man bellowed.

Grae gripped Meric's arm, pulling him up and forward. His leg burned—a rush of blood running down the limb. He groaned, but didn't slow down. Evelyn and Anya ran with Sou far ahead of him and Grae. Lian cradled Retia as she sprinted beside them. Evelyn looked back as the sound of wood slamming against stone echoed down the tunnel. Her red eyes grew wide with fear.

The tunnel shook with a violent tremor as dust from the trapdoor spilled across the floor. Meric looked back to see black wings flapping towards them. The younger raptor was ardent in its pursuit. Saiya's eyes gleaming in the darkness with a malicious blood hunger.

Sou turned around and thrust his hands up and down, creating a wall of wind that collected dust and rock. It threw Grae and Meric to the ground, his body screaming as his leg crashed against stone. Lian was flung from her feet, landing near the wall, her body curled over Retia as Sou's storm flung Saiya to the ground. The tunnel vibrated with a violent quake.

The walls rumbled with what was a damning sign of an imminent collapse. Meric dragged Grae to his feet, pushing his legs to the brink of exhaustion, hearing Lian panting behind him as she followed. Rocks fell and boulders clashed, shattering into splinters of jagged stone. Lian cried out, agony laced in her voice. Meric turned around and saw the woman had fallen to the floor, her leg crushed underneath a large boulder. He and Grae turned back, hands pushing against the stone, teeth bared as their strength failed to move it even a hairs breadth.

"Take her!" she said, lifting Retia and thrusting her into Grae's arms.

"No. We won't abandon you again," Grae said, clutching Retia to his chest. Rocks split onto the ground, dust coalescing about them. Meric glanced at the end of the tunnel, the shapes of Sou, Anya, and Evelyn nothing but fogged figures in the brightness. Sou couldn't clear it for risk of collapsing the tunnel faster and Anya and Evelyn couldn't even see them. He heard Evelyn calling out his name.

"You didn't," Lian said, lines of tears running down her dust coated face. "You came back for us. Now save her! Remind her that she was loved," she said with a sob, pushing her hand against Grae's chest.

Grae opened his mouth to argue when a rock trembled above them, rumbling and cracking. Meric gripped Grae by the shoulder and pulled him back, hurtling them both to the floor. Debris shuffled about them, pebbles digging into the side of his face. Meric sat up and Lian was gone, her body lost under the rubble. Grae stood, grief stricken, staring at the pile of stones that became Lian's tomb.

Meric tugged Grae's arm as the rest of the tunnel collapsed around them. His friend tightened his embrace around Retia, who had remained unconscious. The blood from her back smeared across Grae's arms. They ran and the tunnel broke, nipping at Meric's heels, scratching the back of his legs as he and Grae tried to outrun the falling boulders.

They were almost there. The dust obscured Sou, Anya, and Evelyn from view, but he knew they made it out. Meric leaped into the light, crying out from the pain in his leg, clawing at the cracks of the cliff. The floor slanted significantly, his body sliding. He feared falling over the edge and into the boiling lake he knew was below. His foot caught a rift in the rock, keeping him from sliding off. He pulled, bringing himself to more even ground, although the floor still slanted. He heard coughing and through the settling dust, saw the rest of his friends. Grae clutched a root twisting from the cliff wall, Retia resting in his arms. Sou, Evelyn, and Anya exchanged looks, staring where they had all come from. The tunnel was blocked by rubble, leaving no space for any kind of return that way. The echoes of its collapse still reverberated in the air around them as Meric cleared his throat of dust.

He stood, turning around to take in the still waters below. Vapor curled across Elm Lake like reaching fingers, coalescing around the thick trunk of the elm standing in the middle of the lake. The elm's roots bent and spiraled in and out of the boiling water like a large serpent, disappearing closer to the lake's edge. The slanting cliffs deposited rocks, falling off unstable ledges, hissing as they fell into the water. Meric thought they may have escaped Devu for now, but it was merely a question of which would kill them faster: the pursuing assassin or the burning lake.

Meric's chest heaved, threatening to implode with the strength of his anger. He screamed, his voice echoing across the vast crater. He spun and took a step towards Evelyn. "Why —" His leg spasmed, collapsing beneath his weight as he fell to the ground. Her arm wrapped around his chest before he hit stone, lowering him gently to his knees. Meric winced and stared into Evelyn's red eyes, burning with tears that would not fall.

His voice ripped from the back of his throat, a barely controlled whisper. "Why is this happening?"

Anya stepped forward; concern etched across her filthy expression. "Meric, there is an explanation, but it isn't —"

"Not from you," he snapped, refusing to tear his gaze away from Evelyn.

"I'm sorry," she said, "I couldn't—I didn't expect to—"

"Expect what? To deceive us as to who the Reticent is truly after until someone like Lian were to die?" Evelyn flinched as though she'd been slapped, removing her arm from around his chest. "What does the Reticent want with me?"

"I don't know," Evelyn said after a long pause. "Breaths deny me, I would tell you if I knew."

Meric groaned, trembling against the pain radiating from his ruined leg to the fraying stitches in his shoulder. Lian's pale features exploded in his mind, pulped beneath the rubble of Isla's Reach. His anger surged, white knuckled fists straining at his sides. Evelyn lied. She lied and people were dead. Apple farmers not fighters. It should not have been their fate have died so cruelly. For what nefarious purpose were Evelyn's Viden gifts being used? Had she seen their deaths? She must have.

You couldn't stop it. You and your people should be dead. What is it you came for?

A trembling breeze swirled around Evelyn, and her red gem-like eyes darkened into a black cavern of grief. Meric was taken aback. He'd never seen such agony in a single expression. It was almost as though she had heard him...

"You, Meric. I came for you," she whispered, eyes no longer wet with tears. "I first heard your name in my mountains, spoken from a voice upon the wind. She bade me to find you and it was then that Oretem, my bondsmate, burned my world to ash..."

CHAPTER 42

WHO HE COULD'VE BEEN

Maun waited behind a boulder, his breath causing white wisps of frozen air to float about his head. He'd been waiting for hours in the cold and snow. There was a peace within the mountains that he couldn't acclimate to. A kind of silence he had never experienced. He hadn't been born in the Solov Waste, but he recalled the humid air of his home on the edge of Elm Lake. It seemed he had always been meant to burn. Devu had spoken true; he'd been in the cold too long.

If he could manifest his emotions, Maun knew that the mountain would melt under the blaze of his wrath. Devu had failed, and not only did Meric escape, but the Viden as well. The others were of little consequence, gnats swarming around his kills. He couldn't hear or see much during the skirmish since the Vagu had Saiya pinned to the ceiling.

As soon as she was set free, she heeded his contempt and nearly had them in the tunnel before it had collapsed. Saiya had been blocked by the rubble, almost joining the woman Devu had captured, pulped into bone and meat under the rocks. Maun had noticed the child was not with the woman's body, and a fleeting sense of solace brushed against his thoughts. He had quickly murdered the feeling, wondering why he should care before commanding Saiya to return to Devu.

Maun heard the tapping of hooves, distracting him from the intruding thoughts of Devu's failure. He narrowed his gaze, grinning at what he'd been waiting for. A babi boar turned over a rock with her tusks, grunting and sniffing for roots and small rodents. Behind the sow were three shoats, their quiet grunts mimicking their mother as they stirred the small pebbles around her. The shoats were eager in their search for food, rubbing the tips of their noses to the sow's snout.

Maun reached into his cloak and revealed himself from behind the boulder. The sow started, growling a warning in the back of her throat. The shoats gathered behind her, short legs trembling as they squeaked in panic. Maun pulled out his dagger, hands steady with anticipation. His chest grew tight, and his temper burned for blood. He widened his stance, feeling the cold combat his rising fury.

He growled back at the sow, an indefinable resentment swallowing him whole as he felt control escape him. The animal was the perfect target for his rage. She didn't fear him. He grinned as she tapped her cloven hooves and lowered her head, charging.

Maun bellowed a mutilated howl and raised his dagger. The beast swiped her head to the side, her tusk grazing the side of Maun's shifting cloak. He ran his blade across her thick shoulder, muscle splitting and spraying blood over the snow-covered rocks, its splatter like the star-filled desert sky he'd grown up under. He spun and slashed his blade at her again, this time cutting her snout clean in half.

The sow squealed in pain, shaking her head. She was still intent on protecting her brood and screamed with a voice that sounded almost human. Maun tasted the boar's blood as he laughed, a sound he hadn't heard in so long, he hardly recognized it. He spun, but the slick ice caused him to slip, and he fell under the boar's sharp hooves. He gasped as the animal stumbled over his body, ripping skin, crushing him under her immense weight. His dagger was pinned behind him, impossible to reach. He gripped the sow's tusk, shoving it upwards as she used her bulk to try and skewer him. Her breath smelled of rotten wood and bile. He stuck his thumb out, shoving his finger into her eye. It erupted like a boiled beet and flowed down his arm. The babi screamed and jerked away, lifting Maun and throwing him against the side of the mountain. The resting snow fell around him as he crashed to the ground.

He stood, body aching with newly formed bruises. The sow lifted her leg, smearing the sludge remnants of her eye across her bloodied snout. She spun in circles, grunting and growling, unable to adjust to her lost vision. He moved forward with slow steps, feeling the snow crunch beneath his boots. He bent over and lifted the dagger, dragging its tip across the ice in a way that grated against his ears before standing upright again.

The boar's entire right side was soaked in blood and her snout was a mess of viscera and fluids. She looked up at him and, for a moment, Maun saw his mother—his true mother. Her dark, pleading expression was reflected in the animal's frailty. Even the beast's black hide brought back memories of her hair cascading down her shoulders. He steeled himself, holding the dagger to his side. Its iron hilt glinted in the snowfall, dripping blood at his feet.

Tears teetered on the rims of his eyes, cutting down his cheeks like shards of glass, burning with the hatred of Meric's escape and Devu's disappointment. But what he hated most of all, the pinnacle of misery that was his wretched life, was what he'd become and who he could've been. Neither could fill the void that grew deeper day by day, and it was ripping him apart. Two women had claimed him as a son, both had loved him in their own way, and both had been murdered. He was raised Reticent and yet, it wasn't what he was born to be. So, who was he, and why was this version of himself so weak?

He snarled and slashed his blade across the babi's throat. The animal gasped and fell to the ground, writhing in breathlessness. She kicked up mists of snow, trembling as she fought the inevitable. He watched her fade as her single eye bore into him with a cry for mercy, a supplication for her children. His scars twisted his lips into a disgusted frown, giving her no indication of clemency. She grunted once more and laid still, dead among the still stones and empty wilderness.

He glanced to a cluster of boulders, where the babi infants huddled together, their sniffing snouts buried in their siblings' hides. The black stripes down their backs made excellent camouflage in the shadows, but it did them little good in Maun's presence. He kneeled beside the shoats, lightly touching a finger over one of their stripes. The small babi squealed and buried itself deeper into its sibling's side.

His rage wasn't quite sated in the fight with the sow, but it was enough. He stared at the blood that stained his palms and brought his fingers together, feeling its slick, warm smoothness. One of the babi's lifted its head and snorted at the air. It backed away from its siblings and nestled itself against Maun's leg, shivering against the cold. Its siblings followed suit until they all trembled against the man who had killed their mother.

Maun lifted his hands and held them in the air, unsure of what to do. He stood, backing away, but the shoats followed him, their little hooves making bird-like tracks in the snow. He passed by their dead mother, and they ran past her body like she'd never existed. Maun's chest heaved, hyperventilating against the onslaught of emotions he had no experience of dealing with.

No, not me. Don't you know your enemy?

The infants had no way of understanding him and they continued to follow without preamble. The babi's huddled at his feet again, softly grunting their contentment. He placed his hands over his head, blood staining his dark hair, trying to squeeze out the confusion and uncertainty. He reminded himself of what was in due process.

Devu knew of Isla's Reach, having traveled through the tunnels during the Evandis. She'd discovered many routes in that time to circumvent the boiling lake. It wasn't until Saiya was flying beneath the ground, chasing after Evelyn and her companions, that Maun had realized what his mother and Aunt Yaya had dug up all those years ago. It brought strength to Falconer's story and a growing curiosity in his mind regarding the elm. Devu was traveling through one of them now. Maun could feel Saiya's apprehension at being below the ground.

The Vagu had broken one of Devu's ribs during the fight, but the woman was resilient. Mulish to the point that Maun had to be the one to remind her to bind her torso before she set out in pursuit. Devu was of no use if her split rib cut an organ. His mentor claimed Maun had no control over his emotions, but had she known how close he'd been to commanding Saiya to ripping her throat out for what she had done, Devu would have praise Maun as the most disciplined of Reticent's. He recalled the swell in his chest as Devu claimed him to be her greatest achievement and the rent in his heart as she confessed her disappointment. It was torture. Why should he feel anything? How could one lost memory change him so entirely? Maun left the cave after Devu's failure, not because he needed to hunt, but because he needed to kill something.

The shoats nibbled at his ankle, their tiny tongues licking the snow from his boots. Maun raised his dagger and the infants fell by his blade, hacked with crude precision. They tried to run, screaming further into the mountain, but he was too fast and thoroughly heartless. He stood in the middle of the massacre, surrounded by the blood of others as he always had been. He fell to his knees, his shapeless tongue wordlessly screaming into the bitter mountain where nothing heard him.

CHAPTER 43

LETTING GO

Meric winced as Anya poured hot water over his leg. It swept and burrowed into his wound with the sadism of a benevolent leech, cutting down infection with blinding pain. It had been two days since his rescue and Anya had already redressed his shoulder, continuing the brutal journey down to his leg, replacing the gauze with a new sheet.

"Sorry," she said, her voice unusually detached.

Meric inclined his head, trying to gain her attention, but she was fixated on his leg. It was a distraction, he realized, a way for her to put aside emotions she had no intention of dealing with. He'd tried to give her space, but she'd become more and more withdrawn. She wouldn't like it and she may curse him for it, but he had to force her into speaking.

"Are you going to tell me?" he said, knowing that should he accept her silence, it would destroy her. Her yellow eyes stared into his, but they were impassive, somehow locked and broken at the same time. Unlike Sou, Meric didn't possess the ability to bring about the darkest of confessions, but he was her friend. She had to know there was nothing she could tell him that would make her any less so. She tied the gauze into a knot and to his surprise, instead of walking away she sat there, her will spent.

"I've never told anyone," she said, jaw clenched, eyes leaving his to stare at her hands as though she'd discovered someone else's blood on them.

"Anya, what harm could there be in telling me what you've spent so long punishing yourself for?" He moved his leg to the side, ignoring the sharp jolt that ran up the limb. Anya met his gaze again, vapor twisting her black hair across a bruised face.

"I lived there once," she whispered. "With my older sister, Eli. Our parents died of the fever that swept through the city. She'd been married by that time, taking me in without thought to the burden of my tempestuous ways." She smiled, thinking fondly on the memory of her younger self. "Her husband, Mirdul, built that house in the early days of the plague, seeing what the rest of the city could not. It worked for a while, but he would still venture into the city for supplies. More than ever once Eli became pregnant. He got sick. It started with weariness, prologued fatigue which grew into a loss of appetite and stomach pains. He became thin, gaunt, and weak. One morning he woke raving, the fever burning his mind to sludge. He was dead the next day."

"I'm sorry," Meric said, feeling sweat roll down his forehead.

"I didn't know if Eli would survive it—his death. She was never the same after, but the child she bore, Calian, gave her a piece of him back. Then rumors spread of tongueless men and women in black cloaks invading villages, stealing children. There is nothing in the world more frightening than the thought of someone coming to take your child. Eli and I grew up with the tale of The Decay of Isla Om, but Eli was convinced that the tunnels existed. I thought she'd seen her grief reflected in the story, so I helped her dig, but I never believed her. Then we found it, right beneath our home. We dug it out and placed a door so that should we need to hide we could, but it was surrounded by rock. We could only make it so deep, and we knew if the time should ever come, one of us had to stay behind."

Meric leaned forward, wrapping his fingers around her hand.

"There was never a discussion between us. Children need their mothers. The Reticent came to our home, of course I didn't know that's what they were called then. They'd just begun to organize, making a name for themselves after the attack on Reva. They kept asking for my nephew, beating me while Calian and Eli hid below. The one we fought, the Reticent bitch that ruined your leg, she was there. She didn't have those scars then, but it was her."

If the lake had turned to sand, Meric wouldn't have been more surprised. What were the chances that the same person that kidnapped Juna's baby, sought to kill Evelyn, destroyed Retia's family, and beat Anya as a young girl were the acts of one woman?

"Her name is Devu. She's the one who took Juna's child back in Reva."

Anya's head snapped up, eyes glowing with a fire that promised violence.

"Did she say anything about what was done with the girl?"

Meric shook his head and Anya's frown deepened, expecting.

"What happened to your sister?" It broke Meric's heart to ask, but he felt the story couldn't be left unfinished. Anya swallowed, brow creasing as though feeling the ache of an old battle wound.

"I don't remember much other than darkness. It was absolute. I was ready to die for my sister. I heard a pop, thinking it was the door below slamming shut, Calian and Eli escaping. But it was my jaw dislocating, my body collapsing. Before the darkness took me, I remember thinking my neck had snapped." She rubbed her jaw moving it in and out of the socket. "I woke sometime later. It was still dark outside, and my sister was dead, her throat slit. I had to close her eyes—turn her over. Calian was gone. He was only two years of age, a babe."

Meric sat, silent and contemplating. Anya's tragic tale was a distraction from the unbearable heat.

"How old were you?"

"I was eleven. I traveled with some Venandi to Reva a few days later. As you can imagine, an experience that traumatic might've had a lasting impression on a growing girl. I'd always been… unique. They thought the discipline of their trade would be a restorative salve for my wild ways." A wry grin spread across her face and Meric chuckled, imagining a young Anya sparing with inexperienced ferocity.

"I was on my own for a long time, hearing whispers about the Reticent, but I never caught any voices concerning my nephew. Then I met you and Grae and… well, I moved on. I wasn't healed, but I wasn't alone anymore, and I thought, surely, Calian is dead. That would be kind, that would be fair, but my life has never been kind nor fair." For a moment her voice broke, but she raised her head, composing herself in a way that was entirely Anya. "I looked into her eyes—Devu's eyes. She remembers me," she said, her voice rough and dangerous.

"She must know where Calian is," Meric said, wiping sweat from his brow.

"I've never known anyone to recover a loved one from them. I'm not foolish enough to believe I am any different."

Meric released her hand and leaned forward, forcing her to look at him. "Yes, you are. To survive what we have survived, we'd have to be fools to believe we could. We can capture her, make that nub in the back of her throat tell you where he is."

Anya smiled, but the joy didn't reach her eyes. She took in a long breath, the frown lines of her mouth deepening. "Devu must die. Even at our full strength we are outmatched by her. You're in no condition to fight and we have Retia to consider now. We are wolves, deadly and fierce together, but what weakens the wolf?" Meric shook his head. "The split of the pack," she said. "She'll pick us off one by one, limb from limb, until there is nothing left but bones and blood. She'll never tell us what happened to Calian, and it doesn't matter because my nephew is dead. You and Grae, Evelyn and Sou and Retia are the new life I've forged. I'll not have Devu take that from me too. She's had quite enough."

Meric was astounded by her reserve. Anya was never a woman of restraint, but the way she looked upon him now had him thinking she was, for the first time, holding onto what she currently had and not what she'd lost. He knew she was right. The assassin must die. Meric recalled the stones Devu had given to Lian and Retia, the dark magic that was used to harm both by torturing only one.

"Devu never touched Retia," Meric said, watching Anya's brows knit in confusion. He explained what Devu had done, whipping Lian and somehow causing Retia the same pain.

"You should ask Sou about these stones. He may know more about them," Anya said, her eyes growing dark. "Why is it when I think I've imagined the worst, there are people like Devu who take it upon themselves to do what I am not capable of imagining?"

"It's not just Devu anymore. Apparently, it never was." Meric was still coming to terms with the knowledge that Evelyn had fled her village with the purpose of finding him. The truth of her Viden heritage and the awareness that she could hear his thoughts should he choose to share them with her. While he'd been trying to protect her, she had been saving him since their first meeting. He regretted the anger he'd thrown at her—lamented that he, of all people, questioned her character.

"We all had our secrets and look how they nearly killed us," Anya said, shaking her head.

"I still don't know what he wants of me, the one called Maun. Devu spoke of his father's death and how I had nothing to do with it. Lian had said Devu questioned her about my parentage. It makes no sense," Meric said, frustrated.

"It is more than Evelyn knew."

"Do you believe that?"

"You sound like Grae," she said, chuckling. "I do believe her. I think she tried the best she could with what was given to her. They're good people, Evelyn, and Sou." Anya rolled her eyes, huffing a sigh. "They're also slow and bothersome. If I hear Sou speak another one of his fishing tales, I'll throw him into the lake myself."

Meric chuckled, bending his knee to stand.

"But Retia so enjoys them," he said, his smile disappearing as he recalled Lian buried in the tunnel, leaving the girl an orphan. Retia had suffered a fever the first night, the wounds on her back burning with grime from the tunnel's collapse. Anya had cleaned the ragged cuts as best she could, but the unspoken fear of her death settled into the hearts of everyone. Meric wasn't optimistic, the heat from the lake surrounding them was brutal and he thought that, combined with the fever, would boil the poor girl alive. Grae refused to sleep, keeping the girl's back as dry as possible. She woke the next day, fever broken, but in an incredible amount of pain. Sou made a sling out of spare tunics for Grae to carry Retia on his back. When his friend grew tired, Sou would take his place, telling stories of creatures that lived in the Idris and Elm Lake. Retia had reverted to her mute state, showing little if any emotion, but hearing the old man's stories always resulted in a smile.

Anya helped Meric to his feet, swinging the pack holding all their healing supplies over her shoulder.

"Yes, that's lovely, but does he not have any other stories than Coral and Claw? Depths drown me, I'll scream if I must sit through another tale of how a fish and a crab defeated Mano the shark through the power of friendship."

As though the old man could tell he was being spoken of, he appeared from the vapor, wet hair sticking to the back of his neck.

"If you're finished, Retia needs to have her bandages changed," Sou said, his voice wearied from walking in the heat. Anya stepped in front of him, making her way into the thick mist. Meric ran a hand over his face, scratching his thick beard and following Sou with a limp.

"There is something I need to tell you," Meric said, walking easier with the new bandages. Sou turned his head, listening as

Meric told him of the stones. His expression glowered, green eyes beaming with a darkness rarely seen in the kindly old man.

"What Devu did is quite rare," Sou said, vapor swirling around his body. "The stones are called Celosia's Glare. I'm not sure where they are found, but it is somewhere within the Eshe Willow Wood. The Reticent strive to be emotionless, relying on baser instincts to achieve their dark ambitions. They exchange the stones with their partners, ensuring that they will not love."

"What do you mean?" Meric said, recalling Devu asking Lian who she loved most in the world.

"Those who wear Celosia's Glare will take on the pain of the one they love the most. It can be as little as a cut or as grievous as a sword thrust through the belly. Should the person wearing Celosia's Glare die, so will the one they love who wears it. It is exceedingly rare for a Reticent to use it in the way Devu did. There is no guarantee that the people she uses the stones on are the ones whom each of them loves the most. The sorcery will not work otherwise. It takes time and a lot of observation, combined with intuition to be confident enough to even attempt it. It is a foul way of torture, but an excellent method of interrogation, turning love into a weapon," Sou's voice was rough, regretful, as though he spoke from experience. Meric's stomach clenched, turning his face from Sou to look into the mist. He wanted to ask how the old man knew all of this, but dreaded to think he would tell him.

"This is a dangerous assassin, even among the Reticent," Sou said, his voice lost in memories Meric had no desire to know.

Meric nodded, distracted by his thoughts of Lian. Her back arching as Devu's whip tore her flesh to strips, Retia screaming in agony. Lian loved her daughter and, in the end, that's what hurt Retia the most. For a few moments Meric's anger ruled him, hands curling into fists.

"My only regret is that the Reticent do not feel fear. I

would like to see it in Devu's eyes before I kill her," Meric said, voice grating in the back of his throat like a growl.

"Oh, they feel," Sou said, a remorseful frown spreading down his lips. "These Depths-damned assassins are just as ruled by their emotions as you or I. Instead of centering their joy on the warmth of baked bread or the embrace of a loved one, they fasten it to pain and misery. They love, but it is a twisted thing. Malnourished and abused. Most of the children who were stolen during the Evandis make up what is the Reticent now. If what you said is true, and Devu served during the war, then she took part in molding those young ones. I know it is easier to think of them as beasts, incapable of the sentiments that make us human, but remember this Meric: it takes so little to become them. What makes the Reticent so forbidding is the simple fact that they *are* human and that they endure the same excruciating losses any of us could suffer. Do not be so quick to revel the fear in the eyes of your enemies when it is just as likely to be the fear in yours. This and this alone, is the thin veil that separates us from becoming our foe. Humility serves to protect us from ourselves, disregarding that will only bring you shame."

Meric glared into the mist, hearing Sou's words, but choosing to remain in his anger. He walked in silence until the camp came into view. In between the rocks sprouted roots curling thick and thin up the cliff face. Meric saw their packs and provisions tied to a few, hanging with a lean. Many roots grew outwards, creating bed-like divots where blankets were being laid. The cliffs were at a constant slant, dipping towards the lake. It made sleeping dangerous as one shift in the wrong direction could send any of them tumbling past the edge. So, they slept in pairs, ensuring that if a branch were to break the other person could pull them to safety.

Grae was unfurling a blanket across one of the webbed roots, Retia strapped to his back. The sling Sou made had loops for Retia to thread her legs through, crisscrossing under her rear and up over her shoulders to wrap around Grae's chest and waist, leaving her back untouched for her injury to heal. Evelyn wiped her brow of sweat, helping him lay down blankets. They'd all abandoned their cloaks in Grae's pack, wearing as little clothing as possible, tearing the sleeves off their tunics and bunching up the legs of their pants. The heavy humidity cost them their stamina, forcing them to take breaks the Venandi otherwise wouldn't have allowed.

Meric shuffled his way to Grae, who had stepped away from camp to drink from his skin of water. He held out his hand and Grae gave him the skin, the onni hide course against his palm. Meric threw his head back and immediately hunched over, biting his lips against the hot water. He coughed, handing the canteen back.

"We've gone through the good water for you and Retia. All we have left is whatever the vapor drips from the roots. Its clean and filtered, but it will burn going down," Grae said, chuckling.

"The burn I'm used to. It tastes bloody awful," Meric said, grimacing. The taste of rock, wood and sweat created a flavor he imagined soiled clothing left out for months in a molded shed would be. Anya walked up to them, the pack of healing supplies still slung over her shoulder. She looked at Retia, brushing a strand of dark hair from the girl's damp face.

"Come, little one. Sou will tell you a story while I take a look at your back," she said, her tone kind and absent of all the resentment she'd previously held. Retia leaned away from Grae's back, holding out her arms. Anya tucked her hands under Retia's legs, scooping her out of the sling, careful not to touch her back. The girl settled into Anya's arms, hands folded against her chest.

Grae mouthed *thank you* to Anya, squeezing her shoulder before she walked away. He watched as she laid Retia in one of the root divots next to Sou, who was also laying on the floor. His mouth moved, features animated to distract Retia as Anya lifted her shirt, pulling back the bloodstained linen. The girl winced; brows creased as the semi-dried blood pulled against her skin, but she didn't cry out. Evelyn sat next to Anya, helping her clean Retia's lacerations. Grae looked down and turned to Meric, anger in his blue eyes.

"She'll carry those scars all her life," Grae said, his voice low and fuming.

"Then she's in good company," Meric said. "You'll show her they're nothing to be ashamed of. Her mother loved her and that is all that matters."

Grae exhaled a heavy sigh, crossing his arms over his chest. Meric knew his friend grappled with the responsibility of caring for a child. He'd done it before with Meric, but Retia was much younger than he was when he had come under Grae's care. It was different. Meric had never seen Grae as a parent; he'd always been a friend. The way Grae cared for Retia was like that of a new father, grasping at straws with inexperience.

His friend wiped a hand over his face, meeting Meric's gaze. "How is your shoulder and leg?" he said, changing the topic.

Meric rolled his shoulder, feeling the firm stitches holding him together.

"Better. I can string a bow now although anything too strenuous will break the stitches. The leg will take longer, but the skin is scabbing well."

"Has she said anything to you?" Grae asked, glancing at Anya with concern.

Meric hesitated, contemplating his next choice of words. His mind flashed to the night Sou had impressed them to unburden, sharing the memories none of them had ever spoken to another soul. He decided Anya's wasn't his memory to share.

"She has, but I'm not a minstrel. I couldn't recite it with the proper details it deserves. I think if you ask, she will tell you. You're the one she probably wants to confess most to," Meric said, hearing the twinge in his voice although he tried to hide it. He wished his friends would give into the desires of their hearts and tell each other how they felt. Every day it seemed like they had less and less time to confess it. Grae nodded with a sad curl of his lip, looking over the lake.

"What in the Depths have we gotten ourselves into, Meric?" his friend said, blue eyes staring into an unknown future.

"Can you imagine where we would be if not here?"

There was no imagining needed. Anya and Grae would've been corpses on the streets of Reva and Meric would either be mad or dead by now below in Fallon's prison. Grae sighed, looking back at the camp where Evelyn and Anya were finishing up. Meric gazed beyond the mist into the calm waters of Elm Lake.

The lake held a solemn presence, a great body of water that seemed to flow against its existence. Had it always boiled with such wrath? Meric could feel the hatred that heated its stillness, waiting and growing. Its only witness was the lonely elm that stood towering apart from the gusts of scalding air that sweated his brow. He was perhaps too far to see clearly, but he couldn't recall a moment the leaves moved. It seemed frozen in its own sadness. Its roots gripped to the cliff's edges to keep itself from sinking. He knew the feeling.

"Sou will take the first watch. Get some rest. We're still a few days from reaching the Rya," Grae said, reminding Meric that there was still more to come. It was not just the lake's unbearable heat that made traveling the cliffs so difficult. Vapor serpents slithered through roots and rock, camouflaging their coiled shapes to look like branches. One bite and death would come as swift as the wind. Retia's and Meric's injuries also hindered their progress and none of them were confident that Devu had quit her pursuit. Even if they did reach the opposite side of the lake safely, the Rya River would be falling into the lake, smoothing out any footholds they might use to climb the cliff. There was no guarantee Meric would have the strength to climb with his lame leg. Again, they were faced with impossible odds.

Grae exhaled a hot breath, blonde hair sticking to his forehead as he walked towards Anya. She had finished dressing

Retia's back, smoothing out the girl's hair in her lap. Grae sat beside her, whispering something into her ear. Anya looked into his eyes and laid her head on his shoulder, speaking words that Meric couldn't hear.

Sou sat on the floor leaning against the cliff, his arm looped around a root that had caused a fissure to crack all the way up the rock wall. A few paces away, Evelyn sat cross-legged in a rooted divot, hair plaited in a damp braid across her bare shoulder. She had her back turned to them, her head resting against the cliff wall.

Meric walked across the camp, standing in front of Sou.

"Who's next on watch?" Meric asked, shifting his stance, involuntarily groaning as he did so. Sou's slanted brows raised, creasing his many wrinkles.

"Most certainly not you. Grae will watch after me, don't you worry lad. I've got just as keen an eye as any of you Venandi and more sense as well. You need rest."

Meric cocked his head to the side, his earring grazing the back of his neck. "If I rested for a year, it wouldn't be enough. I need a new body," Meric said, wincing as he stretched his shoulder.

"Oh, you'll live. The young heal fast. In any case, she'll make sure you do. She's a wonderfully stubborn girl," Sou chuckled as he glanced at Evelyn.

"It makes sense, her being Viden."

"Being Viden has nothing to do with it," Sou said, his gaze glowing with amusement. "When she was a child, she once tried to cross the Omya on the back of her three-month-old bena wolf. They both almost drowned, and you know what she told me when I pulled her from the river? *Put me back, I nearly had it.*"

Meric couldn't help the smile that spread across his face. He inclined his head and turned away, walking towards Evelyn. He would be bunking with her this night. It wasn't until he was within arm's reach that he noticed her shoulders shaking, tears flowing as she stared at her hands. Meric sat beside her, a groan escaping his lips as his leg protested. She started, turning as though to face an enemy. That's when he noticed the blood on her hands—Retia's blood. Her ruby eyes glistened, hollowed out by an exhaustion that threatened to hold her under. She held her hands aloft, fingers trembling. He'd seen her in tears before, but they had been long-suffering, quickly cast away by a need to keep moving. These tears carried the grief of far too many people, and she was drowning in them. He wondered when was the last time anyone had tried to pull her out. He took Evelyn's hands in his, feeling Retia's blood slip between their intertwined fingers. There was an irony in that mingling, and he nearly turned away with the shame of it.

He dipped her hands under a root dripping with vapor water, cleaning the blood from her fingers until she was free of it. She met his eyes, twin rubies confessing what she could not say. He wrapped his arms around her, pulling her into his chest. She stiffened, holding her breath.

"I'm sorry," he whispered into her ear. "I'm sorry for what I said—for what I thought. Let go. You don't have to be so Depths-damned strong all the time." He felt her body crumble into his embrace, arms curling around his shoulders, face buried into the crook of his neck.

"I can't stop what I see," she said, shuddering

He gripped her arms, releasing her from his embrace so he could look at her. Her hair wisped in strands around her face, sticking to the sweat at her brow. He wiped the tears from her cheeks, his fingers lingering on the skin of her jaw. What could he do? Her burdens were her own, but perhaps instead of lifting them for her, he could lift her.

Then do not stop seeing me, he thought, knowing she would hear him.

A breeze gently caressed the fabric of her torn shirt. She sighed, leaning her head to the side with the shadow of a smile. He pulled her back into his arms, not caring that their bodies were wet and sticky with sweat. They remained in silence for a time, parting to lay down beside each other for the night. The heat had exhausted Meric so much the previous nights—his body refusing to rest for more than a few hours, that he found no trouble in finding sleep now.

It wasn't until morning, when the sun's rays filtered through the fog, had he felt the back of Evelyn's hand touching his. His skin grazed the surface of hers, touching, but still sundered by the different worlds they'd come from. He flexed a finger, threading it in between hers. He wondered if there would ever be a time for this. She shifted in her sleep, her fingers moving over his as though wondering the same.

CHAPTER 44

DON'T LOSE ME

"You lie," Grae said, shaking his head at Sou. Evelyn peered in between the two with a curled lip, enjoying the light conversation. Retia was strapped to Sou's back, head leaning against his shoulder with interest. The old man shrugged, gripping his shirt as he beat it back and forth, trying to cool himself with hot air.

"It's true. That dreadful fish nearly pulled me into Idris Stream, but I saw it before the cord snapped. Black as tar it was and it shone like oil, its mouth wide enough for my head," Sou said, arms spread wide for Retia's amusement. She smiled and it warmed Evelyn's heart to see it. Her calves burned as she leaned against the cliff slant, but her muscles were growing used to the posture. As they approached the end of their third day following the path around Elm Lake, Evelyn thought she might have a hard time adjusting to standing upright again.

"An Ignis Gulper living within *that*?" Grae said, gesturing to the steaming lake. "No, nothing lives in these boiling waters. It's just another one of your Vagu myths."

"What is an Innis — Igis —" Anya said, sighing her way into a permanent frown. "Whatever the Depths that animal is called?"

"Gulper. Ignis Gulper," Meric said beside her, running a

528

hand over his damp hair. It stuck to the back of his neck and forehead, sweat running down his cheeks.

Anya gave him a sharp look. He only shrugged in response.

"If it is a myth, it's one he's been telling for a long time," Evelyn said, recalling this particular story being told to her many times as a child. "At first it was the size of a man, then the measure of a field. The last time I'd heard the story I believe it could fill the halls of a great cathedral." She glanced at Sou who rolled his eyes, dismissively waving his hand at her.

"When I saw the beast, I was a young man. The fish grows with the story and surely is now the size of the elm herself," Sou said, pointing at the great elm's vaporous shape in the distance. Retia turned her head, looking down the cliff, searching for this fabled creature.

"Apparently it is quite long. Its head is the largest part of its body, growing thin towards the tail. It's finless like an eel and when it opens its mouth it can swallow ships whole," Evelyn said, turning towards Retia with her mouth wide, chomping down, teeth bared. The grey in Retia's eyes brightened and she redoubled her efforts in scouring the lake, pulling against the straps that held her to Sou's back.

Sou glanced behind him, meeting Evelyn's eyes with a sweaty scowl.

"Now, that's ridiculous. Not ships lass, but smaller fishing vessels of course." His voice was collected, matter of fact. He tapped Retia's hand on his shoulder and the girl turned towards him. "The only way to spot one is to search for geysers," Sou said, shooting his fingers into the sky. "This creature spits out a jet of boiling water to incapacitate its prey. It also uses it for defense. It is how it escaped my fishing line."

Retia's eyes narrowed with determination, turning her head once more to Elm Lake. Grae glanced over the cliff ledge and peered into the water, scoffing.

"Superstition," he muttered.

"Only to those who haven't seen it," Sou said, patting the blonde Venandi on the shoulder.

Grae grunted and Sou wrapped an arm around the young man pulling him into a very one-sided hug. The Venandi cried out and lost his balance, nearly falling to the floor, but Sou held on, dragging Grae's feet, not losing a single stride. Retia turned from the lake, glancing at the top of Grae's head trapped under Sou's arm with concern.

"Get off me," Grae said, struggling against Sou's hold.

Meric ran ahead and picked up Grae's feet, a mischievous smile spreading across his lips. At first, Meric struggled with Grae's weight and Evelyn almost told him to not exert himself in fear of his shoulder reopening, but the obvious joy emitting from Sou and Meric stopped her from doing so. Together, the two men held Grae as if he were a pig being carried on a spit. They had such little opportunity to smile, and she thought Grae's weight wasn't so strenuous. It would do Meric good to stretch the muscles to prevent atrophy of the limb and hearing him laugh brought a grin to her own lips.

Anya touched her on the arm, a hand over her mouth as she chuckled. Evelyn wiped sweat that had dripped down her neck, joining the Venandi in her laughter.

"How about we throw him in? Perhaps the beast needs a fresh meal to reveal itself," Meric said, leaning his head towards the cliff's ledge. Sou bit his lip with a smile, his crinkled eyes bunched in laughter lines. Retia let out a high-pitched squeal.

"Retia!" Grae said, mocked surprise in his voice when he realized Retia, who had not spoken a word since the tunnel's collapse, was laughing. "You would allow me to become fish food? For shame."

Retia rested her head against Sou's neck, plump red cheeks spread in a humorous smile.

"I want to see it, but I don't think you'd be very tasty," she said, her voice small and hoarse from disuse. The collective sigh of relief at hearing Retia talk was palpable and Evelyn felt herself walk easier as though a weight had been lifted.

"He smells far too much like the backend of a horse to be a temptation," Anya said, agreeing with Retia.

"We *all* smell like the backends of horses," Grae said, snapping like an upturned turtle.

"Yes, but it was I who woke when you decided to lift your arms while sleeping. I've never been woken by a smell before," Anya said, raising her hands above her head. Evelyn turned away, covering her nose. The aroma of trapped sweat mingling with the hot air wasn't a combination that inspired thoughts of perfumed flowers. Retia grimaced, looking down at Grae.

"I woke too," she said. "You do smell bad." Retia glanced back at Anya who raised her brows at Grae, satisfied she had won the argument. Grae jerked once more, unable to break the hold of Sou's and Meric's arms, eventually resigning to his fate of being carried.

"How long must I endure this?" he said, hair swinging across his damp forehead.

"You're much more accommodating this way. Answer a few questions and you'll be released," Sou said, looking onward into the steams of mist that hid the path they walked.

"How does that make any kind of sense?"

"It's true, I think it might be the way your face turns red upside down. It's much less intimidating. I suspect with all that blood going to your head, your brain might actually work better as well," Evelyn said, enjoying the look of annoyance he shot at her. Anya cocked her head, as though contemplating if he were less intimidating in his current state.

"To the Depths with all of you," Grae muttered, his cheeks puffing as he hung his head in the air.

Meric glanced over his shoulder at Evelyn, honey eyes beaming with mirth. Her chest tightened as she smiled back, unable to stop the flutter in her stomach as memories of Birdie and Adel resurfaced, Meric's eyes reminding her of the way they used to look at each other.

A hot wind blew across the cliff face, and she gasped, dizziness sweeping through her body. Despite the slanting cliffs, vapor serpents and the constant threat of falling into the boiling water below, it was the hot gusts of wind were the most dangerous part of Elm Lake. They consumed and burned the eyes, locking limbs and softening the mind. Sou had to be caught by Grae earlier in the morning due to an especially searing breeze. This one quickly passed, but a silence cut through the laughter, reminding them of where they were. Sou heaved, loosening his grip on Grae. Meric panted, slowly returning Grae's feet to the ground. He lined his lips with a grimace, limping and holding his bandaged shoulder. Evelyn quickened her pace, placing a hand over his. His fingers parted so that hers fit in between his.

"Did it open?" she said looking over the gauze. It was still clean and, although slightly damp from the air, no blood seeped through.

"No. It's only sore," he said, brushing his finger over hers. A tremor ran through her arm and up her spine at his touch. She lowered her hand from his. He looked at her a moment, the line of his mouth twisting up, slight and nearly invisible. "Grae's just grown fat," he said as the Venandi made an obscene gesture in response.

Evelyn recalled Meric cleaning Retia's blood from her fingers, telling her to let go. She could still feel his embrace, the strength of his arms lifting her from the torturous thoughts of everything she hadn't the power to change. It had been so long since she had been held and never in the way Meric had. How could this have happened? When had she allowed her heart to rule her mind? There was no time for this, but she couldn't deny what Meric did to her. The way his autumn eyes melted the winter in her, warming the tundra of her grief so she could glimpse into the realm of what could be. She could not allow herself to consider the possibility, to hope. She thought back on her vision, the death reflected in Meric's eyes as Maun's dagger fell. She couldn't stop it. She hadn't been able to prevent the deaths of her village, of Lian and Isaad. She recalled reaching out to the poor soul burning in the lake. Only Sou knew of what she had seen. Although with what she had said to Meric last night, she suspected that he had an idea of what she grappled with.

Grae came up behind Sou, who appeared to be struggling

with Retia's weight, and lifted the girl from the sling. He placed the wrappings around his back, but she shook her head as he lifted her, preferring to walk instead of being held. Evelyn thought this was a good sign that the girl was healing, her mother's defiant look reflecting in her eyes.

"You had questions," Grae said, marching alongside Sou, who dipped his head in exhaustion. The day was diminishing to the rise of the moon, and they'd need to make camp soon.

"How long until we see the Rya? As much as I enjoy the steam, I really would love to feel dry again, lad," Sou said, hair dripping rivulets of sweat down the back of his neck.

Anya swayed her head in agreement, mouth open as she continued to try and regain a steady breath. Meric limped beside her, his leg tiring now that the end of the day had been reached.

"We should be at the fall of the Rya River by evening tomorrow. I've never traveled below the cliffs. I've only seen them from above, so it'll be a matter of finding a reasonable place to climb. Then we'll follow the river and in about two days we should see the outline of Birny across the horizon," Grae said, huffing. He lifted a hand to wipe his face, but Retia gripped his fingers, tugging on them.

"I have a question," she said.

"You may ask whatever you like," Grae said, encouraging the girl to talk.

"Is mama dead?" Retia said, grey eyes meeting his, intelligent beyond her years. Evelyn's breath caught in her throat and Anya stifled a painful groan. Grae stopped walking, kneeling beside Retia, who stood with the strength of someone far older than she.

"Yes," he said, gripping her hand. "She and your uncle are dead, but do you know what never dies?" Retia shook her head. "Love. The love of Isa and your mama. It is the steel that does not bend. The mountain that cannot break. It is as enduring as the wind and more powerful than your fear. It is a thing no one can take from you. It is yours and no matter what happens in your long, long life, it will always be yours."

The wind coalesced around Grae, blue light enveloping the man as though the spirits who rode it were trying to convince him of his own words. Evelyn's eyes shone with tears, feeling the love of Tansey swell within her heart. Suddenly realizing how long it had been there without her noticing. A tear slipped from Retia's eye, a small smile forming across her sad expression.

"We should make camp there," Meric said, his voice rough as though straining against an emotion he didn't want shown. Evelyn noticed some roots many paces ahead, beckoning safe sleep with their intertwined branches. Sou grunted in agreement, clearing his throat.

Once arrived, they tossed their blankets over the roots, listening to Sou tell another fishing tale. Grae fell asleep, snoring quietly beside Anya who looked over the lake, disinterested in another story of Coral and Claw. When Sou had finished, he slept, his torso tucked under a thick root. Retia was awake in between Anya and Grae, rummaging through Grae's pack as he snored. Evelyn rested within a net of roots beside Meric, watching the girl reach into the pack, pulling out one of Evelyn's throwing knives. She only had three left; the others having been abandoned when they fought Devu on the Greens. The knife fit inside Retia's hand perfectly, the throwing weapon becoming a simple dagger in her fist.

"Do you know how to use it?" Evelyn said, sitting up on an elbow. Anya turned her head, reaching out a hand. Retia flipped the blade, placing the hilt in Anya's hand. Evelyn raised a brow, impressed that Retia showed such dexterity for one so young.

"Mama said to cut them with the sharp side," Retia said, running a finger across the steel when Anya had finished inspecting the knife, handing it back. "She was speaking of apples when said that."

"The same concept applies," Evelyn said, caught between pride and heartsickness that this girl should be so rational. "Keep it. I will teach you how to throw it in the morning."

"And I shall teach you how to slice flesh with it," Anya said.

Retia's eyes grew wide, and she tucked the knife into the belt of her tunic, holding onto the hilt as though it gave her comfort. A darkness colored the grey in her eyes, thunder striking within her gaze as Evelyn imagined Retia thinking on the Reticent, perhaps driving the knife in her hand through her heart.

"Thank you," she said, laying her head on Anya's lap who stroked the girl's hair. Evelyn exchanged a look with Anya, feeling the weight of responsibility grow heavier.

Evelyn settled herself beside Meric, who had already laid down with a contented sigh, stretching out his leg. His dark hair swept past his face, brown beard catching beads of sweat dripping down his temples.

"How's your leg?" she said, tucking her arm against her cheek.

Meric placed his hands on his stomach and turned his head to her, eyes searching.

"I'll live, Evelyn," he said, her name quiet on his lips. "It seems pointless to say not to worry given we're being hunted by a deranged assassin and slowly smothering to death within the bowels of this lake, but I'll say it anyway because that's what people do. Stop worrying."

She exhaled a short breath and gave him a pointed stare at what she knew to be an impossible task for her. He chuckled at her defiant expression. He was doing that more often, smiling and laughing. The rare bird stretching out its wings beyond the confines of golden leaves.

"Have you decided what you will do in Birny?" Meric said, his voice a whisper so the others couldn't hear.

After rescuing Meric she had explained what she'd been through and the decisions that led them together. She told Meric of Oretem and his madness, her decision to mend the bond and her fears of his fury being released upon Iona. She hadn't confessed that she wanted to visit Edewor, the Vagu capitol to search for any ancient knowledge that could help her save Oretem and recover her loss of Iona's Breath. She was certain that the answers wouldn't be found in Birny. The home of the first Videns, deep within the Eshe Willow Wood, was where she needed to go. They must have histories and accounts of the dragon bonds, some book or wise Vagu had the answers she searched for. Now as she was thinking on it, she recalled the original purpose to her arrival.

"My father and my sister are in Birny," she said, that emptiness filling her chest whenever she thought of them. "I have no memory of either one, so I imagine it might be like meeting them for the first time."

"In a way that's true," Meric said, tucking his good arm behind his head.

Evelyn shifted a little closer, trying to find a comfortable position within the roots, but it was impossible. She found a small divot where her legs fit, but was much closer to Meric than she'd anticipated.

"Their blood runs in my veins. They're family. I should feel... something, but I don't, and that frightens me," she said, confessing more than she expected to. She hadn't thought of her sister or father since Sou had told her their names, weeks ago in Reva. Had she been too occupied in her efforts to stay alive? Or had her heart turned so cold that it would not even warm at the thought of knowing Ranvir and Era waited for her? Meric turned over so that he was on his side, facing her. He grunted as his shoulder stiffened then relaxed, settling into position.

"Blood sustains a bond, this is true, but if you have not experienced life with the people you share it with, then it is vicarious. You had not even the opportunity to imagine that life, and so how could you be expected to feel a bond to those who are strangers to you? It doesn't mean you are iron-hearted; it means you are human," Meric said, his voice low and kind. "Your feelings might change when you meet them. Coming from someone who has no blood, only the disembodied voice of a dead mother and even that isn't certain, it's different when you know the marrow of your bones lives on in more than just yourself."

Evelyn remembered the night of Meric's confession. The childhood he could barely recall except the old woman decomposing before his eyes. Surviving on the streets of Reva with no one to look after him, starving and abandoned by those who were supposed to love him. She shouldn't have spoken so casually of the blessing she'd received in knowing she had family, but Meric seemed to take no offence by it.

Only sadness marked his features. She had told him of the voice in the mountains, its echoing plea for her to find him. Days ago, he had asked her who it was that spoke with her, and it broke her heart to tell him she didn't know. They both had the same hope, that their mothers were watching over them. He displayed the same stoic understanding in his eyes as he did then, sinking into a cavernous sadness she didn't know how to lift him from.

"I know," she paused trying to collect her thoughts. "I suppose there's no knowing until I am faced with them. I just…" she trailed off, her chest expanding with a truth she feared to speak.

"Tell me," Meric said, taking her hand in his own. She squeezed his fingers, hating herself for how much she savored his touch.

"I am afraid to love them," she whispered, voice trembling. "Everything I have ever loved, all that I have touched, has died. What if they do not recognize me? Will they be disappointed in what they see? If I do not love them, then they cannot not hurt me. But I fear that I will. I fear that I already do."

"Grae did not lie when he said that love is the steel that does not break, but love can also be too finely tempered. A blade heated for too long, placed in water too soon. Even a master blacksmith cannot predict the temperament of every metal. It is a gamble and sometimes that gamble results in cracked steel," Meric, said, his thumb caressing the back of her hand.

There was a shift in the air, a stillness that seemed to only effect the space between them. Evelyn gazed into his eyes, autumn driving away the winter. She took her hand from his grasp, feeling unnaturally cold in the lake's heat.

No. This cannot be. I am the thing that breaks. I cannot love you.

"I saw you die," she whispered. It was incredible how a single sentence could leave her mouth raw, her tongue thick.

Meric's brows knit together, his expression more curious than surprised.

"Was it quick?" he said, lowering his head. Evelyn's frown deepened, anger overcoming all other emotions.

"I saw you *die*, Meric. Do you care so little for yourself?" she said, bewildered by his response. How could he be so casual about it? Why wouldn't he bother to think of what that would do to Grae and Anya, or her?

"Of course. How is it to be done then?" he said, turning to lay on his back.

"You'll be stabbed," Evelyn tried to keep her voice even, but the images returned. Combined with her rising anger she turned away, flashes of their violence rushing across her mind. "I thought it was a Reticent blade, but perhaps it just might've been my own."

Meric smiled, but its presence only made her want to rip the stitches out of his shoulder.

"I do not fear death," he said, staring into the night sky.

"Then fear for those you leave behind." Her voice grew in volume, enraged that Meric would consider himself so disposable. "You would greet death so happily in the place of one you care for, but what about that same person who must live with what you did? The one who would be forced to face each dawn, knowing you were not there to see it too. You are not so special to have no one mourn your passing. Do you believe Retia will not blame herself for what happened to her family? People live on, Meric, and while you ride the wind, they suffer in their endeavor to survive."

Meric twisted his head to stare at her, his expression bemused by her words. She turned away for fear of what else she might confess to him.

"You must stop this," he whispered. "You are drowning, Evelyn. It is not enough to just survive. You must live. Those who have passed, the ones who loved you, would want that."

Evelyn chuckled a sob, tears running down her temples. She watched the night sky, following the wisps of blue light dancing above her. When had they ceased being so beautiful?

"I am drowning," she said, exhausted from pretending like she wasn't. "I have these visions and there's nothing I can do to stop them. I saw the tunnel collapse before it happened, my village destroyed. There's more, but the images are shapeless. I can't make sense of what I see, and I can't stop all the deaths that follow. It's madness. Perhaps that's what truly killed the Videns, watching their visions come to life without the capability of stopping them."

A hot breeze flew over them, lighting the night in blue.

"If you cannot stop them, then why try? What is it you fight against?"

She turned towards him, contemplating the question she hadn't thought to ask herself.

"I fight against what I haven't seen yet. The end of all things," she said, thinking of Oretem and the chaos he would unleash on the world if she were to do nothing.

"That seems a worthy endeavor. If we are choosing to live, then the end of all things will certainly make that far harder to do."

She huffed a chuckle, releasing the tension in her shoulders.

"I've killed people, Meric," she said, the compulsion to unburden too strong. "I never thought in all my life I'd be the cause of someone's death. The death of my village," she paused, letting the words fall like blood droplets from a seeping wound. "I didn't set the flame, I know. But they burned all the same because I couldn't protect them. It is said that there is always a choice. A fork in the path to decide whether to spill blood or choose peace. I was not made for such a choice, and I don't know how to survive now that I've made it. It is simple to say that the choice was not mine to make. That forces beyond my control bent my hand to its will, but this is my hand. I chose to lift it and I chose to strike. There is blood still on it that only I can see, and I cannot find a way to make it clean again."

She was no longer speaking of her village as Kiev's blank, dead stare sprung from her memory. The guard she'd killed in Fallon's courtyard, Isaad's bodyless head squelching at her feet as it fell from the sky. Some she had personally dealt the death blow to, others she had lent an unsuspecting helping hand. She felt all their deaths like a deep bruise that was unwilling to heal. It hadn't mattered whether they deserved their end or not. She had caused them and somehow must learn to live with it. Meric lined his lips, weighted because she knew he couldn't help her.

"I know what it is to be haunted by the people you've failed," he said, eyes lost in memories that seemed painful. "I used to think that forgiveness was a lie. An illusion to make terrible people feel like they're good. I'm not a good person. Perhaps that's the key to obtaining it. Accepting what you've done and doing what you can to make it right."

He was telling her what he wished he could do, what he felt he could not. She decided that she would once again have to prove him wrong. It felt like a hollow choice, but it wasn't one of peace or bloodshed, it was a choice of her own. She was seeking redemption, and he forgiveness. The two were fused, two blades made of the same steel. She was always meant to find him.

Her mind filled with imaginations of Sou tending a new garden, Anya arm-wrestling in a tavern while Grae and Retia cheered on from the crowd. Meric holding her close, lips kissing the hollow of her neck. Oretem soaring into the sky, free of madness. Maun and Devu cold and dead in the ground. That was what she sought after, that was the future she envisioned, the only one worth fighting for.

"Do you remember what you told me in the Reva? When the raptor had come upon us," she said, feeling the red in her eyes burn with the intensity of her resolve. Meric kept her gaze, locked in the power of her stare.

"I remember," he said.

"Say it," she whispered, fighting the urge to touch him.

"Don't lose me."

"I won't," she repeated. Her voice like granite, a promise etched into the words as though she had sworn them in blood. She would not lose him to a world he deemed was better off without him and she would not allow herself to crumble beneath the magnitude of her grief. He was right. She would do all she could to make things right again. It was all either of them were capable of.

CHAPTER 45

ALL SHE FEARED

Evelyn watched with approval as Retia twisted the blade in her hand, bending her wrist to imitate a throw. The girl walked in between Anya and Grae, leaning her body against the cliff's heavy slant to maintain balance. Anya nodded, reaching out a hand to bend Retia's arm.

"Don't stretch your arm so far. You're small, use that to your advantage. Aim for the joints, elbows, and the back of the knees," Anya said, releasing Retia's arm. The girl flipped the blade in her hand, twisting into a crouch. She winced, the pain in her back causing her foot to slide. The flat of the blade landed lower onto Anya's calf, but the cut would've still caused a considerable amount of pain.

"Better," the Venandi said. "It's hard to consider your form while we're walking, but we'll have time for that when we've surfaced from this Depths-damned lake."

Retia continued to practice, focusing on a steady breath as Evelyn had taught her that morning. Weaving her wrist into a forward and backwards spin to train the body that the blade was an extension of the flesh. It was one of the first lessons Tansey had taught Evelyn. She remembered standing in the snow for hours, spinning the blade in her hand, irritated that Tansey would teach her something so mundane. It wasn't until years later that Evelyn appreciated the training.

"I recognize that move," Sou said, walking beside her. "For the longest time you would spin all sorts of objects. Spoons, sticks, even my gardening rake."

"I wanted to be good," Evelyn said, watching Retia slice the blade up as if stabbing into an imaginary jaw.

"You are. Retia has excellent teachers in you and Anya," he said, his mouth curling into a fond smile. Evelyn nodded, the awkward pause creating a silence between them.

She hadn't been able to truly speak with Sou since leaving Reva. They were almost always within the company of the Venandi and with the constant threat of Devu and her raptors it seemed like conversation wasn't important. Now, with the others walking ahead it was the first time since Ciar she felt alone with her old friend. She could hear the faint rush of water echoing across the cliffs, a sign that they were coming upon where the Rya fell into Elm Lake. They were close.

"It must be a great relief to be returning home," she said, too fast in her attempt to fill in the silence. Sou raised his head to the sky, squinting against the sun peeking in through the mist.

"It is. There are many I am eager to see again." Sou's voice was soft with a deep sense of longing. Evelyn's chest tightened, wondering which was worse: knowing your home was destroyed or wandering with the knowledge that it was still there, living on without you. She recalled how angry she was in Reva when Sou had revealed his true identity. Looking back, after all they had gone through, it seemed so trivial a confession.

"Sou..." she paused, and he met her gaze. His green eyes were free of expectation, absolved of forgiveness because he didn't believe he deserved it. He was perfectly content to allow Evelyn to remain in her anger. She wanted to be free of it. "I'm sorry," she said, looking away. "I'm sorry for all of it. Staying angry with you is too heavy a burden, and I miss you."

"Lass," he said, voice hitched. "I never left."

Evelyn raised her head, looking at him with tears in her eyes.

"I know," she whispered, biting her trembling lip. "I'm sorry that I did."

Sou wrapped an arm around her shoulders, pulling her in close. She leaned her head against his shoulder as they walked, closing her eyes briefly in the warmth of his embrace.

"You have nothing to apologize for. I'm just a stubborn old fool who has plenty to say, but no ears with which to listen. My own small wisdoms cannot penetrate this thick skull," he tapped the side of his head, grinning.

"When it comes to the thickness of your skull on that we can agree," Evelyn said, shrugging out of Sou's embrace as a hot gale swept over the lake. "You do not look nearly as wise as you sound." Sou laughed, his slanted brows lifting with mirth.

They walked on in companionable silence, listening to Grae and Anya argue about the best way for Retia to hold a blade. Meric interjected with his own opinions, although he would revert to an annoyed, silent glare when the two ignored him. Evelyn looked up into the sky, keeping a close eye on the wind. Her neck was sore by how many times she watched Iona's Breath, making sure to notice the slightest change in direction. She didn't want to be caught off guard like she was in the Greens. She'd seen these cliffs in her vision and whether the person falling from them and into the lake was friend or foe, she couldn't be sure. Her gut recoiled at the thought of any one of them burning in the boiling waters. The faint rumble of the Rya meeting Elm Lake was growing louder, the mist becoming thicker. Every step Evelyn took heightened her anxiety and she peered at the sky again, seeing nothing but the rays of sun shining through the vapor.

"We'll be fine, lass. We're almost there," Sou said, feeling her concern through the impressions of the wind.

"That's what I fear," she said, continuing to search the sky.

"You fear nothing," he said with a scoff.

"You know that isn't true. I fear everything. I am not as brave as you think," she lowered her head with a grimace, rubbing the back of her neck.

"Perhaps you're right." He side-glanced at her with a knowing smile. "Exaggeration is one of my many aimable qualities, but I digress. Bravery and fear are like trees that need fire to multiply."

"I assume you see me as the tree," Evelyn said, brows raised. Sou surprised her by shaking his head, looking at her as though she were missing the obvious.

"The tree is your fear, Evelyn. It stands and it grows, taller and stronger. Immovable and stagnant. The fire is courage, propagating your fear. That's the beauty of it. Fear isn't something that fades with bravery. It spreads, creating forests of all you fear to lose. It is difficult to burn so much, each time a tree burns a new one grows. But burn it must or it will thicken, spreading its branches too high for the flames to reach. The fire will need to burn hotter and longer, and eventually it will collapse, and the tree will remain, undying and alone. To grow you must burn."

Sou stared at her for a moment, his expression somber. It was the longest he'd ever looked upon her since her bond, his green eyes not leaving hers. A trail of blue light floated into being around his head, almost invisible as if frightened by its own formation. It crept towards her timid, but resilient as it battled the strong wind of the lake.

Come, she thought, *be not afraid.*

Sou's thought faded into the vapor, pulled back by his reluctance. She hid her disappointment, knowing there was still more that Sou was not ready to share with her. Evelyn wondered if all would be revealed once they reached Birny. Would Sou finally feel safe enough to share the things he'd spent so long hiding? She thought of Grae, Retia, and Anya.

Meric...

When they reached Birny, the Venandi would no longer be bound to her. Their contract would end, and they would go their separate ways. Grae would take Retia and she knew Meric would follow. How could he not? Anya and Grae were his family. What twisted her gut was that they had become her family as well. She could already feel her heart collapsing at the inevitability of having to let them go.

"It's hard to believe how we all found each other. How close we've become," Evelyn said, looking over at the Venandi who were wrapped up in conversation.

Sou followed her line of sight, a caring smile creasing the skin around his mouth.

"I'm glad I was wrong about them," Sou said. "I hope they will stay in Birny. I would be sad to see them leave."

"As would I," Evelyn said, her gaze drifting over to Meric.

"We're here," Grae called out in front of them.

Before them, hidden in the hot mist, was a wall of stone and roots. The branches twisted and warped from the stone like hands, desperate in their attempt to escape being crushed beneath the jagged boulders. Their small twigs-like fingers grasped towards empty air and Evelyn was suddenly reminded of Lian. She blinked and the hands became roots again, sinister in appearance—but only roots. They grew far, their tips brushing against the thick barricade of water that fell into Elm Lake. The waterfall was loud, its roar akin to the bellows of crashing rocks, rumbling, and growling. The fall created a cool breeze, a glimpse to the surface Evelyn had forgotten existed. She sighed, lifting her hands as droplets of the Rya chilled her hot skin. She moved closer to the spray and noticed another opening to Isla's Reach under the waterfall, its entrance dark and wet.

Evelyn looked up, taking in the full height of the cliff. There were no paths to walk or divots to cling too. Pebbles fell to the ground around her feet as the Rya broke loose the worn stones. All they had any hope of climbing were the roots reaching out through the cliff's rocky face.

"There has to be another way," Grae said in a quiet murmur, his eyes searching the cliff for a safer route. Anya stared up without a twitch in her features, damp hair blowing behind her.

"This is it. We must climb here," she said, lowering her

head and meeting Sou's resigned eyes. Retia belted her blade, staring into the waterfall.

"I don't see much of a choice," Sou said, sighing. "We should follow one after the other, stepping on the same branches. We can't tell what's rotten through and if whoever leads falls, they can be caught by the one beneath them."

Meric lined his lips and rolled his shoulder, trying to mask the transparent pain that was still plaguing him. Evelyn held a breath, wondering how he was going to make it up the rock wall without the use of his leg and a barely healed shoulder. He surprised her when he shook his hands at his side, inhaled, and said, "I should lead."

Grae gave him an incredulous look, his tunic soaked in the spraying mist of the waterfall.

"You've only just started bearing weight on that leg," Grae said, waving his hand at the limb with splayed fingers. "Celosia's Depths, this isn't the time for you to prove anything."

"That isn't why I'll do it," Meric said, his tone abiding, but firm. "I am the weakest among us. I'll be the most likely to fall and if I do, I'll have four times more chance of being caught. If any of you fall, there's little chance I could hold on with any certainty. The ascent will be slow, but it's the best chance we have at everyone making it to the top."

His gaze flowed between them all, imploring his decision. As much as Evelyn wanted to disagree with Meric, she couldn't. The logic was sound, and she hadn't a better plan to speak of.

"He's right," Sou said, reaching for a root, fingers caressing the grooves of the bark. "I'll follow him, then Anya, and Evelyn. Grae, you carry Retia."

Grae turned and gripped Retia's hand. The girl's body was facing Grae, but her gaze was still set on the Rya rushing into the lake. Her brows furrowed into a hard crease as though she were trying to make out a shape from within. Grae tugged on her arm and her head jerked upwards, meeting Grae's eyes with worry as she looked over the height of the cliff.

"I can't climb that," she said, ashamed.

"You won't have to," Grae told her, shifting the pack holding all their supplies and cloaks across his chest so that the sling Retia had been using less and less was draped across his back. She frowned, rolling her shoulders with a wince, knowing her back prevented her independence.

"Let's get on with it," Anya clapped, rubbing her hands together. "I'm ready for clear skies again." She glanced upwards into the vaporous sky, swirling in a smoke-like dance.

Meric gripped a root, pulling himself up with a grunt. He used his injured arm like an elosi tail, balancing him instead of taking the brunt of his weight. He climbed several more spans up, placing his leg on the branch he'd gripped before. Meric pulled against two roots then stopped, looking upwards, his head leaning to the side.

"What is it?" Evelyn said, stretching her neck to see what he was looking at.

He pointed at a twisted network of broken roots, the bark torn and splintered as if pulled downwards. Evelyn thought it didn't look any different from the thousands of others around it that had been crushed by falling rocks. Then she noticed the three distinct lacerations that cut deep into the root, the fractured edges like split flesh.

"Tell me I'm wrong," Meric said, his voice wearied with dread.

The silence was only accompanied by the waterfall, drowning out everything but the fear that settled into Evelyn's chest. Anya and Grae looked at each other, their expressions hard with unease. Retia took out her blade, releasing Grae's hand to face the waterfall. The mist above Meric spun, blue wisps condensing against the natural breeze. It pumped up and down, gaining in speed, invisible to everyone but Evelyn.

"Meric!" she screamed, but her voice was drowned out by the piercing caw of the raptor, descending from the mist like the pouring of black tar. Its talons stretched outward, golden eyes wide with bloodlust. Before he could react, Meric was thrown from the cliff, his body slamming onto the stone below with a hard thud, slipping towards the cliff's edge.

Evelyn ran towards him, breath staggering in her throat. A dark shape threw her to the ground, scaled talons raking the stone on either side of her body. Evelyn's fingers gripped the cracks in the floor, taking all her weight so she would not slide off the ledge. An'gan stood above her, screaming in her face. His breath sour, red tongue curled, and faded feathers erect.

She reached for the daggers in the pocket of her trousers when the animal hunched over with a painful cry, turning around, an arrow in his shoulder. Anya stood with Meric, her face eager and dark with resentment as she held his waist, providing the balance he needed to shoot his weapon. Meric had another arrow nocked, his face bloodied from the fall. The raptor turned away from Evelyn, leaping in short bursts of flight towards Meric and Anya.

Sou stood beside Grae, raising his hands as a burst of wind tore through the air. The gale swept low across the path, but An'gan beat his wings, soaring above Iona's Breath. The wind crashed into Meric and Anya, blowing them from their feet. They clawed at the ground until Sou lowered his hands, stopping the wind. The old man looked up, watching An'gan descend with frightening speed. Sou raised his hands again, throwing wind at the creature who dodged the storm with agile twists. An'gan kept flying low, making it impossible for Sou to use the wind against the raptor without also threatening to careen Anya and Meric from the cliff's ledge. Sou bared his teeth, his kind mouth contorted into a snarl. He gripped a root and began to climb, trying to gain a better vantage point to use his power.

Evelyn felt small hands pulling her own. Retia's grip was as tight as any iron shackles. The girl helped Evelyn to her feet, looking back at the waterfall with a confident stare. Grae stood beneath Sou, rapier in hand. Retia followed a dark shape inside the waterfall, its form creating a figure of mist where the tunnel began.

"Grae, move!" Evelyn screamed. Retia ran to the Venandi, arms outstretched to push him out of the way.

Evelyn saw the curve of blue tendrils spinning in a direction she knew to be unnatural. Something shined from within the falling Rya—steel. She gripped the hilt of her throwing dagger, casting it from her hand with a grunt. Retia crashed into Grae and her arms wrapped around his stomach. He stumbled just after Evelyn's blade shrieked across the steel of another throwing blade; its path diverted from Grae's throat. The dagger's black hilt stuck from a crack in the ground and Evelyn's broke within the crevasse of the cliff wall. Grae wrapped one arm around Retia and pointed his rapier towards the waterfall with the other.

Devu emerged from the blackness of the tunnel, walking out from under the waterfall. Her black cloak was missing, sweat soaking through the dark clothes she wore. The whip at her belt swayed in the breeze, Lian's blood still upon it. She stared at Retia, scars stretching across her cruel face as she smiled. The grin was empty, voided of the emotion accompanied by a smile. A spray of water flew over them as the other raptor, Saiya, flew from the tunnel, her smaller frame no less intimidating than her older companion. Rage flooded Evelyn's veins as she remembered the sound of Saiya's talons breaking the neck of her beloved wolf. A rush of wind blew from above Evelyn, her loose braid uncoiling. Saiya shrieked, wings beating against a furious wind that threw her out towards the lake.

Evelyn glanced up to see Sou had climbed the wall, feet straddling two thick roots, hands outstretched. He looked down at An'gan, who had cornered Meric against the cliff face. Sou lifted his palm, creating a vortex of wind that gulfed upwards, shooting An'gan into the air with an inhuman scream. Tendrils of Iona's Breath swirled around Sou, the old man bathed in blue light.

Evelyn turned back to Devu and saw the faces of those she had killed. Lian and Isaad stared back through the assassin's eyes as though she had trapped them there, screaming for their freedom. Evelyn felt the dragon rise within her, stoking a fire that had but one way to be quelled. Devu must die. There was no escaping this time. The assassin would either kill them all, sealing Meric's horrifying fate, or she would fall. The Reticent glanced up at Sou then back at Evelyn, a slight curve peeking on the edge of her mouth. Devu darted to the side, towards the cliff face, reaching for the roots to climb. Evelyn ran after her, but Grae was closer. Retia ripped herself from Grae's arms, stepping into the path of the Reticent, blade swinging. The Venandi grabbed Retia's arm, tossing her to the side as Devu's blade thrust into empty air where the girl's chest once was. Retia's back scraped across roots as she fell, screaming with a blind rage Evelyn had never heard from the quiet girl.

Grae chopped his rapier down across a root, narrowly missing the Reticent's hand. Devu let no emotion escape her features as she crouched and lunged, her blade meeting Grae's in sparks of red that flew across the cliff's surface. Devu cracked her metal plated arm against Grae's jaw, blood seeping from a cut that formed across his cheek as he stumbled back. The assassin made her way to a hunched Retia, who was still finding her balance. Evelyn had one dagger left—she threw it just as Devu raised her steel to cut down the girl. It sunk deep into the Reticent's arm, causing her to pause and allowing Retia time to climb into a network of roots. Devu made no sound as she bared her teeth and pulled the blade from her flesh, blood dripping from the steel. She spun it in her hand and threw it at Evelyn before she could blink.

Evelyn leaned to the side as far as she could, but the blade still managed to cut across her thigh, disappearing into the lake below. She fell to a knee, groaning against the pain. She prodded the cut, her hands coming away bloody. It had not cut the main artery, but it burned in the hot air. Evelyn regained her balance and pulled the dagger that Sou had given her in Reva from its sheath.

Grae came up behind Devu and she whirled around, slashing the air with a series of blade swipes and forceful kicks. Evelyn joined the fray, blocking where she could and stabbing at every open opportunity. There was something different about Devu this time. The woman she had fought on the Greens hadn't the care to apply her true prowess, but now her pride had been wounded. Evelyn noticed the twitch in her eye when she bent at the waist, stretching the ribs she had broken in the house where she kept Meric imprisoned. There was a desperation in her movements, as though she knew she couldn't perform at her best.

Devu's scars puckered across her skin, misshaping her face into a soundless snarl. Evelyn came in close, slamming her elbow into the Reticent's face. Devu bared her teeth and spat blood into Evelyn's eyes. She cried out, the blood burning and blurring her vision. A fist burrowed into her gut and Evelyn doubled over, feeling the uncontrollable urge to retch. Grae screamed, steel meeting, rocks creaking, and feet shuffling. She opened her eyes, blinking against the pain until she could bear to keep them open. Grae had led the Reticent away from her, closer to the cliff's edge where the slant was the worst.

She took a step forward and heard a startling cry behind her. Anya was pinned to the ground by An'gan, her arms thrashing against his weight. Meric nocked an arrow, but couldn't hold the bow steady. His hands shook as he stretched the string, unable to pull it far enough. His dressing was soaked in blood, the stitches obviously torn and tearing apart the freshly healed skin. She glanced up at Sou who was conjuring powerful winds to keep Saiya in the middle of the lake, unable to cast An'gan from Anya without harming her. Grae and Devu parried around each other. Grae's skill was outmatched by the Reticent's as his rapier struggled to deflect the assassin's blows. Retia huddled in the shadowed canopy of roots, watching Grae fight with an agonized glare. The blood stain on her back spreading, crippling her from helping.

No... no, no, no.

This was all she'd feared. Everything she had left to lose was here. Tansey's face filled her mind, Birdie and Maysom, Alen and Izel. Broken and bloody, burnt, and frozen. She had lived through so many devastating losses in the aftermath of one catastrophe; she could not bear to live through another. Evelyn's fingers tightened around the dagger in her hand, fury igniting a whirlpool of vengeance she hadn't known rumbled within her. She reached for the pocket of her cloak, but the garb was wrapped in Grae's pack. Oretem's scale resided within to make sure she wouldn't use it again. Evelyn growled in frustration, having to decide who was in most need of her help. Tears fell unbidden down her cheek as she turned her back on Grae, praying to the Breaths and Depths that her friend would hold his own until she could return. Evelyn sped up behind An'gan, increasing her stride as she ran. She was going to need every bit of strength for the terrible idea that came to her.

CHAPTER 46

THE PRICE OF VENGEANCE

Meric forced his shoulder to comply, groaning against the pain of his flesh ripping apart. Anya was beneath An'gan's talons, slashing her blade across his reptile-like claws. Blood fell around her, splattering her face and staining the ground in ruddy red, but the raptor would not concede so easily. The arrow Meric nocked fell from the bow, his fingers shaking too much to pull the string back.

Depths drown me!

He couldn't fight properly, and Anya was about to pay the price for his weakness. He reached for one of the curved blades at the end of his bow and stopped short as he saw a figure from behind the beast leap into the air, brown hair billowing, red eyes streaming tears of blood.

Evelyn landed on the raptor's back, clinging to his faded feathers with white knuckles. An'gan reared, flapping his massive wings, whirling a breeze that threatened to knock him over. Evelyn's body thrashed against An'gan's, his head twisting as he tried to pluck her from his back as he would a stuck feather. Meric feared she'd be tossed into the empty air, falling towards a burning death. He limped forward, gripping Anya by the arm, pulling her from beneath An'gan's scraping talons.

Anya stumbled to her feet beside Meric as Evelyn lifted her

dagger, steel glinting in the foggy air. She gripped a handful of feathers on An'gan's face, dragging the raptor's head towards her dagger. She plunged the steel into his eye, blood pouring as An'gan released a guttural cry. She pulled the dagger free, ichor dripping from the blade and moved to stab down again, but An'gan jerked his wing, slamming Evelyn's head into the back of his. She lost her grip and with a final thrust, was thrown from the raptor's back. Her body crashed against the cliff wall, a mass of rotten roots breaking as she fell. Meric held his breath as Evelyn landed on a collection of roots strong enough to hold her weight. Her arms were cut to ribbons, blood trickling across her skin. She lifted herself, straddling the roots beneath her and met his eyes. Her features were blood stained, sunk, and wearied. Exhaustion passed over her expression with a curved lip which turned into a painful grimace. Her failed attempt to reassure him of her well-being.

Breaths and Depths, she amazes me.

Anya shook her head, yellow eyes transfixed on An'gan, who flew overhead.

"The beast is about as weak as he will ever be," she said, turning the blade over in her hand to throw it. Meric placed a hand over hers, pulling it down.

"You'll be left without a weapon. We must wait for him to come to us."

"You can barely stand," she said taking his arm, steading him as he swayed. His leg screamed against the weight of his body, shoulder throbbing.

He looked ahead to see Grae in the thick of battle with Devu, the scarred woman's features vacant and bored. Anya grew silent beside Meric, a bestial anger rising in her eyes. She released his arm and ran to Grae's side, allowing the heat of her fury to release in flares instead of all at once. She protected Grae where he was vulnerable and blocked the blows that he couldn't reach in time, fighting with him instead of for him.

Meric ignored the rising pain in his leg, feeling blood run down his trousers. He squeezed the handles of his blades, finding comfort in the curve of their hilts. Devu narrowed her hollowed eyes, bored expression turning into one of focus now that she faced three opponents. Grae climbed onto a root and leaped, bringing down his rapier to slice through the Reticent's shoulder. Anya's dagger speared towards Devu's gut, but the woman used her wrist to swipe Anya's attack, crashing her elbow into her cheek while lifting her blade to meet Grae's. The blow was so swift and smooth Meric couldn't help but admire Devu's skill. Blades met, but the blow Grae dealt carried too much weight and the sharp edge of his steel ripped through the fabric of the Reticent's leather, sawing into Devu's shoulder as blood strewed across her neck.

The scars on Devu's face contracted as she grimaced a silent howl. Meric parried behind the Reticent and slashed his curved blade across her back. Devu's tunic opened like a cut grape, splitting and spilling crimson over roots and stone. The woman snarled between clenched teeth and tore herself away from beneath Grae's rapier. The blade only cut deeper into her shoulder as she moved. Meric met the Reticent's falling blade, the pain in his shoulder causing him to bite his lip.

Devu twisted her hands, thumb and forefinger gripping the hilt of Meric's dagger as the rest of her fingers latched themselves onto his wrist. She pulled him forward and rammed her forehead into his face. Something crunched and breath cleared Meric's chest, leaving him gasping. The skin on Devu's forehead split as blood swelled down her cheek, creating a halo around black eyes that were wide with apathy. The assassin raised her blade to skewer Meric through the heart when a small figure glided behind Devu, the assassin's knee buckling beneath her. Retia was crouched by a system of roots, the blade Evelyn had gifted her slick with Devu's blood. The Reticent limped towards the girl; malice raged in her features when the tip of a blade burst through the woman's shoulder. Anya's resentful sneer appeared next to the assassin's head, lips close to her ear.

"Where is he?" she whispered, voice trembling with a combination of anger and desperation. Evidently, she had not resigned herself to Calian's death, and Meric never thought she would.

Devu looked up smiling, teeth stained red. Meric glanced up to see the faded feathers of An'gan diving towards them, bloody talons outstretched, his ruined eye dripping blood. It was far too late to move out of the way. Meric raised his dagger, preparing for the inevitable death that was about to befall him when a gust of wind tore through the air. An'gan screamed as he was tossed to the middle of the lake where Saiya had remained stuck, barred by the constant tempest Sou had conjured. He glanced up at the old man who stood firm high on the cliff wall, Evelyn beside him.

Devu's shoulders shook and a huffing, bubbling sound escaped her lips. He thought the Reticent was choking, but realized that she was laughing. The sound unsettled him more than the assassin's silence. Devu spun, backhanding Anya who collided with Retia, crashing into rotten roots and pools of heated water. The assassin ripped the dagger from her shoulder, letting the blood flow without concern.

What kind of creature is this to feel such pain and endure it?

Anya stood without a weapon, pushing Retia behind her even as the girl glowered through her brows. Anya balled her hands into fists, careening towards Devu, dodging the two blades she now wielded. Grae stood beside Anya, swiping his blade across Devu's. Their steel screeched, joining the cries of the raptors trapped on the lake. Devu fought as though the injuries she sustained were mere bruises, her deadpan expression not revealing a single twitch of pain. Meric moved to help, but his head pounded, and he wondered if his brain wasn't seeping out through his ears.

Grae raised his blade just as the Reticent did, but at the last moment he bent his leg at the knee, his free hand reaching inside his boot. Blades clashed with a thunderous chime over the Venandi's head as he pulled out a small knife, slashing at the Reticent's ankle. The ease at which Grae performed the move brought back memories of his confession, cutting his childhood friend down at the well. Meric saw the agonized recognition in his friend's angry glare. He'd done it before, and he'd perfected its effectiveness.

Devu's expression transformed from indifference to surprise. She crumbled against the cliff wall, looping her arm around a root to keep her steady. There was hardly a woman under all the blood and slashes, her body littered with wounds that would've felled anyone else with a weaker will. Devu's scars stretched across her marred face, trembling against the wall. She panted, sliding down to her knees, hands palms down onto the stone floor. Anya strode over and gripped her white hair in her fist, jerking the assassin's head up to face her. She bent over, her nose mere breadths from hers.

"Where is he?" Anya said again, the corner of her mouth quivering.

The assassin smiled wide, displaying bloody teeth that almost looked like fangs. Retia appeared beside Anya, grey eyes a storm of emotion. Devu spoke, but the sound was garbled, incoherent without a tongue. She glared at the Venandi with a sneer that turned Meric's stomach, as if she had answered Anya's question, knowing she couldn't understand her.

Anya sobbed a heavy breath and picked up the dagger Devu had dropped. She raised it and Grae reached out a hand to stop her. He was too late. A blade pierced through the Reticent's jaw, a small hand holding the bloody hilt. Anya gasped, still holding the dagger in the air, staring at Retia as she twisted her blade, burrowing it deeper into the Devu's flesh until the woman spit up blood. The small girl bared her teeth, releasing a pained wail as she ripped the dagger free with a sick squelch.

The assassin had no expression as she gurgled, spit rippling with suffocated breath, drowning in her own blood. She fell to the floor with nothing to vacate the life in her eyes. As voided as they were when living, they remained so in death, as if she had no soul to travel back to Iona with.

CHAPTER 47

A TERRIBLE COMING TO PASS

From above the world, all Evelyn could see was blood. It covered the ground below in cascading ripples, dripping into random pools of heated water, creating a metallic taste in the air. She was reminded of red snow, flowing and widening as crimson stained the path to her home.

The blood of her enemy dripped from the dagger Retia had pulled from Devu's jaw, but the Reticent's demise left Evelyn hollow. Her previous anger drifted from her, replaced by the sickening emptiness of wasted life, even for one as cruel as Devu. A sense of profound sadness seized Evelyn's heart as she listened to Retia scream. The girl had fallen to her knees, stabbing Devu's dead corpse in the back over and over.

"Bring them back! Bring mama and Isa back!" she cried, blood splattering her face and arms. Grae lifted Retia to her feet, wrapping his arms around the small girl, weeping. She stilled in his embrace, blade still raised, blood-soaked in her grief. Her hand trembled and she dropped the throwing knife, becoming limp in his embrace like she was the one who had died. Raw tears streamed down her face, and she wept like the child she was for the family she had avenged. Evelyn felt sick. She recognized the embrace. This was all vengeance bought, blood and regret.

Sou groaned beside her and as Evelyn met his exhausted

gaze, she was filled with sudden panic. The green in his eyes was darker, lids fluttering, form swaying. His legs gave out from beneath him and if Evelyn hadn't been there to catch him, he'd have fallen headfirst down the cliff. He leaned against her, a tired grin forming across his aged face.

"You've always been so strong, lass," he said, his voice drifting.

Evelyn clutched Sou's arm around her shoulder, realizing her hair was no longer whipping against her face. The air had suddenly grown stagnant, and she looked to where the raptors had once been only to find empty air and mist. Terror ate its way through her body as she looked down at her friends below. Meric turned towards the lake, then back at her with the kind of fear in his eyes that stopped time from progressing. She was stuck in the horror of his expression, reminding her of Alen as he was being eaten by Oretem.

"Evelyn!" Meric screamed, his voice raw with desperation.

She looked up to see faded feathers and an open, dagger-like beak flying towards her with all the speed of a painful death. She reached for the pocket of her cloak, knowing she wasn't wearing it, Oretm's scale far beyond her reach in Grae's pack. Sou gasped and he folded her into a tight embrace.

An'gan screamed and somehow the cry was mournful, an echo of Retia's grief. His talons reached, mere moments from skewering both she and Sou, when an arrow appeared through the raptor's skull. The shaft entered up his jaw, spraying brain matter as the tip ripped through the top of his head, eerily similar to his master. Anya lowered Meric's bow, an arrow missing from the quiver at his back. An'gan's momentum carried him just above them, crashing into the cliff wall with a deafening blast, then sliding and tearing his way to the floor. The cliff trembled, rocks and branches crashing around Evelyn and Sou. An'gan's body fell past them, shattering the roots they stood on. Evelyn dropped and clung to another thick branch, hanging with Sou, feet barely touching a root beneath her. A slew of boulders crashed below, burying the old raptor with Devu's body. Retia was thrust from Grae's grasp, clawing at the floor as she slid toward the cliff's edge. Anya caught the girl's wrist, using Meric's bow she had wedged between a crack in the floor. Meric clung to a root some paces away, his nose bent and bloody, arm bent over his head as rocks smashed around him.

Evelyn looked up and a massive boulder cracked its way towards her, breaking the branch she and Sou held. The root collapsed beneath her, and Evelyn was catapulting to the stone floor, branches and rock tearing her apart as she fell. She tried to grab whatever she could, but she was falling too fast. The palms of her hands tore at the effort it took to avert her descent. Sou grunted beneath her, attempting to do much of the same. Black and grey clouded her vision as her body met the stone surface of the cliff's slanted edge. Breath escaped her body, ribs throbbing against deep forming bruises, but she was still moving. She tumbled and spun, unable to stop, fingers scratching the stone until she found a handhold, blood welling under her nails.

She looked to the cliff's edge and Sou still slid. Evelyn let go, tumbling over the edge, reaching for him. His fingers curl around her wrist, desperate and tight. She flung her hand out in a despairing reach for a root that peeked just over the edge. Her fingers clasped the branch, but she lost her grip as a stone scraped against her face with stinging force. She was falling and there was nothing left to reach for.

A strong hand gripped hers as she swung suspended in the air. Her fingers held firm around Sou's wrist who hung beneath her, vapor swirling around him. Meric's body was half over the cliff's edge, his bloodied shoulder straining to keep the weight of both her and Sou. The dressing was ripped to shreds, unveiling the torn flesh that had split during the fight. How he fought against such miserable pain, Evelyn couldn't know. Meric's eyes were closed tight, teeth bared. He tried to lift her, but the weight of both she and Sou was too much. His limbs trembled with the effort, blood running down his arm.

Anya and Grae were trapped beyond the rocks that had fallen over the dead raptor. They could only watch as Evelyn swung suspended in between two men who had little strength to be of any aid. Grae had an arm wrapped around Anya, who had pulled Retia up, holding her against her chest. Anya's yellow eyes widened, holding up Meric's bow, but realizing she had no arrow to shoot.

"Meric! Pull them up!" Anya screamed, pointing out onto the lake.

Saiya appeared from the fog, her golden eyes manic with a sorrow that looked human. There was nothing to be done. Evelyn could only watch as the raptor flew closer, wings pumping with malicious intent. The water stirred beneath Saiya, bubbling as a whirlpool of spraying water flew into the air, sprouting as if from a geyser. The spear of boiling water hit the young raptor, steaming her flesh as feathers erupted from her body. Saiya screeched in pain as a colossal black mouth broke the boiling surface of Elm Lake. The creature was immeasurable in size, but Evelyn could see its open jaws surpassing its eel-like body that hid beneath the surface. It was sleek, glistening in the mist with steam rising from its hot, oily skin. Evelyn gaped at the incredible beast of legend, confident that they were the creature's next meal.

Saiya beat her wings, but the water had burned off her flight feathers. She fell into the fish's open mouth, disappearing within its black void. The carnivorous beast closed its jaws and threw itself backwards, creating a wave and spraying hot mist onto Evelyn's skin, stinging with heat. The fish disappeared beneath the surface; the only sign of its presence were Saiya's feathers scattering in the wind.

Sou huffed an exhausted chuckle.

"I told you it was real," he said.

Evelyn tightened her grip as the breeze swung them. Meric growled, fingers slipping just a hairs breadth.

"Meric, hold on," Evelyn said, her voice urgent. He grunted in response, unable to form words. Her body drifted lower as Meric's hold onto her weakened. He was trying so hard, but it wasn't going to be enough. Sou loosened his fingers on Evelyn's wrist, letting his palm hang limp. She looked down, her eyes wide with alarm.

"What are you doing?" she said, voice trembling.

No… no. Not Sou.

"It's not your fault, lass. Tell the others it's not theirs either," Sou said, glancing over at Anya and Grae who were throwing rocks aside in their rush to help. Retia stared back, shaking her head, tears falling as though she knew.

"Meric, now! Pull us up *now*! Sou… please. Call upon Iona's Breath. You've the strength." Evelyn heard the desperation in her voice. She lost sense of her surroundings, focusing only on Sou and what he dangled over. She had to stop this.

Not Sou. Breaths and Depths, I beg of you, not Sou!

Meric gritted his teeth, grimacing his pain. He growled Sou's name, pleading. The ferryman lifted a hand, blue wind faint around trembling fingers. The light dissipated and Iona's Breath left Sou as his body sunk further into complete exhaustion.

I am an old man, lass, he had said, and it wasn't until now — when she needed him to be stronger than he'd ever been — was she forced to realize he couldn't be.

"Find your father and your sister. Tell them I did my best. Evelyn… I'm so sorry it's me," Sou's voice was anguished, words strangled in fear and grief.

"I can hold on! Don't let go," she begged, tears running down her cheeks. Had Evelyn the use of her arms she'd demand Iona of her Breath. She'd draw it forth like poison from a wound, forcing it to obey her commands although she knew it would be of no use. She was as powerless as he was. Sou was right. The whole of the world was too large to protect. She only needed to save one. Just one. Why couldn't she save only one? The corners of Sou's green eyes crinkled as he wept, a trembling smile spreading across his kind face.

"I know, lass. But he can't." He nodded to Meric who groaned again in protest, limbs straining, ready to fail at any moment.

"Please... don't—I can hold on. Soup, please!" Evelyn sobbed, vision blurring.

"The finest meal to be, my dearest lass. I'll try not to scream."

With those words, Sou jerked his hand free of her grip, falling without a sound. Evelyn felt something inside her break, ripped from her being as though torn by some unseen hand. It left her gasping, suddenly emptied from what had made life worthwhile. The shattering of a person is no mere pain. It echoes across voids, reaps in the darkness, and lives forever. Evelyn had shattered, the broken pieces of her cutting down every new growth she had cultivated, skewering all she had done to rebuild herself. It was gone, and so was Sou. She reached out for him, but he had sunk into the water, his face a mask of terrible pain. She howled his name as she was pulled up, solid ground beneath her.

Something resonated across the lake—screaming. Excruciating, torturous screaming. Evelyn covered her ears, trying to drown out Sou's cries of pain. She was being held, her body crushed against a familiar warmth. Meric's body shook, whether from pain or grief she couldn't tell. Within the depths of her shattering, Sou's screams stopped. His silence was louder than his death and Evelyn wailed, trapped in the emptiness he'd left behind.

CHAPTER 48

THE KINDEST OF PEOPLE

Meric's feet dragged through the streets of Birny, limbs sore and downtrodden in more ways than what was physical. It had been four days since Sou's death. He recalled the slow ascent from Elm Lake, reaching the surface to see green pastures covering the flat land, clustered with willow trees that had left the Eshe as seedlings, finding ground to grow far from the main forest. The Rya flowed next to them, calm and serene. Nothing like the violence it exhibited below. The beauty of the landscape was lost to him, the joy of surfacing nonexistent. They'd been so close to making it out together. Sou had been so close. The guilt crushed Meric, bending and twisting his insides as sharply as a knife, eviscerating the light Sou once lit within him. He kept telling himself he could've done it. That had Sou held on just a moment longer, he would be here with them in Birny now. But he knew the words to be bitter and false. If Sou hadn't let go when he did, Meric would've dropped them both and if Grae hadn't broken through the wall of stones separating them, he'd have dropped Evelyn as well. He cursed his weakness and the darkness it brought upon them. Evelyn had hardly spoken a word since, vacant eyes staring into nothing.

Meric wondered where the voices of their dead loved ones were in their hour of need. The voice Evelyn heard in her mountains had never made another appearance. He remembered the faint tune of a voice singing to him when he woke after his capture. He attributed it to his subconscious rousing him to wake but in the days since Sou's death, he wondered. He recalled the flash of a fading blue light, wisps of smoke-like tendrils dissipating from his blurred vision. Had it been real? Why hadn't the voice helped? He felt the burn of anger rise in him. He let it simmer, then smothered it as he continued forward, passing the townsfolk that stared with curious but cautious eyes.

Traveling to Birny was only meant to be a two-day trek, but the emotional weight of Sou's demise combined with the injuries they'd sustained gave them the speed of a broken anchor, pulling them under without the relief of oblivion. Meric recalled once saying that there weren't good people in the world, that there never were. He was wrong then, but now... in the absence of Sou's light, the days were longer and somehow diminished in what had once made them bright.

Anya remained as stoic as she could, but she always woke in the morning with red, tear brimmed eyes, as if her unconscious allowed her to express the grief she barred herself from when awake. He knew she blamed herself the same as he did. She had torn the bow from his grip and felled An'gan, her aim impeccable and true. He remembered the look of utter despair in her eyes as she realized the consequences of her actions. She'd saved Evelyn and Sou only to condemn them again. Meric hadn't tried to convince her of her faultlessness, just as she hadn't tried to persuade him. They both knew they'd never believe the other.

Grae was a rock, immovable and stubborn. When they surfaced the cliffs, he went to wash the blood from his hands in the river, spending an unnecessary amount of time scrubbing his hands until they puckered with blisters. Only then, as he scrubbed his blisters open, had he wept and hadn't shed a single tear since. Despite being so young, Retia was a child no longer. The girl's features had hardened, her strength carrying the rest of the company. Regardless of the wounds in her back reopening, she refused to be carried. She continued to practice her blade skills, and often offered to take a watch. They'd refused, but it didn't stop her from staying up anyway. On a night Meric had kept watch he noticed Retia up with him, wiping away a tear from Anya's face as she slept. The girl watched over the woman, often looking out over the Rya with grey eyes devoid of whatever happiness she had hoped to gain in killing Devu. She wasn't broken by it, but it seemed that the act hadn't mended what was broken to begin with.

Evelyn had separated herself from sleeping with the rest of the group, keeping her back to them as she laid awake. Meric had noticed the deepening bags under her ruby eyes growing darker with each passing day. On the second night he settled behind her and wrapped his arm around her. She felt strong, hard muscles taut from the physical toll of their trek, but he knew that meant nothing. He feared she'd toss him aside, scream and shout of his failure, but she hadn't pulled away. Instead, he heard for the first time the soft breath of her slumber. It wasn't for long and she always woke much sooner than the rest of them, but it was better than before. If it was of any comfort to her, she wouldn't speak of it. So, he continued to hold her at night, listening to her fight sleep only to succumb with the restful rise and fall of her chest.

Evelyn walked beside him now, cloaked within her dark green hood, features gaunt from exhaustion. Grae and Anya trailed ahead with Retia in between them, making a path through the small crowd of people in the road.

Birny rested on the edge the Rya, giving the town a fishing and swamp-like appearance. Small sailing vessels rested against the sides of the meager homes, wood made and carved with expert skill. The buildings consisted mostly of stone and willow as the Eshe Willow Wood was only a few thousand paces from the town. He could smell the blooming flowers that the forest was famous for. People traveling the road alongside them wore reed caps and leather gloves, carrying fishing poles, nets, and gutting tools. Butcher shops lined the street, gliding with the smell of dead river creatures. Anya and Grae stopped on the side of the road, glancing in between the village folk that paid them wary glances.

"Did Sou tell you where your family lived?" Anya said, her voice trembling against the Vagu's name. Evelyn's throat tightened, forcing herself to speak.

"He told me of an inn. The Mire, he called it." The pain in Evelyn's voice was still raw and Meric ached to take it from her.

"We are travelers. It shouldn't be too much to ask for directions to the inn," Grae said, turning towards a group of people who took one look at his silver earring and ventured to the opposite side of the street. Anya sighed, bringing a hand to her own ear, fingers grazing the silver chain.

"We'll have to find it on our own. Retia, you'll come with Grae and I. Try to look as innocent as you can," Anya said as the girl's brows furrowed in annoyance. "Evelyn, go with Meric. Keep your hood up."

Evelyn's sunken eyes were darkened under her hood, giving her a sickly appearance. Meric understood Anya's goal was for the townspeople to take pity on the people traveling with Venandi, not the Venandi themselves. Evelyn told them the names of her father and sister, and they parted ways. Meric conversed with a butcher, fisherman, and a local brewer but either they didn't know Era and Ranvir or the cautious looks they'd given his earring was their way of staying out of Venandi business. Evelyn's presence did nothing to soften the hearts of those they spoke with.

"I could take the earring off, but too many have seen it already. I'm sure word has spread. We might have to wander until we see the inn," he said, fingers pulling against his ear.

"I don't mind wandering," Evelyn said, her voice stronger. "This place... it's like walking in a dream."

"You recognize it?" Meric said, confused. He had thought Verbena was her place of birth.

"Sou and my mother brought me to Verbena when I was a child. I was born here. It's more familiar than recognizable. Like a song I'd forgotten the words to."

Evelyn's demeanor had changed. She was still weighed by the loss of Sou, but being in a place that felt familiar to her had brought some color back into her features. She wiped strands of hair from her forehead and glanced at a home across from them. Its roof was badly patched, wooden pillars splintered with age. An old woman sat in a chair, staring at Evelyn as though she'd seen an old friend. The woman pointed at her, turning her hand inward, beckoning. Meric exchanged a puzzled glance with Evelyn, and they made their way to where the old woman sat.

She wore a faded green dress hanging over her thin body without much shape to the garment. Her hands peeked through the sleeves like frightened turtles. A sharp nose complimented her high cheekbones, wrinkles adorning the corners of her dark eyes as she flashed a wide smile. It was a pleasant smile that brought out the beauty the woman surely was in her youth.

"Nakesha, you promised me those tomatoes in your garden some time ago. I haven't forgotten," the old woman said, wagging her finger in the air.

Meric glanced at Evelyn, whose red eyes showed not the slightest twitch at the mention of her mother's name. She met Meric's gaze, swallowing then crouching next to the woman. Her lips curved into a grin he hadn't seen in days.

"I'm waiting for them to ripen. I only wish to give you the best," she said, patting the old woman's hand.

"Oh, you said that last week. Could you send Dorion back when you've returned home? I know he and Eve have such fun together, but I'm making supper and we have a long day of fishing in the morning." The old woman's voice creaked, her demeanor cheerful, but there was something missing. A certain awareness that she seemed to lack about her surroundings.

569

"Of course. As soon as I can track down Ranvir and Era. Do you happen to know where they are?"

The woman brows creased, and she chuckled.

"Well, my friend, I don't see how they could be anywhere else but Mire Inn. Dinner is still being served, is it not? I'm sure you just missed them in the kitchen." The old woman leaned back into her chair, blissfully unaware that it was morning. Evelyn opened her mouth to speak again when a figure opened the door, standing at the threshold of the home.

The man was probably the same age as Grae, his ocean-colored eyes matching the old woman in all the familiarity of a son. His auburn hair corkscrewed atop a narrow face, bronzed and clean shaven. His eyes met Evelyn's with the slightest wave of familiarity but discarded as he turned to the old woman.

"Louve, are these people bothering you?" he said, casting a wary eye where Meric's earring hung.

"Dorion," Louve said with exasperation. "Be polite to Nakesha. She's been kind enough to share the growings of her garden in exchange for your services in watching little Evelyn, show some respect."

Dorion sighed, his shoulders drooping as though he'd had this conversation before. He glanced back between Evelyn and Meric, but with a more apologetic demeanor. Evelyn stood still, her face showing no thought to her name being so casually mentioned.

"I've made breakfast, come inside," Dorion said.

"Breakfast, at this hour?" Louve looked into the sky as she stood.

"It's morning, Louve. Don't worry, it'll come back," he said with a kindness that masked the disbelief his tone suggested. The old woman looked back at Evelyn and Meric, her eyes searching for the recognition that was so present only a moment ago. She touched her temple with confusion then slipped through the door, Dorian watching her go.

"I apologize for my mother. She isn't well. I hope she didn't disturb your routine." His voice was considerate, but prying.

"You do look strikingly similar to an old friend of hers. I don't believe we've met. I'm Dorion," he said, extending his arm, palm up towards the sky.

It seemed a curious way for a handshake, but Evelyn only paused a moment, ruby eyes gleaming with understanding. She reached out her own arm, passing her hand over Dorion's until resting it at the base of his elbow, clasping it tightly in the way Meric had never seen before.

Dorion squinted and inclined his head, expression resigned.

"You've been here before. I thought with the eyes…" he trailed off, studying Evelyn's red irises. He squeezed her arm once, then released her. "Ah, no matter. You can always tell when an outsider has come to Birny. They'll usually try to shake my hand." He waved his fingers in the air.

"It's been a long time. I forgot that I knew," she said, her voice soft. "Can you direct us to Mire Inn? We've had a long journey."

"Follow this road until you hear the tall tales of old river folk and can no longer smell fish entrails. There'll be a sign on your right, ask for Ranvir. He'll set you up with a warm bed and Era will make sure you get plenty to eat. I'd direct you myself but," Dorion cocked his head towards the house, still looking over Evelyn as if trying to connect a thought with a memory.

"Please, I wouldn't inconvenience you. You've been most helpful." Evelyn turned and gestured for Meric to follow her as she stepped from the threshold.

"This is a peaceful town, sir," Dorion called out. Meric turned around to see the young man leaning a muscled arm on a pillar, gaze fixed on him. "You'll find the kindest of people and little work if that's what you're here for."

It was apparent Dorion had listened to stories of the Venandi and hadn't liked what he'd heard. Meric didn't believe the man was violent, but he was sure Dorion would let everyone know exactly who was lodging at Mire Inn. Meric inclined his head in a slight bow.

"I've not much experience with the kindest of people, as you put it. If our meeting is an indication of that kindness then look forward to the peace," Meric said, watching Dorion's features relax as he pushed himself off the pillar and returned inside the house.

Meric followed Evelyn on the road—wincing against the sharp pain of his healing leg—until, to his surprise, the smell of decaying fish had faded and the sounds of men exchanging fishing tales grew loud from within a tall building. It was several stories high and kept up with freshly sapped wood. A sign swung above him, its hinges creaking, bold lettering reflecting the morning light. The sweet smell of ale traveled across the air, but it glided through the senses instead of forcing its way. Evelyn stared at the open door where figures of laughing villagers and candlelight beckoned a welcoming atmosphere, where even children's shrieking could be heard inside.

There was no way to conceive the anticipation of meeting loved ones thought to be dead. The line between curses and blessings were interchangeable and Meric wondered which one Evelyn thought she'd been bestowed. Questions of her family's potential refusal to accept her, her worthiness to return, their inability to recognize her and so many others were probably raging in her head like a captured vapor serpent, spiting hot poisonous thoughts.

He'd seen fear in her before; it was always in place for the well-being of another. She never thought of her own needs and for the first time, he was seeing genuine fright within those bright eyes. He grazed his fingers against hers, feeling a tremble course through them. She started, looking up at him as though she had forgotten his presence. He reached up, running the back of his hand across her cheek, her skin warm and smooth. There were no words he could speak to comfort her, so he thought instead, as he'd done when he wiped Retia's blood from her hands.

Fear offers the opportunity for strength. Embrace it for its encouragement.

He thought back on what Sou had spoken to them when all was well, and the stars lit the sky with promise. Even beyond the grave, Sou was ever present in their lives. A small breeze tousled Evelyn's hair and she squeezed his hand. Her anxiety was palpable, but no longer debilitating. Together they stepped inside Mire Inn.

CHAPTER 49

TO BE INFINITE

The differences between Decorum and Mire Inn could not be more apparent if the establishments were neighbors. The Mire's pristine, dark willow floors shone with cleanliness that the brothel had sorely lacked. Across the ceiling were chandeliers of unlit torches, iron railings casting shadows from three open windows that poured light into the mess hall. Families gathered with their children, eating clam soup and various river fish mixed with grown vegetables of carrots and hardy potatoes. The smell was incredible, drifting up Evelyn's nose with seductive gentility. She had the sudden realization that she hadn't eaten much the last four days.

Her stomach ached in a way she had never felt, ribs threatening to tear through her skin as her belly screamed for sustenance. She stared at a table where a woman was holding a small boy, only a few years into life. She dipped her spoon into a bowl of fish stew and placed the steaming, chunky liquid into her mouth. She chewed then placed her forefinger and thumb against her lips, spitting out a small piece of mushy fish, placing it in the toddler's eager open mouth. It was a simple sight, one that for some reason reminded her of Sou. He and Lyn had built this place and she could feel his essence in the fabric of the wood beneath her feet.

"Good morning," a high-pitched voice exclaimed.

Evelyn turned her head and looked down at a young boy around ten years, wearing a black apron smudged with whatever he'd been chopping in the kitchen. His light brown hair fell about his shoulders, wavy with youth as his sea blue eyes blinked, awaiting her response.

"Good morning," she said smiling, the act unfamiliar and oppressed with guilt. How could she smile in a world without Sou?

"Welcome to the Mire Inn. Are you in need of a room? Oh wait," he snapped his fingers. "I'm supposed to ask if you'd like a meal first. Are you hungry?"

The boy bounced up and down on the balls of his feet, waiting for a response. Meric grunted behind her and reached into his pocket for a silver piece. He placed it in the boy's hand and gestured to a table in the corner.

"Starving. We'll be sitting there when the food is ready," Meric said, talking to the boy as though he were grown.

The boy smiled, revealing a large gap between his bottom teeth, white peeking from the gums. He fingered the silver in his small hand, grinning all the while.

"Thank you, sir! We have a menu. Shall I fetch it?"

"No need," Meric said, softening his voice. "Bring us what your favorite meal is. You have the look of someone who knows the taste of excellent food."

The boy bounced once more and raced to the end of the room where he disappeared behind a door. It swung open momentarily, revealing a group of three or four people toiling at various hearths, skinning fish and stirring pots.

Evelyn made her way to the table, sitting on the sturdy bench. At the end of the table was a large conch spiraled with sand-colored ridges and white spots. Inside the shell were three white flowers, the petals dripping down as though they were meant to grow towards the earth. Evelyn held her breath, recognizing the shape of the flower, its petals mirroring the ones she had dreamt of so long ago. When Tansey was alive, and the world was simple. She reached out her hand and with her finger traced the curve of the petal, its soft surface as alive as her own skin.

Meric sat next to her, his arm brushing against hers. She lowered her hand and looked at him, watching his eyes travel throughout the room, alert and conditioned to watch for trouble. The corners of her mouth turned involuntarily as he glanced at her.

"What?" Meric said, hazel eyes gleaming.

"That was kind of you," she said, interlocking her fingers on the table.

"What was?"

"What you said to the boy. I don't think he's been asked his favorite meal before. He seemed quite excited." Evelyn's grin widened as Meric shrugged, his confusion amusing.

"Would you have rather me demand my order from the tip of my arrow? Behave like a typical Venandi?"

She sighed, imagining the spectacle that would've caused.

"I'm not sure that would've made for a good first impression. I'm grateful for your restraint," she said, squeezing his hand. Meric grinned, returning his gaze back to the inn's many occupants.

"Do you suppose she works here, your sister?" he said.

When the kitchen door had opened, there was not enough time to search the faces of those within. Dorion had mentioned to ask Era for a hot meal, so she was probably one of the cooks.

"I think so. We can ask the boy once he returns," she said, noticing two figures walking in, their Venandi earrings glimmering in the sunlight. Meric waved Anya and Grae over, Retia following close behind. The three sat across from them, eyes swimming with hunger.

"Have you ordered already?" Grae said, glancing at the hot meals being carried down the aisles.

"Yes, but only for the two of us. When the food comes you may order. I gave him coin enough for all of us," Meric said. Grae frowned at having to wait while Anya drummed her fingers on the table.

"How did you find the place?" Evelyn said, curious as to their meeting up.

"I told an especially stout man that Retia's father was Ranvir. He was quite insistent that I must be mistaken but, after some colorful descriptions, I managed to convince him. He told me I could find him here." Her voice was melodic as though she were singing the song of a great legendary tale. Evelyn gaped and looked at Retia, who glared at the Venandi.

"You did not tell me that was the plan," the girl said, crossing her arms.

"I did not need to. I said, look as innocent as possible, and you did. Now you get a hot meal," Anya said, as though it were a reasonable exchange.

"Anya," Evelyn said through her teeth. "Why would you say such a thing? This is a small village, that sort of story will be told to everyone by nightfall and it's not fair to Retia."

"This place could use a little gossip and Retia is fine." Anya glance at the girl who continued to scowl. "Oh, don't look at me like that. You can take your vengeance when we spar this evening. So, until then, frown at something else."

Retia huffed and looked away, staring at a bowl of soup at another table. Evelyn kept Anya's eyes; she wasn't a child for the woman to berate.

"Very well," Anya said, sighing. "I'll confess my sins once we find your father. Celosia's Depths drown us all if I have a little fun." She scoffed in annoyance, leaning on the back of the bench, her gaze shifting back to a blank stare of thought.

"Perhaps a less severe rumor would've been more appropriate, but I admit would be far less humorous," Evelyn said, wanting to lessen the severity of her response. Anya returned her gaze with a mischievous grin, pulling away the dark thoughts that had threatened to overtake her.

"Did this *stout* man say anything else?" Evelyn turned to Grae whose jaw hung loose, staring at the adjacent table's steaming buttered bread.

"All we know is that Ranvir and Era work here, no one else seemed to want to speak with us. Which is to be expected.

It's a small town, I'm sure they've heard stories," Grae said, still focused on the food.

Meric nodded beside Evelyn, most likely thinking back on Dorion's wary comments.

"They seem friendly enough. Just don't start a brawl," Meric said, shifting his accusatory gaze to Anya, who was biting her fingertips. She shrugged and spat a piece of her nail across the table. It bounced off the wood, disappearing somewhere on the floor. Retia flinched, looking at Anya with disgust.

"We can take you nowhere, can we?" Evelyn said, shaking her head. Anya beat her hands against the table, pumping to an unknown tune. Grief manifested itself in a variety of ways and Anya was only trying to suppress hers. The Venandi's overtly gleeful demeanor was masking a deep sorrow that Evelyn supposed was better than sinking in it as she was.

The blue-eyed boy appeared from Grae's side, his small hands balancing two bowls on a wide wooden plate with expert precision. He placed the bowls in the center of the table, wisps of steam rising from the hot meal. The bowls contained white fish meat, glistening in broth with a variety of herbs Evelyn had no names for. Floating at the top were onions and leeks, small bits of potato and a large boiled egg.

"It's the egg that makes it the best. It can't be boiled for too long. I like it to ooze. No one else does that but me," the boy said proudly, lifting his chest. He looked over Anya and Grae, eyes lingering on Retia. "Welcome to Mire Inn. Would you like a menu?"

"I'll have that," Retia said, grabbing the bowl and shoving a large piece of fish into her mouth. Grae nodded, his mouth open as he gripped the second bowl before Anya could.

"Yes, please. More of this," Anya said, scowling at Grae.

The boy inclined his head, perplexed by the situation. Evelyn exchanged an irritated glance with Meric as their meals were ravenously stolen from them. Grae leaned over the table, looking at Retia's bowl.

"Does yours have garlic? I haven't had garlic in—Oy, wait for your own!" Grae said as Anya dipped her hand into the stew, stealing a piece of potato. She laughed as she chewed, fingers dripping as she continued to take more from his bowl. The frown he flashed was almost lost in his endeavor to place as much stew in his mouth as possible.

The boy pushed hair from his face, smiling in appreciation. He clutched the wooden plate to his chest, showcasing the gap in his teeth.

"I'll be back with three more bowls," he said with excitement. Evelyn reached out her hand before he could scamper away.

"Just a moment. Do you know Era? May we speak with her?" she said, trying to still her trembling.

The boy looked in between them, his smile disappearing into one of trepidation. He fingered the plate in his hand nervously as though he'd been caught stealing.

"Is it the egg? I didn't tell ma to put the egg in the stew. I did that. I can bring you one without it if you'd like. You won't tell her, will you? She doesn't like it when I tinker with the flavors." He peered at her through worried brows, emitting an innocence that made her heart ache.

Whatever Evelyn had planned to say next was caught in her throat. She would've never known. There was nothing in the boy that was familiar to her. She beheld the shape of his eyes, the curve of his lips and the build of his physique. Nothing. There was nothing she could recognize, and it broke her heart to realize that had he not said anything, she would've never known he was her nephew. She tried to speak, but her lips refused to move. She could feel the tears forming, an apprehensive confusion shifting over the boy's expression.

"Of course we won't. We only want to thank her for her hospitality," Grae said, his mouth half-full of stew, looking at Evelyn with a quiet concern.

"She's quite busy at the moment, but I can fetch my grandfather. He's the innkeeper and will tell my ma of your gratitude," the boy said, the tension rising from his small shoulders. Evelyn looked about the inn with new eyes, taking in the grandeur and simplicity of its hospitable ambiance. Her father had maintained the inn all these years.

"That will do," Meric said, squeezing Evelyn's hand under the table.

The boy turned his heel and began to walk away when Evelyn suddenly found her voice.

"What is your name?" she said, louder than she had intended.

"Kaleb, ma'am," he said with a slight bow of his head.

"Thank you, Kaleb."

The boy gave another toothless grin, his bird-like feet pattering back towards the kitchen. Anya leaned over the table, wiping her mouth of broth.

"You're here and that's all Sou ever wanted," she said, her voice calm with sympathy.

Evelyn stared into her tattooed eyes, gathering her strength for the moment she'd hardly thought of since leaving Verbena. So much had happened, so much had changed. The woman who danced around the burning fire of an Oathbearing celebration was a far distant woman, unrecognizable. How could she expect her father to know her when she didn't even know herself?

There was a sudden clatter of metal against wood beside her, echoing through the room loud enough to silence the crowd within the inn. Evelyn turned towards the sound to see a man standing before her, bowls of stew splattered and cracked across the floor. The man paid them no mind. His black hair, peppered with grey, grew to his temples, matching his thick slanted brows, and green eyes wide with astonishment. His full lips matched her own, lined with wrinkles that spoke to years of laughter and surrounded by a thin black and grey beard. He wore the same dark apron Kaleb donned, but it was far cleaner than the young boy's. His form was strong and lean, as though he spent his days in a constant state of movement.

She met his eyes, her gaze searching his, finding the familiarity she couldn't in Kaleb. This man was her father. She could see it, feel it in her bones. Words escaped her again, chest tightening against everything that was left unsaid. She'd come so far just to see this man's face. Endured so much to find a place to belong. Would he deny her? Had he forgotten her? She stood, her head a foot shorter than his. She gulped. Her throat was dry as though she'd been screaming for hours on end. She blocked out the thoughts of the room, ignoring all the tendrils of light surrounding them.

Ranvir tilted his head, shoulders slumping as though drained of strength. He blinked tears and gasped, taking in his first breath since he'd laid eyes on her.

"Eve. You're a woman," he said, his voice breaking as he collapsed into sobs reaching out for her. She fell apart in his arms, fragmenting all her fears and laying them to waste upon the floor with the cracked bowls of stew. Had she bones to keep her standing? She felt sunken, flattened by her anxiety that melted away as Ranvir whispered her name.

He knew her. He knew her the moment he saw her, and she could feel his unconditional love as his tears fell upon her head. She cried against his chest, burying her face into the crook of his neck, feeling the warmth of his parental embrace. There was no passing of time as she was held. She was infinite in the love of a father. He released her, holding her at arm's length, looking over her features with a tear-streaked smile. Ranvir cupped her cheek, wiping a rogue tear from her jaw.

"How long I have waited for you to come home," he said, his deep voice thick with joy.

Home. The word cradled her heart, lulling it with the safety of refuge. She sniffed and smiled at how impossibly happy she was. Ranvir glanced at the Venandi, who had stood from their seats. Retia remained sitting, eating her stew as she watched.

"I would know your names at my table tonight. Thank you for bringing her home," Ravir said, holding out his hand palm up. Anya and Grae stared at his hand, confused by the gesture, but Meric took her father's arm in the Birny way, shaking his head.

"We merely guided the way," Meric said, with Grae and Anya nodding their agreement. Ranvir looked over their faces as though searching for someone. He turned his head, checking the surrounding tables, then shifted his gaze back to Evelyn.

"I suppose Sou grew impatient for my arrival and left to look for me?" his voice lifted with excited humor. "Perhaps he found Kaleb in the kitchen, he hasn't met him yet. I'm sure he's thrilled at the prospect of gaining *great* status for his current grandfather title."

And just like that, Evelyn's world corroded, tainted in a new darkness that overshadowed all the joy she had felt.

"Grandfather?" she whispered.

"Is he still Soup to you? He always loved that. He would insist upon the nickname when your mother tried to correct you. *It's a fine meal to be,* he'd say," Ranvir said, chuckling.

Evelyn's legs went numb, and she wondered how she was still standing. Ranvir's smile turned into a concerned frown, eyes searching for the bright daughter he saw only a moment ago. That woman was an illusion, a façade to cover the truth of who she'd become.

"Eve, my father—where is he?" Ranvir said, a rising dread in his voice. Meric strode over to Evelyn's side, placing a comforting hand on her shoulder. She shrugged him off, angry grief overtaking her sorrow.

No. Enough! Where does sadness go when there is nowhere left for it to live? I'm spent. It is eating me alive.

She could feel it threatening to erupt, ensuring her death. She straightened her stance, breathing heavily against the weight of the words that were about to pass through her lips.

"He never told me. I didn't—" Evelyn's voice broke, the words ripping her apart as they escaped. "I didn't know."

Ranvir backed away, staring at her in disbelief. His expression one of fury, angry tears brimming the green in his eyes.

"What has that old Depths-damned fool done now?" Ranvir's voice was almost a growl.

Evelyn met with each of the Venandi's expressions, their features marred with confusion and pity, as if they'd known all along. How could they know and not she? Grae stepped forward lifting his arm as if to embrace her, but he thought better of it and stepped back.

"We just assumed..." Grae said, glancing at Ranvir whose features remained fixed on Evelyn.

Everything had suddenly snapped into place. The moments when Sou said nothing, held back by an unseen force, unwilling to say what he longed to. She recalled his attentiveness and protective nature, the pain in his eyes when she had told him he was a stranger to her. How could she have not seen it?

"Come. All of you," Ranvir said, his voice severe. Retia stood from her seat, walking next to Grae. Ranvir turned back, glancing at the small girl, then to Grae, his mouth a hard line.

"I can place the girl in the kitchens while we speak. She need not be present for any unpleasant talk." Ranvir's voice softened somewhat, and Retia clasped her hand in Grae's.

"I am no stranger to unpleasantness. I go where they do," Retia said, and Ranvir's brows knit together.

"Very well. This way."

Ranvir led them across the mess hall and up a staircase, ushering them inside a small room where a simple desk stood in the corner. Scrolls of paper spread across the desk, quills and splattered ink staining the wood. Ranvir turned, leaning on the desk with arms folded. His expression was stern, but the green in his eyes reflected a sad compassion she knew all too well.

"Tell me all that's happened," Ranvir said, a tremor lining the words.

Evelyn's eyes burned, feeling the weight of Oretem's scale resting in the pouch of her cloak. She looked inward, recalling all she'd been though and everyone she had lost. She felt the presence of Retia, Meric, Anya, and Grae behind her, the suffocating oppression of their own losses. She was not alone. Not anymore. She would not lose herself to the anguish of grief that fought so hard to destroy her. The blackness shifted in her mind's eye, reflecting oiled figures that blinked with blue eyes, brown eyes... green eyes. Her anger dissipated; grief quenched as she stared down the blackness of her suffering.

Hello, old friend. Let us battle.

CHAPTER 50

THE CHOICE TO BURN

Maun was in the belly of the beast, heaving and spitting up blood. His fingers stretched and contorted as he closed his eyes against the intense heat that had plagued him for weeks. Had it been weeks or days? Saiya was still alive under the boiling lake, her body broken and burnt, slowly dying in the stomach of the lake creature that had swallowed her whole. He could feel everything that was happening to her, the decay of her flesh as the creatures' stomach acid burned her remaining feathers, bones peeking from melted skin.

She was too weak to writhe and so, laid still in her agony. Maun never left her, no matter how intense the pain. He wouldn't allow her to be alone in so dark a place. She was comforted by his presence, but often forgot he was there, opening her beak in a weak cry as more of her withered away. Maun felt the wall of the cave closing in around him, Oretem's hot breath swirling as he entered his thoughts. The dragon's mind sympathized with Maun, knowing the pain of sharing a partner's slow death. Maun wanted no sympathy. He coveted anger—earth-shattering anger. He beat at the dragon's mind until his compassion withdrew to a more sinister disposition, a fire stoking in Oretem to accompany the madness that was ever present.

Maun's breath shortened, giving way to emptiness. It was so dark. He couldn't see anything as he lifted his head, wheezing for fresh air that would never come. He was alone in the dark and then he was thrust into it. The world exploded into blackness where a great nothing consumed all.

Maun returned to his body with the violence of a beating. His body trembled from the aftereffects of experiencing Saiya's last breath. She had died having felt alone. He curled his hands into fists, fingernails digging into his palms. Oretem growled, his graveled tone filling the cave. The roots overhead shook with the force.

What have I left but my vengeance? This world has taken all else from me.

Devu claimed the Reticent had no need for vengeance. Perhaps that was once true, but no longer. It was all Maun had now. Devu and An'gan rotted beneath stone, entombed within the bowels of Elm Lake. All of Maun's life, Devu had been there. She watched as Eli's throat was split open, lifted him from the pool of Ovia's blood. She trained him, berated him, fed him, made him into the man he was now. Devu was his constant, and now she was gone. He'd been so angry with her. Where was that anger now? He was no longer Reticent, but neither was he Calian. He was born anew, crushed by all the emotions he'd been taught to suppress. This worthless world was full of hate and pain, endless sorrow, and the bleak emptiness of solitude.

IN THE END, EVERYONE DIES ALONE. Oretem's voice filled his mind, and suddenly Saiya's absence was too much to bear.

Evelyn's and Meric's faces appeared before him, their companions staring at him through the haze of his grief. He would kill them all. Their cries would be heard across Iona. He would stain the dirt with their blood, cursing the ground they died on. He wouldn't stop until he felt the earth bleed.

Oretem's anger grew, but this time Maun didn't sate it. He let it rise, soaring over him like wildfire. He could feel the flames in his veins, coursing through his body, burning, scouring everything he used to be. He had begun as an ember, glowing with nothing more than a name. One single name that became two, then five and now names didn't matter. He still didn't matter. Saiya was gone. Left inside the black belly of a lake beast to crumble and digest, and become more food for passing water creatures to eat the beast's waste. Devu was gone. His mother was gone.

Everyone was *gone*.

He lifted his head to the ceiling, fire becoming his sky as Oretem threw open his jaws, releasing flames across the canopy of roots. Maun screamed, his tongueless mouth bellowing a despair that shook the cave walls. Oretem roared, rocks crumbling, ears ringing. Maun almost believed he was the one tearing the boulders away, raking his claws through stone — bringing down a mountain. The crushing sound of the cave collapsing paled in comparison to the rage that Oretem unveiled. His jaws snapped; teeth bared into a vicious snarl. The mountain quaked under the madness of the dragon, encircling Maun with light as boulders fell around him.

The cold sizzled against the burning stone, releasing steam as snow fell among the ashes of burnt roots. Frost settled across the Oretem's great body, melting under his heat, red scales glistening in the white backdrop of a frozen wasteland. Rocks the size of homes tumbled down the side of the mountain, tearing and ripping apart stone that hadn't been touched in centuries.

A shadow loomed over Maun's head, and he arched his neck as Oretem's wing unfurled above him, turning the sky into the color of blood, adorned with scars and veins. The beast stretched his neck, crimson eyes wide with derangement. Maun felt as if his chest would explode from the magnitude of Oretem's insanity, but it mirrored his own, making what he'd lost bearable. Maun looked ahead at the peaceful landscape of the snow-covered horizon. The sun peeked over the desert frost, coloring the ice in red and yellow. He was above it all and he hated the sight of it. Oretem roared, shaking the settled snow as his voice echoed through Maun's mind.

BURN... The dragon's graveled, bestial voice reverberated

within every living thing, silencing the entire mountain. Maun fingered Celosia's Glare in his pocket, relishing in the freedom of control. Or rather, the loss of it.

He stared at the rising sun, knowing he had its power. Vengeance would be his on the world that had done nothing but break him. Eli's dead eyes stared through him, Ovia's shattered face crumpling before him. Both women combined to become one awful memory of what he'd been too weak to prevent. For as long as he could remember Maun woke with the expectation of violence. Pain and blood were all he knew; love and hate were interchangeable. The choice was never his and today, he would be free of it all. Today, he imagined a world on fire, soaring through the ashes on dragon back.

Today, he chose to burn.

Postlude

REACH. HOLD. EMBRACE.

20 YEARS AGO...

The mantra of Isla's final thought chimed in her head like the far distant sound of rain. It echoed through the ages, her everlasting companion, whispering the impossible.

Reach. Hold. Embrace.

It was impossible. She held the world and the world fought against her, thrashing towards the end of all things. She could feel it, the battle surrounding her. She felt the heat of dragon fire grazing her leaves that never fell. The rumble of ships reverberated through the boiled heat of her sister's wrath. The sister she loved, the sister who betrayed her.

Isla had no eyes other than the ones she already possessed, closed, resting. There was nothing to see inside her elm — inside herself. If she opened her eyes, she'd only see what had been left behind. What *he* had left behind. His name was Omya, and he was beautiful. She could still see his face, eyes a window into the sky.

Memory is an affliction, diseased with heartache and sudden gales of violent loneliness.

She was ever swept out of reach, kept below water without the mercy of drowning. Omya's absence was a breath denied. But it was her sister Isla felt the most within the deepest throes of her sadness, burning beneath her. She recalled a time when she cherished that warmth, a mountain of fire turned to flesh when they'd emerged from the sea, embraced as they had never been before. Isla tried to curl her fingers into fists, but her fingers had grown, far to the edges of the Solov Waste. She could remember making the sand, how Celosia had lifted it from the sea and how she had dragged it back in her wrath.

Isla lifted her head, the movement awkward within the complex growth of branches stretching from her mortal form. How long had it been since she had a true thought? Too long. This world of flame and blood was not what she'd created. These were not the people she had ached to walk among. She could feel him. Om's blue irises staring at her through close lids, pleading with her to save them. How could she? She hadn't been able to save him. He had already descended, drowning in earth, crying out her name. She still could hear him. The storm thundered through the sky, swirling through her branches, whispering from his unmade grave.

Gone, my love. I have gone.

He spoke. After all this time... he spoke. Her roots rolled, twisting through the gaps of stone and dirt in the farthest reaches of the land. Isla felt the life above her, the souls of those she held. She knew every drop of blood spilt in the boiling lake, absorbed through the rough bark of her skin. The battle raged, the dead and dying sinking to where her sister laid. She felt hands curling around what used to be her feet, bone peeking from the melted flesh. A great roar broke through the air—dragons were fighting in the sky. No more. She could bear it no more. The world was too heavy a burden and Isla had only wanted to save one.

"Om," she whispered, her voice hoarse. She hadn't spoken in many, many years.

Isla...

She gasped. Her name. It was a word of no substance, made up of the same rotting meat many of her roots had become within her sister's roiling lake. But spoken from the same lips that had once kissed her so deeply, it was the origin of light; the cradle from which stars were born.

"Omya," she breathed, his name as vital as air. "Where are you?"

I... am... here...

Through the canopy of her branches, a torrent breeze ripped through the tunnels of her roots, swirling the inside of her elm, enclosing her in an embrace she hadn't felt in so long. The echo of the battle grew quiet, fading into distant screaming that eventually silenced. Isla opened her eyes and Iona's Breath gathered before her into a globe of light, wisps of smoke-like tendrils dripping with what appeared to be steaming vapor.

I... am... here...

The voice crept from the globe as if exhausted beyond measure, and it was not Omya. It pulsed and with its rhythm, slowly disappeared. Isla viewed the prison she'd created, moon beams drifting in shadows from her open canopy across a vast emptiness. Vines and stems, bare branches and chiseled bark littered the hollow of her elm — the hollow of herself.

She nearly closed her eyes again when she saw something. A flash of lightning strewn across one of her roots, illuminating a reaching hand. The skin was blistered, shrouded in open sores that wept with blood. Isla lifted her root, twisting around the arm until she had curled herself across the body entirely. The fragility of flesh had always amazed Isla and even now, she bore witness to its resilience to escape death as she place the body below her suspended form.

A woman. Her dark hair was wet, most of it burned from her scalp that simmered in the cool breeze. Isla's root hovered above the woman's face, feeling the unsteady breath escaping a body trying so hard to live. She turned towards the tunnel she'd pulled the woman from, and a dragon's head emerged, white and dripping with boiling water. The beast was long, a blue and white membrane trailing from her tail as she crawled to the woman's side. The dragon's belly was slit with deep gashes, her wing shattered from its glass-like membrane.

YOU LIVE, the dragon whispered, her voice drained of all strength. She had not noticed Isla looking down from the confines of her branched suspension. The dragon curled her neck around the woman, broken wing unfurled as blood pooled beneath her.

Isla watched as they slept, listening to the rise and fall of their breath. This was what Celosia had birthed in her wrath. This was what was never meant to be. Tears fell from her cheeks, running along the bark of her skin. She felt the shared soul of the dragon and her Viden—broken. The same as she was. Isla stared into the cavern of her elm and saw that she was no longer empty. She twisted her roots to embrace these shared souls as she did the world, knowing once they woke there would be much to say. The woman groaned, white eyes wide as Isla lifted the bark of her roots, sap-like blood coating the woman's burns.

"Eliam. Where is Meric? It..." the woman swallowed, blinking rapidly with sightless eyes. "It is... dark. He must be hungry." Isla hushed the woman, continuing to lather the dragon and Viden until all their wounds were covered, numbed by her sap. They were not beyond repair, but they would never be as they once were. The woman hung limp in Isla's embrace, falling into merciful unconsciousness. She held them close, remembering what it once was to be so free. Even in her pain, Isla envied the Viden. To feel such agony and still cling to life—what was she living for?

What do I live for?

Isla lifted her chin, gazing past the open canopy of her branches, listening to the thrum of Celosia's boil. Her sister was never meant for the realms of mortality. She could not help her nature any more than Isla could her own. She burned and within that burning there was still love. Isla held the world in the face of inevitability. One day her strength would fail, and the world would die. But one day was not this day and as she twisted her roots, embracing inevitability, Isla smiled.

ACKNOWLEDGMENTS

As a reader, I had never given much thought to this portion of a book. The story is over, and all my favorite characters are dead. So, in truth, I didn't give a single tooth or nail at who the author had to thank to break my heart. Now that I've written my own heartbreaker, I suppose this acknowledgment is somewhat of a published diary entry. Something personal that not everyone will read, but makes me feel better.

To my readers, thank you for picking up *Isla's Reach*. It means a lot to the little girl who at twelve years old wrote her first unpublished book within a three-prong folder on wide-ruled paper with a pencil that refused to sharpen. It is my hope that you enjoyed *Isla's Reach,* and perhaps, once you've stopped cursing my name, you'll be curious enough to pick up book 2 and the many other projects I have planned for the future.

To my friends and family, not to sound cliché, but I could've totally done this without you. Sarcasm is more of an auditory experience, so just imagine the voice inflection for the sentence above. Your love and support are invaluable, and I couldn't thank you enough for believing in me.

Now I'd like to take a moment to thank my college English Professor Jeremy, who once said he demanded credit from any of his students who ever published work. I would not be where I am as a writer without your tutelage and anarchic opinions on adverbs. A huge thank you to Felix Ortiz for the incredible cover art he created and to Hillary Sames for her editing sorcery.

I ask only one thing and that is for a review. Whether that be on Goodreads, Amazon, or wherever you leave reviews.

This is the sharpest tool a writer possesses, and it is entirely within the readers hands. Thank you to everyone who helped me make this dream a reality. I look forward to sharing more stories in the future with you.